ŚRĪMAD BHĀGAVATAM

Fifth Canto
"The Creative Impetus"

(Part Two—Chapters 14-26)

With the Original Sanskrit Text, Its Roman Transliteration, Synonyms, Translation and Elaborate Purports by

His Divine Grace
A.C. Bhaktivedanta Swami Prabhupāda
Founder-*Ācārya* of the International Society for Krishna Consciousness

THE BHAKTIVEDANTA BOOK TRUST
New York · Los Angeles · London · Bombay

Readers interested in the subject matter of this book
are invited by the International Society for Krishna Consciousness
to correspond with its Secretary.

International Society for Krishna Consciousness
3764 Watseka Avenue
Los Angeles, California 90034

Library of Congress Catalogue Card Number: 73-169353
International Standard Book Number: 0-912776-79-x

First printing, 1975: 20,000 copies

Printed in the United States of America

Table of Contents

CHAPTER NINETEEN
A Description of the Island of Jambūdvīpa

CHAPTER TWENTY
Studying the Structure of the Universe

Preface

We must know the present need of human society. And what is that need? Human society is no longer bounded by geographical limits to particular countries or communities. Human society is broader than in the Middle Ages, and the world tendency is toward one state or one human society. The ideals of spiritual communism, according to *Śrīmad-Bhāgavatam,* are based more or less on the oneness of the entire human society, nay, on the entire energy of living beings. The need is felt by great thinkers to make this a successful ideology. *Śrīmad-Bhāgavatam* will fill this need in human society. It begins, therefore, with the aphorism of Vedānta philosophy (*janmādy asya yataḥ*) to establish the ideal of a common cause.

Human society, at the present moment, is not in the darkness of oblivion. It has made rapid progress in the field of material comforts, education and economic development throughout the entire world. But there is a pinprick somewhere in the social body at large, and therefore there are large-scale quarrels, even over less important issues. There is need of a clue as to how humanity can become one in peace, friendship and prosperity with a common cause. *Śrīmad-Bhāgavatam* will fill this need, for it is a cultural presentation for the re-spiritualization of the entire human society.

Śrīmad-Bhāgavatam should be introduced also in the schools and colleges, for it is recommended by the great student devotee Prahlāda Mahārāja in order to change the demonic face of society.

kaumāra ācaret prājño
dharmān bhāgavatān iha
durlabhaṁ mānuṣaṁ janma
tad apy adhruvam arthadam
(*Bhāg.* 7.6.1)

Disparity in human society is due to lack of principles in a godless civilization. There is God, or the Almighty One, from whom everything emanates, by whom everything is maintained and in whom everything is merged to rest. Material science has tried to find the ultimate source of creation very insufficiently, but it is a fact that there is one ultimate source of everything that be. This ultimate source is explained rationally and authoritatively in the beautiful *Bhāgavatam* or *Śrīmad-Bhāgavatam.*

Śrīmad-Bhāgavatam is the transcendental science not only for knowing the ultimate source of everything but also for knowing our relation with Him and our duty towards perfection of the human society on the basis of this perfect knowledge. It is powerful reading matter in the Sanskrit language, and it is now rendered into English elaborately so that simply by a careful reading one will know God perfectly well, so much so that the reader will be sufficiently educated to defend himself from the onslaught of atheists. Over and above this, the reader will be able to convert others to accept God as a concrete principle.

Śrīmad-Bhāgavatam begins with the definition of the ultimate source. It is a bona fide commentary on the *Vedānta-sūtra* by the same author, Śrīla Vyāsadeva, and gradually it develops into nine cantos up to the highest state of God realization. The only qualification one needs to study this great book of transcendental knowledge is to proceed step by step cautiously and not jump forward haphazardly as with an ordinary book. It should be gone through chapter by chapter, one after another. The reading matter is so arranged with its original Sanskrit text, its English transliteration, synonyms, translation and purports so that one is sure to become a God realized soul at the end of finishing the first nine cantos.

The Tenth Canto is distinct from the first nine cantos, because it deals directly with the transcendental activities of the Personality of Godhead Śrī Kṛṣṇa. One will be unable to capture the effects of the Tenth Canto without going through the first nine cantos. The book is complete in twelve cantos, each independent, but it is good for all to read them in small installments one after another.

I must admit my frailties in presenting *Śrīmad-Bhāgavatam,* but still I am hopeful of its good reception by the thinkers and leaders of society on the strength of the following statement of *Śrīmad-Bhāgavatam.*

tad vāg-visargo janatāgha-viplavo
yasmin pratiślokam abaddhavaty api

nāmāny anantasya yaśo 'nkitāni yac
chṛṇvanti gāyanti gṛṇanti sādhavaḥ
(*Bhāg.* 1.5.11)

"On the other hand, that literature which is full with descriptions of the transcendental glories of the name, fame, form and pastimes of the unlimited Supreme Lord is a transcendental creation meant to bring about a revolution in the impious life of a misdirected civilization. Such transcendental literatures, even though irregularly composed, are heard, sung and accepted by purified men who are thoroughly honest."

Oṁ tat sat

A. C. Bhaktivedanta Swami

Introduction

"This *Bhāgavata Purāṇa* is as brilliant as the sun, and it has arisen just after the departure of Lord Kṛṣṇa to His own abode, accompanied by religion, knowledge, etc. Persons who have lost their vision due to the dense darkness of ignorance in the age of Kali shall get light from this *Purāṇa*." (*Śrīmad-Bhāgavatam* 1.3.43)

The timeless wisdom of India is expressed in the *Vedas*, ancient Sanskrit texts that touch upon all fields of human knowledge. Originally preserved through oral tradition, the *Vedas* were first put into writing five thousand years ago by Śrīla Vyāsadeva, the "literary incarnation of God." After compiling the *Vedas*, Vyāsadeva set forth their essence in the aphorisms known as *Vedānta-sūtras*. *Śrīmad-Bhāgavatam* is Vyāsadeva's commentary on his own *Vedānta-sūtras*. It was written in the maturity of his spiritual life under the direction of Nārada Muni, his spiritual master. Referred to as "the ripened fruit of the tree of Vedic literature," *Śrīmad-Bhāgavatam* is the most complete and authoritative exposition of Vedic knowledge.

After compiling the *Bhāgavatam*, Vyāsa impressed the synopsis of it upon his son, the sage Śukadeva Gosvāmī. Śukadeva Gosvāmī subsequently recited the entire *Bhāgavatam* to Mahārāja Parīkṣit in an assembly of learned saints on the bank of the Ganges at Hastināpura (now Delhi). Mahārāja Parīkṣit was the emperor of the world and was a great *rājarṣi* (saintly king). Having received a warning that he would die within a week, he renounced his entire kingdom and retired to the bank of the Ganges to fast until death and receive spiritual enlightenment. The *Bhāgavatam* begins with Emperor Parīkṣit's sober inquiry to Śukadeva Gosvāmī:

> "You are the spiritual master of great saints and devotees. I am therefore begging you to show the way of perfection for all persons, and especially for one who is about to die. Please let me know what a man should hear, chant, remember and worship, and also what he should not do. Please explain all this to me."

Śukadeva Gosvāmī's answer to this question, and numerous other questions posed by Mahārāja Parīkṣit, concerning everything from the nature of the self to the origin of the universe, held the assembled sages in rapt attention continuously for the seven days leading to the King's death. The sage Sūta Gosvāmī, who was present on the bank of the Ganges when Śukadeva Gosvāmī first recited *Śrīmad-Bhāgavatam,* later repeated the *Bhāgavatam* before a gathering of sages in the forest of Naimiṣāraṇya. Those sages, concerned about the spiritual welfare of the people in general, had gathered to perform a long, continuous chain of sacrifices to counteract the degrading influence of the incipient age of Kali. In response to the sages' request that he speak the essence of Vedic wisdom, Sūta Gosvāmī repeated from memory the entire eighteen thousand verses of *Śrīmad-Bhāgavatam,* as spoken by Śukadeva Gosvāmī to Mahārāja Parīkṣit.

The reader of *Śrīmad-Bhāgavatam* hears Sūta Gosvāmī relate the questions of Mahārāja Parīkṣit and the answers of Śukadeva Gosvāmī. Also, Sūta Gosvāmī sometimes responds directly to questions put by Śaunaka Ṛṣi, the spokesman for the sages gathered at Naimiṣāraṇya. One therefore simultaneously hears two dialogues: one between Mahārāja Parīkṣit and Śukadeva Gosvāmī on the bank of the Ganges, and another at Naimiṣāraṇya between Sūta Gosvāmī and the sages at Naimiṣāraṇya Forest, headed by Śaunaka Ṛṣi. Furthermore, while instructing King Parīkṣit, Śukadeva Gosvāmī often relates historical episodes and gives accounts of lengthy philosophical discussions between such great souls as the saint Maitreya and his disciple Vidura. With this understanding of the history of the *Bhāgavatam,* the reader will easily be able to follow its intermingling of dialogues and events from various sources. Since philosophical wisdom, not chronological order, is most important in the text, one need only be attentive to the subject matter of *Śrīmad-Bhāgavatam* to appreciate fully its profound message.

It should also be noted that the volumes of the *Bhāgavatam* need not be read consecutively, starting with the first and proceeding to the last. The translator of this edition compares the *Bhāgavatam* to sugar candy—wherever you taste it, you will find it equally sweet and relishable.

This edition of the *Bhāgavatam* is the first complete English translation of this important text with an elaborate commentary, and it is the first widely available to the English-speaking public. It is the product of the scholarly and devotional effort of His Divine Grace A. C. Bhaktivedanta Swami Prabhupāda, the world's most distinguished teacher of Indian religious and philosophical thought. His consummate Sanskrit scholarship and intimate familiarity with Vedic culture and thought as well as the modern way of life combine to reveal to the West a magnificent exposition of this important classic.

Readers will find this work of value for many reasons. For those interested in the classical roots of Indian civilization, it serves as a vast reservoir of detailed information on virtually every one of its aspects. For students of comparative philosophy and religion, the *Bhāgavatam* offers a penetrating view into the meaning of India's profound spiritual heritage. To sociologists and anthropologists, the *Bhāgavatam* reveals the practical workings of a peaceful and scientifically organized Vedic culture, whose institutions were integrated on the basis of a highly developed spiritual world view. Students of literature will discover the *Bhāgavatam* to be a masterpiece of majestic poetry. For students of psychology, the text provides important perspectives on the nature of consciousness, human behavior and the philosophical study of identity. Finally, to those seeking spiritual insight, the *Bhāgavatam* offers simple and practical guidance for attainment of the highest self-knowledge and realization of the Absolute Truth. The entire multivolume text, presented by the Bhaktivedanta Book Trust, promises to occupy a significant place in the intellectual, cultural and spiritual life of modern man for a long time to come.

—The Publishers

His Divine Grace
A. C. Bhaktivedanta Swami Prabhupāda
Founder-Ācārya of the International Society for Krishna Consciousness

CHART ONE

This map shows the Bhū-maṇḍala planetary system as viewed from above. Bhū-maṇḍala is like a lotus, and its seven islands (*dvīpas*) resemble its whorl. In the middle of the central island, Jambūdvīpa, stands Mount Sumeru, a mountain of solid gold. Jambūdvīpa is surrounded by an ocean of salt water, which is surrounded by the next island, Plakṣadvīpa. Each island is thus surrounded by an ocean and then another island.

The outermost island, Puṣkaradvīpa, is divided in two by a great mountain named Mānasottara. The sun orbits on top of this mountain and thus encircles Mount Sumeru. On Mānasottara Mountain, in the four directions, are the residential quarters of four prominent demigods.

Beyond the outermost ocean and a land made of gold stands Lokāloka Mountain, which is extremely high and which blocks the sunlight so that Aloka-varṣa, the land beyond it, is dark and uninhabited.

This map is not drawn to scale. In reality, the innermost island, Jambūdvīpa, is 800,000 miles wide. Each ocean is as broad as the island it surrounds, and each succeeding island is twice as broad as the one before it. The total diameter of the universe is four billion miles. Thus if the entire map were drawn to the same scale as Jambūdvīpa, the distance from the center of the map to its outermost edge would have to be almost half a mile.

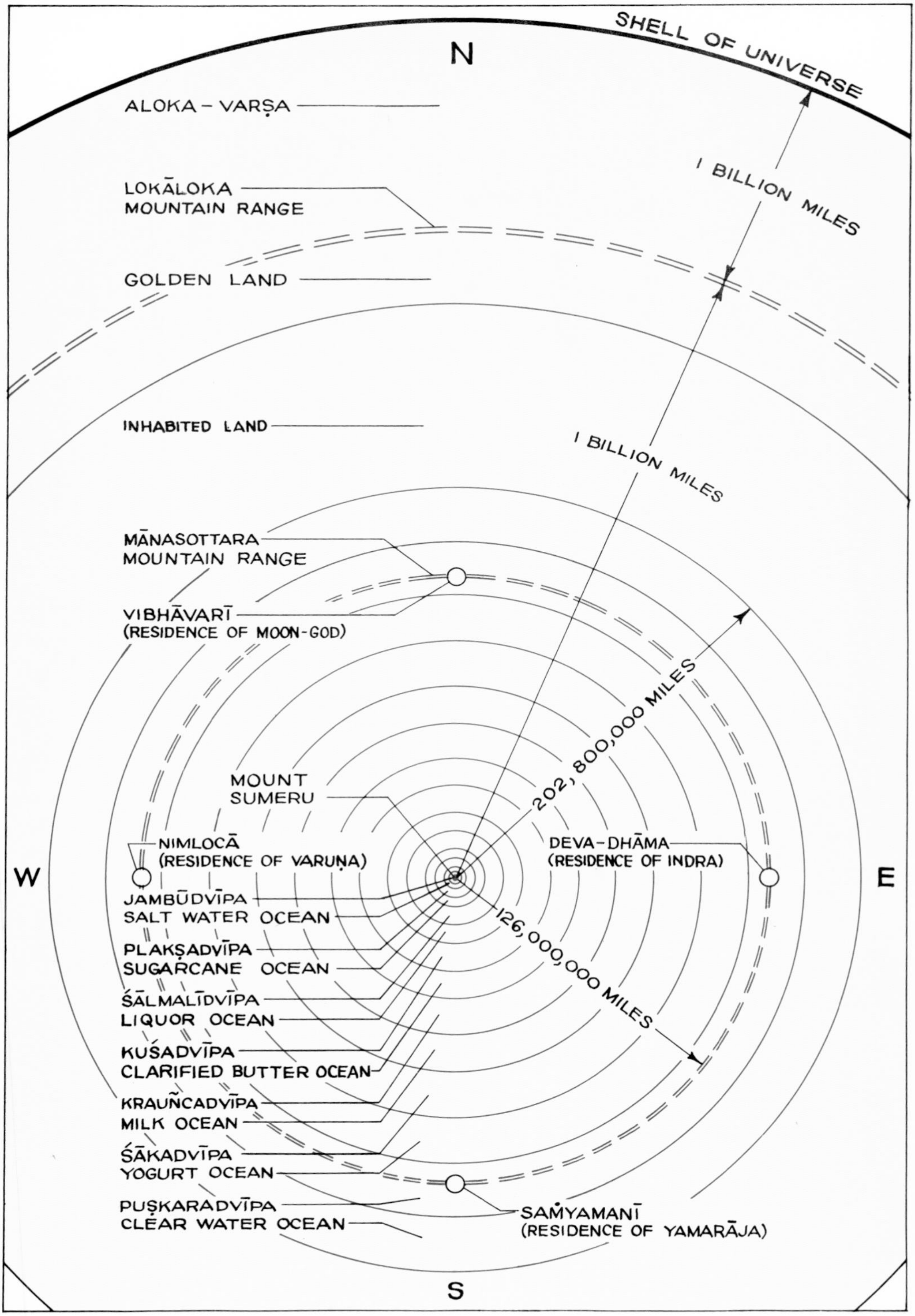

SHELL OF UNIVERSE
N
ALOKA-VARṢA
LOKĀLOKA MOUNTAIN RANGE
1 BILLION MILES
GOLDEN LAND
INHABITED LAND
1 BILLION MILES
MĀNASOTTARA MOUNTAIN RANGE
VIBHĀVARĪ (RESIDENCE OF MOON-GOD)
202,800,000 MILES
MOUNT SUMERU
NIMLOCĀ (RESIDENCE OF VARUṆA)
DEVA-DHĀMA (RESIDENCE OF INDRA)
W
E
JAMBŪDVĪPA
SALT WATER OCEAN
126,000,000 MILES
PLAKṢADVĪPA
SUGARCANE OCEAN
ŚĀLMALĪDVĪPA
LIQUOR OCEAN
KUŚADVĪPA
CLARIFIED BUTTER OCEAN
KRAUÑCADVĪPA
MILK OCEAN
ŚĀKADVĪPA
YOGURT OCEAN
PUṢKARADVĪPA
CLEAR WATER OCEAN
SAṀYAMANĪ (RESIDENCE OF YAMARĀJA)
S

CHART TWO

Moving with the great wheel of time, the stars and constellations travel clockwise around the polestar, and the sun travels with them. The sun, however, encircles the polestar in its own counterclockwise orbit around Sumeru, and therefore the sun's motion is seen to be different from that of the wheel of time itself. Passing through twelve months, the sun comes in touch with the twelve different signs of the zodiac and assumes twelve different names according to those signs. The aggregate of those twelve months is called a *saṁvatsara,* or an entire year.

The sun travels at different speeds. When it travels in its northern course, it travels slowly during the day and quickly at night, thus increasing the duration of the daytime and decreasing the duration of night. When it travels in its southern course, the exact opposite is true—the duration of the day decreases, and the duration of the night increases.

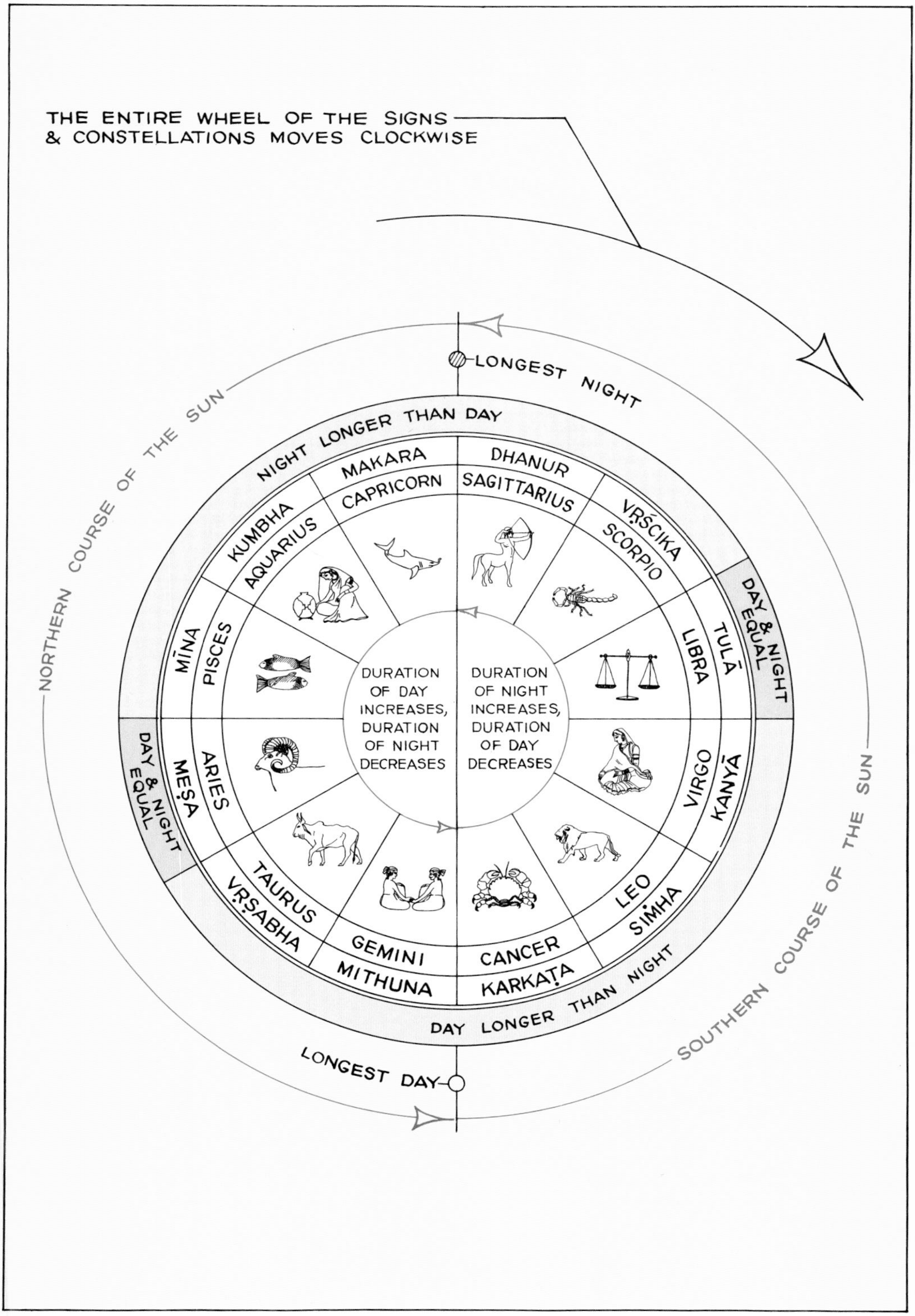
THE ENTIRE WHEEL OF THE SIGNS & CONSTELLATIONS MOVES CLOCKWISE
LONGEST NIGHT
NIGHT LONGER THAN DAY
NORTHERN COURSE OF THE SUN
SOUTHERN COURSE OF THE SUN
DAY & NIGHT EQUAL
DAY & NIGHT EQUAL
MAKARA
CAPRICORN
DHANUR
SAGITTARIUS
VṚŚCIKA
SCORPIO
KUMBHA
AQUARIUS
MĪNA
PISCES
TULĀ
LIBRA
DURATION OF DAY INCREASES, DURATION OF NIGHT DECREASES
DURATION OF NIGHT INCREASES, DURATION OF DAY DECREASES
MEṢA
ARIES
VIRGO
KANYĀ
TAURUS
VṚṢABHA
LEO
SIṀHA
GEMINI
MITHUNA
CANCER
KARKAṬA
DAY LONGER THAN NIGHT
LONGEST DAY

CHART THREE

This scale drawing shows a basic cross-section of the universe in which we live. For simplicity, the planets are represented in a straight line, one above another, although the *Bhāgavatam* describes that the sun, the moon and the other planets are actually revolving around the polestar in their own orbits and at various speeds. These planets are revolving in obedience to the will of the Supreme Personality of Godhead, for the great machinery of the universe is all working according to His order. The area between the planet Saturn and the Garbhodaka Ocean has also been depicted in a larger scale in the box on the right of the illustration. The drawing does not attempt to represent accurately the relative sizes of the planets, nor does it show the full depth of the Garbhodaka Ocean—249,800,000 *yojanas* (nearly half the universe). The total height of the universe, from top to bottom, is 510,000,000 *yojanas*, or 4,080,000,000 miles. This is but one of the innumerable universes in the material world, which constitutes only a small fraction of the creation of the Supreme Personality of Godhead. Since one cannot understand the details of even one universe in the vast material creation, certainly one cannot estimate the expansiveness of the spiritual world.

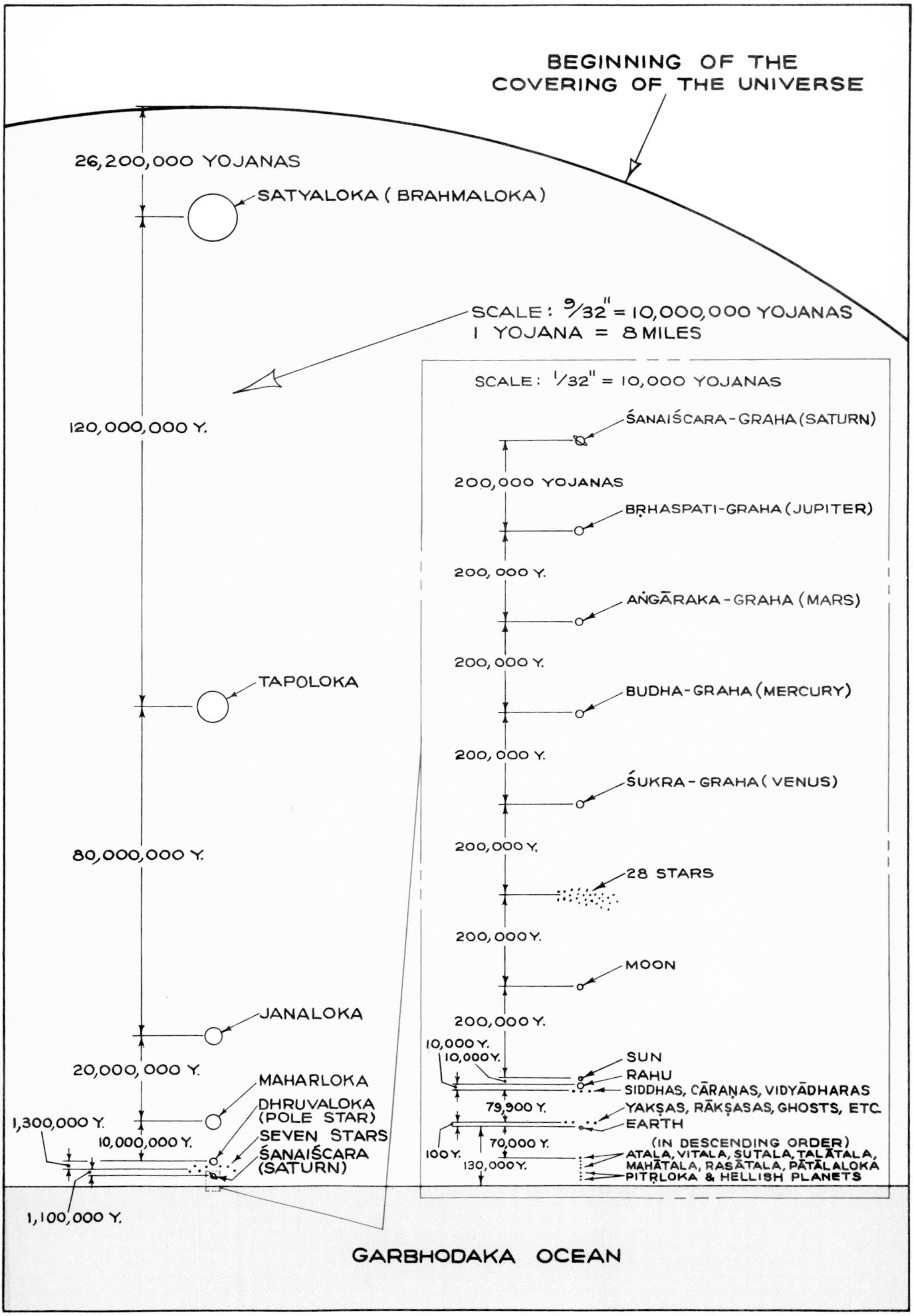

BEGINNING OF THE
COVERING OF THE UNIVERSE
26,200,000 YOJANAS
SATYALOKA (BRAHMALOKA)
SCALE: 9/32" = 10,000,000 YOJANAS
1 YOJANA = 8 MILES
120,000,000 Y.
TAPOLOKA
80,000,000 Y.
JANALOKA
20,000,000 Y.
MAHARLOKA
DHRUVALOKA
(POLE STAR)
SEVEN STARS
ŚANAIŚCARA
(SATURN)
1,300,000 Y.
10,000,000 Y.
1,100,000 Y.
SCALE: 1/32" = 10,000 YOJANAS
ŚANAIŚCARA-GRAHA (SATURN)
200,000 YOJANAS
BṚHASPATI-GRAHA (JUPITER)
200,000 Y.
AṄGĀRAKA-GRAHA (MARS)
200,000 Y.
BUDHA-GRAHA (MERCURY)
200,000 Y.
ŚUKRA-GRAHA (VENUS)
200,000 Y.
28 STARS
200,000 Y.
MOON
200,000 Y.
10,000 Y.
10,000 Y.
SUN
RAHU
SIDDHAS, CĀRAṆAS, VIDYĀDHARAS
79,900 Y.
YAKṢAS, RĀKṢASAS, GHOSTS, ETC.
EARTH
100 Y.
70,000 Y.
130,000 Y.
(IN DESCENDING ORDER)
ATALA, VITALA, SUTALA, TALĀTALA,
MAHĀTALA, RASĀTALA, PĀTĀLALOKA
PITṚLOKA & HELLISH PLANETS
GARBHODAKA OCEAN

PLATE ONE

"In the tract of land known as Ilāvṛta-varṣa, the only male person is Lord Śiva, the most powerful demigod. Goddess Durgā, the wife of Lord Śiva, does not like any man to enter that land. If any foolish man dares to do so, she immediately turns him into a woman. In Ilāvṛta-varṣa, Lord Śiva is always encircled by ten billion maidservants of goddess Durgā, who minister to him. The quadruple expansion of the Supreme Lord is composed of Vāsudeva, Pradyumna, Aniruddha and Saṅkarṣaṇa. Saṅkarṣaṇa, the fourth expansion, is certainly transcendental, but because His activities of destruction in the material world are in the mode of ignorance, He is known as *tamasi*, the Lord's form in the mode of ignorance. Lord Śiva knows that Saṅkarṣaṇa is the original cause of his own existence, and thus he always meditates upon Him in trance." *(pp.142–143)*

PLATE TWO

"Bhadraśravā, the son of Dharmarāja, rules the tract of land known as Bhadrāśva-varṣa. Just as Lord Śiva worships Saṅkarṣaṇa in Ilāvṛta-varṣa, Bhadraśravā, accompanied by his intimate servants and all the residents of the land, worships the plenary expansion of Vāsudeva known as Hayaśīrṣa (also called Hayagrīva). Lord Hayaśīrṣa is very dear to the devotees, and He is the director of all religious principles. Fixed in the topmost trance, Bhadraśravā and his associates offer their respectful obeisances to the Lord and chant the following prayers with careful pronunciation: 'At the end of the millennium, ignorance personified assumed the form of a demon, stole all the *Vedas* and took them down to the planet of Rasātala. The Supreme Lord, however, in His form of Hayagrīva, retrieved the *Vedas* and returned them to Lord Brahmā when he begged for them. I offer my respectful obeisances unto the Supreme Lord, whose determination never fails.' " *(pp.157–163)*

PLATE THREE

"The Supreme Lord in His boar incarnation, who accepts all sacrificial offerings, lives in the northern part of Jambūdvīpa. There, in the tract of land known as Uttarakuru-varṣa, mother earth and all the other inhabitants worship Him with unfailing devotional service by repeatedly chanting the following *Upaniṣad mantra:* 'O Lord, we offer our respectful obeisances unto You as the gigantic person. Simply by chanting *mantras*, we shall be able to understand You fully. You are *yajña* (sacrifice), and You are the *kratu* (ritual). Therefore all the ritualistic ceremonies of sacrifice are part of Your transcendental body, and You are the only enjoyer of all sacrifices. My Lord, as the original boar within this universe, You fought and killed the great demon Hiraṇyākṣa. Then You lifted me (the earth) from the Garbhodaka Ocean on the end of Your tusk, exactly as a sporting elephant plucks a lotus flower from the water. I bow down before You.' " *(pp.212–220)*

PLATE FOUR

"In Kimpuruṣa-varṣa the great devotee Hanumān is always engaged with the inhabitants of that land in devotional service to Lord Rāmacandra, the elder brother of Lakṣmaṇa and dear husband of Sītādevī. A host of Gandharvas is always engaged in chanting the glories of Rāmacandra. That chanting is always extremely auspicious. Hanumānjī and Ārṣṭiṣeṇa, the chief person in Kimpuruṣa-varṣa, constantly hear those glories with complete attention. Hanumān chants the following *mantras:* 'Let me please Your Lordship by chanting the *bīja-mantra, oṁkāra.* I wish to offer my respectful obeisances unto the Supreme Personality of Godhead, who is the best among the most elevated personalities. Your Lordship is the reservoir of all good qualities. Your character and behavior are always consistent, and You always control Your senses and mind. Acting just like an ordinary human being, You exhibit exemplary character to teach others how to behave. It was ordained that Rāvaṇa, chief of the Rākṣasas, could not be killed by anyone but a man, and for this reason Lord Rāmacandra, the Supreme Personality of Godhead, appeared in the form of a human being to kill Rāvaṇa.' " *(pp.223–229)*

PLATE FIVE

"Lord Śrī Ananta is worshiped by all the uncontaminated devotees. He has thousands of hoods and is the reservoir of all devotional service. Simply due to the glance of Lord Ananta, the three modes of nature interact and produce creation, maintenance and annihilation. These modes of nature appear again and again. Lord Anantadeva is known as Śeṣa (the unlimited end) because He ends our passage through this material world. Simply by chanting His glories everyone can be liberated. At the time of devastation, when Lord Anantadeva desires to destroy the entire creation, He becomes slightly angry. Then from between His two eyebrows appears three-eyed Rudra, carrying a trident. This Rudra, who is known as Saṅkarṣaṇa, is the embodiment of the eleven Rudras, or incarnations of Lord Śiva. He appears in order to devastate the entire creation." *(pp.412–423)*

PLATE SIX

"All the hellish planets are situated in the intermediate space between the three worlds and the Garbhodaka Ocean. The king of the *pitās* is Yamarāja, the very powerful son of the sun-god. He resides in Pitṛloka with his personal assistants and, while abiding by the rules and regulations set down by the Supreme Lord, has his agents, the Yamadūtas, bring all the sinful men to him immediately upon their death. After bringing them within his jurisdiction, he properly judges them according to their specific sinful activities and sends them to one of the many hellish planets for suitable punishments. In the province of Yamarāja there are hundreds and thousands of hellish planets. All impious people must enter these various planets according to the degree of their impiety.

"For the maintenance of their bodies and the satisfaction of their tongues, cruel persons cook poor animals and birds alive. Such persons are condemned even by man-eaters. In their next lives, they are carried by the Yamadūtas to the hell known as Kumbhīpāka, where they are cooked in boiling oil.

"A human being endowed with knowledge certainly commits sin if he kills or torments insignificant creatures, who have no discrimination. The Supreme Lord punishes such a man by putting him into the hell known as Andhakūpa, where he is attacked by all the birds and beasts, reptiles, mosquitos, lice, worms, flies, and any other creatures he tormented during his life. They attack him from all sides, robbing him of the pleasure of sleep. Unable to rest, he constantly wanders about in the darkness. Thus in Andhakūpa his suffering is just like that of a creature in the lower species.

"In his next life, a sinful king or governmental representative who punishes an innocent person, or who inflicts corporal punishment upon a *brāhmaṇa*, is taken by the Yamadūtas to a hell known as Śūkharamukha, where the most powerful assistants of Yamarāja crush him exactly as one crushes sugarcane to squeeze out juice. The sinful living entity cries very pitiably and faints, just like an innocent man undergoing punishment. This is the result of punishing a faultless person." *(pp.437–453)*

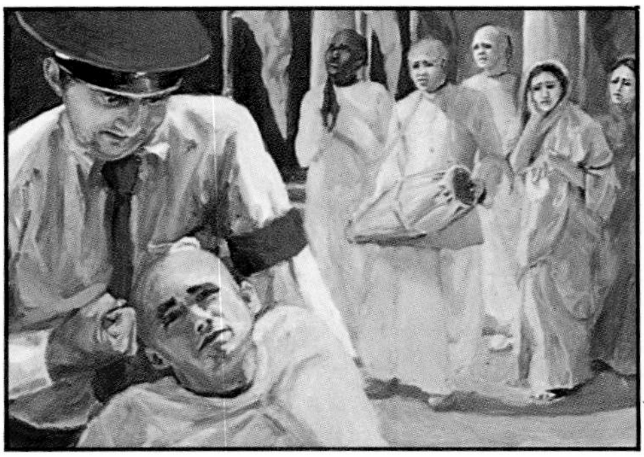

PLATE SEVEN

"A man or woman who indulges in sexual intercourse with an unworthy member of the opposite sex is punished after death by the assistants of Yamarāja in the hell known as Taptaśūrmi. There such men and women are beaten with whips. The man is forced to embrace a red-hot iron form of a woman, and the woman is forced to embrace a similar form of a man. Such is the punishment for illicit sex.

"Any *brāhmaṇa* or *brāhmaṇa's* wife who drinks liquor is taken by the agents of Yamarāja to the hell known as Ayaḥpāna. The hell also awaits any *kṣatriya, vaiśya,* or a person under a vow who in illusion drinks *soma-rasa.* In Ayaḥpāna the agents of Yamarāja stand on their chests and pour hot melted iron into their mouths.

"One who in this world or in this life is very proud of his wealth always thinks, 'I am so rich. Who can equal me?' His vision is twisted, and he is always afraid that someone will take his wealth. Indeed, he even suspects his superiors. His face and heart dry up at the thought of losing his wealth, and therefore he always looks like a wretched fiend. He is not in any way able to obtain actual happiness, and he does not know what it is to be free from anxiety. Because of these sinful things he does to earn money, augment his wealth and protect it, he is put into the hell known as Sūcimūkha, where the officials of Yamarāja punish him by stitching thread through his entire body like weavers manufacturing cloth." *(pp.456–474)*

CHAPTER FOURTEEN

The Material World as the Great Forest of Enjoyment

The direct meaning of the forest of material existence is given in this chapter. Merchants sometimes enter the forest to collect many rare things and sell them at a good profit in the city, but the forest path is always bedecked with dangers. When the pure soul wants to give up the Lord's service to enjoy the material world, Kṛṣṇa certainly gives him a chance to enter the material world. As stated in the *Prema-vivarta: kṛṣṇa-bahirmukha hañā bhoga vāñchā kare.* This is the reason the pure spirit soul falls down to the material world. Due to his activities under the influence of the three modes of material nature, the living entity takes different positions in different species. Sometimes he is a demigod in the heavenly planets and sometimes a most insignificant creature in the lower planetary systems. In this regard, Śrīla Narottama dāsa Ṭhākura says, *nānā yoni sadā phire:* the living entity passes through various species. *Kardarya bhakṣaṇa kare:* he is obliged to eat and enjoy abominable things. *Tāra janma adhaḥ-pāte yāya:* in this way his whole life is spoiled. Without the protection of an all-merciful Vaiṣṇava, the conditioned soul cannot get out of the clutches of *māyā.* As stated in *Bhagavad-gītā* (*manaḥ ṣaṣṭhānīndriyāṇi prakṛti-sthāni karṣati*), the living entity begins material life with his mind and the five knowledge-acquiring senses, and with these he struggles for existence within the material world. These senses are compared to rogues and thieves within the forest. They take away a man's knowledge and place him in a network of nescience. Thus the senses are like rogues and thieves that plunder his spiritual knowledge. Over and above this, there are family members, wife and children, who are exactly like ferocious animals in the forest. The business of such ferocious animals is to eat a man's flesh. The living entity allows himself to be attacked by jackals and foxes (wife and children), and thus his real spiritual life is finished. In the forest of material life, everyone is envious like mosquitoes, and rats and mice are always creating disturbances. Everyone in this material world is placed in many awkward positions and surrounded by envious people and disturbing animals. The result is that the living entity in the material world is always plundered and bitten by many living entities. Nonetheless, despite these disturbances, he does not want to give up his family life, and he continues his fruitive activities in an attempt to become happy in the future. He thus becomes more and more entangled in the results of *karma*, and thus he is forced to act impiously. His witnesses are the sun during the day and the moon during the night. The demigods also witness, but the conditioned soul thinks that his attempts at sense gratification are not being witnessed by anyone. Sometimes, when he is detected, he temporarily renounces everything, but due to his great attachment for the body, his renunciation is given up before he can attain perfection.

In this material world there are many envious people. There is the tax-exacting government, which is compared to an owl, and there are invisible crickets that create unbearable sounds. The conditioned soul is certainly greatly harassed by the agents of material nature, but his intelligence is lost due to undesirable association. In an attempt to gain relief from the disturbances of material existence, he falls victim to so-called *yogīs, sādhus* and incarnations who can display some magic but who do not understand devotional service. Sometimes the conditioned soul is bereft of all money, and consequently he becomes unkind to his family members. In this material world there is not a pinch of actual happiness, for which the conditioned soul is longing life after life. The government officials are like carnivorous Rākṣasas who exact heavy taxes for the maintenance of the government. The hard-working conditioned soul is very saddened due to these heavy taxes.

The path of fruitive activities leads to difficult mountains, and sometimes the conditioned soul wants to cross these mountains, but he is never successful, and consequently he becomes more and more aggrieved and disappointed. Becoming materially and financially embarrassed, the conditioned soul unnecessarily chastises his family. In the material condition there are four principal needs, out of which sleep is compared to a python. When asleep, the conditioned soul completely forgets his real existence, and in sleep he does not feel the tribulations of material life. Sometimes, being in need of money, the conditioned soul steals and cheats, although he may apparently be associated with devotees for spiritual advancement. His only business is getting out of the clutches of *māyā*, but due to improper guidance he becomes more and more entangled in material dealings. This material world is simply an embarrassment and is composed of tribulations presented as happiness, distress, attachment, enmity and envy. On the whole it is simply full of tribulation and misery. When a person loses his intelligence due to attachment to wife and sex, his entire consciousness becomes polluted. He thus only thinks of the association of women. The time factor, which is like a serpent, takes away everyone's life, including that of Lord Brahmā and the insignificant ant. Sometimes the conditioned soul tries to save himself from inexorable time and thus takes shelter of some bogus savior. Unfortunately, the bogus savior cannot even save himself. How, then, can he protect others? The bogus saviors do not care for bona fide knowledge received from qualified *brāhmaṇas* and Vedic sources. Their only business is indulging in sex and recommending sexual freedom even for widows. Thus they are like monkeys in the forest. Śrīla Śukadeva Gosvāmī thus explains the material forest and its difficult path to Mahārāja Parīkṣit.

TEXT 1

स होवाच

य एष देहात्ममानिनां सत्त्वादिगुणविशेषविकल्पितकुशलाकुशलसमवहार-
विनिर्मितविविधदेहावलिभिर्वियोगसंयोगाद्यनादिसंसारानुभवस्य द्वार-
भूतेनषडिन्द्रियवर्गेण तस्मिन्दुर्गाध्ववदसुगमेऽध्वन्यापतित ईश्वरस्य भगवतो
विष्णोर्वशवर्तिन्या मायया जीवलोकोऽयं यथा वणिक्सार्थोऽर्थपरः
स्वदेहनिष्पादितकर्मानुभवः श्मशानवदशिवतमायां संसाराटव्यां गतो नाद्यापि
विफलबहुप्रतियोगेहस्तत्तापोपशमनीं हरिगुरुचरणारविन्दमधुकरानुपदवीम
वरुन्धे ॥१॥

sa hovāca

sa eṣa dehātma-mānināṁ sattvādi-guṇa-viśeṣa-vikalpita-kuśalākuśala-samavahāra-vinirmita-vividha-dehāvalibhir viyoga-saṁyogādy-anādi-saṁsārānubhavasya dvāra-bhūtena ṣaḍ-indriya-vargeṇa tasmin durgādhvavad asugame 'dhvany āpatita īśvarasya bhagavato viṣṇor vaśa-vartinyā māyayā jīva-loko 'yaṁ yathā vaṇik-sārtho 'rtha-paraḥ sva-deha-niṣpādita-karmānubhavaḥ śmaśānavad aśivatamāyāṁ saṁsārāṭavyāṁ gato nādyāpi viphala-bahu-pratiyogehas tat-tāpopaśamanīṁ hari-guru-caraṇāravinda-madhukarānupadavīm avarundhe.

saḥ—the self-realized devotee (Śrī Śukadeva Gosvāmī); *ha*—indeed; *uvāca*—spoke; *saḥ*—he (the conditioned soul); *eṣaḥ*—this one; *deha-ātma-māninām*—of those who foolishly take the body to be the self; *sattva-ādi*—of *sattva, rajaḥ* and *tamaḥ; guṇa*—by the modes; *viśeṣa*—particular; *vikalpita*—falsely constituted; *kuśala*—sometimes by favorable actions; *akuśala*—sometimes by very unfavorable actions; *samavahāra*—by a mixture of both; *vinirmita*—obtained; *vividha*—various types; *deha-āvalibhiḥ*—by the series of bodies; *viyoga-saṁyoga-ādi*—symptomized by giving up one type of body (*viyoga*) and accepting another (*saṁyoga*); *anādi-saṁsāra-anubhavasya*—of the perception of the beginningless process of transmigration; *dvāra-bhūtena*—existing as the doorways; *ṣaṭ-indriya-vargeṇa*—by these six senses (the mind and five knowledge-acquiring senses, namely the eyes, ears, tongue, nose and skin); *tasmin*—on that; *durga-adhva-vat*—like a path that is very difficult to traverse; *asugame*—being difficult to pass through; *adhvani*—on a path in the forest; *āpatitaḥ*—happened; *īśvarasya*—of the controller; *bhagavataḥ*—the Supreme Personality of Godhead; *viṣṇoḥ*—of Lord Viṣṇu; *vaśa-vartinyā*—acting under the control; *māyayā*—by the material energy; *jīva-lokaḥ*—the conditioned living entity; *ayam*—this; *yathā*—exactly like; *vaṇik*—a merchant; *sa-arthaḥ*—having an object; *artha-paraḥ*—who is very attached to money; *sva-deha-niṣpādita*—performed by his own body; *karma*—the fruits of activities; *anubhavaḥ*—who experiences; *śmaśāna-vat aśivatamāyām*—like an inauspicious cemetery or place of burial; *saṁsāra-aṭavyām*—in the forest of material life; *gataḥ*—having entered; *na*—not; *adya api*—until now; *viphala*—unsuccessful; *bahu-pratiyoga*—full of great difficulties and varieties of miserable conditions; *īhaḥ*—whose activities here in this material world; *tat-tāpa-upaśamanīm*—which pacifies the miseries of the forest of material life; *hari-guru-caraṇa-aravinda*—to the lotus feet of the Lord and His devotee;

madhukara-anupadavīm—the road followed in pursuance of devotees who are attached like bumblebees; *avarundhe*—gain.

TRANSLATION

When King Parīkṣit asked Śukadeva Gosvāmī about the direct meaning of the material forest, Śukadeva Gosvāmī replied as follows: My dear King, a man belonging to the mercantile community [vaṇik] is always interested in earning money. Sometimes he enters the forest to acquire some cheap commodities like wood and earth and sell them in the city at good prices. Similarly, the conditioned soul, being greedy, enters this material world for some material profit. Gradually he enters the deepest part of the forest, not really knowing how to get out. Having entered the material world, the pure soul becomes conditioned by the material atmosphere, which is created by the external energy under the control of Lord Viṣṇu. Thus the living entity comes under the control of the external energy, daivī māyā. Living independently and bewildered in the forest, he does not attain the association of devotees who are always engaged in the service of the Lord. Once in the bodily conception, he gets different types of bodies one after the other under the influence of material energy and impelled by the modes of material nature [sattva-guṇa, rajo-guṇa and tamo-guṇa]. In this way the conditioned soul goes sometimes to the heavenly planets, sometimes to the earthly planets and sometimes to the lower planets and lower species. Thus he suffers continuously due to different types of bodies. These sufferings and pains are sometimes mixed. Sometimes they are very severe, and sometimes they are not. These bodily conditions are acquired due to the conditioned soul's mental speculation. He uses his mind and five senses to acquire knowledge, and these bring about the different bodies and different conditions. Using the senses under the control of the external energy, māyā, the living entity suffers the miserable conditions of material existence. He is actually searching for relief, but he is generally baffled, although sometimes he is relieved after great difficulty. Struggling for existence in this way, he cannot get

the shelter of pure devotees, who are like bumblebees engaged in loving service at the lotus feet of Lord Viṣṇu.

PURPORT

The most important information in this verse is *hari-guru-caraṇa-aravinda-madhukara-anupadavīm.* In this material world the conditioned souls are baffled by their activities, and sometimes they are relieved after great difficulty. On the whole the conditioned soul is never happy. He simply struggles for existence. Actually his only business is to accept the spiritual master, the *guru,* and through him he must accept the lotus feet of the Lord. This is explained by Śrī Caitanya Mahāprabhu: *guru-kṛṣṇa-prasāde pāya bhakti-latā-bīja.* People struggling for existence in the forests or cities of the material world are not actually enjoying life. They are simply suffering different pains and pleasures, generally pains that are always inauspicious. They try to gain release from these pains, but they cannot due to ignorance. For them it is stated in the *Vedas: tad-vijñānārthaṁ sa gurum evābhigacchet.* When the living entity is lost in the forest of the material world, in the struggle for existence, his first business is to find a bona fide *guru* who is always engaged at the lotus feet of the Supreme Personality of Godhead, Viṣṇu. After all, if he is at all eager to be relieved of the struggle for existence, he must find a bona fide *guru* and take instructions at his lotus feet. In this way he can get out of the struggle.

Since the material world is compared herein to a forest, it may be argued that in Kali-yuga modern civilization is mainly situated in the cities. A great city, however, is like a great forest. Actually city life is more dangerous than life in the forest. If one enters an unknown city without friend or shelter, living in that city is more difficult than living in a forest. There are many big cities all over the surface of the globe, and wherever one looks he sees the struggle for existence going on twenty-four hours a day. People rush about in cars going seventy and eighty miles an hour, constantly coming and going, and this sets the scene of the great struggle for existence. One has to rise early in the morning and travel in that car at breakneck speed. There is always the danger of an accident, and one has to take great care. In his automobile, the living entity is full of anxieties, and his struggle is not at all auspicious. Apart from human beings, other species like cats and dogs are also struggling very hard day and night for existence. Thus the struggle for existence continues, and the conditioned soul changes from one position to another. For a while, he is a child, but he has to become a boy. From a boy, he has to change into a youth, and from youth to manhood and old age. Finally, when the body is no longer workable, he has to accept a new body in a different species. Giving up the body is called death, and accepting another body is called birth. The human form is an opportunity to take shelter of the bona fide spiritual master and, through him, the Supreme Lord. This Kṛṣṇa consciousness movement has been started to give an opportunity to all the members of human society, who are misled by foolish leaders. No one can get out of this struggle for existence, which is full of miseries, without accepting a pure devotee of the Lord. The material attempt changes from one position to another, and no one actually gains relief from the struggle for existence. The only resort is the lotus feet of a bona fide spiritual master, and, through him, the lotus feet of the Lord.

TEXT 2

यस्यामु ह वा एते षडिन्द्रियनामानः कर्मणा दस्यव एव ते। तद्यथा पुरुषस्य
धनं यत्किञ्चिद्धर्मौपयिकं बहुकृच्छ्राधिगतं साक्षात्परमपुरुषाराधनलक्षणो योऽसौ
धर्मस्तं तु साम्पराय उदाहरन्ति। तद्धर्म्यं धनं दर्शनस्पर्शनश्रवणा-
स्वादनावघ्राणसङ्कल्पव्यवसायगृहग्राम्योपभोगेन कुनाथस्याजितात्मनो यथा
सार्थस्य विलुम्पन्ति ॥ २ ॥

yasyām u ha vā ete ṣaḍ-indriya-nāmānaḥ karmaṇā dasyava eva te. tad yathā puruṣasya dhanaṁ yat kiñcid dharmaupayikaṁ bahu-kṛcchrādhigataṁ sākṣāt parama-puruṣārādhana-lakṣaṇo yo 'sau dharmas taṁ tu sāmparāya udāharanti. tad-dharmyaṁ dhanaṁ darśana-sparśana-śravaṇāsvādanāvaghrāṇa-saṅkalpa-vyavasāya-gṛha-grāmyopabhogena kunāthasyājitātmano yathā sārthasya vilumpanti.

yasyām—in which; *u ha*—certainly; *vā*—or; *ete*—all these; *ṣaṭ-indriya-nāmānaḥ*—who are named the six senses (the mind and the five knowledge-acquiring senses); *karmaṇā*—by their activity; *dasyavaḥ*—the plunderers; *eva*—certainly; *te*—they; *tat*—that; *yathā*—as; *puruṣasya*—of a person; *dhanam*—the wealth; *yat*—whatever; *kiñcit*—something; *dharma-aupayikam*—which is a means to religious principles; *bahu-kṛcchra-adhigatam*—earned after much hard labor; *sākṣāt*—directly; *parama-puruṣa-ārādhana-lakṣaṇaḥ*—whose symptoms are worship of the Supreme Lord by performance of sacrifices and so on; *yaḥ*—which; *asau*—that; *dharmaḥ*—religious principles; *tam*—that; *tu*—but; *sāmparāye*—for the benefit of the living entity after death; *udāharanti*—the wise declare; *tat-dharmyam*—religious (relating to the prosecution of the *varṇāśrama-dharma*); *dhanam*—wealth; *darśana*—by seeing; *sparśana*—by touching; *śravaṇa*—by hearing; *āsvādana*—by tasting; *avaghrāṇa*—by smelling; *saṅkalpa*—by determination; *vyavasāya*—by a conclusion; *gṛha*—in the material home; *grāmya-upabhogena*—by material sense gratification; *kunāthasya*—of the misguided conditioned soul; *ajita-ātmanaḥ*—who has not controlled himself; *yathā*—just as; *sārthasya*—of the living entity interested in sense gratification; *vilumpanti*—they plunder.

TRANSLATION

In the forest of material existence, the uncontrolled senses are like plunderers. The conditioned soul may earn some money for the advancement of Kṛṣṇa consciousness, but unfortunately the uncontrolled senses plunder his money through sense gratification. The senses are plunderers because they make one spend his money unnecessarily for seeing, smelling, tasting, touching, hearing, desiring and willing. In this way the conditioned soul is obliged to gratify his senses, and thus all his money is spent. This money is actually acquired for the execution of religious principles, but it is taken away by the plundering senses.

PURPORT

Pūrva-jamnārjitā vidyā pūrva-janmārjitaṁ dhanaṁ agre dhāvati dhāvati. By following the principles of the *varṇāśrama-dharma,* one attains a better position in the material world. One may be rich, learned, beautiful or highborn. One who has all these assets should know that they are all meant for the advancement of Kṛṣṇa consciousness. Unfortunately, when a person is misguided he misuses his high position for sense gratification. Therefore the uncontrolled senses are considered plunderers. The good position one attains by executing religious principles is wasted as the plundering senses take it away. By executing religious principles under the laws of *varṇāśrama-dharma*, one is placed in a comfortable position. One may very easily use his assets for the further advancement of Kṛṣṇa consciousness. One should understand that the wealth and opportunity one gets in the material world should not be squandered in sense gratification. They are meant for the advancement of Kṛṣṇa consciousness. This Kṛṣṇa consciousness movement is therefore teaching people to control the mind and five knowledge-acquiring senses by a definite process. One should practice a little austerity and not spend money on anything other than the regulative life of devotional service. The senses demand that one see beautiful things; therefore money should be spent for decorating the Deity in the temple. Similarly, the tongue has to taste good food, which should be bought and offered to the Deity. The nose can be utilized in smelling the flowers offered to the Deity, and the hearing can be utilized by listening to the vibration of the Hare Kṛṣṇa *mantra*. In this way the senses can be regulated and utilized to advance Kṛṣṇa consciousness. Thus a good position might not be spoiled by material sense gratification in the form of illicit sex, meat-eating, intoxication and gambling. One spoils an opulent position in the material world by driving cars, spending time in nightclubs or tasting abominable food in restaurants. In these ways, the plundering senses take away all the assets that the conditioned soul has acquired with great difficulty.

TEXT 3

अथ च यत्र कौटुम्बिका दारापत्यादयो नाम्ना कर्मणा वृकसृगाला एवानिच्छतोऽपि कदर्यस्य कुटुम्बिन उरणकवत्संरक्ष्यमाणं मिषतोऽपि हरन्ति ॥ ३ ॥

atha ca yatra kauṭumbikā dārāpatyādayo nāmnā karmaṇā vṛka-sṛgālā
evānicchato 'pi kadaryasya kuṭumbina uraṇakavat saṁrakṣyamāṇaṁ
miṣato 'pi haranti.

atha—in this way; *ca*—also; *yatra*—in which; *kauṭumbikāḥ*—the family members; *dāra-apatya-ādayaḥ*—beginning with the wife and children; *nāmnā*—by name only; *karmaṇā*—by their behavior; *vṛka-sṛgālāḥ*—tigers and jackals; *eva*—certainly; *anicchataḥ*—of one who does not desire to spend his wealth; *api*—certainly; *kadaryasya*—being too miserly; *kuṭumbinaḥ*—who is surrounded by family members; *uraṇaka-vat*—like a lamb; *saṁrakṣyamāṇam*—although protected; *miṣataḥ*—of one who is observing; *api*—even; *haranti*—they forcibly take away.

TRANSLATION

My dear King, family members in this material world go under the names of wife and children, but actually they behave like tigers and jackals. A herdsman tries to protect his sheep to the best of his ability, but the tigers and foxes take them away by force. Similarly, although a miserly man wants to guard his money very carefully, his family members take away all his assets forcibly, even though he is very vigilant.

PURPORT

One Hindi poet has sung: *din kā dakinī rāt kā bāghinī pālak pālak rahu cuse.* During the daytime, the wife is compared to a witch, and at night she is compared to a tigress. Her only business is sucking the blood of her husband both day and night. During the day there are household expenditures, and the money earned by the husband at the cost of his blood is taken away. At night, due to sex pleasure, the husband discharges blood in the form of semen. In this way he is bled by his wife both day and night, yet he is so crazy that he very carefully maintains her. Similarly, the children are also like tigers, jackals and foxes. As tigers, jackals and foxes take away lambs despite the herdsman's vigilant protection, children take away the father's money, although the father supervises the money himself. Thus family members may be called wives and children, but actually they are plunderers.

TEXT 4

यथा ह्यनुवत्सरं कृष्यमाणमप्यदग्धबीजं क्षेत्रं पुनरेवावपनकाले गुल्मतृणवीरुद्भिर्गह्वरमिव भवत्येवमेव गृहाश्रमः कर्मक्षेत्रं यस्मिन्न हि कर्माण्युत्सीदन्ति यदयं कामकरण्ड एष आवसथः ॥ ४ ॥

yathā hy anuvatsaraṁ kṛṣyamāṇam apy adagdha-bījaṁ kṣetraṁ punar evāvapana-kāle gulma-tṛṇa-vīrudbhir gahvaram iva bhavaty evam eva gṛhāśramaḥ karma-kṣetraṁ yasmin na hi karmāṇy utsīdanti yad ayaṁ kāma-karaṇḍa eṣa āvasathaḥ.

yathā—just as; *hi*—certainly; *anuvatsaram*—every year; *kṛṣyamāṇam*—being plowed; *api*—although; *adagdha-bījam*—in which the seeds are not burned; *kṣetram*—the field; *punaḥ*—again; *eva*—certainly; *āvapana-kāle*—at the times for sowing the seeds; *gulma*—by bushes; *tṛṇa*—by grasses; *vīrudbhiḥ*—by the creepers; *gahvaram iva*—like a bower; *bhavati*—becomes; *evam*—thus; *eva*—certainly; *gṛha-āśramaḥ*—family life; *karma-kṣetram*—the field of activities; *yasmin*—in which; *na*—not; *hi*—certainly; *karmāṇi utsīdanti*—fruitive activities disappear; *yat*—therefore; *ayam*—this; *kāma-karaṇḍaḥ*—the storehouse of fruitive desire; *eṣaḥ*—this; *āvasathaḥ*—abode.

TRANSLATION

Every year the plowman plows over his grain field, completely uprooting all weeds. Nonetheless, the seeds lie there and, not being completely burned, again come up with the plants sown in the field. Even after being plowed under, the weeds come up densely. Similarly, the gṛhastha-āśrama [family life] is a field of fruitive activity. Unless the desire to enjoy family life is completely burned out, it grows up again and again. Even though camphor may be removed from a pot, the pot nonetheless retains the aroma of camphor. As long as the seeds of desire are not destroyed, fruitive activities are not destroyed.

PURPORT

Unless one's desires are completely transferred to the service of the Supreme Personality of Godhead, the desire for family life continues, even after one has taken *sannyāsa*. Sometimes in our society, ISKCON, a person out of sentiment may take *sannyāsa*, but because his desires are not burned completely, he again takes to family life, even at the risk of losing his prestige and disgracing his good name. These strong desires can be burned out completely when one fully engages in the service of the Lord in devotional service.

TEXT 5

तत्रगतो दंशमशकसमापसदैर्मनुजैः शलभशकुन्ततस्करमूषकादिभिरुपरुध्यमानबहिःप्राणः क्वचित् परिवर्तमानोऽस्मिन्नध्वन्यविद्याकामकर्मभिरुपरक्तमनसानुपपन्नार्थं नरलोकं गन्धर्वनगरमुपपन्नमिति मिथ्यादृष्टिरनुपश्यति ॥ ५ ॥

tatra gato daṁśa-maśaka-samāpasadair manujaiḥ śalabha-śakunta-taskara-mūṣakādibhir uparudhyamāna-bahiḥ-prāṇaḥ kvacit parivartamāno 'sminn adhvany avidyā-kāma-karmabhir uparakta-manasānupapannārthaṁ nara-lokaṁ gandharva-nagaram upapannam iti mithyā-dṛṣṭir anupaśyati.

tatra—to that household life; *gataḥ*—gone; *daṁśa*—gadflies; *maśaka*—mosquitoes; *sama*—equal to; *apasadaiḥ*—who are low-class; *manu-jaiḥ*—by men; *śalabha*—locusts; *śakunta*—a large bird of prey; *taskara*—thieves; *mūṣaka-ādibhiḥ*—by rats and so on; *uparudhyamāna*—being disturbed; *bahiḥ-prāṇaḥ*—the external life air in the form of wealth and so on; *kvacit*—sometimes; *parivartamānaḥ*—wandering; *asmin*—in this; *adhvani*—path of material existence; *avidyā-kāma*—by ignorance and lust; *karmabhiḥ*—and by fruitive activities; *uparakta-manasā*—due to the mind's being influenced; *anupapanna-artham*—in which the desired results are never obtained; *nara-lokam*—this material world; *gandharva-nagaram*—a will-o'-the-wisp city; *upapannam*—existing; *iti*—taking it as; *mithyā-dṛṣṭiḥ*—he whose vision is mistaken; *anupaśyati*—observes.

TRANSLATION

Sometimes the conditioned soul in household life, being attached to material wealth and possessions, is disturbed by gadflies and mosquitoes, and sometimes locusts, birds of prey and rats give him trouble. Nonetheless, he still wanders down the path of material existence. Due to ignorance he becomes lusty and engages in fruitive activity. Because his mind is absorbed in these activities, he sees the material world as permanent, although it is temporary like a phantasmagoria, a house in the sky.

PURPORT

The following song is sung by Narottama dāsa Ṭhākura:

ahaṅkāre matta hañā, nitāi-pada pāsariyā,
asatyere satya kari māni

Due to forgetting the lotus feet of Lord Nityānanda and being puffed up by material possessions, wealth and opulence, one thinks the false, temporary material world to be an actual fact. This is the material disease. The living entity is eternal and blissful, but despite miserable material conditions, he thinks the material world to be real and factual due to his ignorance.

TEXT 6

तत्र च क्वचिदातपोदकनिभान् विषयानुपधावति पानभोजनव्यवायादि-
व्यसनलोलुपः ॥ ६ ॥

tatra ca kvacid ātapodaka-nibhān viṣayān upadhāvati pāna-bhojana-vyavāyādi-vyasana-lolupaḥ.

tatra—there (in this phantom place); *ca*—also; *kvacit*—sometimes; *ātapa-udaka-nibhān*—like the water in a mirage in the desert; *viṣayān*—the objects of sense enjoyment; *upadhāvati*—runs after; *pāna*—to drinking; *bhojana*—to eating; *vyavāya*—to sex life; *ādi*—and so on; *vyasana*—with addiction; *lolupaḥ*—a debauchee.

TRANSLATION

Sometimes in this house in the sky [gandharva-pura] the conditioned soul drinks, eats and has sex. Being overly attached, he chases after the objects of the senses just as a deer chases a mirage in the desert.

PURPORT

There are two worlds—the spiritual and the material. The material world is false like a mirage in the desert. In the desert, animals think they see water, but actually there is none. Similarly, those who are animalistic try to find peace within the desert of material life. It is repeatedly said in different *śāstras* that there is no pleasure in this material world. Furthermore, even if we agree to live without pleasure, we are not allowed to do so. In *Bhagavad-gītā*, Lord Kṛṣṇa says that the material world is not only full of miseries (*duḥkhālayam*) but also temporary (*aśāśvatam*). Even if we want to live here amid miseries, material nature will not allow us to do so. It will oblige us to change bodies and enter another atmosphere full of miserable conditions.

TEXT 7

क्वचिच्चाशेषदोषनिषदनं पुरीषविशेषं तद्वर्णगुणनिर्मितमतिः सुवर्णमुपादित्सत्यग्निकामकातर इवोल्मुकपिशाचम् ॥७॥

kvacic cāśeṣa-doṣa-niṣadanaṁ purīṣa-viśeṣaṁ tad-varṇa-guṇa-nirmita-matiḥ suvarṇam upāditsaty agni-kāma-kātara ivolmuka-piśācam.

kvacit—sometimes; *ca*—also; *aśeṣa*—unlimited; *doṣa*—of faults; *niṣadanam*—the source of; *purīṣa*—of stool; *viśeṣam*—a particular type; *tat-varṇa-guṇa*—whose color is the same as that of the mode of passion (reddish); *nirmita-matiḥ*—whose mind is absorbed in that; *suvarṇam*—gold; *upāditsati*—desiring to get; *agni-kāma*—by the desire for fire; *kāturaḥ*—who is troubled; *iva*—like; *ulmuka-piśācam*—a phosphorescent light known as a will-o'-the-wisp, which is sometimes mistaken for a ghost.

TRANSLATION

Sometimes the living entity is interested in the yellow stool known as gold and runs after it. That gold is the source of material opulence and envy, and it can enable one to afford illicit sex, gambling, meat-eating and intoxication. Those whose minds are overcome by the mode of passion are attracted by the color of gold, just as a man suffering from cold in the forest runs after a phosphorescent light in a marshy land, considering it to be fire.

PURPORT

Parīkṣit Mahārāja told Kali-yuga to leave his kingdom immediately and reside in four places: brothels, liquor shops, slaughterhouses and gambling casinos. However, Kali-yuga requested him to give him only one place where these four places are included, and Parīkṣit Mahārāja gave him the place where gold is stored. Gold encompasses the four principles of sin, and therefore, according to spiritual life, gold should be avoided as far as possible. If there is gold, there is certainly illicit sex, meat-eating, gambling and intoxication. Because people in the Western world have a great deal of gold, they are victims of these four sins. The color of gold is very glittering, and a materialistic person becomes very much attracted by its yellow color. However, this gold is actually a type of stool. A person with a bad liver generally passes yellow stool. The color of this stool attracts a materialistic person, just as the will-o'-the-wisp attracts one who needs heat.

TEXT 8

अथ कदाचिन्निवासपानीयद्रविणाद्यनेकात्मोपजीवनाभिनिवेश एतस्यां
संसाराटव्यामितस्ततः परिधावति ॥८॥

atha kadācin nivāsa-pānīya-draviṇādy-anekātmopajīvanābhiniveśa
etasyāṁ saṁsārāṭavyām itas tataḥ paridhāvati.

atha—in this way; *kadācit*—sometimes; *nivāsa*—residence; *pānīya*—water; *draviṇa*—wealth; *ādi*—and so on; *aneka*—in various items; *ātma-upajīvana*—which are considered necessary to maintain body and soul together; *abhiniveśaḥ*—a person fully absorbed; *etasyām*—in this; *saṁsāra-aṭavyām*—the material world, which is like a great forest; *itaḥ tataḥ*—here and there; *paridhāvati*—runs around.

TRANSLATION

Sometimes the conditioned soul is absorbed in finding residential quarters or apartments and getting a supply of water and riches to maintain his body. Absorbed in acquiring a variety of

necessities, he forgets everything and perpetually runs around the forest of material existence.

PURPORT

As originally mentioned, a poor man belonging to the mercantile community goes to the forest to get some cheap goods to bring back to the city to sell at a profit. He is so absorbed in the thought of maintaining body and soul together that he forgets his original relationship with Kṛṣṇa and seeks only the bodily comforts. Thus material activities are the conditioned soul's only engagement. Not knowing the aim of life, the materialist perpetually wanders in material existence, struggling to get the necessities of life. Not understanding the aim of life, even though he acquires sufficient necessities, he manufactures artificial necessities and thus becomes more and more entangled. He creates a mental situation whereby he needs greater and greater comforts. The materialist does not know the secret of nature's ways. As confirmed in *Bhagavad-gītā* (3.27):

prakṛteḥ kriyamāṇāni
guṇaiḥ karmāṇi sarvaśaḥ
ahaṅkāra-vimūḍhātmā
kartāham iti manyate

"The bewildered spirit soul, under the influence of the three modes of material nature, thinks himself to be the doer of activities which are in actuality carried out by nature." Due to lusty desire, the living entity creates a certain mental situation whereby he wants to enjoy this material world. He thus becomes entangled, enters different bodies and suffers in them.

TEXT 9

क्वचिच्च वात्यौपम्यया प्रमदयाऽऽरोहमारोपितस्तत्कालरजसा रजनीभूत इवासाधुमर्यादो रजस्वलाक्षोऽपि दिग्देवता अतिरजस्वलमतिर्न विजानाति ॥ ९ ॥

kvacic ca vātyaupamyayā pramadayāroham āropitas tat-kāla-rajasā rajanī-bhūta ivāsādhu-maryādo rajas-valākṣo 'pi dig-devatā atirajas-vala-matir na vijānāti.

kvacit—sometimes; *ca*—also; *vātyā aupamyayā*—compared to a whirlwind; *pramadayā*—by a beautiful woman; *āroham āropitaḥ*—raised onto the lap for sex enjoyment; *tat-kāla-rajasā*—by the passion of lusty desires at that moment; *rajanī-bhūtaḥ*—the darkness of night; *iva*—like; *asādhu-maryādaḥ*—who is without proper respect for the higher witnesses; *rajaḥ-vala-akṣaḥ*—blinded by strong lusty desires; *api*—certainly; *dik-devatāḥ*—the demigods in charge of different directions, like the sun and the moon; *atirajaḥ-vala-matiḥ*—whose mind is overcome by lust; *na vijānāti*—he does not know (that witnesses all around take note of his impudent sexual act).

TRANSLATION

Sometimes, as if blinded by the dust of a whirlwind, the conditioned soul sees the beauty of the opposite sex, which is called pramadā. Being thus bewildered, he is raised upon the lap of a woman, and at that time his good senses are overcome by the force of passion. He thus becomes almost blind with lusty desire and disobeys the rules and regulations governing sex life. He does not know that his disobedience is witnessed by different demigods, and he enjoys illicit sex in the dead of night, not seeing the future punishment awaiting him.

PURPORT

In *Bhagavad-gītā* (7.11) it is said: *dharmāviruddho bhūteṣu kāmo 'smi bharatarṣabha.* Sex is allowed only for the begetting of children, not for enjoyment. One can indulge in sex to beget a good child for the benefit of the family, society and world. Otherwise, sex is against the rules and regulations of religious life. A materialistic person does not believe that everything is managed in nature, and he does not know that if one does something wrong, he is witnessed by different demigods. A person enjoys illicit sex, and due to his blind, lusty desire, he thinks that no one can see him, but this illicit sex is thoroughly observed by the agents of the Supreme Personality of Godhead. Therefore the person is punished in so many ways. Presently in Kali-yuga there are many pregnancies due to illicit sex, and sometimes abortions ensue. These sinful activities are witnessed by the agents of the Supreme Personality of Godhead, and a man and woman who create such a situation are punished in the future by the stringent laws of material nature (*daivī hy eṣā guṇamayī mama māyā duratyayā*). Illicit sex is never excused, and those who indulge in it are punished life after life. As confirmed in *Bhagavad-gītā* (16.20):

āsurīṁ yonim āpannā
mūḍhā janmani janmani
mām aprāpyaiva kaunteya
tato yānty adhamāṁ gatim

"Attaining repeated birth among the species of demoniac life, such persons can never approach Me. Gradually they sink down to the most abominable type of existence."

The Supreme Personality of Godhead does not allow anyone to act against the stringent laws of material nature; therefore illicit sex is punished life after life. Illicit sex creates pregnancies, and these unwanted pregnancies lead to abortion. Those involved become implicated in these sins, so much so that they are punished in the same way the next life. Thus in the next life they also enter the womb of a mother and are killed in the same way. All these things can be avoided by remaining on the transcendental platform of Kṛṣṇa consciousness. In this way one does not commit sinful activity. Illicit sex is the most prominent sin due to lusty desire. When one associates with the mode of passion, he is implicated in suffering life after life.

TEXT 10

क्वचित्सकृदवगतविषयवैतथ्यः स्वयं पराभिध्यानेन विभ्रंशितस्मृतिस्तयैव मरीचितोयप्रायांस्तानेवाभिधावति ॥१०॥

kvacit sakṛd avagata-viṣaya-vaitathyaḥ svayaṁ parābhidhyānena
vibhraṁśita-smṛtis tayaiva marīci-toya-prāyāṁs tān evābhidhāvati.

kvacit—sometimes; *sakṛt*—once; *avagata-viṣaya-vaitathyaḥ*—becoming conscious of the uselessness of enjoying material sense gratification; *svayam*—himself; *para-abhidhyānena*—by the bodily concept of the self; *vibhraṁśita*—destroyed; *smṛtiḥ*—whose remembrance; *tayā*—by that; *eva*—certainly; *marīci-toya*—water in a mirage; *prāyān*—similar to; *tān*—those sense objects; *eva*—certainly; *abhidhāvati*—runs after.

TRANSLATION

The conditioned soul sometimes personally appreciates the futility of sense enjoyment in the material world, and he sometimes considers material enjoyment to be full of miseries. However, due to his strong bodily conception, his memory is destroyed, and again and again he runs after material enjoyment, just as an animal runs after a mirage in the desert.

PURPORT

The main disease in material life is the bodily conception. Being baffled again and again in material activity, the conditioned soul temporarily thinks of the futility of material enjoyment, but he again tries the same thing. By the association of devotees, a person may become convinced of the material futility, but he cannot give up his engagement, although he is very eager to return home, back to Godhead. Under these circumstances, the Supreme Personality of Godhead, who is situated in everyone's heart, compassionately takes away all the material possessions of such a devotee. As stated in *Śrīmad-Bhāgavatam* (10.88.8): *yasyāham anugṛhṇāmi hariṣye tad-dhanaṁ śanaiḥ.* Lord Kṛṣṇa says that He takes everything away from the devotee whom He especially favors when that devotee is overly attached to material possessions. When everything is taken away, the devotee feels helpless and frustrated in society, friendship and love. He feels that his family does not care for him any longer, and he therefore completely surrenders unto the lotus feet of the Supreme Lord. This is a special favor granted by the Lord to a devotee who cannot fully surrender to the Lord due to a strong bodily conception. As explained in *Caitanya-caritāmṛta* (*Madhya* 22.39): *āmi——vijña, ei mūrkhe 'viṣaya' kene diba.* The Lord understands the devotee who hesitates to engage in the Lord's service, not knowing whether he should again try to revive his material life. After repeated attempts and failures, he fully surrenders to the lotus feet of the Lord. The Lord then gives him directions, and, attaining happiness, he forgets all material engagement.

TEXT 11

क्वचिदुलूकझिल्लीस्वनवदतिपरुषरभसाटोपं प्रत्यक्षं परोक्षं वा रिपुराजकुल-
निर्भर्त्सितेनातिव्यथितकर्णमूलहृदयः ॥ ११ ॥

kvacid ulūka-jhillī-svanavad ati-paruṣa-rabhasāṭopaṁ pratyakṣaṁ parokṣaṁ vā ripu-rāja-kula-nirbhartsitenāti-vyathita-karṇa-mūla-hṛdayaḥ.

kvacit—sometimes; *ulūka*—of the owl; *jhillī*—and the cricket; *svana-vat*—exactly like intolerable sounds; *ati-paruṣa*—extremely piercing; *rabhasa*—by perseverance; *āṭopam*—agitation; *pratyakṣam*—directly; *parokṣam*—indirectly; *vā*—or; *ripu*—of enemies; *rāja-kula*—and of government officers; *nirbhartsitena*—by chastisement; *ati-vyathita*—very aggrieved; *karṇa-mūla-hṛdayaḥ*—whose ear and heart.

TRANSLATION

Sometimes the conditioned soul is very aggrieved by the chastisement of his enemies and government servants, who use harsh words against him directly or indirectly. At that time his heart and ears become very saddened. Such chastisement may be compared to the sounds of owls and crickets.

PURPORT

There are different types of enemies within this material world. The government chastises one due to not paying income taxes. Such criticism, direct or indirect, saddens one, and sometimes the conditioned soul tries to counteract that chastisement. Unfortunately, he cannot do anything.

TEXT 12

स यदा दुग्धपूर्वसुकृतस्तदा कारस्करकाकतुण्डाद्यपुण्यद्रुमलताविषोदपानवदुभयार्थशून्यद्रविणान् जीवन्मृतान् स्वयं जीवन्म्रियमाण उपधावति ॥१२॥

sa yadā dugdha-pūrva-sukṛtas tadā kāraskara-kākatuṇḍādy-apuṇya-druma-latā-viṣoda-pānavad ubhayārtha-śūnya-draviṇān jīvan-mṛtān svayaṁ jīvan-mriyamāṇa upadhāvati.

saḥ—that conditioned soul; *yadā*—when; *dugdha*—exhausted; *pūrva*—previous; *sukṛtaḥ*—pious activities; *tadā*—at that time; *kāraskara-kākatuṇḍa-ādi*—named *kāraskara, kākatuṇḍa,* etc.; *apuṇya-druma-latā*—impious trees and creepers; *viṣa-uda-pāna-vat*—like wells with poisonous water; *ubhaya-artha-śūnya*—which cannot give happiness either in this life or in the next; *draviṇān*—those who possess wealth; *jīvat-mṛtān*—who are dead, although apparently alive; *svayam*—he himself; *jīvat*—living; *mriyamāṇaḥ*—being dead; *upadhāvati*—approaches for material acquisition.

TRANSLATION

Due to his pious activities in previous lives, the conditioned soul attains material facilities in this life, but when they are finished, he takes shelter of wealth and riches, which cannot help him in this life or the next. Because of this, he approaches the living dead who possess these things. Such people are compared to impure trees, creepers and poisonous wells.

PURPORT

The wealth and riches acquired through previous pious activities should not be misused for sense gratification. Enjoying them for sense gratification is like enjoying the fruits of a poisonous tree. Such activities will not help the conditioned soul in any way, neither in this life nor the next. However, if one engages his possessions in the service of the Lord under the guidance of a proper spiritual master, he will attain happiness both in this life and the next. Unless he does so, he eats a forbidden apple and thereby loses his paradise. Lord Śrī Kṛṣṇa therefore advises that one's possessions should be given unto Him.

yat karoṣi yad aśnāsi
yaj juhoṣi dadāsi yat
yat tapasyasi kaunteya
tat kuruṣva mad-arpaṇam

"O son of Kuntī, all that you do, all that you eat, all that you offer and give away, as well as all austerities that you may perform, should be done as an offering unto Me." (Bg. 9.27) Material wealth and opulence attained through previous pious activities can be fully utilized for one's benefit in this life and the next if one is Kṛṣṇa conscious. One should not try to possess more than he needs for the bare necessities. If one gets more than is needed, the surplus should be fully engaged in the Lord's service. That will make the conditioned soul, the world and Kṛṣṇa happy, and this is the aim of life.

TEXT 13

एकदासत्प्रसङ्गान्निकृतमतिर्व्युदकस्रोतःस्खलनवदुभयतोऽपि दुःखदं पाखण्डमभियाति ॥१३॥

ekadāsat-prasaṅgān nikṛta-matir vyudaka-srotaḥ-skhalanavad
ubhayato 'pi duḥkhadaṁ pākhaṇḍam abhiyāti.

ekadā—sometimes; *asat-prasaṅgāt*—by association of nondevotees who are against the Vedic principles and who manufacture different paths of religion; *nikṛta-matiḥ*—whose intelligence has been brought to the abominable status of defying the authority of the Supreme Personality of Godhead; *vyudaka-srotaḥ*—into rivers without sufficient water; *skhalana-vat*—like jumping; *ubhayataḥ*—from both sides; *api*—although; *duḥkha-dam*—giving distress; *pākhaṇḍam*—the atheistic path; *abhiyāti*—he approaches.

TRANSLATION

Sometimes, to mitigate distresses in this forest of the material world, the conditioned soul receives cheap blessings from atheists.

He then loses all intelligence in their association. This is exactly like jumping in a shallow river. As a result one simply breaks his head. He is not able to mitigate his sufferings from the heat, and in both ways he suffers. The misguided conditioned soul also approaches so-called sādhus and svāmīs who preach against the principles of the Vedas. He does not receive benefit from them, either in the present or in the future.

PURPORT

Cheaters are always there to manufacture their own way of spiritual realization. To get some material benefit, the conditioned soul approaches these pseudo *sannyāsīs* and *yogīs* for cheap blessings, but he does not receive any benefit from them, either spiritual or material. In this age there are many cheaters who show some jugglery and magic. They even create gold to amaze their followers, and their followers accept them as God. This type of cheating is very prominent in Kali-yuga. Viśvanātha Cakravatī Ṭhākura describes the real *guru* in this way.

saṁsāra-dāvānala-līḍha-loka-
trāṇāya kāruṇya-ghanāghanatvam
prāptasya kalyāṇa-guṇārṇavasya
vande guroḥ śrī-caraṇāravindam

One should approach a *guru* who can extinguish the blazing fire of this material world, the struggle for existence. People want to be cheated, and therefore they go to *yogīs* and *svāmīs* who play tricks, but tricks do not mitigate the miseries of material life. If being able to manufacture gold is a criterion for becoming God, then why not accept Kṛṣṇa, the proprietor of the entire universe, wherein there are countless tons of gold? As mentioned before, the color of gold is compared to the will-o'-the-wisp or yellow stool; therefore one should not be allured by gold-manufacturing *gurus* but should sincerely approach a devotee like Jaḍa Bharata. Jaḍa Bharata instructed Rahūgaṇa Mahārāja so well that the King was relieved from the bodily conception. One cannot become happy by accepting a false *guru*. A *guru* should be accepted as advised in *Śrīmad-Bhāgavatam* (11.3.21). *Tasmād guruṁ prapadyeta jijñāsuḥ śreya uttamam:* One should approach a bona fide *guru* to inquire about the highest benefit of life. Such a *guru* is described as follows: *śābde pare ca niṣṇātam.* Such a *guru* does not manufacture gold or juggle words. He is well versed in the conclusions of Vedic knowledge (*vedaiś ca sarvair aham eva vedyaḥ*). He is freed from all material contamination and is fully engaged in Kṛṣṇa's service. If one is able to obtain the dust of the lotus feet of such a *guru*, his life becomes successful. Otherwise he is baffled both in this life and in the next.

TEXT 14

यदा तु परबाधयान्ध आत्मने नोपनमति तदा हि पितृपुत्रबर्हिष्मतः पितृपुत्रान् वा स खलु भक्षयति ॥१४॥

yadā tu para-bādhayāndha ātmane nopanamati tadā hi pitṛ-putra-barhiṣmataḥ pitṛ-putrān vā sa khalu bhakṣayati.

yadā—when; *tu*—but (because of misfortune); *para-bādhayā*—in spite of exploiting all others; *andhaḥ*—blind; *ātmane*—for himself; *na upanamati*—does not fall into one's share; *tadā*—at that time; *hi*—certainly; *pitṛ-putra*—of the father or sons; *barhiṣmataḥ*—as insignificant as a piece of grass; *pitṛ-putrān*—father or sons; *vā*—or; *saḥ*—he (the conditioned soul); *khalu*—indeed; *bhakṣayati*—gives trouble to.

TRANSLATION

In this material world, when the conditioned soul cannot arrange for his own maintenance, despite exploiting others, he tries to exploit his own father or son, taking away that relative's possessions, although they may be very insignificant. If he cannot acquire things from his father, son or other relatives, he is prepared to give them all kinds of trouble.

PURPORT

Once we actually saw a distressed man steal ornaments from his daughter just to maintain himself. As the English proverb goes, necessity knows no law. When a conditioned soul needs something, he forgets his relationship with his relatives and exploits his own father or son. We also receive information from *Śrīmad-Bhāgavatam* that in this age of Kali the time is quickly approaching when a relative will kill another relative for a small farthing. Without Kṛṣṇa consciousness, people will deteriorate further and further into a hellish condition wherein they will perform abominable acts.

TEXT 15

कचिदासाद्य गृहं दाववत्प्रियार्थविधुरमसुखोदर्कं शोकाग्निना दह्यमानो भृशं निर्वेदमुपगच्छति ॥१५॥

kvacid āsādya gṛhaṁ dāvavat priyārtha-vidhuram asukhodarkaṁ
śokāgninā dahyamāno bhṛśaṁ nirvedam upagacchati.

kvacit—sometimes; *āsādya*—experiencing; *gṛham*—the home life; *dāva-vat*—exactly like a blazing fire in the forest; *priya-artha-vidhuram*—without any beneficial object; *asukha-udarkam*—resulting only in more and more unhappiness; *śoka-agninā*—by the fire of lamentation; *dahyamānaḥ*—being burned; *bhṛśam*—very great; *nirvedam*—disappointment; *upagacchati*—he obtains.

TRANSLATION

In this world, family life is exactly like a blazing fire in the forest. There is not the least happiness, and gradually one becomes more and more implicated in unhappiness. In household life, there is nothing favorable for perpetual happiness. Being implicated in home life, the conditioned soul is burned by the fire of lamentation. Sometimes he condemns himself as being very unfortunate, and sometimes he claims that he suffers because he performed no pious activities in his previous life.

PURPORT

In the *Gurv-aṣṭaka*, Śrīla Viśvanātha Cakravatī Ṭhākura has sung:

saṁsāra-dāvānala-līḍha-loka-
trāṇāya kāruṇya-ghanāghanatvam

A life in this material world is exactly like a blazing forest fire. No one goes to set fire to the forest, yet the fire takes place. Similarly, everyone wants to be happy in the material world, but the miserable conditions of material life simply increase. Sometimes a person caught in the blazing fire of material existence condemns himself, but due to his bodily conception he cannot get out of the entanglement, and thus he suffers more and more.

TEXT 16

क्वचित्कालविषमितराजकुलरक्षसापहृतप्रियतमधनासुः प्रमृतक इव विगतजीवलक्षण आस्ते॥ १६॥

kvacit kāla-viṣa-mita-rāja-kula-rakṣasāpahṛta-priyatama-dhanāsuḥ pramṛtaka iva vigata-jīva-lakṣaṇa āste.

kvacit—sometimes; *kāla-viṣa-mita*—made crooked by time; *rāja-kula*—the government men; *rakṣasā*—by those who are like carnivorous human beings; *apahṛta*—being plundered; *priya-tama*—most dear; *dhana*—in the form of wealth; *asuḥ*—whose life air; *pramṛtakaḥ*—dead; *iva*—like; *vigata-jīva-lakṣaṇaḥ*—bereft of all signs of life; *āste*—he remains.

TRANSLATION

Government men are always like carnivorous demons called Rākṣasas [man-eaters]. Sometimes these government men turn against the conditioned soul and take away all his accumulated wealth. Being bereft of his life's reserved wealth, the conditioned soul loses all enthusiasm. Indeed, it is as though he loses his life.

PURPORT

The word *rāja-kula-rakṣasā* is very significant. *Śrīmad-Bhāgavatam* was compiled about five thousand years ago, yet government men are referred to as Rākṣasas, or carnivorous demons. If government men are opposed to a person, that person will be bereft of all his riches, which he has accumulated with great care over a long period of time. Actually no one wants to pay income taxes—even government men themselves try to avoid these taxes—but at unfavorable times income taxes are exacted forcibly, and the taxpayers become very morose.

TEXT 17

कदाचिन्मनोरथोपगतपितृपितामहाद्यसत्सदिति स्वप्ननिर्वृतिलक्षणमनुभवति॥१७॥

kadācin manorathopagata-pitṛ-pitāmahādy asat sad iti svapna-nirvṛti-lakṣaṇam anubhavati.

kadācit—sometimes; *manoratha-upagata*—obtained by mental concoction; *pitṛ*—the father; *pitā-maha-ādi*—or grandfather and others; *asat*—although long dead (and although no one knows that the soul has gone); *sat*—again the father or grandfather has come; *iti*—thus thinking; *svapna-nirvṛti-lakṣaṇam*—the kind of happiness found in dreams; *anubhavati*—the conditioned soul feels.

TRANSLATION

Sometimes the conditioned soul imagines that his father or grandfather has again come in the form of his son or grandson. In this way he feels the happiness one sometimes feels in a dream, and the conditioned soul sometimes takes pleasure in such mental concoctions.

PURPORT

Due to ignorance of the real existence of the Lord, the conditioned soul imagines many things. Influenced by fruitive activity, he comes together with his relatives, fathers, sons and grandfathers, exactly as straws gather together in a moving stream. In a moment the straws are thrown everywhere, and they lose contact. In conditional life, the living entity is temporarily with many other conditioned souls. They gather together as family members, and the material affection is so strong that even after a father or grandfather passes away, one takes pleasure in thinking that they return to the family in different forms. Sometimes this may happen. but in any case the conditioned soul likes to take pleasure in such concocted thoughts.

TEXT 18

क्वचिद् गृहाश्रमकर्मचोदनातिभरगिरिमारुरुक्षमाणो लोकव्यसनकर्षितमनाः कण्टकशर्कराक्षेत्रं प्रविशन्निव सीदति ॥१८॥

kvacid gṛhāśrama-karma-codanāti-bhara-girim āurukṣamāṇo loka-vyasana-karṣita-manāḥ kaṇṭaka-śarkarā-kṣetraṁ praviśann iva sīdati.

kvacit—sometimes; *gṛha-āśrama*—in householder life; *karma-codana*—of the rules of fruitive activity; *ati-bhara-girim*—the big hill; *ārurukṣamāṇaḥ*—desiring to ascend; *loka*—material; *vyasana*—to pursuits; *karṣita-manāḥ*—whose mind is attracted; *kaṇṭaka-śarkarā-kṣetram*—a field covered with thorns and sharp pebbles; *praviśan*—entering; *iva*—like; *sīdati*—he laments.

TRANSLATION

In household life one is ordered to execute many yajñas and fruitive activities, especially the vivāha-yajña [the marriage ceremony for sons and daughters] and the sacred thread ceremony. These are all the duties of a gṛhastha, and they are very extensive and troublesome to execute. They are compared to a big hill over which one must cross when one is attached to material activities. A person desiring to cross over these ritualistic ceremonies certainly feels pains like the piercing of thorns and pebbles endured by one attempting to climb a hill. Thus the conditioned soul suffers unlimitedly.

PURPORT

There are many social functions for keeping a prestigious position in society. In different countries and societies there are various festivals and rituals. In India, the father is supposed to get his children married. When he does so, his responsibility to the family is complete. Arranging marriages is very difficult, especially in these days. At the present moment no one can perform the proper ritual of sacrifice, nor can anyone afford to pay for the marriage ceremony of sons and daughters. Therefore householders are very much distressed when they are confronted by these social duties. It is as though they were pierced by thorns and hurt by pebbles. Material attachment is so strong that despite the suffering, one cannot give it up. Prahlāda Mahārāja therefore recommends (*Bhāg.* 7.5.5):

hitvātma-pātaṁ gṛham andha-kūpaṁ
vanaṁ gato yad dharim āśrayeta

The so-called comfortable family position is compared to a dark well in a field. If one falls in a dark well covered by grass, his life is lost, despite his cry for rescue. Highly advanced spiritualists therefore recommend that one should not enter the *gṛhastha-āśrama.* It is better to prepare oneself in the *brahmacarya-āśrama* for austerities and remain a pure *brahmacārī* throughout one's life so that one will not feel the piercing thorns of material life in the *gṛhastha-āśrama.* In the *gṛhastha-āśrama* one has to accept invitations from friends and relatives and perform ritualistic ceremonies. By so doing, one becomes captivated by such things, although he may not have sufficient resources to continue them. To maintain the *gṛhastha* life-style, one has to work very hard to acquire money. Thus one is implicated in material life, and he suffers the thorn pricks.

TEXT 19

क्वचिच्च दुःसहेन कायाभ्यन्तरवह्निना गृहीतसारः स्वकुटुम्बाय क्रुध्यति ॥१९॥

kvacic ca duḥsahena kāyābhyantara-vahninā gṛhīta-sāraḥ sva-kuṭumbāya krudhyati.

kvacit ca—and sometimes; *duḥsahena*—unbearable; *kāya-abhyantara-vahninā*—because of the fire of hunger and thirst within the body; *gṛhīta-sāraḥ*—whose patience is exhausted; *sva-kuṭumbāya*—unto his own family members; *krudhyati*—he becomes angry.

TRANSLATION

Sometimes, due to bodily hunger and thirst, the conditioned soul becomes so disturbed that he loses his patience and becomes angry with his own beloved sons, daughters and wife. Thus, being unkind to them, he suffers all the more.

PURPORT

Śrīla Vidyāpati Ṭhākura has sung:

tātala saikate, vāri-bindu-sama,
suta-mita-ramaṇī-samāje

The happiness of family life is compared to a drop of water in the desert. No one can be happy in family life. According to the Vedic civilization, one cannot give up the responsibilities of family life, but today everyone is giving up family life by divorce. This is due to the miserable condition experienced in the family. Sometimes, due to misery, one becomes very hardened toward his affectionate sons, daughters and wife. This is but part of the blazing fire of the forest of material life.

TEXT 20

स एव पुनर्निद्राजगरगृहीतोऽन्धे तमसि मग्नः शून्यारण्य इव शेते नान्यत्किञ्चन वेद शव इवापविद्धः ॥ २० ॥

sa eva punar nidrājagara-gṛhīto 'ndhe tamasi magnaḥ śūnyāraṇya iva śete nānyat-kiñcana veda śava ivāpaviddhaḥ.

saḥ—that conditioned soul; *eva*—certainly; *punaḥ*—again; *nidrā-ajagara*—by the python of deep sleep; *gṛhītaḥ*—being devoured; *andhe*—in deep darkness; *tamasi*—in ignorance; *magnaḥ*—being absorbed; *śūnya-araṇye*—in the isolated forest; *iva*—like; *śete*—he lies down; *na*—not; *anyat*—else; *kiñcana*—anything; *veda*—knows; *śavaḥ*—a dead body; *iva*—like; *apaviddhaḥ*—thrown away.

TRANSLATION

Śukadeva Gosvāmī continued speaking to Mahārāja Parīkṣit: My dear King, sleep is exactly like a python. Those who wander in the forest of material life are always devoured by the python of sleep. Being bitten by this python, they always remain in the darkness of ignorance. They are like dead bodies thrown in a distant forest. Thus the conditioned souls cannot understand what is going on in life.

PURPORT

Material life means being fully absorbed in eating, sleeping, mating and defending. Out of these, sleep is taken very seriously. While asleep, one completely forgets the object of life and what to do. For spiritual realization, one should try to avoid sleep as much as possible. The Gosvāmīs of Vṛndāvana practically did not sleep at all. Of course, they slept some, for the body requires sleep, but they slept only about two hours, and sometimes not even that. They always engaged in spiritual cultivation. *Nidrāhāra-vihārakādi-vijitau.* Following in the footsteps of the Gosvāmīs, we should try to reduce sleeping, eating, mating and defending.

TEXT 21

कदाचिद्भग्नमानदंष्ट्रो दुर्जनदन्दशूकैरलब्धनिद्राक्षणो व्यथित-
हृदयेनानुक्षीयमाणविज्ञानोऽन्धकूपेऽन्धवत्पतति ॥ २१ ॥

kadācid bhagna-māna-daṁṣṭro durjana-danda-śūkair alabdha-nidrā-kṣaṇo vyathita-hṛdayenānukṣīyamāṇa-vijñāno 'ndha-kūpe 'ndhavat patati.

kadācit—sometimes; *bhagna-māna-daṁṣṭraḥ*—whose teeth of pride are broken; *durjana-danda-śūkaiḥ*—by the envious activities of evil men, who are compared to a kind of serpent; *alabdha-nidrā-kṣaṇaḥ*—who does not get an opportunity to sleep; *vyathita-hṛdayena*—by a disturbed mind; *anukṣīyamāṇa*—gradually being decreased; *vijñānaḥ*—whose real consciousness; *andha-kūpe*—in a blind well; *andha-vat*—like illusion; *patati*—he falls down.

TRANSLATION

In the forest of the material world, the conditioned soul is sometimes bitten by envious enemies, which are compared to serpents and other creatures. Through the tricks of the enemy, the conditioned soul falls from his prestigious position. Being anxious, he cannot even sleep properly. He thus becomes more and more unhappy, and he gradually loses his intelligence and

consciousness. In that state he becomes almost perpetually like a blind man who has fallen into a dark well of ignorance.

TEXT 22

कर्हि स्म चित्काममधुलवान् विचिन्वन् यदा परदारपरद्रव्याण्यवरुन्धानो
राज्ञा स्वामिभिर्वा निहतः पतत्यपारे निरये ॥२२॥

karhi sma cit kāma-madhu-lavān vicinvan yadā para-dāra-para-drav-yāṇy avarundhāno rājñā svāmibhir vā nihataḥ pataty apāre niraye.

karhi sma cit—sometimes; *kāma-madhu-lavān*—little drops of honeylike sense gratification; *vicinvan*—searching after; *yadā*—when; *para-dāra*—another's wife, or a woman other than his own wife; *para-dravyāṇi*—another's money and possessions; *avarundhānaḥ*—taking as his own property; *rājñā*—by the government; *svāmibhiḥ vā*—or by the husband or relatives of the woman; *nihataḥ*—severely beaten; *patati*—he falls down; *apāre*—into unlimitedly; *niraye*—hellish conditions of life (the government's prison for criminal activities like rape, kidnapping or theft of others' property).

TRANSLATION

The conditioned soul is sometimes attracted to the little happiness derived from sense gratification. Thus he has illicit sex or steals another's property. At such a time he may be arrested by the government or chastised by the woman's husband or protector. Thus simply for a little material satisfaction, he falls into a hellish condition and is put into jail for rape, kidnapping, theft and so forth.

PURPORT

Material life is such that due to indulgence in illicit sex, gambling, intoxication and meat-eating, the conditioned soul is always in a dangerous condition. Meat-eating and intoxication excite the senses more and more, and the conditioned soul falls victim to women. In order to keep women, money is required, and to acquire money, one begs, borrows or steals. Indeed, he commits abominable acts that cause him to suffer both in this life and in the next. Consequently illicit sex must be stopped by those who are spiritually inclined or who are on the path of spiritual realization. Many devotees fall down due to illicit sex. They may steal money and even fall down from the highly honored renounced order. Then for a livelihood they accept menial services and become beggars. It is therefore said in the *śāstras, yan maithunādi-gṛhamedhi-sukhaṁ hi tuccham:* materialism is based on sex, whether licit or illicit. Sex is full of dangers even for those who are addicted to household life. Whether one has a license for sex or not, there is great trouble. *Bahu-duḥkha-bhāk:* after one indulges in sex, many volumes of miseries ensue. One suffers more and more in material life. A miserly person cannot properly utilize the wealth he has, and similarly a materialistic person misuses the human form. Instead of using it for spiritual emancipation, he uses the body for sense gratification. Therefore he is called a miser.

TEXT 23

अथ च तस्मादुभयथापि हि कर्मास्मिन्नात्मनः संसारावपनमुदाहरन्ति ॥२३॥

atha ca tasmād ubhayathāpi hi karmāsminn ātmanaḥ saṁsārāvapanam udāharanti.

atha—now; *ca*—and; *tasmāt*—because of this; *ubhayathā api*—both in this life and in the next; *hi*—undoubtedly; *karma*—fruitive activities; *asmin*—on this path of sense enjoyment; *ātmanaḥ*—of the living entity; *saṁsāra*—of material life; *āvapanam*—the cultivation ground or source; *udāharanti*—the authorities of the *Vedas* say.

TRANSLATION

Learned scholars and transcendentalists therefore condemn the materialistic path of fruitive activity because it is the original source and breeding ground of material miseries, both in this life and in the next.

PURPORT

Not knowing the value of life, *karmīs* create situations whereby they suffer in this life and the next. Unfortunately, *karmīs* are very attached to material sense gratification, and they cannot appreciate the miserable condition of material life, neither in this life nor in the next. Therefore the *Vedas* enjoin that one should awaken to spiritual consciousness and utilize all his activities to attain the favor of the Supreme Personality of Godhead. The Lord Himself says in *Bhagavad-gītā* (9.27):

yat karoṣi yad aśnāsi
yaj juhoṣi dadāsi yat
yat tapasyasi kaunteya
tat kuruṣva mad-arpaṇam

"O son of Kuntī, all that you do, all that you eat, all that you offer and give away, as well as all austerities that you may perform, should be done as an offering unto Me."

The results of all one's activities should be utilized not for sense gratification but for the mission of the Supreme Personality of Godhead. The Supreme Lord gives all information in *Bhagavad-gītā* about the aim of life, and at the end of *Bhagavad-gītā* He demands surrender unto Him. People do not generally like this demand, but one who cultivates spiritual knowledge for many births eventually surrenders unto the lotus feet of the Lord (*bahūnāṁ janmanām ante jñānavān māṁ prapadyate*).

TEXT 24

मुक्तस्ततो यदि बन्धाद्देवदत्त उपाच्छिनत्ति तस्मादपि विष्णुमित्र इत्यनवस्थितिः ॥ २४ ॥

muktas tato yadi bandhād devadatta upācchinatti tasmād api viṣṇumitra ity anavasthitiḥ.

muktaḥ—liberated; *tataḥ*—from that; *yadi*—if; *bandhāt*—from the government imprisonment or being beaten by the protector of the woman; *deva-dattaḥ*—person named Devadatta; *upācchinatti*—takes the money from him; *tasmāt*—from the person named Devadatta; *api*—again; *viṣṇu-mitraḥ*—a person named Viṣṇumitra; *iti*—thus; *anavasthitiḥ*—the riches do not stay in one place but pass from one hand to another.

TRANSLATION

Stealing or cheating another person out of his money, the conditioned soul somehow or other keeps it in his possession and escapes punishment. Then another man, named Devadatta, cheats him and takes the money away. Similarly, another man, named Viṣṇumitra, steals the money from Devadatta and takes it away. In any case, the money does not stay in one place. It passes from one hand to another. Ultimately no one can enjoy the money, and it remains the property of the Supreme Personality of Godhead.

PURPORT

Riches come from Lakṣmī, the goddess of fortune, and the goddess of fortune is the property of Nārāyaṇa, the Supreme Personality of Godhead. The goddess of fortune cannot stay anywhere but by the side of Nārāyaṇa; therefore another of her names is Cañcalā, restless. She cannot be peaceful unless she is in the company of her husband, Nārāyaṇa. For example, Lakṣmī was carried away by the materialistic Rāvaṇa. Rāvaṇa kidnapped Sītā, the goddess of fortune belonging to Lord Rāma. As a result, Rāvaṇa's entire family, opulence and kingdom were smashed, and Sītā, the goddess of fortune, was recovered from his clutches and reunited with Lord Rāma. Thus all property, riches and wealth belong to Kṛṣṇa. As stated in *Bhagavad-gītā* (5.29):

bhoktāraṁ yajña-tapasāṁ
sarva-loka-maheśvaram

"The Supreme Personality of Godhead is the true beneficiary of all sacrifices and austerities, and He is the supreme proprietor of all the planetary systems."

Foolish materialistic people collect money and steal from other thieves, but they cannot keep it. In any case, it must be spent. One person cheats another, and another person cheats someone else; therefore the best way to possess Lakṣmī is to keep her by the side of Nārāyaṇa. This is the point of the Kṛṣṇa consciousness movement. We worship Lakṣmī (Rādhārāṇī) along with Nārāyaṇa (Kṛṣṇa). We collect money from various sources, but that money does not belong to anyone but Rādhā and Kṛṣṇa (Lakṣmī-

Nārāyaṇa). If money is utilized in the service of Lakṣmī-Nārāyaṇa, the devotee automatically lives in an opulent way. However, if one wants to enjoy Lakṣmī the way Rāvaṇa did, he will be vanquished by the laws of nature, and whatever few possessions he has will be taken away. Finally death will take everything away, and death is the representative of Kṛṣṇa.

TEXT 25

क्वचिच्च शीतवाताद्यनेकाधिदैविकभौतिकात्मीयानां दशानां प्रतिनिवारणेऽकल्पो दुरन्तचिन्तया विषण्ण आस्ते ॥२५॥

kvacic ca śīta-vātādy-anekādhidaivika-bhautikātmīyānāṁ daśānāṁ pratinivāraṇe 'kalpo duranta-cintayā viṣaṇṇa āste.

kvacit—sometimes; *ca*—also; *śīta-vāta-ādi*—such as cold and strong wind; *aneka*—various; *adhidaivika*—created by the demigods; *bhautika*—*adhibhautika,* created by other living beings; *ātmīyānām*—*adhyātmika,* created by the body and mind; *daśānām*—of conditions of misery; *pratinivāraṇe*—in the counteracting; *akalpaḥ*—unable; *duranta*—very severe; *cintayā*—by anxieties; *viṣaṇṇaḥ*—morose; *āste*—he remains.

TRANSLATION

Being unable to protect himself from the threefold miseries of material existence, the conditioned soul becomes very morose and lives a life of lamentation. These threefold miseries are miseries suffered by mental calamity at the hands of the demigods [such as freezing wind and scorching heat], miseries offered by other living entities, and miseries arising from the mind and body themselves.

PURPORT

The so-called happy materialistic person is constantly having to endure the threefold miseries of life, called *adhidaivika, adhyātmika* and *adhibhautika.* Actually no one can counteract these threefold miseries. All three may assail one at one time, or one misery may be absent and the other present. Thus the living entity is full of anxiety, fearing misery from one side or the other. The conditioned soul must be disturbed by at least one of these three miseries. There is no escape.

TEXT 26

क्वचिन्मिथो व्यवहरन् यत्किञ्चिद्धनमन्येभ्यो वा काकिणिकामात्रमप्यपहरन्
यत्किञ्चिद्वा विद्वेषमेति वित्तशाठ्यात् ॥ २६ ॥

kvacin mitho vyavaharan yat kiñcid dhanam anyebhyo vā kākiṇikā-mātram apy apaharan yat kiñcid vā vidveṣam eti vitta-śāṭhyāt.

kvacit—sometimes; *mithaḥ*—with one another; *vyavaharan*—trading; *yat kiñcit*—whatever little bit; *dhanam*—money; *anyebhyaḥ*—from others; *vā*—or; *kākiṇikā-mātram*—a very small amount (twenty cowries); *api*—certainly; *apaharan*—taking away by cheating; *yat kiñcit*—whatever small amount; *vā*—or; *vidveṣam eti*—creates enmity; *vitta-śāṭhyāt*—because of cheating.

TRANSLATION

As far as transactions with money are concerned, if one person cheats another by a farthing or less, they become enemies.

PURPORT

This is called *saṁsāra-dāvānala.* Even in ordinary transactions between two people, there is invariably cheating because the conditioned soul is defective in four ways—he is illusioned, he commits mistakes, his knowledge is imperfect, and he has a propensity to cheat. Unless one is liberated from material conditioning, these four defects must be there. Consequently every man has a cheating propensity, which is employed in business or money transactions. Although two friends may be living peacefully together, due to their propensity to cheat they become enemies when there is a transaction between them. A philosopher accuses an economist of being a cheater, and an economist may accuse a philosopher of being a cheater when he comes in contact with money. In any case, this is the condition of material life. One may profess a high philosophy, but when one is in need of money, he becomes a cheater. In this material world, so-called scientists, philosophers and economists are nothing but cheaters in one way or another. The scientists are cheaters because they present so many bogus things in the name of science. They propose going to the moon, but actually they end up cheating the entire public of large sums of money for their experiments. They cannot do anything useful. Unless one can find a person transcendental to the four basic defects, one should not accept advice and become a victim of the material condition. The best process is to take the advice and instructions of Śrī Kṛṣṇa or His bona fide representative. In this way one can be happy in this life and the next.

TEXT 27

**अध्वन्यमुष्मिन्निम उपसर्गास्तथा सुखदुःखरागद्वेषभयाभिमानप्रमादोन्माद-
शोकमोहलोभमात्सर्येर्ष्यावमानक्षुत्पिपासाधिव्याधिजन्मजरामरणादयः॥२७॥**

adhvany amuṣminn ima upasargās tathā sukha-duḥkha-rāga-dveṣa-bhayābhimāna-pramādonmāda-śoka-moha-lobha-mātsaryerṣyāva-māna-kṣut-pipāsādhi-vyādhi-janma-jarā-maraṇādayaḥ.

adhvani—on the path of material life; *amuṣmin*—on that; *ime*—all these; *upasargāḥ*—eternal difficulties; *tathā*—so much also; *sukha*—so-called happiness; *duḥkha*—unhappiness; *rāga*—attachment; *dveṣa*—hate; *bhaya*—fear; *abhimāna*—false prestige; *pramāda*—illusion; *un-māda*—madness; *śoka*—lamentation; *moha*—bewilderment; *lobha*—greed; *mātsarya*—envy; *īrṣya*—enmity; *avamāna*—insult; *kṣut*—hunger; *pipāsā*—thirst; *ādhi*—tribulations; *vyādhi*—disease; *janma*—birth; *jarā*—old age; *maraṇa*—death; *ādayaḥ*—and so on.

TRANSLATION

In this materialistic life, there are many difficulties, as I have just mentioned, and all of these are insurmountable. In addition, there are difficulties arising from so-called happiness, distress, attachment, hate, fear, false prestige, illusion, madness, lamentation, bewilderment, greed, envy, enmity, insult, hunger, thirst, tribulation, disease, birth, old age and death. All these combine

together to give the materialistic conditioned soul nothing but misery.

PURPORT

The conditioned soul has to accept all these conditions simply to enjoy sense gratification in this world. Although people declare themselves great scientists, economists, philosophers, politicians and sociologists, they are actually nothing but rascals. Therefore they have been described as *mūḍhas* and *narādhamas* in *Bhagavad-gītā* (7.15):

na māṁ duṣkṛtino mūḍhāḥ
prapadyante narādhamāḥ
māyayāpahṛta-jñānā
āsuraṁ bhāvam āśritāḥ

"Those miscreants who are grossly foolish, lowest among mankind, whose knowledge is stolen by illusion, and who partake of the atheistic nature of demons, do not surrender unto Me."

Due to their foolishness, all these materialists are described in *Bhagavad-gītā* as *narādhamas.* They have attained the human form in order to get released from material bondage, but instead of doing so, they become further embarrassed amid the miserable material conditions. Therefore they are *narādhamas,* the lowest of men. One may ask whether scientists, philosophers, economists and mathematicians are also *narādhamas,* the lowest of men, and the Supreme Personality of Godhead replies that they are because they have no actual knowledge. They are simply proud of their false prestige and position. Actually they do not know how to get relief from the material condition and renovate their spiritual life of transcendental bliss and knowledge. Consequently they waste time and energy in the search for so-called happiness. These are the qualifications of the demons. In *Bhagavad-gītā* it says that when one has all these demonic qualities, he becomes a *mūḍha.* Due to this, he envies the Supreme Personality of Godhead; therefore birth after birth he is born into a demonic family, and he transmigrates from one demonic body to another. Thus he forgets his relationship with Kṛṣṇa and remains a *narādhama* in an abominable condition life after life.

TEXT 28

क्वापि देवमायया स्त्रिया भुजलतोपगूढः प्रस्कन्नविवेकविज्ञानो यद्विहारगृहारम्भाकुलहृदयस्तदाश्रयावसक्तसुतदुहितृकलत्रभाषितावलोकविचेष्टितापहृतहृदय आत्मानमजितात्मापारेऽन्धे तमसि प्रहिणोति॥२८॥

kvāpi deva-māyayā striyā bhuja-latopagūḍhaḥ praskanna-viveka-vijñāno yad-vihāra-gṛhārambhākula-hṛdayas tad-āśrayāvasakta-suta-duhitṛ-kalatra-bhāṣitāvaloka-viceṣṭitāpahṛta-hṛdaya ātmānam ajitātmāpāre 'ndhe tamasi prahiṇoti.

kvāpi—somewhere; *deva-māyayā*—by the influence of the illusory energy; *striyā*—in the form of one's girl friend or wife; *bhuja-latā*—by beautiful arms, which are compared to tender creepers in the forest; *upagūḍhaḥ*—being deeply embarrassed; *praskanna*—lost; *viveka*—all intelligence; *vijñānaḥ*—scientific knowledge; *yat-vihāra*—for the enjoyment of the wife; *gṛha-ārambha*—to find a house or apartment; *ākula-hṛdayaḥ*—whose heart becomes engrossed; *tat*—of that house; *āśraya-avasakta*—who are under the shelter; *suta*—of sons; *duhitṛ*—of daughters; *kalatra*—of the wife; *bhāṣita-avaloka*—by the conversations and by their beautiful glances; *viceṣṭita*—by activities; *apahṛta-hṛdayaḥ*—whose consciousness is taken away; *ātmānam*—himself; *ajita*—uncontrolled; *ātmā*—whose self; *apāre*—in unlimited; *andhe*—blind darkness; *tamasi*—in hellish life; *prahiṇoti*—he hurls.

TRANSLATION

Sometimes the conditioned soul is attracted by illusion personified (his wife or girl friend) and becomes eager to be embraced by a woman. Thus he loses his intelligence as well as knowledge of life's goal. At that time, no longer attempting spiritual cultivation, he becomes overly attached to his wife or girl friend and tries to provide her with a suitable apartment. Again, he becomes very busy under the shelter of that home and is captivated by the talks, glances and activities of his wife and children. In this way he loses his Kṛṣṇa consciousness and throws himself in the dense darkness of material existence.

PURPORT

When the conditioned soul is embraced by his beloved wife, he forgets everything about Kṛṣṇa consciousness. The more he becomes attached to his wife, the more he becomes implicated in family life. One Bengali poet, Bankim Chandra, says that to the eyes of the lover the beloved is always very beautiful, even though ugly. This attraction is called *deva-māyā*. The attraction between man and woman is the cause of bondage for both. Actually both belong to the *parā prakṛti*, the superior energy of the Lord, but both are actually *prakṛti* (female). However, because both want to enjoy one another, they are sometimes described as *puruṣa* (male). Actually neither is *puruṣa*, but both can be superficially described as *puruṣa*. As soon as man and woman are united, they become attached to home, hearth, land, friendship and money. In this way they are both entrapped in material existence. The word *bhuja-latā-upagūḍha*, meaning "being embraced by beautiful arms which are compared to creepers," describes the way the conditioned soul is bound within this material world. The products of sex life—sons and daughters—certainly follow. This is the way of material existence.

TEXT 29

कदाचिदीश्वरस्य भगवतो विष्णोश्चक्रात्परमाण्वादिद्विपरार्धापवर्ग-
कालोपलक्षणात्परिवर्तितेन वयसा रंहसा हरत आब्रह्मतृणस्तम्बादीनां भूताना-
मनिमिषतो मिषतां वित्रस्तहृदयस्तमेवेश्वरं कालचक्रनिजायुधं साक्षाद्भगवन्तं
यज्ञपुरुषमनादृत्य पाखण्डदेवताः कङ्कगृध्रबकवटप्राया आर्यसमयपरिहृताः
साङ्केत्येनाभिधत्ते ॥२९॥

kadācid īśvarasya bhagavato viṣṇoś cakrāt paramāṇv-ādi-dvi-parārdhāpavarga-kālopalakṣaṇāt parivartitena vayasā raṁhasā harata ābrahma-tṛṇa-stambādīnāṁ bhūtānām animiṣato miṣatāṁ vitrasta-hṛdayas tam eveśvaraṁ kāla-cakra-nijāyudhaṁ sākṣād bhagavantaṁ yajña-puruṣam anādṛtya pākhaṇḍa-devatāḥ kaṅka-gṛdhra-baka-vaṭa-prāyā ārya-samaya-parihṛtāḥ sāṅketyenābhidhatte.

kadācit—sometimes; *īśvarasya*—of the Supreme Lord; *bhagavataḥ*—of the Supreme Personality of Godhead; *viṣṇoḥ*—of Lord Viṣṇu;

cakrāt—from the disc; *paramāṇu-ādi*—beginning from the time of minute atoms; *dvi-parārdha*—the duration of the life of Brahmā; *apavarga*—ending; *kāla*—of time; *upalakṣaṇāt*—having the symptoms; *parivartitena*—revolving; *vayasā*—by the chronological order of ages; *raṁhasā*—swiftly; *harataḥ*—taking away; *ā-brahma*—beginning from Lord Brahmā; *tṛṇa-stamba-ādīnām*—down to the small clumps of grass; *bhūtānām*—of all living entities; *animiṣataḥ*—without blinking the eyes (without fail); *miṣatām*—before the eyes of the living entities (without their being able to stop it); *vitrasta-hṛdayaḥ*—being afraid in the heart; *tam*—Him; *eva*—certainly; *īśvaram*—the Supreme Lord; *kāla-cakra-nija-āyudham*—whose personal weapon is the disc of time; *sākṣāt*—directly; *bhagavantam*—the Supreme Personality of Godhead; *yajña-puruṣam*—who accepts all kinds of sacrificial ceremonies; *anādṛtya*—without caring for; *pākhaṇḍa-devatāḥ*—concocted incarnations of God (man-made gods or demigods); *kaṅka*—buzzards; *gṛdhra*—vultures; *baka*—herons; *aṭa-prāyāḥ*—like crows; *ārya-samaya-parihṛtāḥ*—who are rejected by authorized Vedic scriptures accepted by the Āryans; *sāṅketyena*—by concoction or with no basis of authority indicated by scripture; *abhidhatte*—he accepts as worshipable.

TRANSLATION

The personal weapon used by Lord Kṛṣṇa, the disc, is called hari-cakra, the disc of Hari. This cakra is the wheel of time. It expands from the beginning of the atoms up to the time of Brahmā's death, and it controls all activities. It is always revolving and spending the lives of the living entities, from Lord Brahmā down to an insignificant blade of grass. Thus one changes from infancy, to childhood, to youth and maturity, and thus one approaches the end of life. It is impossible to check this wheel of time. This wheel is very exacting because it is the personal weapon of the Supreme Personality of Godhead. Sometimes the conditioned soul, fearing the approach of death, wants to worship someone who can save him from imminent danger. Yet he does not care for the Supreme Personality of Godhead, whose weapon is the indefatigable time factor. The conditioned soul instead takes shelter of a man-made god described in unauthorized scriptures. Such gods are like

buzzards, vultures, herons and crows. Vedic scriptures do not refer to them. Imminent death is like the attack of a lion, and neither vultures, buzzards, crows nor herons can save one from such an attack. One who takes shelter of unauthorized man-made gods cannot be saved from the clutches of death.

PURPORT

It is stated: *hariṁ vinā mṛtiṁ na taranti.* No one can save himself from the cruel hands of death without being favored by Hari, the Supreme Personality of Godhead. In *Bhagavad-gītā* it is stated, *mām eva ye prapadyante māyām etāṁ taranti te:* whoever fully surrenders unto Kṛṣṇa can be saved from the cruel hands of material nature. The conditioned soul, however, sometimes wants to take shelter of a demigod, man-made god, pseudo incarnation or bogus *svāmī* or *yogī.* All these cheaters claim to follow religious principles, and all this has become very popular in this age of Kali. There are many *pāṣaṇḍīs* who, without referring to the *śāstras,* pose themselves as incarnations, and foolish people follow them. Kṛṣṇa, the Supreme Personality of Godhead, has left behind Him *Śrīmad-Bhāgavatam* and *Bhagavad-gītā.* Not referring to these authorized scriptures, rascals take shelter of man-made scriptures and try to compete with Lord Kṛṣṇa. That is the greatest difficulty one encounters when trying to promote spiritual consciousness in human society. The Kṛṣṇa consciousness movement is trying its best to bring people back to Kṛṣṇa consciousness in its pure form, but the *pāṣaṇḍīs* and atheists, who are cheaters, are so numerous that sometimes we become perplexed and wonder how to push this movement forward. In any case, we cannot accept the unauthorized ways of so-called incarnations, gods, cheaters and bluffers, who are described here as crows, vultures, buzzards and herons.

TEXT 30

यदा पाखण्डिभिरात्मवञ्चितैस्तैरुरु वञ्चितो ब्रह्मकुलं समावसंस्तेषां शील-
मुपनयनादिश्रौतस्मार्तकर्मानुष्ठानेन भगवतो यज्ञपुरुषस्याराधनमेव तदरोचयन्
शूद्रकुलं भजते निगमाचारेऽशुद्धितो यस्य मिथुनीभावः कुटुम्बभरणं
यथा वानरजातेः ॥ ३० ॥

yadā pākhaṇḍibhir ātma-vañcitais tair uru vañcito brahma-kulaṁ samāvasaṁs teṣāṁ śīlam upanayanādi-śrauta-smārta-karmānuṣṭhānena bhagavato yajña-puruṣasyārādhanam eva tad arocayan śūdra-kulaṁ bhajate nigamācāre 'śuddhito yasya mithunī-bhāvaḥ kuṭumba-bharaṇaṁ yathā vānara-jāteḥ.

yadā—when; *pākhaṇḍibhiḥ*—by *pāṣaṇḍīs* (godless atheists); *ātma-vañcitaiḥ*—who themselves are cheated; *taiḥ*—by them; *uru*—more and more; *vañcitaḥ*—being cheated; *brahma-kulam*—the bona fide *brāhmaṇas* strictly following the Vedic culture; *samāvasan*—settling among them to advance spiritually; *teṣām*—of them (the *brāhmaṇas* who strictly follow Vedic principles); *śīlam*—the good character; *upanayana-ādi*—beginning with offering the sacred thread or training the conditioned soul to qualify as a bona fide *brāhmaṇa; śrauta*—according to the Vedic principles; *smārta*—according to the authorized scriptures derived from the *Vedas; karma-anuṣṭhānena*—the performance of activities; *bhagavataḥ*—of the Supreme Personality of Godhead; *yajña-puruṣasya*—who is worshiped by Vedic ritualistic ceremonies; *ārādhanam*—the process of worshiping Him; *eva*—certainly; *tat arocayan*—not finding pleasure in it due to its being difficult for unscrupulous persons to perform; *śūdra-kulam*—the society of *śūdras; bhajate*—he turns to; *nigama-ācāre*—in behaving according to Vedic principles; *aśuddhitaḥ*—not purified; *yasya*—of whom; *mithunī-bhāvaḥ*—sex enjoyment or the materialistic way of life; *kuṭumba-bharaṇam*—the maintenance of the family; *yathā*—as it is; *vānara-jāteḥ*—of the society of monkeys, or the descendants of the monkey.

TRANSLATION

The pseudo svāmīs, yogīs and incarnations who do not believe in the Supreme Personality of Godhead are known as pāṣaṇḍīs. They themselves are fallen and cheated because they do not know the real path of spiritual advancement, and whoever goes to them is certainly cheated in his turn. When one is thus cheated, he sometimes takes shelter of the real followers of Vedic principles [brāhmaṇas or those in Kṛṣṇa consciousness], who teach everyone how to worship the Supreme Personality of Godhead according to the Vedic rituals. However, being unable to stick to these princi-

ples, these rascals again fall down and take shelter among śūdras who are very expert in making arrangements for sex indulgence. Sex is very prominent among animals like monkeys, and such people who are enlivened by sex may be called descendants of monkeys.

PURPORT

By fulfilling the process of evolution from the aquatics to the animal platform, a living entity eventually reaches the human form. The three modes of material nature are always working in the evolutionary process. Those who come to the human form through the quality of *sattva-guṇa* were cows in their last animal incarnation. Those who come to the human form through the quality of *rajo-guṇa* were lions in their last animal incarnation. And those who come to the human form through the quality of *tamo-guṇa* were monkeys in their last animal incarnation. In this age, those who come through the monkey species are considered by modern anthropologists like Darwin to be descendants of monkeys. We receive information herein that those who are simply interested in sex are actually no better than monkeys. Monkeys are very expert in sexual enjoyment, and sometimes sex glands are taken from monkeys and placed in the human body so that a human being can enjoy sex in old age. In this way modern civilization has advanced. Many monkeys in India were caught and sent to Europe so that their sex glands could serve as replacements for those of old people. Those who actually descend from the monkeys are interested in expanding their aristocratic families through sex. In the *Vedas* there are also certain ceremonies especially meant for sexual improvement and promotion to higher planetary systems, where the demigods are enjoying sex. The demigods are also very much inclined toward sex because that is the basic principle of material enjoyment.

First of all, the conditioned soul is cheated by so-called *svāmīs*, *yogīs* and incarnations when he approaches them to be relieved of material miseries. When the conditioned soul is not satisfied with them, he comes to devotees and pure *brāhmaṇas* who try to elevate him for final liberation from material bondage. However, the unscrupulous conditioned soul cannot rigidly follow the principles prohibiting illicit sex, intoxication, gambling and meat-eating. Thus he falls down and takes shelter of people who are like monkeys. In the Kṛṣṇa consciousness movement these monkey disciples, being unable to follow the strict regulative principles, sometimes fall down and try to form societies based on sex. This is proof that such people are descendants of monkeys, as confirmed by Darwin. In this verse it is therefore clearly stated: *yathā vānara-jāteḥ.*

TEXT 31

तत्रापि निरवरोधः स्वैरेण विहरन्नतिकृपणबुद्धिरन्योन्यमुख-
निरीक्षणादिना ग्राम्यकर्मणैव विस्मृतकालावधिः ॥ ३१ ॥

tatrāpi niravarodhaḥ svaireṇa viharann ati-kṛpaṇa-buddhir anyonya-mukha-nirīkṣaṇādinā grāmya-karmaṇaiva vismṛta-kālāvadhiḥ.

tatra api—in that condition (in the society of human beings descended from monkeys); *niravarodhaḥ*—without hesitation; *svaireṇa*—independently, without reference to the goal of life; *viharan*—enjoying like monkeys; *ati-kṛpaṇa-buddhiḥ*—whose intelligence is dull because he does not properly utilize his assets; *anyonya*—of one another; *mukha-nirīkṣaṇa-ādinā*—by seeing the faces (when a man sees the beautiful face of a woman and the woman sees the strong build of the man's body, they always desire one another); *grāmya-karmaṇā*—by material activities for sense gratification; *eva*—only; *vismṛta*—forgotten; *kāla-avadhiḥ*—the limited span of life (after which one's evolution may be degrading or elevating).

TRANSLATION

In this way the descendants of the monkeys intermingle with each other, and they are generally known as śūdras. Without hesitating, they live and move freely, not knowing the goal of life. They are captivated simply by seeing the faces of one another, which remind them of sense gratification. They are always engaged in material activities, known as grāmya-karma, and they work hard for material benefit. Thus they forget completely that one day their small life spans will be finished and they will be degraded in the evolutionary cycle.

PURPORT

Materialistic people are sometimes called *śūdras*, or descendants of monkeys, due to their monkeylike intelligence. They do not care to know how the evolutionary process is taking place, nor are they eager to know what will happen after they finish their small human life span. This is the attitude of *śūdras*. Śrī Caitanya Mahāprabhu's mission, this Kṛṣṇa consciousness movement, is trying to elevate *śūdras* to the *brāhmaṇa* platform so that they will know the real goal of life. Unfortunately, being overly attached to sense gratification, materialists are not serious in helping this movement. Instead, some of them try to suppress it. Thus it is the business of monkeys to disturb the activities of the *brāhmaṇas*. The descendants of monkeys completely forget that they have to die, and they are very proud of scientific knowledge and the progress of material civilization. The word *grāmya-karmaṇā* indicates activities meant only for the improvement of bodily comforts. Presently all human society is engaged in improving economic conditions and bodily comforts. People are not interested in knowing what is going to happen after death, nor do they believe in the transmigration of the soul. When one scientifically studies the evolutionary theory, one can understand that human life is a junction where one may take the path of promotion or degradation. As stated in *Bhagavad-gītā* (9.25):

yānti deva-vratā devān
pitṝn yānti pitṛ-vratāḥ
bhūtāni yānti bhūtejyā
yānti mad-yājino 'pi mām

"Those who worship the demigods will take birth among the demigods; those who worship ghosts and spirits will take birth among such beings; those who worship ancestors go to the ancestors; and those who worship Me will live with Me."

In this life we have to prepare ourselves for promotion to the next life. Those who are in the mode of *rajo-guṇa* are generally interested in being promoted to the heavenly planets. Some, unknowingly, are degraded to lower animal forms. Those in the mode of goodness can engage in devotional service, and after that they can return home, back to Godhead (*yānti mad-yājino 'pi mām*). That is the real purpose of human life. This

Kṛṣṇa consciousness movement is trying to bring intelligent human beings to the platform of devotional service. Instead of wasting time trying to attain a better position in material life, one should simply endeavor to return home, back to Godhead. Then all problems will be solved. As stated in *Śrīmad-Bhāgavatam* (1.2.17):

śṛṇvatāṁ sva-kathāḥ kṛṣṇaḥ
puṇya-śravaṇa-kīrtanaḥ
hṛdy antaḥ-stho hy abhadrāṇi
vidhunoti su-hṛt-satām

"Śrī Kṛṣṇa, the Personality of Godhead, who is the Paramātmā [Supersoul] in everyone's heart and the benefactor of the truthful devotee, cleanses the desire for material enjoyment from the heart of the devotee who relishes His messages, which are in themselves virtuous when properly heard and chanted."

One simply has to follow the regulative principles, act like a *brāhmaṇa*, chant the Hare Kṛṣṇa *mantra* and read *Bhagavad-gītā* and *Śrīmad-Bhāgavatam*. In this way one purifies himself of the baser material modes (*tamo-guṇa* and *rajo-guṇa*) and, becoming freed from the greed of these modes, can attain complete peace of mind. In this way one can understand the Supreme Personality of Godhead and one's relationship with Him and thus be promoted to the highest perfection (*siddhiṁ paramāṁ gatāḥ*).

TEXT 32

क्वचिद् द्रुमवदैहिकार्थेषु गृहेषु रंस्यन् यथा वानरः सुतदारवत्सलो व्यवायक्षणः ॥३२॥

kvacid drumvad aihikārtheṣu gṛheṣu raṁsyan yathā vānaraḥ suta-dāra-vatsalo vyavāya-kṣaṇaḥ.

kvacit—sometimes; *druma-vat*—like trees (as monkeys jump from one tree to another, the conditioned soul transmigrates from one body to another); *aihika-artheṣu*—simply to bring about better worldly comforts; *gṛheṣu*—in houses (or bodies); *raṁsyan*—delighting (in one body after another, either in animal life, human life or demigod life); *yathā*—exactly as; *vānaraḥ*—the monkey; *suta-dāra-vatsalaḥ*—very affectionate to the children and wife; *vyavāya-kṣaṇaḥ*—whose leisure time is spent in sex pleasure.

TRANSLATION

Just as a monkey jumps from one tree to another, the conditioned soul jumps from one body to another. As the monkey is ultimately captured by the hunter and is unable to get out of captivity, the conditioned soul, being captivated by momentary sex pleasure, becomes attached to different types of bodies and is encaged in family life. Family life affords the conditioned soul a festival of momentary sex pleasure, and thus he is completely unable to get out of the material clutches.

PURPORT

As stated in *Śrīmad-Bhāgavatam* (11.9.29): *viṣayaḥ khalu sarvataḥ syāt.* Bodily necessities—eating, sleeping, mating and defending—are all very easily available in any form of life. It is stated here that the *vānara* (monkey) is very much attracted to sex. Each monkey keeps at least two dozen wives, and he jumps from one tree to another to capture the female monkeys. Thus he immediately engages in sexual intercourse. In this way the monkey's business is to jump from one tree to another and enjoy sex with his wives. The conditioned soul is doing the same thing, transmigrating from one body to another and engaging in sex. He thus completely forgets how to become free from the clutches of material encagement. Sometimes the monkey is captured by a hunter, who sells its body to doctors so that its glands can be removed for the benefit of another monkey. All this is going on in the name of economic development and improved sex life.

TEXT 33

एवमध्वन्यवरुन्धानो मृत्युगजभयात्तमसि गिरिकन्दरप्राये ॥ ३३ ॥

evam adhvany avarundhāno mṛtyu-gaja-bhayāt tamasi giri-kandara-prāye.

evam—in this way; *adhvani*—on the path of sense gratification; *avarundhānaḥ*—being confined, he forgets the real purpose of life; *mṛtyu-gaja-bhayāt*—out of fear of the elephant of death; *tamasi*—in the darkness; *giri-kandara-prāye*—similar to the dark caves in the mountains.

TRANSLATION

In this material world, when the conditioned soul forgets his relationship with the Supreme Personality of Godhead and does not care for Kṛṣṇa consciousness, he simply engages in different types of mischievous and sinful activities. He is then subjected to the threefold miseries, and, out of fear of the elephant of death, he falls into the darkness found in a mountain cave.

PURPORT

Everyone is afraid of death, and however strong a materialistic person may be, when there is disease and old age one must certainly accept death's notice. The conditioned soul becomes very morose to receive notice of death. His fear is compared to the fear experienced upon entering a dark mountain cave, and death is compared to a great elephant.

TEXT 34

क्वचिच्छीतवाताद्यनेकदैविकभौतिकात्मीयानां दुःखानां प्रति-
निवारणेऽकल्पो दुरन्तविषयविषण्ण आस्ते ॥३४॥

kvacic chīta-vātādy-aneka-daivika-bhautikātmīyānāṁ duḥkhānāṁ pratinivāraṇe 'kalpo duranta-viṣaya-viṣaṇṇa āste.

kvacit—sometimes; *śīta-vāta-ādi*—such as extreme cold or wind; *aneka*—many; *daivika*—offered by the demigods or powers beyond our control; *bhautika*—offered by other living entities; *ātmīyānām*—offered by the conditioned material body and mind; *duḥkhānām*—the many miseries; *pratinarārane*—in counteracting; *akalpaḥ*—being unable; *duranta*—insurmountable; *viṣaya*—from connection with sense gratification; *viṣaṇṇaḥ*—morose; *āste*—he remains.

TRANSLATION

The conditioned soul suffers many miserable bodily conditions, such as being affected by severe cold and strong winds. He also suffers due to the activities of other living beings and due to natural disturbances. When he is unable to counteract them and has to remain in a miserable condition, he naturally becomes very morose because he wants to enjoy material facilities.

TEXT 35

क्वचिन्मिथो व्यवहरन् यत्किञ्चिद्धनमुपयाति वित्तशाठ्येन ॥३५॥

kvacin mitho vyavaharan yat kiñcid dhanam upayāti vitta-śāṭhyena.

kvacit—sometimes or somewhere; *mithaḥ vyavaharan*—transacting with each other; *yat*—whatever; *kiñcit*—little bit; *dhanam*—material benefit or wealth; *upayāti*—he obtains; *vitta-śāṭhyena*—by means of cheating someone of his wealth.

TRANSLATION

Sometimes conditioned souls exchange money, but in due course of time, enmity arises because of cheating. Although there may be a tiny profit, the conditioned souls cease to be friends and become enemies.

PURPORT

As stated in *Śrīmad-Bhāgavatam* (5.5.8):

puṁsaḥ striyā mithunī-bhāvam etaṁ
tayor mitho hṛdaya-granthim āhuḥ
ato gṛha-kṣetra-sutāpta-vittair
janasya moho 'yam ahaṁ mameti

The monkeylike conditioned soul first becomes attached to sex, and when intercourse actually takes place he becomes more attached. He then requires some material comforts—apartment, house, food, friends, wealth and so on. In order to acquire these things he has to cheat others, and this creates enmity even among the most intimate friends. Sometimes this enmity is created between the conditioned soul and the father or spiritual master. Unless one is firmly fixed in the regulative principles, one may perform mischievous acts, even if one is a member of the Kṛṣṇa consciousness movement. We therefore advise our disciples to strictly follow the regulative principles; otherwise the most important movement for the upliftment of humanity will be hampered due to dissension among its members. Those who are serious about pushing forward this Kṛṣṇa consciousness movement should remember this and strictly follow the regulative principles so that their minds will not be disturbed.

TEXT 36

क्वचित्क्षीणधनः शय्यासनाशनाद्युपभोगविहीनो यावदप्रतिलब्धमनोरथोपगता-
दानेऽवसितमतिस्ततस्ततोऽवमानादीनि जनादभिलभते ॥३६॥

kvacit kṣīṇa-dhanaḥ śayyāsanāśanādy-upabhoga-vihīno yāvad
apratilabdha-manorathopagatādāne 'vasita-matis tatas tato
'vamānādīni janād abhilabhate.

kvacit—sometimes; *kṣīṇa-dhanaḥ*—not having sufficient money; *śayyā-āsana-aśana-ādi*—accommodations for sleeping, sitting or eating; *upabhoga*—of material enjoyment; *vihīnaḥ*—being bereft; *yāvat*—as long as; *apratilabdha*—not achieved; *manoratha*—by his desire; *upagata*—obtained; *ādāne*—in seizing by unfair means; *avasita-matiḥ*—whose mind is determined; *tataḥ*—because of that; *tataḥ*—from that; *avamāna-ādīni*—insults and punishment; *janāt*—from the people in general; *abhilabhate*—he gets.

TRANSLATION

Sometimes, having no money, the conditioned soul does not get sufficient accommodations. Sometimes he doesn't even have a place to sit, nor does he have the other necessities. In other words, he falls into scarcity, and at that time, when he is unable to secure the necessities by fair means, he decides to seize the property of

others unfairly. When he cannot get the things he wants, he simply receives insults from others and thus becomes very morose.

PURPORT

It is said that necessity knows no law. When the conditioned soul needs money to acquire life's bare necessities, he adopts any means. He begs, borrows or steals. Instead of receiving these things, he is insulted and chastised. Unless one is very well organized, one cannot accumulate riches by unfair means. Even if one acquires riches by unfair means, he cannot avoid punishment and insult from the government or the general populace. There are many instances of important people's embezzling money, getting caught and being put in prison. One may be able to avoid the punishment of prison, but one cannot avoid the punishment of the Supreme Personality of Godhead, who works through the agency of material nature. This is described in *Bhagavad-gītā* (7.14): *daivī hy eṣā guṇamayī mama māyā duratyayā.* Nature is very cruel. She does not excuse anyone. When people do not care for nature, they commit all kinds of sinful activities, and consequently they have to suffer.

TEXT 37

**एवं वित्तव्यतिषङ्गविवृद्धवैरानुबन्धोऽपि पूर्ववासनया मिथ उद्वहत्यथा-
पवहति ॥३७॥**

evaṁ vitta-vyatiṣaṅga-vivṛddha-vairānubandho 'pi pūrva-vāsanayā mitha udvahaty athāpavahati.

evam—in this way; *vitta-vyatiṣaṅga*—because of monetary transactions; *vivṛddha*—increased; *vaira-anubandhaḥ*—having relationships of enmity; *api*—although; *pūrva-vāsanayā*—by the fructifying results of previous impious activities; *mithaḥ*—with each other; *udvahati*—become united by means of the marriage of sons and daughters; *atha*—thereafter; *apavahati*—they give up the marriage or get a divorce.

TRANSLATION

Although people may be enemies, in order to fulfill their desires again and again, they sometimes get married. Unfortunately, these

marriages do not last very long, and the people involved are separated again by divorce or other means.

PURPORT

As stated previously, every conditioned soul has the propensity to cheat, even in marriage. Everywhere in this material world, one conditioned soul is envious of another. For the time being, people may remain friends, but eventually they become enemies again and fight over money. Sometimes they marry and then separate by divorce or other means. On the whole, unity is never permanent. Due to the cheating propensity, both parties always remain envious. Even in Kṛṣṇa consciousness, separation and enmity take place due to the prominence of material propensities.

TEXT 38

एतस्मिन् संसाराध्वनि नानाक्लेशोपसर्गबाधित आपन्नविपन्नो यत्र
यस्तमु ह वावेतरस्तत्र विसृज्य जातं जातमुपादाय शोचन्मुह्यन्
बिभ्यद्विवदन्क्रन्दन् संहृष्यन् गायन्नह्यमानः साधुवर्जितो नैवावर्ततेऽद्यापि
यत आरब्ध एष नरलोकसार्थो यमध्वनः पारमुपदिशन्ति ॥३८॥

etasmin saṁsārādhvani nānā-kleśopasarga-bādhita āpanna-vipanno yatra yas tam u ha vāvetaras tatra visṛjya jātaṁ jātam upādāya śocan muhyan bibhyad-vivadan krandan saṁhṛṣyan gāyan nahyamānaḥ sādhu-varjito naivāvartate 'dyāpi yata ārabdha eṣa nara-loka-sārtho yam adhvanaḥ pāram upadiśanti.

etasmin—on this; *saṁsāra*—of miserable conditions; *adhvani*—path; *nānā*—various; *kleśa*—by miseries; *upasarga*—by the troubles of material existence; *bādhitaḥ*—disturbed; *āpanna*—sometimes having gained; *vipannaḥ*—sometimes having lost; *yatra*—in which; *yaḥ*—who; *tam*—him; *u ha vāva*—or; *itaraḥ*—someone else; *tatra*—thereupon; *visṛjya*—giving up; *jātam jātam*—newly born; *upādāya*—accepting; *śocan*—lamenting; *muhyan*—being illusioned; *bibhyat*—fearing; *vivadan*—sometimes exclaiming loudly; *krandan*—sometimes crying; *saṁhṛṣyan*—sometimes being pleased; *gāyan*—singing;

nahyamānaḥ—being bound; *sādhu-varjitaḥ*—being away from saintly persons; *na*—not; *eva*—certainly; *āvartate*—achieves; *adya api*—even until now; *yataḥ*—from whom; *ārabdhaḥ*—commenced; *eṣaḥ*—this; *nara-loka*—of the material world; *sa-arthaḥ*—the self-interested living entities; *yam*—whom (the Supreme Personality of Godhead); *adhvanaḥ*—of the path of material existence; *pāram*—the other end; *upadiśanti*—saintly persons indicate.

TRANSLATION

The path of this material world is full of material miseries, and various troubles disturb the conditioned souls. Sometimes he loses, and sometimes he gains. In either case, the path is full of danger. Sometimes the conditioned soul is separated from his father by death or other circumstances. Leaving him aside he gradually becomes attached to others, such as his children. In this way, the conditioned soul is sometimes illusioned and afraid. Sometimes he cries loudly out of fear. Sometimes he is happy maintaining his family, and sometimes he is overjoyed and sings melodiously. In this way he becomes entangled and forgets his separation from the Supreme Personality of Godhead since time immemorial. Thus he traverses the dangerous path of material existence, and on this path he is not at all happy. Those who are self-realized simply take shelter of the Supreme Personality of Godhead in order to get out of this dangerous material existence. Without accepting the devotional path, one cannot get out of the clutches of material existence. The conclusion is that no one can be happy in material life. One must take to Kṛṣṇa consciousness.

PURPORT

By thoroughly analyzing the materialistic way of life, any sane man can understand that there is not the least happiness in this world. However, due to continuing on the path of danger from time immemorial and not associating with saintly persons, the conditioned soul, under illusion, wants to enjoy this material world. Material energy sometimes gives him a chance at so-called happiness, but the conditioned soul is perpetually being punished by material nature. It is therefore said: *daṇḍya-*

jane rājā yena nadīte cubāya (Cc. *Madhya* 20.118). Materialistic life means continuous unhappiness, but sometimes we accept happiness as it appears between the gaps. Sometimes a condemned person is submerged in water and hauled out. Actually all of this is meant for punishment, but he feels a little comfort when he is taken out of the water. This is the situation with the conditioned soul. All the *śāstras* therefore advise that one associate with devotees and saintly people.

> *'sādhu-saṅga', 'sādhu-saṅga'——sarva-śāstre kaya*
> *lava-mātra sādhu-saṅge sarva-siddhi haya*
> (Cc. *Madhya* 22.54)

Even by a little association with devotees, the conditioned soul can get out of this miserable material condition. This Kṛṣṇa consciousness movement is therefore trying to give everyone a chance to associate with saintly people. Therefore all the members of this Kṛṣṇa consciousness society must themselves be perfect *sādhus* in order to give a chance to fallen conditioned souls. This is the best humanitarian work.

TEXT 39

यदिदं योगानुशासनं न वा एतदवरुन्धते यन्न्यस्तदण्डा मुनय उपशमशीला उपरतात्मानः समवगच्छन्ति ॥ ३९ ॥

yad idaṁ yogānuśāsanaṁ na vā etad avarundhate yan nyasta-daṇḍā munaya upaśama-śīlā uparatātmānaḥ samavagacchanti.

yat—which; *idam*—this ultimate abode of the Supreme Personality of Godhead; *yoga-anuśāsanam*—only to be achieved by practicing devotional service; *na*—not; *vā*—either; *etat*—this path of liberation; *avarundhate*—obtain; *yat*—therefore; *nyasta-daṇḍāḥ*—persons who have given up envying others; *munayaḥ*—saintly persons; *upaśama-śīlāḥ*—who are now situated in a most peaceful existence; *uparata-ātmānaḥ*—who have control over the mind and senses; *samavagacchanti*—very easily obtain.

TRANSLATION

Saintly persons, who are friends to all living entities, have a peaceful consciousness. They have controlled their senses and minds, and they easily attain the path of liberation, the path back to Godhead. Being unfortunate and attached to the miserable material conditions, a materialistic person cannot associate with them.

PURPORT

The great saint Jaḍa Bharata described both the miserable condition and the means to get out. The only way out of it is association with devotees, and this association is very easy. Although unfortunate people also get this opportunity, due to their great misfortune they cannot take shelter of pure devotees, and consequently they continuously suffer. Nonetheless, this Kṛṣṇa consciousness movement insists that everyone take to this path by adopting the chanting of the Hare Kṛṣṇa *mahā-mantra*. The preachers of Kṛṣṇa consciousness go from door to door to inform people how they can be relieved from the miserable conditions of material life. As stated by Śrī Caitanya Mahāprabhu, *guru-kṛṣṇa-prasāde pāya bhakti-latā-bīja:* by the mercy of Kṛṣṇa and *guru*, one can get the seed of devotional service. If one is a little intelligent, he can cultivate Kṛṣṇa consciousness and be freed from the miserable conditions of material life.

TEXT 40

यदपि दिगिभजयिनो यज्विनो ये वै राजर्षयः किं तु परं मृधे
शयीरन्नस्यामेव ममेयमिति कृतवैरानुबन्धायां विसृज्य स्वयमुपसंहृताः ॥४०॥

yad api dig-ibha-jayino yajvino ye vai rājarṣayaḥ kiṁ tu paraṁ mṛdhe
śayīrann asyām eva mameyam iti kṛta-vairānubandhāyāṁ visṛjya
svayam upasaṁhṛtāḥ.

yat api—although; *dik-ibha-jayinaḥ*—who are victorious in all directions; *yajvinaḥ*—expert in performing great sacrifices; *ye*—all of whom; *vai*—indeed; *rāja-ṛṣayaḥ*—very great saintly kings; *kim tu*—but; *param*—only this earth; *mṛdhe*—in battle; *śayīran*—lying down; *asyām*—on this (earth); *eva*—indeed; *mama*—mine; *iyam*—this; *iti*—considering in that way; *kṛta*—on which is created; *vaira-anu-bandhāyām*—a relationship of enmity with others; *visṛjya*—giving up; *svayam*—his own life; *upasaṁhṛtāḥ*—being killed.

TRANSLATION

There were many great saintly kings who were very expert in performing sacrificial rituals and very competent in conquering other kingdoms, yet despite their power they could not attain the loving service of the Supreme Personality of Godhead. This is because those great kings could not even conquer the false consciousness of "I am this body, and this is my property." Thus they simply created enmity with rival kings, fought with them and died without having discharged life's real mission.

PURPORT

The real mission of life for the conditioned soul is to reestablish the forgotten relationship with the Supreme Personality of Godhead and engage in devotional service so that he may revive Kṛṣṇa consciousness after giving up the body. One doesn't have to give up his occupation as a *brāhmaṇa, kṣatriya, vaiśya, śūdra* or whatever. In any position, while discharging his prescribed duty, one can develop Kṛṣṇa consciousness simply by associating with devotees who are representatives of Kṛṣṇa and who can teach this science. Regretfully, the big politicians and leaders in the material world simply create enmity and are not interested in spiritual advancement. Material advancement may be very pleasing to an ordinary man, but ultimately he is defeated because he identifies himself with the material body and considers everything related to it to be his property. This is ignorance. Actually nothing belongs to him, not even the body. By one's *karma*, one gets a particular body, and if he does not utilize his body to please the Supreme Personality of Godhead, all his activities are frustrated. The real purpose of life is stated in *Śrīmad-Bhāgavatam* (1.2.13):

ataḥ pumbhir dvija-śreṣṭhā
varṇāśrama-vibhāgaśaḥ

svanuṣṭhitasya dharmasya
saṁsiddhir hari-toṣaṇam

It really doesn't matter what activity a man engages in. If he can simply satisfy the Supreme Lord, his life is successful.

TEXT 41

कर्मवल्लीमवलम्ब्य तत आपदः कथञ्चिन्नरकाद्विमुक्तः पुनरप्येवं
संसाराध्वनि वर्तमानो नरलोकसार्थमुपयाति एवमुपरि गतोऽपि ॥४१॥

karma-vallīm avalambya tata āpadaḥ kathañcin narakād vimuktaḥ punar apy evaṁ saṁsārādhvani vartamāno nara-loka-sārtham upayāti evam upari gato 'pi.

karma-vallīm—the creeper of fruitive activities; *avalambya*—taking shelter of; *tataḥ*—from that; *āpadaḥ*—dangerous or miserable condition; *kathañcit*—somehow or other; *narakāt*—from the hellish condition of life; *vimuktaḥ*—being freed; *punaḥ api*—again; *evam*—in this way; *saṁsāra-adhvani*—on the path of material existence; *vartamānaḥ*—existing; *nara-loka-sa-artham*—the field of self-interested material activities; *upayāti*—he enters; *evam*—thus; *upari*—above (in the higher planetary systems); *gataḥ api*—although promoted.

TRANSLATION

When the conditioned soul accepts the shelter of the creeper of fruitive activity, he may be elevated by his pious activities to higher planetary systems and thus gain liberation from hellish conditions, but unfortunately he cannot remain there. After reaping the results of his pious activities, he has to return to the lower planetary systems. In this way he perpetually goes up and comes down.

PURPORT

In this regard Śrī Caitanya Mahāprabhu says:

brahmāṇḍa bhramite kona bhāgyavān jīva
guru-kṛṣṇa-prasāde pāya bhakti-latā-bīja
(Cc. *Madhya* 19.151)

Even if one wanders for many millions of years, from the time of creation until the time of annihilation, one cannot get free from the path of material existence unless one receives shelter at the lotus feet of a pure devotee. As a monkey takes shelter of the branch of a banyan tree and thinks he is enjoying, the conditioned soul, not knowing the real interest of his life, takes shelter of the path of *karma-kāṇḍa*, fruitive activities. Sometimes he is elevated to the heavenly planets by such activities, and sometimes he again descends to earth. This is described by Śrī Caitanya Mahāprabhu as *brahmāṇḍa bhramite.* However, if by Kṛṣṇa's grace one is fortunate enough to come under the shelter of the *guru,* by the mercy of Kṛṣṇa he receives lessons on how to execute devotional service to the Supreme Lord. In this way he receives a clue of how to get out of his continuous struggle up and down within the material world. Therefore the Vedic injunction is that one should approach a spiritual master. The *Vedas* declare: *tad-vijñānārthaṁ sa gurum evābhigacchet* (*Muṇḍaka Upaniṣad* 1.2.12). Similarly in *Bhagavad-gītā* (4.34) the Supreme Personalty of Godhead advises:

tad viddhi praṇipātena
paripraśnena sevayā
upadekṣyanti te jñānaṁ
jñāninas tattva-darśinaḥ

"Just try to learn the truth by approaching a spiritual master. Inquire from him submissively and render service unto him. The self-realized soul can impart knowledge unto you because he has seen the truth." *Śrīmad-Bhāgavatam* (11.3.21) gives similar advice:

tasmād guruṁ prapadyeta
jijñāsuḥ śreya uttamam
śābde pare ca niṣṇātaṁ
brahmaṇy upaśamāśrayam

"Any person who seriously desires to achieve real happiness must seek out a bona fide spiritual master and take shelter of him by initiation. The qualification of his spiritual master is that he must have realized the conclusion of the scriptures by deliberation and be able to convince others of these conclusions. Such great personalities, who have taken shelter of the Supreme Godhead, leaving aside all material considerations, are to be understood as bona fide spiritual masters." Similarly, Viśvanātha Cakravartī, a great Vaiṣṇava, also advises, *yasya prasādād bhagavat-prasādaḥ:* "By the mercy of the spiritual master one receives the mercy of Kṛṣṇa." This is the same advice given by Śrī Caitanya Mahāprabhu (*guru-kṛṣṇa-prasāde pāya bhakti-latā-bīja*). This is essential. One must come to Kṛṣṇa consciousness, and therefore one must take shelter of a pure devotee. Thus one can become free from the clutches of matter.

TEXT 42

तस्येदमुपगायन्ति—
आर्षभस्येह राजर्षेर्मनसापि महात्मनः ।
नानुवर्त्मार्हति नृपो मक्षिकेव गरुत्मतः ॥४२॥

tasyedam upagāyanti—
ārṣabhasyeha rājarṣer
manasāpi mahātmanaḥ
nānuvartmārhati nṛpo
makṣikeva garutmataḥ

tasya—of Jaḍa Bharata; *idam*—this glorification; *upagāyanti*—they sing; *ārṣabhasya*—of the son of Ṛṣabhadeva; *iha*—here; *rāja-ṛṣeḥ*—of the great saintly King; *manasā api*—even by the mind; *mahā-ātmanaḥ*—of the great personality Jaḍa Bharata; *na*—not; *anuvartma arhati*—able to follow the path; *nṛpaḥ*—any king; *makṣikā*—a fly; *iva*—like; *garutmataḥ*—of Garuḍa, the carrier of the Supreme Personality of Godhead.

TRANSLATION

Having summarized the teachings of Jaḍa Bharata, Śukadeva Gosvāmī said: My dear King Parīkṣit, the path indicated by Jaḍa Bharata is like the path followed by Garuḍa, the carrier of the Lord, and ordinary kings are just like flies. Flies cannot follow the

path of Garuḍa, and to date none of the great kings and victorious leaders could follow this path of devotional service, not even mentally.

PURPORT

As Kṛṣṇa says in *Bhagavad-gīta* (7.3):

manuṣyāṇāṁ sahasreṣu
kaścid yatati siddhaye
yatatām api siddhānāṁ
kaścin māṁ vetti tattvataḥ

"Out of many thousands among men, one may endeavor for perfection, and of those who have achieved perfection, hardly one knows Me in truth." The path of devotional service is very difficult, even for great kings who have conquered many enemies. Although these kings were victorious on the battlefield, they could not conquer the bodily conception. There are many big leaders, *yogīs, svāmīs* and so-called incarnations who are very much addicted to mental speculation and who advertise themselves as perfect personalities, but they are not ultimately successful. The path of devotional service is undoubtedly very difficult to follow, but it becomes very easy if the candidate actually wants to follow the path of the *mahājana*. In this age there is the path of Śrī Caitanya Mahāprabhu, who appeared to deliver all fallen souls. This path is so simple and easy that everyone can take to it by chanting the holy name of the Lord.

harer nāma harer nāma
harer nāmaiva kevalam
kalau nāsty eva nāsty eva
nāsty eva gatir anyathā

We are very satisfied that this path is being opened by this Kṛṣṇa consciousness movement because so many European amd American boys and girls are taking this philosophy seriously and gradually attaining perfection.

TEXT 43

यो दुस्त्यजान्दारसुतान् सुहृद्राज्यं हृदिस्पृशः ।
जहौ युवैव मलवदुत्तमश्लोकलालसः ॥४३॥

yo dustyajān dāra-sutān
suhṛd rājyaṁ hṛdi-spṛśaḥ
jahau yuvaiva malavad
uttamaśloka-lālasaḥ

yaḥ—the same Jaḍa Bharata who was formerly Mahārāja Bharata, the son of Mahārāja Ṛṣabhadeva; *dustyajān*—very difficult to give up; *dāra-sutān*—the wife and children or the most opulent family life; *suhṛt*—friends and well-wishers; *rājyam*—a kingdom that extended all over the world; *hṛdi-spṛśaḥ*—that which is situated within the core of one's heart; *jahau*—he gave up; *yuvā eva*—even as a young man; *mala-vat*—like stool; *uttama-śloka-lālasaḥ*—who was so fond of serving the Supreme Personality of Godhead, known as Uttamaśloka.

TRANSLATION

While in the prime of life, the great Mahārāja Bharata gave up everything because he was fond of serving the Supreme Personality of Godhead, Uttamaśloka. He gave up his beautiful wife, nice children, great friends and an enormous empire. Although these things were very difficult to give up, Mahārāja Bharata was so exalted that he gave them up just as one gives up stool after evacuating. Such was the greatness of His Majesty.

PURPORT

The name of God is Kṛṣṇa, because He is so attractive that the pure devotee can give up everything within this material world on His behalf. Mahārāja Bharata was an ideal king, instructor and emperor of the world. He possessed all the opulences of the material world, but Kṛṣṇa is so attractive that He attracted Mahārāja Bharata from all his material possessions. Yet somehow or other, the King became affectionate to a little deer and, falling from his position, had to accept the body of a deer in his next life. Due to Kṛṣṇa's great mercy upon him, he could not forget his position, and he could understand how he had fallen. Therefore in the next life, as Jaḍa Bharata, Mahārāja Bharata was careful not to spoil his energy, and therefore he presented himself as a deaf and dumb person. In this way he could concentrate on his devotional service. We have to learn from the great King Bharata how to become cautious in cultivating Kṛṣṇa consciousness. A little inattention will retard our devotional service for the time being. Yet any service rendered to the Supreme Personality of Godhead is never lost: *svalpam apy asya dharmasya trāyate mahato bhayāt* (Bg. 2.40). A little devotional service rendered sincerely is a permanent asset. As stated in *Śrīmad-Bhāgavatam* (1.5.17):

tyaktvā sva-dharmaṁ caraṇāmbujaṁ harer
bhajann apakvo 'tha patet tato yadi
yatra kva vābhadram abhūd amuṣya kiṁ
ko vārtha āpto 'bhajatāṁ sva-dharmataḥ

Somehow or other, if one is attracted to Kṛṣṇa, whatever he does in devotional service is a permanent asset. Even if one falls down due to immaturity or bad association, his devotional assets are never lost. There are many examples of this—Ajāmila, Mahārāja Bharata, and many others. This Kṛṣṇa consciousness movement is giving everyone a chance to engage in devotional service for at least some time. A little service will give one an impetus to advance and thus make one's life successful.

In this verse the Lord is described as Uttamaśloka. *Uttama* means "the best," and *śloka* means "reputation." Lord Kṛṣṇa is full in six opulences, one of which is reputation. *Aiśvaryasya samagrasya vīryasya yaśasaḥ śriyaḥ.* Kṛṣṇa's reputation is still expanding. We are spreading the glories of Kṛṣṇa by pushing forward this Kṛṣṇa consciousness movement. Kṛṣṇa's reputation, five thousand years after the Battle of Kurukṣetra, is still expanding throughout the world. Every important individual within this world must have heard of Kṛṣṇa, especially at the present moment, due to the Kṛṣṇa consciousness movement. Even people who do not like us and want to suppress the movement are also somehow or other chanting Hare Kṛṣṇa. They say, "The Hare Kṛṣṇa people should be chastised." Such foolish people do not realize the true value of this movement, but the mere fact that they want to criticize it gives them a chance to chant Hare Kṛṣṇa, and this is its success.

TEXT 44

यो दुस्त्यजान् क्षितिसुतस्वजनार्थदारान्
प्रार्थ्यां श्रियं सुरवरैः सदयावलोकाम् ।
नैच्छन्नृपस्तदुचितं महतां मधुद्विट्-
सेवानुरक्तमनसामभवोऽपि फल्गुः ॥४४॥

yo dustyajān kṣiti-suta-svajanārtha-dārān
prārthyāṁ śriyaṁ sura-varaiḥ sadayāvalokām
naicchan nṛpas tad-ucitaṁ mahatāṁ madhudviṭ-
sevānurakta-manasām abhavo 'pi phalguḥ

yaḥ—who; *dustyajān*—very difficult to give up; *kṣiti*—the earth; *suta*—children; *sva-jana-artha-dārān*—relatives, riches and a beautiful wife; *prārthyām*—desirable; *śriyam*—the goddess of fortune; *sura-varaiḥ*—by the best of the demigods; *sa-daya-avalokām*—whose merciful glance; *na*—not; *aicchat*—desired; *nṛpaḥ*—the King; *tat-ucitam*—this is quite befitting him; *mahatām*—of great personalities (*mahātmās*); *madhu-dviṭ*—of Lord Kṛṣṇa, who killed the demon Madhu; *sevā-anurakta*—attracted by the loving service; *manasām*—of those whose minds; *abhavaḥ api*—even the position of liberation; *phalguḥ*—insignificant.

TRANSLATION

Śukadeva Gosvāmī continued: My dear King, the activities of Bharata Mahārāja are wonderful. He gave up everything difficult for others to give up. He gave up his kingdom, his wife and his family. His opulence was so great that even the demigods envied it, yet he gave it up. It was quite befitting a great personality like him to be a great devotee. He could renounce everything because he was so attracted to the beauty, opulence, reputation, knowledge, strength and renunciation of the Supreme Personality of Godhead, Kṛṣṇa. Kṛṣṇa is so attractive that one can give up all desirable things for His sake. Indeed, even liberation is considered insignificant for those whose minds are attracted to the loving service of the Lord.

PURPORT

This verse confirms Kṛṣṇa's all-attractiveness. Mahārāja Bharata was so attracted to Kṛṣṇa that he gave up all his material possessions. Generally materialistic people are attracted by such possessions.

ato gṛha-kṣetra-sutāpta-vittair
janasya moho 'yam ahaṁ mameti
(*Bhāg.* 5.5.8)

"One becomes attracted to his body, home, property, children, relatives and wealth. In this way one increases life's illusions and thinks in terms of 'I and mine.' " The attraction for material things is certainly due to illusion. There is no value in attraction to material things, for the conditioned soul is diverted by them. One's life is successful if he is absorbed in the attraction of Kṛṣṇa's strength, beauty and pastimes as described in the Tenth Canto of *Śrīmad-Bhāgavatam.* The Māyāvādīs are attracted to merging into the existence of the Lord, but Kṛṣṇa is more attractive than the desire to merge. The word *abhavaḥ* means "not to take birth again in this material world." A devotee doesn't care whether he is going to be reborn or not. He is simply satisfied with the Lord's service in any condition. That is real *mukti.*

īhā yasya harer dāsye
karmaṇā manasā girā
nikhilāsv apy avasthāsu
jīvan-muktaḥ sa ucyate

"One who acts to serve Kṛṣṇa with his body, mind, intelligence and words is a liberated person, even within this material world." (*Bhakti-rasāmṛta-sindhu* 1.2.187) A person who always desires to serve Kṛṣṇa is interested in ways to convince people that there is a Supreme Personality of Godhead and that the Supreme Personality of Godhead is Kṛṣṇa. That is his ambition. It doesn't matter whether he is in heaven or in hell. This is called *uttamaśloka-lālasa.*

TEXT 45

यज्ञाय धर्मपतये विधिनैपुणाय
योगाय सांख्यशिरसे प्रकृतीश्वराय ।

नारायणाय हरये नम इत्युदारं
हास्यन्मृगत्वमपि यः समुदाजहार ॥४५॥

yajñāya dharma-pataye vidhi-naipuṇāya
yogāya sāṅkhya-śirase prakṛtīśvarāya
nārāyaṇāya haraye nama ity udāraṁ
hāsyan mṛgatvam api yaḥ samudājahāra

yajñāya—unto the Supreme Personality of Godhead, who enjoys the results of all great sacrifices; *dharma-pataye*—unto the master or propounder of religious principles; *vidhi-naipuṇāya*—who gives the devotee the intelligence to follow the regulative principles expertly; *yogāya*—the personification of mystic *yoga; sāṅkhya-śirase*—who taught the Sāṅkhya philosophy or who actually gives knowledge of Sāṅkhya to the people of the world; *prakṛti-īśvarāya*—the supreme controller of this cosmic manifestation; *nārāyaṇāya*—the resting place of the innumerable living entities (*nara* means the living entities, and *ayana* means the shelter); *haraye*—unto the Supreme Personality of Godhead, known as Hari; *namaḥ*—respectful obeisances; *iti*—thus; *udāram*—very loudly; *hāsyan*—smiling; *mṛgatvam api*—although in the body of a deer; *yaḥ*—who; *samudājahāra*—chanted.

TRANSLATION

Even though in the body of a deer, Mahārāja Bharata did not forget the Supreme Personality of Godhead; therefore when he was giving up the body of a deer, he loudly uttered the following prayer: "The Supreme Personality of Godhead is sacrifice personified. He gives the results of ritualistic activity. He is the protector of religious systems, the personification of mystic yoga, the source of all knowledge, the controller of the entire creation, and the Supersoul in every living entity. He is beautiful and attractive. I am quitting this body offering obeisances unto Him and hoping that I may perpetually engage in His transcendental loving service." Uttering this, Mahārāja Bharata left his body.

PURPORT

The entire *Vedas* are meant for the understanding of *karma, jñāna* and *yoga*—fruitive activity, speculative knowledge and mystic *yoga*. Whatever way of spiritual realization we accept, the ultimate goal is Nārāyaṇa, the Supreme Personality of Godhead. The living entities are eternally connected with Him via devotional service. As stated in *Śrīmad-Bhāgavatam, ante nārāyaṇa-smṛtiḥ:* the perfection of life is to remember Nārāyaṇa at the time of death. Although Bharata Mahārāja had to accept the body of a deer, he could remember Nārāyaṇa at the time of death. Consequently he took birth as a perfect devotee in a *brāhmaṇa* family. This confirms the statement of *Bhagavad-gītā* (6.41), *śucīnāṁ śrīmatāṁ gehe yoga-bhraṣṭo 'bhijāyate:* "One who falls from the path of self-realization takes birth in a family of *brāhmaṇas* or wealthy aristocrats." Although Mahārāja Bharata appeared in the royal family, he became neglectful and took birth as a deer. Because he was very cautious within his deer body, he took birth in a *brāhmaṇa* family as Jaḍa Bharata. During this lifetime, he remained perfectly Kṛṣṇa conscious and preached the gospel of Kṛṣṇa consciousness directly, beginning with his instructions to Mahārāja Rahūgaṇa. In this regard, the word *yogāya* is very significant. The purpose of *aṣṭāṅga-yoga*, as stated by Madhvācārya, is to link or connect with the Supreme Personality of Godhead. The goal is not to display some material perfections.

TEXT 46

य इदं भागवतसभाजितावदातगुणकर्मणो राजर्षेर्भरतस्यानुचरितं स्वस्त्ययनमायुष्यं धन्यं यशस्यं स्वर्ग्यापवर्ग्यं वानुशृणोत्याख्यास्यत्यभिनन्दति च सर्वा एवाशिष आत्मन आशास्ते न काञ्चन परत इति ॥४६॥

ya idaṁ bhāgavata-sabhājitāvadāta-guṇa-karmaṇo rājarṣer
bharatasyānucaritaṁ svasty-ayanam āyuṣyaṁ dhanyaṁ yaśasyaṁ
svargyāpavargyaṁ vānuśṛṇoty ākhyāsyaty abhinandati ca sarvā evāśiṣa
ātmana āśāste na kāñcana parata iti.

yaḥ—anyone who; *idam*—this; *bhāgavata*—by exalted devotees; *sabhājita*—greatly worshiped; *avadāta*—pure; *guṇa*—whose qualities; *karmaṇaḥ*—and activities; *rāja-ṛṣeḥ*—of the great saintly King;

bharatasya—of Bharata Mahārāja; *anucaritam*—the narration; *svasti-ayanam*—the abode of auspiciousness; *āyuṣyam*—which increases one's duration of life; *dhanyam*—increases one's fortune; *yaśasyam*—bestows reputation; *svargya*—gives promotion to the higher planetary systems (the goal of the *karmīs*); *apavargyam*—gives liberation from this material world and enables one to merge into the Supreme (the goal of the *jñānīs*); *vā*—or; *anuśṛṇoti*—always hears, following the path of devotional service; *ākhyāsyati*—describes for the benefit of others; *abhinandati*—glorifies the characteristics of devotees and the Supreme Lord; *ca*—and; *sarvāḥ*—all; *eva*—certainly; *āśiṣaḥ*—blessings; *ātmanaḥ*—for himself; *āśāste*—he achieves; *na*—not; *kāñcana*—anything; *parataḥ*—from anyone else; *iti*—thus.

TRANSLATION

Devotees interested in hearing and chanting [śravaṇaṁ kīrtanam] regularly discuss the pure characteristics of Bharata Mahārāja and praise his activities. If one submissively hears and chants about the all-auspicious Mahārāja Bharata, one's life span and material opulences certainly increase. One can become very famous and easily attain promotion to the heavenly planets, or attain liberation by merging into the existence of the Lord. Whatever one desires can be attained simply by hearing, chanting and glorifying the activities of Mahārāja Bharata. In this way, one can fulfill all his material and spiritual desires. One does not have to ask anyone else for these things, for simply by studying the life of Mahārāja Bharata, one can attain all desirable things.

PURPORT

The forest of material existence is summarized in this Fourteenth Chapter. The word *bhavāṭavī* refers to the path of material existence. The merchant is the living entity who comes to the forest of material existence to try to make money for sense gratification. The six plunderers are the senses—eyes, ears, nose, tongue, touch and mind. The bad leader is diverted intelligence. Intelligence is meant for Kṛṣṇa consciousness, but due to material existence we divert all our intelligence to achieve material facilities. Everything belongs to Kṛṣṇa, the Supreme Personality of Godhead, but due to our perverted mind and senses, we plunder the property of the Lord and engage in satisfying our senses. The jackals and tigers in the forest are our family members, and the herbs and creepers are our material desires. The mountain cave is our happy home, and the mosquitoes and serpents are our enemies. The rats, beasts and vultures are different types of thieves who take away our possessions, and the *gandharva-pura* is the phantasmagoria of the body and home. The will-o'-the-wisp is our attraction for gold and its color, and material residence and wealth are the ingredients for our material enjoyment. The whirlwind is our attraction for our wife, and the dust storm is our blinding passion experienced during sex. The demigods control the different directions, and the cricket is the harsh words spoken by our enemy during our absence. The owl is the person who directly insults us, and the impious trees are impious men. The waterless river represents atheists who give us trouble in this world and the next. The meat-eating demons are the government officials, and the pricking thorns are the impediments of material life. The little taste experienced in sex is our desire to enjoy another's wife, and the flies are the guardians of women, like the husband, father-in-law, mother-in-law and so forth. The creeper itself is women in general. The lion is the wheel of time, and the herons, crows and vultures are so-called demigods, pseudo *svāmīs, yogīs* and incarnations. All of these are too insignificant to give one relief. The swans are the perfect *brāhmaṇas,* and the monkeys are the extravagant *śūdras* engaged in eating, sleeping, mating and defending. The trees of the monkeys are our households, and the elephant is ultimate death. Thus all the constituents of material existence are described in this chapter.

Thus end the Bhaktivedanta purports of the Fifth Canto, Fourteenth Chapter, of the Śrīmad-Bhāgavatam, *entitled "The Material World as the Great Forest of Enjoyment."*

CHAPTER FIFTEEN

The Glories of the Descendants of King Priyavrata

In this chapter the descendants of Bharata Mahārāja and many other kings are described. The son of Mahārāja Bharata was named Sumati. He followed the path of liberation given by Ṛṣabhadeva. Some people mistakenly thought Sumati to be the direct incarnation of Lord Buddha. The son of Sumati was Devatājit, and his son was Devadyumna. Devadyumna's son was Parameṣṭhī, and his son was Pratīha. Pratīha was a very great devotee of Lord Viṣṇu, and he had three sons, named Pratihartā, Prastotā and Udgātā. Pratihartā had two sons, Aja and Bhūmā. The son of Bhūmā was Udgītha, and the son of Udgītha was Prastāva. The son of Prastāva was Vibhu, and the son of Vibhu was Pṛthuṣeṇa, whose son was Nakta. The wife of Nakta, Druti, gave birth to Gaya, who was a very famous and saintly king. Actually King Gaya was a partial incarnation of Lord Viṣṇu, and because of his great devotion to Lord Viṣṇu he received the title Mahāpuruṣa. King Gaya had sons named Citraratha, Sumati and Avarodhana. The son of Citraratha was the emperor Samrāṭ, and his son was Marīci, whose son was Bindu. Bindu's son was Madhu, and Madhu's son was Vīravrata. Vīravrata's two sons were Manthu and Pramanthu, and the son of Manthu was Bhauvana. The son of Bhauvana was Tvaṣṭā, and the son of Tvaṣṭā was Viraja, who glorified the whole dynasty. Viraja had one hundred sons and one daughter. Of these, the son named Śatajit became very famous.

TEXT 1

श्रीशुक उवाच

भरतस्यात्मजः सुमतिर्नामाभिहितो यमु ह वाव केचित्पाखण्डिन ऋषभपदवीमनुवर्तमानं चानार्या अवेदसमाम्नातां देवतां स्वमनीषया पापीयस्या कलौ कल्पयिष्यन्ति ॥ १ ॥

śrī-śuka uvāca
bharatasyātmajaḥ sumatir nāmābhihito yam u ha vāva kecit
pākhaṇḍina ṛṣabha-padavīm anuvartamānaṁ cānāryā aveda-
samāmnātāṁ devatāṁ sva-manīṣayā pāpīyasyā kalau kalpayiṣyanti.

śrī-śukaḥ uvāca—Śrī Śukadeva Gosvāmī continued to speak; *bharatasya*—of Bharata Mahārāja; *ātma-jaḥ*—the son; *sumatiḥ nāma-abhihitaḥ*—named Sumati; *yam*—unto whom; *u ha vāva*—indeed; *kecit*—some; *pākhaṇḍinaḥ*—atheists, men without Vedic knowledge; *ṛṣabha-padavīm*—the path of King Ṛṣabhadeva; *anuvartamānam*—following; *ca*—and; *anāryāḥ*—not belonging to the Āryans who strictly follow the Vedic principles; *aveda-samāmnātām*—not enumerated in the *Vedas; devatām*—to be Lord Buddha or a similar Buddhist deity; *sva-manīṣayā*—by their own mental speculation; *pāpīyasyā*—most sinful; *kalau*—in this age of Kali; *kalpayiṣyanti*—will imagine.

TRANSLATION

Śrīla Śukadeva Gosvāmī continued: The son of Mahārāja Bharata known as Sumati followed the path of Ṛṣabhadeva, but some unscrupulous people imagined him to be Lord Buddha himself. These people, who were actually atheistic and of bad character, took up the Vedic principles in an imaginary, infamous way to support their activities. Thus these sinful people accepted Sumati as Lord Buddhadeva and propagated the theory that everyone should follow the principles of Sumati. In this way they were carried away by mental concoction.

PURPORT

Those who are Āryans strictly follow the Vedic principles, but in this age of Kali a community has sprung up known as the *ārya-samāja*, which is ignorant of the import of the *Vedas* in the *paramparā* system. Their leaders decry all bona fide *ācāryas*, and they pose themselves as the real followers of the Vedic principles. These *ācāryas* who do not follow the Vedic principles are presently known as the *ārya-samājas*, or the Jains. Not only do they not follow the Vedic principles, but they have no relationship with Lord Buddha. Imitating the behavior of Sumati, they claim to be the descendants of Ṛṣabhadeva. Those who are Vaiṣṇavas carefully avoid their company because they are ignorant of the path of the *Vedas*. In *Bhagavad-gītā* (15.15) Kṛṣṇa says, *vedaiś ca sarvair aham eva vedyaḥ:* "The real purpose of the *Vedas* is to understand Me." This is the injunction of all Vedic literatures. One who does not know the greatness of Lord Kṛṣṇa cannot be accepted as an Āryan. Lord Buddha, an incarnation of Lord Kṛṣṇa, adopted a particular means to propagate the philosophy of *bhāgavata-dharma*. He preached almost exclusively among atheists. Atheists do not want any God, and Lord Buddha therefore said that there is no God, but he adopted the means to instruct his followers for their benefit. Therefore he preached in a duplicitous way, saying that there is no God. Nonetheless, he himself was an incarnation of God.

TEXT 2

तस्माद् वृद्धसेनायां देवताजिन्नाम पुत्रोऽभवत् ॥ २ ॥

tasmād vṛddhasenāyāṁ devatājin-nāma putro 'bhavat.

tasmāt—from Sumati; *vṛddha-senāyām*—in the womb of his wife, named Vṛddhasenā; *devatājit-nāma*—named Devatājit; *putraḥ*—a son; *abhavat*—was born.

TRANSLATION

From Sumati, a son named Devatājit was born by the womb of his wife named Vṛddhasenā.

TEXT 3

अथासुर्यां तत्तनयो देवद्युम्नस्ततो धेनुमत्यां सुतः परमेष्ठी तस्य सुवर्चलायां प्रतीह उपजातः ॥ ३ ॥

athāsuryāṁ tat-tanayo devadyumnas tato dhenumatyāṁ sutaḥ
parameṣṭhī tasya suvarcalāyāṁ pratīha upajātaḥ.

atha—thereafter; *āsuryām*—in the womb of his wife, named Āsurī; *tat-tanayaḥ*—one son of Devatājit; *deva-dyumnaḥ*—named

Devadyumna; *tataḥ*—from Devabhyumna; *dhenu-matyām*—in the womb of Dhenumatī, the wife of Devadyumna; *sutaḥ*—one son; *parameṣṭhī*—named Parameṣṭhī; *tasya*—of Parameṣṭhī; *suvar-calāyām*—in the womb of his wife, named Suvarcalā; *patrīhaḥ*—the son named Pratīha; *upajātaḥ*—appeared.

TRANSLATION

Thereafter, in the womb of Āsurī, the wife of Devatājit, a son named Devadyumna was begotten. Devadyumna begot in the womb of his wife, Dhenumatī, a son named Parameṣṭhī. Parameṣṭhī begot a son named Pratīha in the womb of his wife, Suvarcalā.

TEXT 4

य आत्मविद्यामाख्याय स्वयं संशुद्धो महापुरुषमनुसस्मार ॥ ४ ॥

ya ātma-vidyām ākhyāya svayaṁ saṁśuddho mahā-puruṣam anusasmāra.

yaḥ—who (King Pratīha); *ātma-vidyām ākhyāya*—after instructing many people about self-realization; *svayam*—personally; *saṁśuddhaḥ*—being very advanced and purified in self-realization; *mahā-puruṣam*—the Supreme Personality of Godhead, Viṣṇu; *anusasmāra*—perfectly understood and always remembered.

TRANSLATION

King Pratīha personally propagated the principles of self-realization. In this way, not only was he purified, but he became a great devotee of the Supreme Person, Lord Viṣṇu, and directly realized Him.

PURPORT

The word *anusasmāra* is very significant. God consciousness is not imaginary or concocted. The devotee who is pure and advanced realizes God as He is. Mahārāja Pratīha did so, and due to his direct realization of Lord Viṣṇu, he propagated self-realization and became a preacher. A real preacher cannot be bogus; he must first of all realize Lord Viṣṇu as He is. As confirmed in *Bhagavad-gītā* (4.34), *upadekṣyanti te jñānaṁ jñāninas tattva-darśinaḥ:* "One who has seen the truth can impart knowledge." The word *tattva-darśī* refers to one who has perfectly realized the Supreme Personality of Godhead. Such a person can become a *guru* and propound Vaiṣṇava philosophy all over the world. The paragon of bona fide preachers and *guru* is King Pratīha.

TEXT 5

प्रतीहात्सुवर्चलायां प्रतिहर्त्रादयस्त्रय आसन्निज्याकोविदाः सूनवः प्रतिहर्तुः
स्तुत्यामजभूमानावजनिषाताम् ॥५॥

pratīhāt suvarcalāyāṁ pratihartrādayas traya āsann ijyā-kovidāḥ
sūnavaḥ pratihartuḥ stutyām aja-bhūmānāv ajaniṣātām.

pratīhāt—from King Pratīha; *suvarcalāyām*—in the womb of his wife, named Suvarcalā; *pratihartṛ-ādayaḥ trayaḥ*—the three sons Pratihartā, Prastotā and Udgātā; *āsan*—came into being; *ijyā-kovidāḥ*—who were all very expert in the ritualistic ceremonies of the *Vedas; sūnavaḥ*—sons; *pratihartuḥ*—from Pratihartā; *stutyām*—in the womb of Stutī, his wife; *aja-bhūmānau*—the two sons Aja and Bhūmā; *ajaniṣātām*—were brought into existence.

TRANSLATION

In the womb of his wife Suvarcalā, Pratīha begot three sons, named Pratihartā, Prastotā and Udgātā. These three sons were very expert in performing Vedic rituals. Pratihartā begot two sons, named Aja and Bhūmā, in the womb of his wife, named Stutī.

TEXT 6

भूम्न ऋषिकुल्यायामुद्गीथस्ततः प्रस्तावो देवकुल्यायां प्रस्तावान्नियुत्सायां
हृदयज आसीद्विभुर्विभो रत्यां च पृथुषेणस्तस्मान्नक्त आकूत्यां जज्ञे
नक्ताद्द्रुतिपुत्रो गयो राजर्षिप्रवर उदारश्रवा अजायत साक्षाद्भगवतो

विष्णोर्जगद् रिरक्षिषया गृहीतसत्त्वस्य कलाऽऽत्मवत्त्वादिलक्षणेन महापुरुषतां प्राप्तः ॥ ६ ॥

bhūmna ṛṣikulyāyām udgīthas tataḥ prastāvo devakulyāyāṁ prastāvān niyutsāyāṁ hṛdayaja āsīd vibhur vibho ratyāṁ ca pṛthuṣeṇas tasmān nakta ākūtyāṁ jajñe naktād druti-putro gayo rājarṣi-pravara udāra-śravā ajāyata sākṣād bhagavato viṣṇor jagad-rirakṣiṣayā gṛhīta-sattvasya kalātmavattvādi-lakṣaṇena mahā-puruṣatāṁ prāptaḥ.

bhūmnaḥ—from King Bhūmā; *ṛṣi-kulyāyām*—in the womb of his wife, named Ṛṣikulyā; *udgīthaḥ*—the son named Udgītha; *tataḥ*—again from King Udgītha; *prastāvaḥ*—the son named Prastāva; *deva-kulyāyām*—his wife, named Devakulyā; *prastāvāt*—from King Prastāva; *niyutsāyām*—in his wife, named Niyutsā; *hṛdaya-jaḥ*—the son; *āsīt*—was begotten; *vibhuḥ*—named Vibhu; *vibhoḥ*—from King Vibhu; *ratyām*—in his wife, named Ratī; *ca*—also; *pṛthu-ṣeṇaḥ*—named Pṛthuṣeṇa; *tasmāt*—from him (King Pṛthuṣeṇa); *naktaḥ*—a son named Nakta; *ākūtyām*—in his wife, named Ākūtī; *jajñe*—was begotten; *naktāt*—from King Nakta; *druti-putraḥ*—a son in the womb of Druti; *gayaḥ*—named King Gaya; *rāja-ṛṣi-pravaraḥ*—most exalted among the saintly royal order; *udāra-śravāḥ*—famous as a very pious king; *ajāyata*—was born; *sākṣāt bhagavataḥ*—of the Supreme Personality of Godhead directly; *viṣṇoḥ*—of Lord Viṣṇu; *jagat-rirakṣiṣayā*—for the purpose of giving protection to the whole world; *gṛhīta*—who is conceived; *sattvasya*—in the *śuddha-sattva* qualities; *kalā-ātma-vattva-ādi*—of being a direct incarnation of the Lord; *lakṣaṇena*—by symptoms; *maha-puruṣatām*—the chief quality of being the leader of the human society (exactly like the chief leader of all living beings, Lord Viṣṇu); *prāptaḥ*—achieved.

TRANSLATION

In the womb of his wife, Ṛṣikulyā, King Bhūmā begot a son named Udgītha. From Udgītha's wife, Devakulyā, a son named Prastāva was born, and Prastāva begot a son named Vibhu through his wife, Niyutsā. In the womb of his wife, Ratī, Vibhu begot a son named Pṛthuṣeṇa. Pṛthuṣeṇa begot a son named Nakta in the

womb of his wife, named Ākūti. Nakta's wife was Druti, and from her womb the great King Gaya was born. Gaya was very famous and pious; he was the best of saintly kings. Lord Viṣṇu and His expansions, who are meant to protect the universe, are always situated in the transcendental mode of goodness, known as viśuddha-sattva. Being the direct expansion of Lord Viṣṇu, King Gaya was also situated in the viśuddha-sattva. Because of this, Mahārāja Gaya was fully equipped with transcendental knowledge. Therefore he was called Mahāpuruṣa.

PURPORT

From this verse it appears that the incarnations of God are various. Some are part and parcel of the direct expansions, and some are direct expansions of Lord Viṣṇu. A direct incarnation of the Supreme Personality of Godhead is called *aṁśa* or *svāṁśa,* whereas an incarnation from *aṁśa* is called *kalā.* Among the *kalās* there are the *vibhinnāṁśa-jīvas,* or living entities. These are counted among the *jīva-tattvas.* Those who come directly from Lord Viṣṇu are called *viṣṇu-tattva* and are sometimes designated as Mahāpuruṣa. Another name for Kṛṣṇa is Mahāpuruṣa, and a devotee is sometimes called *mahā-pauruṣika.*

TEXT 7

स वै स्वधर्मेण प्रजापालन पोषणप्रीणनोपलालनानुशासनलक्षणेनेज्यादिना च
भगवति महापुरुषे परावरे ब्रह्मणि सर्वात्मनार्पितपरमार्थलक्षणेन
ब्रह्मविच्चरणानुसेवयाऽऽपादितभगवद्भक्तियोगेन चाभीक्ष्णशः परिभाविता-
तिशुद्ध मतिरुपरतानात्म्य आत्मनि स्वयमुपलभ्यमानब्रह्मात्मानुभवोऽपि
निरभिमान एवावनिमजूगुपत् ॥७॥

sa vai sva-dharmeṇa prajā-pālana-poṣaṇa-prīṇanopalālanānuśāsana-lakṣaṇenejyādinā ca bhagavati mahā-puruṣe parāvare brahmaṇi sarvātmanārpita-paramārtha-lakṣaṇena brahmavic-caraṇānusevayāpādita-bhagavad-bhakti-yogena cābhīkṣṇaśaḥ paribhāvitāti-śuddha-matir uparatānātmya ātmani svayam upalabhyamāna-brahmātmānubhavo 'pi nirabhimāna evāvanim ajūgupat.

saḥ—that King Gaya; *vai*—indeed; *sva-dharmeṇa*—by his own duty; *prajā-pālana*—of protecting the subjects; *poṣaṇa*—of maintaining them; *prīṇana*—of making them happy in all respects; *upalālana*—of treating them as sons; *anuśāsana*—of sometimes chastising them for their mistakes; *lakṣaṇena*—by the symptoms of a king; *ijyā-ādinā*—by performing the ritualistic ceremonies as recommended in the *Vedas; ca*—also; *bhagavati*—unto the Supreme Personality of Godhead, Viṣṇu; *mahā-puruṣe*—the chief of all living entities; *para-avare*—the source of all living entities, from the highest, Lord Brahmā, to the lowest, like the insignificant ants; *brahmaṇi*—unto Parabrahman, the Supreme Personality of Godhead, Vāsudeva; *sarva-ātmanā*—in all respects; *arpita*—of being surrendered; *parama-artha-lakṣaṇena*—with spiritual symptoms; *brahma-vit*—of self-realized, saintly devotees; *caraṇa-anusevayā*—by the service of the lotus feet; *āpādita*—achieved; *bhagavat-bhakti-yogena*—by the practice of devotional service to the Lord; *ca*—also; *abhīkṣṇaśaḥ*—continuously; *paribhāvita*—saturated; *ati-śuddha-matiḥ*—whose completely pure consciousness (full realization that the body and mind are separate from the soul); *uparata-anātmye*—wherein identification with material things was stopped; *ātmani*—in his own self; *svayam*—personally; *upalabhyamāna*—being realized; *brahma-ātma-anubhavaḥ*—perception of his own position as the Supreme Spirit; *api*—although; *nirabhimānaḥ*—without false prestige; *eva*—in this way; *avanim*—the whole world; *ajūgupat*—ruled strictly according to the Vedic principles.

TRANSLATION

King Gaya gave full protection and security to the citizens so that their personal property would not be disturbed by undesirable elements. He also saw that there was sufficient food to feed all the citizens. [This is called poṣaṇa.] He would sometimes distribute gifts to the citizens to satisfy them. [This is called prīṇana.] He would sometimes call meetings and satisfy the citizens with sweet words. [This is called upalālana.] He would also give them good instructions on how to become first-class citizens. [This is called anuśāsana.] Such were the characteristics of King Gaya's royal order. Besides all this, King Gaya was a householder who strictly

observed the rules and regulations of household life. He performed sacrifices and was an unalloyed pure devotee of the Supreme Personality of Godhead. He was called Mahāpuruṣa because as a king he gave the citizens all facilities, and as a householder he executed all his duties so that at the end he became a strict devotee of the Supreme Lord. As a devotee, he was always ready to give respect to other devotees and to engage in the devotional service of the Lord. This is the bhakti-yoga process. Due to all these transcendental acitivites, King Gaya was always free from the bodily conception. He was full in Brahman realization, and consequently he was always jubilant. He did not experience material lamentation. Although he was perfect in all respects, he was not proud, nor was he anxious to rule the kingdom.

PURPORT

As Lord Kṛṣṇa states in *Bhagavad-gītā,* when He descends on earth, He has two types of business—to give protection to the faithful and annihilate the demons (*paritrāṇāya sādhūnāṁ vināśāya ca duṣkṛtām*). Since the king is the representative of the Supreme Personality of Godhead, he is sometimes called *nara-deva,* that is, the Lord as a human being. According to the Vedic injunctions, he is worshiped as God on the material platform. As a representative of the Supreme Lord, the king had the duty to protect the citizens in a perfect way so that they would not be anxious for food and protection and so that they would be jubilant. The king would supply everything for their benefit, and because of this he would levy taxes. If the king or government otherwise levies taxes on the citizens, he becomes responsible for the sinful activities of the citizens. In Kali-yuga, monarchy is abolished because the kings themselves are subjected to the influence of Kali-yuga. It is understood from the *Rāmāyaṇa* that when Bibhīṣaṇa became friends with Lord Rāmacandra, he promised that if by chance or will he broke the laws of friendship with Lord Rāmacandra, he would become a *brāhmaṇa* or a king in Kali-yuga. In this age, as Bibhīṣaṇa indicated, both *brāhmaṇas* and kings are in a wretched condition. Actually there are no kings or *brāhmaṇas* in this age, and due to their absence the whole world is in a chaotic condition and is always in distress. Compared to present standards, Mahārāja Gaya was a true representative of Lord Viṣṇu; therefore he was known as Mahāpuruṣa.

TEXT 8

तस्येमां गाथां पाण्डवेय पुराविद उपगायन्ति॥८॥

tasyemāṁ gāthāṁ pāṇḍaveya purāvida upagāyanti.

tasya—of King Gaya; *imām*—these; *gāthām*—poetic verses of glorification; *pāṇḍaveya*—O Mahārāja Parīkṣit; *purā-vidaḥ*—those learned in the historical events of the *Purāṇas; upagāyanti*—sing.

TRANSLATION

My dear King Parīkṣit, those who are learned scholars in the histories of the Purāṇas eulogize and glorify King Gaya with the following verses.

PURPORT

The historical references to exalted kings serve as a good example for present rulers. Those who are ruling the world at the present moment should take lessons from King Gaya, King Yudhiṣṭhira and King Pṛthu and rule the citizens so that they will be happy. Presently the governments are levying taxes without improving the citizens in any cultural, religious, social or political way. According to the *Vedas*, this is not recommended.

TEXT 9

गयं नृपः कः प्रतियाति कर्मभि-
र्यज्वाभिमानी बहुविद्धर्मगोप्ता ।
समागतश्रीः सदसस्पतिः सतां
सत्सेवकोऽन्यो भगवत्कलामृते ॥ ९ ॥

gayaṁ nṛpaḥ kaḥ pratiyāti karmabhir
yajvābhimānī bahuvid dharma-goptā

samāgata-śrīḥ sadasas-patiḥ satāṁ
sat-sevako 'nyo bhagavat-kalām ṛte

gayam—King Gaya; *nṛpaḥ*—king; *kaḥ*—who; *pratiyāti*—is a match for; *karmabhiḥ*—by his execution of ritualistic ceremonies; *yajvā*—who performed all sacrifices; *abhimānī*—so widely respected all over the world; *bahu-vit*—fully aware of the conclusion of Vedic literature; *dharma-goptā*—protector of the occupational duties of everyone; *samāgata-śrīḥ*—possessing all kinds of opulence; *sadasaḥ-patiḥ satām*—the dean of the assembly of great persons; *sat-sevakaḥ*—servant of the devotees; *anyaḥ*—anyone else; *bhagavat-kalām*—the plenary incarnation of the Supreme Personality of Godhead; *ṛte*—besides.

TRANSLATION

The great King Gaya used to perform all kinds of Vedic rituals. He was highly intelligent and expert in studying all the Vedic literatures. He maintained the religious principles and possessed all kinds of opulence. He was a leader among gentlemen and a servant of the devotees. He was a totally qualified plenary expansion of the Supreme Personality of Godhead. Therefore who could equal him in the performance of gigantic ritualistic ceremonies?

TEXT 10

यमभ्यषिञ्चन् परया मुदा सतीः
सत्याशिषो दक्षकन्याः सरिद्भिः ।
यस्य प्रजानां दुदुहे धराऽऽशिषो
निराशिषो गुणवत्सस्नुतोधाः ॥१०॥

yam abhyaṣiñcan parayā mudā satīḥ
satyāśiṣo dakṣa-kanyāḥ saridbhiḥ
yasya prajānāṁ duduhe dharāśiṣo
nirāśiṣo guṇa-vatsa-snutodhāḥ

yam—whom; *abhyaṣiñcan*—bathed; *parayā*—with great; *mudā*—satisfaction; *satīḥ*—all chaste and devoted to their husbands; *satya*—

true; *āśiṣaḥ*—whose blessings; *dakṣa-kanyāḥ*—the daughters of King Dakṣa; *saridbhiḥ*—with sanctified water; *yasya*—whose; *prajānām*—of the citizens; *duduhe*—fulfilled; *dharā*—the planet earth; *āśiṣaḥ*—of all desires; *nirāśiṣaḥ*—although personally having no desire; *guṇa-vatsa-snuta-udhāḥ*—earth becoming like a cow whose udders flowed upon seeing Gaya's qualities in ruling over the citizens.

TRANSLATION

All the chaste and honest daughters of Mahārāja Dakṣa, such as Śraddhā, Maitrī and Dayā, whose blessings were always effective, bathed Mahārāja Gaya with sanctified water. Indeed, they were very satisfied with Mahārāja Gaya. The planet earth personified came as a cow, and, as though she saw her calf, she delivered milk profusely when she saw all the good qualities of Mahārāja Gaya. In other words, Mahārāja Gaya was able to derive all benefits from the earth and thus satisfy the desires of his citizens. However, he personally had no desire.

PURPORT

The earth over which Mahārāja Gaya ruled is compared to a cow. The good qualities whereby he maintained and ruled the citizens are compared to the calf. A cow delivers milk in the presence of her calf; similarly the cow, or earth, fulfilled the desires of Mahārāja Gaya, who was able to utilize all the resources of the earth to benefit his citizens. This was possible because he was bathed in sanctified water by the honest daughters of Dakṣa. Unless a king or ruler is blessed by authorities, he cannot rule the citizens very satisfactorily. Through the good qualities of the ruler, the citizens become very happy and well qualified.

TEXT 11

छन्दांस्यकामस्य च यस्य कामान्
दुदूहुराजहुरथो बलिं नृपाः ।
प्रत्यञ्चिता युधि धर्मेण विप्रा
यदाशिषां षष्ठमंशं परेत्य ॥११॥

chandāṁsy akāmasya ca yasya kāmān
dudūhur ājahrur atho baliṁ nṛpāḥ
pratyañcitā yudhi dharmeṇa viprā
yadāśiṣāṁ ṣaṣṭham aṁśaṁ paretya

chandāṁsi—all the different parts of the *Vedas; akāmasya*—of one who has no desire for personal sense gratification; *ca*—also; *yasya*—whose; *kāmān*—all desirables; *dudūhuḥ*—yielded; *ājahruḥ*—offered; *atho*—thus; *balim*—presentation; *nṛpāḥ*—all the kings; *pratyañcitāḥ*—being satisfied by his fighting in opposition; *yudhi*—in the war; *dharmeṇa*—by religious principles; *viprāḥ*—all the *brāhmaṇas; yadā*—when; *āśiṣām*—of blessings; *ṣaṣṭham aṁśam*—one sixth; *paretya*—in the next life.

TRANSLATION

Although King Gaya had no personal desire for sense gratification, all his desires were fulfilled by virtue of his performance of Vedic rituals. All the kings with whom Mahārāja Gaya had to fight were forced to fight on religious principles. They were very satisfied with his fighting, and they would present all kinds of gifts to him. Similarly, all the brāhmaṇas in his kingdom were very satisfied with King Gaya's munificent charities. Consequently the brāhmaṇas contributed a sixth of their pious activities for King Gaya's benefit in the next life.

PURPORT

As a *kṣatriya* or emperor, Mahārāja Gaya sometimes had to fight with subordinate kings to maintain his government, but the subordinate kings were not dissatisfied with him because they knew that he fought for religious principles. Consequently they accepted their subordination and offered all kinds of gifts to him. Similarly, the *brāhmaṇas* who performed Vedic rituals were so satisfied with the King that they very readily agreed to part with a sixth of their pious activities for his benefit in the next life. Thus the *brāhmaṇas* and *kṣatriyas* were all satisfied with Mahārāja Gaya because of his proper administration. In other words, Mahārāja Gaya satisfied the *kṣatriya* kings by his fighting and satisfied the *brāhmaṇas* by his charities. The *vaiśyas* were also encouraged by kind words and affectionate dealings, and due to Mahārāja Gaya's constant sacrifices, the *śūdras* were satisfied by sumptuous food and charity. In this way Mahārāja Gaya kept all the citizens very satisfied. When *brāhmaṇas* and saintly persons are honored, they part with their pious activities, giving them to those who honor them and render them service. Therefore, as stated in *Bhagavad-gītā* (4.34), *tad viddhi praṇipātena paripraśnena sevayā:* one should try to approach a spiritual master submissively and render service unto him.

TEXT 12

यस्याध्वरे भगवानध्वरात्मा
मघोनि माद्यत्युरुसोमपीथे ।
श्रद्धाविशुद्धाचलभक्तियोग-
समर्पितेज्याफलमाजहार ॥१२॥

yasyādhvare bhagavān adhvarātmā
maghoni mādyaty uru-soma-pīthe
śraddhā-viśuddhācala-bhakti-yoga-
samarpitejyā-phalam ājahāra

yasya—of whom (King Gaya); *adhvare*—in his different sacrifices; *bhagavān*—the Supreme Personality of Godhead; *adhvara-ātmā*—the supreme enjoyer of all sacrifices, the *yajña-puruṣa; maghoni*—when King Indra; *mādyati*—intoxicated; *uru*—greatly; *soma-pīthe*—drinking the intoxicant called *soma; śraddhā*—by devotion; *viśuddha*—purified; *acala*—and steady; *bhakti-yoga*—by devotional service; *samarpita*—offered; *ijyā*—of worshiping; *phalam*—the result; *ājahāra*—accepted personally.

TRANSLATION

In Mahārāja Gaya's sacrifices, there was a great supply of the intoxicant known as soma. King Indra used to come and become intoxicated by drinking large quantities of soma-rasa. Also, the Supreme Personality of Godhead, Lord Viṣṇu [the yajña-puruṣa]

also came and personally accepted all the sacrifices offered unto Him with pure and firm devotion in the sacrificial arena.

PURPORT

Mahārāja Gaya was so perfect that he satisfied all the demigods, who were headed by the heavenly King Indra. Lord Viṣṇu Himself also personally came to the sacrificial arena to accept the offerings. Although Mahārāja Gaya did not want them, he received all the blessings of the demigods and the Supreme Lord Himself.

TEXT 13

यत्प्रीणनाद्बर्हिषि देवतिर्यङ्-
मनुष्यवीरुत्तृणमाविरिञ्चात् ।
प्रीयेत सद्यः स ह विश्वजीवः
प्रीतः स्वयं प्रीतिमगाद्गयस्य ॥१३॥

yat-prīṇanād barhiṣi deva-tiryaṅ-
manuṣya-vīrut-tṛṇam āviriñcāt
prīyeta sadyaḥ sa ha viśva-jīvaḥ
prītaḥ svayaṁ prītim agād gayasya

yat-prīṇanāt—because of pleasing the Supreme Personality of Godhead; *barhiṣi*—in the sacrificial arena; *deva-tiryak*—the demigods and lower animals; *manuṣya*—human society; *vīrut*—the plants and trees; *tṛṇam*—the grass; *ā-viriñcāt*—beginning from Lord Brahmā; *prīyeta*—becomes satisfied; *sadyaḥ*—immediately; *saḥ*—that Supreme Personality of Godhead; *ha*—indeed; *viśva-jīvaḥ*—maintains the living entities all over the universe; *prītaḥ*—although naturally satisfied; *svayam*—personally; *prītim*—satisfaction; *agāt*—he obtained; *gayasya*—of Mahārāja Gaya.

TRANSLATION

When the Supreme Lord is pleased by a person's actions, automatically all the demigods, human beings, animals, birds, bees, creepers, trees, grass and all other living entities, beginning with

Lord Brahmā, are pleased. The Supreme Personality of Godhead is the Supersoul of everyone, and He is by nature fully pleased. Nonetheless, He came to the arena of Mahārāja Gaya and said, "I am fully pleased."

PURPORT

It is explicitly stated herein that simply by satisfying the Supreme Personality of Godhead, one satisfies the demigods and all other living entities without differentiation. If one pours water on the root of a tree, all the branches, twigs, flowers and leaves are nourished. Although the Supreme Lord is self-satisfied, He was so pleased with the behavior of Mahārāja Gaya that He personally came to the sacrificial arena and said, "I am fully satisfied." Who can compare to Mahārāja Gaya?

TEXTS 14-15

**गयाद्गयन्त्यां चित्ररथः सुगतिरवरोधन इति त्रयः पुत्रा बभूवुश्चि-
त्ररथादूर्णायां सम्राडजनिष्ट तत उत्कलायां मरीचिर्मरीचे ॥१४॥
बिन्दुमत्यां बिन्दुमानुदपद्यत तस्मात्सरघायां मधुर्नामाभवन्मधोः सुमनसि
वीरव्रतस्ततो भोजायां मन्थुप्रमन्थू जज्ञाते मन्थोः सत्यायां भौवनस्ततो
दूषणायां त्वष्टाजनिष्ट त्वष्टुर्विरोचनायां विरजो विरजस्य शतजित्प्रवरं
पुत्रशतं कन्या च विषूच्यां किल जातम् ॥१५॥**

gayād gayantyāṁ citrarathaḥ sugatir avarodhana iti trayaḥ putrā babhūvuś citrarathād ūrṇāyāṁ samrāḍ ajaniṣṭa. tata utkalāyāṁ marīcir marīcer bindumatyāṁ bindum ānudapadyata tasmāt saraghāyāṁ madhur nāmābhavan madhoḥ sumanasi vīravratas tato bhojāyāṁ manthu-pramanthū jajñāte manthoḥ satyāyāṁ bhauvanas tato dūṣaṇāyāṁ tvaṣṭājaniṣṭa tvaṣṭur virocanāyāṁ virajo virajasya śatajit-pravaraṁ putra-śataṁ kanyā ca viṣūcyāṁ kila jātam.

gayāt—from Mahārāja Gaya; *gayantyām*—in his wife, named Gayantī; *citra-rathaḥ*—named Citraratha; *sugatiḥ*—named Sugati;

avarodhanaḥ—named Avarodhana; *iti*—thus; *trayaḥ*—three; *putrāḥ*—sons; *babhūvuḥ*—were born; *citrarathāt*—from Citraratha; *ūrṇāyām*—in the womb of Ūrṇā; *samrāṭ*—named Samrāṭ; *ajaniṣṭa*—was born; *tataḥ*—from him; *utkalāyām*—in his wife named Utkalā; *marīciḥ*—named Marīci; *marīceḥ*—from Marīci; *bindu-matyām*—in the womb of his wife Bindumatī; *bindum*—a son named Bindu; *ānudapadyata*—was born; *tasmāt*—from him; *saraghāyām*—in the womb of his wife Saraghā; *madhuḥ*—Madhu; *nāma*—named; *abhavat*—was born; *madhoḥ*—from Mahdu; *sumanasi*—in the womb of his wife, Sumanā; *vīra-vrataḥ*—a son named Vīravrata; *tataḥ*—from Vīravrata; *bhojāyām*—in the womb of his wife Bhojā; *manthu-pramanthū*—two sons named Manthu and Pramanthu; *jajñāte*—were born; *manthoḥ*—from Manthu; *satyāyām*—in his wife, Satyā; *bhauvanaḥ*—a son named Bhauvana; *tataḥ*—from him; *dūṣaṇāyām*—in the womb of his wife Dūṣaṇā; *tvaṣṭā*—one son named Tvaṣṭā; *ajaniṣṭa*—was born; *tvaṣṭuḥ*—from Tvaṣṭā; *virocanāyām*—in his wife named Virocanā; *virajaḥ*—a son named Viraja; *virajasya*—of King Viraja; *śatajit-pravaram*—headed by Śatajit; *putra-śatam*—one hundred sons; *kanyā*—a daughter; *ca*—also; *viṣūcyām*—in his wife Viṣūcī; *kila*—indeed; *jātam*—took birth.

TRANSLATION

In the womb of Gayantī, Mahārāja Gaya begot three sons, named Citraratha, Sugati and Avarodhana. In the womb of his wife Ūrṇā, Citraratha begot a son named Samrāṭ. The wife of Samrāṭ was Utkalā, and in her womb Samrāṭ begot a son named Marīci. In the womb of his wife Bindumatī, Marīci begot a son named Bindu. In the womb of his wife Saraghā, Bindu begot a son named Madhu. In the womb of his wife named Sumanā, Madhu begot a son named Vīravrata. In the womb of his wife Bhojā, Vīravrata begot two sons named Manthu and Pramanthu. In the womb of his wife Satyā, Manthu begot a son named Bhauvana, and in the womb of his wife Dūṣaṇā, Bhauvana begot a son named Tvaṣṭā. In the womb of his wife Virocanā, Tvaṣṭā begot a son named Viraja. The wife of Viraja was Viṣūcī, and in her womb Viraja begot one hundred sons and one daughter. Of all these sons, the son named Śatajit was predominant.

TEXT 16

तत्रायं श्लोकः—
प्रैयव्रतं वंशमिमं विरजश्चरमोद्भवः ।
अकरोदत्यलं कीर्त्या विष्णुः सुरगणं यथा ॥१६॥

tatrāyaṁ ślokaḥ——
praiyavrataṁ vaṁśam imaṁ
virajaś caramodbhavaḥ
akarod aty-alaṁ kīrtyā
viṣṇuḥ sura-gaṇaṁ yathā

tatra—in that connection; *ayam ślokaḥ*—there is this famous verse; *praiyavratam*—coming from King Priyavrata; *vaṁśam*—the dynasty; *imam*—this; *virajaḥ*—King Viraja; *carama-udbhavaḥ*—the source of one hundred sons (headed by Śatajit); *akarot*—decorated; *ati-alam*—very greatly; *kīrtyā*—by his reputation; *viṣṇuḥ*—Lord Viṣṇu, the Supreme Personality of Godhead; *sura-gaṇam*—the demigods; *yathā*—just as.

TRANSLATION

There is a famous verse about King Viraja. "Because of his high qualities and wide fame, King Viraja became the jewel of the dynasty of King Priyavrata, just as Lord Viṣṇu, by His transcendental potency, decorates and blesses the demigods."

PURPORT

Within a garden, a flowering tree attains a good reputation because of its fragrant flowers. Similarly, if there is a famous man in a family, he is compared to a fragrant flower in a forest. Because of him, an entire family can become famous in history. Because Lord Kṛṣṇa took birth in the Yadu dynasty, the Yadu dynasty and the Yādavas have remained famous for all time. Because of King Viraja's appearance, the family of Mahārāja Priyavrata has remained famous for all time.

Thus end the Bhaktivedanta purports of the Fifth Canto, Fifteenth Chapter of the Śrīmad-Bhāgavatam, *"The Glories of the Descendants of King Priyavrata."*

CHAPTER SIXTEEN

A Description of Jambūdvīpa

While describing the character of Mahārāja Priyavrata and his descendants, Śukadeva Gosvāmī also described Meru Mountain and the planetary system known as Bhū-maṇḍala. Bhū-maṇḍala is like a lotus flower, and its seven islands are compared to the whorl of the lotus. The place known as Jambūdvīpa is in the middle of that whorl. In Jambūdvīpa there is a mountain known as Sumeru, which is made of solid gold. The height of this mountain is 84,000 *yojanas*, of which 16,000 *yojanas* are below the earth. Its width is estimated to be 32,000 *yojanas* at its summit and 16,000 *yojanas* at its foot. (One *yojana* equals approximately eight miles.) This king of mountains, Sumeru, is the support of the planet earth.

On the southern side of the land known as Ilāvṛta-varṣa are the mountains known as Himavān, Hemakūṭa and Niṣadha, and on the northern side are the mountains Nīla, Śveta and Śṛṅga. Similarly, on the eastern and western side there are Mālyavān and Gandhamādana, two large mountains. Surrounding Sumeru Mountain are four mountains known as Mandara, Merumandara, Supārśva and Kumuda, each 10,000 *yojanas* long and 10,000 *yojanas* high. On these four mountains there are trees 1,100 *yojanas* high—a mango tree, a rose apple tree, a *kadamba* tree and a banyan tree. There are also lakes full of milk, honey, sugarcane juice and pure water. These lakes can fulfill all desires. There are also gardens named Nandana, Citraratha, Vaibhrājaka and Sarvatobhadra. On the side of Supārśva Mountain is a *kadamba* tree with streams of honey flowing from its hollows, and on Kumuda Mountain there is a banyan tree named Śatavalśa, from whose roots flow rivers containing milk, yogurt and many other desirable things. Surrounding Sumeru Mountain like filaments of the whorl of a lotus are twenty mountain ranges such as Kuraṅga, Kurara, Kusumbha, Vaikaṅka and Trikūṭa. To the east of Sumeru are the mountains Jaṭhara and Devakūṭa, to the west are Pavana and Pāriyātra, to the south are Kailāsa and Karavīra, and to the north are Triśṛṅga and Makara. These eight mountains are about 18,000 *yojanas* long, 2,000 *yojanas* wide and 2,000 *yojanas* high. On the summit of

Mount Sumeru is Brahmapurī, the residence of Lord Brahmā. Each of its four sides is 10,000 *yojanas* long. Surrounding Brahmapurī are the cities of King Indra and seven other demigods. These cities are one fourth the size of Brahmapurī.

TEXT 1

राजोवाच

उक्तस्त्वया भूमण्डलायामविशेषो यावदादित्यस्तपति यत्र चासौ ज्योतिषां गणैश्चन्द्रमा वा सह दृश्यते ॥ १ ॥

rājovāca
uktas tvayā bhū-maṇḍalāyāma-viśeṣo yāvad ādityas tapati yatra cāsau jyotiṣāṁ gaṇaiś candramā vā saha dṛśyate.

rājā uvāca—Mahārāja Parīkṣit said; *uktaḥ*—already been said; *tvayā*—by you; *bhū-maṇḍala*—of the planetary system known as Bhū-maṇḍala; *āyāma-viśeṣaḥ*—the specific length of the radius; *yāvat*—as far as; *ādityaḥ*—the sun; *tapati*—heats; *yatra*—wherever; *ca*—also; *asau*—that; *jyotiṣām*—of the luminaries; *gaṇaiḥ*—with hordes; *candramā*—the moon; *vā*—either; *saha*—with; *dṛśyate*—is seen.

TRANSLATION

King Parīkṣit said to Śukadeva Gosvāmī: O brāhmaṇa, you have already informed me that the radius of Bhū-maṇḍala extends as far as the sun spreads its light and heat and as far as the moon and all the stars can be seen.

PURPORT

In this verse it is stated that the planetary system known as Bhū-maṇḍala extends to the limits of the sunshine. According to modern science, the sunshine reaches earth from a distance of 93,000,000 miles. If we calculate according to this modern information, 93,000,000 miles can be considered the radius of Bhū-maṇḍala. In the Gāyatrī *mantra*, we chant *oṁ bhūr bhuvaḥ svaḥ*. The word *bhūr* refers to Bhū-maṇḍala. *Tat savitur vareṇyam:* the sunshine spreads throughout Bhū-maṇḍala. Therefore the sun is worshipable. The stars, which are known as *nakṣatra*, are not different suns, as modern astronomers suppose. From *Bhagavad-gītā* (10.21) we understand that the stars are similar to the moon (*nakṣatrāṇām ahaṁ śaśī*). Like the moon, the stars reflect the sunshine. Apart from our modern distinguished estimations of where the planetary systems are located, we can understand that the sky and its various planets were studied long, long before *Śrīmad-Bhāgatavam* was compiled. Śukadeva Gosvāmī explained the location of the planets, and this indicates that the information was known long, long before Śukadeva Gosvāmī related it to Mahārāja Parīkṣit. The location of the various planetary systems was not unknown to the sages who flourished in the Vedic age.

TEXT 2

तत्रापि प्रियव्रतरथचरणपरिखातैः सप्तभिः सप्त सिन्धव उपक्लृप्ता यत
एतस्याः सप्तद्वीपविशेषविकल्पस्त्वया भगवन् खलु सूचित एतदेवाखिलमहं
मानतो लक्षणतश्च सर्वं विजिज्ञासामि ॥ २ ॥

tatrāpi priyavrata-ratha-caraṇa-parikhātaiḥ saptabhiḥ sapta sindhava upakḷptā yata etasyāḥ sapta-dvīpa-viśeṣa-vikalpas tvayā bhagavan khalu sūcita etad evākhilam ahaṁ mānato lakṣaṇataś ca sarvaṁ vijijñāsāmi.

tatra api—in that Bhū-maṇḍala; *priyavrata-ratha-caraṇa-parikhātaiḥ*—by the ditches made by the wheels of the chariot used by Priyavrata Mahārāja while circumambulating Sumeru behind the sun; *saptabhiḥ*—by the seven; *sapta*—seven; *sindhavaḥ*—oceans; *upakḷptāḥ*—created; *yataḥ*—because of which; *etasyāḥ*—of this Bhū-maṇḍala; *sapta-dvīpa*—of the seven islands; *viśeṣa-vikalpaḥ*—the mode of the construction; *tvayā*—by you; *bhagavan*—O great saint; *khalu*—indeed; *sūcitaḥ*—described; *etat*—this; *eva*—certainly; *akhilam*—whole subject; *aham*—I; *mānataḥ*—from the point of view of measurement; *lakṣaṇataḥ*—and from symptoms; *ca*—also; *sarvam*—everything; *vijijñāsāmi*—wish to know.

TRANSLATION

My dear Lord, the rolling wheels of Mahārāja Priyavrata's chariot created seven ditches, in which the seven oceans came into existence. Because of these seven oceans, Bhū-maṇḍala is divided into seven islands. You have given a very general description of their measurement, names and characteristics. Now I wish to know of them in detail. Kindly fulfill my desire.

TEXT 3

भगवतो गुणमये स्थूलरूप आवेशितं मनो ह्यगुणेऽपि सूक्ष्मतम आत्मज्योतिषि परे ब्रह्मणि भगवति वासुदेवाख्ये क्षममावेशितुं तदु हैतद् गुरोऽर्हस्यनुवर्णयितुमिति ॥ ३ ॥

bhagavato guṇamaye sthūla-rūpa āveśitaṁ mano hy aguṇe 'pi
sūkṣmatama ātma-jyotiṣi pare brahmaṇi bhagavati vāsudevākhye
kṣamam āveśituṁ tad u haitad guro 'rhasy anuvarṇayitum iti.

bhagavataḥ—of the Supreme Personality of Godhead; *guṇa-maye*—into the external features, consisting of the three modes of material nature; *sthūla-rūpe*—the gross form; *āveśitam*—entered; *manaḥ*—the mind; *hi*—indeed; *aguṇe*—transcendental; *api*—although; *sūkṣma-tame*—in His smaller form as Paramātmā within the heart; *ātma-jyotiṣi*—who is full of Brahman effulgence; *pare*—the supreme; *brahmaṇi*—spiritual entity; *bhagavati*—the Supreme Personality of Godhead; *vāsudeva-ākhye*—known as Bhagavān Vāsudeva; *kṣamam*—suitable; *āveśitum*—to absorb; *tat*—that; *u ha*—indeed; *etat*—this; *guro*—O my dear spiritual master; *arhasi anuvarṇayitum*—please describe factually; *iti*—thus.

TRANSLATION

When the mind is fixed upon the Supreme Personality of Godhead in His external feature made of the material modes of nature—the gross universal form—it is brought to the platform of pure goodness. In that transcendental position, one can understand the Supreme Personality of Godhead, Vāsudeva, who in His

subtler form is self-effulgent and beyond the modes of nature. O my lord, please describe vividly how that form, which covers the entire universe, is perceived.

PURPORT

Mahārāja Parīkṣit had already been advised by his spiritual master, Śukadeva Gosvāmī, to think of the universal form of the Lord, and therefore, following the advice of his spiritual master, he continuously thought of that form. The universal form is certainly material, but because everything is an expansion of the energy of the Supreme Personality of Godhead, ultimately nothing is material. Therefore Parīkṣit Mahārāja's mind was saturated with spiritual consciousness. Śrīla Rūpa Gosvāmī has stated:

prāpañcikatayā buddhyā
hari-sambandhi-vastunaḥ
mumukṣubhiḥ parityāgo
vairāgyaṁ phalgu kathyate

Everything, even that which is material, is connected with the Supreme Personality of Godhead. Therefore everything should be engaged in the service of the Lord. Śrīla Bhaktisiddhānta Sarasvatī Ṭhākura translates this verse as follows:

hari-sevāya yāhā haya anukūla
viṣaya baliyā tāhāra tyāge haya bhula

"One should not give up anything connected with the Supreme Personality of Godhead, thinking it material or enjoyable for the material senses." Even the senses, when purified, are spiritual. When Mahārāja Parīkṣit was thinking of the universal form of the Lord, his mind was certainly situated on the transcendental platform. Therefore although he might not have had any reason to be concerned with detailed information of the universe, he was thinking of it in relationship with the Supreme Lord, and therefore such geographical knowledge was not material but transcendental. Elsewhere in *Śrīmad-Bhāgavatam* (1.5.20) Nārada Muni has said, *idaṁ hi viśvaṁ bhagavān ivetaraḥ:* the entire universe is also the Supreme Personality of Godhead, although it appears different from Him. Therefore although Parīkṣit Mahārāja had no need for geographical knowledge of this universe, that knowledge was also spiritual and transcendental because he was thinking of the entire universe as an expansion of the energy of the Lord.

In our preaching work also, we deal with so much property and money and so many books bought and sold, but because these dealings all pertain to the Kṛṣṇa consciousness movement, they should never be considered material. That one is absorbed in thoughts of such management does not mean that he is outside of Kṛṣṇa consciousness. If one rigidly observes the regulative principle of chanting sixteen rounds of the *mahā-mantra* every day, his dealings with the material world for the sake of spreading the Kṛṣṇa consciousness movement are not different from the spiritual cultivation of Kṛṣṇa consciousness.

TEXT 4

ऋषिरुवाच

न वै महाराज भगवतो मायागुणविभूतेः काष्ठां मनसा वचसा वाधिगन्तुमलं विबुधायुषापि पुरुषस्तस्मात्प्राधान्येनैव भूगोलकविशेषं नाम-रूप मानलक्षणतो व्याख्यास्यामः ॥ ४ ॥

ṛṣir uvāca
na vai mahārāja bhagavato māyā-guṇa-vibhūteḥ kāṣṭhāṁ manasā vacasā vādhigantum alaṁ vibudhāyuṣāpi puruṣas tasmāt prādhān-yenaiva bhū-golaka-viśeṣaṁ nāma-rūpa-māna-lakṣaṇato vyākhyāsyāmaḥ.

ṛṣiḥ uvāca—Śrī Śukadeva Gosvāmī continued to speak; *na*—not; *vai*—indeed; *mahā-rāja*—O great King; *bhagavataḥ*—of the Supreme Personality of Godhead; *māyā-guṇa-vibhūteḥ*—of the transformation of the qualities of the material energy; *kāṣṭhām*—the end; *manasā*—by the mind; *vacasā*—by words; *vā*—either; *adhigantum*—to understand fully; *alam*—capable; *vibudha-āyuṣā*—with a duration of life like that of Brahmā; *api*—even; *puruṣaḥ*—a person; *tasmāt*—therefore; *prādhānyena*—by a general description of the chief places; *eva*—certainly; *bhū-golaka-viśeṣam*—the particular description of Bhūloka; *nāma-rūpa*—names and forms; *māna*—measurements; *lakṣaṇataḥ*—according to symptoms; *vyākhyāsyāmaḥ*—I shall try to explain.

TRANSLATION

The great ṛṣi Śukadeva Gosvāmī said: My dear King, there is no limit to the expansion of the Supreme Personality of Godhead's material energy. This material world is a transformation of the material qualities [sattva-guṇa, rajo-guṇa and tamo-guṇa], yet no one could possibly explain it perfectly, even in a lifetime as long as that of Brahmā. No one in the material world is perfect, and an imperfect person could not describe this material universe accurately, even after continued speculation. O King, I shall nevertheless try to explain to you the principal regions, such as Bhū-golaka [Bhūloka], with their names, forms, measurements and various symptoms.

PURPORT

The material world is only one fourth of the Supreme Personality of Godhead's creation, but it is unlimited and impossible for anyone to know or describe, even with the qualification of a life as long as that of Brahmā, who lives for millions and millions of years. Modern scientists and astronomers try to explain the cosmic situation and the vastness of space, and some of them believe that all the glittering stars are different suns. From *Bhagavad-gītā*, however, we understand that all these stars (*nakṣatras*) are like the moon, in that they reflect the sunshine. They are not independent luminaries. Bhūloka is explained to be that portion of outer space through which the heat and light of the sun extend. Therefore it is natural to conclude that this universe extends in space as far as we can see and encompasses the glittering stars. Śrīla Śukadeva Gosvāmī admitted that to give full details of this expansive material universe would be impossible, but nevertheless he wanted to give the King as much knowledge as he had received through the *paramparā* system. We should conclude that if one cannot comprehend the material expansions of the Supreme Personality of Godhead, one certainly cannot estimate the expansiveness of the spiritual world. The *Brahma-saṁhitā* (5.33) confirms this:

advaitam acyutam anādim ananta-rūpam
ādyaṁ purāṇa-puruṣaṁ nava-yauvanaṁ ca

The limits of the expansions of Govinda, the Supreme Personality of Godhead, cannot be estimated by anyone, even a person as perfect as Brahmā, not to speak of tiny scientists whose senses and instruments are all imperfect and who cannot give us information of even this one universe. We should therefore be satisfied with the information obtainable from Vedic sources as spoken by authorities like Śukadeva Gosvāmī.

TEXT 5

यो वायं द्वीपः कुवलयकमलकोशाभ्यन्तरकोशो नियुतयोजन विशालः समवर्तुलो यथा पुष्करपत्रम् ॥ ५ ॥

yo vāyaṁ dvīpaḥ kuvalaya-kamala-kośābhyantara-kośo niyuta-yojana-viśālaḥ samavartulo yathā puṣkara-patram.

yaḥ—which; *vā*—either; *ayam*—this; *dvīpaḥ*—island; *kuvalaya*—the Bhūloka; *kamala-kośa*—of the whorl of a lotus flower; *abhyantara*—inner; *kośaḥ*—whorl; *niyuta-yojana-viśālaḥ*—one million *yojanas* (eight million miles) wide; *samavartulaḥ*—equally round, or having a length and breadth of the same measurement; *yathā*—like; *puṣkara-patram*—a lotus leaf.

TRANSLATION

The planetary system known as Bhū-maṇḍala resembles a lotus flower, and its seven islands resemble the whorl of that flower. The length and breadth of the island known as Jambūdvīpa, which is situated in the middle of the whorl, are one million yojanas [eight million miles]. Jambūdvīpa is round like the leaf of a lotus flower.

TEXT 6

यस्मिन्नव वर्षाणि नवयोजनसहस्रायामान्यष्टभिर्मर्यादागिरिभिः सुविभक्तानि भवन्ति ॥६॥

yasmin nava varṣāṇi nava-yojana-sahasrāyāmāny aṣṭabhir maryādā-giribhiḥ suvibhaktāni bhavanti.

yasmin—in that Jambūdvīpa; *nava*—nine; *varṣāṇi*—divisions of land; *nava-yojana-sahasra*—72,000 miles in length; *āyāmāni*—measuring; *aṣṭabhiḥ*—by eight; *maryādā*—indicating the boundaries; *giribhiḥ*—by mountains; *suvibhaktāni*—nicely divided from one another; *bhavanti*—are.

TRANSLATION

In Jambūdvīpa there are nine divisions of land, each with a length of 9,000 yojanas [72,000 miles]. There are eight mountains that mark the boundaries of these divisions and separate them nicely.

PURPORT

Śrīla Viśvanātha Cakravartī Ṭhākura gives the following quotation from the *Vāyu Purāṇa*, wherein the locations of the various mountains, beginning with the Himalayas, are described.

dhanurvat saṁsthite jñeye dve varṣe dakṣiṇottare. dīrghāṇi tatra catvāri caturasram ilāvṛtam iti dakṣiṇottare bhāratottara-kuru-varṣe catvāri kiṁpuruṣa-harivarṣa-ramyaka-hiraṇmayāni varṣāṇi nīla-niṣadhayos tiraścinībhūya samudra-praviṣṭayoḥ saṁlagnatvam aṅgīkṛtya bhadrāśva-ketumālayor api dhanur-ākṛtitvam. atas tayor dairghyata eva madhye saṅkucitatvena nava-sahasrāyāmatvam. ilāvṛtasya tu meroḥ sakāśāt catur-dikṣu nava-sahasrāyāmatvaṁ saṁbhavet vastutas tv ilāvṛta-bhadrāśva-ketumālānāṁ catus-triṁśat-sahasrāyāmatvaṁ jñeyam.

TEXT 7

एषां मध्ये इलावृतं नामाभ्यन्तरवर्षं यस्य नाभ्यामवस्थितः सर्वतः सौवर्णः कुलगिरिराजो मेरुर्द्वीपायामसमुन्नाहः कर्णिकाभूतः कुवलयकमलस्य मूर्धनि द्वात्रिंशत् सहस्र योजनविततो मूले षोडशसहस्रं तावतान्तर्भूम्यां प्रविष्टः ॥ ७ ॥

eṣāṁ madhye ilāvṛtaṁ nāmābhyantara-varṣaṁ yasya nābhyām avasthitaḥ sarvataḥ sauvarṇaḥ kula-giri-rājo merur dvīpāyāma-samunnāhaḥ karṇikā-bhūtaḥ kuvalaya-kamalasya mūrdhani dvā-triṁśat sahasra-yojana-vitato mūle ṣoḍaśa-sahasraṁ tāvat āntar-bhūmyāṁ praviṣṭaḥ.

eṣām—all these divisions of Jambūdvīpa; *madhye*—among; *ilāvṛtam nāma*—named Ilāvṛta-varṣa; *abhyantara-varṣam*—the inner division; *yasya*—of which; *nābhyām*—in the navel; *avasthitaḥ*—situated; *sarvataḥ*—entirely; *sauvarṇaḥ*—made of gold; *kula-giri-rājaḥ*—the most famous among famous mountains; *meruḥ*—Mount Meru; *dvīpa-āyāma-samunnāhaḥ*—whose height is the same measurement as the width of Jambūdvīpa; *karṇikā-bhūtaḥ*—existing as the pericarp; *kuvalaya*—of this planetary system; *kamalasya*—like a lotus flower; *mūrdhani*—on the top; *dvā-triṁśat*—thirty-two; *sahasra*—thousand; *yojana*—*yojanas* (eight miles each); *vitataḥ*—expanded; *mūle*—at the base; *ṣoḍaśa-sahasram*—sixteen thousand *yojanas; tāvat*—so much; *āntaḥ-bhūmyām*—within the earth; *praviṣṭaḥ*—entered.

TRANSLATION

Amidst these divisions, or varṣas, is the varṣa named Ilāvṛta, which is situated in the middle of the whorl of the lotus. Within Ilāvṛta-varṣa is Sumeru Mountain, which is made of gold. Sumeru Mountain is like the pericarp of the lotuslike Bhū-maṇḍala planetary system. The mountain's height is the same as the width of Jambūdvīpa—or, in other words, 100,000 yojanas [800,000 miles]. Of that, 16,000 yojanas [128,000 miles] are within the earth, and therefore the mountain's height above the earth is 84,000 yojanas [672,000 miles]. The mountain's width is 32,000 yojanas [256,000 miles] at its summit and 16,000 yojanas at its base.

TEXT 8

उत्तरोत्तरेणेलावृतं नीलः श्वेतः शृङ्गवानिति त्रयो रम्यकहिरण्मयकुरूणां वर्षाणां
मर्यादागिरयः प्रागायता उभयतः क्षारोदावधयो द्विसहस्रपृथव एकैकशः
पूर्वस्मात्पूर्वस्मादुत्तर उत्तरो दशांशाधिकांशेन दैर्घ्य एव ह्रसन्ति ॥ ८ ॥

uttarottareṇelāvṛtaṁ nīlaḥ śvetaḥ śṛṅgavān iti trayo ramyaka-hiraṇmaya-kurūṇāṁ varṣāṇāṁ maryādā-girayaḥ prāg-āyatā ubhayataḥ kṣārodāvadhayo dvi-sahasra-pṛthava ekaikaśaḥ pūrvasmāt pūrvasmād uttara uttaro daśāṁśādhikāṁśena dairghya eva hrasanti.

uttara-uttareṇa ilāvṛtam—further and further north of Ilāvṛta-varṣa; *nīlaḥ*—Nīla; *śvetaḥ*—Śveta; *śṛṅgavān*—Śṛṅgavān; *iti*—thus; *trayaḥ*—three mountains; *ramyaka*—Ramyaka; *hiraṇmaya*—Hiraṇmaya; *kurūṇām*—of the Kuru division; *varṣāṇām*—of the *varṣas; maryādā-girayaḥ*—the mountains marking the borders; *prāk-āyatāḥ*—extended on the eastern side; *ubhayataḥ*—to the east and the west; *kṣāroda*—the ocean of salt water; *avadhayaḥ*—extending to; *dvi-sahasra-pṛthavaḥ*—which are two thousand *yojanas* wide; *eka-ekaśaḥ*—one after another; *pūrvasmāt*—than the former; *pūrvasmāt*—than the former; *uttaraḥ*—further north; *uttaraḥ*—further north; *daśa-aṁśa-adhika-aṁśena*—by one tenth of the former; *dairghyaḥ*—in length; *eva*—indeed; *hrasanti*—become shorter.

TRANSLATION

Just north of Ilāvṛta-varṣa—and going further northward, one after another—are three mountains named Nīla, Śveta and Śṛṅgavān. These mark the borders of the three varṣas named Ramyaka, Hiraṇmaya and Kuru and separate them from one another. The width of these mountains is 2,000 yojanas [16,000 miles]. Lengthwise, they extend east and west to the beaches of the ocean of salt water. Going from south to north, the length of each mountain is one tenth that of the previous mountain, but the height of them all is the same.

PURPORT

In this regard, Madhvācārya quotes the following verses from the *Brahmāṇḍa Purāṇa:*

yathā bhāgavate tūktaṁ
bhauvanaṁ kośa-lakṣaṇam
tasyāvirodhato yojyam
anya-granthāntare sthitam

maṇḍode puraṇaṁ caiva
vyatyāsaṁ kṣīra-sāgare
rāhu-soma-ravīṇāṁ ca
maṇḍalād dvi-guṇoktitām
vinaiva sarvam unneyaṁ
yojanābhedato 'tra tu

It appears from these verses that aside from the sun and moon, there is an invisible planet called Rāhu. The movements of Rāhu cause both solar and lunar eclipses. We suggest that the modern expeditions attempting to reach the moon are mistakenly going to Rāhu.

TEXT 9

एवं दक्षिणेनेलावृतं निषधो हेमकूटो हिमालय इति प्रागायता यथा नीलादयो-
ऽयुतयोजनोत्सेधा हरिवर्षकिम्पुरुषभारतानां यथासंख्यम् ॥९॥

evaṁ dakṣiṇenelāvṛtaṁ niṣadho hemakūṭo himālaya iti prāg-āyatā yathā nīlādayo 'yuta-yojanotsedhā hari-varṣa-kimpuruṣa-bhāratānāṁ yathā-saṅkhyam.

evam—thus; *dakṣiṇena*—by degrees to the southern side; *ilāvṛtam*—of Ilāvṛta-varṣa; *niṣadhaḥ hema-kūṭaḥ himālayaḥ*—three mountains named Niṣadha, Hemakūṭa and Himālaya; *iti*—thus; *prāk-āyatāḥ*—extended to the east; *yathā*—just as; *nīla-ādayaḥ*—the mountains headed by Nīla; *ayuta-yojana-utsedhāḥ*—ten thousand *yojanas* high; *hari-varṣa*—the division named Hari-varṣa; *kimpuruṣa*—the division named Kimpuruṣa; *bhāratānām*—the division named Bhārata-varṣa; *yathā-saṅkhyam*—according to number.

TRANSLATION

Similarly, south of Ilāvṛta-varṣa and extending from east to west are three great mountains named (from north to south) Niṣadha, Hemakūṭa and Himālaya. Each of them is 10,000 yojanas [80,000 miles] high. They mark the boundaries of the three varṣas named Hari-varṣa, Kimpuruṣa-varṣa and Bhārata-varṣa [India].

TEXT 10

तथैवेलावृतमपरेण पूर्वेण च माल्यवद्गन्धमादनावानीलनिषधायतौ द्विसहस्रं पप्रथतुः केतुमालभद्राश्वयोः सीमानं विदधाते ॥ १० ॥

tathaivelāvṛtam apareṇa pūrveṇa ca mālyavad-gandhamādanāv ānīla-niṣadhāyatau dvi-sahasraṁ paprathatuḥ ketumāla-bhadrāśvayoḥ sīmānaṁ vidadhāte.

tathā eva—exactly like that; *ilāvṛtam apareṇa*—on the western side of Ilāvṛta-varṣa; *pūrveṇa ca*—and on the eastern side; *mālyavad-gandha-mādanau*—the demarcation mountains of Mālyavān on the west and Gandhamādana on the east; *ā-nīla-niṣada-āyatau*—on the northern side up to the mountain known as Nīla and on the southern side up to the mountain known as Niṣadha; *dvi-sahasram*—two thousand *yojanas; paprathatuḥ*—they extend; *ketumāla-bhadrāśvayoḥ*—of the two *varṣas* named Ketumāla and Bhadrāśva; *sīmānam*—the border; *vidadhāte*—establish.

TRANSLATION

In the same way, west and east of Ilāvṛta-varṣa are two great mountains named Mālyavān and Gandhamādana respectively. These two mountains, which are 2,000 yojanas [16,000 miles] high, extend as far as Nīla Mountain in the north and Niṣadha in the south. They indicate the borders of Ilāvṛta-varṣa and also the varṣas known as Ketumāla and Bhadrāśva.

PURPORT

There are so many mountains, even on this planet earth. We do not think that the measurements of all of them have actually been calculated. While passing over the mountainous region from Mexico to Caracas, we actually saw so many mountains that we doubt whether their height, length and breadth have been properly measured. Therefore, as indicated in *Śrīmad-Bhāgavatam* by Śukadeva Gosvāmī, we should not try to comprehend the greater mountainous areas of the universe merely by our calculations. Śukadeva Gosvāmī has already stated that such calculations would be very difficult even if one had a duration of life like that of Brahmā. We should simply be satisfied with the statements of authorities like Śukadeva Gosvāmī and appreciate how the entire cosmic manifestation has been made possible by the external energy of the Supreme Personality of Godhead. The measurements given herein, such as 10,000 *yojanas* or 100,000 *yojanas*, should be considered correct because they have been given by Śukadeva Gosvāmī. Our experimental knowledge can neither verify nor disprove the statements of *Śrīmad-Bhāgavatam.* We should simply hear these statements from the authorities. If we can appreciate the extensive energy of the Supreme Personality of Godhead, that will benefit us.

TEXT 11

मन्दरो मेरुमन्दरः सुपार्श्वः कुमुद इत्ययुतयोजनविस्तारोन्नाहा मेरो-श्चतुर्दिशमवष्टम्भगिरय उपक्लृप्ताः ॥ ११ ॥

mandaro merumandaraḥ supārśvaḥ kumuda ity ayuta-yojana-
vistāronnāhā meroś catur-diśam avaṣṭambha-giraya upakḷptāḥ.

mandaraḥ—the mountain named Mandara; *meru-mandaraḥ*—the mountain named Merumandara; *supārśvaḥ*—the mountain named Supārśva; *kumudaḥ*—the mountain named Kumuda; *iti*—thus; *ayuta-yojana-vistāra-unnāhāḥ*—which measure ten thousand *yojanas* high and wide; *meroḥ*—of Sumeru; *catuḥ-diśam*—the four sides; *avaṣṭambha-girayaḥ*—mountains that are like the belts of Sumeru; *upakḷptāḥ*—situated.

TRANSLATION

On the four sides of the great mountain known as Sumeru are four mountains—Mandara, Merumandara, Supārśva and Kumuda—which are like its belts. The length and height of these mountains are calculated to be 10,000 yojanas [80,000 miles].

TEXT 12

चतुर्ष्वेतेषु चूतजम्बूकदम्बन्यग्रोधाश्चत्वारः पादप प्रवराः पर्वतकेतव इवाधि-सहस्रयोजनोन्नाहास्तावद् विटपविततयः शतयोजनपरिणाहाः ॥ १२ ॥

caturṣv eteṣu cūta-jambū-kadamba-nyagrodhāś catvāraḥ pādapa-pravarāḥ parvata-ketava ivādhi-sahasra-yojanonnāhās tāvad viṭapa-vitatayaḥ śata-yojana-pariṇāhāḥ.

caturṣu—on the four; *eteṣu*—on these mountains, beginning with Mandara; *cūta-jambū-kadamba*—of trees such as the mango, rose apple and *kadamba; nyagrodhāḥ*—and the banyan tree; *catvāraḥ*—four kinds; *pādapa-pravarāḥ*—the best of trees; *parvata-ketavaḥ*—the flagstaffs on the mountains; *iva*—like; *adhi*—over; *sahasra-yojana-un-nāhāḥ*—one thousand *yojanas* high; *tāvat*—so much also; *viṭapa-vitatayaḥ*—the length of the branches; *śata-yojana*—one hundred *yojanas; pariṇāhāḥ*—wide.

TRANSLATION

Standing like flagstaffs on the summits of these four mountains are a mango tree, a rose apple tree, a kadamba tree and a banyan tree. Those trees are calculated to have a width of 100 yojanas [800 miles] and a height of 1,100 yojanas [8,800 miles]. Their branches also spread to a radius of 1,100 yojanas.

TEXTS 13-14

ह्रदाश्चत्वारः पयोमध्विक्षुरसमृष्टजला यदुपस्पर्शिन उपदेवगणा योगैश्वर्याणि स्वाभाविकानि भरतर्षभ धारयन्ति ॥ १३ ॥ देवोद्यानानि च भवन्ति चत्वारि नन्दनं चैत्ररथं वैभ्राजकं सर्वतोभद्रमिति ॥१४॥

hradāś catvāraḥ payo-madhv-ikṣurasa-mṛṣṭa-jalā yad-upasparśina upadeva-gaṇā yogaiśvaryāṇi svābhāvikāni bharatarṣabha dhārayanti. devodyānāni ca bhavanti catvāri nandanaṁ caitrarathaṁ vaibhrājakaṁ sarvatobhadram iti.

hradāḥ—lakes; *catvāraḥ*—four; *payaḥ*—milk; *madhu*—honey; *ikṣu-rasa*—sugarcane juice; *mṛṣṭa-jalāḥ*—filled with pure water; *yat*—of which; *upasparśinaḥ*—those who use the liquids; *upadeva-gaṇāḥ*—the demigods; *yoga-aiśvaryāṇi*—all the perfections of mystic *yoga; svābhāvikāni*—without being tried for; *bharata-ṛṣabha*—O best of the

Bharata dynasty; *dhārayanti*—possess; *deva-udyānāni*—celestial gardens; *ca*—also; *bhavanti*—there are; *catvāri*—four; *nandanam*—of the Nandana garden; *caitra-ratham*—Caitraratha garden; *vaibhrājakam*—Vaibhrājaka garden; *sarvataḥ-bhadram*—Sarvatobhadra garden; *iti*—thus.

TRANSLATION

O Mahārāja Parīkṣit, best of the Bharata dynasty, between these four mountains are four huge lakes. The water of the first tastes just like milk; the water of the second, like honey; and that of the third, like sugarcane juice. The fourth lake is filled with pure water. The celestial beings such as the Siddhas, Cāraṇas and Gandharvas, who are also known as demigods, enjoy the facilities of those four lakes. Consequently they have the natural perfections of mystic yoga, such as the power to become smaller than the smallest or greater than the greatest. There are also four celestial gardens named Nandana, Caitraratha, Vaibhrājaka and Sarvatobhadra.

TEXT 15

येष्वमर परिवृढाः सह सुरललनाललामयूथपतय उपदेवगणैरुपगीयमानमहिमानः किल विहरन्ति ॥ १५ ॥

yeṣv amara-parivṛḍhāḥ saha sura-lalanā-lalāma-yūtha-pataya
upadeva-gaṇair upagīyamāna-mahimānaḥ kila viharanti.

yeṣu—in which; *amara-parivṛḍhāḥ*—the best of the demigods; *saha*—with; *sura-lalanā*—of the wives of all the demigods and semi-demigods; *lalāma*—of those women who are like ornaments; *yūtha-patayaḥ*—the husbands; *upadeva-gaṇaiḥ*—by the semi-demigods (the Gandharvas); *upagīyamāna*—being chanted; *manimānaḥ*—whose glories; *kila*—indeed; *viharanti*—they enjoy sports.

TRANSLATION

The best of the demigods, along with their wives, who are like ornaments of heavenly beauty, meet together and enjoy within

those gardens, while their glories are sung by lesser demigods known as Gandharvas.

TEXT 16

मन्दरोत्सङ्ग एकादशशतयोजनोत्तुङ्गदेवचूतशिरसो गिरिशिखरस्थूलानि फलान्यमृतकल्पानि पतन्ति ॥१६॥

mandarotsaṅga ekādaśa-śata-yojanottuṅga-devacūta-śiraso giri-śikhara-sthūlāni phalāny amṛta-kalpāni patanti.

mandara-utsaṅge—on the lower slopes of Mandara Mountain; *ekādaśa-śata-yojana-uttuṅga*—1,100 *yojanas* high; *devacūta-śirasaḥ*—from the top of a mango tree named Devacūta; *giri-śikhara-sthūlāni*—which are as fat as mountain peaks; *phalāni*—fruit; *amṛta-kalpāni*—as sweet as nectar; *patanti*—fall down.

TRANSLATION

On the lower slopes of Mandara Mountain is a mango tree named Devacūta. It is 1,100 yojanas high. Mangoes as big as mountain peaks and as sweet as nectar fall from the top of this tree for the enjoyment of the denizens of heaven.

PURPORT

In the *Vāyu Purāṇa* there is also a reference to this tree by great learned sages:

aratnīnāṁ śatāny aṣṭāv
eka-ṣaṣṭy-adhikāni ca
phala-pramāṇam ākhyātam
ṛṣibhis tattva-darśibhir

TEXT 17

तेषां विशीर्यमाणानामतिमधुरसुरभिसुगन्धि बहुलारुणरसोदेनारुणोदा नाम नदी मन्दरगिरिशिखरान्निपतन्ती पूर्वेणेलावृतमुपप्लावयति ॥१७॥

teṣāṁ viśīryamāṇānām ati-madhura-surabhi-sugandhi-bahulāruṇa-rasodenāruṇodā nāma nadī mandara-giri-śikharān nipatantī pūrveṇelāvṛtam upaplāvayati.

teṣām—of all the mangoes; *viśīryamāṇānām*—being broken because of falling from the top; *ati-madhura*—very sweet; *surabhi*—fragrant; *sugandhi*—scented with other aromas; *bahula*—large quantities; *aruṇa-rasa-udena*—by reddish juice; *aruṇodā*—Aruṇodā; *nāma*—named; *nadī*—the river; *mandara-giri-śikharāt*—from the top of Mandara Mountain; *nipatantī*—falling down; *pūrveṇa*—on the eastern side; *il-āvṛtam*—through Ilāvṛta-varṣa; *upaplāvayati*—flows.

TRANSLATION

When all those solid fruits fall from such a height, they break, and the sweet, fragrant juice within them flows out and becomes increasingly more fragrant as it mixes with other scents. That juice cascades from the mountain in waterfalls and becomes a river called Aruṇodā, which flows pleasantly through the eastern side of Ilāvṛta.

TEXT 18

यदुपजोषणाद्भवान्या अनुचरीणां पुण्यजनवधूनामवयवस्पर्शसुगन्धवातो
दशयोजनं समन्तादनुवासयति ॥१८॥

yad-upajoṣaṇād bhavānyā anucarīṇāṁ puṇya-jana-vadhūnām
avayava-sparśa-sugandha-vāto daśa-yojanaṁ samantād anuvāsayati.

yat—of which; *upajoṣaṇāt*—because of using the fragrant water; *bhavānyāḥ*—of Bhavānī, the wife of Lord Śiva; *anucarīṇām*—of attendant maidservants; *puṇya-jana-vadhūnām*—who are wives of the most pious Yakṣas; *avayava*—of the bodily limbs; *sparśa*—from contact; *sugandha-vātaḥ*—the wind, which becomes fragrant; *daśa-yojanam*—up to ten *yojanas* (about eighty miles); *samantāt*—all around; *anuvāsayati*—makes fragrant.

TRANSLATION

The pious wives of the Yakṣas act as personal maidservants to assist Bhavānī, the wife of Lord Śiva. Because they drink the water of the River Aruṇodā, their bodies become fragrant, and as the air carries away that fragrance, it perfumes the entire atmosphere for eighty miles around.

TEXT 19

एवं जम्बूफलानामत्युच्चनिपातविशीर्णानामनस्थिप्रायाणामिभकायनिभानां रसेन जम्बू नाम नदी मेरुमन्दरशिखरादयुतयोजनादवनितले निपतन्ती दक्षिणेनात्मानं यावदिलावृतमुपस्यन्दयति ॥१९॥

evaṁ jambū-phalānām atyucca-nipāta-viśīrṇānām anasthi-prāyāṇām ibha-kāya-nibhānāṁ rasena jambū nāma nadī meru-mandara-śikharād ayuta-yojanād avani-tale nipatantī dakṣiṇenātmānaṁ yāvad ilāvṛtam upasyandayati.

evam—similarly; *jambū-phalānām*—of the fruits called *jambū* (the rose apple); *ati-ucca-nipāta*—because of falling from a great height; *viśīrṇānām*—which are broken to pieces; *anasthi-prāyāṇām*—having very small seeds; *ibha-kāya-nibhānām*—and which are as large as the bodies of elephants; *rasena*—by the juice; *jambū nāma nadī*—a river named Jambū-nadī; *meru-mandara-śikharāt*—from the top of Meru-mandara Mountain; *ayuta-yojanāt*—ten thousand *yojanas* high; *avani-tale*—on the ground; *nipatantī*—falling; *dakṣiṇena*—on the southern side; *ātmānam*—itself; *yāvat*—the whole; *ilāvṛtam*—Ilāvṛta-varṣa; *upasyandayati*—flows through.

TRANSLATION

Similarly, the fruits of the jambū tree, which are full of pulp and have very small seeds, fall from a great height and break to pieces. Those fruits are the size of elephants, and the juice gliding from them becomes a river named Jambū-nadī. This river falls a distance of 10,000 yojanas, from the summit of Merumandara to

the southern side of Ilāvṛta, and floods the entire land of Ilāvṛta with juice.

PURPORT

We can only imagine how much juice there might be in a fruit that is the size of an elephant but has a very tiny seed. Naturally the juice from the broken *jambū* fruits forms waterfalls and floods the entire land of Ilāvṛta. That juice produces an immense quantity of gold, as will be explained in the next verses.

TEXTS 20-21

तावदुभयोरपि रोधसोर्या मृत्तिका तद्रसेनानुविध्यमाना वाय्वर्कसंयोगविपाकेन सदामरलोकाभरणं जाम्बूनदं नाम सुवर्णं भवति ॥२०॥ यदु ह वाव विबुधादयः सह युवतिभिर्मुकुटकटककटिसूत्राद्याभरणरूपेण खलु धारयन्ति ॥२१॥

tāvad ubhayor api rodhasor yā mṛttikā tad-rasenānuvidhyamānā vāyv-arka-saṁyoga-vipākena sadāmara-lokābharaṇaṁ jāmbū-nadaṁ nāma suvarṇaṁ bhavati. yad u ha vāva vibudhādayaḥ saha yuvatibhir mukuṭa-kaṭaka-kaṭi-sūtrādy-ābharaṇa-rūpeṇa khalu dhārayanti.

tāvat—entirely; *ubhayoḥ api*—of both; *rodhasoḥ*—of the banks; *yā*—which; *mṛttikā*—the mud; *tat-rasena*—with the juice of the *jambū* fruits that flows in the river; *anuvidhyamānā*—being saturated; *vāyu-arka-saṁyoga-vipākena*—because of a chemical reaction with the air and sunshine; *sadā*—always; *amara-loka-ābharaṇam*—which is used for the ornaments of the demigods, the denizens of the heavenly planets; *jāmbū-nadam nāma*—named Jāmbū-nada; *suvarṇam*—gold; *bhavati*—becomes; *yat*—which; *u ha vāva*—indeed; *vibudha-ādayaḥ*—the great demigods; *saha*—with; *yuvatibhiḥ*—their everlastingly youthful wives; *mukuṭa*—crowns; *kaṭaka*—bangles; *kaṭi-sūtra*—belts; *ādi*—and so on; *ābharaṇa*—of all kinds of ornaments; *rūpeṇa*—in the form; *khalu*—indeed; *dhārayanti*—they possess.

TRANSLATION

The mud on both banks of the River Jambū-nadī, being moistened by the flowing juice and then dried by the air and the

sunshine, produces huge quantities of gold called Jāmbū-nada. The denizens of heaven use this gold for various kinds of ornaments. Therefore all the inhabitants of the heavenly planets and their youthful wives are fully decorated with golden helmets, bangles and belts, and thus they enjoy life.

PURPORT

By the arrangement of the Supreme Personality of Godhead, the rivers on some planets produce gold on their banks. The poor inhabitants of this earth, because of their incomplete knowledge, are captivated by a so-called *bhagavān* who can produce a small quantity of gold. However, it is understood that in a higher planetary system in this material world, the mud on the banks of the Jambū-nadī mixes with *jambū* juice, reacts with the sunshine in the air, and automatically produces huge quantities of gold. Thus the men and women are decorated there by various golden ornaments, and they look very nice. Unfortunately, on earth there is such a scarcity of gold that the governments of the world try to keep it in reserve and issue paper currency. Because that currency is not backed up by gold, the paper they distribute as money is worthless, but nevertheless the people on earth are very proud of material advancement. In modern times, girls and ladies have ornaments made of plastic instead of gold, and plastic utensils are used instead of golden ones, yet people are very proud of their material wealth. Therefore the people of this age are described as *mandāḥ sumanda-matayo manda-bhāgyā hy upadrutāḥ* (*Bhāg.* 1.1.10). In other words, they are extremely bad and slow to understand the opulence of the Supreme Personality of Godhead. They have been described as *sumanda-matayaḥ* because their conceptions are so crippled that they accept a bluffer who produces a little gold to be God. Because they have no gold in their possession, they are actually poverty-stricken, and therefore they are considered unfortunate.

Sometimes these unfortunate people want to be promoted to the heavenly planets to achieve fortunate positions, as described in this verse, but pure devotees of the Lord are not at all interested in such opulence. Indeed, devotees sometimes compare the color of gold to that of bright golden stool. Śrī Caitanya Mahāprabhu has instructed devotees not to be allured by golden ornaments and beautifully decorated women. *Na dhanaṁ na janaṁ na sundarīm:* a devotee should not be allured by gold.

beautiful women or the prestige of having many followers. Śrī Caitanya Mahāprabhu, therefore, confidentially prayed, *mama janmani janmanīśvare bhavatād bhaktir ahaitukī tvayi:* "My Lord, please bless Me with Your devotional service. I do not want anything else." A devotee may pray to be delivered from this material world. That is his only aspiration.

ayi nanda-tanuja kiṅkaraṁ
patitaṁ māṁ viṣame bhavāmbudhau
kṛpayā tava pāda-paṅkaja-
sthita-dhūlī-sadṛśam vicintaya

The humble devotee simply prays to the Lord, "Kindly pick me up from the material world, which is full of varieties of material opulence, and keep me under the shelter of Your lotus feet."

Śrīla Narottama dāsa Ṭhākura prays:

hā hā prabhu nanda-suta, vṛṣabhānu-sutā-yuta,
karuṇā karaha ei-bāra
narottama-dāsa kaya, nā ṭheliha rāṅgā-pāya,
tomā vine ke āche āmāra

"O my Lord, O son of Nanda Mahārāja, now You are standing before me with Your consort, the daughter of Vṛṣabhānu, Śrīmatī Rādhārāṇī. Kindly accept me as the dust of Your lotus feet. Please do not kick me away, for I have no other shelter."

Similarly, Prabodhānanda Sarasvatī indicates that the position of the demigods, who are decorated with golden helmets and other ornaments, is no better than a phantasmagoria (*tri-daśa-pūr ākāśa-puṣpāyate*). A devotee is never allured by such opulences. He simply aspires to become the dust of the lotus feet of the Lord.

TEXT 22

यस्तु महाकदम्बः सुपार्श्वनिरूढो यास्तस्य कोटरेभ्यो विनिःसृताः पञ्चायामपरिणाहाः पञ्च मधुधाराः सुपार्श्वशिखरात्पतन्त्योऽपरेणात्मानमिलावृतमनुमोदयन्ति ॥२२॥

yas tu mahā-kadambaḥ supārśva-nirūḍho yās tasya koṭarebhyo viniḥsṛtāḥ pañcāyāma-pariṇāhāḥ pañca madhu-dhārāḥ supārśva-śikharāt patantyo 'pareṇātmānam ilāvṛtam anumodayanti.

yaḥ—which; *tu*—but; *mahā-kadambaḥ*—the tree named Mahākadamba; *supārśva-nirūḍhaḥ*—which stands on the side of the mountain known as Supārśva; *yāḥ*—which; *tasya*—of that; *koṭarebhyaḥ*—from the hollows; *viniḥsṛtāḥ*—flowing; *pañca*—five; *āyāma*—*vyāma*, a unit of measurement of about eight feet; *pariṇāhāḥ*—whose measurement; *pañca*—five; *madhu-dhārāḥ*—flows of honey; *supārśva-śikharāt*—from the top of Supārśva Mountain; *patantyaḥ*—flowing down; *apareṇa*—on the western side of Sumeru Mountain; *ātmānam*—the whole of; *ilāvṛtam*—Ilāvṛta-varṣa; *anumodayanti*—make fragrant.

TRANSLATION

On the side of Supārśva Mountain stands a big tree called Mahākadamba, which is very celebrated. From the hollows of this tree flow five rivers of honey, each about five vyāmas wide. This flowing honey falls incessantly from the top of Supārśva Mountain and flows all around Ilāvṛta-varṣa, beginning from the western side. Thus the whole land is saturated with the pleasing fragrance.

PURPORT

The distance between one hand and another when one spreads both his arms is called a *vyāma*. This comes to about eight feet. Thus each of the rivers was about forty feet wide, making a total of about two hundred feet.

TEXT 23

या ह्युपयुञ्जानानां मुखनिर्वासितो वायुः समन्ताच्छतयोजनमनुवासयति ॥२३॥

yā hy upayuñjānānāṁ mukha-nirvāsito vāyuḥ samantāc chata-yojanam anuvāsayati.

yāḥ—which (those flows of honey); *hi*—indeed; *upayuñjānānām*—of those who drink; *mukha-nirvāsitaḥ vāyuḥ*—the air emanating from the mouths; *samantāt*—all around; *śata-yojanam*—up to one hundred *yojanas* (eight hundred miles); *anuvāsayati*—makes sweetly flavored.

TRANSLATION

The air carrying the scent from the mouths of those who drink that honey perfumes the land for a hundred yojanas around.

TEXT 24

एवं कुमुदनिरूढो यः शतवल्शो नाम वटस्तस्य स्कन्धेभ्यो नीचीनाः पयोदधिमधुघृतगुडान्नाद्यम्बरशय्यासनाभरणादयः सर्व एव कामदुघा नदाः कुमुदाग्रात्पतन्तस्तमुत्तरेणेलावृतमुपयोजयन्ति ॥२४॥

evaṁ kumuda-nirūḍho yaḥ śatavalśo nāma vaṭas tasya skandhebhyo nīcīnāḥ payo-dadhi-madhu-ghṛta-guḍānnādy-ambara-śayyāsanābharaṇādayaḥ sarva eva kāma-dughā nadāḥ kumudāgrāt patantas tam uttareṇelāvṛtam upayojayanti.

evam—thus; *kumuda-nirūḍhaḥ*—having grown on Kumuda Mountain; *yaḥ*—that; *śata-valśaḥ nāma*—the tree named Śatavalśa (because of having hundreds of trunks); *vaṭaḥ*—a banyan tree; *tasya*—of it; *skandhebhyaḥ*—from the thick branches; *nīcīnāḥ*—flowing down; *payaḥ*—milk; *dadhi*—yogurt; *madhu*—honey; *ghṛta*—clarified butter; *guḍa*—molasses; *anna*—food grains; *ādi*—and so on; *ambara*—clothing; *śayyā*—bedding; *āsana*—sitting places; *ābharaṇa-ādayaḥ*—carrying ornaments and so on; *sarve*—everything; *eva*—certainly; *kāma-dughāḥ*—fulfilling all desires; *nadāḥ*—big rivers; *kumuda-agrāt*—from the top of Kumuda Mountain; *patantaḥ*—flowing; *tam*—to that; *uttareṇa*—on the northern side; *ilāvṛtam*—the land known as Ilāvṛta-varṣa; *upayojayanti*—give happiness.

TRANSLATION

Similarly, on Kumuda Mountain there is a great banyan tree, which is called Śatavalśa because it has a hundred main branches. From those branches come many roots, from which many rivers are flowing. These rivers flow down from the top of the mountain

to the northern side of Ilāvṛta-varṣa for the benefit of those who live there. Because of these flowing rivers, all the people have ample supplies of milk, yogurt, honey, clarified butter [ghee], molasses, food grains, clothes, bedding, sitting places and ornaments. All the objects they desire are sufficiently supplied for their prosperity, and therefore they are very happy.

PURPORT

The prosperity of humanity does not depend on a demoniac civilization that has no culture and no knowledge but has only gigantic skyscrapers and huge automobiles always rushing down the highways. The products of nature are sufficient. When there is a profuse supply of milk, yogurt, honey, food grains, ghee, molasses, dhotis, saris, bedding, sitting places and ornaments, the residents are actually opulent. When a profuse supply of water from the river inundates the land, all these things can be produced, and there will not be scarcity. This all depends, however, on the performance of sacrifice as described in the Vedic literature.

annād bhavanti bhūtāni
parjanyād anna-sambhavaḥ
yajñād bhavati parjanyo
yajñaḥ karma-samudbhavaḥ

"All living bodies subsist on food grains, which are produced from rains. Rains are produced by performance of *yajña* [sacrifice], and *yajña* is born of prescribed duties." These are the prescriptions given in *Bhagavad-gītā* (3.14). If people follow these principles in full Kṛṣṇa consciousness, human society will be prosperous, and they will be happy both in this life and in the next.

TEXT 25

यानुपजुषाणानां न कदाचिदपि प्रजानां बलीपलितक्लमस्वेददौर्गन्ध्यजरामय-
मृत्युशीतोष्णवैवर्ण्योपसर्गादयस्तापविशेषा भवन्ति यावज्जीवं सुखं निरतिशयमेव
॥ २५ ॥

yān upajuṣāṇānāṁ na kadācid api prajānāṁ valī-palita-klama-sveda-daurgandhya-jarāmaya-mṛtyu-śītoṣṇa-vaivarṇyopasargādayas tāpa-viśeṣā bhavanti yāvaj jīvaṁ sukhaṁ niratiśayam eva.

yān—which (all the products produced because of the flowing rivers mentioned above); *upajuṣāṇānām*—of persons who are fully utilizing; *na*—not; *kadācit*—at any time; *api*—certainly; *prajānām*—of the citizens; *valī*—wrinkles; *palita*—grey hair; *klama*—fatigue; *sveda*—perspiration; *daurgandhya*—bad odors because of unclean perspiration; *jarā*—old age; *āmaya*—disease; *mṛtyu*—untimely death; *śīta*—severe cold; *uṣṇa*—scorching heat; *vaivarṇya*—fading of the luster of the body; *upasarga*—troubles; *ādayaḥ*—and so on; *tāpa*—of sufferings; *viśeṣāḥ*—varieties; *bhavanti*—are; *yāvat*—as long as; *jīvam*—life; *sukham*—happiness; *niratiśayam*—unlimited; *eva*—only.

TRANSLATION

The residents of the material world who enjoy the products of these flowing rivers have no wrinkles on their bodies and no grey hair. They never feel fatigue, and perspiration does not give their bodies a bad odor. They are not afflicted by old age, disease or untimely death, they do not suffer from chilly cold or scorching heat, nor do their bodies lose their luster. They all live very happily, without anxieties, until death.

PURPORT

This verse hints at the perfection of human society even within this material world. The miserable conditions of this material world can be corrected by a sufficient supply of milk, yogurt, honey, ghee, molasses, food grains, ornaments, bedding, sitting places and so on. This is human civilization. Ample food grains can be produced through agricultural enterprises, and profuse supplies of milk, yogurt and ghee can be arranged through cow protection. Abundant honey can be obtained if the forests are protected. Unfortunately, in modern civilization, men are busy killing the cows that are the source of yogurt, milk and ghee, they are cutting down all the trees that supply honey, and they are opening factories to manufacture nuts, bolts, automobiles and wine instead of engaging in agriculture. How can the people be happy? They must suffer from all the misery of materialism. Their bodies become wrinkled and gradually deteriorate until they become almost like dwarves, and a bad odor emanates from their bodies because of unclean perspiration resulting from eating all kinds of nasty things. This is not human civilization. If people actually want happiness in this life and want to prepare for the best in the next life, they must adopt a Vedic civilization. In a Vedic civilization, there is a full supply of all the necessities mentioned above.

TEXT 26

कुरङ्गकुररकुसुम्भवैकङ्कत्रिकूटशिशिरपतङ्गरुचकनिषधशिनीवासकपिलशङ्ख-वैदूर्यजारुधिहंसर्षभनागकालञ्जरनारदादयो विंशतिगिरयो मेरोः कर्णिकाया इव केसरभूता मूलदेशे परित उपक्लृप्ताः ॥ २६ ॥

kuraṅga-kurara-kusumbha-vaikaṅka-trikūṭa-śiśira-pataṅga-rucaka-niṣadha-śinīvāsa-kapila-śaṅkha-vaidūrya-jārudhi-haṁsa-ṛṣabha-nāga-kālañjara-nāradādayo viṁśati-girayo meroḥ karṇikāyā iva kesara-bhūtā mūla-deśe parita upakḷptāḥ.

kuraṅga—Kuraṅga; *kurara*—Kurara; *kusumbha-vaikaṅka-trikūṭa-śiśira-pataṅga-rucaka-niṣadha-śinīvāsa-kapila-śaṅkha-vaidūrya-jārudhi-haṁsa-ṛṣabha-nāga-kālañjara-nārada*—the names of mountains; *ādayaḥ*—and so on; *viṁśati-girayaḥ*—twenty mountains; *meroḥ*—of Sumeru Mountain; *karṇikāyāḥ*—of the whorl of the lotus; *iva*—like; *kesara-bhūtāḥ*—as filaments; *mūla-deśe*—at the base; *paritaḥ*—all around; *upakḷptāḥ*—arranged by the Supreme Personality of Godhead.

TRANSLATION

There are other mountains beautifully arranged around the foot of Mount Meru like the filaments around the whorl of a lotus flower. Their names are Kuraṅga, Kurara, Kusumbha, Vaikaṅka, Trikūṭa, Śiśira, Pataṅga, Rucaka, Niṣadha, Sinīvāsa, Kapila, Śaṅkha, Vaidūrya, Jārudhi, Haṁsa, Ṛṣabha, Nāga, Kālañjara and Nārada.

TEXT 27

जठरदेवकूटौ मेरुं पूर्वेणाष्टादशयोजनसहस्रमुदगायतौ द्विसहस्रं पृथुतुङ्गौ भवतः । एवमपरेण पवनपारियात्रौ दक्षिणेन कैलासकरवीरौ प्रागाय-
तावेवमुत्तरतस्त्रिशृङ्गमकरावष्टभिरेतैः परिसृतोऽग्निरिव परितश्चकास्तिकाञ्चन-
गिरिः ॥२७॥

jaṭhara-devakūṭau meruṁ purveṇāṣṭādaśa-yojana-sahasram udagāyatau dvi-sahasraṁ pṛthu-tuṅgau bhavataḥ. evam apareṇa pavana-pāriyātrau dakṣiṇena kailāsa-karavīrau prāg-āyatāv evam uttaratas triśṛṅga-makarāv aṣṭabhir etaiḥ parisṛto 'gnir iva paritaś cakāsti kāñcana-giriḥ.

jaṭhara-devakūṭau—two mountains named Jaṭhara and Devakūṭa; *merum*—Sumeru Mountain; *pūrveṇa*—on the eastern side; *aṣṭādaśa-yojana-sahasram*—eighteen thousand *yojanas; udgāyatau*—stretching from north to south; *dvi-sahasram*—two thousand *yojanas; pṛthu-tuṅgau*—in width and height; *bhavataḥ*—there are; *evam*—similarly; *apareṇa*—on the western side; *pavana-pāriyātrau*—two mountains named Pavana and Pāriyātra; *dakṣiṇena*—on the southern side; *kailāsa-karavīrau*—two mountains named Kailāsa and Karavīra; *prāk-āyatau*—expanding east and west; *evam*—similarly; *uttarataḥ*—on the northern side; *triśṛṅga-makarau*—two mountains named Triśṛṅga and Makara; *aṣṭabhiḥ etaiḥ*—by these eight mountains; *parisṛtaḥ*—surrounded; *agniḥ iva*—like fire; *paritaḥ*—all over; *cakāsti*—brilliantly shines; *kāñcana-giriḥ*—the golden mountain named Sumeru, or Meru.

TRANSLATION

On the eastern side of Sumeru Mountain are two mountains named Jaṭhara and Devakūṭa, which extend to the north and south for 18,000 yojanas [144,000 miles]. Similarly, on the western side of Sumeru are two mountains named Pavana and Pāriyātra, which also extend north and south for the same distance. On the southern side of Sumeru are two mountains named Kailāsa and Karavīra, which extend east and west for 18,000 yojanas, and on the northern side of Sumeru, extending for the same distance east and west, are two mountains named Triśṛṅga and Makara. The

width and height of all these mountains is 2,000 yojanas [16,000 miles]. Sumeru, a mountain of solid gold shining as brilliantly as fire, is surrounded by these eight mountains.

TEXT 28

मेरोर्मूर्धनि भगवत आत्मयोनेर्मध्यत उपक्लृप्तां पुरीमयुतयोजनसाहस्रीं समचतुरस्रां शातकौम्भीं वदन्ति ॥ २८ ॥

meror mūrdhani bhagavata ātma-yoner madhyata upakḷptāṁ purīm ayuta-yojana-sāhasrīṁ sama-caturasrāṁ śātakaumbhīṁ vadanti.

meroḥ—of Sumeru Mountain; *mūrdhani*—on the head; *bhagavataḥ*—of the most powerful being; *ātma-yoneḥ*—of Lord Brahmā; *madhyataḥ*—in the middle; *upakḷptām*—situated; *purīm*—the great township; *ayuta-yojana*—ten thousand *yojanas; sāhasrīm*—one thousand; *sama-caturasrām*—of the same length on all sides; *śāta-kaumbhīm*—made entirely of gold; *vadanti*—the great learned sages say.

TRANSLATION

In the middle of the summit of Meru is the township of Lord Brahmā. Each of its four sides is calculated to extend for ten million yojanas [eighty million miles]. It is made entirely of gold, and therefore learned scholars and sages call it Śātakaumbhī.

TEXT 29

तामनुपरितो लोकपालानामष्टानां यथादिशं यथारूपं तुरीयमानेन पुरोऽष्टावुपक्लृप्ताः ॥२९॥

tām anuparito loka-pālānām aṣṭānāṁ yathā-diśaṁ yathā-rūpaṁ turīya-mānena puro 'ṣṭāv upakḷptāḥ.

tām—that great township named Brahmapurī; *anuparitaḥ*—surrounding; *loka-pālānām*—of the governors of the planets; *aṣṭānām*—eight; *yathā-diśam*—according to the directions; *yathā-rūpam*—in exact conformity with the township of Brahmapurī; *turīya-mānena*—by measurement only one fourth; *puraḥ*—townships; *aṣṭau*—eight; *upakḷptāḥ*—situated.

TRANSLATION

Surrounding Brahmapurī in all directions are the residences of the eight principal governors of the planetary systems, beginning with King Indra. These abodes are similar to Brahmapurī but are one fourth the size.

PURPORT

Śrīla Viśvanātha Cakravartī Ṭhākura confirms that the townships of Lord Brahmā and the eight subordinate governors of the planetary systems, beginning with Indra, are mentioned in other *Purāṇas.*

merau nava-pūrāṇi syur
manovaty amarāvatī
tejovatī saṁyamanī
tathā kṛṣṇāṅganā parā
śraddhāvatī gandhavatī
tathā cānyā mahodayā
yaśovatī ca brahmendra
bahyādīnāṁ yathā-kramam

Brahmā's township is known as Manovatī, and those of his assistants such as Indra and Agni are known as Amarāvatī, Tejovatī, Saṁyamanī, Kṛṣṇāṅganā, Śraddhāvatī, Gandhavatī, Mahodayā and Yaśovatī. Brahmapurī is situated in the middle, and the other eight *purīs* surround it in all directions.

Thus end the Bhaktivedanta purports of the Fifth Canto, Sixteenth Chapter of the Śrīmad-Bhāgavatam, *entitled, "A Description of Jambūdvīpa."*

CHAPTER SEVENTEEN

The Descent of the River Ganges

The Seventeenth Chapter describes the origin of the Ganges River and how it flows in and around Ilāvṛta-varṣa. There is also a description of the prayers Lord Śiva offers to Lord Saṅkarṣaṇa, part of the quadruple expansions of the Supreme Personality of Godhead. Lord Viṣṇu once approached Bali Mahārāja while the King was performing a sacrifice. The Lord appeared before him as Trivikrama, or Vāmana, and begged alms from the King in the form of three steps of land. With two steps, Lord Vāmana covered all three planetary systems and pierced the covering of the universe with the toes of His left foot. A few drops of water from the Causal Ocean leaked through this hole and fell on the head of Lord Śiva, where they remained for one thousand millenniums. These drops of water are the sacred Ganges River. It first flows onto the heavenly planets, which are located on the soles of Lord Viṣṇu's feet. The Ganges River is known by many names, such as the Bhāgīrathī and the Jāhnavī. It purifies Dhruvaloka and the planets of the seven sages because both Dhruva and the sages have no other desire than to serve the Lord's lotus feet.

The Ganges River, emanating from the lotus feet of the Lord, inundates the heavenly planets, especially the moon, and then flows through Brahmapurī atop Mount Meru. Here the river divides into four branches (known as Sītā, Alakanandā, Cakṣu and Bhadrā), which then flow down to the ocean of salt water. The branch known as Sītā flows through Śekhara-parvata and Gandhamādana-parvata and then flows down to Bhadrāśva-varṣa, where it mixes with the ocean of salt water in the West. The Cakṣu branch flows through Mālyavān-giri and, after reaching Ketumāla-varṣa, mixes with the ocean of salt water in the West. The branch known as Bhadrā flows onto Mount Meru, Mount Kumuda, and the Nīla, Śveta and Śṛṅgavān mountains before it reaches Kuru-deśa, where it flows into the ocean of salt water in the north. The Alakanandā branch flows through Brahmālaya, crosses over many mountains, including Hemakūṭa and Himakūṭa, and then reaches Bhārata-varṣa, where it flows into the southern side of the ocean of salt water. Many other rivers and their branches flow through the nine *varṣas.*

The tract of land known as Bhārata-varṣa is the field of activities, and the other eight *varṣas* are for persons who are meant to enjoy heavenly comfort. In each of these eight beautiful provinces, the celestial denizens enjoy various standards of material comfort and pleasure. A different incarnation of the Supreme Personality of Godhead distributes His mercy in each of the nine *varṣas* of Jambūdvīpa.

In the Ilāvṛta-varṣa, Lord Śiva is the only male. There he lives with his wife, Bhavānī, who is attended by many maidservants. If any other male enters that province, Bhavānī curses him to become a woman. Lord Śiva worships Lord Saṅkarṣaṇa by offering various prayers, one of which is as follows: "My dear Lord, please liberate all Your devotees from material life and bind all the nondevotees to the material world. Without Your mercy, no one can be released from the bondage of material existence."

TEXT 1

श्रीशुक उवाच

तत्र भगवतः साक्षाद्यज्ञलिङ्गस्य विष्णोर्विक्रमतो वामपादाङ्गुष्ठनखनिर्भिन्नो-
र्ध्वाण्डकटाहविवरेणान्तःप्रविष्टा या बाह्यजलधारा तच्चरणपङ्कजावनेजना-
रुणकिञ्जल्कोपरञ्जिताखिलजगदघमलापहोपस्पर्शनामला साक्षाद्भगवत्पदीत्य
नुपलक्षितवचोऽभिधीयमानातिमहता कालेन युगसहस्रोपलक्षणेन दिवो
मूर्धन्यवततार यत्तद्विष्णुपदमाहुः ॥१॥

śrī-śuka uvāca

tatra bhagavataḥ sākṣād yajña-liṅgasya viṣṇor vikramato vāma-pādāṅguṣṭha-nakha-nirbhinnordhvāṇḍa-kaṭāha-vivareṇāntaḥ-praviṣṭā yā bāhya-jala-dhārā tac-caraṇa-paṅkajāvanejanāruṇa-kiñjalkoparañjitākhila-jagad-agha-malāpahopasparśanāmalā sākṣād bhagavat-padīty anupalakṣita-vaco 'bhidhīyamānāti-mahatā kālena yuga-sahasropalakṣaṇena divo mūrdhany avatatāra yat tad viṣṇu-padam āhuḥ.

śrī-śukaḥ uvāca—Śrī Śukadeva Gosvāmī said; *tatra*—at that time; *bhagavataḥ*—of the incarnation of the Supreme Personality of Godhead; *sākṣāt*—directly; *yajña-liṅgasya*—the enjoyer of the results of all sacrifices; *viṣṇoḥ*—of Lord Viṣṇu; *vikramataḥ*—while taking His second step; *vāma-pāda*—of His left leg; *aṅguṣṭha*—of the big toe; *nakha*—by the nail; *nirbhinna*—pierced; *ūrdhva*—upper; *aṇḍa-kaṭāha*—the covering of the universe (consisting of seven layers—earth, water, fire, etc.); *vivareṇa*—through the hole; *antaḥ-praviṣṭā*—having entered the universe; *yā*—which; *bāhya-jala-dhārā*—the flow of water from the Causal Ocean outside the universe; *tat*—of Him; *caraṇa-paṅkaja*—of the lotus feet; *avanejana*—by the washing; *aruṇa-kiñjalka*—by reddish powder; *uparañjitā*—being colored; *akhila-jagat*—of the whole world; *agha-mala*—the sinful activities; *apahā*—destroys; *upasparśana*—the touching of which; *amalā*—completely pure; *sākṣāt*—directly; *bhagavat-padī*—emanating from the lotus feet of the Supreme Personality of Godhead; *iti*—thus; *anupalakṣita*—described; *vacaḥ*—by the name; *abhidhīyamānā*—being called; *ati-mahatā kālena*—after a long time; *yuga-sahasra-upalakṣaṇena*—consisting of one thousand milleniums; *divaḥ*—of the sky; *mūrdhani*—on the head (Dhruvaloka); *avatatāra*—descended; *yat*—which; *tat*—that; *viṣṇu-padam*—the lotus feet of Lord Viṣṇu; *āhuḥ*—they call.

TRANSLATION

Śukadeva Gosvāmī said: My dear King, Lord Viṣṇu, the enjoyer of all sacrifices, appeared as Vāmanadeva in the sacrificial arena of Bali Mahārāja. Then He extended His left foot to the end of the universe and pierced a hole in its covering with the nail of His big toe. Through the hole, the pure water of the Causal Ocean entered this universe as the Ganges River. Having washed the lotus feet of the Lord, which are covered with reddish powder, the water of the Ganges acquired a very beautiful pink color. Every living being can immediately purify his mind of material contamination by touching the transcendental water of the Ganges, yet its waters remain ever pure. Because the Ganges directly touches the lotus feet of the Lord before descending within this universe, she is known as Viṣṇupadī. Later she received other names like Jāhnavī

and Bhāgīrathī. After one thousand millenniums, the water of the Ganges descended on Dhruvaloka, the topmost planet in this universe. Therefore all learned sages and scholars proclaim Dhruvaloka to be Viṣṇupada ["situated on Lord Viṣṇu's lotus feet"].

PURPORT

In this verse, Śukadeva Gosvāmī describes the glories of the Ganges River. The water of the Ganges is called *patita-pāvanī*, the deliverer of all sinful living beings. It is a proven fact that a person who regularly bathes in the Ganges is purified both externally and internally. Externally his body becomes immune to all kinds of disease, and internally he gradually develops a devotional attitude toward the Supreme Personality of Godhead. Throughout India, many thousands of people live on the banks of the Ganges, and by regularly bathing in her waters, they are undoubtedly being purified both spiritually and materially. Many sages, including Śaṅkarācārya, have composed prayers in praise of the Ganges, and the land of India itself has become glorious because such rivers as the Ganges, Yamunā, Godāvarī, Kāverī, Kṛṣṇā and Narmadā flow there. Anyone living on the land adjacent to these rivers is naturally advanced in spiritual consciousness. Śrīla Madhvācārya says:

vārāhe vāma-pādaṁ tu
tad-anyeṣu tu dakṣiṇam
pādaṁ kalpeṣu bhagavān
ujjahāra trivikramaḥ

Standing on His right foot and extending His left to the edge of the universe, Lord Vāmana became known as Trivikrama, the incarnation who performed three heroic deeds.

TEXT 2

यत्र ह वाव वीरव्रत औत्तानपादिः परमभागवतोऽस्मत्कुलदेवताचरणारविन्दो-
दकमिति यामनुसवनमुत्कृष्यमाणभगवद्भक्तियोगेन दृढं क्लिद्यमानान्तर्हृदय
औत्कण्ठ्यविवशामीलितलोचनयुगलकुड्मलविगलितामलबाष्पकलयाभिव्यज्य-
मानरोमपुलककुलकोऽधुनापि परमादरेण शिरसा बिभर्ति ॥ २ ॥

yatra ha vāva vīra-vrata auttānapādiḥ parama-bhāgavato 'smat-kula-devatā-caraṇāravindodakam iti yām anusavanam utkṛṣyamāṇa-bhagavad-bhakti-yogena dṛḍhaṁ klidyamānāntar-hṛdaya autkaṇṭhya-vivaśāmīlita-locana-yugala-kuḍmala-vigalitāmala-bāṣpa-kalayābhivyajyamāna-roma-pulaka-kulako 'dhunāpi paramādareṇa śirasā bibharti.

yatra ha vāva—in Dhruvaloka; *vīra-vrataḥ*—firmly determined; *auttānapādiḥ*—the famous son of Mahārāja Uttānapāda; *parama-bhāgavataḥ*—the most exalted devotee; *asmat*—our; *kula-devatā*—of the family Deity; *caraṇa-aravinda*—of the lotus feet; *udakam*—in the water; *iti*—thus; *yām*—which; *anusavanam*—constantly; *utkṛṣyamāṇa*—being increased; *bhagavat-bhakti-yogena*—by devotional service unto the Lord; *dṛḍham*—greatly; *klidyamāna-antaḥ-hṛdayaḥ*—being softened within the core of his heart; *autkaṇṭhya*—by great anxiety; *vivaśa*—spontaneously; *amīlita*—slightly open; *locana*—of eyes; *yugala*—pair; *kuḍmala*—from the flowerlike; *vigalita*—emanating; *amala*—uncontaminated; *bāṣpa-kalayā*—with tears; *abhivyajyamāna*—being manifested; *roma-pulaka-kulakaḥ*—whose symptoms of ecstasy on the body; *adhunā api*—even now; *parama-ādareṇa*—with great reverence; *śirasā*—by the head; *bibharti*—he bears.

TRANSLATION

Dhruva Mahārāja, the famous son of Mahārāja Uttānapāda, is known as the most exalted devotee of the Supreme Lord because of his firm determination in executing devotional service. Knowing that the sacred Ganges water washes the lotus feet of Lord Viṣṇu, Dhruva Mahārāja, situated on his own planet, to this very day accepts that water on his head with great devotion. Because he constantly thinks of Kṛṣṇa very devoutly within the core of his heart, he is overcome with ecstatic anxiety. Tears flow from his half-open eyes, and eruptions appear on his entire body.

PURPORT

When a person is firmly fixed in devotional service to the Supreme Personality of Godhead, he is described as *vīra-vrata*, fully determined.

Such a devotee increases his ecstasy in devotional service more and more. Thus as soon as he remembers Lord Viṣṇu, his eyes fill with tears. This is a symptom of a *mahā-bhāgavata*. Dhruva Mahārāja maintained himself in that devotional ecstasy, and Śrī Caitanya Mahāprabhu also gave us a practical example of transcendental ecstasy when He lived at Jagannātha Purī. His pastimes there are fully narrated in *Caitanya-caritāmṛta*.

TEXT 3

**ततः सप्त ऋषयस्तत्प्रभावाभिज्ञा यां ननु तपसआत्य-
न्तिकी सिद्धिरेतावती भगवति सर्वात्मनि वासुदेवेऽनुपरतभक्ति-
योगलाभेनैवोपेक्षितान्यार्थात्मगतयो मुक्तिमिवागतां मुमुक्षव इव
सबहुमानमद्यापि जटाजूटैरुद्वहन्ति ॥३॥**

tataḥ sapta ṛṣayas tat prabhāvābhijñā yāṁ nanu tapasa ātyantikī siddhir etāvatī bhagavati sarvātmani vāsudeve 'nuparata-bhakti-yoga-lābhenaivopekṣitānyārthātma-gatayo muktim ivāgatāṁ mumukṣava iva sabahu-mānam adyāpi jaṭā-jūṭair udvahanti.

tataḥ—thereafter; *sapta ṛṣayaḥ*—the seven great sages (beginning with Marīci); *tat prabhāva-abhijñāḥ*—who knew very well the influence of the Ganges River; *yām*—this Ganges water; *nanu*—indeed; *tapasaḥ*—of our austerities; *ātyantikī*—the ultimate; *siddhiḥ*—perfection; *etāvatī*—this much; *bhagavati*—the Supreme Personality of Godhead; *sarva-ātmani*—in the all-pervading; *vāsudeve*—Kṛṣṇa; *anuparata*—continuous; *bhakti-yoga*—of the mystic process of devotional service; *lābhena*—simply by achieving this platform; *eva*—certainly; *upekṣita*—neglected; *anya*—other; *artha-ātma-gatayaḥ*—all other means of perfection (namely religion, economic development, sense gratification and liberation); *muktim*—liberation from material bondage; *iva*—like; *āgatām*—obtained; *mumukṣavaḥ*—persons desiring liberation; *iva*—like; *sa-bahu-mānam*—with great honor; *adya api*—even now; *jaṭā-jūṭaiḥ*—with matted locks of hair; *udvahanti*—they carry.

TRANSLATION

The seven great sages [Marīci, Vasiṣṭha, Atri and so on] reside on planets beneath Dhruvaloka. Well aware of the influence of the water of the Ganges, to this day they keep Ganges water on the tufts of hair on their heads. They have concluded that this is the ultimate wealth, the perfection of all austerities, and the best means of prosecuting transcendental life. Having obtained uninterrupted devotional service to the Supreme Personality of Godhead, they neglect all other beneficial processes like religion, economic development, sense gratification and even merging into the Supreme. Just as jñānīs think that merging into the existence of the Lord is the highest truth, these seven exalted personalities accept devotional service as the perfection of life.

PURPORT

Transcendentalists are divided into two primary groups: the *nirviśeṣa-vādīs*, or impersonalists, and the *bhaktas*, or devotees. The impersonalists do not accept spiritual varieties of life. They want to merge into the existence of the Supreme Lord in His Brahman feature (the *brahma-jyoti*). The devotees, however, desire to take part in the transcendental activities of the Supreme Lord. In the upper planetary system, the topmost planet is Dhruvaloka, and beneath Dhruvaloka are the seven planets occupied by the great sages, beginning with Marīci, Vasiṣṭha and Atri. All these sages regard devotional service as the highest perfection of life. Therefore they all carry the holy water of the Ganges on their heads. This verse proves that for one who has achieved the platform of pure devotional service, nothing else is important, even so-called liberation (*kaivalya*). Śrīla Śrīdhara Svāmī states that only by achieving pure devotional service of the Lord can one give up all other engagements as insignificant. Prabodhānanda Sarasvatī confirms his statement as follows:

kaivalyaṁ narakāyate tri-daśa-pūr ākāśa-puṣpāyate
durdāntendriya-kāla-sarpa-paṭalī protkhāta-daṁṣṭrāyate
viśvaṁ pūrṇa-sukhāyate vidhi-mahendrādiś ca kīṭāyate
yat kāruṇya-kaṭākṣa-vaibhavavatāṁ taṁ gauram eva stumaḥ

Śrī Caitanya Mahāprabhu has perfectly enunciated and broadcast the process of *bhakti-yoga*. Consequently, for one who has taken shelter at the lotus feet of Śrī Caitanya Mahāprabhu, the highest perfection of the Māyāvādīs, *kaivalya*, or becoming one with the Supreme, is considered hellish, to say nothing of the *karmīs'* aspiration to be promoted to the heavenly planets. Devotees consider such goals to be worthless phantasmagoria. There are also *yogīs*, who try to control their senses, but they can never succeed without coming to the stage of devotional service. The senses are compared to poisonous snakes, but the senses of a *bhakta* engaged in the service of the Lord are like snakes with their poisonous fangs removed. The *yogī* tries to suppress his senses, but even great mystics like Viśvāmitra fail in the attempt. Viśvāmitra was conquered by his senses when he was captivated by Menakā during his meditation. She later gave birth to Śakuntalā. The wisest persons in the world, therefore, are the *bhakti-yogīs*, as Lord Kṛṣṇa confirms in *Bhagavad-gītā* (6.47):

yoginām api sarveṣāṁ
mad-gatenāntarātmanā
śraddhāvān bhajate yo māṁ
sa me yuktatamo mataḥ

"Of all *yogīs*, he who always abides in Me with great faith, worshiping Me in transcendental loving service, is most intimately united with Me in *yoga* and is the highest of all."

TEXT 4

ततोऽनेकसहस्रकोटिविमानानीकसङ्कुलदेवयानेनावतरन्तीन्दुमण्डलमावार्य ब्रह्म सदने निपतति ॥ ४ ॥

tato 'neka-sahasra-koṭi-vimānānīka-saṅkula-deva-yānenāvatar-antīndu maṇḍalam āvārya brahma-sadane nipatati.

tataḥ—after purifying the seven planets of the seven great sages; *aneka*—many; *sahasra*—thousands; *koṭi*—of millions; *vimāna-anīka*—with contingents of airplanes; *saṅkula*—congested; *deva-yānena*—by the spaceways of the demigods; *avatarantī*—descending; *indu-maṇ-*

ḍalam—the moon planet; *āvārya*—inundated; *brahma-sadane*—to the abode of Lord Brahmā atop Sumeru-parvata; *nipatati*—falls down.

TRANSLATION

After purifying the seven planets near Dhruvaloka [the polestar], the Ganges water is carried through the spaceways of the demigods in billions of celestial airplanes. Then it inundates the moon [Candraloka] and finally reaches Lord Brahmā's abode atop Mount Meru.

PURPORT

We should always remember that the Ganges River comes from the Causal Ocean, beyond the covering of the universe. After the water of the Causal Ocean leaks through the hole created by Lord Vāmanadeva, it flows down to Dhruvaloka (the polestar) and then to the seven planets beneath Dhruvaloka. Then it is carried to the moon by innumerable celestial airplanes, and then it falls to the top of Mount Meru, which is known as Sumeru-parvata. In this way, the water of the Ganges finally reaches the lower planets and the peaks of the Himalayas, and from there it flows through Hardwar and throughout the plains of India, purifying the entire land. How the Ganges water reaches the various planets from the top of the universe is explained herein. Celestial airplanes carry the water from the planets of the sages to other planets. So-called advanced scientists of the modern age are trying to go to the higher planets, but at the same time they are experiencing a power shortage on earth. If they were actually capable scientists, they could personally go by airplane to other planets, but this they are unable to do. Having now given up their moon excursions, they are attempting to go to other planets, but without success.

TEXT 5

तत्र चतुर्धा भिद्यमाना चतुर्भिर्नामभिश्चतुर्दिशमभिस्पन्दन्ती
नदनदीपतिमेवाभिनिविशति सीतालकनन्दा चक्षुर्भद्रेति ॥ ५ ॥

tatra caturdhā bhidyamānā caturbhir nāmabhiś catur-diśam abhispandantī nada-nadī-patim evābhiniviśati sītālakanandā cakṣur bhadreti.

tatra—there (on top of Mount Meru); *caturdhā*—into four branches; *bhidyamānā*—being divided; *caturbhiḥ*—with four; *nāmabhiḥ*—names; *catuḥ-diśam*—the four directions (east, west, north and south); *abhispandantī*—profusely flowing; *nada-nadī-patim*—the reservoir of all great rivers (the ocean); *eva*—certainly; *abhiniviśati*—enters; *sītā-alakanandā*—Sītā and Alakanandā; *cakṣuḥ*—Cakṣu; *bhadrā*—Bhadrā; *iti*—known by these names.

TRANSLATION

On top of Mount Meru, the Ganges divides into four branches, each of which gushes in a different direction [east, west, north and south]. These branches, known by the names Sītā, Alakanandā, Cakṣu and Bhadrā, flow down to the ocean.

TEXT 6

सीता तु ब्रह्मसदनात्केसराचलादिगिरिशिखरेभ्यो ऽधोऽधः प्रस्रवन्ती गन्धमादनमूर्धसु पतित्वान्तरेण भद्राश्ववर्षं प्राच्यां दिशि क्षारसमुद्रमभिप्रविशति ॥ ६ ॥

sītā tu brahma-sadanāt kesarācalādi-giri-śikharebhyo 'dho 'dhaḥ prasravantī gandhamādana-mūrdhasu patitvāntareṇa bhadrāśva-varṣaṁ prācyāṁ diśi kṣāra-samudram abhipraviśati.

sītā—the branch known as Sītā; *tu*—certainly; *brahma-sadanāt*—from Brahmapurī; *kesarācala-ādi*—of Kesarācala and of other great mountains; *giri*—hills; *śikharebhyaḥ*—from the tops; *adhaḥ adhaḥ*—downward; *prasravantī*—flowing; *gandhamādana*—of Gandhamādana Mountain; *mūrdhasu*—on the top; *patitvā*—falling down; *antareṇa*—within; *bhadrāśva-varṣam*—the province known as Bhadrāśva; *prācyām*—in the western; *diśi*—direction; *kṣāra-samudram*—the ocean of salt water; *abhipraviśati*—enters.

TRANSLATION

The branch of the Ganges known as the Sītā flows through Brahmapurī atop Mount Meru, and from there it runs down to the

nearby peaks of the Kesarācala Mountains, which stand almost as high as Mount Meru itself. These mountains are like a bunch of filaments around Mount Meru. From the Kesarācala Mountains, the Ganges falls to the peak of Gandhamādana Mountain and then flows into the land of Bhadrāśva-varṣa. Finally it reaches the ocean of salt water in the west.

TEXT 7

एवं माल्यवच्छिखरान्निष्पतन्ती ततो ऽनुपरतवेगा केतुमालमभि चक्षुः प्रतीच्यां दिशि सरित्पतिं प्रविशति ॥७॥

evaṁ mālyavac-chikharān niṣpatantī tato 'nuparata-vegā ketumālam abhi cakṣuḥ pratīcyāṁ diśi sarit-patiṁ praviśati.

evam—in this way; *mālyavat-śikharāt*—from the top of Mālyavān Mountain; *niṣpatantī*—falling down; *tataḥ*—thereafter; *anuparata-vegā*—whose force is uninterrupted; *ketumālam abhi*—into the land known as Ketumāla-varṣa; *cakṣuḥ*—the branch known as Cakṣu; *pratīcyām*—in the West; *diśi*—direction; *sarit-patim*—the ocean; *pra-viśati*—enters into.

TRANSLATION

The branch of the Ganges known as Cakṣu falls onto the summit of Mālyavān Mountain and from there cascades onto the land of Ketumāla-varṣa. The Ganges flows incessantly through Ketumāla-varṣa and in this way also reaches the ocean of salt water in the West.

TEXT 8

भद्रा चोत्तरतो मेरुशिरसो निपतिता गिरिशिखराद्गिरिशिखरमतिहाय शृङ्गवतः शृङ्गादवस्यन्दमाना उत्तरांस्तु कुरूनभित उदीच्यां दिशि जलधिमभिप्रविशति ॥८॥

bhadrā cottarato meru-śiraso nipatitā giri-śikharād giri-śikharam atihāya śṛṅgavataḥ śṛṅgād avasyandamānā uttarāṁs tu kurūn abhita udīcyāṁ diśi jaladhim abhipraviśati.

bhadrā—the branch known as Bhadrā; *ca*—also; *uttarataḥ*—to the northern side; *meru-śirasaḥ*—from the top of Mount Meru; *nipatitā*—having fallen; *giri-śikharāt*—from the peak of Kumuda Mountain; *giri-śikharam*—to the peak of Nīla Mountain; *atihāya*—passing over as if not touching; *śṛṅgavataḥ*—of the mountain known as Śṛṅgavān; *śṛṅgāt*—from the peak; *avasyandamānā*—flowing; *uttarān*—the northern; *tu*—but; *kurūn*—the land known as Kuru; *abhitaḥ*—on all sides; *udīcyām*—in the northern; *diśi*—direction; *jaladhim*—the ocean of salt water; *abhipraviśati*—enters into.

TRANSLATION

The branch of the Ganges known as Bhadrā flows from the northern side of Mount Meru. Its waters fall onto the peaks of Kumuda Mountain, Mount Nīla, Śveta Mountain and Śṛṅgavān Mountain in succession. Then it runs down into the province of Kuru and, after crossing through that land, flows into the salt-water ocean in the north.

TEXT 9

तथैवालकनन्दा दक्षिणेन ब्रह्मसदनाद्बहूनि गिरिकूटान्यतिक्रम्य हेमकूटाद्धैमकूटान्यतिरभसतररंहसा लुठयन्ती भारतमभिवर्षं दक्षिणस्यां दिशि जलधिमभिप्रविशति यस्यां स्नानार्थं चागच्छतः पुंसः पदे पदेऽश्वमेधराजसूयादीनां फलं न दुर्लभमिति ॥९॥

tathaivālakanandā dakṣiṇena brahma-sadanād bahūni giri-kūṭāny atikramya hemakūṭād dhaimakūṭāny ati-rabhasatara-raṁhasā luṭhayantī bhāratam abhivarṣaṁ dakṣiṇasyāṁ diśi jaladhim abhipraviśati yasyāṁ snānārthaṁ cāgacchataḥ puṁsaḥ pade pade 'śvamedha-rājasūyādīnāṁ phalaṁ na durlabham iti.

tathā eva—similarly; *alakanandā*—the branch known as Alakanandā; *dakṣiṇena*—by the southern side; *brahma-sadanāt*—from the city known as Brahmapurī; *bahūni*—many; *giri-kūṭāni*—the tops of mountains; *atikramya*—crossing over; *hemakūṭāt*—from Hemakūṭa Mountain; *haimakūṭāni*—and Himakūṭa; *ati-rabhasatara*—more fiercely; *raṁhasā*—with great force; *luṭhayantī*—plundering; *bhāratam abhivarṣam*—on all sides of Bhārata-varṣa; *dakṣiṇasyām*—in the southern; *diśi*—direction; *jaladhim*—the ocean of salt water; *abhipraviśati*—enters into; *yasyām*—in which; *snāna-artham*—for bathing; *ca*—and; *āgacchataḥ*—of one who is coming; *puṁsaḥ*—a person; *pade pade*—at every step; *aśvamedha-rājasūya-ādīnām*—of great sacrifices like the Aśvamedha *yajña* and Rājasūya *yajña; phalam*—the result; *na*—not; *durlabham*—very difficult to obtain; *iti*—thus.

TRANSLATION

Similarly, the branch of the Ganges known as Alakanandā flows from the southern side of Brahmapurī [Brahma-sadana]. Passing over the tops of mountains in various lands, it falls down with fierce force upon the peaks of the mountains Hemakūṭa and Himakūṭa. After inundating the tops of those mountains, the Ganges falls down onto the tract of land known as Bhārata-varṣa, which she also inundates. Then the Ganges flows into the ocean of salt water in the south. Persons who come to bathe in this river are fortunate. It is not very difficult for them to achieve with every step the results of performing great sacrifices like the Rājasūya and Aśvamedha yajñas.

PURPORT

The place where the Ganges flows into the salt water of the Bay of Bengal is still known as Gaṅgā-sāgara, or the meeting place of the Ganges and the Bay of Bengal. On Makara-saṅkrānti, in the month of January-February, thousands of people still go there to bathe, hoping to be liberated. That they can actually be liberated in this way is confirmed herein. For those who bathe in the Ganges at any time, the results of great sacrifices like the Aśvamedha and Rājasūya *yajñas* are not at all difficult to achieve. Most people in India are still inclined to bathe in the Ganges, and there are many places where they can do so. At Prayāga (Allahabad), many thousands of people gather during the month of January to bathe in the confluence of the Ganges and Yamunā. Afterward, many of them go to the confluence of the Bay of Bengal and the Ganges to take bath there. Thus it is a special facility for all the people of India that they can bathe in the water of the Ganges at so many places of pilgrimage.

TEXT 10

अन्ये च नदा नद्यश्च वर्षे वर्षे सन्ति बहुशो मेर्वादिगिरिदुहितरः शतशः ॥ १० ॥

anye ca nadā nadyaś ca varṣe varṣe santi bahuśo merv-ādi-giri-duhitaraḥ śataśaḥ.

anye—many others; *ca*—also; *nadāḥ*—rivers; *nadyaḥ*—small rivers; *ca*—and; *varṣe varṣe*—in each tract of land; *santi*—are; *bahuśaḥ*—of many varieties; *meru-ādi-giri-duhitaraḥ*—daughters of the mountains beginning with Meru; *śataśaḥ*—in the hundreds.

TRANSLATION

Many other rivers, both big and small, flow from the top of Mount Meru. These rivers are like daughters of the mountain, and they flow to the various tracts of land in hundreds of branches.

TEXT 11

तत्रापि भारतमेव वर्षं कर्मक्षेत्रमन्यान्यष्ट वर्षाणि स्वर्गिणां पुण्यशेषोपभोगस्थानानि भौमानि स्वर्गपदानि व्यपदिशन्ति ॥ ११ ॥

tatrāpi bhāratam eva varṣaṁ karma-kṣetram anyāny aṣṭa varṣāṇi svargiṇāṁ puṇya-śeṣopabhoga-sthānāni bhaumāni svarga-padāni vyapadiśanti.

tatra api—out of all of them; *bhāratam*—known as Bhārata-varṣa; *eva*—certainly; *varṣam*—the tract of land; *karma-kṣetram*—the field of activities; *anyāni*—the others; *aṣṭa varṣāṇi*—eight tracts of land; *svargiṇām*—of the living entities elevated to the heavenly planets by extraordinary pious activities; *puṇya*—of the results of pious activities; *śeṣa*—of the remainder; *upabhoga-sthānāni*—the places for material enjoyment; *bhaumāni svarga-padāni*—as the heavenly places on earth; *vyapadiśanti*—they designate.

TRANSLATION

Among the nine varṣas, the tract of land known as Bhārata-varṣa is understood to be the field of fruitive activities. Learned scholars and saintly persons declare the other eight varṣas to be meant for very highly elevated pious persons. After returning from the heavenly planets, they enjoy the remaining results of their pious activities in these eight earthly varṣas.

PURPORT

The heavenly places of enjoyment are divided into three groups: the celestial heavenly planets, the heavenly places on earth, and the *bila* heavenly places, which are found in the lower regions. Among these three classes of heavenly places (*bhauma-svarga-padāni*), the heavenly places on earth are the eight *varṣas* other than Bhārata-varṣa. In *Bhagavad-gītā* (9.21) Kṛṣṇa says, *kṣīṇe puṇye martya-lokaṁ viśanti:* when the persons living in the heavenly planets exhaust the results of their pious activities, they return to this earth. In this way, they are elevated to the heavenly planets, and then they again fall to the earthly planets. This process is known as *brahmāṇḍa bhramaṇa*, wandering up and down throughout the universes. Those who are intelligent—in other words, those who have not lost their intelligence—do not involve themselves in this process of wandering up and down. They take to the devotional service of the Lord so that they can ultimately penetrate the covering of this universe and enter the spiritual kingdom. Then they are situated on one of the planets known as Vaikuṇṭhaloka or, still higher, Kṛṣṇaloka (Goloka Vṛndāvana). A devotee is never caught in the process of being promoted to the heavenly planets and again coming down. Therefore Śrī Caitanya Mahāprabhu says:

ei rūpe brahmāṇḍa bhramite kona bhāgyavān jīva
guru-kṛṣṇa-prasāde pāya bhakti-latā-bīja

Among all the living entities wandering throughout the universe, one who is most fortunate comes in contact with a representative of the Supreme Personality of Godhead and thus gets the opportunity to execute devotional service. Those who are sincerely seeking the favor of

Kṛṣṇa come in contact with a *guru,* a bona fide representative of Kṛṣṇa. The Māyāvādīs indulging in mental speculation and the *karmīs* desiring the results of their actions cannot become *gurus.* A *guru* must be a direct representative of Kṛṣṇa who distributes the instructions of Kṛṣṇa without any change. Thus only the most fortunate persons come in contact with the *guru.* As confirmed in the Vedic literatures, *tad-vijñānārthaṁ sa gurum evābhigacchet:* one has to search out a *guru* to understand the affairs of the spiritual world. *Śrīmad-Bhāgavatam* also confirms this point. *Tasmād guruṁ prapadyeta jijñāsuḥ śreya uttamam:* one who is very interested in understanding the activities in the spiritual world must search out a *guru*— a bona fide representative of Kṛṣṇa. From all angles of vision, therefore, the word *guru* is especially meant for the bona fide representative of Kṛṣṇa and no one else. *Padma Purāṇa* states, *avaiṣṇavo gurur na syāt:* one who is not a Vaiṣṇava, or who is not a representative of Kṛṣṇa, cannot be a *guru.* Even the most qualified *brāhmaṇa* cannot become a *guru* if he is not a representative of Kṛṣṇa. *Brāhmaṇas* are supposed to acquire six kinds of auspicious qualifications: they become very learned scholars (*paṭhana*) and very qualified teachers (*pāṭhana*); they become expert in worshiping the Lord or the demigods (*yajana*), and they teach others how to execute this worship (*yājana*); they qualify themselves as bona fide persons to receive alms from others (*pratigraha*), and they distribute the wealth in charity (*dāna*). Yet even a *brāhmaṇa* possessing these qualifications cannot become a *guru* unless he is the representative of Kṛṣṇa (*gurur na syāt*). *Vaiṣṇavaḥ śva-paco guruḥ:* but a Vaiṣṇava, a bona fide representative of the Supreme Personality of Godhead, Viṣṇu, can become a *guru,* even if he is *śva-paca,* a member of a family of dog-eaters. Of the three divisions of heavenly planets (*svarga-loka*), *bhauma-svarga* is sometimes accepted as the tract of land in Bhārata-varṣa known as Kashmir. In this region there are certainly good facilities for material sense enjoyment, but this is not the business of a pure transcendentalist. Rūpa Gosvāmī describes the engagement of a pure transcendentalist as follows:

anyābhilāṣitā-śūnyaṁ
jñāna-karmādy-anāvṛtam
ānukulyena kṛṣṇānu-
śīlanaṁ bhaktir uttamā

"One should render transcendental loving service to the Supreme Lord Kṛṣṇa favorably and without desire for material profit or gain through fruitive activities or philosophical speculation. That is called pure devotional service." Those who fully engage in devotional service to Kṛṣṇa just to please Him are not interested in the three divisions of heavenly places, namely, *divya-svarga*, *bhauma-svarga* and *bila-svarga*.

TEXT 12

एषु पुरुषाणामयुतपुरुषायुर्वर्षाणां देवकल्पानां नागायुतप्राणानां
वज्रसंहननबलवयोमोदप्रमुदितमहासौरतमिथुनव्यवायापवर्गवर्षधृतैकगर्भ कल-
त्राणां तत्र तु त्रेतायुगसमः कालो वर्तते ।१२।

eṣu puruṣāṇām ayuta-puruṣāyur-varṣāṇāṁ deva-kalpānāṁ nāgāyuta-prāṇānāṁ vajra-saṁhanana-bala-vayo-moda-pramudita-mahā-saurata-mithuna-vyavāyāpavarga-varṣa-dhṛtaika-garbha-kalatrāṇāṁ tatra tu tretā-yuga-samaḥ kālo vartate.

eṣu—in these (eight) *varṣas*, or tracts of land; *puruṣāṇām*—of all the men; *ayuta*—ten thousand; *puruṣa*—by the measure of men; *āyuḥ-varṣāṇām*—of those whose years of life; *deva-kalpānām*—who are like the demigods; *nāga-ayuta-prāṇānām*—having the strength of ten thousand elephants; *vajra-saṁhanana*—by bodies as solid as thunderbolts; *bala*—by bodily strength; *vayaḥ*—by youth; *moda*—by abundant sense enjoyment; *pramudita*—being excited; *mahā-saurata*—a great deal of sexual; *mithuna*—combinations of man and woman; *vyavāya-apavarga*—at the end of their period of sexual enjoyment; *varṣa*—in the last year; *dhṛta-eka-garbha*—who conceive one child; *kalatrāṇām*—of those who have wives; *tatra*—there; *tu*—but; *tretā-yuga-samaḥ*—exactly like the Tretā-yuga (when there is no tribulation); *kālaḥ*—time; *vartate*—exists.

TRANSLATION

In these eight varṣas, or tracts of land, human beings live ten thousand years according to earthly calculations. All the inhabitants are almost like demigods. They have the bodily strength of ten thousand elephants. Indeed, their bodies are as sturdy as

thunderbolts. The youthful duration of their lives is very pleasing, and both men and women enjoy sexual union with great pleasure for a long time. After years of sensual pleasure—when a balance of one year of life remains—the wife conceives a child. Thus the standard of pleasure for the residents of these heavenly regions is exactly like that of the human beings who lived during Tretā-yuga.

PURPORT

There are four *yugas:* Satya-yuga, Tretā-yuga, Dvāpara-yuga and Kali-yuga. During the first *yuga*, Satya-yuga, people were very pious. Everyone practiced the mystic *yoga* system for spiritual understanding and realization of God. Because everyone was always absorbed in *samādhi*, no one was interested in material sense enjoyment. During Tretā-yuga, people enjoyed sense pleasure without tribulations. Material miseries began in Dvāpara-yuga, but they were not very stringent. Stringent material miseries really began from the advent of Kali-yuga.

Another point in this verse is that in all eight of these heavenly *varṣas*, although men and women enjoy sex pleasure, there is no pregnancy. Pregnancy takes place only in lower-grade life. For example, animals like dogs and hogs become pregnant twice a year, and each time they beget at least half a dozen offspring. Even lower species of life such as snakes give birth to hundreds of young at one time. This verse informs us that in grades of life higher than ours, pregnancy occurs once in a lifetime. People still have sex life, but there is no pregnancy. In the spiritual world, people are not very attracted to sex life, due to their exalted devotional attitude. Practically speaking, there is no sex life in the spiritual world, but even if sometimes it does occur, there is no pregnancy at all. On the planet earth, however, human beings do become pregnant, although the tendency is to avoid having children. In this sinful age of Kali, people have even taken to the process of killing the child in the womb. This is the most degraded practice; it can only perpetuate the miserable material conditions of those who perform it.

TEXT 13

यत्र ह देवपतयः स्वैः स्वैर्गणनायकैर्विहितमहार्हणाः सर्वर्तुकुसुम-
स्तबकफलकिसलयश्रियाऽऽनम्यमानविटपलता विटपिभिरुपशुम्भमानरुचिर-

काननाश्रमायतनवर्षगिरिद्रोणीषु तथा चामलजलाशयेषु विकचविविधनववन-
रुहामोदमुदितराजहंसजलकुक्कुटकारण्डवसारसचक्रवाकादिभिर्मधुकरनिकराकृति-
भिरुपकूजितेषु जलक्रीडादिभिर्विचित्रविनोदैः सुललितसुरसुन्दरीणां
कामकलिलविलासहासलीलावलोकाकृष्टमनोदृष्टयः स्वैरं विहरन्ति ॥ १३ ॥

yatra ha deva-patayaḥ svaiḥ svair gaṇa-nāyakair vihita-mahārhaṇāḥ sarvartu-kusuma-stabaka-phala-kisalaya-śriyānamyamāna-viṭapa-latā-viṭapibhir upaśumbhamāna-rucira-kānanāśramāyatana-varṣa-giri-droṇīṣu tathā cāmala-jalāśayeṣu vikaca-vividha-nava-vanaruhāmoda-mudita-rāja-haṁsa-jala-kukkuṭa-kāraṇḍava-sārasa-cakravākādibhir madhukara-nikarākṛtibhir upakūjiteṣu jala-krīḍādibhir vicitra-vinodaiḥ sulalita-sura-sundarīṇāṁ kāma-kalila-vilāsa-hāsa-līlāvalokākṛṣṭa-mano-dṛṣṭayaḥ svairaṁ viharanti.

yatra ha—in those eight tracts of land; *deva-patayaḥ*—the lords of the demigods, such as Lord Indra; *svaiḥ svaiḥ*—by their own respective; *gaṇa-nāyakaiḥ*—leaders of the servants; *vihita*—furnished with; *mahā-arhaṇāḥ*—valuable gifts, such as sandalwood pulp and garlands; *sarva-ṛtu*—in all seasons; *kusuma-stabaka*—of bunches of flowers; *phala*—of fruits; *kisalaya-śriyā*—by the opulences of shoots; *ānamyamāna*—being bent down; *viṭapa*—whose branches; *latā*—and creepers; *viṭapibhiḥ*—by many trees; *upaśumbhamāna*—being fully decorated; *rucira*—beautiful; *kānana*—gardens; *āśrama-āyatana*—and many hermitages; *varṣa-giri-droṇīṣu*—the valleys between the mountains designating the borders of the tracts of land; *tathā*—as well as; *ca*—also; *amala-jala-āśayeṣu*—in lakes with clear water; *vikaca*—just fructified; *vividha*—varieties; *nava-vanaruha-āmoda*—by the fragrance of lotus flowers; *mudita*—enthused; *rāja-haṁsa*—great swans; *jala-kukkuṭa*—water fowl; *kāraṇḍava*—aquatic birds called *kāraṇḍavas; sārasa*—cranes; *cakravāka-ādibhiḥ*—by birds known as *cakravākas* and so on; *madhukara-nikara-ākṛtibhiḥ*—by the bumblebees; *upakūjiteṣu*—which were made to resound; *jala-krīḍā-ādibhiḥ*—such as water sports; *vicitra*—various; *vinodaiḥ*—by pastimes; *su-lalita*—attractive; *sura-sundarīṇām*—of the women of the demigods; *kāma*—from lust; *kalila*—born; *vilāsa*—pastimes; *hāsa*—

smiling; *līlā-avaloka*—by playful glances; *ākṛṣṭa-manaḥ*—whose minds are attracted; *dṛṣṭayaḥ*—and whose vision is attracted; *svairam*—very freely; *viharanti*—engage in sportive enjoyment.

TRANSLATION

In each of those tracts of land, there are many gardens filled with flowers and fruits according to the season, and there are beautifully decorated hermitages as well. Between the great mountains demarcating the borders of those lands lie enormous lakes of clear water filled with newly grown lotus flowers. Aquatic birds such as swans, ducks, water chickens, and cranes become greatly excited by the fragrance of lotus flowers, and the charming sound of bumblebees fills the air. The inhabitants of those lands are important leaders among the demigods. Always attended by their respective servants, they enjoy life in gardens alongside the lakes. In this pleasing situation, the wives of the demigods smile playfully at their husbands and look upon them with lusty desires. All the demigods and their wives are constantly supplied with sandalwood pulp and flower garlands by their servants. In this way, all the residents of the eight heavenly varṣas enjoy, attracted by the activities of the opposite sex.

PURPORT

Here is a description of the lower heavenly planets. The inhabitants of those planets enjoy life in a pleasing atmosphere of clear lakes filled with newly grown lotus flowers and gardens filled with fruits, flowers, various kinds of birds and humming bees. In that atmosphere they enjoy life with their very beautiful wives, who are always sexually stimulated. Nonetheless, they are all devotees of the Supreme Personality of Godhead, as will be explained in subsequent verses. The inhabitants of this earth also desire such heavenly enjoyment, but when they somehow or other achieve imitation pleasures like sex and intoxication, they completely forget the service of the Supreme Lord. In the heavenly planets, however, although the residents enjoy superior sense gratification, they never forget their positions as eternal servants of the Supreme Being.

TEXT 14

नवस्वपि वर्षेषु भगवान्नारायणो महापुरुषः पुरुषाणां तदनुग्रहायात्मतत्त्व
व्यूहेनात्मनाद्यापि संनिधीयते ॥ १४ ॥

navasv api varṣeṣu bhagavān nārāyaṇo mahā-puruṣaḥ puruṣāṇāṁ tad-anugrahāyātma-tattva-vyūhenātmanādyāpi sannidhīyate.

navasu—in the nine; *api*—certainly; *varṣeṣu*—tracts of land known as *varṣas; bhagavān*—the Supreme Personality of Godhead; *nārāyaṇaḥ*—Lord Viṣṇu; *mahā-puruṣaḥ*—the Supreme Person; *puruṣāṇām*—unto His various devotees; *tat-anugrahāya*—to show His mercy; *ātma-tattva-vyūhena*—by expansions of Himself in the quadruple forms Vāsudeva, Saṅkarṣaṇa, Pradyumna and Aniruddha; *ātmanā*—personally; *adya api*—until now; *sannidhīyate*—is near the devotees for accepting their services.

TRANSLATION

To show mercy to His devotees in each of these nine tracts of land, the Supreme Personality of Godhead known as Nārāyaṇa expands Himself in His quadruple principles of Vāsudeva, Saṅkarṣaṇa, Pradyumna and Aniruddha. In this way He remains near His devotees to accept their service.

PURPORT

In this connection, Viśvanātha Cakravartī Ṭhākura informs us that the demigods worship the Supreme Lord in His various Deity forms (*arcā-vigraha*) because except in the spiritual world, the Supreme Personality of Godhead cannot be directly worshiped in person. In the material world, the Lord is always worshiped as the *arcā-vigraha*, or Deity in the temple. There is no difference between the *arcā-vigraha* and the original person, and therefore those who are engaged in worshiping the Deity in the temple in full opulence, even on this planet, should be understood to be directly in touch with the Supreme Personality of Godhead without a doubt. As enjoined in the *śāstras, arcye viṣṇau śilā-dhīr guruṣu nara-matiḥ:* "No one should treat the Deity in the temple as stone or metal, nor should one think that the spiritual master is an ordinary human being." One should strictly follow this śāstric injunction and worship the Deity, the Supreme Personality of Godhead, without offenses. The spiritual master is the direct representative of the Lord, and no one should consider him an ordinary human being. By avoiding offenses against the Deity and the spiritual master, one can advance in spiritual life, or Kṛṣṇa consciousness.

In this regard, the following quotation appears in the *Laghu-bhāgavatāmṛta:*

pādme tu parama-vyomnaḥ
pūrvādye dik-catuṣṭaye
vāsudevādayo vyūhaś
catvāraḥ kathitāḥ kramāt

tathā pāda-vibhūtau ca
nivasanti kramādi me
jalāvṛti-stha-vaikuṇṭha-
sthita vedavatī-pure

satyordhve vaiṣṇave loke
nityākhye dvārakā-pure
śuddhodād uttare śveta-
dvīpe cairāvatī-pure

kṣīrāmbudhi-sthitānte
kroḍa-paryaṅka-dhāmani
sātvatīye kvacit tantre
nava vyūhāḥ prakīrtitāḥ
catvāro vāsudevādyā
nārāyaṇa-nṛsiṁhakau

hayagrīvo mahā-kroḍo
brahmā ceti navoditāḥ
tatra brahmā tu vijñeyaḥ
pūrvokta-vidhayā hariḥ

"In the *Padma Purāṇa* it is said that in the spiritual world the Lord personally expands in all directions and is worshiped as Vāsudeva, Saṅkarṣaṇa, Pradyumna and Aniruddha. The same God is represented by the Deity in this material world, which is only one quarter of His creation. Vāsudeva, Saṅkarṣaṇa, Pradyumna and Aniruddha are also present in the four directions of this material world. There is a Vaikuṇṭhaloka covered with water in this material world, and on that planet is a place called Vedavatī, where Vāsudeva is located. Another planet known as Viṣṇuloka is situated above Satyaloka, and there Saṅkarṣaṇa is present. Similarly, in Dvārakā-purī, Pradyumna is the predominator. On the island known as Śvetadvīpa, there is an ocean of milk, and in the midst of that ocean is a place called Airāvatī-pura, where Aniruddha lies on Ananta. In some of the *sātvata-tantras*, there is a description of the nine *varṣas* and the predominating Deity worshiped in each: (1) Vāsudeva, (2) Saṅkarṣaṇa, (3) Pradyumna, (4) Aniruddha, (5) Nārāyaṇa, (6) Nṛsiṁha, (7) Hayagrīva, (8) Mahāvarāha, and (9) Brahmā." The Lord Brahmā mentioned in this connection is the Supreme Personality of Godhead. When there is no fit human being to empower as Lord Brahmā, the Lord Himself takes the position of Lord Brahmā. *Tatra brahmā tu vijñeyaḥ pūrvokta-vidhayā hariḥ.* That Brahmā mentioned here is Hari Himself.

TEXT 15

इलावृते तु भगवान् भव एक एव पुमान्न ह्यन्यस्तत्रापरो निर्विशति
भवान्याः शापनिमित्तज्ञो यत्प्रवेक्ष्यतः स्त्रीभावस्तत्पश्चाद्वक्ष्यामि ॥ १५ ॥

ilāvṛte tu bhagavān bhava eka eva pumān na hy anyas tatrāparo
nirviśati bhavānyāḥ śāpa-nimitta-jño yat-pravekṣyataḥ strī-bhāvas tat
paścād vakṣyāmi.

ilāvṛte—in the tract of land known as Ilāvṛta-varṣa; *tu*—but; *bhagavān*—the most powerful; *bhavaḥ*—Lord Śiva; *eka*—only; *eva*—certainly; *pumān*—male person; *na*—not; *hi*—certainly; *anyaḥ*—any other; *tatra*—there; *aparaḥ*—besides; *nirviśati*—enters; *bhavānyāḥ śāpa-nimitta-jñaḥ*—who knows the cause of the curse by Bhavānī, the wife of Lord Śiva; *yat-pravekṣyataḥ*—of one who forcibly enters that tract of land; *strī-bhāvaḥ*—transformation into a female; *tat*—that; *paścāt*—later; *vakṣyāmi*—I shall explain.

TRANSLATION

Śukadeva Gosvāmī said: In the tract of land known as Ilāvṛta-varṣa, the only male person is Lord Śiva, the most powerful demigod. Goddess Durgā, the wife of Lord Śiva, does not like any man to enter that land. If any foolish man dares to do so, she immediately turns him into a woman. I shall explain this later [in the Ninth Canto of Śrīmad-Bhāgavatam].

TEXT 16

भवानीनाथैः स्त्रीगणार्बुदसहस्रै रवरुध्यमानो भगवतश्चतुर्मूर्तेर्महापुरुषस्य
तुरीयां तामसीं मूर्तिं प्रकृतिमात्मनः सङ्कर्षणसंज्ञामात्मसमाधिरूपेण
संनिधाप्यैतदभिगृणन् भव उपधावति ॥ १६ ॥

bhavānī-nāthaiḥ strī-gaṇārbuda-sahasrair avarudhyamāno bhagavataś catur-mūrter mahā-puruṣasya turīyāṁ tāmasīṁ mūrtiṁ prakṛtim ātmanaḥ saṅkarṣaṇa-saṁjñām ātma-samādhi-rūpeṇa sannidhāpyaitad abhigṛṇan bhava upadhāvati.

bhavānī-nāthaiḥ—by the company of Bhavānī; *strī-gaṇa*—of females; *arbuda-sahasraiḥ*—by ten billion; *avarudhyamānaḥ*—always being served; *bhagavataḥ catuḥ-mūrteḥ*—the Supreme Personality of Godhead, who is expanded in four; *mahā-puruṣasya*—of the Supreme Person; *turīyām*—the fourth expansion; *tāmasīm*—related to the mode of ignorance; *mūrtim*—the form; *prakṛtim*—as the source; *ātmanaḥ*—of himself (Lord Śiva); *saṅkarṣaṇa-saṁjñām*—known as Saṅkarṣaṇa; *ātma-samādhi-rūpeṇa*—by meditating upon Him in trance; *sannidhāpya*—bringing Him near; *etat*—this; *abhigṛṇan*—clearly chanting; *bhavaḥ*—Lord Śiva; *upadhāvati*—worships.

TRANSLATION

In Ilāvṛta-varṣa, Lord Śiva is always encircled by ten billion maidservants of goddess Durgā, who minister to him. The quadru-

ple expansion of the Supreme Lord is composed of Vāsudeva, Pradyumna, Aniruddha and Saṅkarṣaṇa. Saṅkarṣaṇa, the fourth expansion, is certainly transcendental, but because his activities of destruction in the material world are in the mode of ignorance, He is known as tāmasī, the Lord's form in the mode of ignorance. Lord Śiva knows that Saṅkarṣaṇa is the original cause of his own existence, and thus he always meditates upon Him in trance by chanting the following mantra.

PURPORT

Sometimes we see a picture of Lord Śiva engaged in meditation. This verse explains that Lord Śiva is always meditating upon Lord Saṅkarṣaṇa in trance. Lord Śiva is in charge of the destruction of the material world. Lord Brahmā creates the material world, Lord Viṣṇu maintains it, and Lord Śiva destroys it. Because destruction is in the mode of ignorance, Lord Śiva and his worshipable Deity, Saṅkarṣaṇa, are technically called *tāmasī*. Lord Śiva is the incarnation of *tamo-guṇa*. Since both Lord Śiva and Saṅkarṣaṇa are always enlightened and situated in the transcendental position, they have nothing to do with the modes of material nature—goodness, passion and ignorance—but because their activities involve them with the mode of ignorance, they are sometimes called *tāmasī*.

TEXT 17

श्रीभगवानुवाच

ॐ नमो भगवते महापुरुषाय सर्वगुणसङ्ख्यानायानन्तायाव्यक्ताय नम इति ॥१७॥

śrī-bhagavān uvāca
oṁ namo bhagavate mahā-puruṣāya sarva-guṇa-saṅkhyānāy-ānantāyāvyaktāya nama iti.

śrī-bhagavān uvāca—the most powerful Lord Śiva says; *om namo bhagavate*—O Supreme Personality of Godhead, I offer my respectful obeisances unto You; *mahā-puruṣāya*—who are the Supreme Person; *sarva-guṇa-saṅkhyānāya*—the reservoir of all transcendental qualities;

anantāya—the unlimited; *avyaktāya*—not manifested within the material world; *namaḥ*—my respectful obeisances; *iti*—thus.

TRANSLATION

The most powerful Lord Śiva says: O Supreme Personality of Godhead, I offer my respectful obeisances unto You in Your expansion as Lord Saṅkarṣaṇa. You are the reservoir of all transcendental qualities. Although You are unlimited, You remain unmanifest to the nondevotees.

TEXT 18

भजे भजन्यारणपादपङ्कजं
भगस्य कृत्स्नस्य परं परायणम् ।
भक्तेष्वलं भावितभूतभावनं
भवापहं त्वा भवभावमीश्वरम् ॥१८॥

bhaje bhajanyāraṇa-pāda-paṅkajaṁ
bhagasya kṛtsnasya paraṁ parāyaṇam
bhakteṣv alaṁ bhāvita-bhūta-bhāvanaṁ
bhavāpahaṁ tvā bhava-bhāvam īśvaram

bhaje—I worship; *bhajanya*—O worshipable Lord; *araṇa-pāda-paṅkajam*—whose lotus feet protect His devotees from all fearful situations; *bhagasya*—of opulences; *kṛtsnasya*—of all different varieties (wealth, fame, strength, knowledge, beauty and renunciation); *param*—the best; *parāyaṇam*—the ultimate shelter; *bhakteṣu*—to the devotees; *alam*—beyond value; *bhāvita-bhūta-bhāvanam*—who manifests His different forms for the satisfaction of His devotees; *bhava-apaham*—who stops the devotees' repetition of birth and death; *tvā*—unto You; *bhava-bhāvam*—who is the origin of the material creation; *īśvaram*—the Supreme Personality of Godhead.

TRANSLATION

O my Lord, You are the only worshipable person, for You are the Supreme Personality of Godhead, the reservoir of all

opulences. Your secure lotus feet are the only source of protection for all Your devotees, whom You satisfy by manifesting Yourself in various forms. O my Lord, You deliver Your devotees from the clutches of material existence. Nondevotees, however, remain entangled in material existence by Your will. Kindly accept me as Your eternal servant.

TEXT 19

न यस्य मायागुणचित्तवृत्तिभि-
निरीक्षतो ह्यण्वपि दृष्टिरज्यते ।
ईशे यथा नोऽजितमन्युरंहसां
कस्तं न मन्येत जिगीषुरात्मनः ॥१९॥

na yasya māyā-guṇa-citta-vṛttibhir
nirīkṣato hy aṇv api dṛṣṭir ajyate
īśe yathā no 'jita-manyu-raṁhasāṁ
kas taṁ na manyeta jigīṣur ātmanaḥ

na—never; *yasya*—whose; *māyā*—of the illusory energy; *guṇa*—in the qualities; *citta*—of the heart; *vṛttibhiḥ*—by the activities (thinking, feeling and willing); *nirīkṣataḥ*—of Him who is glancing; *hi*—certainly; *aṇu*—slightly; *api*—even; *dṛṣṭiḥ*—vision; *ajyate*—is affected; *īśe*—for the purpose of regulating; *yathā*—as; *naḥ*—of us; *ajita*—who have not conquered; *manyu*—of anger; *raṁhasām*—the force; *kaḥ*—who; *tam*—unto Him (the Supreme Lord); *na*—not; *manyeta*—would worship; *jigīṣuḥ*—aspiring to conquer; *ātmanaḥ*—the senses.

TRANSLATION

We cannot control the force of our anger. Therefore when we look at material things, we cannot avoid feeling attraction or repulsion for them. But the Supreme Lord is never affected in this way. Although He glances over the material world for the purpose of creating, maintaining and destroying it, He is not affected, even to the slightest degree. Therefore, one who desires to conquer the force of the senses must take shelter of the lotus feet of the Lord. Then he will be victorious.

PURPORT

The Supreme Personality of Godhead is always equipped with inconceivable potencies. Although creation takes place by His glancing over the material energy, He is not affected by the modes of material nature. Because of His eternally transcendental position, when the Supreme Personality of Godhead appears in this material world, the modes of material nature cannot affect Him. Therefore the Supreme Lord is called Transcendence, and anyone who wants to be secure from the influence of the modes of material nature must take shelter of Him.

TEXT 20

असद्दृशो यः प्रतिभाति मायया
क्षीबेव मध्वासवताम्रलोचनः ।
न नागवध्वोऽर्हण ईशिरे ह्रिया
यत्पादयोः स्पर्शनधर्षितेन्द्रियाः ॥२०॥

asad-dṛśo yaḥ pratibhāti māyayā
kṣībeva madhv-āsava-tāmra-locanaḥ
na nāga-vadhvo 'rhaṇa īśire hriyā
yat-pādayoḥ sparśana-dharṣitendriyāḥ

asat-dṛśaḥ—for a person with polluted vision; *yaḥ*—who; *pratibhāti*—appears; *māyayā*—the influence of *māyā; kṣībaḥ*—one who is inebriated or angry; *iva*—like; *madhu*—by honey; *āsava*—and liquor; *tāmra-locanaḥ*—having eyes reddish like copper; *na*—not; *nāga-vadhvaḥ*—the wives of the serpent demon; *arhaṇe*—in worshiping; *īśire*—were unable to proceed; *hriyā*—because of bashfulness; *yat-pādayoḥ*—of whose lotus feet; *sparśana*—by the touching; *dharṣita*—agitated; *indriyāḥ*—whose senses.

TRANSLATION

For persons with impure vision, the Supreme Lord's eyes appear like those of someone who indiscriminately drinks intoxicating beverages. Thus bewildered, such unintelligent persons become angry at the Supreme Lord, and due to their angry mood the Lord

Himself appears angry and very fearful. However, this is an illusion. When the wives of the serpent demon were agitated by the touch of the Lord's lotus feet, due to shyness they could proceed no further in their worship of Him. Yet the Lord remained unagitated by their touch, for He is equipoised in all circumstances. Therefore who will not worship the Supreme Personality of Godhead?

PURPORT

Anyone who remains unagitated, even in the presence of cause for agitation, is called *dhīra*, or equipoised. The Supreme Personality of Godhead, being always in a transcendental position, is never agitated by anything. Therefore someone who wants to become *dhīra* must take shelter of the lotus feet of the Lord. In *Bhagavad-gītā* (2.13) Kṛṣṇa says, *dhīras tatra na muhyati:* a person who is equipoised in all circumstances is never bewildered. Prahlāda Mahārāja is a perfect example of a *dhīra.* When the fierce form of Nṛsiṁhadeva appeared in order to kill Hiraṇyakaśipu, Prahlāda was unagitated. He remained calm and quiet, whereas others, including even Lord Brahmā, were frightened by the features of the Lord.

TEXT 21

यमाहुरस्य स्थितिजन्मसंयमं
त्रिभिर्विहीनं यमनन्तमृषयः ।
न वेद सिद्धार्थमिव क्वचित्स्थितं
भूमण्डलं मूर्धसहस्रधामसु ॥२१॥

yam āhur asya sthiti-janma-saṁyamaṁ
tribhir vihīnaṁ yam anantam ṛṣayaḥ
na veda siddhārtham iva kvacit sthitaṁ
bhū-maṇḍalaṁ mūrdha-sahasra-dhāmasu

yam—whom; *āhuḥ*—they said; *asya*—of the material world; *sthiti*—the maintenance; *janma*—creation; *saṁyamam*—annihilation; *tribhiḥ*—these three; *vihīnam*—without; *yam*—which; *anantam*—

unlimited; *ṛṣayaḥ*—all the great sages; *na*—not; *veda*—feels; *siddha-artham*—a mustard seed; *iva*—like; *kvacit*—where; *sthitam*—situated; *bhū-maṇḍalam*—the universe; *mūrdha-sahasra-dhāmasu*—on the hundreds and thousands of hoods of the Lord.

TRANSLATION

Lord Śiva continued: All the great sages accept the Lord as the source of creation, maintenance and destruction, although He actually has nothing to do with these activities. Therefore the Lord is called unlimited. Although the Lord in His incarnation as Śeṣa holds all the universes on His hoods, each universe feels no heavier than a mustard seed to Him. Therefore, what person desiring perfection will not worship the Lord?

PURPORT

The incarnation of the Supreme Personality of Godhead known as Śeṣa or Ananta has unlimited strength, fame, wealth, knowledge, beauty and renunciation. As described in this verse, Ananta's strength is so great that the innumerable universes rest on His hoods. He has the bodily features of a snake with thousands of hoods, and since His strength is unlimited, all the universes resting on His hoods feel no heavier than mustard seeds. We can just imagine how insignificant a mustard seed is on the hood of a serpent. In this connection, the reader is referred to *Śrī Caitanya-caritāmṛta, Ādi-līlā,* Chapter Five, verses 117-125. There it is stated that Lord Viṣṇu's incarnation as the serpentine Ananta Śeṣa Nāga supports all the universes on His hoods. By our calculation, a universe may be very, very heavy, but because the Lord is *ananta* (unlimited), He feels the weight to be no heavier than a mustard seed.

TEXTS 22-23

यस्याद्य आसीद् गुणविग्रहो महान्
विज्ञानधिष्ण्यो भगवानजः किल ।
यत्सम्भवोऽहं त्रिवृता स्वतेजसा
वैकारिकं तामसमैन्द्रियं सृजे ॥२२॥

एते वयं यस्य वशे महात्मनः
स्थिताः शकुन्ता इव सूत्रयन्त्रिताः ।
महानहं वैकृततामसेन्द्रियाः
सृजाम सर्वे यदनुग्रहादिदम् ॥२३॥

yasyādya āsīd guṇa-vigraho mahān
vijñāna-dhiṣṇyo bhagavān ajaḥ kila
yat-sambhavo 'haṁ tri-vṛtā sva-tejasā
vaikārikaṁ tāmasam aindriyaṁ sṛje

ete vayaṁ yasya vaśe mahātmanaḥ
sthitāḥ śakuntā iva sūtra-yantritāḥ
mahān ahaṁ vaikṛta-tāmasendriyāḥ
sṛjāma sarve yad-anugrahād idam

yasya—from whom; *ādyaḥ*—the beginning; *āsīt*—there was; *guṇa-vigrahaḥ*—the incarnation of the material qualities; *mahān*—the total material energy; *vijñāna*—of full knowledge; *dhiṣṇyaḥ*—the reservoir; *bhagavān*—the most powerful; *ajaḥ*—Lord Brahmā; *kila*—certainly; *yat*—from whom; *sambhavaḥ*—born; *aham*—I; *tri-vṛtā*—having three varieties according to the three modes of nature; *sva-tejasā*—by my material strength; *vaikārikam*—all the demigods; *tāmasam*—material elements; *aindriyam*—the senses; *sṛje*—I create; *ete*—all of these; *vayam*—we; *yasya*—of whom; *vaśe*—under the control; *mahā-āt-manaḥ*—great personalities; *sthitāḥ*—situated; *śakuntāḥ*—vultures; *iva*—like; *sūtra-yantritāḥ*—bound by rope; *mahān*—the *mahat-tattva;* *aham*—I; *vaikṛta*—the demigods; *tāmasa*—the five material elements; *indriyāḥ*—senses; *sṛjāmaḥ*—we create; *sarve*—all of us; *yat*—of whom; *anugrahāt*—by the mercy; *idam*—this material world.

TRANSLATION

From that Supreme Personality of Godhead appears Lord Brahmā, whose body is made from the total material energy, the reservoir of intelligence predominated by the passionate mode of material nature. From Lord Brahmā, I myself am born as a

representation of false ego known as Rudra. By my own power I create all the other demigods, the five elements and the senses. Therefore, I worship the Supreme Personality of Godhead, who is greater than any of us and under whose control are situated all the demigods, material elements and senses, and even Lord Brahmā and I myself, like birds bound by a rope. Only by the Lord's grace can we create, maintain and annihilate the material world. Therefore I offer my respectful obeisances unto the Supreme Being.

PURPORT

A summary of creation is given in this verse. From Saṅkarṣaṇa, Mahā-Viṣṇu expands, and from Mahā-Viṣṇu, Garbhodakaśāyī Viṣṇu expands. Lord Brahmā, who was born of Garbhodakaśāyī Viṣṇu, fathers Lord Śiva, from whom all the other demigods gradually evolve. Lord Brahmā, Lord Śiva and Lord Viṣṇu are incarnations of the different material qualities. Lord Viṣṇu is actually above all material qualities, but He accepts control of *sattva-guṇa* (the mode of goodness) to maintain the universe. Lord Brahmā is born from the *mahat-tattva.* Brahmā creates the entire universe, Lord Viṣṇu maintains it, and Lord Śiva annihilates it. The Supreme Personality of Godhead controls all the most important demigods—especially Lord Brahmā and Lord Śiva—exactly as the owner of a bird controls it by binding it with a rope. Sometimes vultures are controlled in this way.

TEXT 24

यन्निर्मितां कर्ह्यपि कर्मपर्वणीं
मायां जनोऽयं गुणसर्गमोहितः ।
न वेद निस्तारणयोगमञ्जसा
तस्मै नमस्ते विलयोदयात्मने ॥२४॥

yan-nirmitāṁ karhy api karma-parvaṇīṁ
māyāṁ jano 'yaṁ guṇa-sarga-mohitaḥ
na veda nistāraṇa-yogam añjasā
tasmai namas te vilayodayātmane

yat—by whom; *nirmitām*—created; *karhi api*—at any time; *karma-parvaṇīm*—which ties the knots of fruitive activity; *māyām*—the illusory energy; *janaḥ*—a person; *ayam*—this; *guṇa-sarga-mohitaḥ*—bewildered by the three modes of material nature; *na*—not; *veda*—knows; *nistāraṇa-yogam*—the process of getting out of material entanglement; *añjasā*—soon; *tasmai*—unto Him (the Supreme); *namaḥ*—respectful obeisances; *te*—unto You; *vilaya-udaya-ātmane*—in whom everything is annihilated and from whom everything is again manifested.

TRANSLATION

The illusory energy of the Supreme Personality of Godhead binds all of us conditioned souls to this material world. Therefore, without being favored by Him, persons like us cannot understand how to get out of that illusory energy. Let me offer my respectful obeisances unto the Lord, who is the cause of creation and annihilation.

PURPORT

Kṛṣṇa clearly states in *Bhagavad-gītā* (7.14):

daivī hy eṣā guṇa-mayī
mama māyā duratyayā
mām eva ye prapadyante
māyām etāṁ taranti te

"This divine energy of Mine, consisting of the three modes of material nature, is difficult to overcome. But those who have surrendered unto Me can easily cross beyond it." All conditioned souls working within the illusory energy of the Lord consider the body to be the self, and thus they continuously wander throughout the universe, taking birth in different species of life and creating more and more problems. Sometimes they become disgusted with the problems and seek out a process by which they can get out of this entanglement. Unfortunately, such so-called research workers are unaware of the Supreme Personality of Godhead and His illusory energy, and thus all of them work only in darkness, never finding a way out. So-called scientists and advanced research scholars are ludicrously trying to find the cause of life. They take no notice of the fact that life is already being produced. What will be their credit if they find out the chemical composition of life? All their chemicals are nothing but different transformations of the five elements—earth, water, fire, air and ether. As stated in *Bhagavad-gītā* (2.20), the living entity is never created (*na jāyate mriyate vā kadācin*). There are five gross material elements and three minor material elements (mind, intelligence and ego), and there are eternal living entities. The living entity desires a certain type of body, and by the order of the Supreme Personality of Godhead, that body is created from material nature, which is nothing but a kind of machine handled by the Supreme Lord. The Lord gives the living entity a particular type of mechanical body, and the living entity must work with it according to the law of fruitive activities. Fruitive activities are described in this verse: *karma-parvanīṁ māyām.* The living entity is seated on a machine (the body), and according to the order of the Supreme Lord, he operates the machine. This is the secret of transmigration of the soul from one body to another. The living entity thus becomes entangled in fruitive activities in this material world. As confirmed in *Bhagavad-gītā* (15.7), *manaḥ ṣaṣṭhānīndriyāṇi prakṛti-sthāni karṣati:* the living entity is struggling very hard against the six senses, which include the mind.

In all the activities of creation and annihilation, the living entity is entangled in fruitive activities, which are executed by the illusory energy, *māyā.* He is exactly like a computer handled by the Supreme Personality of Godhead. The so-called scientists say that nature acts independently, but they cannot explain what nature is. Nature is nothing but a machine operated by the Supreme Personality of Godhead. When one understands the operator, his problems of life are solved. As Kṛṣṇa says in *Bhagavad-gītā* (7.19):

bahūnāṁ janmanām ante
jñānavān māṁ prapadyate
vāsudevaḥ sarvam iti
sa mahātmā sudurlabhaḥ

"After many births and deaths, he who is actually in knowledge surrenders unto Me, knowing Me to be the cause of all causes and all that is.

Such a great soul is very rare." A sane man, therefore, surrenders to the Supreme Personality of Godhead and thus gets out of the clutches of the illusory energy, *māyā.*

Thus end the Bhaktivedanta purports of the Fifth Canto, Seventeenth Chapter of the Śrīmad-Bhāgavatam, *entitled "The Descent of the River Ganges."*

CHAPTER EIGHTEEN

The Prayers Offered to the Lord by the Residents of Jambūdvīpa

In this chapter Śukadeva Gosvāmī describes the different *varṣas* of Jambūdvīpa and the incarnation of the Supreme Lord worshiped in each. The predominating ruler of Bhadrāśva-varṣa is Bhadraśravā. He and his many servants always worship the incarnation known as Lord Hayagrīva. At the end of each *kalpa*, when the demon Ajñāna steals the Vedic knowledge, Lord Hayagrīva appears and preserves it. Then He delivers it to Lord Brahmā. In the land known as Hari-varṣa, the exalted devotee Prahlāda Mahārāja worships Lord Nṛsiṁhadeva. (The appearance of Lord Nṛsiṁhadeva is described in the Seventh Canto of *Śrīmad-Bhāgavatam.*) Following in the footsteps of Prahlāda Mahārāja, the inhabitants of Hari-varṣa always worship Lord Nṛsiṁhadeva to receive from Him the benediction of being engaged in His loving service. In the tract of land known as Ketumāla-varṣa, the Supreme Personality of Godhead (Lord Hṛṣīkeśa) appears in the form of Cupid. The goddess of fortune and the demigods living there engage in His service day and night. Manifesting Himself in sixteen parts, Lord Hṛṣīkeśa is the source of all encouragement, strength and influence. The conditioned living entity has the defect of being always fearful, but simply by the mercy of the Supreme Personality of Godhead, he can rid himself of this defect of material life. Therefore the Lord alone can be addressed as master. In the tract of land known as Ramyaka-varṣa, Manu and all the inhabitants worship Matsyadeva to this very day. Matsyadeva, whose form is pure goodness, is the ruler and maintainer of the whole universe, and as such He is the director of all the demigods, headed by King Indra. In Hiraṇmaya-varṣa Lord Viṣṇu has assumed the form of a tortoise (Kūrma *mūrti*) and is worshiped there by Aryamā, along with all the other residents. Similarly, in the tract of land known as Uttarakuru-varṣa, Lord Śrī Hari has assumed the form of a boar, and in that form He accepts service from all the inhabitants living there.

All the information in this chapter can be fully realized by one who associates with devotees of the Lord. Therefore in the *śāstras* it is recommended that one associate with devotees. This is better than residing on the banks of the Ganges. In the hearts of pure devotees reside all good sentiments as well as all the superior qualities of the demigods. In the hearts of nondevotees, however, there cannot be any good qualities, for such people are simply enchanted by the external, illusory energy of the Lord. Following in the footsteps of devotees, one should know that the Supreme Personality of Godhead is the only worshipable Deity. Everyone should accept this proposal and worship the Lord. As stated in *Bhagavad-gītā* (15.15), *vedaiś ca sarvair aham eva vedyaḥ:* the purpose of studying all Vedic literature is to worship the Supreme Personality of Godhead, Kṛṣṇa. If after studying all the Vedic literature, one does not awaken his dormant love for the Supreme Lord, it is to be understood that he has labored for nothing. He has simply wasted his time. Lacking attachment for the Supreme Personality of Godhead, he remains attached to family life in this material world. Thus the lesson of this chapter is that one should get out of family life and completely take shelter of the lotus feet of the Lord.

TEXT 1

श्रीशुक उवाच

तथा च भद्रश्रवा नाम धर्मसुतस्तत्कुलपतयः पुरुषा भद्राश्ववर्षे साक्षाद्भगवतो वासुदेवस्य प्रियां तनुं धर्ममयीं हयशीर्षाभिधानां परमेण समाधिना संनिधाप्येदमभिगृणन्त उपधावन्ति ॥ १ ॥

śrī-śuka uvāca

tathā ca bhadraśravā nāma dharma-sutas tat-kula-patayaḥ puruṣā bhadrāśva-varṣe sākṣād bhagavato vāsudevasya priyāṁ tanuṁ dharmamayīṁ hayaśīrṣābhidhānām parameṇa samādhinā sannidhāpyedam abhigṛṇanta upadhāvanti.

śrī-śukaḥ uvāca—Śukadeva Gosvāmī said; *tathā ca*—similarly (just as Lord Śiva worships Saṅkarṣaṇa in Ilāvṛta-varṣa); *bhadra-śravā*—Bhadraśravā; *nāma*—known as; *dharma-sutaḥ*—the son of Dharmarāja; *tat*—of him; *kula-patayaḥ*—the chiefs of the dynasty; *puruṣāḥ*—all the residents; *bhadrāśva-varṣe*—in the land known as Bhadrāśva-varṣa; *sākṣāt*—directly; *bhagavataḥ*—of the Supreme Personality of Godhead; *vāsudevasya*—of Lord Vāsudeva; *priyām tanum*—very dear form; *dharma-mayīm*—the director of all religious principles; *hayaśīrṣa-abhidhānām*—the Lord's incarnation named Hayaśīrṣa (also called Hayagrīva); *paramena samādhinā*—with the highest form of trance; *sannidhāpya*—coming near; *idam*—this; *abhigṛṇantaḥ*—chanting; *upadhāvanti*—they worship.

TRANSLATION

Śrī Śukadeva Gosvāmī said: Bhadraśravā, the son of Dharmarāja, rules the tract of land known as Bhadrāśva-varṣa. Just as Lord Śiva worships Saṅkarṣaṇa in Ilāvṛta-varṣa, Bhadraśravā, accompanied by his intimate servants and all the residents of the land, worships the plenary expansion of Vāsudeva known as Hayaśīrṣa. Lord Hayaśīrṣa is very dear to the devotees, and He is the director of all religious principles. Fixed in the topmost trance, Bhadraśravā and his associates offer their respectful obeisances to the Lord and chant the following prayers with careful pronunciation.

TEXT 2

भद्रश्रवस ऊचुः
ॐ नमो भगवते धर्मायात्मविशोधनाय नम इति ॥ २ ॥

bhadraśravasa ūcuḥ
oṁ namo bhagavate dharmāyātma-viśodhanāya nama iti.

bhadraśravasaḥ ūcuḥ—the ruler Bhadraśravā and his intimate associates said; *om*—O Lord; *namaḥ*—respectful obeisances; *bhagavate*—unto the Supreme Personality of Godhead; *dharmāya*—the source of all religious principles; *ātma-viśodhanāya*—who purifies us of material contamination; *namaḥ*—our obeisances; *iti*—thus.

TRANSLATION

The ruler Bhadraśravā and his intimate associates utter the following prayer: We offer our respectful obeisances unto the

Supreme Personality of Godhead, the reservoir of all religious principles, who cleanses the heart of the conditioned soul in this material world. Again and again we offer our respectful obeisances unto Him.

PURPORT

Foolish materialistic persons do not know how they are being controlled and punished at every step by the laws of nature. They think they are very happy in the conditioned state of material life, not knowing the purpose of repeated birth, death, old age and disease. Therefore in *Bhagavad-gītā* (7.15) Lord Kṛṣṇa describes such materialistic persons as *mūḍhas* (rascals): *na māṁ duṣkṛtino mūḍhāḥ prapadyante narādhamāḥ.* These *mūḍhas* do not know that if they want to purify themselves, they must worship Lord Vāsudeva (Kṛṣṇa) by performing penances and austerities. This purification is the aim of human life. This life is not meant for blind indulgence in sense gratification. In the human form, the living being must engage himself in Kṛṣṇa consciousness to purify his existence: *tapo divyaṁ putrakā yena sattvaṁ śuddhyet.* This is the instruction of King Ṛṣabhadeva to His sons. In the human form of life, one must undergo all kinds of austerities to purify his existence. *Yasmād brahma-saukhyaṁ tv anantam.* We are all seeking happiness, but because of our ignorance and foolishness, we cannot know what unobstructed happiness really is. Unobstructed happiness is called *brahma-saukhya,* spiritual happiness. Although we may get some so-called happiness in this material world, that happiness is temporary. The foolish materialists cannot understand this. Therefore Prahlāda Mahārāja points out, *māyā-sukhāya bharam udvahato vimūḍhān:* merely for temporary materialistic happiness, these rascals are making huge arrangements, and thus they are baffled life after life.

TEXT 3

अहो विचित्रं भगवद्विचेष्टितं
घ्नन्तं जनोऽयं हि मिषन्न पश्यति ।
ध्यायन्नसद्यर्हि विकर्म सेवितुं
निर्हृत्य पुत्रं पितरं जिजीविषति ॥ ३ ॥

aho vicitraṁ bhagavad-viceṣṭitaṁ
ghnantaṁ jano 'yaṁ hi miṣan na paśyati
dhyāyann asad yarhi vikarma sevituṁ
nirhṛtya putraṁ pitaraṁ jijīviṣati

aho—alas; *vicitram*—wonderful; *bhagavat-viceṣṭitam*—the pastimes of the Lord; *ghnantam*—death; *janaḥ*—a person; *ayam*—this; *hi*—certainly; *miṣan*—although seeing; *na paśyati*—does not see; *dhyāyan*—thinking about; *asat*—material happiness; *yarhi*—because; *vikarma*—forbidden activities; *sevitum*—to enjoy; *nirhṛtya*—burning; *putram*—sons; *pitaram*—the father; *jijīviṣati*—desires a long life.

TRANSLATION

Alas! How wonderful it is that the foolish materialist does not heed the great danger of impending death! He knows that death will surely come, yet he is nevertheless callous and neglectful. If his father dies, he wants to enjoy his father's property, and if his son dies, he wants to enjoy his son's possessions as well. In either case, he heedlessly tries to enjoy material happiness with the acquired money.

PURPORT

Material happiness means to have good facilities for eating, sleeping, sexual intercourse and defense. Within this world, the materialistic person lives only for these four principles of sense gratification, not caring for the impending danger of death. After his father's death, a son tries to inherit his money and use it for sense gratification. Similarly, one whose son dies tries to enjoy the possessions of his son. Sometimes the father of a dead son even enjoys his son's widow. Materialistic persons behave in this way. Thus Śukadeva Gosvāmī says, "How wonderful are these pastimes of material happiness transacted by the will of the Supreme Personality of Godhead!" In other words, materialistic persons want to commit all kinds of sinful activities, but without the sanction of the Supreme Personality of Godhead, no one can do anything. Why does the Supreme Personality of Godhead permit sinful activities? The Supreme Lord does not want any living being to act sinfully, and He begs him through his good conscience to refrain from sin. But when someone insists upon acting sinfully, the Supreme Lord gives him the sanction to act at his own risk (*mattaḥ smṛtir jñānam apohanaṁ ca*). No one can do anything without the sanction of the Lord, but He is so kind that when the conditioned soul persists in doing something, the Lord permits the individual soul to act at his own risk.

According to Srīla Viśvanātha Cakravartī Ṭhākura, sons always outlive their fathers in other planetary systems and other lands in this universe, especially on Svargaloka. However, on this planet earth a son often dies before his father, and the materialistic father is pleased to enjoy the possessions of his son. Neither the father nor the son can see the reality—that both of them are awaiting death. When death comes, however, all their plans for material enjoyment are finished.

TEXT 4

वदन्ति विश्वं कवयः स्म नश्वरं
पश्यन्ति चाध्यात्मविदो विपश्चितः ।
तथापि मुह्यन्ति तवाज मायया
सुविस्मितं कृत्यमजं नतोऽस्मि तम् ॥ ४ ॥

vadanti viśvaṁ kavayaḥ sma naśvaraṁ
paśyanti cādhyātmavido vipaścitaḥ
tathāpi muhyanti tavāja māyayā
suvismitaṁ kṛtyam ajaṁ nato 'smi tam

vadanti—they say authoritatively; *viśvam*—the entire material creation; *kavayaḥ*—great learned sages; *sma*—certainly; *naśvaram*—perishable; *paśyanti*—they see in trance; *ca*—also; *adhyātma-vidaḥ*—who have realized spiritual knowledge; *vipaścitaḥ*—very learned scholars; *tathā api*—still; *muhyanti*—become illusioned; *tava*—your; *aja*—O unborn one; *māyayā*—by the illusory energy; *su-vismitam*—most wonderful; *kṛtyam*—activity; *ajam*—unto the supreme unborn one; *nataḥ asmi*—I offer my obeisances; *tam*—unto Him.

TRANSLATION

O unborn one, learned Vedic scholars who are advanced in spiritual knowledge certainly know that this material world is

perishable, as do other logicians and philosophers. In trance they realize the factual position of this world, and they preach the truth as well. Yet even they are sometimes bewildered by Your illusory energy. This is Your own wonderful pastime. Therefore, I can understand that Your illusory energy is very wonderful, and I offer my respectful obeisances unto You.

PURPORT

Not only does the illusory energy of the Supreme Personality of Godhead act on the conditioned soul within this material world, but sometimes it also acts on the most advanced learned scholars, who factually know the constitutional position of this material world through realization. As soon as someone thinks, "I am this material body (*ahaṁ mameti*) and everything in relationship with this material body is mine," he is in illusion (*moha*). This illusion caused by the material energy acts especially on the conditioned souls, but it sometimes also acts on liberated souls as well. A liberated soul is a person who has sufficient knowledge of this material world and is therefore unattached to the bodily conception of life. But because of association with the modes of material nature for a very long time, even liberated souls sometimes become captivated by the illusory energy due to inattentiveness in the transcendental position. Therefore Lord Kṛṣṇa says in *Bhagavad-gītā* (7.14), *mām eva ye prapadyante māyām etāṁ taranti te:* "Only those who surrender unto Me can overcome the influence of the material energy." Therefore no one should think of himself as a liberated person immune to the influence of *māyā.* Everyone should very cautiously execute devotional service by rigidly following regulative principles. Thus he will remain fixed at the lotus feet of the Lord. Otherwise, a little inattention will create havoc. We have already seen an example of this in the case of Mahārāja Bharata. Mahārāja Bharata was undoubtedly a great devotee, but because he turned his attention slightly toward a small deer, he had to suffer two more births, one as a deer and another as the *brāhmaṇa* Jaḍa Bharata. Afterward he was liberated and went back home, back to Godhead.

The Lord is always prepared to excuse His devotee, but if a devotee takes advantage of the Lord's leniency and purposefully commits mistakes again and again, the Lord will certainly punish him by letting him fall down into the clutches of the illusory energy. In other words, theoretical knowledge acquired by studying the *Vedas* is insufficient to protect one from the clutches of *māyā*. One must strongly adhere to the lotus feet of the Lord in devotional service. Then one's position is secure.

TEXT 5

विश्वोद्भवस्थाननिरोधकर्म ते
ह्यकर्तुरङ्गीकृतमप्यपावृतः ।
युक्तं न चित्रं त्वयि कार्यकारणे
सर्वात्मनि व्यतिरिक्ते च वस्तुतः ॥ ५ ॥

viśvodbhava-sthāna-nirodha-karma te
hy akartur aṅgīkṛtam apy apāvṛtaḥ
yuktaṁ na citraṁ tvayi kārya-kāraṇe
sarvātmani vyatirikte ca vastutaḥ

viśva—of the whole universe; *udbhava*—of the creation; *sthāna*—of the maintenance; *nirodha*—of the annihilation; *karma*—these activities; *te*—of You (O dear Lord); *hi*—indeed; *akartuḥ*—aloof; *aṅgīkṛtam*—still accepted by the Vedic literature; *api*—although; *apāvṛtaḥ*—untouched by all these activities; *yuktam*—befitting; *na*—not; *citram*—wonderful; *tvayi*—in You; *kārya-kāraṇe*—the original cause of all effects; *sarva-ātmani*—in all respects; *vyatirikte*—set apart; *ca*—also; *vastutaḥ*—the original substance.

TRANSLATION

O Lord, although You are completely detached from the creation, maintenance and annihilation of this material world and are not directly affected by these activities, they are all attributed to You. We do not wonder at this, for Your inconceivable energies perfectly qualify You to be the cause of all causes. You are the active principle in everything, although You are separate from everything. Thus we can realize that everything is happening because of Your inconceivable energy.

TEXT 6

वेदान् युगान्ते तमसा तिरस्कृतान्
रसातलाद्यो नृतुरङ्गविग्रहः ।
प्रत्याददे वै कवयेऽभियाचते
तस्मै नमस्तेऽवितथेहिताय इति ॥ ६ ॥

vedān yugānte tamasā tiraskṛtān
rasātalād yo nṛ-turaṅga-vigrahaḥ
pratyādade vai kavaye 'bhiyācate
tasmai namas te 'vitathehitāya iti

vedān—the four *Vedas; yuga-ante*—at the end of the millennium; *tamasā*—by the demon of ignorance personified; *tiraskṛtān*—stolen away; *rasātalāt*—from the lowest planetary system (Rasātala); *yaḥ*—who (the Supreme Personality of Godhead); *nṛ-turaṅga-vigrahaḥ*—assuming the form of half-horse, half-man; *pratyādade*—returned; *vai*—indeed; *kavaye*—to the supreme poet (Lord Brahmā); *abhiyācate*—when he asked for them; *tasmai*—unto Him (the form of Hayagrīva); *namaḥ*—my respectful obeisances; *te*—to You; *avitatha-īhitāya*—whose resolution never fails; *iti*—thus.

TRANSLATION

At the end of the millennium, ignorance personified assumed the form of a demon, stole all the Vedas and took them down to the planet of Rasātala. The Supreme Lord, however, in His form of Hayagrīva retrieved the Vedas and returned them to Lord Brahmā when he begged for them. I offer my respectful obeisances unto the Supreme Lord, whose determination never fails.

PURPORT

Although Vedic knowledge is imperishable, within this material world it is sometimes manifest and sometimes not. When the people of this material world become too absorbed in ignorance, the Vedic knowledge disappears. Lord Hayagrīva or Lord Matsya, however, always protects the Vedic knowledge, and in due course of time it is again distributed through the medium of Lord Brahmā. Brahmā is the trustworthy representative of the Supreme Lord. Therefore when he again asked for the treasure of Vedic knowledge, the Lord fulfilled his desire.

TEXT 7

हरिवर्षे चापि भगवान्नरहरिरूपेणास्ते । तद्रूपग्रहणनिमित्तमुत्तरत्राभिधास्ये । तद्दयितं रूपं महापुरुषगुणभाजनो महाभागवतो दैत्यदानवकुलतीर्थीकरणशीलाचरितः प्रह्लादोऽव्यवधानानन्यभक्तियोगेन सह तद्वर्षपुरुषैरुपास्ते इदं चोदाहरति ॥७॥

hari-varṣe cāpi bhagavān nara-hari-rūpeṇāste. tad-rūpa-grahaṇa-nimittam uttaratrābhidhāsye. tad dayitaṁ rūpaṁ mahā-puruṣa-guṇa-bhājano mahā-bhāgavato daitya-dānava-kula-tīrthīkaraṇa-śīlā-caritaḥ prahlādo 'vyavadhānānanya-bhakti-yogena saha tad-varṣa-puruṣair upāste idaṁ codāharati.

hari-varṣe—in the tract of land known as Harivarṣa; *ca*—also; *api*—indeed; *bhagavān*—the Supreme Personality of Godhead; *nara-hari-rūpeṇa*—His form of Nṛsiṁhadeva; *āste*—is situated; *tat-rūpa-grahaṇa-nimittam*—the reason why Lord Kṛṣṇa (Keśava) assumed the form of Nṛsiṁha; *uttaratra*—in later chapters; *abhidhāsye*—I shall describe; *tat*—that; *dayitam*—most pleasing; *rūpam*—form of the Lord; *mahā-puruṣa-guṇa-bhājanaḥ*—Prahlāda Mahārāja, who is the abode of all the good qualities of great personalities; *mahā-bhāgavataḥ*—the topmost devotee; *daitya-dānava-kula-tīrthī-karaṇa-śīlā-caritaḥ*—whose activities and character were so exalted that he delivered all the *daityas* (demons) born in his family; *prahlādaḥ*—Mahārāja Prahlāda; *avyavadhāna-ananya-bhakti-yogena*—by uninterrupted and unflinching devotional service; *saha*—with; *tat-varṣa-puruṣaiḥ*—the inhabitants of Hari-varṣa; *upāste*—offers obeisances to and worships; *idam*—this; *ca*—and; *udāharati*—chants.

TRANSLATION

Śukadeva Gosvāmī continued: My dear King, Lord Nṛsiṁhadeva resides in the tract of land known as Hari-varṣa. In the Seventh

Canto of Śrīmad-Bhāgavatam, I shall describe to you how Prahlāda Mahārāja caused the Lord to assume the form of Nṛsiṁhadeva. Prahlāda Mahārāja, the topmost devotee of the Lord, is a reservoir of all the good qualities of great personalities. His character and activities have delivered all the fallen members of his demoniac family. Lord Nṛsiṁhadeva is very dear to this exalted personality. Thus Prahlāda Mahārāja, along with his servants and all the denizens of Hari-varṣa, worships Lord Nṛsiṁhadeva by chanting the following mantra.

PURPORT

Jayadeva Gosvāmī's ten prayers worshiping the incarnations of Lord Kṛṣṇa (Keśava) contain His name in every stanza. For example, *keśava dhṛta-nara-hari-rūpa jaya jagad-īśa hare, keśava dhṛta-mīna-śarīra jaya jagad-īśa hare,* and *keśava dhṛta-vāmana-rūpa jaya jagad-īśa hare.* The word *jagad-īśa* refers to the proprietor of all the universes. His original form is the two-handed form of Lord Kṛṣṇa, standing with a flute in His hands and engaged in tending the cows. As stated in *Brahma-saṁhitā:*

cintāmaṇi-prakara-sadmasu kalpa-vṛkṣa-
lakṣāvṛteṣu surabhīr abhipālayantam
lakṣmī-sahasra-śata-sambhrama-sevyamānaṁ
govindam ādi-puruṣaṁ tam ahaṁ bhajāmi

"I worship Govinda, the primeval Lord, the first progenitor, who is tending the cows, yielding all desires, in abodes built with spiritual gems and surrounded by millions of purpose trees. He is always served with great reverence and affection by hundreds and thousands of goddesses of fortune." From this verse we learn that Govinda, or Kṛṣṇa, is the *ādi-puruṣa* (the original person). The Lord has innumerable incarnations, exactly like the innumerable waves of a flowing river, but the original form is Kṛṣṇa, or Keśava.

Śukadeva Gosvāmī refers to Nṛsiṁhadeva because of Prahlāda Mahārāja. Prahlāda Mahārāja was put into great distress by his powerful father, the demon Hiraṇyakaśipu. Apparently helpless before him, Prahlāda Mahārāja called on the Lord, who immediately assumed the gigantic form of Nṛsiṁhadeva, half-lion and half-man, to kill the gigantic demon. Although Kṛṣṇa is the original person, one without a second, He assumes different forms just to satisfy His devotees or to execute a specific purpose. Therefore Jayadeva Gosvāmī always repeats the name of Keśava, the original Personality of Godhead, in his prayers describing the Lord's different incarnations for different purposes.

TEXT 8

ॐ नमो भगवते नरसिंहाय नमस्तेजस्तेजसे आविराविर्भव वज्रनख वज्रदंष्ट्र कर्माशयान् रन्धय रन्धय तमो ग्रस ग्रस ॐ स्वाहा । अभयमभयमात्मनि भूयिष्ठा ॐ क्ष्रौम् ॥ ८ ॥

oṁ namo bhagavate narasiṁhāya namas tejas-tejase āvir-āvirbhava vajra-nakha vajra-daṁṣṭra karmāśayān randhaya randhaya tamo grasa grasa oṁ svāhā. abhayam abhayam ātmani bhūyiṣṭhā oṁ kṣraum.

om—O Lord; *namaḥ*—my respectful obeisances; *bhagavate*—unto the Supreme Personality of Godhead; *nara-siṁhāya*—known as Lord Nṛsiṁha; *namaḥ*—obeisances; *tejaḥ-tejase*—the power of all power; *āviḥ-āvirbhava*—please be fully manifest; *vajra-nakha*—O You who possess nails like thunderbolts; *vajra-daṁṣṭra*—O You who possess teeth like thunderbolts; *karma-āśayān*—demoniac desires to be happy by material activities; *randhaya randhaya*—kindly vanquish; *tamaḥ*—ignorance in the material world; *grasa*—kindly drive away; *grasa*—kindly drive away; *om*—O my Lord; *svāhā*—respectful oblations; *abhayam*—fearlessness; *abhayam*—fearlessness; *ātmani*—in my mind; *bhūyiṣṭhāḥ*—may You appear; *om*—O Lord; *kṣraum*—the *bīja*, or seed, of *mantras* offering prayers to Lord Nṛsiṁha.

TRANSLATION

I offer my respectful obeisances unto Lord Nṛsiṁhadeva, the source of all power. O my Lord who possesses nails and teeth just like thunderbolts, kindly vanquish our demonlike desires for fruitive activity in this material world. Please appear in our hearts and drive away our ignorance so that by Your mercy we may

become fearless in the struggle for existence in this material world.

PURPORT

In *Śrīmad-Bhāgavatam* (4.22.39) Sanat-kumāra speaks the following words to Mahārāja Pṛthu:

yat-pāda-paṅkaja-palāśa-vilāsa-bhaktyā
karmāśayaṁ grathitam udgrathayanti santaḥ
tadvan na rikta-matayo yatayo 'pi ruddha-
srotogaṇās tam araṇaṁ bhaja vāsudevam

"Devotees always engaged in the service of the toes of the Lord's lotus feet can very easily become free from hard-knotted desires for fruitive activities. Because this is very difficult, the nondevotees—the *jñānīs* and *yogīs*—cannot stop the waves of sense gratification, although they try to do so. Therefore you are advised to engage in the devotional service of Kṛṣṇa, the son of Vasudeva."

Every living being within this material world has a strong desire to enjoy matter to his fullest satisfaction. For this purpose, the conditioned soul must accept one body after another, and thus his strongly fixed fruitive desires continue. One cannot stop the repetition of birth and death without being completely desireless. Therefore Śrīla Rūpa Gosvāmī describes pure *bhakti* (devotional service) as follows:

anyābhilāṣitā-śūnyaṁ
jñāna-karmādy-anāvṛtam
ānukulyena kṛṣṇānu-
śīlanaṁ bhaktir uttamā

"One should render transcendental loving service to the Supreme Lord Kṛṣṇa favorably and without desire for material profit or gain through fruitive activities or philosophical speculation. That is called pure devotional service." Unless one is completely freed of all material desires, which are caused by the dense darkness of ignorance, one cannot fully engage in the devotional service of the Lord. Therefore we should always offer our prayers to Lord Nṛsiṁhadeva, who killed Hiraṇyakaśipu, the personification of material desire. *Hiraṇya* means "gold," and *kaśipu* means "a soft cushion or bed." Materialistic persons always desire to make the body comfortable, and for this they require huge amounts of gold. Thus Hiraṇyakaśipu was the perfect representative of materialistic life. He was therefore the cause of great disturbance to the topmost devotee, Prahlāda Mahārāja, until Lord Nṛsiṁhadeva killed him. Any devotee aspiring to be free of material desires should offer his respectful prayers to Nṛsiṁhadeva as Prahlāda Mahārāja did in this verse.

TEXT 9

स्वस्त्यस्तु विश्वस्य खलः प्रसीदतां
ध्यायन्तु भूतानि शिवं मिथो धिया।
मनश्च भद्रं भजतादधोक्षजे
आवेश्यतां नो मतिरप्यहैतुकी ॥ ९ ॥

svasty astu viśvasya khalaḥ prasīdatāṁ
dhyāyantu bhūtāni śivaṁ mitho dhiyā
manaś ca bhadraṁ bhajatād adhokṣaje
āveśyatāṁ no matir apy ahaitukī

svasti—auspiciousness; *astu*—let there be; *viśvasya*—of the entire universe; *khalaḥ*—the envious (almost everyone); *prasīdatām*—let them be pacified; *dhyāyantu*—let them consider; *bhūtāni*—all the living entities; *śivam*—auspiciousness; *mithaḥ*—mutual; *dhiyā*—by their intelligence; *manaḥ*—the mind; *ca*—and; *bhadram*—calmness; *bhajatāt*—let it experience; *adhokṣaje*—in the Supreme Personality of Godhead, who is beyond the perception of mind, intelligence and senses; *āveśyatām*—let it be absorbed; *naḥ*—our; *matiḥ*—intelligence; *api*—indeed; *ahaitukī*—without any motive.

TRANSLATION

May there be good fortune throughout the universe, and may all envious persons be pacified. May all living entities become calm by practicing bhakti-yoga, for by accepting devotional service they will think of each other's welfare. Therefore let us all engage in

the service of the supreme transcendence, Lord Śrī Kṛṣṇa, and always remain absorbed in thought of Him.

PURPORT

The following verse describes a Vaiṣṇava:

vāñchā-kalpa-tarubhyaś ca
kṛpā-sindhubhya eva ca
patitānāṁ pāvanebhyo
vaiṣṇavebhyo namo namaḥ

Just like a desire tree, a Vaiṣṇava can fulfill all the desires of anyone who takes shelter of his lotus feet. Prahlāda Mahārāja is a typical Vaiṣṇava. He prays not for himself, but for all living entities—the gentle, the envious and the mischievous. He always thought of the welfare of mischievous persons like his father, Hiraṇyakaśipu. Prahlāda Mahārāja did not ask for anything for himself; rather, he prayed for the Lord to excuse his demoniac father. This is the attitude of a Vaiṣṇava, who always thinks of the welfare of the entire universe.

Śrīmad-Bhāgavatam and *bhāgavata-dharma* are meant for persons who are completely free of envy (*parama-nirmatsarāṇām*). Therefore Prahlāda Mahārāja prays in this verse, *khalaḥ prasīdatām*: "May all the envious persons be pacified." The material world is full of envious persons, but if one frees himself of envy, he becomes liberal in his social dealings and can think of others' welfare. Anyone who takes up Kṛṣṇa consciousness and engages himself completely in the service of the Lord cleanses his mind of all envy (*manaś ca bhadraṁ bhajatād adhokṣaje*). Therefore we should pray to Lord Nṛsiṁhadeva to sit in our hearts. We should pray, *bahir nṛsiṁho hṛdaye nṛsiṁhaḥ:* "Let Lord Nṛsiṁhadeva sit in the core of my heart, killing all my bad propensities. Let my mind become clean so that I may peacefully worship the Lord and bring peace to the entire world."

Śrīla Viśvanātha Cakravartī Ṭhākura has given us a very fine purport in this regard. Whenever one offers a prayer to the Supreme Personality of Godhead, one always requests some benediction from Him. Even pure (*niṣkāma*) devotees pray for some benediction, as instructed by Lord Śrī Caitanya Mahāprabhu in His *Śikṣāṣṭaka:*

ayi nanda-tanuja kiṅkaraṁ
patitaṁ māṁ viṣame bhavāmbudhau
kṛpayā tava pāda-paṅkaja-
sthiti-dhūlī-sadṛśaṁ vicintaya

"O son of Mahārāja Nanda [Kṛṣṇa], I am Your eternal servitor, yet somehow or other I have fallen into the ocean of birth and death. Please pick Me up from the ocean of death and place Me as one of the atoms at Your lotus feet." In another prayer Lord Caitanya says, *mama janmani janmanīśvare bhavatād bhaktir ahaitukī tvayi:* "Life after life, kindly let Me have unalloyed love and devotion at Your Lordship's lotus feet." When Prahlāda Mahārāja chants *oṁ namo bhagavate narasiṁhāya,* he prays for a benediction from the Lord, but because he is also an exalted Vaiṣṇava, he wants nothing for his personal sense gratification. The first desire expressed in his prayer is *svasty astu viśvasya:* "Let there be good fortune throughout the entire universe." Prahlāda Mahārāja thus requested the Lord to be merciful to everyone, including his father, a most envious person. According to Cāṇakya Paṇḍita, there are two kinds of envious living entities: one is a snake, and the other is the man like Hiraṇyakaśipu, who is by nature envious of everyone, even of his father or son. Hiraṇyakaśipu was envious of his little son Prahlāda, but Prahlāda Mahārāja asked a benediction for the benefit of his father. Hiraṇyakaśipu was very envious of devotees, but Prahlāda wished that his father and other demons like him would give up their envious nature by the grace of the Lord and stop harassing the devotees (*khalaḥ prasīdatām*). The difficulty is that the *khala* (envious living entity) is rarely pacified. One kind of *khala,* the snake, can be pacified simply by *mantras* or by the action of a particular herb (*mantrauṣadhi-vaśaḥ sarpaḥ khalakena nivāryate*). An envious person, however, cannot be pacified by any means. Therefore Prahlāda Mahārāja prays that all envious persons may undergo a change of heart and think of the welfare of others.

If the Kṛṣṇa consciousness movement spreads all over the world, and if by the grace of Kṛṣṇa everyone accepts it, the thinking of envious people will change. Everyone will think of the welfare of others. Therefore Prahlāda Mahārāja prays, *śivaṁ mitho dhiyā.* In material activities, everyone is envious of others, but in Kṛṣṇa consciousness, no one is envious of anyone else; everyone thinks of the welfare of others. Therefore Prahlāda Mahārāja prays that everyone's mind may become gentle by being fixed at the lotus feet of Kṛṣṇa (*bhajatād adhokṣaje*). As indicated elsewhere in *Śrīmad-Bhāgavatam* (*sa vai manaḥ kṛṣṇa-padāravindayoḥ*) and as advised by Lord Kṛṣṇa in *Bhagavad-gītā* (18.65), *man-manā bhava mad-bhaktaḥ,* one should constantly think of the lotus feet of Lord Kṛṣṇa. Then one's mind will certainly be cleansed (*ceto-darpaṇa-mārjanam*). Materialists always think of sense gratification, but Prahlāda Mahārāja prays that the Lord's mercy will change their minds and they will stop thinking of sense gratification. If they think of Kṛṣṇa always, everything will be all right. Some people argue that if everyone thought of Kṛṣṇa in that way, the whole universe would be vacated because everyone would go back home, back to Godhead. However, Śrīla Viśvanātha Cakravatī Ṭhākura says that this is impossible because the living entities are innumerable. If one set of living entities is actually delivered by the Kṛṣṇa consciousness movement, another set will fill the entire universe.

TEXT 10

मागारदारात्मजवित्तबन्धुषु
सङ्गो यदि स्याद्भगवत्प्रियेषु नः ।
यः प्राणवृत्त्या परितुष्ट आत्मवान्
सिद्ध्यत्यदूरान्न तथेन्द्रियप्रियः ॥१०॥

māgāra-dārātmaja-vitta-bandhuṣu
saṅgo yadi syād bhagavat-priyeṣu naḥ
yaḥ prāṇa-vṛttyā parituṣṭa ātmavān
siddhyaty adūrān na tathendriya-priyaḥ

mā—not; *agāra*—house; *dāra*—wife; *ātma-ja*—children; *vitta*—bank balance; *bandhuṣu*—among friends and relatives; *saṅgaḥ*—association or attachment; *yadi*—if; *syāt*—there must be; *bhagavat-priyeṣu*—among persons to whom the Supreme Personality of Godhead is very dear; *naḥ*—of us; *yaḥ*—anyone who; *prāṇa-vṛttyā*—by the bare necessities of life; *parituṣṭaḥ*—satisfied; *ātma-vān*—who has controlled his mind and realized his self; *siddhyati*—becomes successful; *adūrāt*—

very soon; *na*—not; *tathā*—so much; *indriya-priyaḥ*—a person attached to sense gratification.

TRANSLATION

My dear Lord, we pray that we may never feel attraction for the prison of family life, consisting of home, wife, children, friends, bank balance, relatives and so on. If we do have some attachment, let it be for devotees, whose only dear friend is Kṛṣṇa. A person who is actually self-realized and who has controlled his mind is perfectly satisfied with the bare necessities of life. He does not try to gratify his senses. Such a person quickly advances in Kṛṣṇa consciousness, whereas others, who are too attached to material things, find advancement very difficult.

PURPORT

When Śrī Kṛṣṇa Caitanya Mahāprabhu was requested to explain the duty of a Vaiṣṇava, a Kṛṣṇa conscious person, He immediately said, *asat-saṅga-tyāga,*——*ei vaiṣṇava-ācāra.* The first business of a Vaiṣṇava is to give up the association of persons who are not devotees of Kṛṣṇa and who are too attached to material things—wife, children, bank balance and so on. Prahlāda Mahārāja also prays to the Personality of Godhead that he may avoid the association of nondevotees attached to the materialistic way of life. If he must be attached to someone, he prays to be attached only to a devotee.

A devotee is not interested in unnecessarily increasing the demands of the senses for gratification. Of course, as long as one is in this material world, one must have a material body, and it must be maintained for executing devotional service. The body can be maintained very easily by eating *kṛṣṇa-prasāda.* As Kṛṣṇa says in *Bhagavad-gītā* (9.26):

patraṁ puṣpaṁ phalaṁ toyaṁ
yo me bhaktyā prayacchati
tad ahaṁ bhakty-upahṛtam
aśnāmi prayatātmanaḥ

"If one offers Me with love and devotion a leaf, a flower, fruit or water, I will accept it." Why should the menu be unnecessarily increased for the satisfaction of the tongue? Devotees should eat as simply as possible. Otherwise, attachment for material things will gradually increase, and the senses, being very strong, will soon require more and more material enjoyment. Then the real business of life—to advance in Kṛṣṇa consciousness—will stop.

TEXT 11

यत्सङ्गलब्धं निजवीर्यवैभवं
तीर्थं मुहुः संस्पृशतां हि मानसम् ।
हरत्यजोऽन्तः श्रुतिभिर्गतोऽङ्गजं
को वै न सेवेत मुकुन्दविक्रमम् ॥११॥

yat-saṅga-labdhaṁ nija-vīrya-vaibhavaṁ
tīrthaṁ muhuḥ saṁspṛśatāṁ hi mānasam
haraty ajo 'ntaḥ śrutibhir gato 'ṅgajaṁ
ko vai na seveta mukunda-vikramam

yat—of whom (the devotees); *saṅga-labdham*—achieved by the association; *nija-vīrya-vaibhavam*—whose influence is uncommon; *tīrtham*—holy places like the Ganges; *muhuḥ*—repeatedly; *saṁspṛśatām*—of those touching; *hi*—certainly; *mānasam*—the dirty things in the mind; *harati*—vanquishes; *ajaḥ*—the supreme unborn one; *antaḥ*—in the core of the heart; *śrutibhiḥ*—by the ears; *gataḥ*—entered; *aṅga-jam*—dirty things or infections of the body; *kaḥ*—who; *vai*—indeed; *na*—not; *seveta*—would serve; *mukunda-vikramam*—the glorious activities of Mukunda, the Supreme Personality of Godhead.

TRANSLATION

By associating with persons for whom the Supreme Personality of Godhead, Mukunda, is the all in all, one can hear of His powerful activities and soon come to understand them. The activities of Mukunda are so potent that simply by hearing of them one immediately associates with the Lord. For a person who constantly and very eagerly hears narrations of the Lord's powerful activities, the Absolute Truth, the Personality of Godhead in the

form of sound vibrations, enters within his heart and cleanses it of all contamination. On the other hand, although bathing in the Ganges diminishes bodily contaminations and infections, this process and the process of visiting holy places can cleanse the heart only after a long time. Therefore who is the sane man who will not associate with devotees to quickly perfect his life?

PURPORT

Bathing in the Ganges can certainly cure one of many infectious diseases, but it cannot cleanse one's materially attached mind, which creates all kinds of contaminations in material existence. However, one who directly associates with the Supreme Lord by hearing of His activities cleanses the dirt from his mind and very soon comes to Kṛṣṇa consciousness. Sūta Gosvāmī confirms this in *Śrīmad-Bhāgavatam* (1.2.17):

śṛṇvatāṁ sva-kathāḥ kṛṣṇaḥ
puṇya-śravaṇa-kīrtanaḥ
hṛdy antaḥ-stho hy abhadrāṇi
vidhunoti suhṛt-satām

The Supreme Lord within everyone's heart becomes very pleased when a person hears narrations of His activities, and He personally cleanses the dirt from the mind of the listener. *Hṛdy antaḥ-stho hy abhadrāni vidhunoti:* He washes off all dirt from the mind. Material existence is caused by dirty things within the mind. If one can cleanse his mind, he immediately comes to his original position of Kṛṣṇa consciousness, and thus his life becomes successful. Therefore all the great saints in the devotional line very strongly recommend the process of hearing. Śrī Caitanya Mahāprabhu introduced the congregational chanting of the Hare Kṛṣṇa *mantra* to give everyone a chance to hear Kṛṣṇa's holy name, for simply by hearing Hare Kṛṣṇa, Hare Kṛṣṇa, Kṛṣṇa Kṛṣṇa, Hare Hare/ Hare Rāma, Hare Rāma, Rāma Rāma, Hare Hare, one becomes purified (*ceto-darpaṇa-mārjanam*). Therefore our Kṛṣṇa consciousness movement is chiefly engaged in chanting the Hare Kṛṣṇa *mantra* all over the world.

After one's mind becomes cleansed by chanting Hare Kṛṣṇa, one gradually comes to the platform of Kṛṣṇa consciousness and then reads books like *Bhagavad-gītā*, *Śrīmad-Bhāgavatam*, *Caitanya-caritāmṛta* and *The Nectar of Devotion*. In this way, one becomes more and more purified of material contamination. As stated in *Śrīmad-Bhāgavatam* (1.2.18):

naṣṭa-prāyeṣv abhadreṣu
nityaṁ bhāgavata-sevayā
bhagavaty uttama-śloke
bhaktir bhavati naiṣṭhikī

"By regularly hearing the *Bhāgavatam* and rendering service unto the pure devotee, all that is troublesome to the heart is practically destroyed, and loving service unto the glorious Lord, who is praised with transcendental songs, is established as an irrevocable fact." In this way, simply by hearing of the powerful activities of the Lord, the devotee's heart becomes almost completely cleansed of material contamination, and thus his original position as an eternal servant who is part and parcel of the Lord becomes manifest. While the devotee engages in devotional service, the passionate and ignorant modes of material nature are gradually vanquished, and then he acts only in the mode of goodness. At that time he becomes happy and gradually advances in Kṛṣṇa consciousness.

All the great *ācāryas* strongly recommend that people be given a chance to hear about the Supreme Lord. Then success is assured. The more we cleanse the dirt of material attachment from our hearts, the more we will be attracted by Kṛṣṇa's name, form, qualities, paraphernalia and activities. This is the sum and substance of the Kṛṣṇa consciousness movement.

TEXT 12

यस्यास्ति भक्तिर्भगवत्यकिञ्चना
सर्वैर्गुणैस्तत्र समासते सुराः ।
हरावभक्तस्य कुतो महद्गुणा
मनोरथेनासति धावतो बहिः ॥१२॥

yasyāsti bhaktir bhagavaty akiñcanā
sarvair guṇais tatra samāsate surāḥ

harāv abhaktasya kuto mahad-guṇā
manorathenāsati dhāvato bahiḥ

yasya—of whom; *asti*—there is; *bhaktiḥ*—devotional service; *bhagavati*—to the Supreme Personality of Godhead; *akiñcanā*—without any motive; *sarvaiḥ*—with all; *guṇaiḥ*—good qualities; *tatra*—there (in that person); *samāsate*—reside; *surāḥ*—all the demigods; *harau*—unto the Supreme Personality of Godhead; *abhaktasya*—of a person who is not devoted; *kutaḥ*—where; *mahat-guṇāḥ*—good qualities; *manorathena*—by mental speculation; *asati*—in the temporary material world; *dhāvataḥ*—who is running; *bahiḥ*—outside.

TRANSLATION

All the demigods and their exalted qualities, such as religion, knowledge and renunciation, become manifest in the body of one who has developed unalloyed devotion for the Supreme Personality of Godhead, Vāsudeva. On the other hand, a person devoid of devotional service and engaged in material activities has no good qualities. Even if he is adept at the practice of mystic yoga or the honest endeavor of maintaining his family and relatives, he must be driven by his own mental speculations and must engage in the service of the Lord's external energy. How can there be any good qualities in such a man?

PURPORT

As explained in the next verse, Kṛṣṇa is the original source of all living entities. This is confirmed in *Bhagavad-gītā* (15.7), wherein Kṛṣṇa says:

mamaivāṁśo jīva-loke
jīva-bhūtaḥ sanātanaḥ
manaḥ ṣaṣṭhānīndriyāṇi
prakṛti-sthāni karṣati

"The living entities in this conditioned world are My eternal, fragmental parts. Due to conditioned life, they are struggling very hard with the six senses, which include the mind." All living entities are part and parcel of Kṛṣṇa, and therefore when they revive their original Kṛṣṇa consciousness, they possess all the good qualities of Kṛṣṇa in a small quantity. When one engages himself in the nine processes of devotional service (*śravaṇaṁ kīrtanaṁ viṣṇoḥ smaraṇaṁ pāda-sevanam/ arcanaṁ vandanaṁ dāsyaṁ sakhyam ātma-nivedanam*), one's heart becomes purified, and he immediately understands his relationship with Kṛṣṇa. He then revives his original quality of Kṛṣṇa consciousness.

In the *Ādi-līlā* of *Caitanya-caritāmṛta*, Chapter Eight, there is a description of some of the qualities of devotees. For example, Śrī Paṇḍita Haridāsa is described as being very well-behaved, tolerant, peaceful, magnanimous and grave. In addition, he spoke very sweetly, his endeavors were very pleasing, he was always patient, he respected everyone, he always worked for everyone's benefit, his mind was free of duplicity, and he was completely devoid of all malicious acitivites. These are all originally qualities of Kṛṣṇa, and when one becomes a devotee they automatically become manifest. Śrī Kṛṣṇadāsa Kavirāja, the author of *Caitanya-caritāmṛta*, says that all good qualities become manifest in the body of a Vaiṣṇava and that only by the presence of these good qualities can one distinguish a Vaiṣṇava from a non-Vaiṣṇava. Kṛṣṇadāsa Kavirāja lists the following twenty-six good qualities of a Vaiṣṇava: (1) He is very kind to everyone. (2) He does not make anyone his enemy. (3) He is truthful. (4) He is equal to everyone. (5) No one can find any fault in him. (6) He is magnanimous. (7) He is mild. (8) He is always clean. (9) He is without possessions. (10) He works for everyone's benefit. (11) He is very peaceful. (12) He is always surrendered to Kṛṣṇa. (13) He has no material desires. (14) He is very meek. (15) He is steady. (16) He controls his senses. (17) He does not eat more than required. (18) He is not influenced by the Lord's illusory energy. (19) He offers respect to everyone. (20) He does not desire any respect for himself. (21) He is very grave. (22) He is merciful. (23) He is friendly. (24) He is poetic. (25) He is expert. (26) He is silent.

TEXT 13

हरिर्हि साक्षाद्भगवान् शरीरिणा-
मात्मा झषाणामिव तोयमीप्सितम् ।

हित्वा महांस्तं यदि सज्जते गृहे
तदा महत्त्वं वयसा दम्पतीनाम् ॥१३॥

harir hi sākṣād bhagavān śarīriṇām
ātmā jhaṣāṇām iva toyam īpsitam
hitvā mahāṁs taṁ yadi sajjate gṛhe
tadā mahattvaṁ vayasā dampatīnām

hariḥ—the Lord; *hi*—certainly; *sākṣāt*—directly; *bhagavān*—the Supreme Personality of Godhead; *śarīriṇām*—of all living entities who have accepted material bodies; *ātmā*—the life and soul; *jhaṣāṇām*—of the aquatics; *iva*—like; *toyam*—the vast water; *īpsitam*—is desired; *hitvā*—giving up; *mahān*—a great personality; *tam*—Him; *yadi*—if; *sajjate*—becomes attached; *gṛhe*—to household life; *tadā*—at that time; *mahattvam*—greatness; *vayasā*—by age; *dam-patīnām*—of the husband and wife.

TRANSLATION

Just as aquatics always desire to remain in the vast mass of water, all conditioned living entities naturally desire to remain in the vast existence of the Supreme Lord. Therefore if someone very great by material calculations fails to take shelter of the Supreme Soul but instead becomes attached to material household life, his greatness is like that of a young, low-class couple. One who is too attached to material life loses all good spiritual qualities.

PURPORT

Although crocodiles are very fierce animals, they are powerless when they venture out of the water onto land. When they are out of the water, they cannot exhibit their original power. Similarly, the all-pervading Supersoul, Paramātmā, is the source of all living entities, and all living entities are part and parcel of Him. When the living entity remains in contact with the all-pervading Vāsudeva, the Personality of Godhead, he manifests his spiritual power, exactly as the crocodile exhibits its strength in the water. In other words, the greatness of the living entity can be perceived when he is in the spiritual world, engaged in spiritual activities. Many householders, although well-educated in the knowledge of the *Vedas*, become attached to family life. They are compared herein to crocodiles out of water, for they are devoid of all spiritual strength. Their greatness is like that of a young husband and wife who, though uneducated, praise one another and become attracted to their own temporary beauty. This kind of greatness is appreciated only by low-class men with no qualifications.

Everyone should therefore seek the shelter of the Supreme Soul, the source of all living entities. No one should waste his time in the so-called happiness of materialistic household life. In the Vedic civilization, this type of crippled life is allowed only until one's fiftieth year, when one must give up family life and enter either the order of *vānaprastha* (independent retired life for cultivation of spiritual knowledge) or *sannyāsa* (the renounced order, in which one completely takes shelter of the Supreme Personality of Godhead).

TEXT 14

तस्माद्रजोरागविषादमन्यु-
मानस्पृहाभयदैन्याधिमूलम् ।
हित्वा गृहं संसृतिचक्रवालं
नृसिंहपादं भजताकुतोभयमिति ॥१४॥

tasmād rajo-rāga-viṣāda-manyu-
māna-spṛhā-bhayadainyādhimūlam
hitvā gṛhaṁ saṁsṛti-cakravālaṁ
nṛsiṁha-pādaṁ bhajatākutobhayam iti

tasmāt—therefore; *rajaḥ*—of passion or material desires; *rāga*—attachment for material things; *viṣāda*—then disappointment; *manyu*—anger; *māna-spṛhā*—the desire to be respectable in society; *bhaya*—fear; *dainya*—of poverty; *adhimūlam*—the root cause; *hitvā*—giving up; *gṛham*—household life; *saṁsṛti-cakravālam*—the cycle of repeated birth and death; *nṛsiṁha-pādam*—the lotus feet of Lord Nṛsiṁhadeva; *bhajata*—worship; *akutaḥ-bhayam*—the shelter of fearlessness; *iti*—thus.

TRANSLATION

Therefore, O demons, give up the so-called happiness of family life and simply take shelter of the lotus feet of Lord Nṛsiṁhadeva, which are the actual shelter of fearlessness. Entanglement in family life is the root cause of material attachment, indefatigable desires, moroseness, anger, despair, fear and the desire for false prestige, all of which result in the repetition of birth and death.

TEXT 15

केतुमालेऽपि भगवान् कामदेवस्वरूपेण लक्ष्म्याः प्रियचिकीर्षया प्रजापतेर्दुहितॄणां पुत्राणां तद्वर्षपतीनां पुरुषायुषाहोरात्रपरिसंख्यानानां यासां गर्भा महापुरुषमहास्त्रतेजसोद्वेजितमनसां विध्वस्ता व्यसवः संवत्सरान्ते विनिपतन्ति ॥१५॥

ketumāle 'pi bhagavān kāmadeva-svarūpeṇa lakṣmyāḥ priya-cikīrṣayā prajāpater duhitṝṇāṁ putrāṇāṁ tad-varṣa-patīnāṁ puruṣāyuṣāho-rātra-parisaṅkhyānānāṁ yāsāṁ garbhā mahā-puruṣa-mahāstra-tejasodvejita-manasāṁ vidhvastā vyasavaḥ saṁvatsarānte vinipatanti.

ketumāle—in the tract of land known as Ketumāla-varṣa; *api*—also; *bhagavān*—the Supreme Personality of Godhead, Lord Viṣṇu; *kāmadeva-svarūpeṇa*—in the form of Kāmadeva (Cupid or Pradyumna); *lakṣmyāḥ*—of the goddess of fortune; *priya-cikīrṣayā*—with a desire to bring about the satisfaction; *prajāpateḥ*—of Prajāpati; *duhitṝṇām*—of the daughters; *putrāṇām*—of the sons; *tat-varṣa-patīnām*—the ruler of that land; *puruṣa-āyuṣā*—in a human lifetime (about one hundred years); *ahaḥ-rātra*—the days and nights; *parisaṅkhyānānām*—which equal in number; *yāsām*—of whom (the daughters); *garbhāḥ*—fetuses; *mahā-puruṣa*—of the Supreme Personality of Godhead; *mahā-astra*—of the great weapon (the disc); *tejasā*—by the effulgence; *udvejita-manasām*—whose minds are agitated; *vidhvastāḥ*—ruined; *vyasavaḥ*—dead; *saṁvatsara-ante*—at the end of the year; *vinipatanti*—fall down.

TRANSLATION

Śukadeva Gosvāmī continued: In the tract of land called Ketumāla-varṣa, Lord Viṣṇu lives in the form of Kāmadeva, only for the satisfaction of His devotees. These include Lakṣmījī [the goddess of fortune], the Prajāpati Saṁvatsara and all of Saṁvatsara's sons and daughters. The daughters of Prajāpati are considered the controlling deities of the nights, and his sons are considered the controllers of the days. The Prajāpati's offspring number 36,000, one for each day and each night in the lifetime of a human being. At the end of each year, the Prajāpati's daughters become very agitated upon seeing the extremely effulgent disc of the Supreme Personality of Godhead, and thus they all suffer miscarriages.

PURPORT

This Kāmadeva, who appears as Kṛṣṇa's son named Pradyumna, is *viṣṇu-tattva.* How this is so is explained by Madhvācārya, who quotes from the *Brahmāṇḍa Purāṇa: kāmadeva-sthitaṁ viṣṇum upāste.* Although this Kāmadeva is *viṣṇu-tattva,* His body is not spiritul but material. Lord Viṣṇu as Pradyumna or Kāmadeva accepts a material body, but He still acts spiritually. It does not make any difference whether He accepts a spiritual or a material body; He can act spiritually in any condition of existence. Māyāvādī philosophers regard even Lord Kṛṣṇa's body as material, but their opinions cannot impede the spiritual activity of the Lord.

TEXT 16

**अतीव सुललितगतिविलासविलसितरुचिरहासलेशावलोकलीलया
किञ्चिदुत्तम्भितसुन्दरभ्रूमण्डलसुभगवदनारविन्दश्रिया रमां
रमयन्निन्द्रियाणि रमयते ॥१६॥**

atīva sulalita-gati-vilāsa-vilasita-rucira-hāsa-leśāvaloka-līlayā kiñcid-uttambhita-sundara-bhrū-maṇḍala-subhaga-vadanāravinda-śriyā ramāṁ ramayann indriyāṇi ramayate.

atīva—very much; *su-lalita*—beautiful; *gati*—with movements; *vilāsa*—by pastimes; *vilasita*—manifested; *rucira*—pleasing; *hāsa-leśa*—mild smiling; *avaloka-līlayā*—by playful glancing; *kiñcit-ut-tambhita*—slightly raised; *sundara*—beautiful; *bhrū-maṇḍala*—by the eyebrows; *subhaga*—auspicious; *vadana-aravinda-śriyā*—with His beautiful lotuslike face; *ramām*—the goddess of fortune; *ramayan*—pleasing; *indriyāṇi*—all the senses; *ramayate*—He pleases.

TRANSLATION

In Ketumāla-varṣa, Lord Kāmadeva [Pradyumna] moves very graciously. His mild smile is very beautiful, and when He increases the beauty of His face by slightly raising His eyebrows and glancing playfully, He pleases the goddess of fortune. Thus He enjoys His transcendental senses.

TEXT 17

तद्भगवतो मायामयं रूपं परमसमाधियोगेन रमा देवी संवत्सरस्य रात्रिषु प्रजापतेर्दुहितृभिरुपेताहःसु च तद्भर्तृभिरुपास्ते इदं चोदाहरति ॥१७॥

tad bhagavato māyāmayaṁ rūpaṁ parama-samādhi-yogena ramā devī saṁvatsarasya rātriṣu prajāpater duhitṛbhir upetāhaḥsu ca tad-bhartṛbhir upāste idaṁ codāharati.

tat—that; *bhagavataḥ*—of the Supreme Personality of Godhead; *māyā-mayam*—full of affection for the devotees; *rūpam*—form; *parama*—highest; *samādhi-yogena*—by absorption of the mind in the service of the Lord; *ramā*—the goddess of fortune; *devī*—divine woman; *saṁvatsarasya*—known as Saṁvatsara; *rātriṣu*—during the nights; *prajāpateḥ*—of Prajāpati; *duhitṛbhiḥ*—with the daughters; *upeta*—combined; *ahaḥsu*—during the days; *ca*—also; *tat-bhartṛbhiḥ*—with the husbands; *upāste*—worships; *idam*—this; *ca*—also; *udāharati*—chants.

TRANSLATION

Accompanied during the daytime by the sons of the Prajāpati [the predominating deities of the days] and accompanied at night

by his daughters [the deities of the nights], Lakṣmīdevī worships the Lord during the period known as the Saṁvatsara in His most merciful form as Kāmadeva. Fully absorbed in devotional service, she chants the following mantras.

PURPORT

The word *māyāmayam* used in this verse should not be understood according to the interpretations of the Māyāvādīs. *Māyā* means affection as well as illusion. When a mother deals with her child affectionately, she is called *māyāmaya.* In whatever form the Supreme Lord Viṣṇu appears, He is always affectionate toward His devotees. Thus the word *māyāmayam* is used here to mean "very affectionate toward the devotees." Śrīla Jīva Gosvāmī writes in this regard that *māyāmayam* can also mean *kṛpā-pracuram,* deeply merciful. Similarly, Śrīla Vīrarāghava says, *māyā-pracuranātmīya-saṅkalpena parigṛhītam ity arthaḥ jñāna-paryāyo 'tra māyā-śabdaḥ:* when one is very affectionate due to an intimate relationship, one is described as *māyāmaya.* Śrīla Viśvanātha Cakravatī Ṭhākura explains *māyāmayam* by dividing it into the words *māyā* and *āmayam.* He explains these words to indicate that because the living entity is covered by the disease of illusion, the Lord is always eager to deliver His devotee from the clutches of *māyā* and cure him of the disease caused by the illusory energy.

TEXT 18

**ॐ ह्रां ह्रीं ह्रूँ ॐ नमो भगवते हृषीकेशाय सर्वगुणविशेषैर्विलक्षितात्मने
आकूतीनां चित्तीनां चेतसां विशेषाणां चाधिपतये
षोडशकलायच्छन्दोमयायान्नमयायामृतमयाय सर्वमयाय सहसे ओजसे
बलाय कान्ताय कामाय नमस्ते उभयत्र भूयात् ॥१८॥**

oṁ hrāṁ hrīṁ hrūṁ oṁ namo bhagavate hṛṣīkeśāya sarva-guṇa-viśeṣair vilakṣitātmane ākūtīnāṁ cittīnāṁ cetasāṁ viśeṣāṇāṁ cādhipataye ṣoḍaśa-kalāya cchando-mayāyānna-mayāyāmṛta-mayāya sarva-mayāya sahase ojase balāya kāntāya kāmāya namas te ubhayatra bhūyāt.

om—O Lord; *hrām hrīm hrūm*—the seeds of the *mantra*, chanted for a successful result; *om*—O Lord; *namaḥ*—respectful obeisances; *bhagavate*—unto the lotus feet of the Supreme Personality of Godhead; *hṛṣīkeśāya*—unto Hṛṣīkeśa, the Lord of the senses; *sarva-guṇa*—with all transcendental qualities; *viśeṣaiḥ*—with all varieties; *vilakṣita*—particularly observed; *ātmane*—unto the soul of all living entities; *ākūtīnām*—of all kinds of activity; *cittīnām*—of all kinds of knowledge; *cetasām*—of the functions of the mind, such as determination and mental effort; *viśeṣāṇām*—of their respective objects; *ca*—and; *adhipataye*—unto the master; *ṣoḍaśa-kalāya*—whose parts are the sixteen original ingredients of creation (namely the five objects of the senses and the eleven senses, including the mind); *chandaḥ-mayāya*—unto the enjoyer of all ritualistic ceremonies; *anna-mayāya*—who maintains all living entities by supplying the necessities of life; *amṛta-mayāya*—who awards eternal life; *sarva-mayāya*—who is all-pervading; *sahase*—the powerful; *ojase*—who supplies strength to the senses; *balāya*—who supplies strength to the body; *kāntāya*—the supreme husband or master of all living entities; *kāmāya*—who supplies all necessities for the devotees; *namaḥ*—respectful obeisances; *te*—unto You; *ubhayatra*—always (during both day and night, or both in this life and the next); *bhūyāt*—may there be all good fortune.

TRANSLATION

Let me offer my respectful obeisances unto the Supreme Personality of Godhead, Lord Hṛṣīkeśa, the controller of all my senses and the origin of everything. As the supreme master of all bodily, mental and intellectual activities, He is the only enjoyer of their results. The five sense objects and eleven senses, including the mind, are His partial manifestations. He supplies all the necessities of life, which are His energy and thus nondifferent from Him, and He is the cause of everyone's bodily and mental prowess, which is also nondifferent from Him. Indeed, He is the husband and provider of necessities for all living entities. The purpose of all the Vedas is to worship Him. Therefore let us all offer Him our respectful obeisances. May He always be favorable toward us in this life and the next.

PURPORT

In this verse the word *māyāmaya* is further explained in regard to how the Lord expands His mercy in different ways. *Parāsya śaktir vividhaiva śrūyate:* the energies of the Supreme Lord are understood in different ways. In this verse He is described as the original source of everything, even our body, senses, mind, activities, prowess, bodily strength, mental strength and determination for securing the necessities of life. Indeed, the Lord's energies can be perceived in everything. As stated in *Bhagavad-gītā* (7.8), *raso 'ham apsu kaunteya:* the taste of water is also Kṛṣṇa. Kṛṣṇa is the active principle of everything we need for our maintenance.

This verse offering respectful obeisances unto the Lord was composed by Ramā, the goddess of fortune, and is full of spiritual power. Under the guidance of a spiritual master, everyone should chant this *mantra* and thus become a complete and perfect devotee of the Lord. One may chant this *mantra* for complete liberation from material bondage, and after liberation one may continue to chant it while worshiping the Supreme Lord in Vaikuṇṭhaloka. All *mantras,* of course, are meant for this life and the next life, as Kṛṣṇa Himself confirms in *Bhagavad-gītā* (9.14):

satataṁ kīrtayanto māṁ
yatantaś ca dṛḍha-vratāḥ
namasyantaś ca māṁ bhaktyā
nitya-yuktā upāsate

"Always chanting My glories, endeavoring with great determination, bowing down before Me, the great souls perpetually worship Me with devotion." A devotee who both in this life and the next chants the *mahā-mantra,* or any *mantra,* is called *nitya-yuktopāsaka.*

TEXT 19

स्त्रियो व्रतैस्त्वा हृषिकेश्वरं स्वतो
ह्याराध्य लोके पतिमाशासतेऽन्यम् ।

तासां न ते वै परिपान्त्यपत्यं
प्रियं धनायूंषि यतोऽस्वतन्त्राः ॥१९॥

striyo vratais tvā hṛṣīkeśvaraṁ svato
hy ārādhya loke patim āśāsate 'nyam
tāsāṁ na te vai paripānty apatyaṁ
priyaṁ dhanāyūṁṣi yato 'sva-tantrāḥ

striyaḥ—all women; *vrataiḥ*—by observing fasting and other vows; *tvā*—you; *hṛṣīkeśvaram*—the Supreme Personality of Godhead, master of the senses; *svataḥ*—of your own accord; *hi*—certainly; *ārādhya*—worshiping; *loke*—in the world; *patim*—a husband; *āśāsate*—ask for; *anyam*—another; *tāsām*—of all those women; *na*—not; *te*—the husbands; *vai*—indeed; *paripānti*—able to protect; *apatyam*—the children; *priyam*—very dear; *dhana*—the wealth; *āyūṁṣi*—or the duration of life; *yataḥ*—because; *asva-tantrāḥ*—dependent.

TRANSLATION

My dear Lord, You are certainly the fully independent master of all the senses. Therefore all women who worship You by strictly observing vows because they wish to acquire a husband to satisfy their senses are surely under illusion. They do not know that such a husband cannot actually give protection to them or their children. Nor can he protect their wealth or duration of life, for he himself is dependent on time, fruitive results and the modes of nature, which are all subordinate to You.

PURPORT

In this verse, Lakṣmīdevī (Ramā) shows compassion toward women who worship the Lord for the benediction of possessing a good husband. Although such women desire to be happy with children, wealth, a long duration of life and everything dear to them, they cannot possibly do so. In the material world, a so-called husband is dependent on the control of the Supreme Personality of Godhead. There are many examples of a woman whose husband, being dependent on the result of his own fruitive actions, cannot maintain his wife, her children, her wealth or her duration of life. Therefore, factually the only real husband of all women is Kṛṣṇa, the supreme husband. Because the *gopīs* were liberated souls, they understood this fact. Therefore they rejected their material husbands and accepted Kṛṣṇa as their real husband. Kṛṣṇa is the real husband not only of the *gopīs,* but of every living entity. Everyone should perfectly understand that Kṛṣṇa is the real husband of all living entities, who are described in the *Bhagavad-gītā* as *prakṛti* (female), not *puruṣa* (male). In *Bhagavad-gītā* (10.12), only Kṛṣṇa is addressed as *puruṣa:*

paraṁ brahma paraṁ dhāma
pavitraṁ paramaṁ bhavān
puruṣaṁ śāśvataṁ divyam
ādi-devam ajaṁ vibhum

"You are the Supreme Brahman, the ultimate, the supreme abode and purifier, the Absolute Truth and the eternal divine person. You are the primal God, transcendental and original, and You are the unborn and all-pervading beauty."

Kṛṣṇa is the original *puruṣa,* and the living entities are *prakṛti.* Thus Kṛṣṇa is the enjoyer, and all living entities are meant to be enjoyed by Him. Therefore any woman who seeks a material husband for her protection, or any man who desires to become the husband of a woman, is under illusion. To become a husband means to maintain a wife and children nicely by supplying wealth and security. However, a material husband cannot possibly do this, for he is dependent on his *karma. Karmaṇā daiva-netreṇa:* his circumstances are determined by his past fruitive activities. Therefore if one proudly thinks he can protect his wife, he is under illusion. Kṛṣṇa is the only husband, and therefore the relationship between a husband and wife in this material world cannot be absolute. Because we have the desire to marry, Kṛṣṇa mercifully allows the so-called husband to possess a wife, and the wife to possess a so-called husband, for mutual satisfaction. In the *Īśopaniṣad* it is said, *tena tyaktena bhuñjīthā:* the Lord provides everyone with his quota. Actually, however, every living entity is *prakṛti,* or female, and Kṛṣṇa is the only husband.

ekale īśvara kṛṣṇa, āra saba bhṛtya
yāre yaiche nācāya, se taiche kare nṛtya
(Cc. *Ādi* 5.142)

Kṛṣṇa is the original master or husband of everyone, and all other living entities, having taken the form of so-called husbands, or wives, are dancing according to His desire. A so-called husband may unite with his wife for sense gratification, but his senses are conducted by Hṛṣīkeśa, the master of the senses, who is therefore the actual husband.

TEXT 20

स वै पतिः स्यादकुतोभयः स्वयं
समन्ततः पाति भयातुरं जनम् ।
स एक एवेतरथा मिथो भयं
नैवात्मलाभादधि मन्यते परम् ॥२०॥

sa vai patiḥ syād akutobhayaḥ svayaṁ
samantataḥ pāti bhayāturaṁ janam
sa eka evetarathā mitho bhayaṁ
naivātmalābhād adhi manyate param

saḥ—he; *vai*—indeed; *patiḥ*—a husband; *syāt*—would be; *akutaḥ-bhayaḥ*—who is not fearful of anyone; *svayam*—self-sufficient; *samantataḥ*—entirely; *pāti*—maintains; *bhaya-āturam*—who is very afraid; *janam*—a person; *saḥ*—therefore he; *ekaḥ*—one; *eva*—only; *itarathā*—otherwise; *mithaḥ*—from one another; *bhayam*—fear; *na*—not; *eva*—indeed; *ātma-lābhāt*—than the attainment of You; *adhi*—greater; *manyate*—is accepted; *param*—other thing.

TRANSLATION

He alone who is never afraid but who, on the contrary, gives complete shelter to all fearful persons can actually become a husband and protector. Therefore, my Lord, you are the only husband, and no one else can claim this position. If you were not the only husband, You would be afraid of others. Therefore persons

learned in all Vedic literature accept only Your Lordship as everyone's master, and they think no one else a better husband and protector than You.

PURPORT

Here the meaning of husband or guardian is clearly explained. People want to become a husband, a guardian, a governor or a political leader without knowing the actual meaning of such a superior position. There are many people all over the world—indeed, throughout the universe—who claim for some time that they are husbands, political leaders or guardians, but in due course of time the Supreme Lord desires their removal from their posts, and their careers are immediately finished. Therefore those who are actually learned and advanced in spiritual life do not accept any leader, husband or maintainer other than the Supreme Personality of Godhead.

Lord Kṛṣṇa personally states in *Bhagavad-gītā* (18.66), *ahaṁ tvāṁ sarva-pāpebhyo mokṣayiṣyāmi:* "I shall deliver you from all sinful reactions." Kṛṣṇa is not afraid of anyone. On the contrary, everyone is afraid of Kṛṣṇa. Therefore He can actually give protection to a subordinate living entity. Since so-called leaders or dictators are completely under the control of material nature, they can never give complete protection to others, although they claim this ability due to false prestige. *Na te viduḥ svārtha-gatiṁ hi viṣṇum:* people do not know that real advancement in life consists of accepting the Supreme Personality of Godhead as one's master. Instead of deceiving themselves and others by pretending to be all-powerful, all political leaders, husbands and guardians should spread the Kṛṣṇa consciousness movement so that everyone can learn how to surrender to Kṛṣṇa, the supreme husband.

TEXT 21

या तस्य ते पादसरोरुहार्हणं
निकामयेत्साखिलकामलम्पटा ।
तदेव रासीप्सितमीप्सितोऽर्चितो
यद्भग्नयाच्ञा भगवन् प्रतप्यते ॥२१॥

yā tasya te pāda-saroruhārhaṇaṁ
nikāmayet sākhila-kāma-lampaṭā
tad eva rāsīpsitam īpsito 'rcito
yad-bhagna-yācñā bhagavan pratapyate

yā—a woman who; *tasya*—of Him; *te*—of You; *pāda-saroruha*—of the lotus feet; *arhaṇam*—the worship; *nikāmayet*—fully desires; *sā*—such a woman; *akhila-kāma-lampaṭā*—although maintaining all kinds of material desire; *tat*—that; *eva*—only; *rāsi*—You award; *īpsitam*—some other desired benediction; *īpsitaḥ*—being looked to for; *arcitaḥ*—worshiped; *yat*—from which; *bhagna-yācñā*—one who desires objects other than Your lotus feet and who thus becomes broken; *bhagavan*—O my Lord; *pratapyate*—is pained.

TRANSLATION

My dear Lord, You automatically fulfill all the desires of a woman who worships Your lotus feet in pure love. However, if a woman worships Your lotus feet for a particular purpose, You also quickly fulfill her desires, but in the end she becomes brokenhearted and laments. Therefore one need not worship Your lotus feet for some material benefit.

PURPORT

Śrīla Rūpa Gosvāmī describes pure devotional service as *anyābhilāṣitā-śūnyaṁ jñāna-karmādy-anāvṛtam.* One should not worship the Supreme Personality of Godhead to fulfill some material desire for success in fruitive activities or mental speculation. To serve the lotus feet of the Lord means to serve Him exactly as He desires. The neophyte devotee is therefore ordered to worship the Lord strictly according to the regulative principles given by the spiritual master and the *śāstras.* By executing devotional service in that way, he gradually becomes attached to Kṛṣṇa, and when his original dormant love for the Lord becomes manifest, he spontaneously serves the Lord without any motive. This condition is the perfect stage of one's relationship with the Lord. The Lord then looks after the comfort and security of His devotee without being asked. Kṛṣṇa promises in *Bhagavad-gītā* (9.22):

ananyāś cintayanto māṁ
ye janāḥ paryupāsate
teṣāṁ nityābhiyuktānāṁ
yoga-kṣemaṁ vahāmy aham

The Supreme Lord personally takes care of anyone who is completely engaged in His devotional service. Whatever he has, the Lord protects, and whatever he needs, the Lord supplies. Therefore why should one bother the Lord for something material? Such prayers are unnecessary.

Śrīla Viśvanātha Cakravartī Ṭhākura explains that even if a devotee wishes the Lord to fulfill a particular desire, the devotee should not be considered a *sakāma-bhakta* (a devotee with some motive). In the *Bhagavad-gītā* (7.16) Kṛṣṇa says:

catur-vidhā bhajante māṁ
janāḥ sukṛtino 'rjuna
ārto jijñāsur arthārthī
jñānī ca bharatarṣabha

"O best among the Bharatas [Arjuna], four kinds of pious men render devotional service unto Me—the distressed, the desirer of wealth, the inquisitive and he who is searching for knowledge of the Absolute." The *ārta* and the *arthārthī*, who approach the Supreme Personality of Godhead for relief from misery or for some money, are not *sakāma-bhaktas*, although they appear to be. Being neophyte devotees, they are simply ignorant. Later in *Bhagavad-gītā* the Lord says, *udārāḥ sarva evaite:* they are all magnanimous (*udārāḥ*). Although in the beginning a devotee may harbor some desire, in due course of time it will vanish. Therefore the *Śrīmad-Bhāgavatam* enjoins:

akāmaḥ sarva-kāmo vā
mokṣa-kāma udāra-dhīḥ
tīvreṇa bhakti-yogena
yajeta puruṣaṁ param

"A person who has broader intelligence, whether he is full of all material desire, is free from material desire, or has a desire for liberation, must by all means worship the supreme whole, the Personality of Godhead." (*Bhāg.* 2.3.10)

Even if one wants something material, he should pray to no one but the Lord to fulfill his desire. If one approaches a demigod for the fulfillment of his desires, he is to be considered *naṣṭa-buddhi,* bereft of all good sense. Kṛṣṇa says in *Bhagavad-gītā* (7.20):

kāmais tais tair hṛta-jñānāḥ
prapadyante 'nya-devatāḥ
taṁ taṁ niyamam āsthāya
prakṛtyā niyatāḥ svayā

"Those whose minds are distorted by material desires surrender unto demigods and follow the particular rules and regulations of worship according to their own natures."

Lakṣmīdevī advises all devotees who approach the Lord with material desires that according to her practical experience, the Lord is Kāmadeva, and thus there is no need to ask Him for anything material. She says that everyone should simply serve the Lord without any motive. Since the Supreme Personality of Godhead is sitting in everyone's heart, He knows everyone's thoughts, and in due course of time He will fulfill all desires. Therefore let us completely depend on the service of the Lord without bothering Him with our material requests.

TEXT 22

मत्प्राप्तयेऽजेशसुरासुरादय-
स्तप्यन्त उग्रं तप ऐन्द्रियेधियः ।
ऋते भवत्पादपरायणान्न मां
विन्दन्त्यहं त्वद्धृदया यतोऽजित ॥२२॥

mat-prāptaye 'jeśa-surāsurādayas
tapyanta ugraṁ tapa aindriye dhiyaḥ
ṛte bhavat-pāda-parāyaṇān na māṁ
vindanty ahaṁ tvad-dhṛdayā yato 'jita

mat-prāptaye—to obtain my mercy; *aja*—Lord Brahmā; *īśa*—Lord Śiva; *sura*—the other demigods, headed by King Indra, Candra and Varuṇa; *asura-ādayaḥ*—as well as the demons; *tapyante*—undergo; *ugram*—severe; *tapaḥ*—austerity; *aindriye dhiyaḥ*—whose minds are absorbed in thoughts of superior sense gratification; *ṛte*—unless; *bhavat-pada-parāyaṇāt*—one who is wholly and solely engaged in the service of the Supreme Lord's lotus feet; *na*—not; *mām*—me; *vindanti*—obtain; *aham*—I; *tvat*—in You; *hṛdayāḥ*—whose hearts; *yataḥ*—therefore; *ajita*—O unconquerable one.

TRANSLATION

O supreme unconquerable Lord, when they become absorbed in thoughts of material enjoyment, Lord Brahmā and Lord Śiva, as well as other demigods and demons, undergo severe penances and austerities to receive my benedictions. But I do not favor anyone, however great he may be, unless he is always engaged in the service of Your lotus feet. Because I always keep You within my heart, I cannot favor anyone but a devotee.

PURPORT

In this verse the goddess of fortune, Lakṣmīdevī, clearly states that she does not bestow her favor on any materialistic person. Although sometimes a materialist becomes very opulent in the eyes of another materialist, such opulence is bestowed upon him by the goddess Durgādevī, a material expansion of the goddess of fortune, not by Lakṣmīdevī herself. Those who desire material wealth worship Durgādevī with the following *mantra: dhanaṁ dehi rūpaṁ dehi rūpa-pati-bhājaṁ dehi.* "O worshipable mother Durgādevī, please give me wealth, strength, fame, a good wife and so on." By pleasing goddess Durgā one can obtain such benefits, but since they are temporary, they result only in *māyā-sukha* (illusory happiness). As stated by Prahlāda Mahārāja, *māyā-sukhāya bharam udvahato vimūḍhān:* those who work very hard for material benefits are *vimūḍhas,* foolish rascals, because such happiness will not endure. On the other hand, devotees like Prahlāda and Dhruva Mahārāja achieved extraordinary material opulences, but such opulences were not *māyā-sukha.* When a devotee acquires unparalleled opulences, they are the direct gifts of the goddess of fortune, who resides in the heart of Nārāyaṇa.

The material opulences a person obtains by offering prayers to the goddess Durgā are temporary. As described in *Bhagavd-gītā* (7.23), *antavat tu phalaṁ teṣāṁ tad bhavaty alpa-medhasām:* men of meager intelligence desire temporary happiness. We have actually seen that one of the disciples of Bhaktisiddhānta Sarasvatī Ṭhākura wanted to enjoy the property of his spiritual master, and the spiritual master, being merciful toward him, gave him the temporary property, but not the power to preach the cult of Caitanya Mahāprabhu all over the world. That special mercy of the power to preach is given to a devotee who does not want anything material from his spiritual master but wants only to serve him. The story of the demon Rāvaṇa illustrates this point. Although Rāvaṇa tried to abduct the goddess of fortune Sītādevī from the custody of Lord Rāmacandra, he could not possibly do so. The Sītādevī he forcibly took with him was not the original Sītādevī, but an expansion of *māyā,* or Durgādevī. As a result, instead of winning the favor of the real goddess of fortune, Rāvaṇa and his whole family were vanquished by the power of Durgādevī (*sṛṣṭi-sthiti-pralaya-sādhana-śaktir ekā*).

TEXT 23

स त्वं ममाप्यच्युत शीर्ष्णि वन्दितं
करा‍म्बुजं यत्त्वदधायि सात्वताम् ।
बिभर्षि मां लक्ष्म वरेण्य मायया
क ईश्वरस्येहितमूहितुं विभुरिति ॥२३॥

sa tvaṁ mamāpy acyuta śīrṣṇi vanditaṁ
karāmbujaṁ yat tvad-adhāyi sātvatām
bibharṣi māṁ lakṣma vareṇya māyayā
ka īśvarasyehitam ūhituṁ vibhur iti

saḥ—that; *tvam*—You; *mama*—of me; *api*—also; *acyuta*—O infallible one; *śīrṣṇi*—on the head; *vanditam*—worshiped; *kara-ambujam*—Your lotus hand; *yat*—which; *tvat*—by You; *adhāyi*—placed; *sāt-*

vatām—on the head of the devotees; *bibharṣi*—You maintain; *mām*—me; *lakṣma*—as an insignia on Your chest; *vareṇya*—O worshipable one; *māyayā*—with deceit; *kaḥ*—who; *īśvarasya*—of the supremely powerful controller; *īhitam*—the desires; *ūhitum*—to understand by reason and argument; *vibhuḥ*—is able; *iti*—thus.

TRANSLATION

O infallible one, Your lotus palm is the source of all benediction. Therefore Your pure devotees worship it, and You very mercifully place Your hand on their heads. I wish that You may also place Your hand on My head, for although You already bear my insignia of golden streaks on Your chest, I regard this honor as merely a kind of false prestige for me. You show Your real mercy to Your devotees, not to me. Of course, You are the supreme absolute controller, and no one can understand Your motives.

PURPORT

In many places, the *śāstras* describe the Supreme Personality of Godhead as being more inclined toward His devotees than toward His wife, who always remains on His chest. In *Śrīmad-Bhāgavatam* (11.14.15) it is stated:

na tathā me priyatama
ātma-yonir na śaṅkaraḥ
na ca saṅkarṣaṇo na śrīr
naivātmā ca yathā bhavān

Here Krsna plainly says that His devotees are more dear to Him than Lord Brahmā, Lord Śiva, Lord Saṅkarṣaṇa (the original cause of creation, the goddess of fortune or even His own Self. Elsewhere in *Śrīmad-Bhāgavatam* (10.9.20) Śukadeva Gosvāmī says,

nemam viriñco na bhavo
na śrīr apy aṅga saṁśrayā
prasādaṁ lebhire gopī
yat tat prāpa vimuktidāt

The Supreme Lord, who can award liberation to anyone, showed more mercy toward the *gopīs* than to Lord Brahmā, Lord Śiva or even the goddess of fortune, who is His own wife and is associated with His body. Similarly, *Śrīmad-Bhāgavatam* (10.47.60) also states:

nāyaṁ śriyo 'ṅga u nitānta-rateḥ prasādaḥ
svar-yoṣitāṁ nalina-gandha-rucāṁ kuto 'nyāḥ
rāsotsave 'sya bhuja-daṇḍa-gṛhīta-kaṇṭha-
labdhāśiṣāṁ ya udagād vraja-sundarīṇām

"The *gopīs* received benedictions from the Lord that neither Lakṣmīdevī nor the most beautiful dancers in the heavenly planets could attain. In the *rāsa* dance, the Lord showed His favor to the most fortunate *gopīs* by placing His arms on their shoulders and dancing with each of them individually. No one can compare with the *gopīs*, who received the causeless mercy of the Lord."

In the *Caitanya-caritāmṛta* it is said that no one can receive the real favor of the Supreme Personality of Godhead without following in the footsteps of the *gopīs*. Even the goddess of fortune could not receive the same favor as the *gopīs*, although she underwent severe austerities and penances for many years. Lord Śrī Caitanya Mahāprabhu discusses this point with Vyeṅkaṭa Bhaṭṭa in *Caitanya-caritāmṛta* (*Madhya* 9.111-131): "The Lord inquired from Vyeṅkaṭa Bhaṭṭa, 'Your worshipable goddess of fortune, Lakṣmī, always remains on the chest of Nārāyaṇa, and she is certainly the most chaste woman in the creation. However, My Lord is Lord Śrī Kṛṣṇa, a cowherd boy engaged in tending cows. Why is it that Lakṣmī, being such a chaste wife, wants to associate with My Lord? Just to associate with Kṛṣṇa, Lakṣmī abandoned all transcendental happiness in Vaikuṇṭha and for a long time accepted vows and regulative principles and performed unlimited austerities.'

"Vyeṅkaṭa Bhaṭṭa replied, 'Lord Kṛṣṇa and Lord Nārāyaṇa are one and the same, but the pastimes of Kṛṣṇa are more relishable due to their sportive nature. They are very pleasing for Kṛṣṇa's *śaktis*. Since Kṛṣṇa and Nārāyaṇa are both the same personality, Lakṣmī's association with Kṛṣṇa did not break her vow of chastity. Rather, it was in great fun that the goddess of fortune wanted to associate with Lord Kṛṣṇa. The goddess of fortune considered that her vow of chastity would not be damaged by her relationship with Kṛṣṇa. Rather, by associating with Kṛṣṇa she could enjoy the benefit of the *rāsa* dance. If she wanted to enjoy herself with Kṛṣṇa what fault is there? Why are you joking so about this?'

"Lord Caitanya Mahāprabhu replied, 'I know that there is no fault in the goddess of fortune, but still she could not enter into the *rāsa* dance. We hear this from revealed scriptures. The authorities of Vedic knowledge met Lord Rāmacandra in Daṇḍakāraṇya, and by their penances and austerities, they were allowed to enter into the *rāsa* dance. But can you tell me why the goddess of fortune, Lakṣmī, could not get that opportunity?'

"To this Vyeṅkaṭa Bhaṭṭa replied, 'I cannot enter into the mystery of this incident. I am an ordinary living being. My intelligence is limited, and I am always disturbed. How can I understand the pastimes of the Supreme Lord? They are deeper than millions of oceans.'

"Lord Caitanya replied, 'Lord Kṛṣṇa has a specific characteristic. He attracts everyone's heart by the mellow of His personal conjugal love. By following in the footsteps of the inhabitants of the planet known as Vrajaloka or Goloka Vṛndāvana, one can attain the shelter of the lotus feet of Śrī Kṛṣṇa. However, the inhabitants of that planet do not know that Lord Kṛṣṇa is the Supreme Personality of Godhead. Unaware that Kṛṣṇa is the Supreme Lord, the residents of Vṛndāvana like Nanda Mahārāja, Yaśodādevī and the *gopīs* treat Kṛṣṇa as their beloved son or lover. Mother Yaśodā accepts Him as her son and sometimes binds Him to a grinding mortar. Kṛṣṇa's cowherd boy friends think He is an ordinary boy and get up on His shoulders. In Goloka Vṛndāvana no one has any desire other than to love Kṛṣṇa.' "

The conclusion is that one cannot associate with Kṛṣṇa unless he has fully received the favor of the inhabitants of Vrajabhūmi. Therefore if one wants to be delivered by Kṛṣṇa directly, he must take to the service of the residents of Vṛndāvana, who are unalloyed devotees of the Lord.

TEXT 24

रम्यके च भगवतः प्रियतमं मात्स्यमवताररूपं तद्वर्षपुरुषस्य मनोः प्राक्प्रदर्शितं स इदानीमपि महता भक्तियोगेनाराधयतीदं चोदाहरति ॥२४॥

ramyake ca bhagavataḥ priyatamaṁ mātsyam avatāra-rūpaṁ tad-varṣa-puruṣasya manoḥ prāk-pradarśitaṁ sa idānīm api mahatā bhakti-yogenārādhayatīdaṁ codāharati.

ramyake ca—also in Ramyaka-varṣa; *bhagavataḥ*—of the Supreme Personality of Godhead; *priya-tamam*—the foremost; *mātsyam*—fish; *avatāra-rūpam*—the form of the incarnation; *tat-varṣa-puruṣasya*—of the ruler of that land; *manoḥ*—Manu; *prāk*—previously (at the end of the Cākṣuṣa-manvantara); *pradarśitam*—exhibited; *saḥ*—that Manu; *idānīm api*—even until now; *mahatā bhakti-yogena*—by dint of advanced devotional service; *ārādhayati*—worships the Supreme Personality of Godhead; *idam*—this; *ca*—and; *udāharati*—chants.

TRANSLATION

Śukadeva Gosvāmī continued: In Ramyaka-varṣa, where Vaivasvata Manu rules, the Supreme Personality of Godhead appeared as Lord Matsya at the end of the last era [the Cākṣuṣa-manvantara]. Vaivasvata Manu now worships Lord Matsya in pure devotional service and chants the following mantra.

TEXT 25

ॐ नमो भगवते मुख्यतमाय नमः सत्त्वाय प्राणायौजसे सहसे बलाय महामत्स्याय नम इति ॥२५॥

oṁ namo bhagavate mukhyatamāya namaḥ sattvāya prāṇāyaujase sahase balāya mahā-matsyāya nama iti.

om—O my Lord; *namaḥ*—respectful obeisances; *bhagavate*—unto the Supreme Personality of Godhead; *mukhya-tamāya*—the first incarnation to appear; *namaḥ*—my respectful obeisances; *sattvāya*—unto the pure transcendence; *prāṇāya*—the origin of life; *ojase*—the source of the potency of the senses; *sahase*—the origin of all mental power; *balāya*—the origin of bodily strength; *mahā-matsyāya*—unto the gigantic fish incarnation; *namaḥ*—respectful obeisances; *iti*—thus.

TRANSLATION

I offer my respectful obeisances unto the Supreme Personality of Godhead, who is pure transcendence. He is the origin of all life, bodily strength, mental power and sensory ability. Known as Matsyāvatāra, the gigantic fish incarnation, He appears first among all the incarnations. Again I offer my obeisances unto Him.

PURPORT

Śrīla Jayadeva Gosvāmī sings:

pralayo payodhi-jale dhṛtavān asi vedaṁ
vihita-vahitra-caritram akhedam
keśava dhṛta-mīna-śarīra jaya jagad-īśa hare

Soon after the cosmic creation, the entire universe was inundated with water. At that time Lord Kṛṣṇa (Keśava) incarnated as a gigantic fish to protect the *Vedas.* Therefore Manu addresses Lord Matsya as *mukhyatama,* the first incarnation to appear. Fish are generally considered a mixture of the modes of ignorance and passion, but we must understand that every incarnation of the Supreme Personality of Godhead is completely transcendental. There is never any deterioration of the Supreme Lord's original transcendental quality. Therefore the word *sattvāya* is used here, meaning pure goodness on the transcendental platform. There are many incarnations of the Supreme Lord: Varāha *mūrti* (the boar form), Kūrma *mūrti* (the tortoise form), Hayagrīva *mūrti* (the form of a horse) and so on. Yet we should never think any of Them material. They are always situated on the platform of *śuddha-sattva,* pure transcendence.

TEXT 26

अन्तर्बहिश्चाखिललोकपालकै-
रदृष्टरूपो विचरस्युरुस्वनः ।
स ईश्वरस्त्वं य इदं वशेऽनय-
न्नाम्ना यथा दारुमयीं नरः स्त्रियम् ॥२६॥

antar bahiś cākhila-loka-pālakair
adṛṣṭa-rūpo vicarasy uru-svanaḥ
sa īśvaras tvaṁ ya idaṁ vaśe 'nayan
nāmnā yathā dārumayīṁ naraḥ striyam

antaḥ—within; *bahiḥ*—without; *ca*—also; *akhila-loka-pālakaiḥ*—by the leaders of the different planets, societies, kingdoms and so on; *adṛṣṭa-rūpaḥ*—not seen; *vicarasi*—You wander; *uru*—very great; *svanaḥ*—whose sounds (Vedic *mantras*); *saḥ*—He; *īśvaraḥ*—the supreme controller; *tvam*—You; *yaḥ*—who; *idam*—this; *vaśe*—under control; *anayat*—has brought; *nāmnā*—by different names like *brāhmaṇa, kṣatriya, vaiśya* and *śūdra; yathā*—exactly like; *dārumayīm*—made of wood; *naraḥ*—a man; *striyam*—a doll.

TRANSLATION

My dear Lord, just as a puppeteer controls his dancing dolls and a husband controls his wife, Your Lordship controls all the living entities in the universe, such as the brāhmaṇas, kṣatriyas, vaiśyas and śūdras. Although You are in everyone's heart as the supreme witness and commander and are outside everyone as well, the so-called leaders of societies, communities and countries cannot realize You. Only those who hear the vibration of the Vedic mantras can appreciate You.

PURPORT

The Supreme Personality of Godhead is *antarbahiḥ*, present within and without everything. One must overcome the delusion caused by the Lord's external energy and realize His presence both externally and internally. In *Śrīmad-Bhāgavatam* (1.8.19) Śrīmatī Kuntīdevī has explained that Kṛṣṇa appears in this world *naṭo nāṭyadharo yathā*, "exactly like an actor dressed as a player." In *Bhagavad-gītā* (18.61) Kṛṣṇa says, *īśvaraḥ sarva-bhūtānāṁ hṛd-deśe 'rjuna tiṣṭhati:* "The Supreme Lord is situated in everyone's heart, O Arjuna." The Lord is situated within everyone's heart, and outside as well. Within the heart He is the Supersoul, the incarnation who acts as the adviser and witness. Yet although God is residing within their hearts, foolish people say, "I cannot see God. Please show Him to me."

Everyone is under the control of the Supreme Personality of Godhead, exactly like dancing dolls controlled by a puppeteer or a woman controlled by her husband. A woman is compared to a doll (*dārumayī*) because she has no independence. She should always be controlled by a man. Still, due to false prestige, a class of women wants to remain independent. What to speak of women, all living entities are *prakṛti* (female) and therefore dependent on the Supreme Lord, as Kṛṣṇa Himself explains in *Bhagavad-gītā* (*apareyam itas tv anyāṁ prakṛtiṁ viddhi me parām*). The living entity is never independent. Under all circumstances, he is dependent on the mercy of the Lord. The Lord creates the social divisions of human society—*brāhmaṇas, kṣatriyas, vaiśyas* and *śūdras*—and ordains that they follow rules and regulations suited to their particular position. In this way, all members of society remain always under the Supreme Lord's control. Still, some people foolishly deny the existence of God.

Self-realization means to understand one's subordinate position in relation to the Lord. When one is thus enlightened, he surrenders to the Supreme Personality of Godhead and is liberated from the clutches of the material energy. In other words, unless one surrenders to the lotus feet of the Lord, the material energy in its many varieties will continue to control him. No one in the material world can deny that he is under control. The Supreme Lord, Nārāyaṇa, who is beyond this material existence, controls everyone. The following Vedic *mantra* confirms this point: *eko ha vai nārāyaṇa āsīt.* Foolish persons think Nārāyaṇa to be on the platform of ordinary material existence. Because they do not realize the natural constitutional position of the living entity, they concoct names like *daridra-nārāyaṇa, svāmi-nārāyaṇa* or *mithyā-nārāyaṇa.* However, Nārāyaṇa is actually the supreme controller of everyone. This understanding is self-realization.

TEXT 27

यं लोकपालाः किल मत्सरज्वरा
हित्वा यतन्तोऽपि पृथक समेत्य च ।
पातुं न शेकुर्द्विपदश्चतुष्पदः
सरीसृपं स्थाणु यदत्र दृश्यते ॥२७॥

yaṁ loka-pālāḥ kila matsara-jvarā
hitvā yatanto 'pi pṛthak sametya ca
pātuṁ na śekur dvi-padaś catuṣ-padaḥ
sarīsṛpaṁ sthāṇu yad atra dṛśyate

yam—whom (You); *loka-pālāḥ*—the great leaders of the universe, beginning with Lord Brahmā; *kila*—what to speak of others; *matsara-jvarāḥ*—who are suffering from the fever of envy; *hitvā*—leaving aside; *yatantaḥ*—endeavoring; *api*—although; *pṛthak*—separately; *sametya*—combined; *ca*—also; *pātum*—to protect; *na*—not; *śekuḥ*—able; *dvi-padaḥ*—two-legged; *catuḥ-padaḥ*—four-legged; *sarīsṛpam*—reptiles; *sthāṇu*—not moving; *yat*—whatever; *atra*—within this material world; *dṛśyate*—is visible.

TRANSLATION

My Lord, from the great leaders of the universe, such as Lord Brahmā and other demigods, down to the political leaders of this world, all are envious of Your authority. Without Your help, however, they could neither separately nor concertedly maintain the innumerable living entities within the universe. You are actually the only maintainer of all human beings, of animals like cows and asses, and of plants, reptiles, birds, mountains and whatever else is visible within this material world.

PURPORT

It is fashionable for materialistic persons to compete with the power of God. When so-called scientists try to manufacture living entities in their laboratories, their only purpose is to defy the talent and ability of the Supreme Personality of Godhead. This is called illusion. It exists even in the higher planetary systems, where great demigods like Lord Brahmā, Lord Śiva and others reside. In this world everyone is puffed up with false prestige despite the failure of all his endeavors. When so-called philanthropists, who supposedly want to help the poor, are approached by members of the Kṛṣṇa consciousness movement, they say, "You are simply wasting your time, while I am feeding vast masses of starving people." Unfortunately, their meager efforts, either singly or together, do not solve anyone's problems.

Sometimes so-called *svāmīs* are very eager to feed poor people, thinking them to be *daridra-nārāyaṇa,* the Lord's incarnations as beggars. They prefer to serve the manufactured *daridra-nārāyaṇa* than the original, supreme Nārāyaṇa. They say, "Don't encourage service to Lord Nārāyaṇa. It is better to serve the starving people of the world." Unfortunately such materialists, either singly or combined in the form of the United Nations, cannot fulfill their plans. The truth is that the many millions of human beings, animals, birds and trees—indeed, all living entities—are maintained solely by the Supreme Personality of Godhead. *Eko bahūnāṁ yo vidadhāti kāmān:* one person, the Supreme Lord, is supplying the necessities of life for all other living entities. To challenge the authority of Nārāyaṇa, the Supreme Personality of Godhead, is the business of *asuras* (demons). Yet sometimes *suras,* or devotees, are also bewildered by the illusory energy and falsely claim to be the maintainer of the entire universe. Such incidents are described in the Tenth Canto of *Śrīmad-Bhāgavatam,* where Śukadeva Gosvāmī tells how Lord Brahmā and King Indra became puffed up and were eventually chastised by Kṛṣṇa.

TEXT 28

भवान् युगान्तार्णव ऊर्मिमालिनि
क्षोणीमिमामोषधिवीरुधां निधिम् ।
मया सहोरु क्रमतेऽज ओजसा
तस्मै जगत्प्राणगणात्मने नम इति ॥२८॥

bhavān yugāntārṇava ūrmi-mālini
kṣoṇīm imām oṣadhi-vīrudhāṁ nidhim
mayā sahoru kramate 'ja ojasā
tasmai jagat-prāṇa-gaṇātmane nama iti

bhavān—Your Lordship; *yuga-anta-arṇave*—in the water of devastation at the end of the millennium; *ūrmi-mālini*—possessing rows of big waves; *kṣoṇīm*—the planet earth; *imām*—this; *oṣadhi-vīrudhām*—of all kinds of herbs and drugs; *nidhim*—the storehouse; *mayā*—me; *saha*—with; *uru*—great; *kramate*—You roamed; *aja*—O unborn one; *ojasā*—with speed; *tasmai*—unto Him; *jagat*—of the entire universe; *prāṇa-gaṇa-ātmane*—the ultimate source of life; *namaḥ*—my respectful obeisances; *iti*—thus.

TRANSLATION

O almighty Lord, at the end of the millennium this planet earth, which is the source of all kinds of herbs, drugs and trees, was inundated by water and drowned beneath the devastating waves. At that time, You protected me along with the earth and roamed the sea with great speed. O unborn one, You are the actual maintainer of the entire universal creation, and therefore You are the cause of all living entities. I offer my respectful obeisances unto You.

PURPORT

Envious persons cannot appreciate how wonderfully the Lord creates, maintains and annihilates the universe, but devotees of the Lord can understand this perfectly well. Devotees can see how the Lord is acting behind the wonderful workings of the material nature. In *Bhagavad-gītā* (9.10) the Lord says:

mayādhyakṣeṇa prakṛtiḥ
sūyate sa-carācaram
hetunānena kaunteya
jagad viparivartate

"This material nature is working under My direction, O son of Kuntī, and it is producing all moving and unmoving beings. By its rule this manifestation is created and annihilated again and again." All the wonderful transformations of nature are happening under the superintendence of the Supreme Personality of Godhead. Envious persons cannot see this, but a devotee, even though very humble and even if uneducated, knows that behind all the activities of nature is the supreme hand of the Supreme Being.

TEXT 29

हिरण्मयेऽपि भगवान्निवसति कूर्मतनुं बिभ्राणस्तस्य तत्प्रियतमां तनुमर्यमा सह वर्षपुरुषैः पितृगणाधिपतिरुपधावति मन्त्रमिमं चानुजपति ॥२९॥

hiraṇmaye 'pi bhagavān nivasati kūrma-tanuṁ bibhrāṇas tasya tat priyatamāṁ tanum aryamā saha varṣa-puruṣaiḥ pitṛ-gaṇādhipatir upadhāvati mantram imaṁ cānujapati.

hiraṇmaye—in Hiraṇmaya-varṣa; *api*—indeed; *bhagavān*—the Supreme Personality of Godhead; *nivasati*—resides; *kūrma-tanum*—the body of a tortoise; *bibhrāṇaḥ*—manifesting; *tasya*—of the Supreme Personality of Godhead; *tat*—that; *priya-tamām*—dearmost; *tanum*—body; *aryamā*—Aryamā, the chief resident of Hiraṇmaya-varṣa; *saha*—with; *varṣa-puruṣaiḥ*—the people of that tract of land; *pitṛ-gaṇa-adhipatiḥ*—who is the chief of the *pitās; upadhāvati*—worships in devotional service; *mantram*—hymn; *imam*—this; *ca*—also; *anujapati*—chants.

TRANSLATION

Śukadeva Gosvāmī continued: In Hiraṇmaya-varṣa, the Supreme Lord, Viṣṇu, lives in the form of a tortoise [kūrma-śarīra]. This most dear and beautiful form is always worshiped there in devotional service by Aryamā, the chief resident of Hiraṇmaya-varṣa, along with the other inhabitants of that land. They chant the following hymns.

PURPORT

The word *priyatama* (dearmost) is very significant in this verse. Each devotee regards a particular form of the Lord as most dear. Because of an atheistic mentality, some people think that the tortoise, boar and fish incarnations of the Lord are not very beautiful. They do not know that any form of the Lord is always the fully opulent Personality of Godhead. Since one of His opulences is infinite beauty, all the Lord's incarnations are very beautiful and are appreciated as such by devotees. Nondevotees, however, think that Lord Kṛṣṇa's incarnations are ordinary material creatures, and therefore they distinguish between the beautiful and the not beautiful. A certain form of the Lord is worshiped by a particular devotee because he loves to see that form of the Lord. As stated in *Brahma-saṁhitā* (5.33): *advaitam acyutam anādim ananta-rūpam ādyam purāṇa-puruṣaṁ nava-yauvanaṁ ca.* The very beautiful form of the Lord is always youthful. Sincere servants of a particular form of the Lord always see that form as very beautiful, and thus they engage in constant devotional service to Him.

TEXT 30

ॐ नमो भगवते अकूपाराय सर्वसत्त्वगुणविशेषणायानुपलक्षितस्थानाय नमो वर्ष्मणे नमो भूम्ने नमो नमोऽवस्थानाय नमस्ते ॥३०॥

oṁ namo bhagavate akūpārāya sarva-sattva-guṇa-viśeṣaṇāyānu-palakṣita-sthānāya namo varṣmaṇe namo bhūmne namo namo 'vasthānāya namas te.

om—O my Lord; *namaḥ*—respectful obeisances; *bhagavate*—unto You, the Supreme Personality of Godhead; *akūpārāya*—in the form of a tortoise; *sarva-sattva-guṇa-viśeṣaṇāya*—whose form consists of *śuddha-sattva,* transcendental goodness; *anupalakṣita-sthānāya*—unto You, whose position is not discernible; *namaḥ*—my respectful obeisances; *varṣmaṇe*—unto You who, although the oldest, are unaffected by time; *namaḥ*—my respectful obeisances; *bhūmne*—to the great one who can go everywhere; *namaḥ namaḥ*—repeated obeisances; *avasthānāya*—the shelter of everything; *namaḥ*—respectful obeisances; *te*—unto You.

TRANSLATION

O my Lord, I offer my respectful obeisances unto You, who have assumed the form of a tortoise. You are the reservoir of all transcendental qualities, and being entirely untinged by matter, You are perfectly situated in pure goodness. You move here and there in the water, but no one can discern Your position. Therefore I offer my respectful obeisances unto You. Because of Your transcendental position, You are not limited by past, present and future. You are present everywhere as the shelter of all things, and therefore I offer my respectful obeisances unto You again and again.

PURPORT

In the *Brahma-saṁhitā* it is said, *goloka eva nivasaty akhilātma-bhūtaḥ:* the Lord always remains in Goloka, the topmost planet in the spiritual world. At the same time, He is all-pervading. This paradox is only possible for the Supreme Personality of Godhead, who is full of all opulences. The Lord's all-pervasiveness is confirmed in *Bhagavad-gītā* (18.61) where Kṛṣṇa states, *īśvaraḥ sarva-bhūtānāṁ hṛd-deśe 'rjuna tiṣṭhati:* "The Supreme Lord is seated in everyone's heart, O Arjuna." Elsewhere in *Bhagavad-gītā* (15.15) the Lord says, *sarvasya cāhaṁ hṛdi sanniviṣṭo mattaḥ smṛtir jñānam apohanaṁ ca:* "I am seated in everyone's heart, and from Me come remembrance, knowledge and forgetfulness." Therefore, although the Lord is present everywhere, He cannot be seen with ordinary eyes. As Aryamā says, the Lord is *anupalakṣita-sthāna:* no one can locate Him. This is the greatness of the Supreme Personality of Godhead.

TEXT 31

यद्रूपमेतन्निजमाययार्पित-
मर्थस्वरूपं बहुरूपरूपितम् ।
संख्या न यस्यास्त्ययथोपलम्भनात्-
तस्मै नमस्तेऽव्यपदेशरूपिणे ॥३१॥

yad-rūpam etan nija-māyayārpitam
artha-svarūpaṁ bahu-rūpa-rūpitam
saṅkhyā na yasyāsty ayathopalambhanāt
tasmai namas te 'vyapadeśa-rūpiṇe

yat—of whom; *rūpam*—the form; *etat*—this; *nija-māyayā ar-pitam*—manifested by Your personal potency; *artha-svarūpam*—this entire visible cosmic manifestation; *bahu-rūpa-rūpitam*—manifested in various forms; *saṅkhyā*—the measurement; *na*—not; *yasya*—of which; *asti*—there is; *ayathā*—falsely; *upalambhanāt*—from perceiving; *tasmai*—unto Him (the Supreme Lord); *namaḥ*—my respectful obeisances; *te*—unto You; *avyapadeśa*—cannot be ascertained by mental speculation; *rūpiṇe*—whose real form.

TRANSLATION

My dear Lord, this visible cosmic manifestation is a demonstration of Your own creative energy. Since the countless varieties

of forms within this cosmic manifestation are simply a display of Your external energy, this virāṭa-rūpa [universal body] is not Your real form. Except for a devotee in transcendental consciousness, no one can perceive Your actual form. Therefore I offer my respectful obeisances unto You.

PURPORT

Māyāvādī philosophers think the universal form of the Lord to be real and His personal form illusory. We can understand their mistake by a simple example. A fire consists of three elements: heat and light, which are the energy of the fire, and the fire itself. Anyone can understand that the original fire is the reality and that the heat and light are simply the fire's energy. Heat and light are the formless energies of fire, and in that sense they are unreal. Only the fire has form, and therefore it is the real form of the heat and light. As Kṛṣṇa states in *Bhagavad-gītā* (9.4), *mayā tatam idaṁ sarvaṁ jagad avyakta-mūrtinā:* "By Me, in My unmanifested form, this entire universe is pervaded." Thus the impersonal conception of the Lord is like the expansion of heat and light from a fire. In *Bhagavad-gītā* the Lord also says, *mat-sthāni sarva-bhūtāni na cāhaṁ teṣv avasthitaḥ:* the entire material creation is resting on Kṛṣṇa's energy, either material, spiritual or marginal, but because His form is absent from the expansion of His energy, He is not personally present. This inconceivable expansion of the Supreme Lord's energy is called *acintya-śakti.* Therefore no one can understand the real form of the Lord without becoming His devotee.

TEXT 32

जरायुजं स्वेदजमण्डजोद्भिदं
चराचरं देवर्षिपितृभूतमैन्द्रियम् ।
द्यौः खं क्षितिः शैलसरित्समुद्र-
द्वीपग्रहर्क्षेत्यभिधेय एकः ॥३२॥

jarāyujaṁ svedajaṁ aṇḍajodbhidaṁ
carācaraṁ devarṣi-pitṛ-bhūtam aindriyam
dyauḥ khaṁ kṣitiḥ śaila-sarit-samudra-
dvīpa-graharkṣety abhidheya ekaḥ

jarāyu-jam—one born from a womb; *sveda-jam*—one born from perspiration; *aṇḍa-ja*—one born from an egg; *udbhidam*—one born of the earth; *cara-acaram*—the moving and the stationary; *deva*—the demigods; *ṛṣi*—the great sages; *pitṛ*—the inhabitants of Pitṛloka; *bhūtam*—the material elements air, fire, water and earth; *aindriyam*—all the senses; *dyauḥ*—the higher planetary systems; *kham*—the sky; *kṣitiḥ*—the earthly planets; *śaila*—the hills and mountains; *sarit*—the rivers; *samudra*—the oceans; *dvīpa*—the islands; *graha-ṛkṣa*—the stars and planets; *iti*—thus; *abhidheyaḥ*—to be variously named; *ekaḥ*—one.

TRANSLATION

My dear Lord, You manifest Your different energies in countless forms: as living entities born from wombs, from eggs and from perspiration; as plants and trees that grow out of the earth; as all living entities, both moving and standing, including the demigods, the learned sages and the pitās; as outer space, as the higher planetary system containing the heavenly planets, and as the planet earth with its hills, rivers, seas, oceans and islands. Indeed, all the stars and planets are simply manifestations of Your different energies, but originally You are one without a second. Therefore there is nothing beyond You. This entire cosmic manifestation is therefore not false but is simply a temporary manifestation of Your inconceivable energy.

PURPORT

This verse completely rejects the theory of *brahma satyaṁ jagan mithyā,* which states that spirit, or Brahman, is real, whereas the manifested material world, with its great variety of things, is false. Nothing is false. One thing may be permanent and another temporary, but both the permanent and the temporary are facts. For example, if someone becomes angry for a certain period, no one can say that his anger is false. It is simply temporary. Everything we experience in our daily lives is of this same character; it is temporary but real.

The different kinds of living entities coming from various sources are very clearly described in this verse. Some are born from a womb and some (like certain insects) from human perspiration. Others hatch from eggs, and still others sprout from the earth. A living entity takes birth under different circumstances according to his past activities (*karma*). Although the body of the living entity is material, it is never false. No one will accept the argument that since a person's material body is false, murder has no repercussions. Our temporary bodies are given to us according to our *karma*, and we must remain in our given bodies to enjoy the pains and pleasures of life. Our bodies cannot be called false; they are only temporary. In other words, the energy of the Supreme Lord is as permanent as the Lord Himself, although His energy is sometimes manifest and sometimes not. As summarized in the *Vedas, sarvaṁ khalv idaṁ brahma:* "Everything is Brahman."

TEXT 33

यस्मिन्नसंख्येयविशेषनाम-
रूपाकृतौ कविभिः कल्पितेयम् ।
संख्या यया तत्त्वदृशापनीयते
तस्मै नमः सांख्यनिदर्शनाय ते इति ॥३३॥

yasminn asaṅkhyeya-viśeṣa-nāma-
rūpākṛtau kavibhiḥ kalpiteyam
saṅkhyā yayā tattva-dṛśāpanīyate
tasmai namaḥ sāṅkhya-nidarśanāya te iti

yasmin—in You (the Supreme Personality of Godhead); *asaṅkhyeya*—innumerable; *viśeṣa*—particular; *nāma*—names; *rūpa*—forms; *ākṛtau*—possessing bodily features; *kavibhiḥ*—by great learned persons; *kalpitā*—imagined; *iyam*—this; *saṅkhyā*—number; *yayā*—by whom; *tattva*—of the truth; *dṛśā*—by knowledge; *apanīyate*—is extracted; *tasmai*—unto Him; *namaḥ*—respectful obeisances; *sāṅkhya-nidarśanāya*—who is the revealer of this numerical knowledge; *te*—unto You; *iti*—thus.

TRANSLATION

O my Lord, Your name, form and bodily features are expanded in countless forms. No one can determine exactly how many forms exist, yet You Yourself, in Your incarnation as the learned scholar Kapiladeva, have analyzed the cosmic manifestation as containing

twenty-four elements. Therefore if one is interested in Sāṅkhya philosophy, by which one can enumerate the different truths, he must hear it from You. Unfortunately, nondevotees simply count the different elements and remain ignorant of Your actual form. I offer my respectful obeisances unto You.

PURPORT

Philosophers and scientists have been trying to study the entire cosmic situation and have been theorizing and calculating in different ways for millions and millions of years. However, the speculative research work of a so-called scientist or philosopher is always interrupted when he dies, and the laws of nature go on without regard for his work.

For billions of years changes take place in the material creation, until at last the whole universe is dissolved and remains in an unmanifested state. Constant change and destruction (*bhūtvā bhūtvā pralīyate*) is perpetually going on in nature, yet the material scientists want to study natural laws without knowing the Supreme Personality of Godhead, who is the background of nature. As Kṛṣṇa states in *Bhagavad-gītā* (9.10):

mayādhyakṣeṇa prakṛtiḥ
sūyate sa-carācaram
hetunānena kaunteya
jagad viparivartate

"This material nature is working under My direction, O son of Kuntī, and it is producing all moving and unmoving beings. By its rule this manifestation is created and annihilated again and again."

Now the material creation is manifest, eventually it will be annihilated and remain for many millions of years in a dormant state, and finally it will again be created. This is the law of nature.

TEXT 34

उत्तरेषु च कुरुषु भगवान् यज्ञपुरुषः कृतवराहरूप आस्ते तं तु देवी हैषा भूः सह कुरुभिरस्खलितभक्तियोगेनोपधावति इमां च परमामुपनिषद-मावर्तयति ॥ ३४ ॥

uttareṣu ca kuruṣu bhagavān yajña-puruṣaḥ kṛta-varāha-rūpa āste taṁ tu devī haiṣā bhūḥ saha kurubhir askhalita-bhakti-yogenopadhāvati imāṁ ca paramām upaniṣadam āvartayati.

uttareṣu—on the northern side; *ca*—also; *kuruṣu*—in the tract of land known as Kuru; *bhagavān*—the Supreme Personality of Godhead; *yajña-puruṣaḥ*—who accepts all results of sacrifices; *kṛta-varāha-rūpaḥ*—having accepted the form of a boar; *āste*—exists eternally; *tam*—Him; *tu*—certainly; *devī*—the goddess; *ha*—certainly; *eṣā*—this; *bhūḥ*—planet earth; *saha*—along with; *kurubhiḥ*—the inhabitants of the land known as Kuru; *askhalita*—unfailing; *bhakti-yogena*—by devotional service; *upadhāvati*—worship; *imām*—this; *ca*—also; *paramām upaniṣadam*—the supreme *Upaniṣad* (the process by which one can approach the Lord); *āvartayati*—chants again and again for the purpose of practice.

TRANSLATION

Śukadeva Gosvāmī said: Dear King, the Supreme Lord in His boar incarnation, who accepts all sacrificial offerings, lives in the northern part of Jambūdvīpa. There, in the tract of land known as Uttarakuru-varṣa, mother earth and all the other inhabitants worship Him with unfailing devotional service by repeatedly chanting the following Upaniṣad mantra.

TEXT 35

ॐ नमो भगवते मन्त्रतत्त्वलिङ्गाय यज्ञक्रतवे महाध्वरावयवाय महापुरुषाय नमः कर्मशुक्लाय त्रियुगाय नमस्ते ॥३५॥

oṁ namo bhagavate mantra-tattva-liṅgāya yajña-kratave mahā-dhvarāvayavāya mahā-puruṣāya namaḥ karma-śuklāya tri-yugāya namas te.

om—O Lord; *namaḥ*—respectful obeisances; *bhagavate*—unto the Supreme Personality of Godhead; *mantra-tattva-liṅgāya*—who is understood in truth by different *mantras; yajña*—in the form of animal sacrifices; *kratave*—and animal sacrifice; *mahā-dhvara*—great sacrifices; *avayavāya*—whose limbs and bodily parts; *mahā-puruṣāya*—unto the Supreme Person; *namaḥ*—respectful obeisances; *karma-śuklāya*—who purifies the fruitive activities of the living entities; *tri-yugāya*—unto the Supreme Personality of Godhead, who is full with six opulences and who appears in three *yugas* (remaining concealed in the fourth *yuga*); *namaḥ*—my respectful obeisances; *te*—unto You.

TRANSLATION

O Lord, we offer our respectful obeisances unto You as the gigantic person. Simply by chanting mantras, we shall be able to understand You fully. You are yajña [sacrifice], and You are the kratu [ritual]. Therefore all the ritualistic ceremonies of sacrifice are part of Your transcendental body, and You are the only enjoyer of all sacrifices. Your form is composed of transcendental goodness. You are known as tri-yuga because in Kali-yuga You appeared as a concealed incarnation and because You always fully possess the three pairs of opulences.

PURPORT

Śrī Caitanya Mahāprabhu is the incarnation for this age of Kali, as confirmed in many places throughout the *Purāṇas*, the *Mahābhārata*, *Śrīmad-Bhāgavatam* and the *Upaniṣads*. The summary of His appearance is given in *Caitanya-caritāmṛta* (*Madhya* 6.99) as follows:

kali-yuge līlāvatāra nā kare bhagavān
ataeva 'tri-yuga' kari' kahi tāra nāma

In this age of Kali, the Supreme Personality of Godhead (Bhagavān) does not appear as a *līlāvatāra*, an incarnation to display pastimes. Therefore He is known as *tri-yuga*. Unlike other incarnations, Lord Śrī Caitanya Mahāprabhu appears in this age of Kali as a devotee of the Lord. Therefore He is called a concealed incarnation (*channāvatāra*).

TEXT 36

यस्य स्वरूपं कवयो विपश्चितो
गुणेषु दारुष्विव जातवेदसम् ।
मथ्नन्ति मथ्ना मनसा दिदृक्षवो
गूढं क्रियार्थैर्नम ईरितात्मने ॥३६॥

yasya svarūpaṁ kavayo vipaścito
guṇeṣu dāruṣv iva jāta-vedasam
mithnanti mathnā manasā didṛkṣavo
gūḍhaṁ kriyārthair nama īritātmane

yasya—whose; *sva-rūpam*—form; *kavayaḥ*—the greatly learned sages; *vipaścitaḥ*—expert in ascertaining the Absolute Truth; *guṇeṣu*—in the material manifestation, consisting of the three modes of nature; *dāruṣu*—in wood; *iva*—like; *jāta*—manifested; *vedasam*—fire; *mithnanti*—stir; *mathnā*—with a piece of wood used for producing fire; *manasā*—by the mind; *didṛkṣavaḥ*—who are inquisitive; *gūḍham*—hidden; *kriyā-arthaiḥ*—by fruitive activities and their results; *namaḥ*—respectful obeisances; *īrita-ātmane*—unto the Lord, who is manifested.

TRANSLATION

By manipulating a fire-generating stick, great saints and sages can bring forth the fire lying dormant within wood. In the same way, O Lord, those expert in understanding the Absolute Truth try to see You in everything—even in their own bodies. Yet you remain concealed. You are not to be understood by indirect processes involving mental or physical activities. Because You are self-manifested, only when You see that a person is wholeheartedly engaged in searching for You do You reveal Yourself. Therefore I offer my respectful obeisances unto You.

PURPORT

The word *kriyārthaiḥ* means "by performing ritualistic ceremonies to satisfy the demigods." The word *vipaścitaḥ* is explained in the *Taittirīya*

Upaniṣad as follows: *satyaṁ jñānam anantaṁ brahma. yo veda nihitaṁ guhāyāṁ parame vyoman. so 'śnute sarvān kāmān saha brahmaṇā vipaściteti.* As Kṛṣṇa states in *Bhagavad-gītā* (7.19), *bahūnāṁ janmanām ante jñānavān māṁ prapadyate:* "After many births and deaths, he who is actually in knowledge surrenders unto Me." When one understands that the Lord is situated in everyone's heart and actually sees the Lord present everywhere, he has perfect knowledge. The word *jāta-vedaḥ* means "fire which is produced by rubbing wood." In Vedic times, learned sages could bring forth fire from wood. *Jāta-vedaḥ* also indicates the fire in the stomach, which digests everything we eat and which produces an appetite. The word *gūḍha* is explained in the *Śvetāśvatara Upaniṣad. Eko devaḥ sarva-bhūteṣu gūḍhaḥ:* The Supreme Personality of Godhead is understood by chanting the Vedic *mantras. Sarva-vyāpī sarva-bhūtāntar-ātmā:* He is all-pervading, and He is within the heart of living entities. *Karmādhyakṣaḥ sarva-bhūtādhivāsaḥ:* He witnesses all activities of the living entity. *Sākṣī cetā kevalo nirguṇaś ca:* The Supreme Lord is the witness as well as the living force, yet He is transcendental to all material qualities.

TEXT 37

द्रव्यक्रियाहेत्वयनेशकर्तृभि-
मार्यागुणैर्वस्तुनिरीक्षितात्मने ।
अन्वीक्षयाङ्गातिशयात्मबुद्धिभि-
र्निरस्तमायाकृतये नमो नमः ॥३७॥

dravya-kriyā-hetv-ayaneśa-kartṛbhir
māyā-guṇair vastu-nirīkṣitātmane
anvīkṣayāṅgātiśayātma-buddhibhir
nirasta-māyākṛtaye namo namaḥ

dravya—by the objects of sense enjoyment; *kriyā*—the activities of the senses; *hetu*—the predominating deities of sensory activities; *ayana*—the body; *īśa*—the predominating time; *kartṛbhiḥ*—by false egotism; *māyā-guṇaiḥ*—by the modes of material nature; *vastu*—as a fact; *nirīkṣita*—being observed; *ātmane*—unto the Supreme Soul;

anvīkṣayā—by careful consideration; *aṅga*—by the limbs of yogic practice; *atiśaya-ātma-buddhibhiḥ*—by those whose intelligence has become fixed; *nirasta*—completely freed from; *māyā*—the illusory energy; *ākṛtaye*—whose form; *namaḥ*—all respectful obeisances; *namaḥ*—respectful obeisances.

TRANSLATION

The objects of material enjoyment [sound, form, taste, touch and smell], the activities of the senses, the controllers of sensory activities [the demigods], the body, eternal time and egotism are all creations of Your material energy. Those whose intelligence has become fixed by perfect execution of mystic yoga can see that all these elements result from the actions of Your external energy. They can also see Your transcendental form as Supersoul in the background of everything. Therefore I repeatedly offer my respectful obeisances unto You.

PURPORT

The objects of material enjoyment, the sensory activities, attachment to sensual pleasure, the body, false egotism and so on are produced by the Lord's external energy, *māyā*. The background of all these activities is the living being, and the director of the living beings is the Supersoul. The living being is not the all in all. He is directed by the Supersoul. In *Bhagavad-gītā* (15.15) Kṛṣṇa confirms this:

sarvasya cāhaṁ hṛdi sanniviṣṭo
mattaḥ smṛtir jñānam apohanaṁ ca

"I am seated in everyone's heart, and from Me come remembrance, knowledge and forgetfulness." The living entity depends on the Supersoul for directions. A person advanced in spiritual knowledge, or a person expert in the practice of mystic *yoga* (*yama*, *niyama*, *āsana* and so on) can understand transcendence either as Paramātmā or as the Supreme Personality of Godhead. The Supreme Lord is the original cause of all natural events. Therefore He is described as *sarva-kāraṇa-kāraṇam*, the cause of all causes. Behind everything visible to our material eyes is some cause, and one who can see the original cause of all causes, Lord Kṛṣṇa, can actually see. Kṛṣṇa, the *sac-cid-ānanda-vigraha*, is the background of everything, as He Himself confirms in *Bhagavad-gītā* (9.10):

mayādhyakṣeṇa prakṛtiḥ
sūyate sa-carācaram
hetunānena kaunteya
jagad viparivartate

"This material nature is working under My direction, O son of Kuntī, and it is producing all moving and unmoving beings. By its rule this manifestation is created and annihilated again and again."

TEXT 38

करोति विश्वस्थितिसंयमोदयं
यस्येप्सितं नेप्सितमीक्षितुर्गुणैः ।
माया यथायो भ्रमते तदाश्रयं
ग्राव्णो नमस्ते गुणकर्मसाक्षिणे ॥३८॥

karoti viśva-sthiti-saṁyamodayaṁ
yasyepsitaṁ nepsitam īkṣitur guṇaiḥ
māyā yathāyo bhramate tad-āśrayaṁ
grāvṇo namas te guṇa-karma-sākṣiṇe

karoti—performing; *viśva*—of the universe; *sthiti*—the maintenance; *saṁyama*—winding up; *udayam*—creation; *yasya*—of whom; *īpsitam*—desired; *na*—not; *īpsitam*—desired; *īkṣituḥ*—of the one glancing over; *guṇaiḥ*—with the modes of material nature; *māyā*—the material energy; *yathā*—as much as; *ayaḥ*—iron; *bhramate*—moves; *tat-āśrayam*—placed near that; *grāvṇaḥ*—a magnetic stone; *namaḥ*—my respectful obeisances; *te*—unto You; *guṇa-karma-sākṣiṇe*—the witness of the actions and reactions of material nature.

TRANSLATION

O Lord, You do not desire the creation, maintenance or annihilation of this material world, but You perform these activities for the conditioned souls by Your creative energy. Exactly as a piece of iron moves under the influence of a lodestone, inert matter moves when You glance over the total material energy.

PURPORT

Sometimes the question arises why the Supreme Lord has created this material world, which is so full of suffering for the living entities entrapped in it. The answer given herein is that the Supreme Personality of Godhead does not wish to create this material world just to inflict suffering on the living entities. The Supreme Lord creates this world only because the conditioned souls want to enjoy it.

The workings of nature are not going on automatically. It is only because the Lord glances over the material energy that it acts in wonderful ways, just as a lodestone causes a piece of iron to move here and there. Because materialistic scientists and so-called Sāṅkhya philosophers do not believe in God, they think that material nature is working without supervision. But that is not the fact. In *Caitanya-caritāmṛta* (*Ādi* 6.18-19) the creation of the material world is explained as follows:

yadyapi sāṅkhya māne 'pradhāna'—kāraṇa
jaḍa ha-ite kabhu nahe jagat-sṛjana

nija-sṛṣṭi-śakti prabhu sañcāre pradhāne
īśvarera śaktye tabe haye ta' nirmāṇe

"Atheistic Sāṅkhya philosophers think that the total material energy causes the cosmic manifestation, but they are wrong. Dead matter has no moving power, and therefore it cannot act independently. The Lord infuses the material ingredients with His own creative potency. Then, by the power of the Lord, matter moves and interacts." Sea waves are moved by the air, the air is created from ether, the ether is produced by the agitation of the three modes of material nature, and the three modes of material nature interact due to the Supreme Lord's glance over the total material energy. Therefore the background of all natural occurrences is the Supreme Personality of Godhead, as confirmed in *Bhagavad-gītā* (*mayādhyakṣeṇa prakṛtiḥ sūyate sa-carācaram*). This is also further explained in *Caitanya-caritāmṛta* (*Ādi* 5.59-61):

jagat-kāraṇa nahe prakṛti jaḍa-rūpā
śakti sañcāriyā tāre kṛṣṇa kare kṛpā

kṛṣṇa-śaktye prakṛti haya gauṇa kāraṇa
agni-śaktye lauha yaiche karaye jāraṇa

ataeva kṛṣṇa mūla-jagat-kāraṇa
prakṛti——kāraṇa yaiche ajā-gala-stana

"Because *prakṛti* [material nature] is dull and inert, it cannot actually be the cause of the material world. Lord Kṛṣṇa shows His mercy by infusing His energy into the dull, inert material nature. Thus *prakṛti*, by the energy of Lord Kṛṣṇa, becomes the secondary cause, just as iron becomes red-hot by the energy of fire. Therefore Lord Kṛṣṇa is the original cause of the cosmic manifestation. *Prakṛti* is like the nipples on the neck of a goat, for they cannot give any milk." Thus it is a great mistake on the part of the material scientists and philosophers to think that matter moves independently.

TEXT 39

प्रमथ्य दैत्यं प्रतिवारणं मृधे
यो मां रसाया जगदादिसूकरः ।
कृत्वाग्रदंष्ट्रे निरगादुदन्वतः
क्रीडन्निवेभः प्रणतास्मि तं विभुमिति ॥ ३९ ॥

pramathya daityaṁ prativāraṇaṁ mṛdhe
yo māṁ rasāyā jagad-ādi-sūkaraḥ
kṛtvāgra-daṁṣṭre niragād udanvataḥ
krīḍann ivebhaḥ praṇatāsmi taṁ vibhum iti

pramathya—after killing; *daityam*—the demon; *prativāraṇam*—most formidable opponent; *mṛdhe*—in the fight; *yaḥ*—He who; *mām*—me (the earth); *rasāyāḥ*—fallen to the bottom of the universe; *jagat*—in this material world; *ādi-sūkaraḥ*—the original form of a boar; *kṛtvā*—keeping it; *agra-daṁṣṭre*—on the end of the tusk; *niragāt*—came out of the water; *udanvataḥ*—from the Garbhodaka Ocean; *krīḍan*—playing; *iva*—like; *ibhaḥ*—elephant; *praṇatā asmi*—I bow down; *tam*—to Him; *vibhum*—the Supreme Lord; *iti*—thus.

TRANSLATION

My Lord, as the original boar within this universe, You fought and killed the great demon Hiraṇyakṣa. Then You lifted me [the earth] from the Garbhodaka Ocean on the end of Your tusk, exactly as a sporting elephant plucks a lotus flower from the water. I bow down before You.

Thus end the Bhaktivedanta purports of the Fifth Canto, Eighteenth Chapter of the Śrīmad-Bhāgavatam, *entitled, "The Prayers Offered to the Lord by the Residents of Jambūdvīpa."*

CHAPTER NINETEEN

A Description of the Island of Jambūdvīpa

This chapter describes the glories of Bhārata-varṣa, and it also describes how Lord Rāmacandra is being worshiped in the tract of land known as Kimpuruṣa-varṣa. The inhabitants of Kimpuruṣa-varṣa are fortunate because they worship Lord Rāmacandra with His faithful servant Hanumān. Lord Rāmacandra exemplifies an incarnation of Godhead who descends for the mission of *paritrāṇāya sādhūnāṁ vināśāya ca duṣkṛtām*—protecting the devotees and destroying the miscreants. Lord Rāmacandra exhibits the actual purpose of an incarnation of the Supreme Personality of Godhead, and the devotees take the opportunity to offer loving transcendental service to Him. One should surrender fully to the Lord, forgetting one's so-called material happiness, opulence and education, which are not at all useful for pleasing the Lord. The Lord is pleased only by the process of surrender unto Him.

When Devarṣi Nārada descended to instruct Sārvaṇi Manu, he described the opulence of Bhārata-varṣa, India. Sārvaṇi Manu and the inhabitants of Bhārata-varṣa engage in devotional service to the Supreme Personality of Godhead, who is the origin of creation, maintenance and annihilation and who is always worshiped by self-realized souls. In the planet known as Bhārata-varṣa there are many rivers and mountains, as there are in other tracts of land, yet Bhārata-varṣa has special significance because in this tract of land there exists the Vedic principle of *varṇāśrama-dharma*, which divides society into four *varṇas* and four *āśramas*. Furthermore, Nārada Muni's opinion is that even if there is some temporary disturbance in the execution of the *varṇāśrama-dharma* principles, they can be revived at any moment. The effect of adhering to the institution of *varṇāśrama* is gradual elevation to the spiritual platform and liberation from material bondage. By following the principles of *varṇāśrama-dharma*, one gets the opportunity to associate with devotees. Such association gradually awakens one's dormant propensity to serve the Supreme Personality of Godhead and frees one from all the basic principles of sinful life. One then gets the opportunity to offer unalloyed devotional service to the Supreme Lord, Vāsudeva. Because of this opportunity, the inhabitants of Bhārata-varṣa are praised even in the heavenly planets. Even in the topmost planet of this universe, Brahmaloka, the position of Bhārata-varṣa is discussed with great relish.

All the conditioned living entities are evolving within the universe in different planets and different species of life. Thus one may be elevated to Brahmaloka, but then one must again descend to earth, as confirmed in *Śrīmad Bhagavad-gītā* (*ābrahma-bhuvanāl lokāḥ punar āvartino 'rjuna*). If those who live in Bhārata-varṣa rigidly follow the principles of *varṇāśrama-dharma* and develop their dormant Kṛṣṇa consciousness, they need not return to this material world after death. Any place where one cannot hear about the Supreme Personality of Godhead from realized souls, even if it be Brahmaloka, is not very congenial to the living entity. If one who has taken birth in the land of Bhārata-varṣa as a human being does not take advantage of the opportunity for spiritual elevation, his position is certainly the most miserable. In the land known as Bhārata-varṣa, even if one is a *sarva-kāma-bhakta*, a devotee seeking the fulfillment of some material desire, he is freed from all material desires by his association with devotees, and ultimately he becomes a pure devotee and returns home, back to Godhead, without difficulty.

At the end of this chapter, Śrī Śukadeva Gosvāmī describes to Mahārāja Parīkṣit the eight sub-islands within the island of Jambūdvīpa.

TEXT 1

श्रीशुक उवाच

किम्पुरुषे वर्षे भगवन्तमादिपुरुषं लक्ष्मणाग्रजं सीताभिरामं रामं तच्चरण-
संनिकर्षाभिरतः परमभागवतो हनुमान् सह किम्पुरुषैरविरतभक्तिरुपास्ते ॥१॥

śrī-śuka uvāca
kimpuruṣe varṣe bhagavantam ādi-puruṣaṁ lakṣmaṇāgrajaṁ
sītābhirāmaṁ rāmaṁ tac-caraṇa-sannikarṣābhirataḥ parama-
bhāgavato hanumān saha kimpuruṣair avirata-bhaktir upāste.

śrī-śukaḥ uvāca—Śrī Śukadeva Gosvāmī continued to speak; *kimpuruṣe varṣe*—the tract of land known as Kimpuruṣa; *bhagavantam*—

the Supreme Personality of Godhead; *ādi-puruṣam*—the original cause of all causes; *lakṣmaṇa-agra-jam*—the elder brother of Lakṣmaṇa; *sītā-abhirāmam*—who is very pleasing to mother Sītā, or who is the husband of Sītādevī; *rāmam*—Lord Rāmacandra; *tat-caraṇa-sannikarṣa-abhirataḥ*—one always engaged in service at the lotus feet of Lord Rāmacandra; *parama-bhāgavataḥ*—the great devotee celebrated throughout the universe; *hanumān*—His Grace Hanumānjī; *saha*—with; *kimpuruṣaiḥ*—the inhabitants of the tract of land known as Kimpuruṣa; *avirata*—continuous; *bhaktiḥ*—who possesses devotional service; *upāste*—worships.

TRANSLATION

Śrīla Śukadeva Gosvāmī said: My dear King, in Kimpuruṣa-varṣa the great devotee Hanumān is always engaged with the inhabitants of that land in devotional service to Lord Rāmacandra, the elder brother of Lakṣmaṇa and dear husband of Sītādevī.

TEXT 2

आर्ष्टिषेणेन सह गन्धर्वैरनुगीयमानां परमकल्याणीं भर्तृभगवत्कथां
समुपशृणोति स्वयं चेदं गायति ॥ २ ॥

ārṣṭiṣeṇena saha gandharvair anugīyamānāṁ parama-kalyāṇīṁ
bhartṛ-bhagavat-kathāṁ samupaśṛṇoti svayaṁ cedaṁ gāyati.

ārṣṭi-ṣeṇena—Ārṣṭiṣeṇa, the chief personality of Kimpuruṣa-varṣa; *saha*—with; *gandharvaiḥ*—by a company of Gandharvas; *anugīyamānām*—being chanted; *parama-kalyāṇīm*—most auspicious; *bhartṛ-bhagavat-kathām*—the glories of his master, who is also the Supreme Personality of Godhead; *samupaśṛṇoti*—he hears with great attention; *svayam ca*—and personally; *idam*—this; *gāyati*—chants.

TRANSLATION

A host of Gandharvas is always engaged in chanting the glories of Lord Rāmacandra. That chanting is always extremely auspicious. Hanumānjī and Ārṣṭiṣeṇa, the chief person in

Kimpuruṣa-varṣa, constantly hear those glories with complete attention. Hanumān chants the following mantras.

PURPORT

In the *Purāṇas* there are two different opinions concerning Lord Rāmacandra. In the *Laghu-bhāgavatāmṛta* (5.34-36) this is confirmed in the description of the incarnation of Manu.

vāsudevādi-rūpāṇām
avatārāḥ prakīrtitāḥ
viṣṇu-dharmottare rāma-
lakṣmaṇādyāḥ kramādamī

pādme tu rāmo bhagavān
nārāyaṇa itīritaḥ
śeṣaś cakraṁ ca śaṅkhaś ca
kramāt syur lakṣmaṇādayaḥ

madhya-deśa-sthitāyodhyā-
pure 'sya vasatiḥ smṛtā
mahā-vaikuṇṭhaloke ca
rāghavedrasya kīrtitā

The *Viṣṇu-dharmottara* describes that Lord Rāmacandra and His brothers—Lakṣmaṇa, Bharata and Śatrughna—are incarnations of Vāsudeva, Saṅkarṣaṇa, Pradyumna and Aniruddha respectively. The *Padma Purāṇa*, however, says that Lord Rāmacandra is an incarnation of Nārāyaṇa and that the other three brothers are incarnations of Śeṣa, Cakra and Śaṅkha. Therefore Śrīla Baladeva Vidyābhūṣaṇa has concluded, *tad idaṁ kalpa-bhedenaiva sambhāvyam.* In other words, these opinions are not contradictory. In some millenniums Lord Rāmacandra and His brothers appear as incarnations of Vāsudeva, Saṅkarṣaṇa, Pradyumna and Aniruddha, and in other millenniums They appear as incarnations of Nārāyaṇa, Śeṣa, Cakra and Śaṅkha. The residence of Lord Rāmacandra on this planet is Ayodhyā. Ayodhyā City is still existing in the district of Hyderabad, which is situated on the northern side of Uttara Pradesh.

TEXT 3

ॐ नमो भगवते उत्तमश्लोकाय नम आर्यलक्षणशीलव्रताय नम उपशिक्षितात्मन उपासितलोकाय नमः साधुवादनिकषणाय नमो ब्रह्मण्यदेवाय महापुरुषाय महाराजाय नम इति ॥ ३ ॥

oṁ namo bhagavate uttamaślokāya nama ārya-lakṣaṇa-śīla-vratāya nama upaśikṣitātmana upāsita-lokāya namaḥ sādhu-vāda-nikaṣaṇāya namo brahmaṇya-devāya mahā-puruṣāya mahā-rājāya nama iti.

om—O my Lord; *namaḥ*—my respectful obeisances; *bhagavate*—unto the Supreme Personality of Godhead; *uttama-ślokāya*—who is always worshiped with selected verses; *namaḥ*—my respectful obeisances; *ārya-lakṣaṇa-śīla-vratāya*—who possesses all the good qualities of advanced personalities; *namaḥ*—my respectful obeisances; *upaśikṣita-ātmane*—unto You whose senses are under control; *upāsita-lokāya*—who is always remembered and worshiped by all the different classes of living entities; *namaḥ*—my respectful obeisances; *sādhu-vāda-nikaṣaṇāya*—to the Lord, who is like a stone for examining all the good qualities of a *sādhu; namaḥ*—my respectful obeisances; *brahmaṇya-devāya*—who is worshiped by the most qualified *brāhmaṇas; mahā-puruṣāya*—unto the Supreme Lord, who is worshiped by the *Puruṣa-sūkta* because of being the cause of this material creation; *mahā-rājāya*—unto the supreme king, or the king of all kings; *namaḥ*—my respectful obeisances; *iti*—thus.

TRANSLATION

Let me please Your Lordship by chanting the bīja-mantra oṁkāra. I wish to offer my respectful obeisances unto the Personality of Godhead, who is the best among the most highly elevated personalities. Your Lordship is the reservoir of all the good qualities of Āryans, people who are advanced. Your character and behavior are always consistent, and You always control Your senses and mind. Acting just like an ordinary human being, You exhibit exemplary character to teach others how to behave. There is a touchstone that can be used to examine the quality of gold, but You are like a touchstone that can verify all good qualities. You are

worshiped by brāhmaṇas who are the foremost of all devotees. You, the Supreme Person, are the King of kings, and therefore I offer my respectful obeisances unto You.

TEXT 4

यत्तद्विशुद्धानुभवमात्रमेकं
स्वतेजसा ध्वस्तगुणव्यवस्थम् ।
प्रत्यक् प्रशान्तं सुधियोपलम्भनं
ह्यनामरूपं निरहं प्रपद्ये ॥ ४ ॥

yat tad viśuddhānubhava-mātram ekaṁ
sva-tejasā dhvasta-guṇa-vyavastham
pratyak praśāntaṁ sudhiyopalambhanaṁ
hy anāma-rūpaṁ nirahaṁ prapadye

yat—which; *tat*—to that supreme truth; *viśuddha*—transcendentally pure, without contamination by material nature; *anubhava*—experience; *mātram*—that *sac-cid-ānanda* transcendental body; *ekam*—the one; *sva-tejasā*—by His own spiritual potency; *dhvasta*—vanquished; *guṇa-vyavastham*—the influence of the modes of material nature; *pratyak*—transcendental, not to be seen with material eyes; *praśāntam*—undisturbed by material agitation; *sudhiyā*—by Kṛṣṇa consciousness, or purified consciousness, uncontaminated by material desires, fruitive activities and speculative philosophy; *upalambhanam*—who can be achieved; *hi*—indeed; *anāma-rūpam*—without a material name and form; *niraham*—without a material ego; *prapadye*—let me offer my respectful obeisances.

TRANSLATION

The Lord, whose pure form [sac-cid-ānanda-vigraha] is uncontaminated by the modes of material nature, can be perceived by pure consciousness. In the Vedānta He is described as being one without a second. Because of His spiritual potency, He is untouched by the contamination of material nature, and because He is not subjected to material vision, He is known as transcendental.

He has no material activities, nor has He a material form or name. Only in pure consciousness, Kṛṣṇa consciousness, can one perceive the transcendental form of the Lord. Let us be firmly fixed at the lotus feet of Lord Rāmacandra, and let us offer our respectful obeisances unto those transcendental lotus feet.

PURPORT

The Supreme Personality of Godhead, Kṛṣṇa, appears in various expansions, as stated in the *Brahma-saṁhitā* (5.39):

rāmādi-mūrtiṣu kalā-niyamena tiṣṭhan
nānāvatāram akarod bhuvaneṣu kintu
kṛṣṇaḥ svayaṁ samabhavat paramaḥ pumān yo
govindam ādi-puruṣaṁ tam ahaṁ bhajāmi

"I worship the Supreme Personality of Godhead, Govinda, who is always situated in various incarnations such as Rāma, Nṛsiṁha and many subincarnations as well, but who is the original Personality of Godhead known as Kṛṣṇa and who incarnates personally also." Kṛṣṇa, who is *viṣṇu-tattva*, has expanded Himself in many Viṣṇu forms, of which Lord Rāmacandra is one. We know that the *viṣṇu-tattva* is carried by the transcendental bird Garuḍa and is equipped with different types of weapons in four hands. Therefore we may doubt whether Lord Rāmacandra could be in the same category, since He was carried by Hanumān, not by Garuḍa, and had neither four hands nor the *śaṅkha, cakra, gadā* and *padma*. Consequently this verse clarifies that Rāmacandra is as good as Kṛṣṇa (*rāmādi-mūrtiṣu kalā*). Although Kṛṣṇa is the original Supreme Personality of Godhead, Rāmacandra is not different from Him. Rāmacandra is unaffected by the modes of material nature, and therefore He is *praśānta*, never disturbed by those modes.

Unless one is saturated with love for the Supreme Personality of Godhead, one cannot appreciate the transcendental value of Lord Rāmacandra; one cannot see Him with material eyes. Because demons like Rāvaṇa have no spiritual vision, they consider Lord Rāmacandra an ordinary *kṣatriya* king. Rāvaṇa therefore attempted to kidnap Lord Rāmacandra's eternal consort, Sītādevī. Actually, however, Rāvaṇa could not carry off Sītādevī in her original form. As soon as she was touched by

Rāvaṇa's hands, she gave him a material form, but she maintained her original form beyond his vision. Therefore in this verse the words *pratyak praśāntam* indicate that Lord Rāmacandra and His potency, the goddess Sītā, keep themselves aloof from the influence of the material energy.

In the *Upaniṣads* it is said: *yam evaiṣa vṛṇute tena labhyaḥ.* The Supreme Lord, Paramātmā, the Personality of Godhead, can be seen or perceived only by persons who are saturated with devotional service. As stated in the *Brahma-saṁhitā* (5.38):

premāñjana-cchurita-bhakti-vilocanena
santaḥ sadaiva hṛdayeṣu vilokayanti
yaṁ śyāmasundaram acintya-guṇa-svarūpaṁ
govindam ādi-puruṣaṁ tam ahaṁ bhajāmi

"I worship the primeval Lord, Govinda, who is always seen by the devotee whose eyes are anointed with the pulp of love. He is seen in His eternal form of Śyāmasundara, situated within the heart of the devotee." Similarly, in the *Chāndogya Upaniṣad* it is stated, *etās tisro devatā anena jīvena.* In this verse of the *Chāndogya Upaniṣad* the word *anena* is used to distinguish the *ātmā* and Paramātmā as two separate identities. The words *tisro devatā* indicate that the body of the living entity is made of three material elements—fire, earth and water. Although the Paramātmā enters the heart of the *jīvātmā,* who is influenced and designated by a material body, the Paramātmā has nothing to do with the *jīvātmā's* body. Because the Paramātmā has no material connections, He is described here as *anāma-rūpaṁ niraham.* The Paramātmā has no material identity, whereas the *jīvātmā* does. The *jīvātmā* may introduce himself as an Indian, American, German and so on, but the Paramātmā has no such material designations, and therefore He has no material name. The *jīvātmā* is different from his name, but the Paramātmā is not; His name and He Himself are one and the same. This is the meaning of *niraham,* which means "without material designations." This word cannot possibly be twisted to mean that the Paramātmā has no *ahaṅkāra,* no "I-ness" or identity. He has His transcendental identity as the Supreme. This is the explanation given by Śrīla Jīva Gosvāmī. According to another interpretation, given by Viśvanātha Cakravartī Ṭhākura, *niraham* means *nirniścayena aham. Niraham* does not mean that the Supreme Lord has no identity. Rather, the stress given by the word *aham* proves strongly that He does have His personal identity because *nir* not only means "negative" but also means "strong ascertainment."

TEXT 5

मर्त्यावतारस्त्विह मर्त्यशिक्षणं
रक्षोवधायैव न केवलं विभोः ।
कुतोऽन्यथा स्याद्रमतः स्व आत्मनः
सीताकृतानि व्यसनानीश्वरस्य ॥ ५ ॥

martyāvatāras tv iha martya-śikṣaṇaṁ
rakṣo-vadhāyaiva na kevalaṁ vibhoḥ
kuto 'nyathā syād ramataḥ sva ātmanaḥ
sītā-kṛtāni vyasanānīśvarasya

martya—as a human being; *avatāraḥ*—whose incarnation; *tu*—however; *iha*—in the material world; *martya-śikṣaṇam*—for teaching all the living entities, especially human beings; *rakṣaḥ-vadhāya*—to kill the demon Rāvaṇa; *eva*—certainly; *na*—not; *kevalam*—only; *vibhoḥ*—of the Supreme Personality of Godhead; *kutaḥ*—from where; *anyathā*—otherwise; *syāt*—there would be; *ramataḥ*—of one enjoying; *sve*—in Himself; *ātmanaḥ*—the spiritual identity of the universe; *sītā*—of the wife of Lord Rāmacandra; *kṛtāni*—appearing due to the separation; *vyasanāni*—all the miseries; *īśvarasya*—of the Supreme Personality of Godhead.

TRANSLATION

It was ordained that Rāvaṇa, chief of the Rākṣasas, could not be killed by anyone but a man, and for this reason Lord Rāmacandra, the Supreme Personality of Godhead, appeared in the form of a human being. Lord Rāmacandra's mission, however, was not only to kill Rāvaṇa but also to teach mortal beings that material happiness centered around sex life or centered around one's wife is the cause of many miseries. He is the self-sufficient Supreme Personality of Godhead, and nothing is lamentable for Him.

Therefore why else could He be subjected to tribulations by the kidnapping of mother Sītā?

PURPORT

When the Lord appears in this universe in the form of a human being, He has two purposes, as stated in *Bhagavad-gītā* (4.9)—*paritrāṇāya sādhūnāṁ vināśāya ca duṣkṛtām:* to destroy the demons and protect the devotees. To protect the devotees, the Lord not only satisfies them by His personal presence but also teaches them so that they will not fall down from devotional service. By His personal example, Lord Rāmacandra taught the devotees that it is better not to enter married life, which is certainly followed by many tribulations. As confirmed in *Śrīmad-Bhāgavatam* (7.9.45):

yan maithunādi-gṛhamedhi-sukhaṁ hi tucchaṁ
kaṇḍūyanena karayor iva duḥkha-duḥkham
tṛpyanti neha kṛpaṇā bahu-duḥkha-bhājaḥ
kaṇḍūtivan manasijaṁ viṣaheta-dhīraḥ

Kṛpaṇas, those who are not advanced in spiritual knowledge and who are therefore just the opposite of *brāhmaṇas,* generally take to family life, which is a concession for sex. Thus they enjoy sex again and again, although that sex is followed by many tribulations. This is a warning to devotees. To teach this lesson to devotees and to human society in general, Lord Śrī Rāmacandra, although the Supreme Personality of Godhead Himself, underwent a series of tribulations because He accepted a wife, mother Sītā. Lord Rāmacandra underwent these austerities, of course, only to instruct us; actually He never has any reason to lament for anything.

Another aspect of the Lord's instructions is that one who accepts a wife must be a faithful husband and give her full protection. Human society is divided into two classes of men—those who strictly follow the religious principles and those who are devotees. By His personal example, Lord Rāmacandra wanted to instruct both of them how to fully adopt the discipline of the religious system and how to be a beloved and dutiful husband. Otherwise He had no reason to undergo apparent tribulations. One who strictly follows religious principles must not neglect to provide all facilities for the complete protection of his wife. There may be some suffering because of this, but one must nevertheless endure it. That is the duty of a faithful husband. By His personal example, Lord Rāmacandra demonstrated this duty. Lord Rāmacandra could have produced hundreds and thousands of Sītās from His pleasure energy, but just to show the duty of a faithful husband, He not only rescued Sītā from the hands of Rāvaṇa but also killed Rāvaṇa and all the members of his family.

Another aspect of the teachings of Lord Rāmacandra is that although Lord Viṣṇu, the Supreme Personality of Godhead, and His devotees may apparently suffer from material tribulations, they have nothing to do with such tribulations. They are *mukta-puruṣas*, liberated persons, under all circumstances. It is therefore said in the *Caitanya-bhāgavata:*

yata dekha vaiṣṇavera vyavahāra duḥkha
niścaya jāniha tāhā paramānanda-sukha

A Vaiṣṇava is always firmly situated in transcendental bliss because of engagement in devotional service. Although he may appear to suffer material pains, his position is called transcendental bliss in separation (*viraha*). The emotions a lover and beloved feel when separated from one another are actually very blissful, although apparently painful. Therefore the separation of Lord Rāmacandra from Sītādevī, as well as the consequent tribulation they suffered, is but another display of transcendental bliss. That is the opinion of Śrīla Viśvanātha Cakravartī Ṭhākura.

TEXT 6

न वै स आत्माऽऽत्मवतां सुहृत्तमः
सक्तस्त्रिलोक्यां भगवान् वासुदेवः ।
न स्त्रीकृतं कश्मलमश्नुवीत
न लक्ष्मणं चापि विहातुमर्हति ॥ ६ ॥

na vai sa ātmātmavatāṁ suhṛttamaḥ
saktas tri-lokyāṁ bhagavān vāsudevaḥ
na strī-kṛtaṁ kaśmalam aśnuvīta
na lakṣmaṇaṁ cāpi vihātum arhati

na—not; *vai*—indeed; *saḥ*—He; *ātmā*—the Supreme Soul; *ātmavatām*—of the self-realized souls; *suhṛt-tamaḥ*—the best friend; *saktaḥ*—attached; *tri-lokyām*—to anything within the three worlds; *bhagavān*—the Supreme Personality of Godhead; *vāsudevaḥ*—the all-pervading Lord; *na*—not; *strī-kṛtam*—obtained because of His wife; *kaśmalam*—sufferings of separation; *aśnuvīta*—would obtain; *na*—not; *lakṣmaṇam*—His younger brother Lakṣmaṇa; *ca*—also; *api*—certainly; *vihātum*—to give up; *arhati*—be able.

TRANSLATION

Since Lord Śrī Rāmacandra is the Supreme Personality of Godhead, Vāsudeva, He is not attached to anything in this material world. He is the most beloved Supersoul of all self-realized souls, and He is their very intimate friend. He is full of all opulences. Therefore He could not possibly have suffered because of separation from His wife, nor could He have given up His wife and Lakṣmaṇa, His younger brother. To give up either would have been absolutely impossible.

PURPORT

In defining the Supreme Personality of Godhead, we say that He is full in all six opulences—wealth, fame, strength, influence, beauty and renunciation. He is called renounced because He is not attached to anything in this material world; He is specifically attached to the spiritual world and the living entities there. The affairs of the material world take place under the superintendence of Durgādevī (*sṛṣṭi-sthiti-pralaya-sādhana-śaktir ekā/ chāyeva yasya bhuvanāni bibharti durgā*). Everything is going on under the strict rules and regulations of the material energy, represented by Durgā. Therefore the Lord is completely detached and need not give attention to the material world. Sītādevī belongs to the spiritual world. Similarly, Lord Lakṣmaṇa, Rāmacandra's younger brother, is a manifestation of Saṅkarṣaṇa, and Lord Rāmacandra Himself is Vāsudeva, the Supreme Personality of Godhead.

Since the Lord is always spiritually qualified, He is attached to servants who always render transcendental loving service unto Him. He is attached to the truth in life, not to brahminical qualities. Indeed, He is never attached to any material qualities. Although He is the Supersoul of all living entities, He is specifically manifest to those who are self-realized, and He is especially dear to the hearts of His transcendental devotees. Because Lord Rāmacandra descended to teach human society how dutiful a king should be, He apparently gave up the company of mother Sītā and Lakṣmaṇa. Factually, however, He could not have given them up. One should therefore learn about the activities of Lord Rāmacandra from a self-realized soul. Then one can understand the transcendental activities of the Lord.

TEXT 7

न जन्म नूनं महतो न सौभगं
न वाङ् न बुद्धिर्नाकृतिस्तोषहेतुः ।
तैर्यद्विसृष्टानपि नो वनौकस-
श्चकार सख्ये बत लक्ष्मणाग्रजः ॥ ७ ॥

na janma nūnaṁ mahato na saubhagaṁ
na vāṅ na buddhir nākṛtis toṣa-hetuḥ
tair yad visṛṣṭān api no vanaukasaś
cakāra sakhye bata lakṣmaṇāgrajaḥ

na—not; *janma*—birth in a very polished, aristocratic family; *nūnam*—indeed; *mahataḥ*—of the Supreme Personality of Godhead; *na*—nor; *saubhagam*—great fortune; *na*—nor; *vāk*—an elegant manner of speaking; *na*—nor; *buddhiḥ*—sharpness of intelligence; *na*—not; *ākṛtiḥ*—features of the body; *toṣa-hetuḥ*—the cause of pleasure to the Lord; *taiḥ*—by all those above-mentioned qualities; *yat*—because; *visṛṣṭān*—rejected; *api*—although; *naḥ*—us; *vana-okasaḥ*—the inhabitants of the forest; *cakāra*—accepted; *sakhye*—in friendship; *bata*—alas; *lakṣaṇa-agra-jaḥ*—Lord Śrī Rāmacandra, the elder brother of Lakṣmaṇa.

TRANSLATION

One cannot establish a friendship with the Supreme Lord Rāmacandra on the basis of material qualities such as one's birth in an aristocratic family, one's personal beauty, one's eloquence, one's sharp intelligence or one's superior race or nation. None of these

qualifications is actually a prerequisite for friendship with Lord Śrī Rāmacandra. Otherwise how is it possible that although we uncivilized inhabitants of the forest have not taken noble births, although we have no physical beauty and although we cannot speak like gentlemen, Lord Rāmacandra has nevertheless accepted us as friends?

PURPORT

In a prayer to Kṛṣṇa expressing her feelings, Śrīmatī Kuntīdevī called Him *akiñcana-gocara.* The prefix *a* means "not," and *kiñcana* "something of this material world." One may be very proud of his prestigious position, material wealth, beauty, education and so on, but although these are certainly good qualifications in material dealings, they are not necessary for achieving friendship with the Supreme Personality of Godhead. One who possesses all these material qualities is expected to become a devotee, and when he actually does, the qualities are properly utilized. Those who are puffed up by a high birth, wealth, education and personal beauty (*janmaiśvarya-śruta-śrī*) unfortunately do not care for developing Kṛṣṇa consciousness, nor does the Supreme Personality of Godhead care about all these material qualifications. The Supreme Lord is achieved by devotion (*bhaktyā mām abhijānāti*). One's devotion and sincere desire to serve the Supreme Personality of Godhead are the only qualifications. Rūpa Gosvāmī has also said that the price for achieving God's favor is simply one's sincere eagerness to have it (*laulyam ekaṁ mūlyam*). In the *Caitanya-bhāgavata* it is said:

kholāvecā sevakera dekha bhāgya-sīmā
brahmā śiva kāṅde yāra dekhiyā mahimā

dhane jane pāṇḍitye kṛṣṇa nāhi pāi
kevala bhaktira vaśa caitanya-gosāñi

"Behold the great fortune of the devotee Kholāvecā. Lord Brahmā and Śiva shed tears upon seeing his greatness. One cannot attain Lord Kṛṣṇa by any amount of wealth, followers, or learning. Śrī Caitanya Mahāprabhu is controlled only by pure devotion." Lord Śrī Caitanya Mahāprabhu had a very sincere devotee whose name was Kholāvecā

Śrīdhara and whose only business was to sell pots made of the skin of banana trees. Whatever income he had, he used fifty percent for the worship of mother Ganges, and with the other fifty percent he provided for his necessities. On the whole, he was so very poor that he lived in a cottage that had a broken roof with many holes in it. He could not afford brass utensils, and therefore he drank water from an iron pot. Nevertheless, he was a great devotee of Lord Śrī Caitanya Mahāprabhu. He is a typical example of how a poor man with no material possessions can become a most exalted devotee of the Lord. The conclusion is that one cannot attain shelter at the lotus feet of Lord Kṛṣṇa or Śrī Caitanya Gosāñi through material opulence; that shelter is attainable only by pure devotional service.

anyābhilāṣitā-śūnyaṁ
jñāna-karmādy-anāvṛtam
ānukūlyena kṛṣṇānu-
śīlanaṁ bhaktir uttamā

"One should render transcendental loving service to the Supreme Lord Kṛṣṇa favorably and without desire for material profit or gain through fruitive activities or philosophical speculation. That is called pure devotional service."

TEXT 8

सुरोऽसुरो वाप्यथ वानरो नरः
सर्वात्मना यः सुकृतज्ञमुत्तमम् ।
भजेत रामं मनुजाकृतिं हरिं
य उत्तराननयत्कोसलान्दिवमिति ॥ ८ ॥

suro 'suro vāpy atha vānaro naraḥ
sarvātmanā yaḥ sukṛtajñam uttamam
bhajeta rāmaṁ manujākṛtiṁ hariṁ
ya uttarān anayat kosalān divam iti

suraḥ—demigod; *asuraḥ*—demon; *vā api*—or; *atha*—therefore; *vā*—or; *anaraḥ*—other than a human being (bird, beast, animal and so on); *naraḥ*—a human being; *sarva-ātmanā*—wholeheartedly; *yaḥ*—

who; *su-kṛtajñam*—easily made grateful; *uttamam*—most highly elevated; *bhajeta*—should worship; *rāmam*—Lord Rāmacandra; *manuja-ākṛtim*—appearing as a human being; *harim*—the Supreme Personality of Godhead; *yaḥ*—who; *uttarān*—of northern India; *anayat*—brought back; *kosalān*—the inhabitants of Kosala-deśa, Ayodhyā; *divam*—to the spiritual world, Vaikuṇṭha; *iti*—thus.

TRANSLATION

Therefore, whether one is a demigod or a demon, a man or a creature other than man, such as a beast or bird, everyone should worship Lord Rāmacandra, the Supreme Personality of Godhead, who appears on this earth just like a human being. There is no need of great austerities or penances to worship the Lord, for He accepts even a small service offered by His devotee. Thus He is satisfied, and as soon as He is satisfied, the devotee is successful. Indeed, Lord Śrī Rāmacandra brought all the devotees of Ayodhyā back home, back to Godhead [Vaikuṇṭha].

PURPORT

Lord Śrī Rāmacandra is so kind and merciful to His devotees that He is very easily satisfied by a little service rendered by anyone, human or not. This is the special advantage of worshiping Lord Rāmacandra, and there is the same advantage in worshiping Lord Śrī Caitanya Mahāprabhu. Lord Kṛṣṇa and Lord Rāmacandra, in the manner of *kṣatriyas*, sometimes showed Their mercy by killing *asuras*, but Lord Śrī Caitanya Mahāprabhu awarded love of God without difficulty even to the *asuras*. All the incarnations of the Supreme Personality of Godhead—but especially Lord Rāmacandra, Lord Kṛṣṇa and, later, Lord Śrī Caitanya Mahāprabhu—delivered many of the living entities present before Them, indeed almost all of them. Śrī Caitanya Mahāprabhu is therefore represented in the six-armed form of *ṣaḍ-bhūja-mūrti*, which is a combination of Lord Rāmacandra, Lord Kṛṣṇa and Lord Śrī Caitanya Mahāprabhu. The best purpose of human life can be fulfilled by worshiping the *ṣaḍ-bhūja-mūrti*, the form of the Lord with six arms—two arms of Rāmacandra, two arms of Kṛṣṇa and two arms of Śrī Caitanya Mahāprabhu.

TEXT 9

भारतेऽपि वर्षे भगवान्नरनारायणाख्य आकल्पान्तमुपचितधर्मज्ञानवैराग्यै-
श्वर्योपशमोपरमात्मोपलम्भनमनुग्रहायात्मवतामनुकम्पया तपोऽव्यक्तगतिश्चरति
॥९॥

bhārate 'pi varṣe bhagavān nara-nārāyaṇākhya ākalpāntam upacita-dharma-jñāna-vairāgyaiśvaryopaśamoparamātmopalambhanam anugrahāyātmavatām anukampayā tapo 'vyakta-gatiś carati.

bhārate—in Bhārata; *api*—also; *varṣe*—the tract of land; *bhagavān*—the Supreme Personality of Godhead; *nara-nārāyaṇa-ākhyaḥ*—known as Nara-Nārāyaṇa; *ā-kalpa-antam*—up to the end of the millennium; *upacita*—increasing; *dharma*—religion; *jñāna*—knowledge; *vairāgya*—renunciation or nonattachment; *aiśvarya*—mystic opulences; *upaśama*—control of the senses; *uparama*—freedom from false ego; *ātma-upalambhanam*—self-realization; *anugrahāya*—to show favor; *ātma-vatām*—unto persons interested in self-realization; *anukampayā*—by causeless mercy; *tapaḥ*—austerities; *avyakta-gatiḥ*—whose glories are inconceivable; *carati*—executes.

TRANSLATION

[Śukadeva Gosvāmī continued:] The glories of the Supreme Personality of Godhead are inconceivable. He has appeared in the form of Nara-Nārāyaṇa in the land of Bhārata-varṣa, at the place known as Badarikāśrama, to favor His devotees by teaching them religion, knowledge, renunciation, spiritual power, sense control and freedom from false ego. He is advanced in the opulence of spiritual assets, and He engages in executing austerity until the end of this millennium. This is the process of self-realization.

PURPORT

People in India may visit the temple of Nara-Nārāyaṇa at Badarikāśrama just to learn how the Supreme Personality of Godhead in His incarnation as Nara-Nārāyaṇa engages in austerities to teach the people of the world how to achieve self-realization. It is impossible to realize oneself simply by absorbing oneself in speculation and material activities. One must be very serious about self-realization and the practice of austerity. Unfortunately, the people of this age of Kali do not even know the meaning of austerity. Under these circumstances, the Lord has appeared as Śrī Caitanya Mahāprabhu to bestow upon the fallen souls the easiest method of self-realization, technically called *ceto-darpaṇa-mārjanam,* cleansing of the dirt from the core of one's heart. This method is extremely simple. Anyone can chant the glorious *kṛṣṇa-saṅkīrtana*—Hare Kṛṣṇa, Hare Kṛṣṇa, Kṛṣṇa Kṛṣṇa, Hare Hare/ Hare Rāma, Hare Rāma, Rāma Rāma, Hare Hare. In this age there are different forms of so-called advanced scientific knowledge, such as anthropology, Marxism, Freudianism, nationalism and industrialism, but if we work very hard under their guidance instead of adopting the process practiced by Nara-Nārāyaṇa, we shall waste our valuable human form of life. Thus we shall certainly be cheated and misled.

TEXT 10

तं भगवान्नारदो वर्णाश्रमवतीभिर्भारतीभिः प्रजाभिर्भगवत्प्रोक्ताभ्यां सांख्ययोगाभ्यां भगवदनुभावोपवर्णनं सावर्णेरुपदेक्ष्यमाणः परम-भक्तिभावेनोपसरति इदं चाभिगृणाति ॥१०॥

taṁ bhagavān nārado varṇāśramavatībhir bhāratībhiḥ prajābhir bhagavat-proktābhyāṁ sāṅkhya-yogābhyāṁ bhagavad-anubhāvopavarṇanaṁ sāvarṇer upadekṣyamāṇaḥ parama-bhakti-bhāvenopasarati idaṁ cābhigṛṇāti.

tam—Him (Nara-Nārāyaṇa); *bhagavān*—the most powerful saintly person; *nāradaḥ*—the great sage Nārada; *varṇa-āśrama-vatībhiḥ*—by followers of the institution of the four *varṇas* and four *āśramas; bhāratībhiḥ*—of the land known as Bhārata-varṣa (India); *prajābhiḥ*—who are the inhabitants; *bhagavat-proktābhyām*—which was stated by the Supreme Personality of Godhead; *sāṅkhya*—by the *sāṅkhya-yoga* system (the analytical study of material conditions); *yogābhyām*—by practice of the *yoga* system; *bhagavat-anubhāva-upavarṇanam*—which describes the process of God realization; *sāvarṇeḥ*—unto Sāvarṇi Manu; *upadekṣyamāṇaḥ*—instructing; *parama-bhakti-bhāvena*—in greatly ecstatic loving service to the Lord; *upasarati*—serves the Lord; *idam*—this; *ca*—and; *abhigṛṇāti*—chants.

TRANSLATION

In his own book, known as Nārada Pañcarātra, Bhagavān Nārada has very vividly described how to work to achieve the ultimate goal of life—devotion—through knowledge and through execution of the mystic yoga system. He has also described the glories of the Lord, the Supreme Personality of Godhead. The great sage Nārada instructed the tenets of this transcendental literature to Sāvarṇi Manu in order to teach those inhabitants of Bhārata-varṣa who strictly follow the principles of varṇāśrama-dharma how to achieve the devotional service of the Lord. Thus Nārada Muni, along with the other inhabitants of Bhārata-varṣa, always engages in the service of Nara-Nārāyaṇa, and he chants as follows.

PURPORT

Śrī Caitanya Mahāprabhu has clearly declared:

bhārata-bhūmite haila manuṣya-janma yāra
janma sārthaka kari' kara para-upakāra

The real success or fulfillment of the mission of human life can be achieved in India, Bhārata-varṣa, because in Bhārata-varṣa the purpose of life and the method for achieving success are evident. People should take advantage of the opportunity afforded by Bhārata-varṣa, and this is especially so for those who are following the principles of *varṇāśrama-dharma.* If we do not take to the principles of *varṇāśrama-dharma* by accepting the four social orders (*brāhmaṇa, kṣatriya, vaiśya* and *śūdra*) and the four orders of spiritual life (*brahmacārī, gṛhastha, vānaprastha* and *sannyāsa*), there can be no question of success in life. Unfortunately, because of the influence of Kali-yuga, everything is now being lost. The inhabitants of Bhārata-varṣa are gradually becoming degraded *mlecchas* and *yavanas.* How then will they teach others? Therefore, this Kṛṣṇa consciousness movement has been started not only for the inhabitants of Bhārata-varṣa but for all the people of the world, as announced by Śrī Caitanya Mahāprabhu. There is still time, and if the inhabitants of

Bhārata-varṣa take this movement of Kṛṣṇa consciousness seriously, the entire world will be saved from gliding down to a hellish condition. The Kṛṣṇa consciousness movement follows the process of *pañcarātrika-vidhi* and that of *bhāgavata-vidhi* simultaneously, so that people can take advantage of the movement and make their lives successful.

TEXT 11

ॐ नमो भगवते उपशमशीलायोपरतानात्म्याय नमोऽकिञ्चनवित्ताय ऋषिऋषभाय नरनारायणाय परमहंसपरमगुरवे आत्मारामाधिपतये नमो नम इति ॥११॥

oṁ namo bhagavate upaśama-śīlāyoparatānātmyāya namo 'kiñcana-vittāya ṛṣi-ṛṣabhāya nara-nārāyaṇāya paramahaṁsa-parama-gurave ātmārāmādhipataye namo nama iti.

om—O Supreme Lord; *namaḥ*—my respectful obeisances; *bhagavate*—unto the Supreme Personality of Godhead; *upaśama-śīlāya*—who has mastered the senses; *uparata-anātmyāya*—having no attachment for this material world; *namaḥ*—my respectful obeisances; *akiñcana-vittāya*—unto the Supreme Personality of Godhead, who is the only asset of persons who have no material possessions; *ṛṣi-ṛṣabhāya*—the most exalted of saintly persons; *nara-nārāyaṇāya*—Nara-Nārāyaṇa; *paramahaṁsa-parama-gurave*—the most exalted spiritual master of all *paramahaṁsas,* liberated persons; *ātmārāma-adhipataye*—the best of self-realized persons; *namaḥ namaḥ*—my respectful obeisances again and again; *iti*—thus.

TRANSLATION

Let me offer my respectful obeisances unto Nara-Nārāyaṇa, the best of all saintly persons, the Supreme Personality of Godhead. He is the most self-controlled and self-realized, He is free from false prestige, and He is the asset of persons who have no material possessions. He is the spiritual master of all paramahaṁsas, who are the most exalted human beings, and He is the master of the self-realized. Let me offer my repeated obeisances at His lotus feet.

TEXT 12

गायति चेदम्—
कर्तास्य सर्गादिषु यो न बध्यते
न हन्यते देहगतोऽपि दैहिकैः ।
द्रष्टुर्न दृग्यस्य गुणैर्विदूष्यते
तस्मै नमोऽसक्तविविक्तसाक्षिणे ॥१२॥

gāyati cedam
kartāsya sargādiṣu yo na badhyate
na hanyate deha-gato 'pi daihikaiḥ
draṣṭur na dṛg yasya guṇair vidūṣyate
tasmai namo 'sakta-vivikta-sākṣiṇe

gāyati—he sings; *ca*—and; *idam*—this; *kartā*—the executor; *asya*—of this cosmic manifestation; *sarga-ādiṣu*—of the creation, maintenance and destruction; *yaḥ*—one who; *na badhyate*—is not attached as the creator, master or proprietor; *na*—not; *hanyate*—is victimized; *deha-gataḥ api*—although appearing as a human being; *daihikaiḥ*—by bodily tribulations such as hunger, thirst and fatigue; *draṣṭuḥ*—of Him who is the seer of everything; *na*—not; *dṛk*—the power of vision; *yasya*—of whom; *guṇaiḥ*—by the material qualities; *vidūṣyate*—is polluted; *tasmai*—unto Him; *namaḥ*—my respectful obeisances; *asakta*—unto the Supreme Person, who is unattached; *vivikta*—without affection; *sākṣiṇe*—the witness of everything.

TRANSLATION

Nārada, the most powerful saintly sage, also worships Nara-Nārāyaṇa by chanting the following mantra: The Supreme Personality of Godhead is the master of the creation, maintenance and annihilation of this visible cosmic manifestation, yet He is completely free from false prestige. Although to the foolish He appears to have accepted a material body like us, He is unaffected by bodily tribulations like hunger, thirst and fatigue. Although He is the witness who sees everything, His senses are unpolluted by the objects He sees. Let me offer my respectful obeisances unto that

unattached, pure witness of the world, the Supreme Soul, the Personality of Godhead.

PURPORT

The Supreme Personality of Godhead, Kṛṣṇa, is described as *sac-cid-ānanda-vigraha,* the body of eternity, transcendental bliss and full knowledge. Now in this verse He is more fully described. Kṛṣṇa is the creator of the entire cosmic manifestation, yet He is unattached to it. If we were to construct a very tall skyscraper, we would be very attached to it, but Kṛṣṇa is so renounced that although He has created everything, He is not attached to anything (*na badhyate*). Furthermore, although Kṛṣṇa has His transcendental form, *sac-cid-ānanda-vigraha,* He is not disturbed by the bodily necessities of life, which are called *daihika;* for example, He is never hungry, thirsty or fatigued (*na hanyate deha-gato 'pi daihikaiḥ*). Then again, since everything is Kṛṣṇa's property, He sees everything and is present everywhere, but because His body is transcendental, He is above vision, the objects of vision and the process of vision. When we see someone beautiful, we are attracted. The sight of a beautiful woman immediately attracts a man, and the sight of a man naturally attracts a woman. Kṛṣṇa, however, is transcendental to all these faults. Although He is the seer of everything, He is not afflicted with faulty vision (*na dṛg yasya guṇair vidūṣyate*). Therefore, although He is the witness and seer, He is aloof from all affection for the activities He sees. He is always unattached and separate; He is only a witness.

TEXT 13

इदं हि योगेश्वर योगनैपुणं
हिरण्यगर्भो भगवाञ्जगाद यत् ।
यदन्तकाले त्वयि निर्गुणे मनो
भक्त्या दधीतोज्झितदुष्कलेवरः ॥१३॥

idaṁ hi yogeśvara yoga-naipuṇaṁ
hiraṇyagarbho bhagavān jagāda yat
yad anta-kāle tvayi nirguṇe mano
bhaktyā dadhītojjhita-duṣkalevaraḥ

idam—this; *hi*—certainly; *yoga-īśvara*—O my Lord, master of all mystic power; *yoga-naipuṇam*—the expert process of executing yogic principles; *hiraṇya-garbhaḥ*—Lord Brahmā; *bhagavān*—the most powerful; *jagāda*—spoke; *yat*—which; *yat*—which; *anta-kāle*—at the time of death; *tvayi*—in You; *nirguṇe*—the transcendence; *manaḥ*—the mind; *bhaktyā*—with a devotional attitude; *dadhīta*—one should place; *ujjhita-duṣkalevaraḥ*—having given up his identification with the material body.

TRANSLATION

O my Lord, master of all mystic yoga, this is the explanation of the yogic process spoken of by Lord Brahmā [Hiraṇyagarbha], who is self-realized. At the time of death, all yogīs give up the material body with full detachment simply by placing their minds at Your lotus feet. That is the perfection of yoga.

PURPORT

Śrīla Madhvācārya says:

yasya samyag bhagavati
jñānaṁ bhaktis tathaiva ca
niścintas tasya mokṣaḥ syāt
sarva-pāpa-kṛto 'pi tu

"For one who very seriously practices devotional service during his lifetime in order to understand the constitutional position of the Supreme Personality of Godhead, liberation from this material world is guaranteed, even if he has previously been addicted to sinful habits." This is also confirmed in *Bhagavad-gītā:*

api cet sudurācāro
bhajate mām ananya bhāk
sādhur eva sa mantavyaḥ
samyag vyavasito hi saḥ

"Even if one commits the most abominable actions, if he is engaged in devotional service he is to be considered saintly because he is properly situated." (Bg. 9.30) The only purpose of life is to be fully absorbed in thoughts of Kṛṣṇa and His form, pastimes, activities and qualities. If one is able to think of Kṛṣṇa in this way, twenty-four hours a day, he is already liberated (*svarūpeṇa vyavasthitiḥ*). Whereas materialists are absorbed in material thoughts and activities, devotees, on the contrary, are always absorbed in thoughts of Kṛṣṇa and Kṛṣṇa's activities. Therefore they are already on the platform of liberation. One has to think of Kṛṣṇa with full absorption at the time of death. Then he will certainly return home, back to Godhead, without a doubt.

TEXT 14

यथैहिकामुष्मिककामलम्पटः
सुतेषु दारेषु धनेषु चिन्तयन् ।
शङ्केत विद्वान् कुकलेवरात्ययाद्
यस्तस्य यत्नः श्रम एव केवलम् ॥१४॥

yathaihikāmuṣmika-kāma-lampaṭaḥ
suteṣu dāreṣu dhaneṣu cintayan
śaṅketa vidvān kukalevarātyayād
yas tasya yatnaḥ śrama eva kevalam

yathā—as; *aihika*—in the present life; *amuṣmika*—in the expected future life; *kāma-lampaṭaḥ*—a person who is very attached to lusty desires for bodily enjoyment; *suteṣu*—children; *dāreṣu*—wife; *dhaneṣu*—wealth; *cintayan*—thinking about; *śaṅketa*—is afraid; *vidvān*—a person advanced in spiritual knowledge; *ku-kalevara*—of this body, which is full of stool and urine; *atyayāt*—because of loss; *yaḥ*—anyone; *tasya*—his; *yatnaḥ*—endeavors; *śramaḥ*—a waste of time and energy; *eva*—certainly; *kevalam*—only.

TRANSLATION

Materialists are generally very attached to their present bodily comforts and to the bodily comforts they expect in the future. Therefore they are always absorbed in thoughts of their wives, children and wealth and are afraid of giving up their bodies, which

are full of stool and urine. If a person engaged in Kṛṣṇa consciousness, however, is also afraid of giving up his body, what is the use of his having labored to study the śāstras? It was simply a waste of time.

PURPORT

At the time of death a materialist thinks of his wife and children. He is absorbed in thinking of how they will live and who will take care of them after he leaves. Consequently he is never prepared to give up his body; rather, he wants to continue to live in his body to serve his society, family, friends and so on. Therefore by practicing the mystic *yoga* system one must become detached from bodily relationships. If despite practicing *bhakti-yoga* and studying all the Vedic literature, one is afraid of giving up his bad body, which is the cause of all his suffering, what is the use of his attempts to advance in spiritual life? The secret of success in practicing *yoga* is to become free from bodily attachments. Śrīla Narottama dāsa Ṭhākura says, *deha-smṛti nāhi yāra, saṁsāra-bandhana kāhāṅ tāra:* one whose practice has freed him from the anxieties of bodily needs is no longer in conditional life. Such a person is freed from conditional bondage. A person in Kṛṣṇa consciousness must fully discharge his devotional duties without material attachment. Then his liberation is guaranteed.

TEXT 15

तन्नः प्रभो त्वं कुकलेवरार्पितां
त्वन्माययाहंममतामधोक्षज ।
भिन्द्याम येनाशु वयं सुदुर्भिदां
विधेहि योगं त्वयि नः स्वभावमिति ॥१५॥

tan naḥ prabho tvaṁ kukalevarārpitāṁ
tvan-māyayāhaṁ-mamatām adhokṣaja
bhindyāma yenāśu vayaṁ sudurbhidāṁ
vidhehi yogaṁ tvayi naḥ svabhāvam iti

tat—therefore; *naḥ*—our; *prabho*—O my Lord; *tvam*—You; *kukalevara-arpitām*—invested in this bad body full of stool and urine;

tvat-māyayā—by Your illusory energy; *aham-mamatām*—the conception of "I and my"; *adhokṣaja*—O Transcendence; *bhindyāma*—may give up; *yena*—by which; *āśu*—very soon; *vayam*—we; *sudurbhidām*—which is very difficult to give up; *vidhehi*—please give; *yogam*—the mystic process; *tvayi*—unto You; *naḥ*—our; *svabhāvam*—which is symptomized by a steady mind; *iti*—thus.

TRANSLATION

Therefore, O Lord, O Transcendence, kindly help us by giving us the power to execute bhakti-yoga so that we can control our restless minds and fix them upon You. We are all infected by Your illusory energy; therefore we are very attached to the body, which is full of stool and urine, and to anything related with the body. Except for devotional service, there is no way to give up this attachment. Therefore kindly bestow upon us this benediction.

PURPORT

The Lord advises in *Bhagavad-gītā: man-manā bhava mad-bhakto mad-yājī māṁ namaskuru.* The perfect *yoga* system consists of always thinking of Kṛṣṇa, always engaging in devotional service, always worshiping Kṛṣṇa and always offering obeisances unto Him. Unless we practice this *yoga* system, our illusory attachment for this bad body, which is full of stool and urine, is impossible to give up. The perfection of *yoga* consists of giving up attachment for this body and bodily relationships and transferring that attachment to Kṛṣṇa. We are very attached to material enjoyment, but when we transfer that same attachment to Kṛṣṇa, we traverse the path of liberation. One has to practice this *yoga* system and none other.

TEXT 16

भारतेऽप्यस्मिन् वर्षे सरिच्छैलाः सन्ति बहवो मलयो मङ्गलप्रस्थो
मैनाकस्त्रिकूट ऋषभः कूटकः कोल्लकः सह्यो देवगिरिर्ऋष्यमूकः श्रीशैलो
वेङ्कटो महेन्द्रो वारिधारो विन्ध्यः शुक्तिमानृक्षगिरिः पारियात्रो
द्रोणश्चित्रकूटो गोवर्धनो रैवतकः ककुभो नीलो गोकामुख इन्द्रकीलः

कामगिरिरिति चान्ये च शतसहस्रशः शैलास्तेषां नितम्बप्रभवा नदा नद्यश्च सन्त्यसङ्ख्याताः ॥१६॥

bhārate 'py asmin varṣe saric-chailāḥ santi bahavo malayo maṅgala-prastho mainākas trikūṭa ṛṣabhaḥ kūṭakaḥ kollakaḥ sahyo devagirir ṛṣyamūkaḥ śrī-śailo veṅkaṭo mahendro vāridhāro vindhyaḥ śuktimān ṛkṣagiriḥ pāriyātro droṇaś citrakūṭo govardhano raivatakaḥ kakubho nīlo gokāmukha indrakīlaḥ kāmagirir iti cānye ca śata-sahasraśaḥ śailās teṣāṁ nitamba-prabhavā nadā nadyaś ca santy asaṅkhyātāḥ.

bhārate—in the land of Bhārata-varṣa; *api*—also; *asmin*—in this; *varṣe*—tract of land; *sarit*—rivers; *śailāḥ*—mountains; *santi*—there are; *bahavaḥ*—many; *malayaḥ*—Malaya; *maṅgala-prasthaḥ*—Maṅgala-prastha; *mainākaḥ*—Maināka; *tri-kūṭaḥ*—Trikūṭa; *ṛṣabhaḥ*—Ṛṣabha; *kūṭakaḥ*—Kūṭaka; *kollakaḥ*—Kollaka; *sahyaḥ*—Sahya; *deva-giriḥ*—Devagiri; *ṛṣya-mūkaḥ*—Ṛṣyamūka; *śrī-śailaḥ*—Śrī-śaila; *veṅkaṭaḥ*—Veṅkaṭa; *mahendraḥ*—Mahendra; *vāri-dhāraḥ*—Vāridhāra; *vindhyaḥ*—Vindhya; *śuktimān*—Śuktimān; *ṛkṣa-giriḥ*—Ṛkṣagiri; *pāriyātraḥ*—Pāriyātra; *droṇaḥ*—Droṇa; *citra-kūṭaḥ*—Citrakūṭa; *govardhanaḥ*—Govardhana; *raivatakaḥ*—Raivataka; *kakubhaḥ*—Kakubha; *nīlaḥ*—Nīla; *gokāmukhaḥ*—Gokāmukha; *in-drakīlaḥ*—Indrakīla; *kāma-giriḥ*—Kāmagiri; *iti*—thus; *ca*—and; *anye*—others; *ca*—also; *śata-sahasraśaḥ*—many hundreds and thousands; *śailāḥ*—mountains; *teṣām*—of them; *nitamba-prabhavāḥ*—born of the slopes; *nadāḥ*—big rivers; *nadyaḥ*—small rivers; *ca*—and; *santi*—there are; *asaṅkhyātāḥ*—innumerable.

TRANSLATION

In the tract of land known as Bhārata-varṣa, as in Ilāvṛta-varṣa, there are many mountains and rivers. Some of the mountains are known as Malaya, Maṅgala-prastha, Maināka, Trikūṭa, Ṛṣabha, Kūṭaka, Kollaka, Sahya, Devagiri, Ṛṣyamūka, Śrī-śaila, Veṅkaṭa, Mahendra, Vāridhāra, Vindhya, Śuktimān, Ṛkṣagiri, Pāriyātra, Droṇa, Citrakūṭa, Govardhana, Raivataka, Kakubha, Nīla, Gokāmukha, Indrakīla and Kāmagiri. Besides these, there are many other hills, with many large and small rivers flowing from their slopes.

TEXTS 17-18

एतासामपो भारत्यः प्रजा नामभिरेव पुनन्तीनामात्मना चोपस्पृशन्ति
॥१७॥ चन्द्रवसा ताम्रपर्णी अवटोदा कृतमाला वैहायसी कावेरी वेणी
पयस्विनी शर्करावर्ता तुङ्गभद्रा कृष्णा वेण्या भीमरथी गोदावरी निर्विन्ध्या
पयोष्णी तापी रेवा सुरसा नर्मदा चर्मण्वती सिन्धुरन्धः शोणश्च नदौ
महानदी वेदस्मृतिर्ऋषिकुल्या त्रिसामा कौशिकी मन्दाकिनी यमुना सरस्वती
दृषद्वती गोमती सरयू रोधस्वती सप्तवती सुषोमा शतद्रूश्चन्द्रभागा मरुद्वृधा
वितस्ता असिक्नी विश्वेति महानद्यः ॥१८॥

etāsām apo bhāratyaḥ prajā nāmabhir eva punantīnām ātmanā copaspṛśanti. candravasā tāmraparṇī avaṭodā kṛtamālā vaihāyasī kāverī veṇī payasvinī śarkarāvartā tuṅgabhadrā kṛṣṇāveṇyā bhīmarathī godāvarī nirvindhyā payoṣṇī tāpī revā surasā narmadā carmaṇvatī sindhur andhaḥ śoṇaś ca nadau mahānadī vedasmṛtir ṛṣikulyā trisāmā kauśikī mandākinī yamunā sarasvatī dṛṣadvatī gomatī sarayū rodhasvatī saptavatī suṣomā śatadrūś candrabhāgā marudvṛdhā vitastā asiknī viśveti mahā-nadyaḥ.

etāsām—of all these; *apaḥ*—water; *bhāratyaḥ*—of Bhārata-varṣa (India); *prajāḥ*—the residents; *nāmabhiḥ*—by the names; *eva*—only; *punantīnām*—are purifying; *ātmanā*—by the mind; *ca*—also; *upaspṛśanti*—touch; *candra-vasā*—Candravasā; *tāmra-parṇī*—Tāmraparṇī; *avaṭodā*—Avaṭodā; *kṛta-mālā*—Kṛtamālā; *vaihāyasī*—Vaihāyasī; *kāverī*—Kāverī; *veṇī*—Veṇī; *payasvinī*—Payasvinī; *śarkarāvartā*—Śarkarāvartā; *tuṅga-bhadrā*—Tuṅgabhadrā; *kṛṣṇā-veṇyā*—Kṛṣṇāveṇyā; *bhīma-rathī*—Bhīmarathī; *godāvarī*—Godāvarī; *nirvindhyā*—Nirvindhyā; *payoṣṇī*—Payoṣṇī; *tāpī*—Tāpī; *revā*—Revā; *surasā*—Surasā; *narmadā*—Narmadā; *carmaṇvatī*—Carmaṇvatī; *sindhuḥ*—Sindhu; *andhaḥ*—Andha; *śoṇaḥ*—Śoṇa; *ca*—and; *nadau*—two rivers; *mahā-nadī*—Mahānadī; *veda-smṛtiḥ*—Vedasmṛti; *ṛṣi-kulyā*—Ṛṣikulyā; *tri-sāmā*—Trisāmā; *kauśikī*—Kauśikī; *mandākinī*—Mandākinī; *yamunā*—Yamunā; *sarasvatī*—Sarasvatī; *dṛṣadvatī*—Dṛṣadvatī; *gomatī*—Gomatī; *sarayū*—Sarayū; *rodhasvatī*—Rodhasvatī; *saptavatī*—Saptavatī; *suṣomā*—Suṣomā; *śata-drūḥ*—Śatadrū; *candra-*

bhāgā—Candrabhāgā; *marudvṛdhā*—Marudvṛdhā; *vitastā*—Vitastā; *asiknī*—Asiknī; *viśvā*—Viśvā; *iti*—thus; *mahā-nadyaḥ*—big rivers.

TRANSLATION

Two of the rivers—the Brahmaputra and the Śoṇa—are called nadas, or main rivers. These are other great rivers that are very prominent: Candravasā, Tāmraparṇī, Avaṭodā, Kṛtamālā, Vaihāyasī, Kāverī, Veṇī, Payasvinī, Śarkarāvartā, Tuṅgabhadrā, Kṛṣṇāveṇyā, Bhīmarathī, Godāvarī, Nirvindhyā, Payoṣṇī, Tāpī, Revā, Surasā, Narmadā, Carmaṇvatī, Mahānadī, Vedasmṛti, Ṛṣikulyā, Trisāmā, Kauśikī, Mandākinī, Yamunā, Sarasvatī, Dṛṣadvatī, Gomatī, Sarayū, Rodhasvatī, Saptavatī, Suṣomā, Śatadrū, Candrabhāgā, Marudvṛdhā, Vitastā, Asiknī and Viśvā. The inhabitants of Bhārata-varṣa are purified because they always remember these rivers. Sometimes they chant the names of these rivers as mantras, and sometimes they go directly to the rivers to touch them and bathe in them. Thus the inhabitants of Bhārata-varṣa become purified.

PURPORT

All these rivers are transcendental. Therefore one can be purified by remembering them, touching them or bathing in them. This practice is still going on.

TEXT 19

अस्मिन्नेव वर्षे पुरुषैर्लब्धजन्मभिः शुक्ललोहितकृष्णवर्णेन स्वारब्धेन कर्मणा दिव्यमानुषनारकगतयो बह्व्य आत्मन आनुपूर्व्येण सर्वा ह्येव सर्वेषां विधीयन्ते यथावर्णविधानमपवर्गश्चापि भवति ॥१९॥

asminn eva varṣe puruṣair labdha-janmabhiḥ śukla-lohita-kṛṣṇa-varṇena svārabdhena karmaṇā divya-mānuṣa-nāraka-gatayo bahvya ātmana ānupūrvyeṇa sarvā hy eva sarveṣāṁ vidhīyante yathā-varṇa-vidhānam apavargaś cāpi bhavati.

asmin eva varṣe—in this tract of land (Bhārata-varṣa); *puruṣaiḥ*—by the people; *labdha-janmabhiḥ*—who have taken birth; *śukla*—of the mode of goodness; *lohita*—of the mode of passion; *kṛṣṇa*—of the mode of ignorance; *varṇena*—according to the division; *sva*—by himself; *ārabdhena*—begun; *karmaṇā*—by activities; *divya*—divine; *mānuṣa*—human; *nāraka*—hellish; *gatayaḥ*—goals; *bahvyaḥ*—many; *ātmanaḥ*—of his own; *ānupūrvyeṇa*—according to acts performed previously; *sarvāḥ*—all; *hi*—certainly; *eva*—indeed; *sarveṣām*—of all of them; *vidhīyante*—are allotted; *yathā-varṇa-vidhānam*—in terms of different castes; *apavargaḥ*—the path of liberation; *ca*—and; *api*—also; *bhavati*—is possible.

TRANSLATION

The people who take birth in this tract of land are divided according to the qualities of material nature—the modes of goodness [sattva-guṇa], passion [rajo-guṇa], and ignorance [tamo-guṇa]. Some of them are born as exalted personalities, some are ordinary human beings, and some are extremely abominable, for in Bhārata-varṣa one takes birth exactly according to one's past karma. If one's position is ascertained by a bona fide spiritual master and one is properly trained to engage in the service of Lord Viṣṇu according to the four social divisions [brāhmaṇa, kṣatriya, vaiśya and śūdra] and the four spiritual divisions [brahmacārī, gṛhastha, vānaprastha and sannyāsa], one's life becomes perfect.

PURPORT

For further information, one should refer to *Bhagavad-gītā* (14.18 and 18.42-45). Śrīla Rāmānujācārya writes in his book *Vedānta-saṅgraha:*

evaṁ-vidha-parābhakti-svarūpa-jñāna-viśeṣasyotpādakaḥ pūrvoktāharahar upacīyamāna-jñāna-pūrvaka-karmānugṛhīta-bhakti-yoga eva; yathoktaṁ bhagavatā parāśareṇa——varṇāśrameti. nikhila-jagad-uddhāraṇāyāvanitale 'vatīrṇaṁ para-brahma-bhūtaḥ puruṣottamaḥ svayam etad uktavān——"svakarma-nirataḥ siddhiṁ yathā vindati tac chṛṇu" "yataḥ pravṛttir bhūtānāṁ yena sarvam idaṁ tatam/ svakarmaṇā tam abhyarcya siddhiṁ vindati mānavaḥ"

Quoting from the *Viṣṇu Purāṇa* (389), the great sage Parāśara Muni has recommended:

varṇāśramācāravatā
puruṣeṇa paraḥ pumān
viṣṇur ārādhyate panthā
nānyat tat-toṣa-kāraṇam

"The Supreme Personality of Godhead, Lord Viṣṇu, is worshiped by the proper execution of prescribed duties in the system of *varṇa* and *āśrama*. There is no other way to satisfy the Lord." In the land of Bhārata-varṣa, the institution of *varṇāśrama-dharma* may be easily adopted. At the present moment, certain demoniac sections of the population of Bhārata-varṣa are disregarding the system of *varṇāśrama-dharma*. Because there is no institution to teach people how to become *brāhmaṇas*, *kṣatriyas*, *vaiśyas* and *śūdras* or *brahmacārīs*, *gṛhasthas*, *vānaprasthas* and *sannyāsīs*, these demons want a classless society. This is resulting in chaotic conditions. In the name of secular government, unqualified people are taking the supreme governmental posts. No one is being trained to act according to the principles of *varṇāśrama-dharma*, and thus people are becoming increasingly degraded and are heading in the direction of animal life. The real aim of life is liberation, but unfortunately the opportunity for liberation is being denied to people in general, and therefore their human lives are being spoiled. The Kṛṣṇa consciousness movement, however, is being propagated all over the world to reestablish the *varṇāśrama-dharma* system and thus save human society from gliding down to hellish life.

TEXT 20

योऽसौ भगवति सर्वभूतात्मन्यनात्म्येऽनिरुक्तेऽनिलयने परमात्मनि वासुदेवे-
ऽनन्यनिमित्तभक्तियोगलक्षणो नानागतिनिमित्ताविद्याग्रन्थिरन्धनद्वारेण
यदा हि महापुरुषपुरुषप्रसङ्गः ॥ २० ॥

yo 'sau bhagavati sarva-bhūtātmany anātmye 'nirukte 'nilayane paramātmani vāsudeve 'nanya-nimitta-bhakti-yoga-lakṣaṇo nānā-gati-nimittāvidyā-granthi-randhana-dvāreṇa yadā hi mahā-puruṣa-puruṣa-prasaṅgaḥ

yaḥ—anyone who; *asau*—that; *bhagavati*—unto the Supreme Personality of Godhead; *sarva-bhūta-ātmani*—the Supersoul of all living entities; *anātmye*—having no attachment; *anirukte*—who is beyond the mind and speech; *anilayane*—not dependent on anything else; *parama-ātmani*—unto the Supreme Soul; *vāsudeve*—Lord Vāsudeva, the son of Vasudeva; *ananya*—without any other; *nimitta*—cause; *bhakti-yoga-lakṣaṇaḥ*—having symptoms of pure devotional service; *nānā-gati*—of varied destinations; *nimitta*—the cause; *avidyā-granthi*—the bondage of ignorance; *randhana*—of cutting; *dvāreṇa*—by means; *yadā*—when; *hi*—indeed; *mahā-puruṣa*—of the Supreme Personality of Godhead; *puruṣa*—with the devotee; *prasaṅgaḥ*—an intimate relationship.

TRANSLATION

After many, many births, when the results of one's pious activities mature, one gets an opportunity to associate with pure devotees. Then one is able to cut the knot of bondage to ignorance, which bound him because of varied fruitive activities. As a result of associating with devotees, one gradually renders service to Lord Vāsudeva, who is transcendental, free from attachment to the material world, beyond the mind and words, and independent of everything else. That bhakti-yoga, devotional service to Lord Vāsudeva, is the real path of liberation.

PURPORT

Brahman realization is the beginning of liberation, and Paramātmā realization is still further advancement toward the realm of liberation, but one achieves real liberation when he understands his position as an eternal servant of the Supreme Personality of Godhead (*muktir hitvānyathā rūpaṁ svarūpeṇa vyavasthitiḥ*). In the material world, in the bodily concept of life, everyone is working in the wrong direction. When one becomes *brahma-bhūta,* spiritually realized, one understands that he is not the body and that working in the bodily concept of life is useless and misdirected. Then his devotional service begins. As Kṛṣṇa says in *Bhagavad-gītā* (18.54):

brahma-bhūtaḥ prasannātmā
na śocati na kāṅkṣati
samaḥ sarveṣu bhūteṣu
mad-bhaktiṁ labhate parām

"One who is thus transcendentally situated realizes the Supreme Brahman and becomes fully joyful. He never laments or desires to have anything; he is equally disposed to every living entity. In that state he attains pure devotional service unto Me." Devotional service is actual liberation. When one is attracted by the beauty of the Supreme Personality of Godhead and his mind is always engaged at the Lord's lotus feet, he is no longer interested in subjects that do not help him in self-realization. In other words, he loses all attraction for material activities. In the *Taittirīya Upaniṣad* (2.7) it is said: *eṣa hy evānandayati. yadā hy evaiṣa etasmin na dṛśye 'nātmye anirukte 'nilayane 'bhayaṁ pratiṣṭhāṁ vindate 'tha so 'bhayaṁ gato bhavati.* A living entity becomes established in spiritual, blissful life when he fully understands that his happiness depends on spiritual self-realization, which is the basic principle of *ānanda* (bliss), and when he is eternally situated in the service of the Lord, who has no other lord above Him.

TEXT 21

एतद्देव हि देवा गायन्ति—
अहो अमीषां किमकारि शोभनं
प्रसन्न एषां स्विदुत स्वयं हरिः ।
यैर्जन्म लब्धं नृषु भारताजिरे
मुकुन्दसेवौपयिकं स्पृहा हि नः ॥२१॥

etad eva hi devā gāyanti—
aho amīṣāṁ kim akāri śobhanaṁ
prasanna eṣāṁ svid uta svayaṁ hariḥ
yair janma labdhaṁ nṛṣu bhāratājire
mukunda-sevaupayikaṁ spṛhā hi naḥ

etat—this; *eva*—indeed; *hi*—certainly; *devāḥ*—all the demigods; *gāyanti*—chant; *aho*—oh; *amīṣām*—of these inhabitants of Bhārata-varṣa; *kim*—what; *akāri*—was done; *śobhanam*—pious, beautiful activities; *prasannaḥ*—pleased; *eṣām*—upon them; *svit*—or; *uta*—it is said; *svayam*—personally; *hariḥ*—the Supreme Personality of Godhead; *yaiḥ*—by whom; *janma*—birth; *labdham*—obtained; *nṛṣu*—in human society; *bhārata-ajire*—in the courtyard of Bhārata-varṣa; *mukunda*—the Supreme Personality of Godhead, who can offer liberation; *sevā-aupayikam*—which is the means of serving; *spṛhā*—desire; *hi*—indeed; *naḥ*—our.

TRANSLATION

Since the human form of life is the sublime position for spiritual realization, all the demigods in heaven speak in this way: How wonderful it is for these human beings to have been born in the land of Bhārata-varṣa. They must have executed pious acts of austerity in the past, or the Supreme Personality of Godhead Himself must have been pleased with them. Otherwise, how could they engage in devotional service in so many ways? We demigods can only aspire to achieve human births in Bhārata-varṣa to execute devotional service, but these human beings are already engaged there.

PURPORT

These facts are further explained in *Caitanya-caritāmṛta* (*Ādi* 9.41):

bhārata-bhūmite haila manuṣya-janma yāra
janma sārthaka kari' kara para-upakāra

"One who has taken his birth as a human being in the land of India [Bhārata-varṣa] should make his life successful and work for the benefit of all other people."

There are many facilities in India, Bhārata-varṣa, for executing devotional service. In Bhārata-varṣa, all the *ācāryas* contributed their experience, and Śrī Caitanya Mahāprabhu personally appeared to teach the people of Bhārata-varṣa how to progress in spiritual life and be fixed in devotional service to the Lord. From all points of view, Bhārata-varṣa is the special land where one can very easily understand the process of devotional service and adopt it to make his life successful. If one makes his life successful in devotional service and then preaches devotional service in other parts of the world, people throughout the world will actually benefit.

TEXT 22

किं दुष्करैर्नः क्रतुभिस्तपोव्रतै-
र्दानादिभिर्वा द्युजयेन फल्गुना ।
न यत्र नारायणपादपङ्कज-
स्मृतिः प्रमुष्टातिशयेन्द्रियोत्सवात् ॥२२॥

kiṁ duṣkarair naḥ kratubhis tapo-vratair
dānādibhir vā dyujayena phalgunā
na yatra nārāyaṇa-pāda-paṅkaja-
smṛtiḥ pramuṣṭātiśayendriyotsavāt

kim—what is the value; *duṣkaraiḥ*—very difficult to perform; *naḥ*—our; *kratubhiḥ*—with performances of sacrifice; *tapaḥ*—with austerities; *vrataiḥ*—vows; *dāna-ādibhiḥ*—with executing charitable activities and so on; *vā*—or; *dyujayena*—with achieving the heavenly kingdom; *phalgunā*—which is insignificant; *na*—no; *yatra*—where; *nārāyaṇa-pāda-paṅkaja*—of the lotus feet of Lord Nārāyaṇa; *smṛtiḥ*—the remembrance; *pramuṣṭa*—lost; *atiśaya*—excessive; *indriya-utsavāt*—due to material sense gratification.

TRANSLATION

The demigods continue: After performing the very difficult tasks of executing Vedic ritualistic sacrifices, undergoing austerities, observing vows and giving charity, we have achieved this position as inhabitants of the heavenly planets. But what is the value of this achievement? Here we are certainly very engaged in material sense gratification, and therefore we can hardly remember the lotus feet of Lord Nārāyaṇa. Indeed, because of our excessive sense gratification, we have almost forgotten His lotus feet.

PURPORT

The land of Bhārata-varṣa is so exalted that by taking birth there one can not only attain the heavenly planets but also go directly back home, back to Godhead. As Kṛṣṇa says in *Bhagavad-gītā* (9.25):

yānti deva-vratā devān
pitṝn yānti pitṛ-vratāḥ
bhūtāni yānti bhūtejyā
yānti mad-yājino 'pi mām

"Those who worship the demigods will take birth among the demigods; those who worship ghosts and spirits will take birth among such beings; those who worship ancestors go to the ancestors; and those who worship Me will live with Me." People in the land of Bhārata-varṣa generally follow the Vedic principles and consequently perform great sacrifices by which they can be elevated to the heavenly planets. However, what is the use of such great attainments? As stated in *Bhagavad-gītā* (9.21), *kṣīṇe puṇye martya-lokaṁ viśanti:* after the results of one's sacrifices, charity and other pious activities expire, one must return to the lower planetary systems and again feel the pangs of birth and death. However, one who becomes Kṛṣṇa conscious can go back to Kṛṣṇa (*yānti-mad-yājino 'pi mām*). Therefore the demigods even regret having been elevated to the higher planetary systems. The denizens of the heavenly planets regret that they could not take full advantage of being born in the land of Bhārata-varṣa. Instead, they became captivated by a higher standard of sense gratification, and therefore they forgot the lotus feet of Lord Nārāyaṇa at the time of death. The conclusion is that one who has taken birth in the land of Bhārata-varṣa must follow the instructions given personally by the Supreme Personality of Godhead. *Yad gatvā na nivartante tad dhāma paramaṁ mama.* One should try to return home, back to Godhead, to the Vaikuṇṭha planets—or to the topmost Vaikuṇṭha planet, Goloka Vṛndāvana—to live eternally in full, blissful knowledge in the company of the Supreme Personality of Godhead.

TEXT 23

कल्पायुषां स्थानजयात्पुनर्भवात्
क्षणायुषां भारतभूजयो वरम् ।
क्षणेन मर्त्येन कृतं मनस्विनः
संन्यस्य संयान्त्यभयं पदं हरेः ॥२३॥

kalpāyuṣāṁ sthānajayāt punar-bhavāt
kṣaṇāyuṣāṁ bhārata-bhūjayo varam
kṣaṇena martyena kṛtaṁ manasvinaḥ
sannyasya saṁyānty abhayaṁ padaṁ hareḥ

kalpa-āyuṣām—of those who have a life duration of many millions of years, like Lord Brahmā; *sthāna-jayāt*—than achievement of the place or planetary systems; *punaḥ-bhavāt*—which is liable to birth, death and old age; *kṣaṇa-āyuṣām*—of persons who have only one hundred years of life; *bhārata-bhū-jayaḥ*—a birth in the land of Bhārata-varṣa; *varam*—more valuable; *kṣaṇena*—for such a short life; *martyena*—by the body; *kṛtam*—the work executed; *manasvinaḥ*—those actually understanding the value of life; *sannyasya*—surrendering unto the lotus feet of Kṛṣṇa; *saṁyānti*—they achieve; *abhayam*—where there is no anxiety; *padam*—the abode; *hareḥ*—of the Supreme Personality of Godhead.

TRANSLATION

A short life in the land of Bharata-varṣa is preferable to a life achieved in Brahmaloka for millions and billions of years because even if one is elevated to Brahmaloka, he must return to repeated birth and death. Although life in Bhārata-varṣa, in a lower planetary system, is very short, one who lives there can elevate himself to full Kṛṣṇa consciousness and achieve the highest perfection, even in this short life, by fully surrendering unto the lotus feet of the Lord. Thus one attains Vaikuṇṭhaloka, where there is neither anxiety nor repeated birth in a material body.

PURPORT

This is further confirmation of the statement given by Lord Caitanya Mahāprabhu:

bhārata-bhūmite haila manuṣya-janma yāra
janma sārthaka kari' kara para-upakāra

One who has taken birth in the land of Bhārata-varṣa has a full opportunity to study the direct instructions given by Kṛṣṇa in *Bhagavad-gītā* and thus finally decide what to do in his human form of life. One should certainly give up all other propositions and surrender to Kṛṣṇa. Kṛṣṇa will then immediately take charge and relieve one of the results of past sinful life (*ahaṁ tvāṁ sarva-pāpebhyo mokṣayiṣyāmi mā śucaḥ*). Therefore one should take to Kṛṣṇa consciousness, as Kṛṣṇa Himself recommends. *Man-manā bhava mad-bhakto mad-yājī māṁ namaskuru:* "Always think of Me, become My devotee, worship Me and offer Me obeisances." This is very easy, even for a child. Why not take this path? One should try to follow the instructions of Kṛṣṇa exactly and thus become fully eligible to be promoted to the kingdom of God (*tyaktvā dehaṁ punar janma naiti mām eti so 'rjuna*). One should go directly to Kṛṣṇa and engage in His service. This is the best opportunity offered to the inhabitants of Bhārata-varṣa. One who is fit to return home, back to Godhead, is no longer liable to the results of *karma*, good or bad.

TEXT 24

न यत्र वैकुण्ठकथासुधापगा
न साधवो भागवतास्तदाश्रयाः ।
न यत्र यज्ञेशमखा महोत्सवाः
सुरेशलोकोऽपि न वै स सेव्यताम् ॥२४॥

na yatra vaikuṇṭha-kathā-sudhāpagā
na sādhavo bhāgavatās tadāśrayāḥ
na yatra yajñeśa-makhā mahotsavāḥ
sureśa-loko 'pi na vai sa sevyatām

na—not; *yatra*—where; *vaikuṇṭha-kathā-sudhā-āpagāḥ*—the nectarean rivers of discussions about the Supreme Personality of Godhead, who is called Vaikuṇṭha, or one who drives away all anxiety; *na*—nor; *sādhavaḥ*—devotees; *bhāgavatāḥ*—always engaged in the service of the Lord; *tat-āśrayāḥ*—who are sheltered by the Supreme Personality of Godhead; *na*—nor; *yatra*—where; *yajña-īśa-makhāḥ*—the performance of devotional service to the Lord of sacrifices; *mahā-utsavāḥ*—which are actual festivals; *sureśa-lokaḥ*—a place inhabited by the denizens of heaven; *api*—although; *na*—not; *vai*—certainly; *saḥ*—that; *sevyatām*—be frequented.

TRANSLATION

An intelligent person does not take interest in a place, even in the topmost planetary system, if the pure Ganges of topics concerning the Supreme Lord's activities does not flow there, if there are not devotees engaged in service on the banks of such a river of piety, or if there are no festivals of saṅkīrtana-yajña to satisfy the Lord [especially since saṅkīrtana-yajña is recommended in this age].

PURPORT

Śrī Caitanya Mahāprabhu appeared in the land of Bhārata-varṣa, specifically in Bengal, in the district of Nadia, where Navadvīpa is situated. It is therefore to be concluded, as stated by Śrīla Bhaktivinoda Ṭhākura, that within this universe, this earth is the best planet, and on this planet the land of Bhārata-varṣa is the best; in the land of Bhārata-varṣa, Bengal is still better, in Bengal the district of Nadia is still better, and in Nadia the best place is Navadvīpa because Śrī Caitanya Mahāprabhu appeared there to inaugurate the performance of the sacrifice of chanting the Hare Kṛṣṇa *mahā-mantra.* The *śāstras* recommend:

kṛṣṇa-varṇaṁ tviṣākṛṣṇaṁ
sāṅgopāṅgāstra-pārṣadam
yajñaiḥ saṅkīrtana-prāyair
yajanti hi sumedhasaḥ

Lord Śrī Caitanya Mahāprabhu is always accompanied by His very confidential associates such as Śrī Nityānanda, Śrī Gadādhara and Śrī Advaita and by many devotees like Śrīvāsa. They are always engaged in chanting the name of the Lord and are always describing Lord Kṛṣṇa. Therefore this is the best among all the places in the universe. The Kṛṣṇa consciousness movement has established its center in Māyāpur, the birthsite of Lord Śrī Caitanya Mahāprabhu, to give men the great opportunity to go there and perform a constant festival of *saṅkīrtana-yajña,* as recommended herein (*yajñeśa-makhā mahotsavāḥ*) and to distribute *prasāda* to millions of hungry people hankering for spiritual emancipation. This is the mission of the Kṛṣṇa consciousness movement. *Caitanya-bhāgavata* confirms this as follows: "One should not desire to be elevated even to a place in the heavenly planetary systems if it has no propaganda to expand the glories of the Supreme Personality of Godhead, no trace of Vaiṣṇavas, pure devotees of the Lord, and no festivals for spreading Kṛṣṇa consciousness. It would be better to live perpetually cramped within the airtight bag of a mother's womb, where one can at least remember the lotus feet of the Lord, than to live in a place where there is no opportunity to remember His lotus feet. I pray not to be allowed to take birth in such a condemned place." Similarly, in *Caitanya-caritāmṛta*, Kṛṣṇadāsa Kavirāja Gosvāmī says that since Śrī Caitanya Mahāprabhu is the inaugurator of the *saṅkīrtana* movement, anyone who performs *saṅkīrtana* to please the Lord is very, very glorious. Such a person has perfect intelligence, whereas others are in the ignorance of material existence. Of all the sacrifices mentioned in the Vedic literatures, the performance of *saṅkīrtana-yajña* is the best. Even the performance of one hundred *aśvamedha* sacrifices cannot compare to the sacrifice of *saṅkīrtana*. According to the author of *Śrī Caitanya-caritāmṛta*, if one compares *saṅkīrtana-yajña* to other *yajñas*, he is a *pāṣaṇḍī*, an infidel, and is liable to be punished by Yamarāja. There are many Māyāvādīs who think that the performance of *saṅkīrtana-yajña* is a pious activity similar to the performance of the *aśvamedha-yajña* and other such pious functions, but this is a *nāma-aparādha*. Chanting of the holy name of Nārāyaṇa and chanting of other names are never equal, despite what Māyāvādīs think.

TEXT 25

प्राप्ता नृजातिं त्विह ये च जन्तवो
ज्ञानक्रियाद्रव्यकलापसम्भृताम् ।
न वै यतेरन्नपुनर्भवाय ते
भूयो वनौका इव यान्ति बन्धनम् ॥२५॥

prāptā nṛ-jātiṁ tv iha ye ca jantavo
jñāna-kriyā-dravya-kalāpa-sambhṛtām
na vai yaterann apunar-bhavāya te
bhūyo vanaukā iva yānti bandhanam

prāptāḥ—who have obtained; *nṛ-jātim*—a birth in human society; *tu*—certainly; *iha*—in this land of Bhārata-varṣa; *ye*—those who; *ca*—also; *jantavaḥ*—the living beings; *jñāna*—with knowledge; *kriyā*—with activities; *dravya*—of ingredients; *kalāpa*—with a collection; *sambhṛtām*—full; *na*—not; *vai*—certainly; *yateran*—endeavor; *apunaḥ-bhavāya*—for the position of immortality; *te*—such persons; *bhūyaḥ*—again; *vanaukāḥ*—birds; *iva*—like; *yānti*—go; *bandhanam*—to bondage.

TRANSLATION

Bhārata-varṣa offers the proper land and circumstances in which to execute devotional service, which can free one from the results of jñāna and karma. If one obtains a human body in the land of Bhārata-varṣa, with clear sensory organs with which to execute the saṅkīrtana-yajña, but in spite of this opportunity he does not take to devotional service, he is certainly like liberated forest animals and birds that are careless and are therefore again bound by a hunter.

PURPORT

In the land of Bhārata-varṣa one can very easily perform the *saṅkīrtana-yajña*, which consists of *śravaṇaṁ kīrtanaṁ viṣṇoḥ*, or one can perform other methods of devotional service, such as *smaraṇaṁ vandanam arcanaṁ dāsyaṁ sakhyam* and *ātma-nivedanam.* In Bhārata-varṣa one has the opportunity to visit many holy places, especially Lord Caitanya's birthsite and Lord Kṛṣṇa's birthsite—Navadvīpa and Vṛndāvana—where there are many pure devotees who have no desire other than to execute devotional service (*anyābhilāṣitā-śūnyaṁ jñāna-karmādy-anāvṛtam*), and one may thus become free from the bondage of material conditions. Other paths, such as the path of *jñāna* and the path of *karma*, are not very profitable. Pious activities can elevate one to the higher planetary systems, and by speculative knowledge one can merge into the Brahman existence, but that is not real profit, for one has to come down again even from the liberated condition of being merged in Brahman, and certainly one must come down from the heavenly kingdom. One should endeavor to go back home, back to

Godhead (*yānti mad-yājino 'pi mām*). Otherwise there is no difference between human life and the lives of jungle animals and birds. Animals and birds also have freedom, but because of their lower birth, they cannot use it. Taking advantage of all the facilities offered him, a human being who has taken birth in the land of Bhārata-varṣa should become a fully enlightened devotee and go back home, back to Godhead. This is the subject matter of the Kṛṣṇa consciousness movement. The inhabitants of places other than Bhārata-varṣa have facilities for material enjoyment, but they do not have the same facility to take to Kṛṣṇa consciousness. Therefore Śrī Caitanya Mahāprabhu has advised that one who has taken birth as a human being in Bhārata-varṣa must first realize himself as a part and parcel of Kṛṣṇa, and after taking to Kṛṣṇa consciousness, he must distribute this knowledge all over the world.

TEXT 26

यैः श्रद्धया बर्हिषि भागशो हवि-
निरुप्तमिष्टं विधिमन्त्रवस्तुतः ।
एकः पृथङ्नामभिराहुतो मुदा
गृह्णाति पूर्णः स्वयमाशिषां प्रभुः ॥२६॥

yaiḥ śraddhayā barhiṣi bhāgaśo havir
niruptam iṣṭaṁ vidhi-mantra-vastutaḥ
ekaḥ pṛthaṅ-nāmabhir āhuto mudā
gṛhṇāti pūrṇaḥ svayam āśiṣāṁ prabhuḥ

yaiḥ—by whom (the inhabitants of Bhārata-varṣa); *śraddhayā*—faith and confidence; *barhiṣi*—in the performance of Vedic ritualistic sacrifices; *bhāgaśaḥ*—by division; *haviḥ*—oblations; *niruptam*—offered; *iṣṭam*—to the desired deity; *vidhi*—by the proper method; *mantra*—by reciting *mantras; vastutaḥ*—with the proper ingredients; *ekaḥ*—that one Supreme Personality of Godhead; *pṛthak*—separate; *nāmabhiḥ*—by names; *āhutaḥ*—called; *mudā*—with great happiness; *gṛhṇāti*—He accepts; *pūrṇaḥ*—the Supreme Lord, who is full in Himself; *svayam*—personally; *āśiṣām*—of all benedictions; *prabhuḥ*—the bestower.

TRANSLATION

In India [Bhārata-varṣa], there are many worshipers of the demigods, the various officials appointed by the Supreme Lord, such as Indra, Candra and Sūrya, all of whom are worshiped differently. The worshipers offer the demigods their oblations, considering the demigods part and parcel of the whole, the Supreme Lord. Therefore the Supreme Personality of Godhead accepts these offerings and gradually raises the worshipers to the real standard of devotional service by fulfilling their desires and aspirations. Because the Lord is complete, He offers the worshipers the benedictions they desire even if they worship only part of His transcendental body.

PURPORT

In *Bhagavad-gītā* (9.13) Lord Kṛṣṇa says:

mahātmānas tu māṁ pārtha
daivīṁ prakṛtim āśritāḥ
bhajanty ananya-manaso
jñātvā bhūtādim avyayam

"O son of Pṛthā, those who are not deluded, the great souls, are under the protection of the divine nature. They are fully engaged in devotional service because they know Me as the Supreme Personality of Godhead, original and inexhaustible." *Mahātmās,* advanced devotees, worship only the Supreme Personality of Godhead. Others, however, who are also sometimes called *mahātmās,* worship the Lord as *ekatvena pṛthaktvena.* In other words, they accept the demigods as different parts of Kṛṣṇa and worship them for various benedictions. Although the devotees of the demigods thus achieve the desired results offered by Kṛṣṇa, they have been described in *Bhagavad-gītā* as *hṛta-jñāna,* not very intelligent. Kṛṣṇa does not desire to be worshiped indirectly through the different parts of His body; Kṛṣṇa wants direct devotional worship. Therefore a devotee who directly worships Lord Kṛṣṇa through staunch devotional service, as recommended in *Śrīmad-Bhāgavatam,* (*tīvreṇa bhakti-yogena yajeta puruṣaṁ param*), is very quickly elevated to the transcendental position. Nevertheless, devotees who worship the demigods, the different parts of the Lord, receive the benedictions they desire because the Lord is the original master of all benedictions. If anyone wants a particular benediction, for the Lord to award it is not at all difficult.

TEXT 27

सत्यं दिशत्यर्थितमर्थितो नृणां
नैवार्थदो यत्पुनरर्थिता यतः ।
स्वयं विधत्ते भजतामनिच्छता-
मिच्छापिधानं निजपादपल्लवम् ॥२७॥

satyaṁ diśaty arthitam arthito nṛṇāṁ
naivārthado yat punar arthitā yataḥ
svayaṁ vidhatte bhajatām anicchatām
icchāpidhānaṁ nija-pāda-pallavam

satyam—certainly; *diśati*—He offers; *arthitam*—the object prayed for; *arthitaḥ*—being prayed to; *nṛṇām*—by the human beings; *na*—not; *eva*—indeed; *artha-daḥ*—the bestower of benedictions; *yat*—which; *punaḥ*—again; *arthitā*—a demand for a benediction; *yataḥ*—from which; *svayam*—personally; *vidhatte*—He gives; *bhajatām*—unto those engaged in His service; *anicchatām*—although not desiring it; *icchā-pidhānam*—which covers all desirable things; *nija-pāda-pallavam*—His own lotus feet.

TRANSLATION

The Supreme Personality of Godhead fulfills the material desires of a devotee who approaches Him with such motives, but He does not bestow benedictions upon the devotee that will cause him to demand more benedictions again. However, the Lord willingly gives the devotee shelter at His own lotus feet, even though such a person does not aspire for it, and that shelter satisfies all his desires. That is the Supreme Personality's special mercy.

PURPORT

The devotees mentioned in the previous verse approach the Supreme Personality of Godhead with material motives, but this verse explains how such devotees are saved from those desires. *Śrīmad-Bhāgavatam* (2.3.10) advises:

akāmaḥ sarva-kāmo vā
mokṣa-kāma udāra-dhīḥ
tīvreṇa bhakti-yogena
yajeta puruṣaṁ param

"Whether one is freed from all material desires, is full of material desires, or desires to become one with the Supreme, he should engage in devotional service." In this way, not only will the devotee's desires be fulfilled, but the day will come when he will have no other desire than to serve the lotus feet of the Lord. One who engages in the service of the Lord with some motive is called a *sakāma-bhakta,* and one who serves the Lord without any motives is called an *akāma-bhakta.* Kṛṣṇa is so merciful that He turns a *sakāma-bhakta* into an *akāma-bhakta.* A pure devotee, an *akāma-bhakta,* who has no material motives, is satisfied simply to serve the lotus feet of the Lord. This is confirmed in *Bhagavad-gītā* (6.22). *Yaṁ labdhvā cāparaṁ lābhaṁ manyate nādhikaṁ tataḥ:* if one engages in the service of the lotus feet of the Lord, he does not want anything more. This is the highest stage of devotional service. The Lord is so kind even to a *sakāma-bhakta,* a motivated devotee, that He satisfies his desires in such a way that one day he becomes an *akāma-bhakta.* Dhruva Mahārāja, for example, became a *bhakta* with the motive of getting a better kingdom than that of his father, but finally he became an *akāma-bhakta* and said to the Lord, *svāmin kṛtārtho 'smi varaṁ na yāce:* "My dear Lord, I am very satisfied simply to serve Your lotus feet. I do not want any material benefits." Sometimes it is found that a small child eats dirty things, but his parents take away the dirty things and offer him a *sandeśa* or some other sweetmeat. Devotees who aspire for material benedictions are compared to such children. The Lord is so kind that He takes away their material desires and gives them the highest benediction. Therefore, even for material motives, one should not worship anyone other than the Supreme Personality of Godhead; one must fully engage himself in the devotional service of the Lord so that all his desires will be fulfilled and at the end he can go back home, back to Godhead. This is explained in *Caitanya-caritāmṛta* (*Madhya* 22.37-39, 41) as follows.

Anyakāmī—a devotee may desire something other than service to the lotus feet of the Lord; *yadi kare kṛṣṇera bhajana*—but if he engages in Lord Kṛṣṇa's service; *nā māgiteha kṛṣṇa tāre dena sva-caraṇa*—Kṛṣṇa gives him shelter at His lotus feet, even though he does not aspire for it. *Kṛṣṇa kahe*—the Lord says; *āmā bhaje*—"He is engaged in My service"; *māge viṣaya-sukha*—"but he wants the benefits of material sense gratification." *Amṛta chāḍi' viṣa māge:* "Such a devotee is like a person who asks for poison instead of nectar." *Ei baḍa mūrkha:* "That is his foolishness." *Āmi——vijña:* "But I am experienced." *Ei mūrkhe 'viṣaya' kene diba:* "Why should I give such a foolish person the dirty things of material enjoyment?" *Sva-caraṇāmṛta:* "It would be better for Me to give him shelter at My lotus feet." *'Viṣaya' bhulāiba:* "I shall cause him to forget all material desires." *Kāma lāgi' kṛṣṇa bhaje*—if one engages in the service of the Lord for sense gratification; *paya kṛṣṇa-rase*—the result is that he ultimately gets a taste for serving the lotus feet of the Lord. *Kāma chāḍi' 'dāsa' haite haya abhilāṣe:* He then gives up all material desires and wants to become an eternal servant of the Lord.

TEXT 28

यद्यत्र नः स्वर्गसुखावशेषितं
स्विष्टस्य सूक्तस्य कृतस्य शोभनम् ।
तेनाजनाभे स्मृतिमज्जन्म नः स्याद्
वर्षे हरिर्यद्भजतां शं तनोति ॥२८॥

yady atra naḥ svarga-sukhāvaśeṣitaṁ
sviṣṭasya sūktasya kṛtasya śobhanam
tenājanābhe smṛtimaj janma naḥ syād
varṣe harir yad-bhajatāṁ śaṁ tanoti

yadi—if; *atra*—in this heavenly planet; *naḥ*—of us; *svarga-sukha-avaśeṣitam*—whatever remains after the enjoyment of heavenly happiness; *su-iṣṭasya*—of a perfect sacrifice; *su-uktasya*—of diligently studying the Vedic literature; *kṛtasya*—of having performed a kind act; *śobhanam*—the resultant actions; *tena*—by such a resultant action; *ajanābhe*—in the land of Bhārata-varṣa; *smṛti-mat janma*—a birth enabling one to remember the lotus feet of the Lord; *naḥ*—of us; *syāt*—

let there be; *varṣe*—in the land; *hariḥ*—the Supreme Personality of Godhead; *yat*—wherein; *bhajatām*—of the devotees; *śam tanoti*—expands the auspiciousness.

TRANSLATION

We are now living in the heavenly planets, undoubtedly as a result of our having performed ritualistic ceremonies, pious activities and yajñas and having studied the Vedas. However, our lives here will one day be finished. We pray that at that time, if any merit remains from our pious activities, we may again take birth in Bhārata-varṣa as human beings able to remember the lotus feet of the Lord. The Lord is so kind that He personally comes to the land of Bhārata-varṣa and expands the good fortune of its people.

PURPORT

It is certainly as a result of pious activities that one takes birth in the heavenly planets, but from those planets one must nevertheless come down again to earth, as stated in *Bhagavad-gītā* (*kṣīṇe puṇye martya-lokaṁ viśanti*). Even the demigods must return to earth to work like ordinary men when the results of their pious activities expire. Nevertheless, the demigods desire to come to the land of Bhārata-varṣa if even a small portion of the merits of their pious activities remains. In other words, to take birth in Bhārata-varṣa, one must perform more pious activities than the demigods. In Bhārata-varṣa one is naturally Kṛṣṇa conscious, and if one further cultivates his Kṛṣṇa consciousness, by the grace of Kṛṣṇa he certainly expands his good fortune by becoming perfect in Kṛṣṇa consciousness and very easily going back home, back to Godhead. In many other places in the Vedic literature it is found that even the demigods want to come to this land of Bhārata-varṣa. A foolish person may desire to be promoted to the heavenly planets as a result of his pious activities, but even the demigods from the heavenly planets want to come to Bhārata-varṣa and achieve bodies that may be very easily used to cultivate Kṛṣṇa consciousness. Therefore Śrī Caitanya Mahāprabhu repeatedly says:

bhārata bhūmite haila manuṣya-janma yāra
janma sārthaka kari' kara para-upakāra

A human being born in the land of Bhārata-varṣa has the special prerogative to develop Kṛṣṇa consciousness. Therefore those already born in Bhārata-varṣa should take lessons from the *śāstras* and *guru* and should fully take advantage of the mercy of Śrī Caitanya Mahāprabhu in order to be fully equipped with Kṛṣṇa consciousness. By taking full advantage of Kṛṣṇa consciousness, one goes back home, back to Godhead (*yānti mad-yājino 'pi mām*). The Kṛṣṇa consciousness movement is therefore spreading this facility to human society by opening many, many centers all over the world so that people may associate with the pure devotees of the Kṛṣṇa consciousness movement, understand the science of Kṛṣṇa consciousness and ultimately go back home, back to Godhead.

TEXTS 29-30

श्रीशुक उवाच

जम्बूद्वीपस्य च राजन्नुपद्वीपानष्टौ हैक उपदिशन्ति सगरात्मजैर-
श्वान्वेषण इमां महीं परितो निखनद्भिरुपकल्पितान् ॥२९॥ तद्यथा स्वर्णप्रस्थ-
श्चन्द्रशुक्ल आवर्तनो रमणको मन्दरहरिणः पाञ्चजन्यः सिंहलो लङ्केति ॥३०॥

śrī-śuka uvāca
jambūdvīpasya ca rājann upadvīpān aṣṭau haika upadiśanti
sagarātmajair aśvānveṣaṇa imāṁ mahīṁ parito nikhanadbhir
upakalpitān. tad yathā svarṇaprasthaś candraśukla āvartano ramaṇako
mandarahariṇaḥ pāñcajanyaḥ siṁhalo laṅketi.

śrī-śukaḥ uvāca—Śrī Śukadeva Gosvāmī continued to speak; *jambūdvīpasya*—of the island known as Jambūdvīpa; *ca*—also; *rājan*—O King; *upadvīpān aṣṭau*—eight subordinate islands; *ha*—certainly; *eke*—some; *upadiśanti*—learned scholars describe; *sagara-ātma-jaiḥ*—by the sons of Mahārāja Sagara; *aśva-anveṣaṇe*—while trying to find their lost horse; *imām*—this; *mahīm*—tract of land; *paritaḥ*—all around; *nikhanadbhiḥ*—digging; *upakalpitān*—created; *tat*—that; *yathā*—as follows; *svarṇa-prasthaḥ*—Svarṇaprastha; *candra-śuklaḥ*—Candraśukla; *āvartanaḥ*—Āvartana; *ramaṇakaḥ*—Ramaṇaka; *mandara-hariṇaḥ*—Mandarahariṇa; *pāñcajanyaḥ*—Pāñcajanya; *siṁhalaḥ*—Siṁhala; *laṅkā*—Laṅkā; *iti*—thus.

TRANSLATION

Śrī Śukadeva Gosvāmī said: My dear King, in the opinion of some learned scholars, eight smaller islands surround Jambūdvīpa. When the sons of Mahārāja Sagara were searching all over the world for their lost horse, they dug up the earth, and in this way eight adjoining islands came into existence. The names of these islands are Svarṇaprastha, Candraśukla, Āvartana, Ramaṇaka, Mandarahariṇa, Pāñcajanya, Siṁhala and Laṅkā.

PURPORT

In the *Kūrma Purāṇa* there is this statement about the desires of the demigods:

anadhikāriṇo devāḥ
svarga-sthā bhāratodbhavam
vāñchanty ātma-vimokṣārtha-
mudrekārthe 'dhikāriṇaḥ

Although the demigods are situated in exalted positions in the heavenly planets, they nevertheless desire to descend to the land of Bhārata-varṣa on the planet earth. This indicates that even the demigods are unfit to reside in Bhārata-varṣa. Therefore if persons already born in Bhārata-varṣa live like cats and dogs, not taking full advantage of their birth in this land, they are certainly unfortunate.

TEXT 31

एवं तव भारतोत्तम जम्बूद्वीपवर्षविभागो यथोपदेशमुपवर्णित इति ॥३१॥

evaṁ tava bhāratottama jambūdvīpa-varṣa-vibhāgo yathopadeśam upavarṇita iti.

evam—thus; *tava*—unto you; *bhārata-uttama*—O best of the descendents of Bharata; *jambūdvīpa-varṣa-vibhāgaḥ*—the divisions of the island of Jambūdvīpa; *yathā-upadeśam*—as much as I am instructed by the authorities; *upavarṇitaḥ*—explained; *iti*—thus.

TRANSLATION

My dear King Parīkṣit, O best of the descendants of Bharata Mahārāja, I have thus described to you, as I myself have been instructed, the island of Bhārata-varṣa and its adjoining islands. These are the islands that constitute Jambūdvīpa.

Thus end the Bhaktivedanta purports of the Fifth Canto, Nineteenth Chapter of the Śrīmad-Bhāgavatam, *entitled "A Description of the Island of Jambūdvīpa."*

CHAPTER TWENTY

Studying the Structure of the Universe

In this chapter there is a description of various islands, beginning with Plakṣadvīpa, and the oceans that surround them. There is also a description of the location and dimensions of the mountain known as Lokāloka. The island of Plakṣadvīpa, which is twice as broad as Jambūdvīpa, is surrounded by an ocean of salt water. The master of this island is Idhmajihva, one of the sons of Mahārāja Priyavrata. The island is divided into seven regions, each with a mountain and a large river.

The second island is called Śālmalīdvīpa. It is surrounded by an ocean of liquor and is 3,200,000 miles wide, twice as wide as Plakṣadvīpa. The master of this island is Yajñabāhu, one of the sons of Mahārāja Priyavrata. Like Plakṣadvīpa, this island is also divided into seven regions, each with a mountain and a very large river. The inhabitants of this island worship the Supreme Personality of Godhead in the form of Candrātmā.

The third island, which is surrounded by an ocean of clarified butter and is also divided into seven regions, is called Kuśadvīpa. Its master is Hiraṇyaretā, another son of Mahārāja Priyavrata, and its inhabitants worship the Supreme Personality of Godhead in the form of Agni, the fire-god. The width of this island is 6,400,000 miles, or, in other words, twice the width of Śālmalīdvīpa.

The fourth island, Krauñcadvīpa, which is surrounded by an ocean of milk, is 12,800,000 miles wide and is also divided, like the others, into seven regions, each with a large mountain and a large river. The master of this island is Ghṛtapṛṣṭha, another son of Mahārāja Priyavrata. The inhabitants of this island worship the Supreme Personality of Godhead in the form of water.

The fifth island, Śākadvīpa, which is 25,600,000 miles wide, is surrounded by an ocean of yogurt. Its master is Medhātithi, another son of Mahārāja Priyavrata. It is also divided into seven regions, each with a large mountain and a large river. Its inhabitants worship the Supreme Personality of Godhead in the form of Vāyu, air.

The sixth island, Puṣkaradvīpa, which is twice as wide as the previous island, is surrounded by an ocean of clear water. Its master is Vītihotra, another son of Mahārāja Priyavrata. The island is divided in two by a large mountain named Mānasottara. The inhabitants of this island worship Svayambhū, another feature of the Supreme Personality of Godhead. Beyond Puṣkaradvīpa there are two islands, one always lit by the sunshine and the other always dark. Between them is a mountain called Lokāloka, which is situated one billion miles from the edge of the universe. Lord Nārāyaṇa, expanding His opulence, resides upon this mountain. The area beyond Lokāloka Mountain is called Aloka-varṣa, and beyond Aloka-varṣa is the pure destination of persons who desire liberation.

Vertically, the sun-globe is situated just in the middle of the universe, in Antarikṣa, the space between Bhūrloka and Bhuvarloka. The distance between the sun and the circumference of Aṇḍa-golaka, the globe of the universe, is estimated to be twenty-five *koṭi yojanas* (two billion miles). Because the sun enters the universe and divides the sky, it is known as Mārtaṇḍa, and because it is produced from Hiraṇyagarbha, the body of the *mahat-tattva*, it is also called Hiraṇyagarbha.

TEXT 1

श्रीशुक उवाच

अतः परं प्लक्षादीनां प्रमाणलक्षणसंस्थानतो वर्षविभाग उपवर्ण्यते ॥ १ ॥

śrī-śuka uvāca

ataḥ paraṁ plakṣādīnāṁ pramāṇa-lakṣaṇa-saṁsthānato varṣa-vibhāga upavarṇyate.

śrī-śukaḥ uvāca—Śukadeva Gosvāmī said; *ataḥ param*—after this; *plakṣa-ādīnām*—of the island named Plakṣa and others; *pramāṇa-lakṣaṇa-saṁsthānataḥ*—from the angle of dimensions, particular characteristics and form; *varṣa-vibhāgaḥ*—the division of the island; *upavarṇyate*—is described.

TRANSLATION

The great sage Śukadeva Gosvāmī said: Hereafter I shall describe the dimensions, characteristics and forms of the six islands beginning with the island of Plakṣa.

TEXT 2

जम्बूद्वीपोऽयं यावत्प्रमाणविस्तारस्तावता क्षारोदधिना परिवेष्टितो यथा मेरुर्जम्ब्वाख्येन लवणोदधिरपि ततो द्विगुणविशालेन प्लक्षाख्येन परिक्षिप्तो यथा परिखा बाह्योपवनेन । प्लक्षो जम्बूप्रमाणो द्वीपाख्याकरो हिरण्मय उत्थितो यत्राग्निरुपास्ते सप्तजिह्वस्तस्याधिपतिः प्रियव्रतात्मज इध्मजिह्वः स्वं द्वीपं सप्तवर्षाणि विभज्य सप्तवर्षनामभ्य आत्मजेभ्य आकलय्य स्वयमात्मयोगेनोपरराम ॥ २ ॥

jambūdvīpo 'yaṁ yāvat-pramāṇa-vistāras tāvatā kṣārodadhinā pariveṣṭito yathā merur jambv-ākhyena lavaṇodadhir api tato dvi-guṇa-viśālena plakṣākhyena parikṣipto yathā parikhā bāhyopavanena. plakṣo jambū-pramāṇo dvīpākhyākaro hiraṇmaya utthito yatrāgnir upāste sapta-jihvas tasyādhipatiḥ priyavratātmaja idhmajihvaḥ svaṁ dvīpaṁ sapta-varṣāṇi vibhajya sapta-varṣa-nāmabhya ātmajebhya ākalayya svayam ātma-yogenopararāma.

jambū-dvīpaḥ—Jambūdvīpa, the island named Jambū; *ayam*—this; *yāvat-pramāṇa-vistāraḥ*—as much as the measure of its width, namely 100,000 *yojanas* (one *yojana* equals eight miles); *tāvatā*—so much; *kṣāra-udadhinā*—by the ocean of salt water; *pariveṣṭitaḥ*—surrounded; *yathā*—just as; *meruḥ*—Sumeru Mountain; *jambū-ākhyena*—by the island named Jambū; *lavaṇa-udadhiḥ*—the ocean of salt water; *api*—certainly; *tataḥ*—thereafter; *dvi-guṇa-viśālena*—which is twice as wide; *plakṣa-ākhyena*—by the island named Plakṣa; *parikṣiptaḥ*—surrounded; *yathā*—like; *parikhā*—a moat; *bāhya*—external; *upavanena*—by a gardenlike forest; *plakṣaḥ*—a *plakṣa* tree; *jambū-pramāṇaḥ*—having the height of the *jambū* tree; *dvīpa-ākhyā-karaḥ*—

causing the name of the island; *hiraṇmayaḥ*—magnificently splendorous; *utthitaḥ*—rising; *yatra*—where; *agniḥ*—a fire; *upāste*—is situated; *sapta-jihvaḥ*—having seven flames; *tasya*—of that island; *adhipatiḥ*—the king or master; *priyavrata-ātmajaḥ*—the son of King Priyavrata; *idhma-jihvaḥ*—named Idhmajihva; *svam*—own; *dvīpam*—island; *sapta*—seven; *varṣāṇi*—tracts of land; *vibhajya*—dividing into; *sapta-varṣa-nāmabhyaḥ*—for whom the seven tracts of land were named; *ātmajebhyaḥ*—to his own sons; *ākalayya*—offering; *svayam*—personally; *ātma-yogena*—by the devotional service of the Lord; *upararāma*—he retired from all material activities.

TRANSLATION

As Sumeru Mountain is surrounded by Jambūdvīpa, Jambūdvīpa is also surrounded by an ocean of salt water. The breadth of Jambūdvīpa is 100,000 yojanas [800,000 miles], and the breadth of the saltwater ocean is the same. As a moat around a fort is sometimes surrounded by gardenlike forest, the saltwater ocean surrounding Jambūdvīpa is itself surrounded by Plakṣadvīpa. The breadth of Plakṣadvīpa is twice that of the saltwater ocean—in other words 200,000 yojanas [1,600,000 miles]. On Plakṣadvīpa there is a tree shining like gold and as tall as the jambū tree on Jambūdvīpa. At its root is a fire with seven flames. It is because this tree is a plakṣa tree that the island is called Plakṣadvīpa. Plakṣadvīpa was governed by Idhmajihva, one of the sons of Mahārāja Priyavrata. He endowed the seven islands with the names of his seven sons, divided the islands among the sons, and then retired from active life to engage in the devotional service of the Lord.

TEXTS 3-4

शिवं यवसं सुभद्रं शान्तं क्षेममममृतमभयमिति वर्षाणि तेषु गिरयो नद्यश्च
सप्तैवाभिज्ञाताः ॥३॥ मणिकूटो वज्रकूट इन्द्रसेनो ज्योतिष्मान् सुपर्णो
हिरण्यष्ठीवो मेघमाल इति सेतुशैलाः । अरुणा नृम्णाऽऽङ्गिरसी सावित्री सुप्रभाता

ऋतम्भरा सत्यम्भरा इति महानद्यः । यासां जलोपस्पर्शनविधूतरजस्तमसो हंसपतङ्गोर्ध्वायनसत्याङ्गसंज्ञाश्चत्वारो वर्णाः सहस्रायुषो विबुधोपमसन्दर्शन-प्रजननाः स्वर्गद्वारं त्रय्या विद्यया भगवन्तं त्रयीमयं सूर्यमात्मानं यजन्ते ॥ ४ ॥

śivaṁ yavasaṁ subhadraṁ śāntaṁ kṣemam amṛtam abhayam iti varṣāṇi teṣu girayo nadyaś ca saptaivābhijñātāḥ. maṇikūṭo vajrakūṭa indraseno jyotiṣmān suparṇo hiraṇyaṣṭhīvo meghamāla iti setu-śailāḥ aruṇā nṛmṇāṅgirasī sāvitrī suptabhātā ṛtambharā satyambharā iti mahā-nadyaḥ. yāsāṁ jalopasparśana-vidhūta-rajas-tamaso haṁsa-pataṅgordhvāyana-satyāṅga-saṁjñāś catvāro varṇāḥ sahasrāyuṣo vibudhopama-sandarśana-prajananāḥ svarga-dvāraṁ trayyā vidyayā bhagavantaṁ trayīmayaṁ sūryam ātmānaṁ yajante.

śivam—Śiva; *yavasam*—Yavasa; *subhadram*—Subhadra; *śāntam*—Śānta; *kṣemam*—Kṣema; *amṛtam*—Amṛta; *abhayam*—Abhaya; *iti*—thus; *varṣāṇi*—the tracts of land according to the names of the seven sons; *teṣu*—in them; *girayaḥ*—mountains; *nadyaḥ ca*—and rivers; *sapta*—seven; *eva*—indeed; *abhijñātāḥ*—are known; *maṇi-kūṭaḥ*—Maṇikūṭa; *vajra-kūṭaḥ*—Vajrakūṭa; *indra-senaḥ*—Indrasena; *jyotiṣ-mān*—Jyotiṣmān; *suparṇaḥ*—Suparṇa; *hiraṇya-ṣṭhīvaḥ*—Hiraṇyaṣṭhīva; *megha-mālaḥ*—Meghamāla; *iti*—thus; *setu-śailāḥ*—the ranges of mountains marking the borders of the *varṣas; aruṇā*—Aruṇā; *nṛmṇā*—Nṛmṇā; *āṅgirasī*—Āṅgirasī; *sāvitrī*—Sāvitrī; *supta-bhātā*—Suptabhātā; *ṛtambharā*—Ṛtambharā; *satyambharā*—Satyambharā; *iti*—thus; *mahā-nadyaḥ*—very large rivers; *yāsām*—of which; *jala-upasparśana*—simply by touching the water; *vidhūta*—washed off; *rajaḥ-tamasaḥ*—whose modes of passion and ignorance; *haṁsa*—Haṁsa; *pataṅga*—Pataṅga; *ūrdhvāyana*—Ūrdhvāyana; *satyāṅga*—Satyāṅga; *saṁjñāḥ*—named; *catvāraḥ*—four; *varṇāḥ*—castes or divisions of men; *sahasra-āyuṣaḥ*—living for one thousand years; *vibudha-upama*—similar to the demigods; *sandarśana*—in having very beautiful forms; *prajananāḥ*—and in producing children; *svarga-dvāram*—the gateway to the heavenly planets; *trayyā vidyayā*—by performing ritualistic ceremonies according to Vedic principles; *bhagavantam*—the Supreme Personality of Godhead; *trayī-mayam*—established in the *Vedas;*

sūryam ātmānam—the Supersoul, represented by the sun-god; *yajante*—they worship.

TRANSLATION

The seven islands [varṣas] are named according to the names of those seven sons—Śiva, Yavasa, Subhadra, Śānta, Kṣema, Amṛta and Abhaya. In those seven tracts of land, there are seven mountains and seven rivers. The mountains are named Maṇikūṭa, Vajrakūṭa, Indrasena, Jyotiṣmān, Suparṇa, Hiraṇyaṣṭhīva and Meghamāla, and the rivers are named Aruṇā, Nṛmṇā, Āṅgirasī, Sāvitrī, Suptabhātā, Ṛtambharā and Satyambharā. One can immediately be free from material contamination by touching or bathing in those rivers, and the four castes of people who live in Plakṣadvīpa—the Haṁsas, Pataṅgas, Ūrdhvāyanas and Satyāṅgas—purify themselves in that way. The inhabitants of Plakṣadvīpa live for one thousand years. They are beautiful like the demigods, and they also beget children like the demigods. By completely performing the ritualistic ceremonies mentioned in the Vedas and by worshiping the Supreme Personality of Godhead as represented by the sun-god, they attain the sun, which is a heavenly planet.

PURPORT

According to general understanding, there are originally three deities—Lord Brahmā, Lord Viṣṇu and Lord Śiva—and people with a poor fund of knowledge consider Lord Viṣṇu no better than Lord Brahmā or Lord Śiva. This conclusion, however, is invalid. As stated in the *Vedas, iṣṭāpūrtaṁ bahudhā jāyamānaṁ viśvaṁ bibharti bhuvanasya nābhiḥ tad evāgnis tad vāyus tat sūryas tad u candramāḥ agniḥ sarvadaivataḥ.* This means that the Supreme Lord, who accepts and enjoys the results of Vedic ritualistic ceremonies (technically called *iṣṭāpūrta*), who maintains the entire creation, who supplies the necessities of all living entities (*eko bahūnāṁ yo vidadhāti kāmān*) and who is the central point of all creation, is Lord Viṣṇu. Lord Viṣṇu expands as the demigods known as Agni, Vāyu, Sūrya and Candra, who are simply parts and parcels of His body. Lord Kṛṣṇa says in *Śrīmad Bhagavad-gītā* (9.23):

ye 'py anya-devatā-bhaktā
yajante śraddhayānvitāḥ

te 'pi mām eva kaunteya
yajanty avidhi-pūrvakam

"Devotees who worship the demigods with firm faith worship Me also, but not according to regulative principles." In other words, if one worships the demigods but does not understand the relationship between the demigods and the Supreme Personality of Godhead, his worship is irregular. Kṛṣṇa also says in *Bhagavad-gītā* (9.24), *ahaṁ hi sarva-yajñānāṁ bhoktā ca prabhur eva ca:* "I am the only enjoyer of ritualistic ceremonies."

It may be argued that the demigods are as important as Lord Viṣṇu because the names of the demigods are different names of Viṣṇu. This, however, is not a sound conclusion, for it is contradicted in the Vedic literatures. The *Vedas* declare:

candramā manaso jātaś cakṣoḥ sūryo ajāyata. śrotrādayaś ca prāṇaś ca mukhād agnir ajāyata. nārāyaṇād brahmā, nārāyaṇād rudro jāyate, nārāyaṇāt prajāpatiḥ jāyate, nārāyaṇād indro jāyate, nārāyaṇād aṣṭau vasavo jāyante, nārāyaṇād ekādaśa rudrā jāyante.

"The demigod of the moon, Candra, came from the mind of Nārāyaṇa, and the sun-god came from His eyes. The controlling deities of hearing and the life air came from Nārāyaṇa, and the controlling deity of fire was generated from His mouth. Prajāpati, Lord Brahmā, came from Nārāyaṇa, Indra came from Nārāyaṇa, and the eight Vasus, the eleven expansions of Lord Śiva and the twelve Ādityas also came from Nārāyaṇa." In the *smṛti* Vedic literature it is also said:

brahmā śambhus tathaivārkaś
candramāś ca śatakratuḥ
evam ādyās tathaivānye
yuktā vaiṣṇava-tejasā

jagat-kāryāvasāne tu
viyujyante ca tejasā
vitejaś ca te sarve
pañcatvam upayānti te

"Brahmā, Śambhu, Sūrya and Indra are all merely products of the power of the Supreme Personality of Godhead. This is also true of the many other demigods whose names are not mentioned here. When the cosmic manifestation is annihilated, these different expansions of Nārāyaṇa's potencies will merge into Nārāyaṇa. In other words, all these demigods will die. Their living force will be withdrawn, and they will merge into Nārāyaṇa."

Therefore it should be concluded that Lord Viṣṇu, not Lord Brahmā or Lord Śiva, is the Supreme Personality of Godhead. As a government officer is sometimes accepted as the entire government although he is actually but a departmental manager, so the demigods, having achieved power of attorney from Viṣṇu, act on His behalf, although they are not as powerful as He. All the demigods must work under the orders of Viṣṇu. Therefore it is said, *ekale īśvara kṛṣṇa, āra saba bhṛtya.* The only master is Lord Kṛṣṇa, or Lord Viṣṇu, and all others are His obedient servants, who act exactly according to His orders. The distinction between Lord Viṣṇu and the demigods is also expressed in *Bhagavad-gītā* (9.25). *Yānti deva-vratā devān. . . yānti mad-yājino 'pi mām:* those who worship the demigods go to the planets of the demigods, whereas the worshipers of Lord Kṛṣṇa and Lord Viṣṇu go to the planets in Vaikuṇṭha. These are the statements of the *smṛti.* Therefore the idea that Lord Viṣṇu is on the same level as the demigods is in contradiction to the *śāstras.* The demigods are not supreme. The supremacy of the demigods is dependent on the mercy of Lord Nārāyaṇa (Viṣṇu, or Kṛṣṇa).

TEXT 5

प्रत्नस्य विष्णो रूपं यत्सत्यस्यर्तस्य ब्रह्मणः ।
अमृतस्य च मृत्योश्च सूर्यमात्मानमीमहीति ॥ ५ ॥

pratnasya viṣṇo rūpaṁ yat
satyasyartasya brahmaṇaḥ
amṛtasya ca mṛtyoś ca
sūryam ātmānam īmahīti

pratnasya—of the oldest person; *viṣṇoḥ*—Lord Viṣṇu; *rūpam*—the form; *yat*—which; *satyasya*—of the Absolute Truth; *ṛtasya*—of *dharma; brahmaṇaḥ*—of the Supreme Brahman; *amṛtasya*—of the auspicious result; *ca*—and; *mṛtyoḥ*—of death (the inauspicious result); *ca*—and; *sūryam*—the demigod Sūrya; *ātmānam*—the Supersoul or origin of all souls; *īmahi*—we approach for shelter; *iti*—thus.

TRANSLATION

[This is the mantra by which the inhabitants of Plakṣadvīpa worship the Supreme Lord.] Let us take shelter of the sun-god, who is a reflection of Lord Viṣṇu, the all-expanding Supreme Personality of Godhead, the oldest of all persons. Viṣṇu is the only worshipable Lord. He is the Vedas, He is religion, and He is the origin of all auspicious and inauspicious results.

PURPORT

Lord Viṣṇu is even the Supreme Lord of death, as confirmed in *Bhagavad-gītā* (*mṛtyuḥ sarva-haraś cāham*). There are two kinds of activity—auspicious and inauspicious—and both are controlled by Lord Viṣṇu. Inauspicious activities are said to be behind Lord Viṣṇu, whereas auspicious activities stand before Him. The auspicious and the inauspicious exist throughout the entire world, and Lord Viṣṇu is the controller of them both.

In regard to this verse, Śrīla Madhvācārya says:

sūrya-somāgni-vārīśa-
vidhātṛṣu yathā-kramam
plakṣādi-dvīpa-saṁsthāsu
sthitaṁ harim upāsate

There are many lands, fields, mountains and oceans throughout the creation, and everywhere the Supreme Personality of Godhead is worshiped by His different names.

Śrīla Vīrarāghava Ācārya explains this verse of *Śrīmad-Bhāgavatam* as follows. The original cause of the cosmic manifestation must be the oldest person and must therefore be beyond material transformations. He is the enjoyer of all auspicious activities and is the cause of conditional life and also liberation. The demigod Sūrya, who is categorized as a very powerful *jīva*, or living entity, is a representation of one of the parts of His body. We are naturally subordinate to powerful living entities, and therefore we can worship the various demigods as living beings who are powerful representatives of the Supreme Personality of Godhead. Although the worship of the sun-god is recommended in this *mantra*, He is worshiped not as the Supreme Personality of Godhead but as His powerful representative.

In the *Kaṭha Upaniṣad* (1.3.1) it is said:

ṛtaṁ pibantau sukṛtasya loke
guhāṁ praviṣṭau parame parārdhe
chāyātapau brahmavido vadanti
pañcāgnayo ye ca tri-ṇāciketāḥ

"O Nāciketā, the expansions of Lord Viṣṇu as the tiny living entity and the Supersoul are both situated within the cave of the heart of this body. Having entered that cavity, the living entity, resting on the chief of the life airs, enjoys the results of activities, and the Supersoul, acting as witness enables him to enjoy them. Those who are well-versed in knowledge of Brahman and those householders who carefully follow the Vedic regulations say that the difference between the two is like the difference between a shadow and the sun."

In the *Śvetāśvatara Upaniṣad* (6.16) it is said:

sa viśvakṛd viśvavidātmayoniḥ
jñaḥ kālākāro guṇī sarvavid yaḥ
pradhāna-kṣetrajña-patir guṇeśaḥ
saṁsāra-mokṣa-sthiti-bandha-hetuḥ

"The Supreme Lord, the creator of this cosmic manifestation, knows every nook and corner of His creation. Although He is the cause of creation, there is no cause for His appearance. He is fully aware of everything. He is the Supersoul, the master of all transcendental qualities, and He is the master of this cosmic manifestation in regard to bondage to the conditional state of material existence and liberation from that bondage."

Similarly, in the *Taittirīya Upaniṣad* (2.8) it is said:

bhīṣāsmād vātaḥ pavate
bhīṣodeti sūryaḥ
bhīṣāsmād agniś cendraś ca
mṛtyur dhāvati pañcamaḥ

"It is out of fear of the Supreme Brahman that the wind is blowing, out of fear of Him that the sun regularly rises and sets, and out of fear of Him that fire acts. It is only due to fear of Him that death and Indra, the King of heaven, perform their respective duties."

As described in this chapter, the inhabitants of the five islands beginning with Plakṣadvīpa worship the sun-god, the moon-god, the fire-god, the air-god and Lord Brahmā respectively. Although they engage in the worship of these five demigods, however, they actually worship Lord Viṣṇu, the Supersoul of all living entities, as indicated in this verse by the words *pratnasya viṣṇo rūpam.* Viṣṇu is *brahma, amṛta, mṛtyu*—the Supreme Brahman and the origin of everything, auspicious and inauspicious. He is situated in the heart of everyone, including all the demigods. As stated in *Bhagavad-gītā* (7.20), *kāmais tais tair hṛta-jñānāḥ prapadyante 'nya devatāḥ:* those whose minds are distorted by material desires surrender unto the demigods. People who are almost blind because of lusty desires are recommended to worship the demigods to have their material desires fulfilled, but actually those desires are not fulfilled by the material demigods. Whatever the demigods do is done with the sanction of Lord Viṣṇu. People who are too lusty worship various demigods instead of worshiping Lord Viṣṇu, the Supersoul of all living entities, but ultimately it is Lord Viṣṇu they worship because He is the Supersoul of all demigods.

TEXT 6

प्लक्षादिषु पञ्चसु पुरुषाणामायुरिन्द्रियमोजः सहो बलं बुद्धिर्विक्रम इति च सर्वेषामौत्पत्तिकी सिद्धिरविशेषेण वर्तते ॥ ६ ॥

plakṣādiṣu pañcasu puruṣāṇām āyur indriyam ojaḥ saho balaṁ buddhir vikrama iti ca sarveṣām autpattikī siddhir aviśeṣeṇa vartate.

plakṣa-ādiṣu—in the islands headed by Plakṣa; *pañcasu*—five; *puruṣāṇām*—of the inhabitants; *āyuḥ*—long duration of life; *indriyam*—soundness of the senses; *ojaḥ*—bodily strength; *sahaḥ*—mental strength; *balam*—physical strength; *buddhiḥ*—intelligence; *vikramaḥ*—bravery; *iti*—thus; *ca*—also; *sarveṣām*—of all of them; *autpattikī*—inborn; *siddhiḥ*—perfection; *aviśeṣeṇa*—without distinction; *vartate*—exists.

TRANSLATION

O King, longevity, sensory prowess, physical and mental strength, intelligence and bravery are naturally and equally manifested in all the inhabitants of the five islands headed by Plakṣadvīpa.

TEXT 7

प्लक्षः स्वसमानेनेक्षुरसोदेनावृतो यथा तथा द्वीपोऽपि
शाल्मलो द्विगुणविशालः समानेन सुरोदेनावृतः परिवृङ्क्ते ॥ ७ ॥

plakṣaḥ sva-samānenekṣu-rasodenāvṛto yathā tathā dvīpo 'pi śālmalo dvi-guṇa-viśālaḥ samānena surodenāvṛtaḥ parivṛṅkte.

plakṣaḥ—the land known as Plakṣadvīpa; *sva-samānena*—equal in width; *ikṣu-rasa*—of sugarcane juice; *udena*—by an ocean; *āvṛtaḥ*—surrounded; *yathā*—just as; *tathā*—similarly; *dvīpaḥ*—another island; *api*—also; *śālmalaḥ*—known as Śālmala; *dvi-guṇa-viśālaḥ*—twice as big; *samānena*—equal in width; *surā-udena*—by an ocean of liquor; *āvṛtaḥ*—surrounded; *parivṛṅkte*—exists.

TRANSLATION

Plakṣadvīpa is surrounded by an ocean of sugarcane juice, equal in breadth to the island itself. Similarly, there is then another island—Śālmalīdvīpa—twice as broad as Plakṣadvīpa [400,000 yojanas, or 3,200,000 miles] and surrounded by an equally broad body of water called Surāsāgara, the ocean that tastes like liquor.

TEXT 8

यत्र ह वै शाल्मली प्लक्षायामा यस्यां वाव किल निलयमाहुर्भगवतश्छन्दः स्तुतः पतत्त्रिराजस्य सा द्वीपहूतये उपलक्ष्यते ॥ ८ ॥

yatra ha vai śālmalī plakṣāyāmā yasyāṁ vāva kila nilayam āhur bhagavataś chandaḥ-stutaḥ patattri-rājasya sā dvīpa-hūtaye upalakṣyate.

yatra—where; *ha vai*—certainly; *śālmalī*—a *śālmalī* tree; *plakṣa-āyāmā*—as big as the *plakṣa* tree (one hundred *yojanas* broad and eleven hundred *yojanas* high); *yasyām*—in which; *vāva kila*—indeed; *nilayam*—rest or living place; *āhuḥ*—they say; *bhagavataḥ*—of the most powerful; *chandaḥ-stutaḥ*—who worships the Lord by Vedic prayers; *patattri-rājasya*—of Garuḍa, the carrier of Lord Viṣṇu; *sā*—that tree; *dvīpa-hūtaye*—for the name of the island; *upalakṣyate*—is distinguished.

TRANSLATION

On Śālmalīdvīpa there is a śālmalī tree, from which the island takes its name. That tree is as broad and tall as the plakṣa tree—in other words 100 yojanas [800 miles] broad and 1,100 yojanas [8,800 miles] tall. Learned scholars say that this gigantic tree is the residence of Garuḍa, the king of all birds and carrier of Lord Viṣṇu. In that tree, Garuḍa offers Lord Viṣṇu his Vedic prayers.

TEXT 9

तद्द्वीपाधिपतिः प्रियव्रतात्मजो यज्ञबाहुः स्वसुतेभ्यः सप्तभ्यस्तन्नामानि सप्तवर्षाणि व्यभजत्सुरोचनं सौमनस्यं रमणकं देववर्षं पारिभद्रमाप्यायनमविज्ञातमिति ॥९॥

tad-dvīpādhipatiḥ priyavratātmajo yajñabāhuḥ sva-sutebhyaḥ saptabhyas tan-nāmāni sapta-varṣāṇi vyabhajat surocanaṁ saumanasyaṁ ramaṇakaṁ deva-varṣaṁ pāribhadram āpyāyanam avijñātam iti.

tat-dvīpa-adhipatiḥ—the master of that island; *priyavrata-ātmajaḥ*—the son of Mahārāja Priyavrata; *yajña-bāhuḥ*—named Yajñabāhu; *sva-sutebhyaḥ*—unto his sons; *saptabhyaḥ*—seven in number; *tat-nāmāni*—having names according to their names; *sapta-varṣāṇi*—seven tracts of land; *vyabhajat*—divided; *surocanam*—Surocana; *saumanasyam*—Saumanasya; *ramaṇakam*—Ramaṇaka; *deva-varṣam*—Deva-varṣa; *pāribhadram*—Pāribhadra; *āpyāyanam*—Āpyāyana; *avijñātam*—Avijñāta; *iti*—thus.

TRANSLATION

The son of Mahārāja Priyavrata named Yajñabāhu, the master of Śālmalīdvīpa, divided the island into seven tracts of land, which he gave to his seven sons. The names of those divisions, which correspond to the names of the sons, are Surocana, Saumanasya, Ramaṇaka, Deva-varṣa, Pāribhadra, Āpyāyana and Avijñāta.

TEXT 10

तेषु वर्षाद्रयो नद्यश्च सप्तैवाभिज्ञाताः स्वरसः शतशृङ्गो वामदेवः कुन्दो मुकुन्दः पुष्पवर्षः सहस्रश्रुतिरिति । अनुमतिः सिनीवाली सरस्वती कुहू रजनी नन्दा राकेति ॥१०॥

teṣu varṣādrayo nadyaś ca saptaivābhijñātāḥ svarasaḥ śataśṛṅgo
vāmadevaḥ kundo mukundaḥ puṣpa-varṣaḥ sahasra-śrutir iti. anumatiḥ
sinīvālī sarasvatī kuhū rajanī nandā rāketi.

teṣu—in those tracts of land; *varṣa-adrayaḥ*—mountains; *nadyaḥ ca*—as well as rivers; *sapta eva*—seven in number; *abhijñātāḥ*—understood; *svarasaḥ*—Svarasa; *śata-śṛṅgaḥ*—Śataśṛṅga; *vāma-devaḥ*—Vāmadeva; *kundaḥ*—Kunda; *mukundaḥ*—Mukunda; *puṣpa-varṣaḥ*—Puṣpa-varṣa; *sahasra-śrutiḥ*—Sahasraśruti; *iti*—thus; *anumatiḥ*—Anumati; *sinīvālī*—Sinīvālī; *sarasvatī*—Sarasvatī; *kuhū*—Kuhū; *rajanī*—Rajanī; *nandā*—Nandā; *rākā*—Rākā; *iti*—thus.

TRANSLATION

In those tracts of land there are seven mountains—Svarasa, Śataśṛṅga, Vāmadeva, Kunda, Mukunda, Puṣpa-varṣa and

Sahasraśruti. There are also seven rivers—Anumati, Sinīvālī, Sarasvatī, Kuhū, Rajanī, Nandā and Rākā. They are still existing.

TEXT 11

तद्वर्षपुरुषाः श्रुतधरवीर्यधरवसुन्धरेषन्धरसंज्ञा भगवन्तं वेदमयं सोममात्मानं वेदेन यजन्ते ॥११॥

tad-varṣa-puruṣāḥ śrutadhara-vīryadhara-vasundhareṣandhara-saṁjñā bhagavantaṁ vedamayaṁ somam ātmānaṁ vedena yajante.

tat-varṣa-puruṣāḥ—the residents of those tracts of land; *śrutadhara*—Śrutadhara; *vīryadhara*—Vīryadhara; *vasundhara*—Vasundhara; *iṣandhara*—Iṣandhara; *saṁjñāḥ*—known as; *bhagavantam*—the Supreme Personality of Godhead; *veda-mayam*—fully conversant with the Vedic knowledge; *somam ātmānam*—represented by the living entity known as Soma; *vedena*—by following the Vedic rules and regulations; *yajante*—they worship.

TRANSLATION

Strictly following the cult of varṇāśrama-dharma, the inhabitants of those islands, who are known as Śrutidharas, Vīryadharas, Vasundharas and Iṣandharas, all worship the expansion of the Supreme Personality of Godhead named Soma, the moon-god.

TEXT 12

स्वगोभिः पितृदेवेभ्यो विभजन् कृष्णशुक्लयोः।
प्रजानां सर्वासां राजान्धः सोमो न आस्त्विति ॥१२॥

sva-gobhiḥ pitṛ-devebhyo
vibhajan kṛṣṇa-śuklayoḥ
prajānāṁ sarvāsāṁ rājā-
ndhaḥ somo na āstv iti

sva-gobhiḥ—by expansion of his own illuminating rays; *pitṛ-devebhyaḥ*—unto the *pitās* and the demigods; *vibhajan*—dividing; *kṛṣṇa-śuklayoḥ*—into the two fortnights, dark and light; *prajānām*—of the citizens; *sarvāsām*—of all; *rājā*—the king; *andhaḥ*—food grains; *somaḥ*—the moon-god; *naḥ*—toward us; *āstu*—let him remain favorable; *iti*—thus.

TRANSLATION

[The inhabitants of Śālmalīdvīpa worship the demigod of the moon in the following words.] By his own rays, the moon-god has divided the month into two fortnights, known as śukla and kṛṣṇa, for the distribution of food grains to the pitās and the demigods. The demigod of the moon is he who divides time, and he is the king of all the residents of the universe. We therefore pray that he may remain our king and guide, and we offer him our respectful obeisances.

TEXT 13

एवं सुरोदाद्बहिस्तद्द्विगुणः समानेनावृतो घृतोदेन यथापूर्वः कुशद्वीपो यस्मिन्
कुशस्तम्बो देवकृतस्तद्द्वीपाख्याकरो ज्वलन इवापरः स्वशष्परोचिषा दिशो
विराजयति ॥१३॥

evaṁ surodād bahis tad-dvi-guṇaḥ samānenāvṛto ghṛtodena yathā-
pūrvaḥ kuśa-dvīpo yasmin kuśa-stambo deva-kṛtas tad-dvīpākhyākaro
jvalana ivāparaḥ sva-śaṣpa-rociṣā diśo virājayati.

evam—thus; *surodāt*—from the ocean of liquor; *bahiḥ*—outside; *tat-dvi-guṇaḥ*—twice that; *samānena*—equal in width; *āvṛtaḥ*—surrounded; *ghṛta-udena*—an ocean of clarified butter; *yathā-pūrvaḥ*—as previously with Śālmalīdvīpa; *kuśa-dvīpa*—the island called Kuśadvīpa; *yasmin*—in which; *kuśa-stambaḥ*—*kuśa* grass; *deva-kṛtaḥ*—created by the supreme will of the Supreme Personality of Godhead; *tat-dvīpa-ākhyā-karaḥ*—giving the island its name; *jvalanaḥ*—fire; *iva*—like; *aparaḥ*—another; *sva-śaṣpa-rociṣā*—by the effulgence of the young sprouting grass; *diśaḥ*—all directions; *virājayati*—illuminates.

TRANSLATION

Outside the ocean of liquor is another island, known as Kuśadvīpa, which is 800,000 yojanas [6,400,000 miles] wide,

twice as wide as the ocean of liquor. As Śālmalīdvīpa is surrounded by a liquor ocean, Kuśadvīpa is surrounded by an ocean of liquid ghee as broad as the island itself. On Kuśadvīpa there are clumps of kuśa grass, from which the island takes its name. This kuśa grass, which was created by the demigods by the will of the Supreme Lord, appears like a second form of fire, but with very mild and pleasing flames. Its young shoots illuminate all directions.

PURPORT

From the descriptions in this verse, we can make an educated guess about the nature of the flames on the moon. Like the sun, the moon must also be full of flames because without flames there cannot be illumination. The flames on the moon, however, unlike those on the sun, must be mild and pleasing. This is our conviction. The modern theory that the moon is full of dust is not accepted in the verses of *Śrīmad-Bhāgavatam.* In regard to this verse, Śrīla Viśvanātha Cakravartī Ṭhākura says, *suśaṣpāṇi sukomala-śikhās teṣāṁ rociṣā:* the *kuśa* grass illuminates all directions, but its flames are very mild and pleasing. This gives some idea of the flames existing on the moon.

TEXT 14

तद्द्वीपपतिः प्रैयव्रतो राजन् हिरण्यरेता नाम स्वं द्वीपं सप्तभ्यः स्वपुत्रेभ्यो यथाभागं विभज्य स्वयं तप आतिष्ठत वसुवसुदानदृढरुचिनाभिगुप्तस्तुत्यव्रतविविक्तवाम-देवनामभ्यः ॥ १४ ॥

tad-dvīpa-patiḥ praiyavrato rājan hiraṇyaretā nāma svaṁ dvīpaṁ saptabhyaḥ sva-putrebhyo yathā-bhāgaṁ vibhajya svayaṁ tapa ātiṣṭhata vasu-vasudāna-dṛḍharuci-nābhigupta-stutyavrata-vivikta-vāmadeva-nāmabhyaḥ.

tat-dvīpa-patiḥ—the master of that island; *praiyavrataḥ*—the son of Mahārāja Priyavrata; *rājan*—O King; *hiraṇyaretā*—Hiraṇyaretā; *nāma*—named; *svam*—his own; *dvīpam*—island; *saptabhyaḥ*—unto seven; *sva-putrebhyaḥ*—his own sons; *yathā-bhāgam*—according to division; *vibhajya*—dividing; *svayam*—himself; *tapaḥ ātiṣṭhata*—

engaged in austerities; *vasu*—unto Vasu; *vasudāna*—Vasudāna; *dṛḍha-ruci*—Dṛḍharuci; *nābhi-gupta*—Nābhigupta; *stutya-vrata*—Stutyavrata; *vivikta*—Vivikta; *vāma-deva*—Vāmadeva; *nāmabhyaḥ*—named.

TRANSLATION

O King, another son of Mahārāja Priyavrata, Hiraṇyaretā, was the king of this island. He divided it into seven parts, which he delivered to his seven sons according to the rights of inheritance. The King then retired from family life to engage in austerities. The names of those sons are Vasu, Vasudāna, Dṛḍharuci, Stutyavrata, Nābhigupta, Vivikta and Vāmadeva.

TEXT 15

**तेषां वर्षेषु सीमागिरयो नद्यश्चाभिज्ञाताः सप्त सप्तैव चक्रश्चतुःशृङ्गः कपि-
लश्चित्रकूटो देवानीक ऊर्ध्वरोमा द्रविण इति रसकुल्या मधुकुल्या मित्रविन्दा
श्रुतविन्दा देवगर्भा घृतच्युता मन्त्रमालेति ॥ १५ ॥**

teṣāṁ varṣeṣu sīmā-girayo nadyaś cābhijñātāḥ sapta saptaiva cakraś catuḥśṛṅgaḥ kapilaś citrakūṭo devānīka ūrdhvaromā draviṇa iti rasakulyā madhukulyā mitravindā śrutavindā devagarbhā ghṛtacyutā mantramāleti.

teṣām—all those sons; *varṣeṣu*—in the tracts of land; *sīmā-girayaḥ*—border mountains; *nadyaḥ ca*—as well as rivers; *abhijñātāḥ*—known; *sapta*—seven; *sapta*—seven; *eva*—certainly; *cakraḥ*—Cakra; *catuḥ-śṛṅgaḥ*—Catuḥśṛṅga; *kapilaḥ*—Kapila; *citra-kūṭaḥ*—Citrakūṭa; *devānīkaḥ*—Devānīka; *ūrdhva-romā*—Ūrdhvaromā; *draviṇaḥ*—Draviṇa; *iti*—thus; *rama-kulyā*—Ramakulyā; *madhu-kulyā*—Madhukulyā; *mitra-vindā*—Mitravindā; *śruta-vindā*—Śrutavindā; *deva-garbhā*—Devagarbhā; *ghṛta-cyutā*—Ghṛtacyutā; *mantra-mālā*—Mantramālā; *iti*—thus.

TRANSLATION

In those seven islands there are seven boundary mountains, known as Cakra, Catuḥśṛṅga, Kapila, Citrakūṭa, Devānīka,

Ūrdhvaromā and Draviṇa. There are also seven rivers, known as Ramakulyā, Madhukulyā, Mitravindā, Śrutavindā, Devagarbhā, Ghṛtacyutā and Mantramālā.

TEXT 16

यासां पयोभिः कुशद्वीपौकसः कुशलकोविदाभियुक्तकुलकसंज्ञा भगवन्तं जातवेदसरूपिणं कर्मकौशलेन यजन्ते ॥ १६ ॥

yāsāṁ payobhiḥ kuśadvīpaukasaḥ kuśala-kovidābhiyukta-kulaka-saṁjñā bhagavantaṁ jātaveda-sarūpiṇaṁ karma-kauśalena yajante.

yāsām—of which; *payobhiḥ*—by the water; *kuśa-dvīpa-okasaḥ*—the inhabitants of the island known as Kuśadvīpa; *kuśala*—Kuśala; *kovida*—Kovida; *abhiyukta*—Abhiyukta; *kulaka*—Kulaka; *saṁjñāḥ*—named; *bhagavantam*—unto the Supreme Personality of Godhead; *jāta-veda*—the demigod of fire; *sa-rūpiṇam*—manifesting the form; *karma-kauśalena*—by expertise in ritualistic ceremonies; *yajante*—they worship.

TRANSLATION

The inhabitants of the island of Kuśadvīpa are celebrated as the Kuśalas, Kovidas, Abhiyuktas and Kulakas. They are like the brāhmaṇas, kṣatriyas, vaiśyas and śūdras respectively. By bathing in the waters of those rivers, they all become purified. They are expert in performing ritualistic ceremonies according to the orders of the Vedic scriptures. Thus they worship the Lord in His aspect as the demigod of fire.

TEXT 17

परस्य ब्रह्मणः साक्षाज्जातवेदोऽसि हव्यवाट् ।
देवानां पुरुषाङ्गानां यज्ञेन पुरुषं यजेति ॥१७॥

parasya brahmaṇaḥ sākṣāj
jāta-vedo 'si havyavāṭ

devānāṁ puruṣāṅgānāṁ
yajñena puruṣaṁ yajeti

parasya—of the Supreme; *brahmaṇaḥ*—Brahman; *sākṣāt*—directly; *jāta-vedaḥ*—O fire-god; *asi*—you are; *havyavāṭ*—the carrier of Vedic offerings of grains and ghee; *devānām*—of all the demigods; *puruṣa-aṅgānām*—who are limbs of the Supreme Person; *yajñena*—by performing the ritualistic sacrifices; *puruṣam*—to the Supreme Person; *yaja*—please carry oblations; *iti*—thus.

TRANSLATION

[This is the mantra by which the inhabitants of Kuśadvīpa worship the fire-god.] O fire-god, you are a part of the Supreme Personality of Godhead, Hari, and you carry to Him all the offerings of sacrifices. Therefore we request you to offer to the Supreme Personality of Godhead the yajñic ingredients we are offering the demigods, for the Lord is the real enjoyer.

PURPORT

The demigods are servants who assist the Supreme Personality of Godhead. If one worships the demigods, the demigods, as servants of the Supreme, carry the sacrificial offerings to the Lord, like tax collectors collecting revenue from the citizens and bringing it to the government's treasury. The demigods cannot accept the sacrificial offerings; they simply carry the offerings to the Supreme Personality of Godhead. As stated by Śrīla Viśvanātha Cakravartī Ṭhākura, *yasya prasādād bhagavat-prasādaḥ:* since the *guru* is a representative of the Supreme Personality of Godhead, he carries to the Lord whatever is offered to him. Similarly, all the demigods, as faithful servants of the Supreme Lord, hand over to the Supreme Lord whatever is offered to them in sacrificial performances. There is no fault in worshiping the demigods with this understanding, but to think that the demigods are independent of the Supreme Personality of Godhead and equal to Him is called *hṛta-jñāna*, a loss of intelligence (*kāmais tais tair hṛta-jñānāḥ*). One who thinks that the demigods themselves are the actual benefactors is mistaken.

TEXT 18

तथा घृतोदाद्बहिः क्रौञ्चद्वीपो द्विगुणः स्वमानेन क्षीरोदेन परित उपक्लृप्तो वृतो यथा कुशद्वीपो घृतोदेन यस्मिन् क्रौञ्चो नाम पर्वतराजो द्वीपनामनिर्वर्तक आस्ते ॥१८॥

tathā ghṛtodād bahiḥ krauñcadvīpo dvi-guṇaḥ sva-mānena kṣīrodena parita upakḷpto vṛto yathā kuśadvīpo ghṛtodena yasmin krauñco nāma parvata-rājo dvīpa-nāma-nirvartaka āste.

tathā—so also; *ghṛta-udāt*—from the ocean of clarified butter; *bahiḥ*—outside; *krauñca-dvīpaḥ*—another island, known as Krauñcadvīpa; *dvi-guṇaḥ*—twice as big; *sa-mānena*—as the same measurement; *ksīra-udena*—by an ocean of milk; *paritaḥ*—all around; *upakḷptaḥ*—surrounded; *vṛtaḥ*—surrounded; *yathā*—like; *kuśa-dvīpaḥ*—the island known as Kuśadvīpa; *ghṛta-udena*—by an ocean of clarified butter; *yasmin*—in which; *krauñcaḥ nāma*—named Krauñca; *parvata-rājaḥ*—a king of mountains; *dvīpa-nāma*—the name of the island; *nirvartakaḥ*—bringing about; *āste*—exists.

TRANSLATION

Outside the ocean of clarified butter is another island, known as Krauñcadvīpa, which has a width of 1,600,000 yojanas [12,800,000 miles], twice the width of the ocean of clarified butter. As Kuśadvīpa is surrounded by an ocean of clarified butter, Krauñcadvīpa is surrounded by an ocean of milk as broad as the island itself. On Krauñcadvīpa there is a great mountain known as Krauñca, from which the island takes its name.

TEXT 19

योऽसौ गुहप्रहरणोन्मथितनितम्बकुञ्जोऽपि क्षीरोदेनासिच्यमानो भगवता वरुणेनाभिगुप्तो विभयो बभूव ॥ १९ ॥

yo 'sau guha-praharaṇonmathita-nitamba-kuñjo 'pi kṣīrodenā-sicyamāno bhagavatā varuṇenābhigupto vibhayo babhūva.

yaḥ—which; *asau*—that (mountain); *guha-praharaṇa*—by the weapons of Kārttikeya, the son of Lord Śiva; *unmathita*—shaken; *nitamba-kuñjaḥ*—whose trees and vegetables along the slopes; *api*—although; *kṣīra-udena*—by the ocean of milk; *āsicyamānaḥ*—being always bathed; *bhagavatā*—by the greatly powerful; *varuṇena*—the demigod known as Varuṇa; *abhiguptaḥ*—protected; *vibhayaḥ babhūva*—has become fearless.

TRANSLATION

Although the vegetables living on the slopes of Mount Krauñca were attacked and devastated by the weapons of Kārttikeya, the mountain has become fearless because it is always bathed on all sides by the ocean of milk and protected by Varuṇadeva.

TEXT 20

तस्मिन्नपि प्रैयव्रतो घृतपृष्ठो नामाधिपतिः स्वे द्वीपे वर्षाणि सप्त विभज्य तेषु पुत्रनामसु सप्त रिक्थादान् वर्षपान्निवेश्य स्वयं भगवान् भगवतः परमकल्याण-यशस आत्मभूतस्य हरेश्चरणारविन्दमुपजगाम ॥ २० ॥

tasminn api praiyavrato ghṛtapṛṣṭho nāmādhipatiḥ sve dvīpe varṣāṇi
sapta vibhajya teṣu putra-nāmasu sapta rikthādān varṣapān niveśya
svayaṁ bhagavān bhagavataḥ parama-kalyāṇa-yaśasa ātma-bhūtasya
hareś caraṇāravindam upajagāma.

tasmin—in that island; *api*—also; *praiyavrataḥ*—the son of Mahārāja Priyavrata; *ghṛta-pṛṣṭhaḥ*—Ghṛtapṛṣṭha; *nāma*—named; *adhipatiḥ*—the king of that island; *sve*—his own; *dvīpe*—in the island; *varṣāṇi*—tracts of land; *sapta*—seven; *vibhajya*—dividing; *teṣu*—in each of them; *putra-nāmasu*—possessing the names of his sons; *sapta*—seven; *rikthā-dān*—sons; *varṣa-pān*—the masters of the *varṣas; niveśya*—appointing; *svayam*—himself; *bhagavān*—very powerful; *bhagavataḥ*—of the Supreme Personality of Godhead; *parama-kalyāṇa-yaśasaḥ*—whose glories are so auspicious; *ātma-bhūtasya*—the soul of all souls; *hareḥ caraṇa-aravindam*—the lotus feet of the Lord; *upajagāma*—took shelter at.

TRANSLATION

The ruler of this island was another son of Mahārāja Priyavrata. His name was Ghṛtapṛṣṭha, and he was a very learned scholar. He also divided his own island among his seven sons. After dividing the island into seven parts, named according to the names of his sons, Ghṛtapṛṣṭha Mahārāja completely retired from family life and took shelter at the lotus feet of the Lord, the soul of all souls, who has all auspicious qualities. Thus he attained perfection.

TEXT 21

**आमो मधुरुहो मेघपृष्ठः सुधामा भ्राजिष्ठो लोहितार्णो वनस्पतिरिति घृतपृष्ठसु-
तास्तेषां वर्षगिरयः सप्त सप्तैव नद्यश्चाभिख्याताः शुक्लो वर्धमानो भोजन
उपबर्हिणो नन्दो नन्दनः सर्वतोभद्र इति अभया अमृतौघा आर्यका तीर्थवती
रूपवती पवित्रवती शुक्लेति ॥ २१ ॥**

āmo madhuruho meghapṛṣṭhaḥ sudhāmā bhrājiṣṭho lohitārṇo vanaspatir iti ghṛtapṛṣṭha-sutās teṣāṁ varṣa-girayaḥ sapta saptaiva nadyaś cābhikhyātāḥ śuklo vardhamāno bhojana upabarhiṇo nando nandanaḥ sarvatobhadra iti abhayā amṛtaughā āryakā tīrthavatī rūpavatī pavitravatī śukleti.

āmaḥ—Āma; *madhu-ruhaḥ*—Madhuruha; *megha-pṛṣṭhaḥ*—Meghapṛṣṭha; *sudhāmā*—Sudhāmā; *bhrājiṣṭhaḥ*—Bhrājiṣṭha; *lohitārṇaḥ*—Lohitārṇa; *vanaspatiḥ*—Vanaspati; *iti*—thus; *ghṛtapṛṣṭha-sutāḥ*—the sons of Ghṛtapṛṣṭha; *teṣām*—of those sons; *varṣa-girayaḥ*—boundary hills of the tracts of land; *sapta*—seven; *sapta*—seven; *eva*—also; *nadyaḥ*—rivers; *ca*—and; *abhikhyātāḥ*—celebrated; *śuklaḥ vardhamānaḥ*—Śukla and Vardhamāna; *bhojanaḥ*—Bhojana; *upabarhiṇaḥ*—Upabarhiṇa; *nandaḥ*—Nanda; *nandanaḥ*—Nandana; *sarvataḥ-bhadraḥ*—Sarvatobhadra; *iti*—thus; *abhayā*—Abhayā; *amṛtaughā*—Amṛtaughā; *āryakā*—Āryakā; *tīrthavatī*—Tīrthavatī; *rūpavatī*—Rūpavatī; *pavitravatī*—Pavitravatī; *śuklā*—Śuklā; *iti*—thus.

TRANSLATION

The sons of Mahārāja Ghṛtapṛṣṭha were named Āma, Madhuruha, Meghapṛṣṭha, Sudhāmā, Bhrājiṣṭha, Lohitārṇa and Vanaspati. In their island there are seven mountains, which indicate the boundaries of the seven tracts of land, and there are also seven rivers. The mountains are named Śukla, Vardhamāna, Bhojana, Upabarhiṇa, Nanda, Nandana and Sarvatobhadra. The rivers are named Abhayā, Amṛtaughā, Āryakā, Tīrthavatī, Rūpavatī, Pavitravatī and Śuklā.

TEXT 22

यासामम्भः पवित्रममलमुपयुञ्जानाः पुरुषऋषभद्रविणदेवकसंज्ञा वर्षपुरुषा आपोमयं देवमपां पूर्णेनाञ्जलिना यजन्ते ॥ २२ ॥

yāsām ambhaḥ pavitram amalam upayuñjānāḥ puruṣa-ṛṣabha-draviṇa-devaka-saṁjñā varṣa-puruṣā āpomayaṁ devam apāṁ pūrṇenāñjalinā yajante.

yāsām—of all the rivers; *ambhaḥ*—the water; *pavitram*—very sanctified; *amalam*—very clean; *upayuñjānāḥ*—using; *puruṣa*—Puruṣa; *ṛṣabha*—Ṛṣabha; *draviṇa*—Draviṇa; *devaka*—Devaka; *saṁjñāḥ*—endowed with the names; *varṣa-puruṣāḥ*—the inhabitants of those *varṣas; āpaḥ-mayam*—Varuṇa, the lord of water; *devam*—as the worshipable deity; *apām*—of water; *pūrṇena*—with full; *añjalinā*—folded palms; *yajante*—do worship.

TRANSLATION

The inhabitants of Krauñcadvīpa are divided into four castes, called the Puruṣas, Ṛṣabhas, Draviṇas and Devakas. Using the waters of those sanctified rivers, they worship the Supreme Personality of Godhead by offering a palmful of water at the lotus feet of Varuṇa, the demigod who has a form of water.

PURPORT

Viśvānatha Cakravartī Ṭhākura says, *āpomayaḥ asmayam:* with joined palms the inhabitants of the various sections of Krauñcadvīpa offer the sanctified waters of the rivers to a deity made of stone or iron.

TEXT 23

आपः पुरुषवीर्याः स्थ पुनन्तीर्भूर्भुवःसुवः ।
ता नः पुनीतामीवघ्नीः स्पृशतामात्मना भुव इति ॥ २३ ॥

āpaḥ puruṣa-vīryāḥ stha
punantīr bhūr-bhuvaḥ-suvaḥ
tā naḥ punītāmīva-ghnīḥ
spṛśatām ātmanā bhuva iti

āpaḥ—O water; *puruṣa-vīryāḥ*—endowed with the energy of the Supreme Personality of Godhead; *stha*—you are; *punantīḥ*—sanctifying; *bhūḥ*—of the planetary system known as Bhūḥ; *bhuvaḥ*—of the Bhuvaḥ planetary system; *suvaḥ*—of the Svaḥ planetary system; *tāḥ*—that water; *naḥ*—of us; *punīta*—purify; *amīva-ghnīḥ*—who destroys sin; *spṛśatām*—of those touching; *ātmanā*—by your constitutional position; *bhuvaḥ*—the bodies; *iti*—thus.

TRANSLATION

[The inhabitants of Krauñcadvīpa worship with this mantra.] O water of the rivers, you have obtained energy from the Supreme Personality of Godhead. Therefore you purify the three planetary systems, known as Bhūloka, Bhuvarloka and Svarloka. By your constitutional nature, you take away sins, and that is why we are touching you. Kindly continue to purify us.

PURPORT

Kṛṣṇa says in *Bhagavad-gītā* (7.4):

bhūmir āpo 'nalo vāyuḥ
khaṁ mano buddhir eva ca
ahaṅkāra itīyaṁ me
bhinnā prakṛtir aṣṭadhā

"Earth, water, fire, air, ether, mind, intelligence and false ego—all together these eight comprise My separated material energies."

The energy of the Lord acts throughout the creation, just as heat and light, the energies of the sun, act within the universe and make everything work. The specific rivers mentioned in the *śāstras* are also energies of the Supreme Personality of Godhead, and people who regularly bathe in them are purified. It can actually be seen that many people are cured of diseases simply by bathing in the Ganges. Similarly, the inhabitants of Krauñcadvīpa purify themselves by bathing in the rivers there.

TEXT 24

एवं पुरस्तात्क्षीरोदात्परित उपवेशितः शाकद्वीपो द्वात्रिंशल्लक्षयोजनायामः समानेन च दधिमण्डोदेन परीतो यस्मिन् शाको नाम महीरुहः स्वक्षेत्रव्यपदेशको यस्य ह महासुरभिगन्धस्तं द्वीपमनुवासयति ॥२४॥

evaṁ purastāt kṣīrodāt parita upaveśitaḥ śākadvīpo dvātriṁśal-lakṣa-yojanāyāmaḥ samānena ca dadhi-maṇḍodena parīto yasmin śāko nāma mahīruhaḥ sva-kṣetra-vyapadeśako yasya ha mahā-surabhi-gandhas taṁ dvīpam anuvāsayati.

evam—thus; *parastāt*—beyond; *kṣīra-udāt*—from the ocean of milk; *paritaḥ*—all around; *upaveśitaḥ*—situated; *śāka-dvīpaḥ*—another island, known as Śākadvīpa; *dvā-triṁśat*—thirty-two; *lakṣa*—100,000; *yojana*—*yojanas;* *āyāmaḥ*—whose measure; *samānena*—of equal length; *ca*—and; *dadhi-maṇḍa-udena*—by an ocean containing water resembling churned yogurt; *parītaḥ*—surrounded; *yasmin*—in which land; *śākaḥ*—*śāka;* *nāma*—named; *mahīruhaḥ*—a fig tree; *sva-kṣetra-vyapadeśakaḥ*—giving the island its name; *yasya*—of which; *ha*—indeed; *mahā-surabhi*—a greatly fragrant; *gandhaḥ*—aroma; *tam dvīpam*—that island; *anuvāsayati*—makes fragrant.

TRANSLATION

Outside the ocean of milk is another island, Śākadvīpa, which has a width of 3,200,000 yojanas [25,600,000 miles]. As Krauñcadvīpa is surrounded by its own ocean of milk, Śākadvīpa is surrounded by an ocean of churned yogurt as broad as the island

itself. In Śākadvīpa there is a big śāka tree, from which the island takes its name. This tree is very fragrant. Indeed, it lends its scent to the entire island.

TEXT 25

तस्यापि प्रैयव्रत एवाधिपतिर्नाम्ना मेधातिथिः सोऽपि विभज्य सप्त वर्षाणि पुत्रनामानि तेषु स्वात्मजान् पुरोजवमनोजवपवमानधूम्रानीकचित्ररेफबहुरूप-विश्वधारसंज्ञान्निधाप्याधिपतीन् स्वयं भगवत्यनन्त आवेशितमतिस्तपोवनं प्रविवेश ॥२५॥

tasyāpi praiyavrata evādhipatir nāmnā medhātithiḥ so 'pi vibhajya sapta varṣāṇi putra-nāmāni teṣu svātmajān purojava-manojava-pavamāna-dhūmrānīka-citrarepha-bahurūpa-viśvadhāra-saṁjñān nidhāpyādhipatīn svayaṁ bhagavaty ananta ā-veśita-matis tapovanaṁ praviveśa.

tasya api—of that island also; *praiyavrataḥ*—a son of Mahārāja Priyavrata; *eva*—certainly; *adhipatiḥ*—the ruler; *nāmnā*—by the name; *medhā-tithiḥ*—Medhātithi; *saḥ api*—he also; *vibhajya*—dividing; *sapta varṣāṇi*—seven divisions of the island; *putra-nāmāni*—possessing the names of his sons; *teṣu*—in them; *sva-ātmajān*—his own sons; *purojava*—Purojava; *manojava*—Manojava; *pavamāna*—Pavamāna; *dhūmrānīka*—Dhūmrānīka; *citra-repha*—Citrarepha; *bahu-rūpa*—Bahurūpa; *viśvadhāra*—Viśvadhāra; *saṁjñān*—having as names; *nidhāpya*—establishing as; *adhipatīn*—the rulers; *svayam*—himself; *bhagavati*—in the Supreme Personality of Godhead; *anante*—in the unlimited; *āveśita-matiḥ*—whose mind was fully absorbed; *tapaḥ-vanam*—in the forest where meditation is performed; *praviveśa*—he entered.

TRANSLATION

The master of this island, also one of the sons of Priyavrata, was known as Medhātithi. He also divided his island into seven sections, named according to the names of his own sons, whom he

made the kings of that island. The names of those sons are Purojava, Manojava, Pavamāna, Dhūmrānīka, Citrarepha, Bahurūpa and Viśvadhāra. After dividing the island and situating his sons as its rulers, Medhātithi personally retired, and to fix his mind completely upon the lotus feet of the Supreme Personality of Godhead, he entered a forest suitable for meditation.

TEXT 26

एतेषां वर्षमर्यादागिरयो नद्यश्च सप्त सप्तैव ईशान उरुशृङ्गो बलभद्रः शतकेसरः सहस्रस्रोतो देवपालो महानस इति अनघाऽऽयुर्दा उभयस्पृष्टिरपराजिता पञ्चपदी सहस्रस्रुतिर्निजधृतिरिति ॥२६॥

eteṣāṁ varṣa-maryādā-girayo nadyaś ca sapta saptaiva īśāna uruśṛṅgo balabhadraḥ śatakesaraḥ sahasrasroto devapālo mahānasa iti anaghāyurdā ubhayaspṛṣṭir aparājitā pañcapadī sahasrasrutir nijadhṛtir iti.

eteṣām—of all these divisions; *varṣa-maryādā*—acting as the boundary limits; *girayaḥ*—the big hills; *nadyaḥ ca*—and the rivers also; *sapta*—seven; *sapta*—seven; *eva*—indeed; *īśānaḥ*—Īśāna; *uru-śṛṅgaḥ*—Uruśṛṅga; *bala-bhadraḥ*—Balabhadra; *śata-kesaraḥ*—Śatakesara; *sahasra-srotaḥ*—Sahasrasrota; *deva-pālaḥ*—Devapāla; *mahānasaḥ*—Mahānasa; *iti*—thus; *anaghā*—Anaghā; *āyurdā*—Āyurdā; *ubhayaspṛṣṭiḥ*—Ubhayaspṛṣṭi; *aparājitā*—Aparājitā; *pañcapadī*—Pañcapadī; *sahasra-srutiḥ*—Sahasrasruti; *nija-dhṛtiḥ*—Nijadhṛti; *iti*—thus.

TRANSLATION

For these lands also, there are seven boundary mountains and seven rivers. The mountains are Īśāna, Uruśṛṅga, Balabhadra, Śatakesara, Sahasrasrota, Devapāla and Mahānasa. The rivers are Anaghā, Āyurdā, Ubhayaspṛṣṭi, Aparājitā, Pañcapadī, Sahasrasruti and Nijadhṛti.

TEXT 27

तद्वर्षपुरुषा ऋतव्रतसत्यव्रतदानव्रतानुव्रतनामानो भगवन्तं वाय्वात्मकं प्राणायामविधूतरजस्तमसः परमसमाधिना यजन्ते ॥२७॥

tad-varṣa-puruṣā ṛtavrata-satyavrata-dānavratānuvrata-nāmāno bhagavantaṁ vāyv-ātmakaṁ prāṇāyāma-vidhūta-rajas-tamasaḥ parama-samādhinā yajante.

tat-varṣa-puruṣāḥ—the inhabitants of those tracts of land; *ṛta-vrata*—Ṛtavrata; *satya-vrata*—Satyavrata; *dāna-vrata*—Dānavrata; *anuvrata*—Anuvrata; *nāmānaḥ*—having the four names; *bhagavan-tam*—the Supreme Personality of Godhead; *vāyu-ātmakam*—represented by the demigod Vāyu; *prāṇāyāma*—by the practice of regulating the airs within the body; *vidhūta*—cleansed away; *rajaḥ-tamasaḥ*—whose passion and ignorance; *parama*—sublime; *samādhinā*—by trance; *yajante*—they worship.

TRANSLATION

The inhabitants of those islands are also divided into four castes—Ṛtavrata, Satyavrata, Dānavrata and Anuvrata—which exactly resemble brāhmaṇa, kṣatriya, vaiśya and śūdra. They practice prāṇāyāma and mystic yoga, and in trance they worship the Supreme Lord in the form of Vāyu.

TEXT 28

अन्तः प्रविश्य भूतानि यो बिभर्त्यात्मकेतुभिः ।
अन्तर्यामीश्वरः साक्षात्पातु नो यद्वशे स्फुटम् ॥२८॥

antaḥ-praviśya bhūtāni
yo bibharty ātma-ketubhiḥ
antaryāmīśvaraḥ sākṣāt
pātu no yad-vaśe sphuṭam

antaḥ-praviśya—entering within; *bhūtāni*—all living entities; *yaḥ*—who; *bibharti*—maintains; *ātma-ketubhiḥ*—by the functions of the inner airs (*prāṇa, apāna,* etc.); *antaryāmī*—the Supersoul within; *īśvaraḥ*—the Supreme Person; *sākṣāt*—directly; *pātu*—please maintain; *naḥ*—us; *yat-vaśe*—under whose control; *sphuṭam*—the cosmic manifestation.

TRANSLATION

[The inhabitants of Śākadvīpa worship the Supreme Personality of Godhead in the form of Vāyu in the following words.] O Supreme Person, situated as the Supersoul within the body, You direct the various actions of the different airs, such as prāṇa, and thus You maintain all living entities. O Lord, O Supersoul of everyone, O controller of the cosmic manifestation under whom everything exists, may You protect us from all dangers.

PURPORT

Through the mystic *yoga* practice called *prāṇāyāma,* the *yogī* controls the airs within the body to maintain the body in a healthy condition. In this way, the *yogī* comes to the point of trance and tries to see the Supersoul within the core of his heart. *Prāṇāyāma* is the means to attain *samādhi,* trance, in order to fully absorb oneself in seeing the Supreme Lord as *antrayāmī,* the Supersoul within the core of the heart.

TEXT 29

एवमेव दधिमण्डोदात्परतः पुष्करद्वीपस्ततो द्विगुणायामः समन्तत
उपकल्पितः समानेन स्वादूदकेन समुद्रेण बहिरावृतो यस्मिन् बृहत्पुष्करं
ज्वलनशिखामलकनकपत्रायुतायुतं भगवतः कमलासनस्याध्यासनं परिकल्पितम्
॥२९॥

evam eva dadhi-maṇḍodāt parataḥ puṣkaradvīpas tato dvi-guṇāyāmaḥ samantata upakalpitaḥ samānena svādūdakena samudreṇa bahir āvṛto yasmin bṛhat-puṣkaraṁ jvalana-śikhāmala-kanaka-patrāyutāyutaṁ bhagavataḥ kamalāsanasyādhyāsanaṁ parikalpitam.

evam eva—thus; *dadhi-maṇḍa-udāt*—the ocean of yogurt; *parataḥ*—beyond; *puṣkara-dvīpaḥ*—another island, named Puṣkaradvīpa; *tataḥ*—than that (Śākadvīpa); *dvi-guṇa-āyāmaḥ*—whose measurement is twice as great; *samantataḥ*—on all sides; *upakalpitaḥ*—surrounded; *samānena*—equal in width; *svādu-udakena*—possessing sweet water; *samudreṇa*—by an ocean; *bahiḥ*—outside; *āvṛtaḥ*—surrounded; *yasmin*—in which; *bṛhat*—very big; *puṣkaram*—lotus flower; *jvalana-śikhā*—like the flames of a blazing fire; *amala*—pure; *kanaka*—gold; *patra*—leaves; *ayuta-ayutam*—possessing 100,000,000; *bhagavataḥ*—greatly powerful; *kamala āsanasya*—of Lord Brahmā, whose sitting place is on the lotus flower; *adhyāsanam*—sitting place; *parikalpitam*—considered.

TRANSLATION

Outside the ocean of yogurt is another island, known as Puṣkaradvīpa, which is 6,400,000 yojanas [51,200,000 miles] wide, twice as wide as the ocean of yogurt. It is surrounded by an ocean of very tasteful water as broad as the island itself. On Puṣkaradvīpa there is a great lotus flower with 100,000,000 pure golden petals, as effulgent as the flames of fire. That lotus flower is considered the sitting place of Lord Brahmā, who is the most powerful living being and who is therefore sometimes called bhagavān.

TEXT 30

**तद्द्वीपमध्ये मानसोत्तरनामैक एवार्वाचीनपराचीनवर्षयोर्मर्यादाचलोऽयुतयोजनो-
च्छ्रायायामो यत्र तु चतसृषु दिक्षु चत्वारि पुराणि लोकपालानामिन्द्रादीनां
यदुपरिष्टात्सूर्यरथस्य मेरुं परिभ्रमतः संवत्सरात्मकं चक्रं देवानामहोरात्राभ्यां
परिभ्रमति ॥३०॥**

tad-dvīpa-madhye mānasottara-nāmaika evārvācīna-parācīna-varṣayor
maryādācalo 'yuta-yojanocchrāyāyāmo yatra tu catasṛṣu dikṣu catvāri
purāṇi loka-pālānām indrādīnāṁ yad-upariṣṭāt sūrya-rathasya meruṁ
paribhramataḥ saṁvatsarātmakaṁ cakraṁ devānām aho-rātrābhyāṁ
paribhramati.

tat-dvīpa-madhye—within that island; *mānasottara*—Mānasottara; *nāma*—named; *ekaḥ*—one; *eva*—indeed; *arvācīna*—on this side; *parācīna*—and beyond, or outside; *varṣayoḥ*—of tracts of land; *maryādā*—indicating the boundary; *acalaḥ*—a great mountain; *ayuta*—ten thousand; *yojana*—eight miles; *ucchrāya-āyāmaḥ*—whose height and width; *yatra*—where; *tu*—but; *catasṛṣu*—in the four; *dikṣu*—directions; *catvāri*—four; *purāṇi*—cities; *loka-pālānām*—of the directors of planetary systems; *indra-ādīnām*—headed by Indra; *yat*—of which; *upariṣṭāt*—on the top; *sūrya-rathasya*—of the chariot of the sun-god; *merum*—Meru Mountain; *paribhramataḥ*—while circumambulating; *saṁvatsara-ātmakam*—consisting of one *saṁvatsara; cakram*—wheel or orbit; *devānām*—of the demigods; *ahaḥ-rātrābhyām*—by the day and night; *paribhramati*—moves around.

TRANSLATION

In the middle of that island is a great mountain named Mānasottara, which forms the boundary between the inner side and the outer side of the island. Its breadth and height are 10,000 yojanas [80,000 miles]. On that mountain, in the four directions, are the residential quarters of demigods such as Indra. In the chariot of the sun-god, the sun travels on the top of the mountain in an orbit called the Saṁvatsara, encircling Mount Meru. The sun's path on the northern side is called Uttarāyaṇa, and its path on the southern side is called Dakṣiṇāyana. One side represents a day for the demigods, and the other represents their night.

PURPORT

The movement of the sun is confirmed in the *Brahma-saṁhitā* (5.52): *yasyājñāya bhramati saṁbhṛta-kāla-cakraḥ.* The sun orbits around Mount Sumeru, for six months on the northern side and for six months on the southern. This adds up to the duration of a day and night of the demigods in the upper planetary systems.

TEXT 31

तद्द्वीपस्याप्यधिपतिः प्रैयव्रतो वीतिहोत्रो नामैतस्यात्मजौ रमणकधातकि-
नामानौ वर्षपती नियुज्य स स्वयं पूर्वजवद्भगवत्कर्मशील एवास्ते ॥३१॥

tad-dvīpasyāpy adhipatiḥ praiyavrato vītihotro nāmaitasyātmajau ramaṇaka-dhātaki-nāmānau varṣa-patī niyujya sa svayaṁ pūrvajavad-bhagavat-karma-śīla evāste.

tat-dvīpasya—of that island; *api*—also; *adhipatiḥ*—the ruler; *praiyavrataḥ*—a son of Mahārāja Priyavrata; *vītihotraḥ nāma*—named Vītihotra; *etasya*—of him; *ātma-jau*—unto the two sons; *ramaṇaka*—Ramaṇaka; *dhātaki*—and Dhātaki; *nāmānau*—having the names; *varṣa-patī*—the rulers of the two tracts of land; *niyujya*—appointing; *saḥ svayam*—himself; *pūrvaja-vat*—like his other brothers; *bhagavat-karma-śīlaḥ*—being absorbed in activities to satisfy the Supreme Personality of Godhead; *eva*—indeed; *āste*—remains.

TRANSLATION

The ruler of this island, the son of Mahārāja Priyavrata named Vītihotra, had two sons named Ramaṇaka and Dhātaki. He granted the two sides of the island to these two sons and then personally engaged himself in activities for the sake of the Supreme Personality of Godhead like his elder brother Medhātithi.

TEXT 32

तद्वर्षपुरुषा भगवन्तं ब्रह्मरूपिणं सकर्मकेण कर्मणाऽऽराधयन्तीदं चोदाहरन्ति ॥३२॥

tad-varṣa-puruṣā bhagavantaṁ brahma-rūpiṇaṁ sakarmakeṇa karmaṇārādhayantīdaṁ codāharanti.

tat-varṣa-puruṣāḥ—the inhabitants of that island; *bhagavantam*—the Supreme Personality of Godhead; *brahma-rūpiṇam*—exhibited as Lord Brahmā being seated on the lotus; *sa-karmakeṇa*—for fulfillment of material desires; *karmaṇā*—by performing ritualistic activities according to the *Vedas; ārādhayanti*—worship; *idam*—this; *ca*—and; *udāharanti*—they chant.

TRANSLATION

For the fulfillment of material desires, the inhabitants of this tract of land worship the Supreme Personality of Godhead as

represented by Lord Brahmā. They offer prayers to the Lord as follows.

TEXT 33

यत्तत्कर्ममयं लिङ्गं ब्रह्मलिङ्गं जनोऽर्चयेत् ।
एकान्तमद्वयं शान्तं तस्मै भगवते नम इति ॥३३॥

yat tat karmamayaṁ liṅgaṁ
brahma-liṅgaṁ jano 'rcayet
ekāntam advayaṁ śāntaṁ
tasmai bhagavate nama iti

yat—which; *tat*—that; *karma-mayam*—obtainable by the Vedic ritualistic system; *liṅgam*—the form; *brahma-liṅgam*—which makes known the Supreme Brahman; *janaḥ*—a person; *arcayet*—must worship; *ekāntam*—who has full faith in the one Supreme; *advayam*—nondifferent; *śāntam*—peaceful; *tasmai*—unto him; *bhagavate*—the most powerful; *namaḥ*—our respects; *iti*—thus.

TRANSLATION

Lord Brahmā is known as karma-maya, the form of ritualistic ceremonies, because by performing ritualistic ceremonies one may attain his position and because the Vedic ritualistic hymns become manifest from him. He is devoted to the Supreme Personality of Godhead without deviation, and therefore in one sense he is not different from the Lord. Nevertheless, he should be worshiped not as the monists worship him, but in duality. One should always remain a servitor of the Supreme Lord, the supreme worshipable Deity. We therefore offer our respectful obeisances unto Lord Brahmā, the form of manifest Vedic knowledge.

PURPORT

In this verse, the word *karma-mayam* ("obtainable by the Vedic ritualistic system") is significant. The *Vedas* say, *svadharma-niṣṭhaḥ śata-janmabhiḥ pumān viriñcatām eti:* "One who strictly follows the principles of *varṇāśrama-dharma* for at least one hundred births will be rewarded with the post of Lord Brahmā." It is also significant that although Lord Brahmā is extremely powerful, he never thinks himself one with the Supreme Personality of Godhead; he always knows that he is an eternal servitor of the Lord. Because the Lord and the servant are identical on the spiritual platform, Brahmā is herein addressed as *bhagavān*. Bhagavān is the Supreme Personality of Godhead, Kṛṣṇa, but if a devotee serves Him with full faith, the meaning of the Vedic literature is revealed to him. Therefore Brahmā is called *brahma-liṅga*, which indicates that his entire form consists of Vedic knowledge.

TEXT 34

ऋषिरुवाच

ततः परस्ताल्लोकालोकनामाचलो लोकालोकयोरन्तराले परित उपक्षिप्तः ॥३४॥

tataḥ parastāl lokāloka-nāmācalo lokālokayor antarāle parita upakṣiptaḥ.

tataḥ—from that ocean of sweet drinking water; *parastāt*—beyond; *lokāloka-nāma*—named Lokāloka; *acalaḥ*—a mountain; *loka-alokayoḥ antarāle*—between the countries full of sunlight and those without sunlight; *paritaḥ*—all around; *upakṣiptaḥ*—exists.

TRANSLATION

Thereafter, beyond the ocean of sweet water and fully surrounding it, is a mountain named Lokāloka, which divides the countries that are full of sunlight from those not lit by the sun.

TEXT 35

यावन्मानसोत्तरमेर्वोरन्तरं तावती भूमिः काञ्चन्यन्याऽऽदर्शतलोपमा यस्यां प्रहितः पदार्थो न कथञ्चित्पुनः प्रत्युपलभ्यते तस्मात्सर्वसत्त्वपरिहृताऽऽसीत् ॥३५॥

yāvan mānasottara-mervor antaraṁ tāvatī bhūmiḥ kāñcany anyādarśa-talopamā yasyāṁ prahitaḥ padārtho na kathañcit punaḥ pratyupalabhyate tasmāt sarva-sattva-parihṛtāsīt.

yāvat—as much as; *mānasottara-mervoḥ antaram*—the land between Mānasottara and Meru (beginning from the middle of Mount Sumeru); *tāvatī*—that much; *bhūmiḥ*—land; *kāñcanī*—made of gold; *anyā*—another; *ādarśa-tala-upamā*—whose surface is just like the surface of a mirror; *yasyām*—on which; *prahitaḥ*—dropped; *padārthaḥ*—a thing; *na*—not; *kathañcit*—in any way; *punaḥ*—again; *pratyupalabhyate*—is found; *tasmāt*—therefore; *sarva-sattva*—by all living entities; *parihṛtā*—abandoned; *āsīt*—was.

TRANSLATION

Beyond the ocean of sweet water is a tract of land as broad as the area between the middle of Mount Sumeru and the boundary of Mānasottara Mountain. In that tract of land there are many living beings. Beyond it, extending to Lokāloka Mountain, is another land, which is made of gold. Because of its golden surface, it reflects light like the surface of a mirror, and any physical article that falls on that land can never be perceived again. All living entities, therefore, have abandoned that golden land.

TEXT 36

लोकालोक इति समाख्या यदनेनाचलेन लोकालोकस्यान्तर्वर्तिनावस्थाप्यते ॥३६॥

lokāloka iti samākhyā yad anenācalena lokālokasyāntarvar-tināvasthāpyate.

loka—with light (or with inhabitants); *alokaḥ*—without light (or without inhabitants); *iti*—in this way; *samākhyā*—designation; *yat*—which; *anena*—by this; *acalena*—mountain; *loka*—of the land inhabited by living entities; *alokasya*—and of the land not inhabited by living entities; *antarvartinā*—which is in the middle; *avasthāpyate*—is established.

TRANSLATION

Between the lands inhabited by living entities and those that are uninhabited stands the great mountain which separates the two and which is therefore celebrated as Lokāloka.

TEXT 37

स लोकत्रयान्ते परित ईश्वरेण विहितो यस्मात्सूर्यादीनां ध्रुवापवर्गाणां ज्योतिर्गणानां गभस्तयोऽर्वाचीनांस्त्रीँल्लोकानावितन्वाना न कदाचित्पराचीना भवितुमुत्सहन्ते तावदुन्नहनायामः ॥३७॥

sa loka-trayānte parita īśvareṇa vihito yasmāt sūryādīnāṁ dhruvāpavargāṇāṁ jyotir-gaṇānāṁ gabhastayo 'rvācīnāṁs trīl lokān āvitanvānā na kadācit parācīnā bhavitum utsahante tāvad unnahanāyāmaḥ.

saḥ—that mountain; *loka-traya-ante*—at the end of the three *lokas* (Bhūrloka, Bhuvarloka and Svarloka); *paritaḥ*—all around; *īśvareṇa*—by the Supreme Personality of Godhead, Kṛṣṇa; *vihitaḥ*—created; *yasmāt*—from which; *sūrya-ādīnām*—of the sun planet; *dhruva-apavargāṇām*—up to Dhruvaloka and other, inferior luminaries; *jyotiḥ-gaṇānām*—of all the luminaries; *gabhastayaḥ*—the rays; *arvācīnān*—on this side; *trīn*—the three; *lokān*—planetary systems; *āvitanvānāḥ*—spreading throughout; *na*—not; *kadācit*—at any time; *parācīnāḥ*—beyond the jurisdiction of that mountain; *bhavitum*—to be; *utsahante*—are able; *tāvat*—that much; *unnahana-āyāmaḥ*—the measure of the height of the mountain.

TRANSLATION

By the supreme will of Kṛṣṇa, the mountain known as Lokāloka has been installed as the outer border of the three worlds—Bhūrloka, Bhuvarloka and Svarloka—to control the rays of the sun throughout the universe. All the luminaries, from the sun up to Dhruvaloka, distribute their rays throughout the three worlds, but only within the boundary formed by this mountain. Because it is extremely high, extending even higher than Dhruvaloka, it blocks the rays of the luminaries, which therefore can never extend beyond it.

PURPORT

When we speak of *loka-traya,* we refer to the three primary planetary systems—Bhūḥ, Bhuvaḥ and Svaḥ—into which the universe is divided.

Surrounding these planetary systems are the eight directions, namely east, west, north, south, northeast, southeast, northwest and southwest. Lokāloka Mountain has been established as the outer boundary of all the *lokas* to distribute the rays of the sun and other luminaries equally throughout the universe.

This vivid description of how the rays of the sun are distributed throughout the different planetary systems of the universe is very scientific. Śukadeva Gosvāmī described these universal affairs to Mahārāja Parīkṣit as he had heard about them from his predecessor. He explained these facts five thousand years ago, but the knowledge existed long, long before because Śukadeva Gosvāmī received it through disciplic succession. Because this knowledge is accepted through the disciplic succession, it is perfect. The history of modern scientific knowledge, on the contrary, does not go back more than a few hundred years. Therefore, even if modern scientists do not accept the other factual presentations of *Śrīmad-Bhāgavatam*, how can they deny the perfect astronomical calculations that existed long before they could imagine such things? There is so much information to gather from *Śrīmad-Bhāgavatam*. Modern scientists, however, have no information of other planetary systems and, indeed, are hardly conversant with the planet on which we are now living.

TEXT 38

एतावाँल्लोकविन्यासो मानलक्षणसंस्थाभिर्विचिन्तितः कविभिः स तु पञ्चाशत्कोटिगणितस्य भूगोलस्य तुरीयभागोऽयं लोकालोकाचलः ॥३८॥

etāvāl loka-vinyāso māna-lakṣaṇa-saṁsthābhir vicintitaḥ kavibhiḥ sa tu pañcāśat-koṭi-gaṇitasya bhū-golasya turīya-bhāgo 'yaṁ lokālokācalaḥ.

etāvān—this much; *loka-vinyāsaḥ*—the placing of the different planets; *māna*—with measurements; *lakṣaṇa*—symptoms; *saṁsthābhiḥ*—as well as with their different situations; *vicintitaḥ*—established by scientific calculations; *kavibhiḥ*—by learned scholars; *saḥ*—that; *tu*—but; *pañcāśat-koṭi*—500,000,000 *yojanas; gaṇitasya*—which is measured at; *bhū-golasya*—of the planetary system known as

Bhūgolaka; *turīya-bhāgaḥ*—one fourth; *ayam*—this; *lokāloka-acalaḥ*—the mountain known as Lokāloka.

TRANSLATION

Learned scholars who are free from mistakes, illusions and propensities to cheat have thus described the planetary systems and their particular symptoms, measurements and locations. With great deliberation, they have established the truth that the distance between Sumeru and the mountain known as Lokāloka is one fourth of the diameter of the universe—or, in other words, 125,000,000 yojanas [1 billion miles].

PURPORT

Śrīla Viśvanātha Cakravartī Ṭhākura has given accurate astronomical information about the location of Lokāloka Mountain, the movements of the sun globe and the distance between the sun and the circumference of the universe. However, the technical terms used in the astronomical calculations given by the *Jyotir Veda* are difficult to translate into English. Therefore to satisfy the reader, we may include the exact Sanskrit statement given by Śrīla Viśvanātha Cakravartī Ṭhākura, which records exact calculations regarding universal affairs.

sa tu lokālokas tu bhū-golakasya bhū-sambandhāṇḍa-golakasyety arthaḥ. sūryasy eva bhuvo 'py aṇḍa-golakayor madhya-vartitvāt kha-golam iva bhū-golam api pañcāśat-koṭi-yojana-pramāṇaṁ tasya turīya-bhāgaḥ sārdha-dvādaśa-koṭi-yojana-vistārocchrāya ity arthaḥ bhūs tu catus-triṁśal-lakṣonapañcāśat-koṭi-pramāṇā jñeyā. yathā meru-madhyān mānasottara-madhya-paryantaṁ sārdha-sapta-pañcāśal-lakṣottara-koṭi-yojana-pramāṇam. mānasottara-madhyāt svādūdaka-samudra-paryantaṁ ṣaṇ-ṇavati-lakṣa-yojana-pramāṇaṁ tataḥ kāñcanī-bhūmiḥ sārdha-sapta-pañcāśal-lakṣottara-koṭi-yojana-pramāṇā evam ekato meru-lokālokayor antarālam ekādaśa-śal-lakṣādhika-catuṣ-koṭi-parimitam anyato 'pi tathatyeto lokālokāl loka-paryantaṁ sthānaṁ dvāviṁśati-lakṣottarāṣṭa-koṭi-parimitaṁ lokālokād bahir apy ekataḥ etāvad eva anyato 'py etāvad eva yad vakṣyate, yo 'ntar-vistāra etena hy aloka-parimāṇaṁ ca vyākhyātaṁ yad-bahir lokālokācalād ity ekato lokālokaḥ sārdha-dvādaśa-koṭi-yojana-parimāṇaḥ anyato 'pi sa tathety evaṁ catus-triṁśal-lakṣonapañcāśat-koṭi-pramāṇā bhūḥ sābdhi-dvīpa-parvatā jñeyā. ata evāṇḍa-golakāt sarvato dikṣu sapta-daśa-lakṣa-yojanāvakāśe vartamāne sati pṛthivyāḥ śeṣa-nāgena dhāraṇaṁ dig-gajaiś ca niścalī-karaṇaṁ sārthakaṁ bhaved anyathā tu vyākhyāntare pañcāśat-koṭi-pramāṇatvād aṇḍa-golaka-lagnatve tat tat sarvam akiñcit-karaṁ syāt cākṣuṣe manvantare cākasmāt majjanaṁ śrī-varāha-devenotthāpanaṁ ca durghaṭaṁ syād ity adikaṁ vivecanīyam.

TEXT 39

तदुपरिष्टाच्चतसृष्वाशास्वात्मयोनिनाखिलजगद्गुरुणाधिनिवेशिता ये द्विरदपतय ऋषभः पुष्करचूडो वामनोऽपराजित इति सकललोकस्थितिहेतवः ॥३९॥

tad-upariṣṭāc catasṛṣv āśāsvātma-yoninākhila-jagad-guruṇādhiniveśitā ye dvirada-pataya ṛṣabhaḥ puṣkaracūḍo vāmano 'parājita iti sakala-loka-sthiti-hetavaḥ.

tat-upariṣṭāt—on the top of Lokāloka Mountain; *catasṛṣu āśāsu*—in the four directions; *ātma-yoninā*—by Lord Brahmā; *akhila-jagat-guruṇā*—the spiritual master of the whole universe; *adhiniveśitāḥ*—established; *ye*—all those; *dvirada-patayaḥ*—the best of elephants; *ṛṣabhaḥ*—Ṛṣabha; *puṣkara-cūḍaḥ*—Puṣkaracūḍa; *vāmanaḥ*—Vāmana; *aparājitaḥ*—Aparājita; *iti*—thus; *sakala-loka-sthiti-hetavaḥ*—the causes of the maintenance of the different planets within the universe.

TRANSLATION

On the top of Lokāloka Mountain are the four gaja-patis, the best of elephants, which were established in the four directions by Lord Brahmā, the supreme spiritual master of the entire universe. The names of those elephants are Ṛṣabha, Puṣkaracūḍa, Vāmana and Aparājita. They are responsible for maintaining the planetary systems of the universe.

TEXT 40

तेषां स्वविभूतीनां लोकपालानां च विविधवीर्योपबृंहणाय भगवान् परममहापुरुषो महाविभूतिपतिरन्तर्याम्यात्मनो विशुद्धसत्त्वं धर्मज्ञानवैराग्यैश्वर्याद्यष्टमहासिद्ध्युपलक्षणं विष्वक्सेनादिभिः स्वपार्षदप्रवरैः परिवारितो निजवरायुधोपशोभितैर्निजभुजदण्डैः सन्धारयमाणस्तस्मिन् गिरिवरे समन्तात्सकललोकस्वस्तय आस्ते ॥४०॥

teṣāṁ sva-vibhūtīnāṁ loka-pālānāṁ ca vividha-vīryopabṛṁhaṇāya bhagavān parama-mahā-puruṣo mahā-vibhūti-patir antaryāmy ātmano viśuddha-sattvaṁ dharma-jñāna-vairāgyaiśvaryādy-aṣṭa-mahā-siddhy-upalakṣaṇaṁ viṣvaksenādibhiḥ sva-pārṣada-pravaraiḥ parivārito nija-varāyudhopaśobhitair nija-bhuja-daṇḍaiḥ sandhārayamāṇas tasmin giri-vare samantāt sakala-loka-svastaya āste.

teṣām—of all of them; *sva-vibhūtīnām*—who are his personal expansions and assistants; *loka-pālānām*—who are entrusted with looking after the universal affairs; *ca*—and; *vividha*—varieties; *vīrya-upabṛṁhaṇāya*—for expanding the powers; *bhagavān*—the Supreme Personality of Godhead; *parama-mahā-puruṣaḥ*—the foremost master of all kinds of opulence, the Supreme Personality of Godhead; *mahā-vibhūti-patiḥ*—the master of all inconceivable potencies; *antaryāmī*—the Supersoul; *ātmanaḥ*—of Himself; *viśuddha-sattvam*—having an existence without contamination by the material modes of nature; *dharma-jñāna-vairāgya*—of religion, pure knowledge and renunciation; *aiśvarya-ādi*—of all kinds of opulence; *aṣṭa*—eight; *mahā-siddhi*—and of great mystic perfections; *upalakṣaṇam*—having the characteristics; *viṣvaksena-ādibhiḥ*—by His expansion known as Viṣvaksena and others; *sva-pārṣada-pravaraiḥ*—the best of personal assistants; *parivāritaḥ*—surrounded; *nija*—His own; *vara-āyudha*—by different types of weapons; *upaśobhitaiḥ*—being decorated; *nija*—own; *bhuja-daṇḍaiḥ*—with stout arms; *sandhārayamāṇaḥ*—manifesting this form; *tasmin*—on that; *giri-vare*—great mountain; *samantāt*—all around; *sakala-loka-svastaye*—for the benefit of all the planetary systems; *āste*—exists.

TRANSLATION

The Supreme Personality of Godhead is the master of all transcendental opulences and the master of the spiritual sky. He is the Supreme Person, Bhagavān, the Supersoul of everyone. The demigods, led by Indra, the King of heaven, are entrusted with seeing to the affairs of the material world. To benefit all living beings in all the varied planets and to increase the power of those elephants and of the demigods, the Lord manifests Himself on top of that mountain in a spiritual body, uncontaminated by the modes of material nature. Surrounded by His personal expansions and

assistants like Viṣvaksena, He exhibits all His perfect opulences, such as religion and knowledge, and His mystic powers such as aṇimā, laghimā and mahimā. He is beautifully situated, and He is decorated by the different weapons in His four hands.

TEXT 41

आकल्पमेवं वेषं गत एष भगवानात्मयोगमायया विरचितविविधलोक-यात्रागोपीयायेत्यर्थः ॥४१॥

ākalpam evaṁ veṣaṁ gata eṣa bhagavān ātma-yogamāyayā viracita-vividha-loka-yātrā-gopīyāyety arthaḥ.

ā-kalpam—for the duration of the time of creation; *evam*—thus; *veṣam*—appearance; *gataḥ*—has accepted; *eṣaḥ*—this; *bhagavān*—the Supreme Personality of Godhead; *ātma-yoga-māyayā*—by His own spiritual potency; *viracita*—perfected; *vividha-loka-yātrā*—the livelihood of the various planetary systems; *gopīyāya*—just to maintain; *iti*—thus; *arthaḥ*—the purpose.

TRANSLATION

The various forms of the Supreme Personality of Godhead, such as Nārāyaṇa and Viṣṇu, are beautifully decorated with different weapons. The Lord exhibits those forms to maintain all the varied planets created by His personal potency, yogamāyā.

PURPORT

In *Bhagavad-gītā* (4.6) Lord Kṛṣṇa says, *sambhavāmy ātma-māyayā:* "I appear by My internal potency." The word *ātma-māyā* refers to the Lord's personal potency, *yogamāyā.* After creating both the material world and spiritual world through *yogamāyā,* the Supreme Personality of Godhead personally maintains them by expanding Himself in different categories as the Viṣṇu *mūrtis* and the demigods. He maintains the material creation from beginning to end, and He personally maintains the spiritual world.

TEXT 42

योऽन्तर्विस्तार एतेन ह्यलोकपरिमाणं च व्याख्यातं यद्बहिर्लोकालोकाचलात्।
ततः परस्ताद्योगेश्वरगतिं विशुद्धामुदाहरन्ति ॥४२॥

yo 'ntar-vistāra etena hy aloka-parimāṇaṁ ca vyākhyātaṁ yad bahir lokālokācalāt. tataḥ parastād yogeśvara-gatiṁ viśuddhām udāharanti.

yaḥ—that which; *antaḥ-vistāraḥ*—the distance inside Lokāloka Mountain; *etena*—by this; *hi*—indeed; *aloka-parimāṇam*—the width of the tract of land known as Aloka-varṣa; *ca*—and; *vyākhyātam*—described; *yat*—which; *bahiḥ*—outside; *lokāloka-acalāt*—beyond Lokāloka Mountain; *tataḥ*—that; *parastāt*—beyond; *yogeśvara-gatim*—the path of Yogeśvara (Kṛṣṇa) in penetrating the coverings of the universe; *viśuddhām*—without material contamination; *udāharanti*—they say.

TRANSLATION

My dear King, outside Lokāloka Mountain is the tract of land known as Aloka-varṣa, which extends for the same breadth as the area within the mountain—in other words, 125,000,000 yojanas [one billion miles]. Beyond Aloka-varṣa is the destination of those who aspire for liberation from the material world. It is beyond the jurisdiction of the material modes of nature, and therefore it is completely pure. Lord Kṛṣṇa took Arjuna through this place to bring back the sons of the brāhmaṇa.

TEXT 43

अण्डमध्यगतः सूर्यो द्यावाभूम्योर्यदन्तरम् ।
सूर्याण्डगोलयोर्मध्ये कोट्यः स्युः पञ्चविंशतिः॥४३॥

aṇḍa-madhya-gataḥ sūryo
dyāv-ābhūmyor yad antaram
sūryāṇḍa-golayor madhye
koṭyaḥ syuḥ pañca-viṁśatiḥ

aṇḍa-madhya-gataḥ—situated in the center of the universe; *sūryaḥ*—the sun globe; *dyāv-ābhūmyoḥ*—the two planetary systems Bhūrloka and Bhuvarloka; *yat*—which; *antaram*—in between; *sūrya*—of the sun; *aṇḍa-golayoḥ*—and the globe of the universe; *madhye*—in the middle; *koṭyaḥ*—groups of ten million; *syuḥ*—are; *pañca-viṁśatiḥ*—twenty-five.

TRANSLATION

The sun is situated [vertically] in the middle of the universe, in the area between Bhūrloka and Bhuvarloka, which is called antarikṣa, outer space. The distance between the sun and the circumference of the universe is twenty-five koṭi yojanas [two billion miles].

PURPORT

The word *koṭi* means ten million, and a *yojana* is eight miles. The diameter of the universe is fifty *koṭi yojanas* (four billion miles). Therefore, since the sun is in the middle of the universe, the distance between the sun and the edge of the universe is calculated to be twenty-five *koṭi yojanas* (two billion miles).

TEXT 44

मृतेऽण्ड एष एतस्मिन् यदभूत्ततो मार्तण्ड इति व्यपदेशः ।
हिरण्यगर्भ इति यद्धिरण्याण्डसमुद्भवः ॥४४॥

mṛte 'ṇḍa eṣa etasmin yad abhūt tato mārtaṇḍa iti vyapadeśaḥ.
hiraṇyagarbha iti yad dhiraṇyāṇḍa-samudbhavaḥ.

mṛte—dead; *aṇḍe*—in the globe; *eṣaḥ*—this; *etasmin*—in this; *yat*—which; *abhūt*—entered personally at the time of creation; *tataḥ*—from that; *mārtaṇḍa*—Mārtaṇḍa; *iti*—thus; *vyapadeśaḥ*—the designation; *hiraṇya-garbhaḥ*—known as Hiraṇyagarbha; *iti*—thus; *yat*—because; *hiraṇya-aṇḍa-samudbhavaḥ*—his material body was created from Hiraṇyagarbha.

TRANSLATION

The sun-god is also known as Vairāja, the total material body for all living entities. Because he entered this dull egg of the universe at the time of creation, he is also called Mārtaṇḍa. He is also known as Hiraṇyagarbha because he received his material body from Hiraṇyagarbha [Lord Brahmā].

PURPORT

The post of Lord Brahmā is meant for very highly elevated, spiritually advanced living beings. When such living beings are unavailable, Lord Viṣṇu, the Supreme Personality of Godhead, expands Himself as Lord Brahmā. This takes place very rarely. Consequently there are two kinds of Brahmās. Sometimes Brahmā is an ordinary living entity, and at other times Brahmā is the Supreme Personality of Godhead. The Brahmā spoken of here is an ordinary living being. Whether Brahmā is the Supreme Personality of Godhead or an ordinary living being, he is known as Vairāja Brahmā and Hiraṇyagarbha Brahmā. Therefore the sun-god is also accepted as Vairāja Brahmā.

TEXT 45

सूर्येण हि विभज्यन्ते दिशः खं द्यौर्मही भिदा ।
स्वर्गापवर्गौ नरका रसौकांसि च सर्वशः ॥४५॥

sūryeṇa hi vibhajyante
diśaḥ khaṁ dyaur mahī bhidā
svargāpavargau narakā
rasaukāṁsi ca sarvaśaḥ

sūryeṇa—by the sun-god within the sun planet; *hi*—indeed; *vibhajyante*—are divided; *diśaḥ*—the directions; *kham*—the sky; *dyauḥ*—the heavenly planets; *mahī*—the earthly planets; *bhidā*—other divisions; *svarga*—the heavenly planets; *apavargau*—and the places for liberation; *narakāḥ*—the hellish planets; *rasaukāṁsi*—such as Atala; *ca*—also; *sarvaśaḥ*—all.

TRANSLATION

O King, the sun-god and the sun planet divide all the directions of the universe. It is only because of the presence of the sun that we can understand what the sky, the higher planets, this world and the lower planets are. It is also only because of the sun that we can understand which places are for material enjoyment, which are for liberation, which are hellish and subterranean.

TEXT 46

देवतिर्यङ्मनुष्याणां सरीसृपसवीरुधाम् ।
सर्वजीवनिकायानां सूर्य आत्मा दृगीश्वरः ॥४६॥

deva-tiryaṅ-manuṣyāṇāṁ
sarīsṛpa-savīrudhām
sarva-jīva-nikāyānāṁ
sūrya ātmā dṛg-īśvaraḥ

deva—of the demigods; *tiryak*—the lower animals; *manuṣyāṇām*—and the human beings; *sarīsṛpa*—the insects and the serpents; *savīrudhām*—and the plants and trees; *sarva-jīva-nikāyānām*—of all groups of living entities; *sūryaḥ*—the sun-god; *ātmā*—the life and soul; *dṛk*—of the eyes; *īśvaraḥ*—the Personality of Godhead.

TRANSLATION

All living entities, including demigods, human beings, animals, birds, insects, reptiles, creepers and trees, depend upon the heat and light given by the sun-god from the sun planet. Furthermore, it is because of the sun's presence that all living entities can see, and therefore he is called dṛg-īśvara, the Personality of Godhead presiding over sight.

PURPORT

In this regard, Śrīla Viśvanātha Cakravartī Ṭhākura says, *sūrya ātmā ātmatvenopāsyaḥ.* The actual life and soul of all living entities within this universe is the sun. He is therefore *upāsya*, worshipable. We worship the sun-god by chanting the Gāyatrī *mantra* (*oṁ bhūr bhuvaḥ svaḥ tat savitur vareṇyaṁ bhargo devasya dhīmahi*). Sūrya is the life and soul of this universe, and there are innumerable universes for which a sun-god is the life and soul, just as the Supreme Personality of Godhead is the life and soul of the entire creation. We have information that Vairāja, Hiraṇyagarbha, entered the great, dull, material globe called the sun. This indicates that the theory held by so-called scientists that no one lives there is wrong. *Bhagavad-gītā* also says that Kṛṣṇa first instructed *Bhagavad-gītā* to the sun-god (*imaṁ vivasvate yogaṁ proktavān aham avyayam*). Therefore the sun is not vacant. It is inhabited by living entities, and the predominating deity is Vairāja, or Vivasvān. The difference between the sun and earth is that the sun is a fiery planet, but everyone there has a suitable body and can live there without difficulty.

Thus end the Bhaktivedanta purports of the Fifth Canto, Twentieth Chapter, of the Śrīmad-Bhāgavatam, *entitled, "Studying the Structure of the Universe."*

CHAPTER TWENTY-ONE

The Movements of the Sun

This chapter informs us of the movements of the sun. The sun is not stationary; it is also moving like the other planets. The sun's movements determine the duration of night and day. When the sun travels north of the equator, it moves slowly during the day and very quickly at night, thus increasing the duration of the daytime and decreasing the duration of night. Similarly, when the sun travels south of the equator, the exact opposite is true—the duration of the day decreases, and the duration of night increases. When the sun enters Karkaṭa-rāśi (Cancer) and then travels to Siṁha-rāśi (Leo) and so on through Dhanuḥ-rāśi (Sagittarius), its course is called Dakṣiṇāyana, the southern way, and when the sun enters Makara-rāśi (Capricorn) and thereafter travels through Kumbha-rāśi (Aquarius) and so on through Mithuna-rāśi (Gemini), its course is called Uttarāyaṇa, the northern way. When the sun is in Meṣa-rāśi (Aries) and Tulā-rāśi (Libra), the duration of day and night are equal.

On Mānasottara Mountain are the abodes of four demigods. East of Sumeru Mountain is Devadhānī, where King Indra lives, and south of Sumeru is Saṁyamanī, the abode of Yamarāja, the superintendent of death. Similarly, west of Sumeru is Nimlocanī, the abode of Varuṇa, the demigod who controls the water, and north of Sumeru is Vibhāvarī, where the demigod of the moon lives. Sunrise, noon, sunset and midnight occur in all these places because of the movements of the sun. Diametrically opposite the place where the sunrise takes places and the sun is seen by human eyes, the sun will be setting and passing away from human vision. Similarly, the people residing diametrically opposite the point where it is midday will be experiencing midnight. The sun rises and sets with all the other planets, headed by the moon and other luminaries.

The entire *kāla-cakra*, or wheel of time, is established on the wheel of the sun-god's chariot. This wheel is known as Saṁvatsara. The seven horses pulling the chariot of the sun are known as Gāyatrī, Bṛhatī,

Uṣṇik, Jagatī, Triṣṭup, Anuṣṭup and Paṅkti. They are harnessed by a demigod known as Aruṇadeva to a yoke 900,000 *yojanas* wide. Thus the chariot carries Ādityadeva, the sun-god. Always staying in front of the sun-god and offering their prayers are sixty thousand sages known as Vālikhilyas. There are fourteen Gandharvas, Apsarās and other demigods, who are divided into seven parties and who perform ritualistic activities every month to worship the Supersoul through the sun-god according to different names. Thus the sun-god travels through the universe for a distance of 95,100,000 *yojanas* (760,800,000 miles) at a speed of 16,004 miles at every moment.

TEXT 1

श्रीशुक उवाच
एतावानेव भूवलयस्य संनिवेशः प्रमाणलक्षणतो व्याख्यातः ॥ १ ॥

śrī-śuka uvāca
etāvān eva bhū-valayasya sanniveśaḥ pramāṇa-lakṣaṇato vyākhyātaḥ.

śrī-śukaḥ uvāca—Śrī Śukadeva Gosvāmī said; *etāvān*—so much; *eva*—certainly; *bhū-valayasya sanniveśaḥ*—the arrangement of the whole universe; *pramāṇa-lakṣaṇataḥ*—according to measurement (fifty crores of *yojanas*, or four billion miles in width and length) and characteristics; *vyākhyātaḥ*—estimated.

TRANSLATION

Śukadeva Gosvāmī said: My dear King, I have thus far described the diameter of the universe [fifty crores of yojanas, or four billion miles] and its general characteristics, according to the estimations of learned scholars.

TEXT 2

एतेन हि दिवो मण्डलमानं तद्विद उपदिशन्ति यथा द्विदलयोर्निष्पावादीनां ते अन्तरेणान्तरिक्षं तदुभयसन्धितम् ॥२॥

etena hi divo maṇḍala-mānaṁ tad-vida upadiśanti yathā dvi-dalayor nispāvādīnāṁ te antareṇāntarikṣaṁ tad-ubhaya-sandhitam.

etena—by this estimation; *hi*—indeed; *divaḥ*—of the upper planetary system; *maṇḍala-mānam*—the measurement of the globe; *tat-vidaḥ*—the experts who know about it; *upadiśanti*—instruct; *yathā*—just as; *dvi-dalayoḥ*—in the two halves; *nispāva-ādīnām*—of grain such as wheat; *te*—of the two divisions; *antareṇa*—in the intervening space; *antarikṣam*—the sky or outer space; *tat*—by the two; *ubhaya*—on both sides; *sandhitam*—where the two parts join.

TRANSLATION

As a grain of wheat is divided into two parts and one can estimate the size of the upper part by knowing that of the lower, so, expert geographers instruct, one can understand the measurements of the upper part of the universe by knowing those of the lower part. The sky between the earthly sphere and heavenly sphere is called antarikṣa, or outer space. It adjoins the top of the sphere of earth and the bottom of that of heaven.

TEXT 3

यन्मध्यगतो भगवांस्तपताम्पतिस्तपन आतपेन त्रिलोकीं प्रतपत्यवभासयत्यात्म-
भासा स एष उदगयनदक्षिणायनवैषुवतसंज्ञाभिर्मान्द्यशैघ्र्यसमानाभिर्गतिभिरारोहण-
ावरोहणसमानस्थानेषु यथासवनमभिपद्यमानो मकरादिषु राशिष्वहोरात्राणि
दीर्घह्रस्वसमानानि विधत्ते ॥३॥

yan-madhya-gato bhagavāṁs tapatām patis tapana ātapena tri-lokīṁ
pratapaty avabhāsayaty ātma-bhāsā sa eṣa udagayana-dakṣiṇāyana-
vaiṣuvata-saṁjñābhir māndya-śaighrya-samānābhir gatibhir
ārohaṇāvarohaṇa-samāna-sthāneṣu yathā-savanam abhipadyamāno
makarādiṣu rāśiṣv aho-rātrāṇi dīrgha-hrasva-samānāni vidhatte.

yat—of which (the intermediate space); *madhya-gataḥ*—being situated in the middle; *bhagavān*—the most powerful; *tapatām patiḥ*—the master of those that heat the whole universe; *tapanaḥ*—the sun; *ātapena*—by heat; *tri-lokīm*—the three worlds; *pratapati*—heats;

avabhāsayati—lights; *ātma-bhāsā*—by its own illuminating rays; *saḥ*—that; *eṣaḥ*—the sun globe; *udagayana*—of passing to the northern side of the equator; *dakṣiṇa-ayana*—of passing to the southern side of the equator; *vaiṣuvata*—or of passing through the equator; *saṁjñābhiḥ*—by different names; *māndya*—characterized by slowness; *śaighrya*—swiftness; *samānābhiḥ*—and by equality; *gatibhiḥ*—by movement; *ārohaṇa*—of rising; *avarohaṇa*—of going down; *samāna*—or of staying in the middle; *sthāneṣu*—in positions; *yathā-savanam*—according to the order of the Supreme Personality of Godhead; *abhipadyamānaḥ*—moving; *makara-ādiṣu*—headed by the sign Makara (Capricorn); *rāśiṣu*—in different signs; *ahaḥ-rātrāṇi*—the days and nights; *dīrgha*—long; *hrasva*—short; *samānāni*—equal; *vidhatte*—makes.

TRANSLATION

In the midst of that region of outer space [antarikṣa] is the most opulent sun, the king of all the planets that emanate heat, such as the moon. By the influence of its radiation, the sun heats the universe and maintains its proper order. It also gives light to help all living entities see. While passing toward the north, toward the south or through the equator, in accordance with the order of the Supreme Personality of Godhead, it is said to move slowly, swiftly or moderately. According to its movements in rising above, going beneath or passing through the equator—and correspondingly coming in touch with various signs of the zodiac, headed by Makara [Capricorn]—days and nights are short, long or equal to one another.

PURPORT

Lord Brahmā prays in his *Brahma-saṁhitā* (5.52):

yac cakṣur eṣa savitā sakala-grahāṇāṁ
rājā samasta-sura-mūrtir aśeṣa-tejāḥ
yasyājñayā bhramati saṁbhṛta-kāla-cakro
govindam ādi-puruṣaṁ tam ahaṁ bhajāmi

"I worship Govinda, the primeval Lord, the Supreme Personality of Godhead under whose control even the sun, which is considered to be the eye of the Lord, rotates within the fixed orbit of eternal time. The sun is the king of all planetary systems and has unlimited potency in heat and light." Although the sun is described as *bhagavān*, the most powerful, and although it is actually the most powerful planet within the universe, it nevertheless has to carry out the order of Govinda, Kṛṣṇa. The sun-god cannot deviate even an inch from the orbit designated to him. Therefore in every sphere of life, the supreme order of the Supreme Personality of Godhead is carried out. The entire material nature carries out His orders. However, we foolishly see the activities of material nature without understanding the supreme order and Supreme Person behind them. As confirmed in *Bhagavad-gītā*, *mayādhyakṣeṇa prakṛtiḥ:* material nature carries out the orders of the Lord, and thus everything is maintained in an orderly way.

TEXT 4

यदा मेषतुलयोर्वर्तते तदाहोरात्राणि समानानि भवन्ति यदा वृषभादिषु पञ्चसु च राशिषु चरति तदाहान्येव वर्धन्ते ह्रसति च मासि मास्येकैका घटिका रात्रिषु ॥४॥

yadā meṣa-tulayor vartate tadāho-rātrāṇi samānāni bhavanti yadā vṛṣabhādiṣu pañcasu ca rāśiṣu carati tadāhāny eva vardhante hrasati ca māsi māsy ekaikā ghaṭikā rātriṣu.

yadā—when; *meṣa-tulayoḥ*—in Meṣa (Aries) and Tulā (Libra); *vartate*—the sun exists; *tadā*—at that time; *ahaḥ-rātrāṇi*—the days and nights; *samānāni*—equal in duration; *bhavanti*—are; *yadā*—when; *vṛṣabha-ādiṣu*—headed by Vṛṣabha (Taurus) and Mithuna (Gemini); *pañcasu*—in the five; *ca*—also; *rāśiṣu*—signs; *carati*—moves; *tadā*—at that time; *ahāni*—the days; *eva*—certainly; *vardhante*—increase; *hrasati*—is diminished; *ca*—and; *māsi māsi*—in every month; *eka-ekā*—one; *ghaṭikā*—half hour; *rātriṣu*—in the nights.

TRANSLATION

When the sun passes through Meṣa [Aries] and Tulā [Libra], the durations of day and night are equal. When it passes through the five signs headed by Vṛṣabha [Taurus], the duration of the days

increases [until Cancer], and then it gradually decreases by half an hour each month, until day and night again become equal [in Libra].

TEXT 5

यदा वृश्चिकादिषु पञ्चसु वर्तते तदाहोरात्राणि विपर्ययाणि भवन्ति ॥ ५ ॥

yadā vṛścikādiṣu pañcasu vartate tadāho-rātrāṇi viparyayāṇi bhavanti.

yadā—when; *vṛścika-ādiṣu*—headed by Vṛścika (Scorpio); *pañcasu*—five; *vartate*—remains; *tadā*—at that time; *ahaḥ-rātrāṇi*—the days and nights; *viparyayāṇi*—the opposite (the duration of the day decreases, and that of night increases); *bhavanti*—are.

TRANSLATION

When the sun passes through the five signs beginning with Vṛścika [Scorpio], the duration of the days decreases [until Capricorn], and then gradually it increases month after month, until day and night become equal [in Aries].

TEXT 6

यावद्दक्षिणायनमहानि वर्धन्ते यावदुदगयनं रात्रयः ॥ ६ ॥

yāvad dakṣiṇāyanam ahāni vardhante yāvad udagayanaṁ rātrayaḥ.

yāvat—until; *dakṣiṇa-ayanam*—the sun passes to the southern side; *ahāni*—the days; *vardhante*—increase; *yāvat*—until; *udagayanam*—the sun passes to the northern side; *rātrayaḥ*—the nights.

TRANSLATION

Until the sun travels to the south the days grow longer, and until it travels to the north the nights grow longer.

TEXT 7

एवं नव कोटय एकपञ्चाशल्लक्षाणि योजनानां मानसोत्तर-
गिरिपरिवर्तनस्योपदिशन्ति तस्मिन्नैन्द्रीं पुरीं पूर्वस्मान्मेरोर्देवधानीं
नाम दक्षिणतो याम्यां संयमनीं नाम पश्चाद्वारुणीं निम्लोचनीं नाम उत्तरतः
सौम्यां विभावरीं नाम तासूदयमध्याह्नास्तमयनिशीथानीति भूतानां प्रवृत्तिनि
वृत्तिनिमित्तानि समयविशेषेण मेरोश्चतुर्दिशम् ॥ ७ ॥

evaṁ nava koṭaya eka-pañcāśal-lakṣāṇi yojanānāṁ mānasottara-giri-parivartanasyopadiśanti tasminn aindrīṁ purīṁ pūrvasmān meror devadhānīṁ nāma dakṣiṇato yāmyāṁ saṁyamanīṁ nāma paścād vāruṇīṁ nimlocanīṁ nāma uttarataḥ saumyāṁ vibhāvarīṁ nāma tāsūdaya-madhyāhnāstamaya-niśīthānīti bhūtānāṁ pravṛtti-nivṛtti-nimittāni samaya-viśeṣeṇa meroś catur-diśam.

evam—thus; *nava*—nine; *koṭayaḥ*—ten millions; *eka-pañcāśat*—fifty-one; *lakṣāṇi*—hundred thousands; *yojanānām*—of the *yojanas; mānasottara-giri*—of the mountain known as Mānasottara; *parivartanasya*—of the circumambulation; *upadiśanti*—they (learned scholars) teach; *tasmin*—on that (Mānasottara Mountain); *aindrīm*—of King Indra; *purīm*—the city; *pūrvasmāt*—on the eastern side; *meroḥ*—of Sumeru Mountain; *devadhānīm*—Devadhānī; *nāma*—of the name; *dakṣiṇataḥ*—on the southern side; *yāmyām*—of Yamarāja; *saṁyamanīm*—Saṁyamanī; *nāma*—named; *paścāt*—on the western side; *vāruṇīm*—of Varuṇa; *nimlocanīm*—Nimlocanī; *nāma*—named; *uttarataḥ*—on the northern side; *saumyām*—of the moon; *vibhāvarīm*—Vibhāvarī; *nāma*—named; *tāsu*—in all of them; *udaya*—rising; *madhyāhna*—midday; *astamaya*—sunset; *niśīthāni*—midnight; *iti*—thus; *bhūtānām*—of the living entities; *pravṛtti*—of activity; *nivṛtti*—and cessation of activity; *nimittāni*—the causes; *samaya-viśeṣeṇa*—by the particular times; *meroḥ*—of Sumeru Mountain; *catuḥ-diśam*—the four sides.

TRANSLATION

Śukadeva Gosvāmī continued; My dear King, as stated before, the learned say that the sun travels over all sides of Mānasottara

Mountain in a circle whose length is 95,100,000 yojanas [760,800,000 miles]. On Mānasottara Mountain, due east of Mount Sumeru, is a place known as Devadhānī, possessed by King Indra. Similarly, in the south is a place known as Saṁyamanī, possessed by Yamarāja, in the west is a place known as Nimlocanī, possessed by Varuṇa, and in the north is a place named Vibhāvarī, possessed by the moon-god. Sunrise, midday, sunset and midnight occur in all those places according to specific times, thus engaging all living entities in their various occupational duties and also making them cease such duties.

TEXTS 8-9

तत्रत्यानां दिवसमध्यङ्गत एव सदाऽऽदित्यस्तपति सव्येनाचलं दक्षिणेन करोति
॥ ८ ॥ यत्रोदेति तस्य ह समानसूत्रनिपाते निम्लोचति यत्र क्वचन
स्यन्देनाभितपति तस्य हैष समानसूत्रनिपाते प्रस्वापयति तत्र गतं न पश्यन्ति
ये तं समनुपश्येरन् ॥ ९ ॥

tatratyānāṁ divasa-madhyaṅgata eva sadādityas tapati savyenācalaṁ dakṣiṇena karoti. yatrodeti tasya ha samāna-sūtra-nipāte nimlocati yatra kvacana syandenābhitapati tasya haiṣa samāna-sūtra-nipāte prasvāpayati tatra gataṁ na paśyanti ye taṁ samanupaśyeran.

tatratyānām—for the living entities residing on Mount Meru; *divasa-madhyaṅgataḥ*—being positioned as at midday; *eva*—indeed; *sadā*—always; *ādityaḥ*—the sun; *tapati*—heats; *savyena*—to the left side; *acalam*—Sumeru Mountain; *dakṣiṇena*—to the right (being forced by wind blowing to the right, the sun moves to the right); *karoti*—moves; *yatra*—the point where; *udeti*—it rises; *tasya*—of that position; *ha*—certainly; *samāna-sūtra-nipāte*—at the diametrically opposite point; *nimlocati*—the sun sets; *yatra*—where; *kvacana*—somewhere; *syandena*—with perspiration; *abhitapati*—heats (at midday); *tasya*—of that; *ha*—certainly; *eṣaḥ*—this (the sun); *samāna-sūtra-nipāte*—at the diametrically opposite point; *prasvāpayati*—the sun causes to sleep (as at midnight); *tatra*—there; *gatam*—gone; *na paśyanti*—do not see; *ye*—who; *tam*—the sunset; *samanupaśyeran*—seeing.

TRANSLATION

The living entities residing on Sumeru Mountain are always very warm, as at midday, because for them the sun is always overhead. Although the sun moves counterclockwise, facing the constellations, with Sumeru Mountain on its left, it also moves clockwise and appears to have the mountain on its right because it is influenced by the dakṣiṇāvarta wind. People living in countries at points diametrically opposite to where the sun is first seen rising will see the sun setting, and if a straight line were drawn from a point where the sun is at midday, the people in countries at the opposite end of the line would be experiencing midnight. Similarly, if people residing where the sun is setting were to go to countries diametrically opposite, they would not see the sun in the same condition.

TEXT 10

यदा चैन्द्र्याः पुर्याः प्रचलते पञ्चदशघटिकाभिर्याम्यां सपादकोटिद्वयं योजनानां सार्धद्वादशलक्षाणि साधिकानि चोपयाति ॥ १० ॥

yadā caindryāḥ puryāḥ pracalate pañcadaśa-ghaṭikābhir yāmyāṁ sapāda-koṭi-dvayaṁ yojanānāṁ sārdha-dvādaśa-lakṣāṇi sādhikāni copayāti.

yadā—when; *ca*—and; *aindryāḥ*—of Indra; *puryāḥ*—from the residence; *pracalate*—it moves; *pañcadaśa*—by fifteen; *ghaṭikābhiḥ*—half hours (actually twenty-four minutes); *yāmyām*—to the residence of Yamarāja; *sapāda-koṭi-dvayam*—two and a quarter crores (22,500,000); *yojanānām*—of *yojanas; sārdha*—and one half; *dvādaśa-lakṣāṇi*—twelve hundred thousand; *sādhikāni*—twenty-five thousand more; *ca*—and; *upayāti*—he passes over.

TRANSLATION

When the sun travels from Devadhānī, the residence of Indra, to Saṁyamanī, the residence of Yamarāja, it travels 23,775,000 yojanas [190,200,000 miles] in fifteen ghaṭikās [six hours].

PURPORT

The distance indicated by the word *sādhikāni* is *pañca-viṁśati-sahasrādhikāni,* or 25,000 *yojanas.* That plus two and a half crores and twelve and a half *lakṣa* of *yojanas* is the distance the sun travels between each two cities. This comes to 23,775,000 *yojanas,* or 190,200,000 miles. The total orbit of the sun is four times that distance, or 95,100,000 *yojanas* (760,800,000 miles).

TEXT 11

एवं ततो वारुणीं सौम्यामैन्द्रीं च पुनस्तथान्ये च ग्रहाः सोमादयो नक्षत्रैः सह ज्योतिश्चक्रे समभ्युद्यन्ति सह वा निम्लोचन्ति ॥११॥

evaṁ tato vāruṇīṁ saumyām aindrīṁ ca punas tathānye ca grahāḥ somādayo nakṣatraiḥ saha jyotiś-cakre samabhyudyanti saha vā nimlocanti.

evam—in this way; *tataḥ*—from there; *vāruṇīm*—to the quarters where Varuṇa lives; *saumyām*—to the quarters where the moon lives; *aindrīṁ ca*—and to the quarters where Indra lives; *punaḥ*—again; *tathā*—so also; *anye*—the others; *ca*—also; *grahāḥ*—planets; *soma-ādayaḥ*—headed by the moon; *nakṣatraiḥ*—all the stars; *saha*—with; *jyotiḥ-cakre*—in the celestial sphere; *samabhyudyanti*—rise; *saha*—along with; *vā*—or; *nimlocanti*—set.

TRANSLATION

From the residence of Yamarāja the sun travels to Nimlocanī, the residence of Varuṇa, from there to Vibhāvarī, the residence of the moon-god, and from there again to the residence of Indra. In a similar way, the moon, along with the other stars and planets, becomes visible in the celestial sphere and then sets and again becomes invisible.

PURPORT

In *Bhagavad-gītā* (10.21) Kṛṣṇa says, *nakṣatrāṇām ahaṁ śaśī:* "Of stars I am the moon." This indicates that the moon is similar to the other stars. The Vedic literature informs us that within this universe there is one sun, which is moving. The Western theory that all the luminaries in the sky are different suns is not confirmed in the Vedic literature. Nor can we assume that these luminaries are the suns of other universes, for each universe is covered by various layers of material elements, and therefore although the universes are clustered together, we cannot see from one universe to another. In other words, whatever we see is within this one universe. In each universe there is one Lord Brahmā, and there are other demigods on other planets, but there is only one sun.

TEXT 12

एवं मुहूर्तेन चतुस्त्रिंशल्लक्षयोजनान्यष्टशताधिकानि सौरो रथस्त्रयीमयोऽसौ चतसृषु
परिवर्तते पुरीषु ॥१२॥

evaṁ muhūrtena catus-triṁśal-lakṣa-yojanāny aṣṭa-śatādhikāni sauro rathas trayīmayo 'sau catasṛṣu parivartate purīṣu.

evam—thus; *muhūrtena*—in a *muhūrta* (forty-eight minutes); *catuḥ-triṁśat*—thirty-four; *lakṣa*—hundred thousands; *yojanāni*—*yojanas;* *aṣṭa-śata-dhikāni*—increased by eight hundred; *sauraḥ rathaḥ*—the chariot of the sun-god; *trayī-mayaḥ*—which is worshiped by the Gāyatrī *mantra* (*oṁ bhūr bhuvaḥ svaḥ tat savitur,* etc.); *asau*—that; *catasṛṣu*—to the four; *parivartate*—he moves; *purīṣu*—through different residential quarters.

TRANSLATION

Thus the chariot of the sun-god, which is trayīmaya, or worshiped by the words oṁ bhūr bhuvaḥ svaḥ, travels through the four residences mentioned above at a speed of 3,400,800 yojanas [27,206,400 miles] in a muhūrta.

TEXT 13

यस्यैकं चक्रं द्वादशारं षण्नेमि त्रिणाभि संवत्सरात्मकं
समामनन्ति तस्याक्षो मेरोर्मूर्धनि कृतो मानसोत्तरे कृतेतरभागो यत्र
प्रोतं रविरथचक्रं तैलयन्त्रचक्रवद् भ्रमन्मानसोत्तरगिरौ परिभ्रमति१३।

yasyaikaṁ cakraṁ dvādaśāraṁ ṣaṇ-nemi tri-ṇābhi saṁvatsarātmakaṁ samāmananti tasyākṣo meror mūrdhani kṛto mānasottare kṛtetara-bhāgo yatra protaṁ ravi-ratha-cakraṁ taila-yantra-cakravad bhraman mānosottara-girau paribhramati.

yasya—of which; *ekam*—one; *cakram*—wheel; *dvādaśa*—twelve; *aram*—spokes; *ṣaṭ*—six; *nemi*—the segments of the rim; *tri-ṇābhi*—the three pieces of the hub; *saṁvatsara-ātmakam*—whose nature is a *saṁvatsara; samāmananti*—they fully describe; *tasya*—the chariot of the sun-god; *akṣaḥ*—the axle; *meroḥ*—of Sumeru Mountain; *mūrdhani*—on the top; *kṛtaḥ*—fixed; *mānasottare*—on the mountain known as Mānasottara; *kṛta*—fixed; *itara-bhāgaḥ*—the other end; *yatra*—where; *protam*—fixed on; *ravi-ratha-cakram*—the wheel of the chariot of the sun-god; *taila-yantra-cakra-vat*—like the wheel of an oil-pressing machine; *bhramat*—moving; *mānasottara-girau*—on Mānasottara Mountain; *paribhramati*—turns.

TRANSLATION

The chariot of the sun-god has only one wheel, which is known as Saṁvatsara. The twelve months are calculated to be its twelve spokes, the six seasons are the sections of its rim, and the three cātur-māsya periods are its three-sectioned hub. One side of the axle carrying the wheel rests upon the summit of Mount Sumeru, and the other rests upon Mānasottara Mountain. Affixed to the outer end of the axle, the wheel continuously rotates on Mānasottara Mountain like the wheel of an oil-pressing machine.

TEXT 14

तस्मिन्नक्षे कृतमूलो द्वितीयोऽक्षस्तुर्यमानेन सम्मितस्तैलयन्त्राक्षवद् ध्रुवे कृतोपरिभागः ॥ १४ ॥

tasminn akṣe kṛtamūlo dvitīyo 'kṣas turyamānena sammitas taila-yantrākṣavad dhruve kṛtopari-bhāgaḥ.

tasmin akṣe—in that axle; *kṛta-mūlaḥ*—whose base is fixed; *dvitīyaḥ*—a second; *akṣaḥ*—axle; *turyamānena*—by one fourth; *sam-*

mitaḥ—measured; *taila-yantra-akṣa-vat*—like the axle of an oil-pressing machine; *dhruve*—to Dhruvaloka; *kṛta*—fixed; *upari-bhāgaḥ*—upper portion.

TRANSLATION

As in an oil-pressing machine, this first axle is attached to a second axle, which is one-fourth as long [3,937,500 yojanas, or 31,500,000 miles]. The upper end of this second axle is attached to Dhruvaloka by a rope of wind.

TEXT 15

रथनीडस्तु षट्त्रिंशल्लक्षयोजनायतस्तत्तुरीयभागविशालस्तावान् रविरथयुगो
यत्र हयाश्छन्दोनामानः सप्तारुणयोजिता वहन्ति देवमादित्यम् ॥१५॥

ratha-nīḍas tu ṣaṭ-triṁśal-lakṣa-yojanāyatas tat-turīya-bhāga-viśālas
tāvān ravi-ratha-yugo yatra hayāś chando-nāmānaḥ saptāruṇa-yojitā
vahanti devam ādityam.

ratha-nīḍaḥ—the interior of the chariot; *tu*—but; *ṣaṭ-triṁśat-lakṣa-yojana-āyataḥ*—3,600,000 *yojanas* long; *tat-turīya-bhāga*—one quarter of that measure (900,000 *yojanas*); *viśālaḥ*—having a width; *tāvān*—so much also; *ravi-ratha-yugaḥ*—the yoke for the horses; *yatra*—where; *hayāḥ*—horses; *chandaḥ-nāmānaḥ*—having the different names of Vedic meters; *sapta*—seven; *aruṇa-yojitāḥ*—hooked up by Aruṇadeva; *vahanti*—carry; *devam*—the demigod; *ādityam*—the sun-god.

TRANSLATION

My dear King, the carriage of the sun-god's chariot is estimated to be 3,600,000 yojanas [28,800,000 miles] long and one-fourth as wide [900,000 yojanas, or 7,200,000 miles]. The chariot's horses, which are named after Gāyatrī and other Vedic meters, are harnessed by Aruṇadeva to a yoke that is also 900,000 yojanas wide. This chariot continuously carries the sun-god.

PURPORT

In the *Viṣṇu Purāṇa* it is stated:

gāyatrī ca bṛhaty uṣṇig
jagatī triṣṭup eva ca
anuṣṭup paṅktir ity uktāś
chandāṁsi harayo raveḥ

The seven horses yoked to the sun-god's chariot are named Gāyatrī, Bṛhati, Uṣṇik, Jagatī, Triṣṭup, Anuṣṭup and Paṅkti. These names of various Vedic meters designate the seven horses that carry the sun-god's chariot.

TEXT 16

पुरस्तात्सवितुररुणः पश्चाच्च नियुक्तः सौत्ये कर्मणि किलास्ते ॥१६॥

purastāt savitur aruṇaḥ paścāc ca niyuktaḥ sautye karmaṇi kilāste.

purastāt—in front; *savituḥ*—of the sun-god; *aruṇaḥ*—the demigod named Aruṇa; *paścāt*—looking backward; *ca*—and; *niyuktaḥ*—engaged; *sautye*—of a charioteer; *karmaṇi*—in the work; *kila*—certainly; *āste*—remains.

TRANSLATION

Although Aruṇadeva sits in front of the sun-god and is engaged in driving the chariot and controlling the horses, he looks backward toward the sun-god.

PURPORT

In the *Vāyu Purāṇa* the position of the horses is described:

saptāśva-rūpa-cchandāṁsī
vahante vāmato ravim
cakra-pakṣa-nibaddhāni
cakre vākṣaḥ samāhitaḥ

Although Aruṇadeva is in the front seat, controlling the horses, he looks back toward the sun-god from his left side.

TEXT 17

तथा वालखिल्या ऋषयोऽङ्गुष्ठपर्वमात्राः षष्टिसहस्राणि पुरतः सूर्यं सूक्तवाकाय नियुक्ताः संस्तुवन्ति ॥ १७ ॥

tathā vālakhilyā ṛṣayo 'ṅguṣṭha-parva-mātrāḥ ṣaṣṭi-sahasrāṇi purataḥ sūryaṁ sūkta-vākāya niyuktāḥ saṁstuvanti.

tathā—there; *vālikhilyāḥ*—Vālikhilyas; *ṛṣayaḥ*—great sages; *aṅguṣṭha-parva-mātrāḥ*—whose size is that of a thumb; *ṣaṣṭi-sahasrāṇi*—sixty thousand; *purataḥ*—in front; *sūryam*—the sun-god; *su-ukta-vākāya*—for speaking eloquently; *niyuktāḥ*—engaged; *saṁstuvanti*—offer prayers.

TRANSLATION

There are sixty thousand saintly persons named Vālikhilyas, each the size of a thumb, who are located in front of the sun-god and who offer him eloquent prayers of glorification.

TEXT 18

तथान्ये च ऋषयो गन्धर्वाप्सरसो नागा ग्रामण्यो यातुधाना देवा इत्येकैकशो गणाः सप्त चतुर्दश मासि मासि भगवन्तं सूर्यमात्मानं नानानामानं पृथङ्नाना नामानः पृथक्कर्मभिर्द्वन्द्वश उपासते ॥१८॥

tathānye ca ṛṣayo gandharvāpsaraso nāgā grāmaṇyo yātudhānā devā ity ekaikaśo gaṇāḥ sapta caturdaśa māsi māsi bhagavantaṁ sūryam ātmānaṁ nānā-nāmānaṁ pṛthaṅ-nānā-nāmānaḥ pṛthak-karmabhir dvandvaśa upāsate.

tathā—similarly; *anye*—others; *ca*—also; *ṛṣayaḥ*—saintly persons; *gandharva-apsarasaḥ*—Gandharvas and Apsarās; *nāgāḥ*—Nāga snakes; *grāmaṇyaḥ*—Yakṣas; *yātudhānāḥ*—Rākṣasas; *devāḥ*—demigods; *iti*—

thus; *eka-ekaśaḥ*—one by one; *gaṇāḥ*—groups; *sapta*—seven; *catur-daśa*—fourteen in number; *māsi māsi*—in every month; *bhagavan-tam*—unto the most powerful demigod; *sūryam*—the sun-god; *āt-mānam*—the life of the universe; *nānā*—various; *nāmānam*—who possesses names; *pṛthak*—separate; *nānā-nāmānaḥ*—having various names; *pṛthak*—separate; *karmabhiḥ*—by ritualistic ceremonies; *dvandvaśaḥ*—in groups of two; *upāsate*—worship.

TRANSLATION

Similarly, fourteen other saints, Gandharvas, Apsarās, Nāgas, Yakṣas, Rākṣasas and demigods, who are divided into groups of two, assume different names every month and continuously perform different ritualistic ceremonies to worship the Supreme Lord as the most powerful demigod Sūryadeva, who holds many names.

PURPORT

In the *Viṣṇu Purāṇa* it is said:

stuvanti munayaḥ sūryaṁ
gandharvair gīyate puraḥ
nṛtyanto 'psaraso yānti
sūryasyānu niśācarāḥ

vahanti pannagā yakṣaiḥ
kriyate 'bhiṣusaṅgrahaḥ
vālikhilyās tathaivainaṁ
parivārya samāsate

so 'yaṁ sapta-gaṇaḥ sūrya-
maṇḍale muni-sattama
himoṣṇa vāri-vṛṣṭīṇāṁ
hetutve samayaṁ gataḥ

Worshiping the most powerful demigod Sūrya, the Gandharvas sing in front of him, the Apsarās dance before the chariot, the Niśācaras follow the chariot, the Pannagas decorate the chariot, the Yakṣas guard the chariot, and the saints called the Vālikhilyas surround the sun-god and offer prayers. The seven groups of fourteen associates arrange the proper times for regular snow, heat and rain throughout the universe.

TEXT 19

लक्षोत्तरं सार्धनवकोटियोजनपरिमण्डलं भूवलयस्य क्षणेन सगव्यूत्युत्तरं द्विसहस्र योजनानि स भुङ्क्ते ॥१९॥

lakṣottaraṁ sārdha-nava-koṭi-yojana-parimaṇḍalaṁ bhū-valayasya kṣaṇena sagavyūty-uttaraṁ dvi-sahasra-yojanāni sa bhuṅkte.

lakṣa-uttaram—increased by 100,000; *sārdha*—with 5,000,000; *nava-koṭi-yojana*—of 90,000,000 *yojanas; parimaṇḍalam*—circumference; *bhū-valayasya*—of the earthly sphere; *kṣaṇena*—in one moment; *sagavyūti-uttaram*—augmented by two *krośas* (four miles); *dvi-sahasra-yojanāni*—2,000 *yojanas; saḥ*—the sun-god; *bhuṅkte*—traverses.

TRANSLATION

My dear King, in his orbit through Bhūmaṇḍala, the sun-god traverses a distance of 95,100,000 yojanas [760,800,000 miles] at the speed of 2,000 yojanas and two krośas [16,004 miles] in a moment.

Thus end the Bhaktivedanta purports of the Fifth Canto, Twenty-first Chapter of the Śrīmad-Bhāgavatam, *entitled, "The Movements of the Sun."*

CHAPTER TWENTY-TWO

The Orbits of the Planets

In this chapter the orbits of the planets are described. According to the movements of the moon and other planets, all the inhabitants of the universe are prone to auspicious and inauspicious situations. This is referred to as the influence of the stars.

The sun-god, who controls the affairs of the entire universe, especially in regard to heat, light, seasonal changes and so on, is considered an expansion of Nārāyaṇa. He represents the three *Vedas—Ṛg, Yajur* and *Sāma*—and therefore he is known as Trayīmaya, the form of Lord Nārāyaṇa. Sometimes the sun-god is also called Sūrya Nārāyaṇa. The sun-god has expanded himself in twelve divisions, and thus he controls the six seasonal changes and causes winter, summer, rain and so on. *Yogīs* and *karmīs* following the *varṇāśrama* institution, who practice *haṭha* or *aṣṭāṅga-yoga* or who perform *agnihotra* sacrifices, worship Sūrya Nārāyaṇa for their own benefit. The demigod Sūrya is always in touch with the Supreme Personality of Godhead, Nārāyaṇa. Residing in outer space, which is in the middle of the universe, between Bhūloka and Bhuvarloka, the sun rotates through the time circle of the zodiac, represented by twelve *rāśis,* or signs, and assumes different names according to the sign he is in. For the moon, every month is divided into two fortnights. Similarly, according to solar calculations, a month is equal to the time the sun spends in one constellation; two months constitute one season, and there are twelve months in a year. The entire area of the sky is divided into two halves, each representing an *ayana,* the course traversed by the sun within a period of six months. The sun travels sometimes slowly, sometimes swiftly and sometimes at a moderate speed. In this way it travels within the three worlds, consisting of the heavenly planets, the earthly planets and outer space. These orbits are referred to by great learned scholars by the names Saṁvatsara, Parivatsara, Iḍāvatsara, Anuvatsara and Vatsara.

The moon is situated 100,000 *yojanas* above the rays of the sunshine. Day and night on the heavenly planets and Pitṛloka are calculated according to its waning and waxing. Above the moon by a distance of 200,000 *yojanas* are some stars, and above these stars is Śukra-graha (Venus), whose influence is always auspicious for the inhabitants of the entire universe. Above Śukra-graha by 200,000 *yojanas* is Budha-graha (Mercury), whose influence is sometimes auspicious and sometimes inauspicious. Next, above Budha-graha by 200,000 *yojanas,* is Aṅgāraka (Mars), which almost always has an unfavorable influence. Above Aṅgāraka by another 200,000 *yojanas* is the planet called Bṛhaspati-graha (Jupiter), which is always very favorable for qualified *brāhmaṇas.* Above Bṛhaspati-graha is the planet Śanaiścara (Saturn), which is very inauspicious, and above Saturn is a group of seven stars occupied by great saintly persons who are always thinking of the welfare of the entire universe. These seven stars circumambulate Dhruvaloka, which is the residence of Lord Viṣṇu within this universe.

TEXT 1

राजोवाच

यदेतद्भगवत आदित्यस्य मेरुं ध्रुवं च प्रदक्षिणेन परिक्रामतो राशीनामभिमुखं प्रचलितं चाप्रदक्षिणं भगवतोपवर्णितममुष्य वयं कथमनुमिमीमहीति ॥ १ ॥

rājocāca

yad etad bhagavata ādityasya meruṁ dhruvaṁ ca pradakṣiṇena
parikrāmato rāśīnām abhimukhaṁ pracalitaṁ cāpradakṣiṇaṁ
bhagavatopavarṇitam amuṣya vayaṁ katham anumimīmahīti.

rājā uvāca—the King (Mahārāja Parīkṣit) inquired; *yat*—which; *etat*—this; *bhagavataḥ*—of the most powerful; *ādityasya*—of the sun (Sūrya Nārāyaṇa); *merum*—the mountain known as Sumeru; *dhruvam ca*—as well as the planet known as Dhruvaloka; *pradakṣiṇena*—by placing on the right; *parikrāmataḥ*—which is going around; *rāśīnām*—the different signs of the zodiac; *abhimukham*—facing toward; *pracalitam*—moving; *ca*—and; *apradakṣiṇam*—placing on the left; *bhagavatā*—by Your Lordship; *upavarṇitam*—described; *amuṣya*—of that; *vayam*—we (the hearer); *katham*—how; *anumimīmahi*—can accept it by argument and inference; *iti*—thus.

TRANSLATION

King Parīkṣit inquired from Śukadeva Gosvāmī: My dear lord, you have already affirmed the truth that the supremely powerful sun-god travels around Dhruvaloka with both Dhruvaloka and Mount Sumeru on his right. Yet at the same time the sun-god faces the signs of the zodiac and keeps Sumeru and Dhruvaloka on his left. How can we reasonably accept that the sun-god proceeds with Sumeru and Dhruvaloka on both his left and right simultaneously?

TEXT 2

स होवाच

यथा कुलालचक्रेण भ्रमता सह भ्रमतां तदाश्रयाणां पिपीलिकादीनां गतिरन्यैव प्रदेशान्तरेष्वप्युपलभ्यमानत्वादेवं नक्षत्रराशिभिरुपलक्षितेन कालचक्रेण ध्रुवं मेरुं च प्रदक्षिणेन परिधावता सह परिधावमानानां तदाश्रयाणां सूर्यादीनां ग्रहाणां गतिरन्यैव नक्षत्रान्तरे राश्यन्तरे चोपलभ्यमानत्वात् ॥ २ ॥

sa hovāca
yathā kulāla-cakreṇa bhramatā saha bhramatāṁ tad-āśrayāṇāṁ pipīlikādīnāṁ gatir anyaiva pradeśāntareṣv apy upalabhyamānatvād evaṁ nakṣatra-rāśibhir upalakṣitena kāla-cakreṇa dhruvaṁ meruṁ ca pradakṣiṇena paridhāvatā saha paridhāvamānānāṁ tad-āśrayāṇāṁ sūryādīnāṁ grahāṇāṁ gatir anyaiva nakṣatrāntare rāśy-antare copalabhyamānatvāt.

saḥ—Śukadeva Gosvāmī; *ha*—very clearly; *uvāca*—answered; *yathā*—just as; *kulāla-cakreṇa*—a potter's wheel; *bhramatā*—turning around; *saha*—with; *bhramatām*—of those turning around; *tat-āśrayāṇām*—being located on that (wheel); *pipīlika-ādīnām*—of small ants; *gatiḥ*—the motion; *anyā*—other; *eva*—certainly; *pradeśa-antareṣu*—in different locations; *api*—also; *upalabhyamānatvāt*—due to being experienced; *evam*—similarly; *nakṣatra-rāśibhiḥ*—by the stars and signs; *upalakṣitena*—being seen; *kāla-cakreṇa*—with the great wheel of time; *dhruvam*—the star known as Dhruvaloka; *merum*—the mountain known as Sumeru; *ca*—and; *pradakṣiṇena*—on the right; *paridhāvatā*—going around; *saha*—with; *paridhāvamānānām*—of those going around; *tat-āśrayāṇām*—whose shelter is that wheel of time; *sūrya-ādīnām*—headed by the sun; *grahāṇām*—of the planets; *gatiḥ*—the motion; *anyā*—other; *eva*—certainly; *nakṣatra-antare*—in different stars; *rāśi-antare*—in different signs; *ca*—and; *upalabhyamānatvāt*—due to being observed.

TRANSLATION

Śrī Śukadeva Gosvāmī clearly answered: When a potter's wheel is moving and small ants located on that big wheel are moving with it, one can see that their motion is different from that of the wheel because they appear sometimes on one part of the wheel and sometimes on another. Similarly, the signs and constellations, with Sumeru and Dhruvaloka on their right, move with the wheel of time, and the antlike sun and other planets move with them. The sun and planets, however, are seen in different signs and constellations at different times. This indicates that their motion is different from that of the zodiac and the wheel of time itself.

TEXT 3

स एष भगवानादिपुरुष एव साक्षान्नारायणो लोकानां स्वस्तय आत्मानं त्रयीमयं कर्मविशुद्धिनिमित्तं कविभिरपि च वेदेन विजिज्ञास्यमानो द्वादशधा विभज्य षट्सु वसन्तादिष्वृतुषु यथोपजोषमृतुगुणान् विदधाति ॥ ३ ॥

sa eṣa bhagavān ādi-puruṣa eva sākṣān nārāyaṇo lokānāṁ svastaya ātmānaṁ trayīmayaṁ karma-viśuddhi-nimittaṁ kavibhir api ca vedena vijijñāsyamāno dvādaśadhā vibhajya ṣaṭsu vasantādiṣv ṛtuṣu yathopa-joṣam ṛtu-guṇān vidadhāti.

saḥ—that; *eṣaḥ*—this; *bhagavān*—the supremely powerful; *ādi-puruṣaḥ*—the original person; *eva*—certainly; *sākṣāt*—directly; *nārāyaṇaḥ*—the Supreme Personality of Godhead, Nārāyaṇa; *lokānām*—of all the planets; *svastaye*—for the benefit; *ātmānam*—

Himself; *trayī-mayam*—consisting of the three *Vedas* (*Sāma*, *Yajur* and *Ṛg*); *karma-viśuddhi*—of purification of fruitive activities; *nimittam*—the cause; *kavibhiḥ*—by great saintly persons; *api*—also; *ca*—and; *vedena*—by Vedic knowledge; *vijijñāsyamānaḥ*—being inquired about; *dvādaśa-dhā*—in twelve divisions; *vibhajya*—dividing; *ṣaṭsu*—in six; *vasanta-ādiṣu*—headed by spring; *ṛtuṣu*—seasons; *yathā-upajoṣam*—according to the enjoyment of their past activities; *ṛtu-guṇān*—the qualities of the different seasons; *vidadhāti*—he arranges.

TRANSLATION

The original cause of the cosmic manifestation is the Supreme Personality of Godhead, Nārāyaṇa. When great saintly persons, fully aware of the Vedic knowledge, offered prayers to the Supreme Person, He descended to this material world in the form of the sun to benefit all the planets and purify fruitive activities. He divided Himself into twelve parts and created seasonal forms, beginning with spring. In this way He created the seasonal qualities, such as heat, cold and so on.

TEXT 4

तमेतमिह पुरुषास्त्रय्या विद्यया वर्णाश्रमाचारानुपथा उच्चावचैः कर्मभिराम्नातै-
र्योगवितानैश्च श्रद्धया यजन्तोऽञ्जसा श्रेयः समधिगच्छन्ति ॥ ४ ॥

tam etam iha puruṣās trayyā vidyayā varṇāśramācārānupathā
uccāvacaiḥ karmabhir āmnātair yoga-vitānaiś ca śraddhayā yajanto
'ñjasā śreyaḥ samadhigacchanti.

tam—Him (the Supreme Personality of Godhead); *etam*—this; *iha*—in this world of mortality; *puruṣāḥ*—all people; *trayyā*—having three divisions; *vidyayā*—by the Vedic knowledge; *varṇa-āśrama-ācāra*—the practices of the *varṇāśrama* system; *anupathāḥ*—following; *ucca-avacaiḥ*—higher or lower according to the different positions in the *varṇāśrama-dharma* (*brāhmaṇa*, *kṣatriya*, *vaiśya* and *śūdra*); *karmabhiḥ*—by their respective activities; *āmnātaiḥ*—handed down; *yoga-vitānaiḥ*—by meditation and other yogic processes; *ca*—and; *śrad-*

dhayā—with great faith; *yajantaḥ*—worshiping; *añjasā*—without difficulty; *śreyaḥ*—the ultimate benefit of life; *samadhigacchanti*—they attain.

TRANSLATION

According to the system of four varṇas and four āśramas, people generally worship the Supreme Personality of Godhead, Nārāyaṇa, who is situated as the sun-god. With great faith they worship the Supreme Personality as the Supersoul according to ritualistic ceremonies handed down in the three Vedas, such as agnihotra and similar higher and lower fruitive acts, and according to the process of mystic yoga. In this way they very easily attain the ultimate goal of life.

TEXT 5

**अथ स एष आत्मा लोकानां द्यावापृथिव्योरन्तरेण नभोवलयस्य काल-
चक्रगतो द्वादश मासान् भुङ्क्ते राशिसंज्ञान् संवत्सरावयवान्मास : पक्षद्वयं दिवा
नक्तं चेति सपादर्क्षद्वयमुपदिशन्ति यावता षष्ठमंशं भुञ्जीत स वै
ऋतुरित्युपदिश्यते संवत्सरावयवः ॥ ५ ॥**

atha sa eṣa ātmā lokānāṁ dyāv-āpṛthivyor antareṇa nabho-valayasya
kālacakra-gato dvādaśa māsān bhuṅkte rāśi-saṁjñān
saṁvatsarāvayavān māsaḥ pakṣa-dvayaṁ divā naktaṁ ceti sapādarkṣa-
dvayam upadiśanti yāvatā ṣaṣṭham aṁśaṁ bhuñjīta sa vai ṛtur ity
upadiśyate saṁvatsarāvayavaḥ.

atha—therefore; *saḥ*—He; *eṣaḥ*—this; *ātmā*—the living force; *lokānām*—of all the three worlds; *dyav-ā-pṛthivyoḥ antareṇa*—between the upper and lower portions of the universe; *nabhaḥ-valayasya*—of outer space; *kāla-cakra-gataḥ*—positioned in the wheel of time; *dvādaśa māsān*—twelve months; *bhuṅkte*—passes; *rāśi-saṁjñān*—named after the zodiac signs; *saṁvatsara-avayavān*—the parts of the whole year; *māsaḥ*—one month; *pakṣa-dvayam*—two fortnights; *divā*—a day; *naktam ca*—and a night; *iti*—thus; *sapāda-ṛkṣa-dvayam*—by stellar calculations, two and a quarter constellations; *upadiśanti*—they instruct; *yāvatā*—by as much time; *ṣaṣṭham aṁśam*—

one sixth of his orbit; *bhuñjīta*—pass; *saḥ*—that portion; *vai*—indeed; *ṛtuḥ*—a season; *iti*—thus; *upadiśyate*—is instructed; *saṁvatsara-avayavaḥ*—a part of a year.

TRANSLATION

The sun-god, who is Nārāyaṇa, or Viṣṇu, the soul of all the worlds, is situated in outer space between the upper and lower portions of the universe. Passing through twelve months on the wheel of time, the sun comes in touch with twelve different signs of the zodiac and assumes twelve different names according to those signs. The aggregate of those twelve months is called a saṁvatsara, or an entire year. According to lunar calculations, two fortnights—one of the waxing moon and the other of the waning—form one month. That same period is one day and night for the planet Pitṛloka. According to stellar calculations, a month equals two and one quarter constellations. When the sun travels for two months, a season passes, and therefore the seasonal changes are considered parts of the body of the year.

TEXT 6

अथ च यावतार्धेन नभोवीथ्यां प्रचरति तं कालमयनमाचक्षते ॥ ६ ॥

atha ca yāvatārdhena nabho-vīthyāṁ pracarati taṁ kālam ayanam ācakṣate.

atha—now; *ca*—also; *yāvatā*—by as long as; *ardhena*—half; *nabhaḥ-vīthyām*—in outer space; *pracarati*—the sun moves; *tam*—that; *kālam*—time; *ayanam*—*ayana;* *ācakṣate*—is said.

TRANSLATION

Thus the time the sun takes to rotate through half of outer space is called an ayana, or its period of movement [in the north or in the south].

TEXT 7

अथ च यावन्नभोमण्डलं सह द्यावापृथिव्योर्मण्डलाभ्यां कार्त्स्न्येन स ह भुञ्जीत तं कालं संवत्सरं परिवत्सरमिडावत्सरमनुवत्सरं वत्सरमिति भानोर्मान्द्यशैघ्र्यसमगतिभिः समामनन्ति ॥ ७ ॥

atha ca yāvan nabho-maṇḍalaṁ saha dyāv-āpṛthivyor maṇḍalābhyāṁ kārtsnyena sa ha bhuñjīta taṁ kālaṁ saṁvatsaraṁ parivatsaram iḍāvatsaram anuvatsaraṁ vatsaram iti bhānor māndya-śaighrya-sama-gatibhiḥ samāmananti.

atha—now; *ca*—also; *yāvat*—as long as; *nabhaḥ-maṇḍalam*—outer space, between the upper and lower world; *saha*—along with; *dyāv*—of the upper world; *āpṛthivyoḥ*—of the lower world; *maṇḍalābhyām*—the spheres; *kārtsnyena*—entirely; *saḥ*—he; *ha*—indeed; *bhuñjīta*—may pass through; *tam*—that; *kālam*—time; *saṁvatsaram*—Saṁvatsara; *parivatsaram*—Parivatsara; *iḍāvatasaram*—Iḍāvatsara; *anuvatsaram*—Anuvatsara; *vatsaram*—Vatsara; *iti*—thus; *bhānoḥ*—of the sun; *mān-dya*—slow; *śaighrya*—speedy; *sama*—and equal; *gatibhiḥ*—by the speeds; *samāmananti*—the experienced scholars describe.

TRANSLATION

The sun-god has three speeds—slow, fast and moderate. The time he takes to travel entirely around the spheres of heaven, earth and space at these three speeds is referred to, by learned scholars, by the five names Saṁvatsara, Parivatsara, Iḍāvatsara, Anuvatsara and Vatsara.

PURPORT

According to solar astronomical calculations, each year extends six days beyond the calendar year, and according to lunar calculations, each year is six days shorter. Therefore, because of the movements of the sun and moon, there is a difference of twelve days between the solar and lunar years. As the Saṁvatsara, Parivatsara, Iḍāvatsara, Anuvatsara and Vatsara pass by, two extra months are added within each five years. This makes a sixth *saṁvatsara*, but because that *saṁvatsara* is extra, the solar system is calculated according to the above five names.

TEXT 8

एवं चन्द्रमा अर्कगभस्तिभ्य उपरिष्टाल्लक्षयोजनत उपलभ्यमानोऽर्कस्य संवत्सरभुक्तिं पक्षाभ्यां मासभुक्तिं सपादर्क्षाभ्यां दिनेनैव पक्षभुक्तिमग्रचारी द्रुततरगमनो भुङ्क्ते ॥८॥

evaṁ candramā arka-gabhastibhya upariṣṭāl lakṣa-yojanata upalabhyamāno 'rkasya saṁvatsara-bhuktiṁ pakṣābhyāṁ māsa-bhuktiṁ sapādarkṣābhyāṁ dinenaiva pakṣa-bhuktim agracārī drutatara-gamano bhuṅkte.

evam—thus; *candramā*—the moon; *arka-gabhastibhyaḥ*—from the rays of the sunshine; *upariṣṭāt*—above; *lakṣa-yojanataḥ*—by a measurement of 100,000 *yojanas; upalabhyamānaḥ*—being situated; *arkasya*—of the sun globe; *saṁvatsara-bhuktim*—the passage of one year of enjoyment; *pakṣābhyām*—by two fortnights; *māsa-bhuktim*—the passage of one month; *sapāda-ṛkṣābhyām*—by two and a quarter days; *dinena*—by a day; *eva*—only; *pakṣa-bhuktim*—the passage of a fortnight; *agracārī*—moving impetuously; *druta-tara-gamanaḥ*—passing more speedily; *bhuṅkte*—passes through.

TRANSLATION

Above the rays of the sunshine by a distance of 100,000 yojanas [800,000 miles] is the moon, which travels at a speed faster than that of the sun. In two lunar fortnights the moon travels through the equivalent of a saṁvatsara of the sun, in two and a quarter days it passes through a month of the sun, and in one day it passes through a fortnight of the sun.

PURPORT

When we take into account that the moon is 100,000 *yojanas,* or 800,000 miles, above the rays of the sunshine, it is very surprising that the modern excursions to the moon could be possible. Since the moon is so distant, how space vehicles could go there is a doubtful mystery. Modern scientific calculations are subject to one change after another, and therefore they are uncertain. We have to accept the calculations of the Vedic literature. These Vedic calculations are steady; the astronomical calculations made long ago and recorded in the Vedic literature are correct even now. Whether the Vedic calculations or modern ones are better may remain a mystery for others, but as far as we are concerned, we accept the Vedic calculations to be correct.

TEXT 9

अथ चापूर्यमाणाभिश्च कलाभिरमराणां क्षीयमाणाभिश्च कलाभिः पितॄणामहोरात्राणि पूर्वपक्षापरपक्षाभ्यां वितन्वानः सर्वजीवनिवहप्राणो जीवश्चैकमेकं नक्षत्रं त्रिंशता मुहूर्तैर्भुङ्क्ते ॥ ९ ॥

atha cāpūryamāṇābhiś ca kalābhir amarāṇāṁ kṣīyamāṇābhiś ca kalābhiḥ pitṝṇām aho-rātrāṇi pūrva-pakṣāpara-pakṣābhyāṁ vitanvānaḥ sarva-jīva-nivaha-prāṇo jīvaś caikam ekaṁ nakṣatraṁ triṁśatā muhūrtair bhuṅkte.

atha—thus; *ca*—also; *āpūryamāṇābhiḥ*—gradually increasing; *ca*—and; *kalābhiḥ*—by the parts of the moon; *amarāṇām*—of the demigods; *kṣīyamānābhiḥ*—by gradually decreasing; *ca*—and; *kalābhiḥ*—by parts of the moon; *pitṝṇām*—of those on the planet known as Pitṛloka; *ahaḥ-rātrāṇi*—the days and nights; *pūrva-pakṣa-apara-pakṣābhyām*—by the period of waxing and waning; *vitanvānaḥ*—distributing; *sarva-jīva-nivaha*—of the total living entities; *prāṇaḥ*—the life; *jīvaḥ*—the chief living being; *ca*—also; *ekam ekam*—one after another; *nakṣatram*—a constellation of stars; *triṁśatā*—by thirty; *muhūrtaiḥ*—*muhūrtas;* *bhuṅkte*—passes through.

TRANSLATION

When the moon is waxing, the illuminating portions of it increase daily, thus creating day for the demigods and night for the pitās. When the moon is waning, however, it causes night for the demigods and day for the pitās. In this way the moon passes through each constellation of stars in thirty muhūrtas [an entire day]. The moon is the source of nectarean coolness that influences the growth of food grains, and therefore the moon-god is con-

sidered the life of all living entities. He is consequently called Jīva, the chief living being within the universe.

TEXT 10

य एष षोडशकलः पुरुषो भगवान्मनोमयोऽन्नमयोऽमृतमयो देवपितृ-मनुष्यभूतपशुपक्षिसरीसृपवीरुधां प्राणाप्यायनशीलत्वात्सर्वमय इति वर्णयन्ति ॥ १० ॥

ya eṣa ṣoḍaśa-kalaḥ puruṣo bhagavān manomayo 'nnamayo 'mṛtamayo deva-pitṛ-manuṣya-bhūta-paśu-pakṣi-sarīsṛpa-vīrudhāṁ prāṇāpy āyana-śīlatvāt sarvamaya iti varṇayanti.

yaḥ—that; *eṣaḥ*—this; *ṣoḍaśa-kalaḥ*—having all sixteen parts (the full moon); *puruṣaḥ*—the person; *bhagavān*—having great power received from the Supreme Personality of Godhead; *manaḥ-mayaḥ*—the predominating deity of the mind; *anna-mayaḥ*—the source of potency for food grains; *amṛta-mayaḥ*—the source of the substance of life; *deva*—of all the demigods; *pitṛ*—of all the inhabitants of Pitṛloka; *manuṣya*—all human beings; *bhūta*—all living entities; *paśu*—of the animals; *pakṣi*—of the birds; *sarīsṛpa*—of the reptiles; *vīrudhām*—of all kinds of herbs and plants; *prāṇa*—life air; *api*—certainly; *āyana-śīlatvāt*—due to refreshing; *sarva-mayaḥ*—all-pervading; *iti*—thus; *varṇayanti*—the learned scholars describe.

TRANSLATION

Because the moon is full of all potentialities, it represents the influence of the Supreme Personality of Godhead. The moon is the predominating deity of everyone's mind, and therefore the moon-god is called Manomaya. He is also called Annamaya because he gives potency to all herbs and plants, and he is called Amṛtamaya because he is the source of life for all living entities. The moon pleases the demigods, pitās, human beings, animals, birds, reptiles, trees, plants and all other living entities. Everyone is satisfied by the presence of the moon. Therefore the moon is also called Sarvamaya [all-pervading].

TEXT 11

तत उपरिष्टाद्द्विलक्षयोजनतो नक्षत्राणि मेरुं दक्षिणेनैव
कालायन ईश्वरयोजितानि सहाभिजिताष्टाविंशतिः ॥११॥

tata upariṣṭād dvi-lakṣa-yojanato nakṣatrāṇi meruṁ dakṣiṇenaiva
kālāyana īśvara-yojitāni sahābhijitāṣṭā-viṁśatiḥ.

tataḥ—from that region of the moon; *upariṣṭāt*—above; *dvi-lakṣa-yojanataḥ*—200,000 *yojanas; nakṣatrāṇi*—many stars; *merum*—Sumeru Mountain; *dakṣiṇena eva*—to the right side; *kāla-ayane*—in the wheel of time; *īśvara-yojitāni*—attached by the Supreme Personality of Godhead; *saha*—with; *abhijitā*—the star known as Abhijit; *aṣṭā-viṁśatiḥ*—twenty-eight.

TRANSLATION

There are many stars located 200,000 yojanas [1,600,000 miles] above the moon. By the supreme will of the Supreme Personality of Godhead, they are fixed to the wheel of time, and thus they rotate with Mount Sumeru on their right, their motion being different from that of the sun. There are twenty-eight important stars, headed by Abhijit.

PURPORT

The stars referred to herein are 1,600,000 miles above the sun, and thus they are 4,000,000 miles above the earth.

TEXT 12

तत उपरिष्टादुशना द्विलक्षयोजनत उपलभ्यते पुरतः पश्चात्सहैव वार्कस्य
शैघ्र्यमान्द्यसाम्याभिर्गतिभिरर्कवच्चरति लोकानां नित्यदानुकूल एव
प्रायेण वर्षयंश्चारेणानुमीयते स वृष्टिविष्टम्भग्रहोपशमनः ॥ १२ ॥

tata upariṣṭād uśanā dvi-lakṣa-yojanata upalabhyate purataḥ paścāt
sahaiva vārkasya śaighrya-māndya-sāmyābhir gatibhir arkavac carati
lokānāṁ nityadānukūla eva prāyeṇa varṣayaṁś cāreṇānumīyate sa
vṛṣṭi-viṣṭambha-grahopaśamanaḥ.

tataḥ—from that bunch of stars; *upariṣṭāt*—above; *uśanā*—Venus; *dvi-lakṣa-yojanataḥ*—200,000 *yojanas* (1,600,000 miles); *upalabh-yate*—is experienced; *purataḥ*—in front; *paścāt*—behind; *saha*—along with; *eva*—indeed; *vā*—and; *arkasya*—of the sun; *śaighrya*—speedy; *māndya*—slow; *sāmyābhiḥ*—equal; *gatibhiḥ*—the movements; *arka-vat*—exactly like the sun; *carati*—rotates; *lokānām*—of all the planets within the universe; *nityadā*—constantly; *anukūlaḥ*—offering favorable conditions; *eva*—indeed; *prāyeṇa*—almost always; *varṣayan*—causing rainfall; *cāreṇa*—by infusing the clouds; *anumīyate*—is perceived; *saḥ*—he (Venus); *vṛṣṭi-viṣṭambha*—obstacles to rainfall; *graha-upaśamanaḥ*—nullifying planets.

TRANSLATION

Some 1,600,000 miles above this group of stars is the planet Venus, which moves at almost exactly the same pace as the sun according to swift, slow and moderate movements. Sometimes Venus moves behind the sun, sometimes in front of the sun and sometimes along with it. Venus nullifies the influence of planets that are obstacles to rainfall. Consequently its presence causes rainfall, and it is therefore considered very favorable for all living beings within this universe. This has been accepted by learned scholars.

TEXT 13

उशनसा बुधो व्याख्यातस्तत उपरिष्टाद् द्विलक्षयोजनतो बुधः।
सोमसुत उपलभ्यमानः प्रायेण शुभकृद्यदार्काद् व्यतिरिच्येत तदातिवाता-
भ्रप्रायानावृष्ट्यादिभयमाशंसते ॥ १३ ॥

uśanasā budho vyākhyātas tata upariṣṭād dvi-lakṣa-yojanato budhaḥ
soma-suta upalabhyamānaḥ prāyeṇa śubha-kṛd yadārkād vyatiricyeta
tadātivātābhra-prāyānāvṛṣṭy-ādi-bhayam āśaṁsate.

uśanasā—with Venus; *budhaḥ*—Mercury; *vyākhyātaḥ*—explained; *tataḥ*—from that (Venus); *upariṣṭāt*—above; *dvi-lakṣa-yojanataḥ*—1,600,000 miles; *budhaḥ*—Mercury; *soma-sutaḥ*—the son of the moon; *upalabhyamānaḥ*—is situated; *prāyeṇa*—almost always; *śubha-kṛt*—

very auspicious to the inhabitants of the universe; *yadā*—when; *arkāt*—from the sun; *vyatiricyeta*—is separated; *tadā*—at that time; *ativāta*—of cyclones and other bad effects; *abhra*—clouds; *prāya*—almost always; *anāvṛṣṭi-ādi*—such as scarcity of rain; *bhayam*—fearful conditions; *āśaṁsate*—expands.

TRANSLATION

Mercury is described to be similar to Venus, in that it moves sometimes behind the sun, sometimes in front of the sun and sometimes along with it. It is 1,600,000 miles above Venus, or 7,200,000 miles above earth. Mercury, which is the son of the moon, is almost always very auspicious for the inhabitants of the universe, but when it does not move along with the sun, it forbodes cyclones, dust, irregular rainfall, and waterless clouds. In this way it creates fearful conditions due to inadequate or excessive rainfall.

TEXT 14

अत ऊर्ध्वमङ्गारकोऽपि योजनलक्षद्वितय उपलभ्यमानस्त्रिभिस्त्रिभिः
पक्षैरेकैकशो राशीन्द्वादशानुभुङ्क्ते यदि न वक्रेणाभिवर्तते प्रायेणाशुभग्रहो-
ऽघशंसः ॥१४॥

ata ūrdhvam aṅgārako 'pi yojana-lakṣa-dvitaya upalabhyamānas
tribhis tribhiḥ pakṣair ekaikaśo rāśīn dvādaśānubhuṅkte yadi na
vakreṇābhivartate prāyeṇāśubha-graho 'gha-śaṁsaḥ.

ataḥ—from this; *ūrdhvam*—above; *aṅgārakaḥ*—Mars; *api*—also; *yojana-lakṣa-dvitaye*—at a distance of 1,600,000 miles; *upalabhyamānaḥ*—is situated; *tribhiḥ tribhiḥ*—with each three and three; *pakṣaiḥ*—fortnights; *eka-ekaśaḥ*—one after another; *rāśīn*—the signs; *dvādaśa*—twelve; *anubhuṅkte*—passes through; *yadi*—if; *na*—not; *vakreṇa*—with a curve; *abhivartate*—approaches; *prāyeṇa*—almost always; *aśubha-grahaḥ*—an unfavorable, inauspicious planet; *agha-śaṁsaḥ*—creating trouble.

TRANSLATION

Situated 1,600,000 miles above Mercury, or 8,800,000 miles above earth, is the planet Mars. If this planet does not travel in a crooked way, it crosses through each sign of the zodiac in three

fortnights and in this way travels through all twelve, one after another. It almost always creates unfavorable conditions in respect to rainfall and other influences.

TEXT 15

तत उपरिष्टाद् द्विलक्षयोजनान्तरगता भगवान् बृहस्पतिरेकैकस्मिन् राशौ परिवत्सरं परिवत्सरं चरति यदि न वक्रः स्यात्प्रायेणानुकूलो ब्राह्मणकुलस्य ॥ १५ ॥

tata upariṣṭād dvi-lakṣa-yojanāntara-gatā bhagavān bṛhaspatir ekaikasmin rāśau parivatsaraṁ parivatsaraṁ carati yadi na vakraḥ syāt prāyeṇānukūlo brāhmaṇa-kulasya.

tataḥ—that (Mars); *upariṣṭāt*—above; *dvi-lakṣa-yojana-antara-gatāḥ*—situated at a distance of 1,600,000 miles; *bhagavān*—the most powerful planet; *bṛhaspatiḥ*—Jupiter; *eka-ekasmin*—in one after another; *rāśau*—sign; *parivatsaram parivatsaram*—for the period of Parivatsara; *carati*—moves; *yadi*—if; *na*—not; *vakraḥ*—curved; *syāt*—becomes; *prāyeṇa*—almost always; *anukūlaḥ*—very favorable; *brāhmaṇa-kulasya*—to the *brāhmaṇas* of the universe.

TRANSLATION

Situated 1,600,000 miles above Mars, or 10,400,000 miles above earth, is the planet Jupiter, which travels through one sign of the zodiac within the period of a Parivatsara. If its movement is not curved, the planet Jupiter is very favorable to the brāhmaṇas of the universe.

TEXT 16

तत उपरिष्टाद्योजनलक्षद्वयात्प्रतीयमानः शनैश्चर एकैकस्मिन् राशौ त्रिंशन्मासान् विलम्बमानः सर्वानेवानुपर्येति तावद्भिरनुवत्सरैः प्रायेण हि सर्वेषामशान्तिकरः ॥१६॥

tata upariṣṭād yojana-lakṣa-dvayāt pratīyamānaḥ śanaiścara ekaikasmin rāśau triṁśan māsān vilambamānaḥ sarvān evānuparyeti tāvadbhir anuvatsaraiḥ prāyeṇa hi sarveṣām aśāntikaraḥ.

tataḥ—that (Jupiter); *upariṣṭāt*—above; *yojana-lakṣa-dvayāt*—by a distance of 1,600,000 miles; *pratīyamānaḥ*—is situated; *śanaiścaraḥ*—the planet Saturn; *eka-ekasmin*—in one after another; *rāśau*—zodiac signs; *triṁśat māsān*—for a period of thirty months in each; *vilambamānaḥ*—lingering; *sarvān*—all twelve signs of the zodiac; *eva*—certainly; *anuparyeti*—passes through; *tāvadbhiḥ*—by so many; *anuvatsaraiḥ*—Anuvatsaras; *prāyeṇa*—almost always; *hi*—indeed; *sarveṣām*—to all the inhabitants; *aśāntikaraḥ*—very troublesome.

TRANSLATION

Situated 1,600,000 miles above Jupiter, or 12,000,000 miles above earth, is the planet Saturn, which passes through one sign of the zodiac in thirty months and covers the entire zodiac circle in thirty Anuvatsaras. This planet is always very inauspicious for the universal situation.

TEXT 17

**तत उत्तरस्मादृषय एकादशलक्षयोजनान्तर उपलभ्यन्ते य एव लोकानां
शमनुभावयन्तो भगवतो विष्णोर्यत्परमं पदं प्रदक्षिणं प्रक्रमन्ति ॥१७॥**

*tata uttarasmād ṛṣaya ekādaśa-lakṣa-yojanāntara upalabhyante ya eva
lokānāṁ śam anubhāvayanto bhagavato viṣṇor yat paramaṁ padaṁ
pradakṣiṇaṁ prakramanti.*

tataḥ—the planet Saturn; *uttarasmāt*—above; *ṛṣayaḥ*—great saintly sages; *ekādaśa-lakṣa-yojana-antare*—at a distance of 1,100,000 *yojanas; upalabhyante*—are situated; *ye*—all of them; *eva*—indeed; *lokānām*—for all the inhabitants of the universe; *śam*—the good fortune; *anubhāvayantaḥ*—always thinking of; *bhagavataḥ*—of the Supreme Personality of Godhead; *viṣṇoḥ*—Lord Viṣṇu; *yat*—which; *paramam padam*—the supreme abode; *pradakṣiṇam*—placing on the right; *prakramanti*—circumambulate.

TRANSLATION

Situated 8,800,000 miles above Saturn, or 20,800,000 miles above earth, are the seven saintly sages, who are always thinking of

the well-being of the inhabitants of the universe. They circumambulate the supreme abode of Lord Viṣṇu, known as Dhruvaloka, the polestar.

PURPORT

Śrīla Madhvācārya quotes the following verse from the *Brahmāṇḍa Purāṇa:*

jñānānandātmano viṣṇuḥ
śiśumāra-vapuṣy atha
ūrdhva-lokeṣu sa vyāpta
ādityādyās tad-āśritā

Lord Viṣṇu, who is the source of knowledge and transcendental bliss, has assumed the form of Śiśumāra in the seventh heaven, which is situated in the topmost level of the universe. All the other planets, beginning with the sun, exist under the shelter of this Śiśumāra planetary system.

Thus end the Bhaktivedanta purports of the Fifth Canto, Twenty-second Chapter of Śrīmad-Bhāgavatam, *entitled "The Orbits of the Planets."*

CHAPTER TWENTY-THREE

The Śiśumāra Planetary System

This chapter describes how all the planetary systems take shelter of the polestar, Dhruvaloka. It also describes the totality of these planetary systems to be Śiśumāra, another expansion of the external body of the Supreme Personality of Godhead. Dhruvaloka, the abode of Lord Viṣṇu within this universe, is situated 1,300,000 *yojanas* from the seven stars. In the planetary system of Dhruvaloka are the planets of the fire-god, Indra, Prajāpati, Kaśyapa and Dharma, all of whom are very respectful to the great devotee Dhruva, who lives on the polestar. Like bulls yoked to a central pivot, all the planetary systems revolve around Dhruvaloka, impelled by eternal time. Those who worship the *virāṭa-puruṣa*, the universal form of the Lord, conceive of this entire rotating system of planets as an animal known as *śiśumāra*. This imaginary *śiśumāra* is another form of the Lord. The head of the *śiśumāra* form is downward, and its body appears like that of a coiled snake. On the end of its tail is Dhruvaloka, on the body of the tail are Prajāpati, Agni, Indra and Dharma, and on the root of the tail are Dhātā and Vidhātā. On its waist are the seven great sages. The entire body of the *śiśumāra* faces toward its right and appears like a coil of stars. On the right side of this coil are the fourteen prominent stars from Abhijit to Punarvasu, and on the left side are the fourteen prominent stars from Puṣyā to Uttarāṣāḍhā. The stars known as Punarvasu and Puṣyā are on the right and left hips of the *śiśumāra*, and the stars known as Ārdrā and Aśleṣā are on the right and left feet of the *śiśumāra*. Other stars are also fixed on different sides of the Śiśumāra planetary system according to the calculations of Vedic astronomers. To concentrate their minds, *yogīs* worship the Śiśumāra planetary system, which is technically known as the *kuṇḍalini-cakra*.

TEXT 1

श्रीशुक उवाच

अथ तस्मात्परतस्त्रयोदशलक्षयोजनान्तरतो यत्तद्विष्णोः परमं पदम-
भिवदन्ति यत्र ह महाभागवतो ध्रुव औत्तानपादिरग्निनेन्द्रेण प्रजापतिना

कश्यपेन धर्मेण च समकालयुग्भिः सबहुमानं दक्षिणतः क्रियमाण
इदानीमपि कल्पजीविनामाजीव्य उपास्ते तस्येहानुभाव उपवर्णितः ॥ १ ॥

śrī-śuka uvāca
atha tasmāt paratas trayodaśa-lakṣa-yojanāntarato yat tad viṣṇoḥ paramaṁ padam abhivadanti yatra ha mahā-bhāgavato dhruva auttānapādir agninendreṇa prajāpatinā kaśyapena dharmeṇa ca samakāla-yugbhiḥ sabahu-mānaṁ dakṣiṇataḥ kriyamāṇa idānīm api kalpa-jīvinām ājīvya upāste tasyehānubhāva upavarṇitaḥ.

śrī-śukaḥ uvāca—Śrī Śukadeva Gosvāmī said; *atha*—thereupon; *tasmāt*—the sphere of the seven stars; *parataḥ*—beyond that; *trayodaśa-lakṣa-yojana-antarataḥ*—another 1,300,000 *yojanas; yat*—which; *tat*—that; *viṣṇoḥ paramam padam*—the supreme abode of Lord Viṣṇu, or the lotus feet of Lord Viṣṇu; *abhivadanti*—the *Ṛg Veda mantras* praise; *yatra*—on which; *ha*—indeed; *mahā-bhāgavataḥ*—the great devotee; *dhruvaḥ*—Mahārāja Dhruva; *auttānapādiḥ*—the son of Mahārāja Uttānapāda; *agninā*—by the fire-god; *indreṇa*—by the heavenly King, Indra; *prajāpatinā*—by the Prajāpati; *kaśyapena*—by Kaśyapa; *dharmeṇa*—by Dharmarāja; *ca*—also; *samakāla-yugbhiḥ*—who are engaged at the time; *sa-bahu-mānam*—always respectfully; *dakṣiṇataḥ*—on the right side; *kriyamāṇaḥ*—being circumambulated; *idānīm*—now; *api*—even; *kalpa-jīvinām*—of the living entities who exist at the end of the creation; *ājīvyaḥ*—the source of life; *upāste*—remains; *tasya*—his; *iha*—here; *anubhāvaḥ*—greatness in discharging devotional service; *upavarṇitaḥ*—already described (in the Fourth Canto of *Śrīmad-Bhāgavatam*).

TRANSLATION

Śukadeva Gosvāmī continued: My dear King, 1,300,000 yojanas [10,400,000 miles] above the planets of the seven sages is the place that learned scholars describe as the abode of Lord Viṣṇu. There the son of Mahārāja Uttānapāda, the great devotee Mahārāja Dhruva, still resides as the life source of all the living entities who live until the end of the creation. Agni, Indra, Prajāpati, Kaśyapa and Dharma all assemble there to offer him honor and respectful

obeisances. They circumambulate him with their right sides toward him. I have already described the glorious activities of Mahārāja Dhruva [in the Fourth Canto of Śrīmad-Bhāgavatam].

TEXT 2

स हि सर्वेषां ज्योतिर्गणानां ग्रहनक्षत्रादीनामनिमिषेणाव्यक्तरंहसा भगवता
कालेन भ्राम्यमाणानां स्थाणुरिवावष्टम्भ ईश्वरेण विहितः शश्वदवभासते।२

sa hi sarveṣāṁ jyotir-gaṇānāṁ graha-nakṣatrādīnām animiṣeṇāvyakta-
raṁhasā bhagavatā kālena bhrāmyamāṇānāṁ sthāṇur ivāvaṣṭambha
īśvareṇa vihitaḥ śaśvad avabhāsate.

saḥ—that planet of Dhruva Mahārāja; *hi*—indeed; *sarveṣām*—of all; *jyotiḥ-gaṇānām*—the luminaries; *graha-nakṣatra-ādīnām*—such as the planets and stars; *animiṣeṇa*—who does not rest; *avyakta*—inconceivable; *raṁhasā*—whose force; *bhagavatā*—the most powerful; *kālena*—by the time factor; *bhrāmyamāṇānām*—being caused to revolve; *sthāṇuḥ iva*—like a post; *avaṣṭambhaḥ*—the pivot; *īśvareṇa*—by the will of the Supreme Personality of Godhead; *vihitaḥ*—established; *śaśvat*—constantly; *avabhāsate*—shines.

TRANSLATION

Established by the supreme will of the Supreme Personality of Godhead, the polestar, which is the planet of Mahārāja Dhruva, constantly shines as the central pivot for all the stars and planets. The unsleeping, invisible, most powerful time factor causes these luminaries to revolve around the polestar without cessation.

PURPORT

It is distinctly stated herein that all the luminaries, the planets and stars, revolve by the influence of the supreme time factor. The time factor is another feature of the Supreme Personality of Godhead. Everyone is under the influence of the time factor, but the Supreme Personality of Godhead is so kind and loves His devotee Mahārāja Dhruva so much that He has placed all the luminaries under the control of Dhruva's planet and has arranged for the time factor to work under him or with his cooperation. Everything is actually done according to the will and direction of the Supreme Personality of Godhead, but to make His devotee Dhruva the most important individual within the universe, the Lord has placed the activities of the time factor under his control.

TEXT 3

यथा मेढीस्तम्भ आक्रमणपशवः संयोजितास्त्रिभिस्त्रिभिः सवनैर्यथास्थानं मण्डलानि चरन्त्येवं भगणा ग्रहादय एतस्मिन्नन्तर्बहिर्योगेन कालचक्र आयोजिता ध्रुवमेवावलम्ब्य वायुनोदीर्यमाणा आकल्पान्तं परिचङ्क्रमन्ति नभसि यथा मेघाः श्येनादयो वायुवशाः कर्मसारथयः परिवर्तन्ते एवं ज्योतिर्गणाः प्रकृतिपुरुषसंयोगानुगृहीताः कर्मनिर्मितगतयो भुवि न पतन्ति ॥ ३ ॥

yathā meḍhīstambha ākramaṇa-paśavaḥ saṁyojitās tribhis tribhiḥ savanair yathā-sthānaṁ maṇḍalāni caranty evaṁ bhagaṇā grahādaya etasminn antar-bahir-yogena kāla-cakra āyojitā dhruvam evāvalambya vāyunodīryamāṇā ākalpāntaṁ paricaṅ kramanti nabhasi yathā meghāḥ śyenādayo vāyu-vaśāḥ karma-sārathayaḥ parivartante evaṁ jyotirgaṇāḥ prakṛti-puruṣa-saṁyogānugṛhītāḥ karma-nirmita-gatayo bhuvi na patanti.

yathā—exactly like; *meḍhīstambhe*—to the pivot post; *ākramaṇa-paśavaḥ*—bulls for threshing rice; *saṁyojitāḥ*—being yoked; *tribhiḥ tribhiḥ*—by three; *savanaiḥ*—movements; *yathā-sthānam*—in their proper places; *maṇḍalāni*—orbits; *caranti*—traverse; *evam*—in the same way; *bha-gaṇāḥ*—the luminaries, like the sun, the moon, Venus, Mercury, Mars and Jupiter; *graha-ādayaḥ*—the different planets; *etasmin*—in this; *antaḥ-bahiḥ-yogena*—by connection with the inner or outer circles; *kāla-cakre*—in the wheel of eternal time; *āyojitāḥ*—fixed; *dhruvam*—Dhruvaloka; *eva*—certainly; *avalambya*—taking support of; *vayunā*—by the wind; *udīryamāṇāḥ*—being propelled; *ā-kalpa-antam*—until the end of the creation; *paricaṅ kramanti*—revolve all around; *nabhasi*—in the sky; *yathā*—exactly like; *meghāḥ*—heavy clouds; *śyena-ādayaḥ*—birds such as the big eagle; *vāyu-vaśāḥ*—controlled by the air; *karma-sārathayaḥ*—whose chariot drivers are the results of their own past activities; *parivartante*—move around; *evam*—in this way; *jyotiḥ-gaṇāḥ*—the luminaries, the planets and stars in the sky; *prakṛti*—of material nature; *puruṣa*—and of the Supreme Personality, Kṛṣṇa; *saṁyoga-anugṛhītāḥ*—supported by the combined efforts; *karma-nirmita*—caused by their own past fruitive activities; *gatayaḥ*—whose movements; *bhuvi*—on the ground; *na*—not; *patanti*—fall down.

TRANSLATION

When bulls are yoked together and tied to a central post to thresh rice, they tread around that pivot without deviating from their proper positions—one bull being closest to the post, another in the middle, and a third on the outside. Similarly, all the planets and all the hundreds and thousands of stars revolve around the polestar, the planet of Mahārāja Dhruva, in their respective orbits, some higher and some lower. Fastened by the Supreme Personality of Godhead to the machine of material nature according to the results of their fruitive acts, they are driven around the polestar by the wind and will continue to be so until the end of creation. These planets float in the air within the vast sky, just as clouds with hundreds of tons of water float in the air or as the great śyena eagles, due to the results of past activities, fly high in the sky and have no chance of falling to the ground.

PURPORT

According to the description of this verse, the hundreds and thousands of stars and the great planets such as the sun, the moon, Venus, Mercury, Mars and Jupiter are not clustered together because of the law of gravity or any similar idea of the modern scientists. These planets and stars are all servants of the Supreme Personality of Godhead, Govinda or Kṛṣṇa, and according to His order they sit in their chariots and travel in their respective orbits. The orbits in which they move are compared to machines given by material nature to the operating deities of the stars and planets, who carry out the orders of the Supreme Personality of

Godhead by revolving around Dhruvaloka, which is occupied by the great devotee Mahārāja Dhruva. This is confirmed in the *Brahma-saṁhitā* (5.52) as follows:

yac-cakṣur eṣa savitā sakala-grahāṇāṁ
rājā samasta-sura-mūrtir aśeṣa-tejāḥ
yasyājñayā bhramati sambhṛta-kāla-cakro
govindam ādi-puruṣaṁ tam ahaṁ bhajāmi

"I worship Govinda, the primeval Lord, the Supreme Personality of Godhead, under whose control even the sun, which is considered to be the eye of the Lord, rotates within the fixed orbit of eternal time. The sun is the king of all planetary systems and has unlimited potency in heat and light." This verse from *Brahma-saṁhitā* confirms that even the largest and most powerful planet, the sun, rotates within a fixed orbit, or *kāla-cakra,* in obedience to the order of the Supreme Personality of Godhead. This has nothing to do with gravity or any other imaginary laws created by the material scientists.

Material scientists want to avoid the ruling government of the Supreme Personality of Godhead, and therefore they imagine different conditions under which they suppose the planets move. The only condition, however, is the order of the Supreme Personality of Godhead. All the various predominating deities of the planets are persons, and the Supreme Personality of Godhead is also a person. The Supreme Personality orders the subordinate persons, the demigods of various names, to carry out His supreme will. This fact is also confirmed in *Bhagavad-gītā* (9.10), wherein Kṛṣṇa says:

mayādhyakṣeṇa prakṛtiḥ
sūyate sa-carācaram
hetunānena kaunteya
jagad viparivartate

"This material nature is working under My direction, O son of Kuntī, and it is producing all moving and unmoving beings. By its rule this manifestation is created and annihilated again and again."

The orbits of the planets resemble the bodies in which all living entities are seated because they are both machines controlled by the Supreme Personality of Godhead. As Kṛṣṇa says in *Bhagavad-gītā* (18.61):

īśvaraḥ sarva-bhūtānāṁ
hṛd-deśe 'rjuna tiṣṭhati
bhrāmayan sarva-bhūtāni
yantrārūḍhāni māyayā

"The Supreme Lord is situated in everyone's heart, O Arjuna, and is directing the wanderings of all living entities, who are seated as on a machine, made of the material energy." The machine given by material nature—whether the machine of the body or the machine of the orbit, or *kāla-cakra*—works according to the orders given by the Supreme Personality of Godhead. The Supreme Personality of Godhead and material nature work together to maintain this great universe, and not only this universe but also the millions of other universes beyond this one.

The question of how the planets and stars are floating is also answered in this verse. It is not because of the laws of gravity. Rather, the planets and stars are enabled to float by manipulations of the air. It is due to such manipulations that big, heavy clouds float and big eagles fly in the sky. Modern airplanes like the 747 jet aircraft work in a similar way: by controlling the air, they float high in the sky, resisting the tendency to fall to earth. Such adjustments of the air are all made possible by the cooperation of the principles of *puruṣa* (male) and *prakṛti* (female). By the cooperation of material nature, which is considered to be *prakṛti*, and the Supreme Personality of Godhead, who is considered the *puruṣa*, all the affairs of the universe are going on nicely in their proper order. *Prakṛti*, material nature, is also described in the *Brahma-saṁhitā* (5.44) as follows:

sṛṣṭi-sthiti-pralaya-sādhana-śaktir ekā
chāyeva yasya bhuvanāni bibharti durgā
icchānurūpam api yasya ca ceṣṭate sā
govindam ādi-puruṣaṁ tam ahaṁ bhajāmi

"The external potency, *māyā,* who is of the nature of the shadow of the *cit* [spiritual] potency, is worshiped by all people as Durgā, the creating, preserving and destroying agency of this mundane world. I adore the primeval Lord Govinda, in accordance with whose will Durgā conducts herself." Material nature, the external energy of the Supreme Lord, is also known as Durgā, or the female energy that protects the great fort of this universe. The word Durgā also means fort. This universe is just like a great fort in which all the conditioned souls are kept, and they cannot leave it unless they are liberated by the mercy of the Supreme Personality of Godhead. The Lord Himself declares in *Bhagavad-gītā* (4.9):

janma karma ca me divyam
evaṁ yo vetti tattvataḥ
tyaktvā dehaṁ punar janma
naiti mām eti so 'rjuna

"One who knows the transcendental nature of My appearance and activities does not, upon leaving the body, take his birth again in this material world, but attains My eternal abode, O Arjuna." Thus simply by Kṛṣṇa consciousness, by the mercy of the Supreme Personality of Godhead, one can be liberated, or, in other words, one can be released from the great fort of this universe and go outside it to the spiritual world.

It is also significant that the predominating deities of even the greatest planets have been offered their exalted posts because of the very valuable pious activities they performed in previous births. This is indicated herein by the words *karma-nirmita-gatayaḥ.* For example, as we have previously discussed, the moon is called *jīva,* which means that he is a living entity like us, but because of his pious activities he has been appointed to his post as the moon-god. Similarly, all the demigods are living entities who have been appointed to their various posts as the masters of the moon, the earth, Venus and so on because of their great service and pious acts. Only the predominating deity of the sun, Sūrya Nārāyaṇa, is an incarnation of the Supreme Personality of Godhead. Mahārāja Dhruva, the predominating deity of Dhruvaloka, is also a living entity. Thus there are two kinds of entities—the supreme entity, the Supreme Personality of Godhead, and the ordinary living entity, the *jīva* (*nityo nityānāṁ cetanaś cetanānām*). All the demigods are engaged in the service of the Lord, and only by such an arrangement are the affairs of the universe going on.

Regarding the great eagles mentioned in this verse, it is understood that there are eagles so big that they can prey on big elephants. They fly so high that they can travel from one planet to another. They start flying in one planet and land in another, and while in flight they lay eggs that hatch into other birds while falling through the air. In Sanskrit such eagles are called *śyena*. Under the present circumstances, of course, we cannot see such huge birds, but at least we know of eagles that can capture monkeys and then throw them down to kill and eat them. Similarly, it is understood that there are gigantic birds that can carry off elephants, kill them and eat them.

The two examples of the eagle and the cloud are sufficient to prove that flying and floating can be made possible through adjustments of the air. The planets, in a similar way, are floating because material nature adjusts the air according to the orders of the Supreme Lord. It could be said that these adjustments constitute the law of gravity, but in any case, one must accept that these laws are made by the Supreme Personality of Godhead. The so-called scientists have no control over them. The scientists can falsely, improperly declare that there is no God, but this is not a fact.

TEXT 4

केचनैतज्ज्योतिरनीकं शिशुमारसंस्थानेन भगवतो वासुदेवस्य योगधारणायामनुवर्णयन्ति ॥ ४ ॥

kecanaitaj jyotir-anīkaṁ śiśumāra-saṁsthānena bhagavato
vāsudevasya yoga-dhāraṇāyām anuvarṇayanti.

kecana—some *yogīs* or learned scholars of astronomy; *etat*—this; *jyotiḥ-anīkam*—great wheel of planets and stars; *śiśumāra-saṁsthānena*—imagine this wheel to be a *śiśumāra* (dolphin); *bhagavataḥ*—of the Supreme Personality of Godhead; *vāsudevasya*—Lord Vāsudeva (the son of Vasudeva), Kṛṣṇa; *yoga-dhāraṇāyām*—in absorption in worship; *anuvarṇayanti*—describe.

TRANSLATION

This great machine, consisting of the stars and planets, resembles the form of a śiśumāra [dolphin] in the water. It is sometimes considered an incarnation of Kṛṣṇa, Vāsudeva. Great yogīs meditate upon Vāsudeva in this form because it is actually visible.

PURPORT

Transcendentalists such as *yogīs* whose minds cannot accommodate the form of the Lord prefer to visualize something very great, such as the *virāṭa-puruṣa*. Therefore some *yogīs* comtemplate this imaginary *śiśumāra* to be swimming in the sky the way a dolphin swims in water. They meditate upon it as the *virāṭa-rūpa*, the gigantic form of the Supreme Personality of Godhead.

TEXT 5

यस्य पुच्छाग्रेऽवाक्शिरसः कुण्डलीभूतदेहस्य ध्रुव उपकल्पितस्तस्य लाङ्गूले प्रजापतिरग्निरिन्द्रो धर्म इति पुच्छमूले धाता विधाता च कट्यां सप्तर्षयः । तस्य दक्षिणावर्तकुण्डलीभूतशरीरस्य यान्युदगयनानि दक्षिणपार्श्वे तु नक्षत्राण्युपकल्पयन्ति दक्षिणायनानि तु सव्ये। यथा शिशुमारस्य कुण्डला-भोगसन्निवेशस्य पार्श्वयोरुभयोरप्यवयवाः समसंख्या भवन्ति । पृष्ठे त्वजवीथी आकाशगङ्गा चोदरतः ॥ ५ ॥

yasya pucchāgre 'vākśirasaḥ kuṇḍalī-bhūta-dehasya dhruva
upakalpitas tasya lāṅgūle prajāpatir agnir indro dharma iti puccha-
mūle dhātā vidhātā ca kaṭyāṁ saptarṣayaḥ. tasya dakṣiṇāvarta-
kuṇḍalī-bhūta-śarīrasya yāny udagayanāni dakṣiṇa-pārśve tu
nakṣatrāṇy upakalpayanti dakṣiṇāyanāni tu savye. yathā śiśumārasya
kuṇḍalā-bhoga-sanniveśasya pārśvayor ubhayor apy avayavāḥ
samasaṅkhyā bhavanti. pṛṣṭhe tv ajavīthī ākāśa-gaṅgā codarataḥ.

yasya—of which; *puccha-agre*—at the end of the tail; *avāk-śirasaḥ*—whose head is downward; *kuṇḍalī-bhūta-dehasya*—whose body, which is coiled; *dhruvaḥ*—Mahārāja Dhruva on his planet, the polestar; *upakalpitaḥ*—is situated; *tasya*—of that; *lāṅgūle*—on the tail;

prajāpatiḥ—of the name Prajāpati; *agniḥ*—Agni; *indraḥ*—Indra; *dharmaḥ*—Dharma; *iti*—thus; *puccha-mūle*—at the base of the tail; *dhātā vidhātā*—the demigods known as Dhātā and Vidhātā; *ca*—also; *kaṭyām*—on the hip; *sapta-ṛṣayaḥ*—the seven saintly sages; *tasya*—of that; *dakṣiṇa-āvarta-kuṇḍalī-bhūta-śarīrasya*—whose body is like a coil turning toward the right side; *yāni*—which; *udagayanāni*—marking the northern courses; *dakṣiṇa-pārśve*—on the right side; *tu*—but; *nakṣatrāṇi*—constellations; *upakalpayanti*—are situated; *dakṣina-āyanāni*—the fourteen stars, from Puṣyā to Uttarāṣāḍhā, marking the northern course; *tu*—but; *savye*—on the left side; *yathā*—just like; *śiśumārasya*—of the dolphin; *kuṇḍalā-bhoga-sanniveśasya*—whose body appears like a coil; *pārśvayoḥ*—on the sides; *ubhayoḥ*—both; *api*—certainly; *avayavāḥ*—the limbs; *samasaṅkhyāḥ*—of equal number (fourteen); *bhavanti*—are; *pṛṣṭhe*—on the back; *tu*—of course; *ajavīthī*—the first three stars marking the southern route (Mūlā, Pūrvaṣāḍhā and Uttarāṣāḍhā); *ākāśa-gaṅgā*—the Ganges in the sky (the Milky Way); *ca*—also; *udarataḥ*—on the abdomen.

TRANSLATION

This form of the śiśumāra has its head downward and its body coiled. On the end of its tail is the planet of Dhruva, on the body of its tail are the planets of the demigods Prajāpati, Agni, Indra and Dharma, and at the base of its tail are the planets of the demigods Dhātā and Vidhātā. Where the hips might be on the śiśumāra are the seven saintly sages like Vasiṣṭha and Aṅgirā. The coiled body of the Śiśumāra-cakra turns toward its right side, on which the fourteen constellations from Abhijit to Punarvasu are located. On its left side are the fourteen stars from Puṣyā to Uttarāṣāḍhā. Thus its body is balanced because its sides are occupied by an equal number of stars. On the back of the śiśumāra is the group of stars known as Ajavīthī, and on its abdomen is the Ganges that flows in the sky [the Milky Way].

TEXT 6

पुनर्वसुपुष्यौ दक्षिणवामयोः श्रोण्योरार्द्राश्लेषे च दक्षिणवामयोः पश्चिमयोः पादयोरभिजिदुत्तराषाढे दक्षिणवामयोर्नासिकयोर्यथासंख्यं श्रवणपूर्वाषाढे

दक्षिणवामयोर्लोचनयोर्धनिष्ठा मूलं च दक्षिणवामयोः कर्णयोर्मघादीन्यष्ट
नक्षत्राणि दक्षिणायनानि वामपार्श्ववङ्क्रिषु युञ्जीत तथैव मृगशीर्षादीन्युदगय
नानि दक्षिणपार्श्ववङ्क्रिषु प्रातिलोम्येन प्रयुञ्जीत शतभिषाज्येष्ठे
स्कन्धयोर्दक्षिणवामयोर्न्यसेत् ॥ ६ ॥

punarvasu-puṣyau dakṣiṇa-vāmayoḥ śroṇyor ārdrāśleṣe ca dakṣiṇa-vāmayoḥ paścimayoḥ pādayor abhijid-uttarāṣāḍhe dakṣiṇa-vāmayor nāsikayor yathā-saṅkhyaṁ śravaṇa-pūrvāṣāḍhe dakṣiṇa-vāmayor locanayor dhaniṣṭhā mūlaṁ ca dakṣiṇa-vāmayoḥ karṇayor maghādīny aṣṭa nakṣatrāṇi dakṣiṇāyanāni vāma-pārśva-vaṅkriṣu yuñjīta tathaiva mṛga-śīrṣādīny udagayanāni dakṣiṇa-pārśva-vaṅkriṣu prātilomyena prayuñjīta śatabhiṣā-jyeṣṭhe skandhayor dakṣiṇa-vāmayor nyaset.

punarvasu—the star named Punarvasu; *puṣyau*—and the star named Puṣyā; *dakṣiṇa-vāmayoḥ*—on the right and left; *śroṇyoḥ*—loins; *ārdrā*—the star named Ārdrā; *aśleṣe*—the star named Aśleṣā; *ca*—also; *dakṣiṇa-vāmayoḥ*—at the right and left; *paścimayoḥ*—behind; *pādayoḥ*—feet; *abhijit-uttarāṣāḍhe*—the stars named Abhijit and Uttarāṣāḍhā; *dakṣiṇa-vāmayoḥ*—on the right and left; *nāsikayoḥ*—nostrils; *yathā-saṅkhyam*—according to numerical order; *śravaṇa-pūrvāṣāḍhe*—the stars named Śravaṇā and Pūrvāṣāḍhā; *dakṣiṇa-vāmayoḥ*—at the right and left; *locanayoḥ*—eyes; *dhaniṣṭhā mūlam ca*—and the stars named Dhaniṣṭhā and Mūla; *dakṣiṇa-vāmayoḥ*—at the right and left; *karṇayoḥ*—ears; *maghā-ādīni*—the stars such as Maghā; *aṣṭa nakṣatrāṇi*—eight stars; *dakṣiṇa-āyanāni*—which mark the southern course; *vāma-pārśva*—of the left side; *vaṅkriṣu*—at the ribs; *yuñjīta*—may place; *tathā eva*—similarly; *mṛga-śīrṣā-ādīni*—such as Mṛgaśīrṣā; *udagayanāni*—marking the northern course; *dakṣiṇa-pārśva-vaṅkriṣu*—on the right side; *prātilomyena*—in the reverse order; *prayuñjīta*—may place; *śatabhiṣā*—Śatabhiṣā; *jyeṣṭhe*—Jyeṣṭhā; *skandhayoḥ*—on the two shoulders; *dakṣiṇa-vāmayoḥ*—right and left; *nyaset*—should place.

TRANSLATION

On the right and left sides of where the loins might be on the Śiśumāra-cakra are the stars named Punarvasu and Puṣyā. Ārdrā

and Aśleṣā are on its right and left feet, Abhijit and Uttarāṣāḍhā are on its right and left nostrils, Śravaṇā and Pūrvāṣāḍhā are at its right and left eyes, and Dhaniṣṭhā and Mūla are on its right and left ears. The eight stars from Maghā to Anurādhā, which mark the southern course, are on the ribs of the left of its body, and the eight stars from Mṛgaśīrṣā to Pūrvabhādra, which mark the northern course, are on the ribs on the right side. Śatabhiṣā and Jyeṣṭhā are on the right and left shoulders.

TEXT 7

उत्तराहनावगस्तिरधराहनौ यमो मुखेषु चाङ्गारकः शनैश्चर उपस्थे बृहस्पतिः ककुदि वक्षस्यादित्यो हृदये नारायणो मनसि चन्द्रो नाभ्यामुशना स्तनयोरश्विनौ बुधः प्राणापानयो राहुर्गले केतवः सर्वाङ्गेषु रोमसु सर्वे तारागणाः ॥ ७ ॥

uttarā-hanāv agastir adharā-hanau yamo mukheṣu cāṅgārakaḥ śanaiścara upasthe bṛhaspatiḥ kakudi vakṣasy ādityo hṛdaye nārāyaṇo manasi candro nābhyām uśanā stanayor aśvinau budhaḥ prāṇāpānayo rahur gale ketavaḥ sarvāṅgeṣu romasu sarve tārā-gaṇāḥ.

uttarā-hanau—on the upper jaw; *agastiḥ*—the star named Agasti; *adharā-hanau*—on the lower jaw; *yamaḥ*—Yamarāja; *mukhe*—on the mouth; *ca*—also; *aṅgārakaḥ*—Mars; *śanaiścaraḥ*—Saturn; *upasthe*—on the genitals; *bṛhaspatiḥ*—Jupiter; *kakudi*—on the back of the neck; *vakṣasi*—on the chest; *ādityaḥ*—the sun; *hṛdaye*—within the heart; *nārāyaṇaḥ*—Lord Nārāyaṇa; *manasi*—in the mind; *candraḥ*—the moon; *nābhyām*—on the navel; *uśanā*—Venus; *stanayoḥ*—on the two breasts; *aśvinau*—the two stars named Aśvin; *budhaḥ*—Mercury; *prāṇāpānayoḥ*—in the inner airs known as *prāṇa* and *apāna; rahuḥ*—the planet Rahu; *gale*—on the neck; *ketavaḥ*—comets; *sarva-aṅgeṣu*—all over the body; *romasu*—in the pores of the body; *sarve*—all; *tārā-gaṇāḥ*—the numerous stars.

TRANSLATION

On the upper chin of the śiśumāra is Agasti; on its lower chin, Yamarāja; on its mouth, Mars; on its genitals, Saturn; on the back

of its neck, Jupiter; on its chest, the sun; and within the core of its heart, Nārāyaṇa. Within its mind is the moon; on its navel, Venus; and on its breasts, the Aśvinīkumāras. Within its life air, which is known as prāṇāpāna, is Mercury, on its neck is Rahu, all over its body are comets, and in its pores are the numerous stars.

TEXT 8

एतदु हैव भगवतो विष्णोः सर्वदेवतामयं रूपमहरहः सन्ध्यायां प्रयतो वाग्यतो निरीक्षमाण उपतिष्ठेत नमो ज्योतिर्लोकाय कालायनायानिमिषां पतये महापुरुषायाभिधीमहीति ॥ ८ ॥

etad u haiva bhagavato viṣṇoḥ sarva-devatāmayaṁ rūpam aharahaḥ sandhyāyāṁ prayato vāgyato nirīkṣamāṇa upatiṣṭheta namo jyotir-lokāya kālāyanāyānimiṣāṁ pataye mahā-puruṣāyābhidhīmahīti.

etat—this; *u ha*—indeed; *eva*—certainly; *bhagavataḥ*—of the Supreme Personality of Godhead; *viṣṇoḥ*—of Lord Viṣṇu; *sarva-devatā-mayam*—consisting of all the demigods; *rūpam*—form; *ahaḥ-ahaḥ*—always; *sandhyāyām*—in the morning, noon and evening; *prayataḥ*—meditating upon; *vāgyataḥ*—controlling the words; *nirīkṣamāṇah*—observing; *upatiṣṭheta*—one should worship; *namaḥ*—respectful obeisances; *jyotiḥ-lokāya*—unto the resting place of all the planetary systems; *kālāyanāya*—in the form of supreme time; *animiṣām*—of the demigods; *pataye*—unto the master; *mahā-puruṣāya*—unto the Supreme Person; *abhidhīmahi*—let us meditate; *iti*—thus.

TRANSLATION

My dear King, the body of the śiśumāra, as thus described, should be considered the external form of Lord Viṣṇu, the Supreme Personality of Godhead. Morning, noon and evening, one should silently observe the form of the Lord as the Śiśumāra-cakra and worship Him with this mantra: "O Lord who has assumed the form of time! O resting place of all the planets moving in different orbits! O master of all demigods, O Supreme Person, I offer my respectful obeisances unto You and meditate upon You."

TEXT 9

ग्रहर्क्षतारामयमाधिदैविकं
पापापहं मन्त्रकृतां त्रिकालम् ।
नमस्यतः स्मरतो वा त्रिकालं
नश्येत तत्कालजमाशु पापम् ॥ ९ ॥

graharkṣatārāmayam ādhidaivikaṁ
pāpāpahaṁ mantra-kṛtāṁ tri-kālam
namasyataḥ smarato vā tri-kālaṁ
naśyeta tat-kālajam āśu pāpam

graha-ṛkṣa-tārā-mayam—consisting of all the planets and stars; *ādhidaivikam*—the leader of all the demigods; *pāpa-apaham*—the killer of sinful reactions; *mantra-kṛtām*—of those who chant the *mantra* mentioned above; *tri-kālam*—three times; *namasyataḥ*—offering obeisances; *smarataḥ*—meditating; *vā*—or; *tri-kālam*—three times; *naśyeta*—destroys; *tat-kāla-jam*—born at that time; *āśu*—very quickly; *pāpam*—all sinful reactions.

TRANSLATION

The body of the Supreme Lord, Viṣṇu, which forms the Śiśumāra-cakra, is the resting place of all the demigods and all the stars and planets. One who chants this mantra to worship that Supreme Person three times a day—morning, noon and evening—will surely be freed from all sinful reactions. If one simply offers his obeisances to this form or remembers this form three times a day, all his recent sinful activities will be destroyed.

PURPORT

Summarizing the entire description of the planetary systems of the universe, Śrīla Viśvanātha Cakravartī Ṭhākura says that one who is able to meditate upon this arrangement as the *virāṭa-rūpa*, or *viśva-rūpa*, the external body of the Supreme Personality of Godhead, and worship Him three times a day by meditation will always be free from all sinful reactions. Viśvanātha Cakravartī Ṭhākura estimates that Dhruvaloka, the polestar, is 3,800,000 *yojanas* above the sun. Above Dhruvaloka by 10,000,000 *yojanas* is Maharloka, above Maharloka by 20,000,000 *yojanas* is Janaloka, above Janaloka by 80,000,000 *yojanas* is Tapoloka, and above Tapoloka by 120,000,000 *yojanas* is Satyaloka. Thus the distance from the sun to Satyaloka is 233,800,000 *yojanas*, or 1,870,400,000 miles. The Vaikuṇṭha planets begin 26,200,000 *yojanas* (209,600,000 miles) above Satyaloka. Thus the *Viṣṇu Purāṇa* describes that the covering of the universe is 260,000,000 *yojanas* (2,080,000,000 miles) away from the sun. The distance from the sun to the earth is 100,000 *yojanas*, and below the earth by 70,000 *yojanas* are the seven lower planetary systems called Atala, Vitala, Sutala, Talātala, Mahātala, Rasātala and Pātāla. Below these lower planets by 30,000 *yojanas*, Śeṣa Nāga is lying on the Garbhodaka Ocean. That ocean is 249,800,000 *yojanas* deep. Thus the total diameter of the universe is approximately 500,000,000 *yojanas*, or 4,000,000,000 miles.

Thus end the Bhaktivedanta purports to the Fifth Canto, Twenty-third Chapter of the Śrīmad-Bhāgavatam, *entitled "The Śiśumāra Planetary System."*

CHAPTER TWENTY-FOUR

The Subterranean Heavenly Planets

This chapter describes the planet Rāhu, which is 10,000 *yojanas* (80,000 miles) below the sun, and it also describes Atala and the other lower planetary systems. Rāhu is situated below the sun and moon. It is between these two planets and the earth. When Rāhu conceals the sun and moon, eclipses occur, either total or partial, depending on whether Rāhu moves in a straight or curving way.

Below Rāhu by another 1,000,000 *yojanas* are the planets of the Siddhas, Cāraṇas and Vidyādharas, and below these are planets such as Yakṣaloka and Rakṣaloka. Below these planets is the earth, and 70,000 *yojanas* below the earth are the lower planetary systems—Atala, Vitala, Sutala, Talātala, Mahātala, Rasātala and Pātāla. Demons and Rakṣasas live in these lower planetary systems with their wives and children, always engaged in sense gratification and not fearing their next births. The sunshine does not reach these planets, but they are illuminated by jewels fixed upon the hoods of snakes. Because of these shining gems there is practically no darkness. Those living in these planets do not become old or diseased, and they are not afraid of death from any cause but the time factor, the Supreme Personality of Godhead.

In the planet Atala, the yawning of a demon has produced three kinds of women, called *svairiṇī* (independent), *kāmiṇī* (lusty) and *puṁścalī* (very easily subdued by men). Below Atala is the planet Vitala, wherein Lord Śiva and his wife Gaurī reside. Because of their presence, a kind of gold is produced called *hāṭaka.* Below Vitala is the planet Sutala, the abode of Bali Mahārāja, the most fortunate king. Bali Mahārāja was favored by the Supreme Personality of Godhead, Vāmanadeva, because of his intense devotional service. The Lord went to the sacrificial arena of Bali Mahārāja and begged him for three paces of land, and on this plea the Lord took from him all his possessions. When Bali Mahārāja agreed to all this, the Lord was very pleased, and therefore the Lord serves as his doorkeeper. The description of Bali Mahārāja appears in the Eighth Canto of *Śrīmad-Bhāgavatam.*

When the Supreme Personality of Godhead offers a devotee material happiness, this is not His real favor. The demigods, who are very puffed up by their material opulence, pray to the Lord only for material happiness, not knowing anything better. Devotees like Prahlāda Mahārāja, however, do not want material happiness. Not to speak of material happiness, they do not want even liberation from material bondage, although one can achieve this liberation simply by chanting the holy name of the Lord, even with improper pronunciation.

Below Sutala is the planet Talātala, the abode of the demon Maya. This demon is always materially happy because he is favored by Lord Śiva, but he cannot achieve spiritual happiness at any time. Below Talātala is the planet Mahātala, where there are many snakes with hundreds and thousands of hoods. Below Mahātala is Rasātala, and below that is Pātāla, where the serpent Vasukī lives with his associates.

TEXT 1

श्रीशुक उवाच

अधस्तात्सवितुर्योजनायुते स्वर्भानुर्नक्षत्रवच्चरतीत्येके योऽसावमरत्वं ग्रहत्वं चालभत भगवदनुकम्पया स्वयमसुरापसदः सैंहिकेयो ह्यतदर्हस्तस्य तात जन्म कर्माणि चोपरिष्टाद्वक्ष्यामः ॥ १ ॥

śrī-śuka uvāca

adhastāt savitur yojanāyute svarbhānur nakṣatravac caratīty eke yo 'sāv amaratvaṁ grahatvaṁ cālabhata bhagavad-anukampayā svayam asurāpasadaḥ saiṁhikeyo hy atad-arhas tasya tāta janma karmāṇi copariṣṭād vakṣyāmaḥ.

śrī-śukaḥ uvāca—Śrī Śukadeva Gosvāmī said; *adhastāt*—below; *savituḥ*—the sun globe; *yojana*—a measurement equal to eight miles; *ayute*—ten thousand; *svarbhānuḥ*—the planet known as Rāhu; *nakṣatra-vat*—like one of the stars; *carati*—is rotating; *iti*—thus; *eke*—some who are learned in the *Purāṇas; yaḥ*—which; *asau*—that; *amaratvam*—a lifetime like those of the demigods; *grahatvam*—a position as one of the chief planets; *ca*—and; *alabhata*—obtained;

bhagavat-anukampayā—by the compassion of the Supreme Personality of Godhead; *svayam*—personally; *asura-apasadaḥ*—the lowest of the *asuras; saiṁhikeyaḥ*—being the son of Siṁhikā; *hi*—indeed; *a-tat-arhaḥ*—not qualified for that position; *tasya*—his; *tāta*—O my dear King; *janma*—birth; *karmāṇi*—activities; *ca*—also; *upariṣṭāt*—later; *vakṣyāmaḥ*—I shall explain.

TRANSLATION

Śrī Śukadeva Gosvāmī said: My dear King, some historians, the speakers of the Purāṇas, say that 10,000 yojanas [80,000 miles] below the sun is the planet known as Rāhu, which moves like one of the stars. The presiding deity of that planet, who is the son of Siṁhikā, is the most abominable of all asuras, but although he is completely unfit to assume the position of a demigod or planetary deity, he has achieved that position by the grace of the Supreme Personality of Godhead. Later I shall speak further about him.

TEXT 2

यददस्तरणेर्मण्डलं प्रतपतस्तद्विस्तरतो योजनायुतमाचक्षते द्वादशसहस्रं सोमस्य त्रयोदशसहस्रं राहोर्यः पर्वणि तद्व्यवधानकृद्वैरानुबन्धः सूर्या-चन्द्रमसावभिधावति ॥ २ ॥

yad adas taraṇer maṇḍalaṁ pratapatas tad vistarato yojanāyutam ācakṣate dvādaśa-sahasraṁ somasya trayodaśa-sahasraṁ rāhor yaḥ parvaṇi tad-vyavadhāna-kṛd vairānubandhaḥ sūryā-candramasāv abhidhāvati.

yat—which; *adaḥ*—that; *taraṇeḥ*—of the sun; *maṇḍalam*—globe; *pratapataḥ*—which is always distributing heat; *tat*—that; *vistarataḥ*—in terms of width; *yojana*—a distance of eight miles; *ayutam*—ten thousand; *ācakṣate*—they estimate; *dvādaśa-sahasram*—20,000 *yojanas* (160,000 miles); *somasya*—of the moon; *trayodaśa*—thirty; *sahasram*—one thousand; *rāhoḥ*—of the planet Rāhu; *yaḥ*—which; *parvaṇi*—on occasion; *tat-vyavadhāna-kṛt*—who created an obstruction to the sun and moon at the time of the distribution of nectar; *vaira-anu-*

bandhaḥ—whose intentions are inimical; *sūryā*—the sun; *candramasau*—and the moon; *abhidhāvati*—runs after them on the full-moon night and the dark-moon day.

TRANSLATION

The sun globe, which is a source of heat, extends for 10,000 yojanas [80,000 miles]. The moon extends for 20,000 yojanas [160,000 miles], and Rāhu extends for 30,000 yojanas [240,000 miles]. Formerly, when nectar was being distributed, Rāhu tried to create dissension between the sun and moon by interposing himself between them. Rāhu is inimical toward both the sun and the moon, and therefore he always tries to cover the sunshine and moonshine on the dark-moon day and full-moon night.

PURPORT

As stated herein, the sun extends for 10,000 *yojanas*, and the moon extends for twice that, or 20,000 *yojanas*. The word *dvādaśa* should be understood to mean twice as much as ten, or twenty. In the opinion of Vijayadhvaja, the extent of Rāhu should be twice that of the moon, or 40,000 *yojanas*. However, to reconcile this apparent contradiction to the text of the *Bhāgavatam*, Vijayadhvaja cites the following quotation concerning Rāhu: *rāhu-soma-ravīṇāṁ tu maṇḍalā dvi-guṇoktitām.* This means that Rāhu is twice as large as the moon, which is twice as large as the sun. This is the conclusion of the commentator Vijayadhvaja.

TEXT 3

तन्निशम्योभयत्रापि भगवता रक्षणाय प्रयुक्तं सुदर्शनं नाम भागवतं
दयितमस्त्रं तत्तेजसा दुर्विषहं मुहुः परिवर्तमानमभ्यवस्थितो मुहूर्तमुद्वि-
जमानश्चकितहृदय आरादेव निवर्तते तदुपरागमिति वदन्ति लोकाः ॥३॥

tan niśamyobhayatrāpi bhagavatā rakṣaṇāya prayuktaṁ sudarśanaṁ
nāma bhāgavataṁ dayitam astraṁ tat tejasā durviṣahaṁ muhuḥ
parivartamānam abhyavasthito muhūrtam udvijamānaś cakita-hṛdaya
ārād eva nivartate tad uparāgam iti vadanti lokāḥ.

tat—that situation; *niśamya*—hearing; *ubhayatra*—around both the sun and moon; *api*—indeed; *bhagavatā*—by the Supreme Personality of Godhead; *rakṣaṇāya*—for their protection; *prayuktam*—engaged; *sudarśanam*—the wheel of Kṛṣṇa; *nāma*—named; *bhāgavatam*—the most confidential devotee; *dayitam*—the most favorite; *astram*—weapon; *tat*—that; *tejasā*—by its effulgence; *durviṣaham*—unbearable heat; *muhuḥ*—repeatedly; *parivartamānam*—moving around the sun and moon; *abhyavasthitaḥ*—situated; *muhūrtam*—for a *muhūrta* (forty-eight minutes); *udvijamānaḥ*—whose mind was full of anxieties; *cakita*—frightened; *hṛdayaḥ*—the core of whose heart; *ārāt*—to a distant place; *eva*—certainly; *nivartate*—flees; *tat*—that situation; *uparāgam*—an eclipse; *iti*—thus; *vadanti*—they say; *lokāḥ*—the people.

TRANSLATION

After hearing from the sun and moon demigods about Rāhu's attack, the Supreme Personality of Godhead, Viṣṇu, engages His disc, known as the Sudarśana cakra, to protect them. The Sudarśana cakra is the Lord's most beloved devotee and is favored by the Lord. The intense heat of its effulgence, meant for killing non-Vaiṣṇavas, is unbearable to Rāhu, and he therefore flees in fear of it. During the time Rāhu disturbs the sun or moon, there occurs what people commonly know as an eclipse.

PURPORT

The Supreme Personality of Godhead, Viṣṇu, is always the protector of His devotees, who are also known as demigods. The controlling demigods are most obedient to Lord Viṣṇu, although they also want material sense enjoyment, and that is why they are called demigods, or almost godly. Although Rāhu attempts to attack both the sun and the moon, they are protected by Lord Viṣṇu. Being very afraid of Lord Viṣṇu's *cakra*, Rāhu cannot stay in front of the sun or moon for more than a *muhūrta* (forty-eight minutes). The phenomenon that occurs when Rāhu blocks the light of the sun or moon is called an eclipse. The attempt of the scientists of this earth to go to the moon is as demoniac as Rāhu's attack. Of course, their attempts will be failures because no one can enter the moon or sun so easily. Like the attack of Rāhu, such attempts will certainly be failures.

TEXT 4

ततोऽधस्तात्सिद्धचारणविद्याधराणां सदनानि तावन्मात्र एव ॥ ४ ॥

tato 'dhastāt siddha-cāraṇa-vidyādharāṇāṁ sadanāni tāvan mātra eva.

tataḥ—the planet Rāhu; *adhastāt*—below; *siddha-cāraṇa*—of the planets known as Siddhaloka and Cāraṇaloka; *vidyādharāṇām*—and the planets of the Vidyādharas; *sadanāni*—the residential places; *tāvat mātra*—only that much distance (eighty thousand miles); *eva*—indeed.

TRANSLATION

Below Rāhu by 10,000 yojanas [80,000 miles] are the planets known as Siddhaloka, Cāraṇaloka and Vidyādhara-loka.

PURPORT

It is said that the residents of Siddhaloka, being naturally endowed with the powers of *yogīs*, can go from one planet to another by their natural mystic powers without using airplanes or similar machines.

TEXT 5

ततोऽधस्ताद्यक्षरक्षःपिशाचप्रेतभूतगणानां विहाराजिरमन्तरिक्षं यावद्वायुः प्रवाति यावन्मेघा उपलभ्यन्ते ॥ ५ ॥

tato 'dhastād yakṣa-rakṣaḥ-piśāca-preta-bhūta-gaṇānāṁ vihārājiram antarikṣaṁ yāvad vāyuḥ pravāti yāvan meghā upalabhyante.

tataḥ adhastāt—beneath the planets occupied by the Siddhas, Cāraṇas and Vidyādharas; *yakṣa-rakṣaḥ-piśāca-preta-bhūta-gaṇānām*—of Yakṣas, Rākṣasas, Piśācas, ghosts and so on; *vihāra-ajiram*—the place of sense gratification; *antarikṣam*—in the sky or outer space; *yāvat*—as far as; *vāyuḥ*—the wind; *pravāti*—blows; *yāvat*—as far as; *meghāḥ*—the clouds; *upalabhyante*—are seen.

TRANSLATION

Beneath Vidyādhara-loka, Cāraṇaloka and Siddhaloka, in the sky called antarikṣa, are the places of enjoyment for the Yakṣas, Rākṣasas, Piśācas, ghosts and so on. Antarikṣa extends as far as the wind blows and the clouds float in the sky. Above this there is no more air.

TEXT 6

ततोऽधस्ताच्छतयोजनान्तर इयं पृथिवी यावद्धंसभासश्येन सुपर्णादयः पतत्त्रिप्रवरा उत्पतन्तीति ॥ ६ ॥

tato 'dhastāc chata-yojanāntara iyaṁ pṛthivī yāvad dhaṁsa-bhāsa-śyena-suparṇādayaḥ patattri-pravarā utpatantīti.

tataḥ adhastāt—beneath that; *śata-yojana*—of one hundred *yojanas; antare*—by an interval; *iyam*—this; *pṛthivī*—planet earth; *yāvat*—as high as; *haṁsa*—swans; *bhāsa*—vultures; *śyena*—eagles; *suparṇa-ādayaḥ*—and other birds; *patattri-pravarāḥ*—the chief among birds; *utpatanti*—can fly; *iti*—thus.

TRANSLATION

Below the abodes of the Yakṣas and Rākṣasas by a distance of 100 yojanas [800 miles] is the planet earth. Its upper limits extend as high as swans, hawks, eagles and similar large birds can fly.

TEXT 7

उपवर्णितं भूमेर्यथासंनिवेशावस्थानमवनेरप्यधस्तात् सप्त भूविवरा एकैकशो योजनायुतान्तरेणायामविस्तारेणोपक्लृप्ता अतलं वितलं सुतलं तलातलं महातलं रसातलं पातालमिति ॥ ७ ॥

upavarṇitaṁ bhūmer yathā-sanniveśāvasthānam avaner apy adhastāt sapta bhū-vivarā ekaikaśo yojanāyutāntareṇāyāma-vistāreṇopakḷptā atalaṁ vitalaṁ sutalaṁ talātalaṁ mahātalaṁ rasātalaṁ pātālam iti.

upavarṇitam—stated previously; *bhūmeḥ*—of the planet earth; *yathā-sanniveśa-avasthānam*—according to the arrangement of the different places; *avaneḥ*—the earth; *api*—certainly; *adhastāt*—beneath; *sapta*—seven; *bhū-vivarāḥ*—other planets; *eka-ekaśaḥ*—in succession, up to the outer limit of the universe; *yojana-ayuta-antareṇa*—with an interval of ten thousand *yojanas* (eighty thousand miles); *āyāma-vistāreṇa*—by width and length; *upakḷptāḥ*—situated; *atalam*—named Atala; *vitalam*—Vitala; *sutalam*—Sutala; *talātalam*—Talātala; *mahātalam*—Mahātala; *rasātalam*—Rasātala; *pātālam*—Pātāla; *iti*—thus.

TRANSLATION

My dear King, beneath this earth are seven other planets, known as Atala, Vitala, Sutala, Talātala, Mahātala, Rasātala and Pātāla. I have already explained the situation of the planetary systems of earth. The width and length of the seven lower planetary systems are calculated to be exactly the same as those of earth.

TEXT 8

एतेषु हि बिलस्वर्गेषु स्वर्गादप्यधिककामभोगैश्वर्यानन्दभूतिविभूतिभिः सुसमृद्धभवनोद्यानाक्रीडविहारेषु दैत्यदानवकाद्रवेया नित्यप्रमुदितानुरक्त-कलत्रापत्यबन्धुसुहृदनुचरा गृहपतय ईश्वरादप्यप्रतिहतकामा मायाविनोदा निवसन्ति ॥ ८ ॥

eteṣu hi bila-svargeṣu svargād apy adhika-kāma-bhogaiśvaryānanda-bhūti-vibhūtibhiḥ susamṛddha-bhavanodyānākrīḍa-vihāreṣu daitya-dānava-kādraveyā nitya-pramuditānurakta-kalatrāpatya-bandhu-suhṛd-anucarā gṛha-pataya īśvarād apy apratihata-kāmā māyā-vinodā nivasanti.

eteṣu—in these; *hi*—certainly; *bila-svargeṣu*—known as the heavenly subterranean worlds; *svargāt*—than the heavenly planets; *api*—even; *adhika*—a greater quantity; *kāma-bhoga*—enjoyment of sense gratification; *aiśvarya-ānanda*—bliss due to opulence; *bhūti*—influence; *vibhūtibhiḥ*—by those things and wealth; *su-samṛddha*—improved; *bhavana*—houses; *udyāna*—gardens; *ākrīḍa-vihāreṣu*—in places for different types of sense gratification; *daitya*—the demons; *dānava*—ghosts; *kādraveyāḥ*—snakes; *nitya*—who are always; *pramudita*—overjoyed; *anurakta*—because of attachment; *kalatra*—to wife; *apatya*—children; *bandhu*—family relations; *suhṛt*—friends; *anucarāḥ*—followers; *gṛha-patayaḥ*—the heads of the households; *īśvarāt*—than those more capable, like the demigods; *api*—even; *apratihata-kāmāḥ*—whose fulfillment of lusty desires is unimpeded; *māyā*—illusory; *vinodāḥ*—who feel happiness; *nivasanti*—live.

TRANSLATION

In these seven planetary systems, which are also known as the subterranean heavens [bila-svarga], there are very beautiful houses, gardens and places of sense enjoyment, which are even more opulent than those in the higher planets because the demons have a very high standard of sensual pleasure, wealth and influence. Most of the residents of these planets, who are known as Daityas, Dānavas and Nāgas, live as householders. Their wives, children, friends and society are all fully engaged in illusory, material happiness. The sense enjoyment of the demigods is sometimes disturbed, but the residents of these planets enjoy life without disturbances. Thus they are understood to be very attached to illusory happiness.

PURPORT

According to the statements of Prahlāda Mahārāja, material enjoyment is *māyā-sukha*, illusory enjoyment. A Vaiṣṇava is full of anxieties for the deliverance of all living entities from such false enjoyment. Prahlāda Mahārāja says, *māyā-sukhāya bharam udvahato vimūḍhān:* these fools (*vimūḍhas*) are engaged in material happiness, which is surely temporary. Whether in the heavenly planets, the lower planets or the earthly planets, people are engrossed in temporary, material happiness, forgetting that in due course of time they have to change their bodies according to the material laws and suffer the repetition of birth, death, old age and disease. Not caring what will happen in the next birth, gross materialists are simply busy enjoying during the present short span of life. A Vaiṣṇava is always anxious to give all such bewildered materialists the real happiness of spiritual bliss.

TEXT 9

येषु महाराज मयेन मायाविना विनिर्मिताः पुरो नानामणिप्रवर-प्रवेकविरचितविचित्रभवनप्राकारगोपुरसभाचैत्यचत्वरायतनादिभिर्नागासुरमिथुनपारावतशुकसारिकाकीर्णकृत्रिमभूमिभिर्विवरेश्वरगृहोत्तमैः समलङ्कृताश्चकासति ॥ ९ ॥

yeṣu mahārāja mayena māyāvinā vinirmitāḥ puro nānā-maṇi-pravara-praveka-viracita-vicitra-bhavana-prākāra-gopura-sabhā-caitya-catvarāyatanādibhir nāgāsura-mithuna-pārāvata-śuka-sārikākīrṇa-kṛtrima-bhūmibhir vivareśvara-gṛhottamaiḥ samalaṅkṛtāś cakāsati.

yeṣu—in those lower planetary systems; *mahā-rāja*—O my dear King; *mayena*—by the demon named Maya; *māyā-vinā*—possessing advanced knowledge in the construction of material comforts; *vinirmitāḥ*—constructed; *puraḥ*—cities; *nānā-maṇi-pravara*—of valuable gems; *praveka*—with excellent; *viracita*—constructed; *vicitra*—wonderful; *bhavana*—houses; *prākāra*—walls; *gopura*—gates; *sabhā*—legislative meeting rooms; *caitya*—temples; *catvara*—schools; *āyatana-ādibhiḥ*—with hotels or recreation halls and so on; *nāga*—of living entities with snakelike bodies; *asura*—of demons, or godless persons; *mithuna*—by couples; *pārāvata*—pigeons; *śuka*—parrots; *sārikā*—mynas; *ākīrṇa*—crowded; *kṛtrima*—artificial; *bhūmibhiḥ*—possessing areas; *vivara-īśvara*—of the leaders of the planets; *gṛha-uttamaiḥ*—with first-class houses; *samalaṅkṛtāḥ*—decorated; *cakāsati*—shine magnificently.

TRANSLATION

My dear King, in the imitation heavens known as bila-svarga there is a great demon named Maya Dānava, who is an expert artist and architect. He has constructed many brilliantly decorated cities. There are many wonderful houses, walls, gates, assembly houses, temples, yards and temple compounds, as well as many hotels serving as residential quarters for foreigners. The houses for the leaders of these planets are constructed with the most valuable jewels, and they are always crowded with living entities known as Nāgas and Asuras, as well as many pigeons, parrots and similar birds. All in all, these imitation heavenly cities are most beautifully situated and attractively decorated.

TEXT 10

उद्यानानि चातितरां मनइन्द्रियानन्दिभिः कुसुमफलस्तबकसुभगकिसलया-
वनतरुचिरविटपविटपिनां लताङ्गालिङ्गितानां श्रीभिः समिथुनविविधविहङ्गम-
जलाशयानाममलजलपूर्णानां झषकुलोल्लङ्घनक्षुभितनीरनीरजकुमुदकुवलयकह्लार-
नीलोत्पललोहितशतपत्रादिवनेषु कृतनिकेतनानामेकविहाराकुलमधुरविविध-
स्वनादिभिरिन्द्रियोत्सवैरमरलोकश्रियमतिशयितानि ॥१०॥

udyānāni cātitarāṁ mana-indriyānandibhiḥ kusuma-phala-stabaka-subhaga-kisalayāvanata-rucira-viṭapa-viṭapināṁ latāṅgāliṅgitānāṁ śrībhiḥ samithuna-vividha-vihaṅgama-jalāśayānām amala-jala-pūrṇānāṁ jhaṣakulollaṅghana-kṣubhita-nīra-nīraja-kumuda-kuvalaya-kahlāra-nīlotpala-lohita-śatapatrādi-vaneṣu kṛta-niketanānām eka-vihārākula-madhura-vividha-svanādibhir indriyotsavair amara-loka-śriyam atiśayitāni.

udyānāni—the gardens and parks; *ca*—also; *atitarām*—greatly; *manaḥ*—to the mind; *indriya*—and to the senses; *ānandibhiḥ*—which cause pleasure; *kusuma*—by flowers; *phala*—of fruits; *stabaka*—bunches; *subhaga*—very beautiful; *kisalaya*—new twigs; *avanata*—bent low; *rucira*—attractive; *viṭapa*—possessing branches; *viṭapinām*—

of trees; *latā-aṅga-āliṅgitānām*—which are embraced by the limbs of creepers; *śrībhiḥ*—by the beauty; *sa-mithuna*—in pairs; *vividha*—varieties; *vihaṅgama*—frequented by birds; *jala-āśayānām*—of reservoirs of water; *amala-jala-pūrṇānām*—full of clear and transparent water; *jhaṣa-kula-ullaṅghana*—by the jumping of different fish; *kṣubhita*—agitated; *nīra*—in the water; *nīraja*—of lotus flowers; *kumuda*—lilies; *kuvalaya*—flowers named *kuvalaya; kahlāra*—*kahlāra* flowers; *nīla-utpala*—blue lotus flowers; *lohita*—red; *śata-patra-ādi*—lotus flowers with a hundred petals and so on; *vaneṣu*—in forests; *kṛta-niketanānām*—of birds that have made their nests; *eka-vihāra-ākula*—full of uninterrupted enjoyment; *madhura*—very sweet; *vividha*—varieties; *svana-ādibhiḥ*—by vibrations; *indriya-utsavaiḥ*—invoking sense enjoyment; *amara-loka-śriyam*—the beauty of the residential places of the demigods; *atiśayitāni*—surpassing.

TRANSLATION

The parks and gardens in the artificial heavens surpass in beauty those of the upper heavenly planets. The trees in those gardens, embraced by creepers, bend with a heavy burden of twigs with fruits and flowers, and therefore they appear extraordinarily beautiful. That beauty could attract anyone and make his mind fully blossom in the pleasure of sense gratification. There are many lakes and reservoirs with clear, transparent water, agitated by jumping fish and decorated with many flowers such as lilies, kuvalayas, kahlāras and blue and red lotuses. Pairs of cakravākas and many other water birds nest in the lakes and always enjoy in a happy mood, making sweet, pleasing vibrations that are very satisfying and conducive to enjoyment of the senses.

TEXT 11

यत्र ह वाव न भयमहोरात्रादिभिः कालविभागैरुपलक्ष्यते ॥११॥

yatra ha vāva na bhayam aho-rātrādibhiḥ kāla-vibhāgair upalakṣyate.

yatra—where; *ha vāva*—certainly; *na*—not; *bhayam*—fearfulness; *ahaḥ-rātra-ādibhiḥ*—because of days and nights; *kāla-vibhāgaiḥ*—the divisions of time; *upalakṣyate*—is experienced.

TRANSLATION

Since there is no sunshine in those subterranean planets, time is not divided into days and nights, and consequently fear produced by time does not exist.

TEXT 12

यत्र हि महाहिप्रवरशिरोमणयः सर्वं तमः प्रबाधन्ते ॥१२॥

yatra hi mahāhi-pravara-śiro-maṇayaḥ sarvaṁ tamaḥ prabādhante.

yatra—where; *hi*—indeed; *mahā-ahi*—of great serpents; *pravara*—of the best; *śiraḥ-maṇayaḥ*—the gems on the hoods; *sarvam*—all; *tamaḥ*—darkness; *prabādhante*—drive away.

TRANSLATION

Many great serpents reside there with gems on their hoods, and the effulgence of these gems dissipates the darkness in all directions.

TEXT 13

न वा एतेषु वसतां दिव्यौषधिरसरसायनान्नपानस्नानादिभिराधयो व्याधयो वलीपलितजरादयश्च देहवैवर्ण्यदौर्गन्ध्यस्वेदक्लमग्लानिरिति वयोऽवस्थाश्च भवन्ति ॥१३॥

na vā eteṣu vasatāṁ divyauṣadhi-rasa-rasāyanānna-pāna-snānādibhir ādhayo vyādhayo valī-palita-jarādayaś ca deha-vaivarṇya-daurgandhya-sveda-klama-glānir iti vayo 'vasthāś ca bhavanti.

na—not; *vā*—either; *eteṣu*—in these planets; *vasatām*—of those residing; *divya*—wonderful; *auṣadhi*—of herbs; *rasa*—the juices; *rasāyana*—and elixirs; *anna*—by eating; *pāna*—drinking; *snāna-ādibhiḥ*—by bathing in and so on; *ādhayaḥ*—mental troubles; *vyādhayaḥ*—diseases; *valī*—wrinkles; *palita*—grey hair; *jarā*—old age; *ādayaḥ*—and so on; *ca*—and; *deha-vaivarṇya*—the fading of bodily luster; *daurgandhya*—bad odor; *sveda*—perspiration; *klama*—

fatigue; *glāniḥ*—lack of energy; *iti*—thus; *vayaḥ avasthāḥ*—miserable conditions due to increasing age; *ca*—and; *bhavanti*—are.

TRANSLATION

Since the residents of these planets drink and bathe in juices and elixirs made from wonderful herbs, they are freed from all anxieties and physical diseases. They have no experience of grey hair, wrinkles or invalidity, their bodily lusters do not fade, their perspiration does not cause a bad smell, and they are not troubled by fatigue or by lack of energy or enthusiasm due to old age.

TEXT 14

न हि तेषां कल्याणानां प्रभवति कुतश्चन मृत्युर्विना भगवत्तेजसश्चक्रा-
पदेशात् ॥१४॥

na hi teṣāṁ kalyāṇānāṁ prabhavati kutaścana mṛtyur vinā bhagavat-tejasaś cakrāpadeśāt.

na hi—not; *teṣām*—of them; *kalyāṇānām*—who are by nature auspicious; *prabhavati*—able to influence; *kutaścana*—from anywhere; *mṛtyuḥ*—death; *vinā*—except; *bhagavat-tejasaḥ*—of the energy of the Supreme Personality of Godhead; *cakra-apadeśāt*—from that weapon named the Sudarśana *cakra.*

TRANSLATION

They live very auspiciously and do not fear death from anything but death's established time, which is the effulgence of the Sudarśana cakra of the Supreme Personality of Godhead.

PURPORT

This is the defect of material existence. Everything in the subterranean heavens is very nicely arranged. There are well situated residential quarters, there is a pleasing atmosphere, and there are no bodily inconveniences or mental anxieties, but nevertheless those who live there have to take another birth according to *karma.* Persons whose minds are dull cannot understand this defect of a materialistic civilization aiming at material comforts. One may make his living conditions very pleasing for the senses, but despite all favorable conditions, one must in due course of time meet death. The members of a demoniac civilization endeavor to make their living conditions very comfortable, but they cannot check death. The influence of the Sudarśana *cakra* will not allow their so-called material happiness to endure.

TEXT 15

यस्मिन् प्रविष्टेऽसुरवधूनां प्रायः पुंसवनानि भयादेव स्रवन्ति
पतन्ति च ॥१५॥

yasmin praviṣṭe 'sura-vadhūnāṁ prāyaḥ puṁsavanāni bhayād eva
sravanti patanti ca.

yasmin—where; *praviṣṭe*—when entered; *asura-vadhūnām*—of the wives of those demons; *prāyaḥ*—almost always; *puṁsavanāni*—fetuses; *bhayāt*—because of fear; *eva*—certainly; *sravanti*—slip out; *patanti*—fall down; *ca*—and.

TRANSLATION

When the Sudarśana disc enters those provinces, the pregnant wives of the demons all have miscarriages due to fear of its effulgence.

TEXT 16

अथातले मयपुत्रोऽसुरो बलो निवसति येन ह वा इह
सृष्टाः षण्णवतिर्मायाः काश्चनाद्यापि मायाविनो धारयन्ति यस्य च जृम्भ-
माणस्य मुखतस्त्रयः स्त्रीगणा उदपद्यन्त स्वैरिण्यः कामिन्यः पुंश्चल्य इति
या वै बिलायनं प्रविष्टं पुरुषं रसेन हाटकाख्येन साधयित्वा स्वविलासा-
वलोकनानुरागस्मितसंलापोपगूहनादिभिः स्वैरं किल रमयन्ति
यस्मिन्नुपयुक्ते पुरुष ईश्वरोऽहं सिद्धोऽहमित्ययुतमहागजबलमात्मानम-
भिमन्यमानः कत्थते मदान्ध इव ॥१६॥

athātale maya-putro 'suro balo nivasati yena ha vā iha sṛṣṭāḥ ṣaṇ-ṇavatir māyāḥ kāścanādyāpi māyāvino dhārayanti yasya ca jṛmbhamāṇasya mukhatas trayaḥ strī-gaṇā udapadyanta svairiṇyaḥ kāminyaḥ puṁścalya iti yā vai bilāyanaṁ praviṣṭaṁ puruṣaṁ rasena hāṭakākhyena sādhayitvā sva-vilāsāvalokanānurāga-smita-saṁlāpopagūhanādibhiḥ svairaṁ kila ramayanti yasminn upayukte puruṣa īśvaro 'ham siddho 'ham ity ayuta-mahā-gaja-balam ātmānam abhimanyamānaḥ katthate madāndha iva.

atha—now; *atale*—on the planet named Atala; *maya-putraḥ asuraḥ*—the demon son of Maya; *balaḥ*—Bala; *nivasati*—resides; *yena*—by whom; *ha vā*—indeed; *iha*—in this; *sṛṣṭāḥ*—propagated; *ṣaṭ-ṇavatiḥ*—ninety-six; *māyāḥ*—varieties of illusion; *kāścana*—some; *adya api*—even today; *māyā-vinaḥ*—those who know the art of magical feats (like manufacturing gold); *dhārayanti*—utilize; *yasya*—of whom; *ca*—also; *jṛmbhamāṇasya*—while yawning; *mukhataḥ*—from the mouth; *trayaḥ*—three; *strī-gaṇāḥ*—varieties of women; *udapadyanta*—were generated; *svairiṇyaḥ*—*svairiṇī* (one who only marries in her same class); *kāminyaḥ*—*kāmiṇī* (one who, being lusty, marries men from any group); *puṁścalyaḥ*—*puṁścalī* (one who wants to go from one husband to another); *iti*—thus; *yāḥ*—who; *vai*—certainly; *bila-ayanam*—the subterranean planets; *praviṣṭam*—entering; *puruṣam*—a male; *rasena*—by a juice; *hāṭaka-ākhyena*—made from an intoxicating herb known as *hāṭaka; sādhayitvā*—making sexually fit; *sva-vilāsa*—for their personal sense gratification; *avalokana*—by glances; *anurāga*—lustful; *smita*—by smiling; *saṁlāpa*—by talking; *upagūhana-ādibhiḥ*—and by embracing; *svairam*—according to their own desire; *kila*—indeed; *ramayanti*—enjoy sex pleasure; *yasmin*—which; *upayukte*—when used; *puruṣaḥ*—a man; *īśvaraḥ aham*—I am the most powerful person; *siddhaḥ aham*—I am the greatest and most elevated person; *iti*—thus; *ayuta*—ten thousand; *mahā-gaja*—of big elephants; *balam*—the strength; *ātmānam*—himself; *abhimanyamānaḥ*—being full of pride; *katthate*—they say; *mada-andhaḥ*—blinded by false prestige; *iva*—like.

TRANSLATION

My dear King, now I shall describe to you the lower planetary systems, one by one, beginning from Atala. In Atala there is a

demon, the son of Maya Dānava named Bala, who created ninety-six kinds of mystic power. Some so-called yogīs and svāmīs take advantage of this mystic power to cheat people even today. Simply by yawning, the demon Bala created three kinds of women, known as svairiṇī, kāmiṇī and puṁścalī. The svairiṇīs like to marry men from their own group, the kāmiṇīs marry men from any group, and the puṁścalīs change husbands one after another. If a man enters the planet of Atala, these women immediately capture him and induce him to drink an intoxicating beverage made with a drug known as hāṭaka [cannabis indica]. This intoxicant endows the man with great sexual prowess, of which the women take advantage for enjoyment. A woman will enchant him with attractive glances, intimate words, smiles of love and then embraces. In this way she induces him to enjoy sex with her to her full satisfaction. Because of his increased sexual power, the man thinks himself stronger than ten thousand elephants and considers himself most perfect. Indeed, illusioned and intoxicated by false pride, he thinks himself God, ignoring impending death.

TEXT 17

ततोऽधस्ताद्वितले हरो भगवान् हाटकेश्वरः स्वपार्षदभूतगणावृतः
प्रजापतिसर्गोपबृंहणाय भवो भवान्या सह मिथुनीभूत आस्ते यतः
प्रवृत्ता सरित्प्रवरा हाटकी नाम भवयोर्वीर्येण यत्र
चित्रभानुर्मातरिश्वना समिध्यमान ओजसा पिबति तन्निष्ठ्यूतं
हाटकाख्यं सुवर्णं भूषणेनासुरेन्द्रावरोधेषु पुरुषाः सह पुरुषीभिर्धारयन्ति
॥ १७ ॥

tato 'dhastād vitale haro bhagavān hāṭakeśvaraḥ sva-pārṣada-bhūta-gaṇāvṛtaḥ prajāpati-sargopabṛṁhaṇāya bhavo bhavānyā saha mithunī-bhūta āste yataḥ pravṛttā sarit-pravarā hāṭakī nāma bhavayor vīryeṇa yatra citrabhānur mātariśvanā samidhyamāna ojasā pibati tan niṣṭhyūtaṁ hāṭakākhyaṁ suvarṇaṁ bhūṣaṇenāsurendrāvarodheṣu puruṣāḥ saha puruṣībhir dhārayanti.

tataḥ—the planet Atala; *adhastāt*—beneath; *vitale*—on the planet; *haraḥ*—Lord Śiva; *bhagavān*—the most powerful personality; *hāṭa-*

keśvaraḥ—the master of gold; *sva-pārṣada*—by his own associates; *bhūta-gaṇa*—who are ghostly living beings; *āvṛtaḥ*—surrounded; *prajāpati-sarga*—of the creation of Lord Brahmā; *upabṛṁhaṇāya*—to increase the population; *bhavaḥ*—Lord Śiva; *bhavānyā saha*—with his wife, Bhavānī; *mithunī-bhūtaḥ*—being united in sex; *āste*—remains; *yataḥ*—from that planet (Vitala); *pravṛttā*—being emanated; *sarit-pravarā*—the great river; *hāṭakī*—Hāṭakī; *nāma*—named; *bhavayoḥ vīryeṇa*—due to the semina and ovum of Lord Śiva and Bhavānī; *yatra*—where; *citra-bhānuḥ*—the fire-god; *mātariśvanā*—by the wind; *samidhyamānaḥ*—being brightly inflamed; *ojasā*—with great strength; *pibati*—drinks; *tat*—that; *niṣṭhyūtam*—spit out with a hissing sound; *hāṭaka-ākhyam*—named Hāṭaka; *suvarṇam*—gold; *bhūṣaṇena*—by different types of ornaments; *asura-indra*—of the great *asuras; avarodheṣu*—in the homes; *puruṣāḥ*—the males; *saha*—with; *puruṣībhiḥ*—their wives and women; *dhārayanti*—wear.

TRANSLATION

The next planet below Atala is Vitala, wherein Lord Śiva, who is known as the master of gold mines, lives with his personal associates, the ghosts and similar living entities. Lord Śiva, as the progenitor, engages in sex with Bhavānī, the progenitress, to produce living entities, and from the mixture of their vital fluid the river named Hāṭakī is generated. When fire, being made to blaze by the wind, drinks of this river and then sizzles and spits it out, it produces gold called Hāṭaka. The demons who live on that planet with their wives decorate themselves with various ornaments made from that gold, and thus they live there very happily.

PURPORT

It appears that when Bhava and Bhavānī, Lord Śiva and his wife, unite sexually, the emulsification of their secretions creates a chemical which when heated by fire can produce gold. It is said that the alchemists of the medieval age tried to prepare gold from base metal, and Śrīla Sanātana Gosvāmī also states that when bell metal is treated with mercury, it can produce gold. Śrīla Sanātana Gosvāmī mentions this in regard to the initiation of low-class men to turn them into *brāhmaṇas.* Sanātana Gosvāmī said:

yathā kāñcanatāṁ yāti
kāṁsyaṁ rasa-vidhānataḥ
tathā dīkṣā-vidhānena
dvijatvaṁ jāyate nṛṇām

"As one can transform *kaṁsa,* or bell metal, into gold by treating it with mercury, one can also turn a lowborn man into a *brāhmaṇa* by initiating him properly into Vaiṣṇava activities." The International Society for Krishna Consciousness is trying to turn *mlecchas* and *yavanas* into real *brāhmaṇas* by properly initiating them and stopping them from engaging in meat-eating, intoxication, illicit sex and gambling. One who stops these four principles of sinful activity and chants the Hare Kṛṣṇa *mahā-mantra* can certainly become a pure *brāhmaṇa* through the process of bona fide initiation, as suggested by Śrīla Sanātana Gosvāmī.

Apart from this, if one takes a hint from this verse and learns how to mix mercury with bell metal by properly heating and melting them, one can get gold very cheaply. The alchemists of the medieval age tried to manufacture gold, but they were unsuccessful, perhaps because they did not follow the right instructions.

TEXT 18

ततोऽधस्तात्सुतले उदारश्रवाः पुण्यश्लोको विरोचनात्मजो बलिर्भगवता महेन्द्रस्य प्रियं चिकीर्षमाणेनादितेर्लब्धकायो भूत्वा वटुवामनरूपेण पराक्षिप्तलोकत्रयो भगवदनुकम्पयैव पुनः प्रवेशित इन्द्रादिष्वविद्यमानया सुसमृद्धया श्रियाभिजुष्टः स्वधर्मेणाराधयंस्तमेव भगवन्तमाराधनीयमपगतसाध्वस आस्तेऽधुनापि ॥१८॥

tato 'dhastāt sutale udāra-śravāḥ puṇya-śloko virocanātmajo balir bhagavatā mahendrasya priyaṁ cikīrṣamāṇenāditer labdha-kāyo bhūtvā vaṭu-vāmana-rūpeṇa parākṣipta-loka-trayo bhagavad-anukampayaiva punaḥ praveśita indrādiṣv avidyamānayā susamṛddhayā śriyābhijuṣṭaḥ sva-dharmeṇārādhayaṁs tam eva bhagavantam ārādhanīyam apagata-sādhvasa āste 'dhunāpi.

tataḥ adhastāt—beneath the planet known as Vitala; *sutale*—on the planet known as Sutala; *udāra-śravāḥ*—very greatly celebrated; *puṇya-ślokaḥ*—very pious and advanced in spiritual consciousness; *virocana-ātmajaḥ*—the son of Virocana; *baliḥ*—Bali Mahārāja; *bhagavatā*—by the Supreme Personality of Godhead; *mahā-indrasya*—of the King of heaven, Indra; *priyam*—the welfare; *cikīrṣamāṇena*—desiring to perform; *āditeḥ*—from Āditi; *labdha-kāyaḥ*—having obtained His body; *bhūtvā*—appearing; *vaṭu—brahmacārī; vāmana-rūpeṇa*—in the form of a dwarf; *parākṣipta*—wrested away; *loka-trayaḥ*—the three worlds; *bhagavat-anukampayā*—by the causeless mercy of the Supreme Personality of Godhead; *eva*—certainly; *punaḥ*—again; *praveśitaḥ*—caused to enter; *indra-ādiṣu*—even among the demigods like the King of heaven; *avidyamānayā*—not existing; *susamṛddhayā*—much enriched by such exalted opulence; *śriyā*—by good fortune; *abhijuṣṭaḥ*—being blessed; *sva-dharmeṇa*—by discharging devotional service; *ārādhayan*—worshiping; *tam*—Him; *eva*—certainly; *bhagavantam*—the Supreme Personality of Godhead; *ārādhanīyam*—who is most worshipable; *apagata-sādhvasaḥ*—without fear; *āste*—remains; *adhunā api*—even today.

TRANSLATION

Below the planet Vitala is another planet, known as Sutala, where the great son of Mahārāja Virocana, Bali Mahārāja, who is celebrated as the most pious king, resides even now. For the welfare of Indra, the King of heaven, Lord Viṣṇu appeared in the form of a dwarf brahmacārī as the son of Āditi and tricked Bali Mahārāja by begging for only three paces of land but taking all the three worlds. Being very pleased with Bali Mahārāja for giving all his possessions, the Lord returned his kingdom and made him richer than the opulent King Indra. Even now, Bali Mahārāja engages in devotional service by worshiping the Supreme Personality of Godhead in the planet of Sutala.

PURPORT

The Supreme Personality of Godhead is described as Uttamaśloka, "He who is worshiped by the best of selected Sanskrit verses," and His devotees such as Bali Mahārāja are also worshiped by *puṇya-śloka*, verses that increase one's piety. Bali Mahārāja offered everything to the Lord—his wealth, his kingdom and even his own body (*sarvātma-nivedane baliḥ*). The Lord appeared before Bali Mahārāja as a *brāhmaṇa* beggar, and Bali Mahārāja gave Him everything he had. However, Bali Mahārāja did not become poor; by donating all his possessions to the Supreme Personality of Godhead, he became a successful devotee and got everything back again with the blessings of the Lord. Similarly, those who give contributions to expand the activities of the Kṛṣṇa consciousness movement and to accomplish its objectives will never be losers; they will get their wealth back with the blessings of Lord Kṛṣṇa. On the other side, those who collect contributions on behalf of the International Society for Krishna Consciousness should be very careful not to use even a farthing of the collection for any purpose other than the transcendental loving service of the Lord.

TEXT 19

नो एवैतत्साक्षात्कारो भूमिदानस्य यत्तद्भगवत्यशेषजीवनिकायानां जीव-
भूतात्मभूते परमात्मनि वासुदेवे तीर्थतमे पात्र उपपन्ने परया श्रद्धया
परमादरसमाहितमनसा सम्प्रतिपादितस्य साक्षादपवर्गद्वारस्य
यद्बिलनिलयैश्वर्यम् ॥१९॥

no evaitat sākṣātkāro bhūmi-dānasya yat tad bhagavaty aśeṣa-jīva-
nikāyānāṁ jīva-bhūtātma-bhūte paramātmani vāsudeve tīrthatame
pātra upapanne parayā śraddhayā paramādara-samāhita-manasā
sampratipāditasya sākṣād apavarga-dvārasya yad bila-nilayaiśvaryam.

no—not; *eva*—indeed; *etat*—this; *sākṣātkāraḥ*—the direct result; *bhūmi-dānasya*—of contribution of land; *yat*—which; *tat*—that; *bhagavati*—unto the Supreme Personality of Godhead; *aśeṣa-jīva-nikāyānām*—of unlimited numbers of living entities; *jīva-bhūta-ātma-*

bhūte—who is the life and the Supersoul; *parama-ātmani*—the supreme regulator; *vāsudeve*—Lord Vāsudeva (Kṛṣṇa); *tīrtha-tame*—who is the best of all places of pilgrimage; *pātre*—the most worthy recipient; *upapanne*—having approached; *parayā*—by the topmost; *śraddhayā*—faith; *parama-ādara*—with great respect; *samāhita-manasā*—with an attentive mind; *sampratipāditasya*—which was given; *sākṣāt*—directly; *apavarga-dvārasya*—the gate of liberation; *yat*—which; *bila-nilaya*—of *bila-svarga*, the imitation heavenly planets; *aiśvaryam*—the opulence.

TRANSLATION

My dear King, Bali Mahārāja donated all his possessions to the Supreme Personality of Godhead, Vāmanadeva, but one should certainly not conclude that he achieved his great worldly opulence in bila-svarga as a result of his charitable disposition. The Supreme Personality of Godhead, who is the source of life for all living entities, lives within everyone as the friendly Supersoul, and under His direction a living entity enjoys or suffers in the material world. Greatly appreciating the transcendental qualities of the Lord, Bali Mahārāja offered everything at His lotus feet. His purpose, however, was not to gain anything material, but to become a pure devotee. For a pure devotee, the door of liberation is automatically opened. One should not think that Bali Mahārāja was given so much material opulence merely because of his charity. When one becomes a pure devotee in love, he may also be blessed with a good material position by the will of the Supreme Lord. However, one should not mistakenly think that the material opulence of a devotee is the result of his devotional service. The real result of devotional service is the awakening of pure love for the Supreme Personality of Godhead, which continues under all circumstances.

TEXT 20

यस्य ह वाव क्षुतपतनप्रस्खलनादिषु विवशः सकृन्नामाभिगृणन् पुरुषः कर्मबन्धनमञ्जसा विधुनोति यस्य हैव प्रतिबाधनं मुमुक्षवोऽन्यथैवोपलभन्ते ॥२०॥

yasya ha vāva kṣuta-patana-praskhalanādiṣu vivaśaḥ sakṛn nāmābhigṛṇan puruṣaḥ karma-bandhanam añjasā vidhunoti yasya haiva pratibādhanaṁ mumukṣavo 'nyathaivopalabhante.

yasya—of whom; *ha vāva*—indeed; *kṣuta*—when in hunger; *patana*—falling down; *praskhalana-ādiṣu*—stumbling and so on; *vivaśaḥ*—being helpless; *sakṛt*—once; *nāma abhigṛṇan*—chanting the holy name of the Lord; *puruṣaḥ*—a person; *karma-bandhanam*—the bondage of fruitive activity; *añjasā*—completely; *vidhunoti*—washes away; *yasya*—of which; *ha*—certainly; *eva*—in this way; *pratibādhanam*—the repulsion; *mumukṣavaḥ*—persons desiring liberation; *anyathā*—otherwise; *eva*—certainly; *upalabhante*—are trying to realize.

TRANSLATION

If one who is embarrassed by hunger or who falls down or stumbles chants the holy name of the Lord even once, willingly or unwillingly, he is immediately freed from the reactions of his past deeds. Karmīs entangled in material activities face many difficulties in the practice of mystic yoga and other endeavors to achieve that same freedom.

PURPORT

It is not a fact that one has to offer his material possessions to the Supreme Personality of Godhead and be liberated before he can engage in devotional service. A devotee automatically attains liberation without separate endeavors. Bali Mahārāja did not get back all his material possessions merely because of his charity to the Lord. One who becomes a devotee, free from material desires and motives, regards all opportunities, both material and spiritual, as benedictions from the Lord, and in this way his service to the Lord is never hampered. *Bhukti,* material enjoyment, and *mukti,* liberation, are only by-products of devotional service. A devotee need not work separately to attain *mukti.* Śrīla Bilvamaṅgala Ṭhākura said, *muktiḥ svayaṁ mukulitāñjaliḥ sevate 'smān:* a pure devotee of the Lord does not have to endeavor separately for *mukti,* because *mukti* is always ready to serve him.

In this regard, *Caitanya-caritāmṛta* (*Antya* 3.177-188) describes Haridāsa Ṭhākura's confirmation of the effect of chanting the holy name of the Lord.

keha bale—'nāma haite haya pāpa-kṣaya'
keha bale—'nāma haite jīvera mokṣa haya'

Some say that by chanting the holy name of the Lord one is freed from all the reactions of sinful life, and others say that by chanting the holy name of the Lord one attains liberation from material bondage.

haridāsa kahena,—"nāmera ei dui phala naya
nāmera phale kṛṣṇa-pade prema upajaya

Haridāsa Ṭhākura, however, said that the desired result of chanting the holy name of the Lord is not that one is liberated from material bondage or freed from the reactions of sinful life. The actual result of chanting the holy name of the Lord is that one awakens his dormant Kṛṣṇa consciousness, his loving service to the Lord.

ānuṣaṅgika phala nāmera—'mukti', 'pāpa-nāśa'
tāhāra dṛṣṭānta yaiche sūryera prakāśa

Haridāsa Ṭhākura said that liberation and freedom from the reactions of sinful activities are only by-products of chanting the holy name of the Lord. If one chants the holy name of the Lord purely, he attains the platform of loving service to the Supreme Personality of Godhead. In this regard Haridāsa Ṭhākura gave an example comparing the power of the holy name to sunshine.

ei ślokera artha kara paṇḍitera gaṇa"
sabe kahe,—'tumi kaha artha-vivaraṇa'

He placed a verse before all the learned scholars present, but the learned scholars asked him to state the purport of the verse.

haridāsa kahena,—"yaiche sūryera udaya
udaya nā haite ārambhe tamera haya kṣaya

Haridāsa Ṭhākura said that as the sun begins to rise, it dissipates the darkness of night, even before the sunshine is visible.

caura-preta-rākṣasādira bhaya haya nāśa
udaya haile dharma-karma-ādi parakāśa

Before the sunrise even takes place, the light of dawn destroys the fear of the dangers of the night, such as disturbances by thieves, ghosts and Rākṣasas, and when the sunshine actually appears, one engages in his duties.

aiche nāmodayārambhe pāpa-ādira kṣaya
udaya kaile kṛṣṇa-pade haya premodaya

Similarly, even before one's chanting of the holy name is pure, one is freed from all sinful reactions, and when he chants purely he becomes a lover of Kṛṣṇa.

'mukti' tuccha-phala haya nāmābhāsa haite
ye mukti bhakta nā laya, se kṛṣṇa cāhe dite"

A devotee never accepts *mukti*, even if Kṛṣṇa offers it. *Mukti*, freedom from all sinful reactions, is obtained even by *nāmābhāsa*, or a glimpse of the light of the holy name before its full light is perfectly visible.

The *nāmābhāsa* stage is between that of *nāma-aparādha*, or chanting of the holy name with offenses, and pure chanting. There are three stages in chanting the holy name of the Lord. In the first stage, one commits ten kinds of offenses while chanting. In the next stage, *nāmābhāsa*, the offenses have almost stopped, and one is coming to the platform of pure chanting. In the third stage, when one chants the Hare Kṛṣṇa *mantra* without offenses, his dormant love for Kṛṣṇa immediately awakens. This is the perfection.

TEXT 21

तद्भक्तानामात्मवतां सर्वेषामात्मन्यात्मद आत्मतयैव ॥२१॥

tad bhaktānām ātmavatāṁ sarveṣām ātmany ātmada ātmatayaiva.

tat—that; *bhaktānām*—of great devotees; *ātma-vatām*—of self-realized persons like Sanaka and Sanātana; *sarveṣām*—of all; *ātmani*—to the Supreme Personality of Godhead, who is the soul; *ātma-de*—who gives Himself without hesitation; *ātmatayā*—who is the Supreme Soul, Paramātmā; *eva*—indeed.

TRANSLATION

The Supreme Personality of Godhead, who is situated in everyone's heart as the Supersoul, sells Himself to His devotees such as Nārada Muni. In other words, the Lord gives pure love to such devotees and gives Himself to those who love Him purely. Great, self-realized mystic yogīs such as the four Kumāras also derive great transcendental bliss from realizing the Supersoul within themselves.

PURPORT

The Lord became Bali Mahārāja's doorkeeper not because of his giving everything to the Lord, but because of his exalted position as a lover of the Lord.

TEXT 22

न वै भगवान्नूनममुष्यानुजग्राह यदुत पुनरात्मानुस्मृतिमोषणं मायामय-
भोगैश्वर्यमेवातनुतेति ॥२२॥

na vai bhagavān nūnam amuṣyānujagrāha yad uta punar ātmānusmṛti-moṣaṇaṁ māyāmaya-bhogaiśvaryam evātanuteti.

na—not; *vai*—indeed; *bhagavān*—the Supreme Personality of Godhead; *nūnam*—certainly; *amuṣya*—unto Bali Mahārāja; *anujagrāha*—showed His favor; *yat*—because; *uta*—certainly; *punaḥ*—again; *ātma-anusmṛti*—of remembrance of the Supreme Personality of Godhead; *moṣaṇam*—which robs one; *māyā-maya*—an attribute of Māyā; *bhoga-aiśvaryam*—the material opulence; *eva*—certainly; *ātanuta*—extended; *iti*—thus.

TRANSLATION

The Supreme Personality of Godhead did not award His mercy to Bali Mahārāja by giving him material happiness and opulence, for these make one forget loving service to the Lord. The result of material opulence is that one can no longer absorb his mind in the Supreme Personality of Godhead.

PURPORT

There are two kinds of opulence. One, which results from one's *karma*, is material, whereas the other is spiritual. A surrendered soul who fully depends upon the Supreme Personality of Godhead does not want material opulence for sense gratification. Therefore when a pure devotee is seen to possess exalted material opulence, it is not due to his *karma*. Rather, it is due to his *bhakti*. In other words, he is in that position because the Supreme Lord wants him to execute service to Him very easily and opulently. The special mercy of the Lord for the neophyte devotee is that he becomes materially poor. This is the Lord's mercy because if a neophyte devotee becomes materially opulent, he forgets the service of the Lord. However, if an advanced devotee is favored by the Lord with opulence, it is not material opulence but a spiritual opportunity. Material opulence offered to the demigods causes forgetfulness of the Lord, but opulence was given to Bali Mahārāja for continuing service to the Lord, which was free from any touch of *māyā*.

TEXT 23

यत्तद्भगवतानधिगतान्योपायेन याच्ञाच्छलेनापहृतस्वशरीरावशेषितलोकत्रयो
वरुणपाशैश्च सम्प्रतिमुक्तो गिरिदर्यां चापविद्ध इति होवाच ॥ २३ ॥

yat tad bhagavatānadhigatānyopāyena yācñā-cchalenāpahṛta-sva-śarīrāvaśeṣita-loka-trayo varuṇa-pāśaiś ca sampratimukto giri-daryāṁ cāpaviddha iti hovāca.

yat—which; *tat*—that; *bhagavatā*—by the Supreme Personality of Godhead; *anadhigata-anya-upāyena*—who is not perceived by other means; *yācñā-chalena*—by a trick of begging; *apahṛta*—taken away;

sva-śarīra-avaśeṣita—with only his own body remaining; *loka-trayaḥ*—the three worlds; *varuṇa-pāśaiḥ*—by the ropes of Varuṇa; *ca*—and; *sampratimuktaḥ*—completely bound; *giri-daryām*—in a cave in a mountain; *ca*—and; *apaviddhaḥ*—being detained; *iti*—thus; *ha*—indeed; *uvāca*—said.

TRANSLATION

When the Supreme Personality of Godhead could see no other means of taking everything away from Bali Mahārāja, He adopted the trick of begging from him and took away all the three worlds. Thus only his body was left, but the Lord was still not satisfied. He arrested Bali Mahārāja, bound him with the ropes of Varuṇa and threw him in a cave in a mountain. Nevertheless, although all his property was taken and he was thrown into a cave, Bali Mahārāja was such a great devotee that he spoke as follows.

TEXT 24

नूनं बतायं भगवानर्थेषु न निष्णातो योऽसाविन्द्रो यस्य सचिवो
मन्त्राय वृत एकान्ततो बृहस्पतिस्तमतिहाय स्वयमुपेन्द्रेणात्मानमयाच-
तात्मनश्चाशिषो नो एव तद्दास्यमतिगम्भीरवयसः कालस्य मन्वन्तर-
परिवृत्तं कियल्लोकत्रयमिदम् ॥२४॥

nūnaṁ batāyaṁ bhagavān artheṣu na niṣṇāto yo 'sāv indro yasya sacivo
mantrāya vṛta ekāntato bṛhaspatis tam atihāya svayam
upendreṇātmānam ayācatātmanaś cāśiṣo no eva tad-dāsyam ati-
gambhīra-vayasaḥ kālasya manvantara-parivṛttaṁ kiyal loka-trayam
idam.

nūnam—certainly; *bata*—alas; *ayam*—this; *bhagavān*—very learned; *artheṣu*—in self-interest; *na*—not; *niṣṇātaḥ*—very experienced; *yaḥ*—who; *asau*—the King of heaven; *indraḥ*—Indra; *yasya*—of whom; *sacivaḥ*—the prime minister; *mantrāya*—for giving instructions; *vṛtaḥ*—chosen; *ekāntataḥ*—alone; *bṛhaspatiḥ*—named Bṛhaspati; *tam*—him; *atihāya*—ignoring; *svayam*—personally;

upendreṇa—by means of Upendra (Lord Vāmanadeva); *ātmānam*—myself; *ayācata*—requested; *ātmanaḥ*—for himself; *ca*—and; *āśiṣaḥ*—blessings (the three worlds); *no*—not; *eva*—certainly; *tat-dāsyam*—the loving service of the Lord; *ati*—very; *gambhīra-vayasaḥ*—having an insurmountable duration; *kālasya*—of time; *manvantara-parivṛttam*—changed by the end of a life of a Manu; *kiyat*—what is the value of; *loka-trayam*—three worlds; *idam*—these.

TRANSLATION

Alas, how pitiable it is for Indra, the King of heaven, that although he is very learned and powerful and although he chose Bṛhaspati as his prime minister to instruct him, he is completely ignorant concerning spiritual advancement. Bṛhaspati is also unintelligent because he did not properly instruct his disciple Indra. Lord Vāmanadeva was standing at Indra's door, but King Indra, instead of begging Him for an opportunity to render transcendental loving service, engaged Him in asking me for alms to gain the three worlds for his sense gratification. Sovereignty over the three worlds is very insignificant because whatever material opulence one may possess lasts only for an age of Manu, which is but a tiny fraction of endless time.

PURPORT

Bali Mahārāja was so powerful that he fought with Indra and took possession of the three worlds. Indra was certainly very advanced in knowledge, but instead of asking Vāmanadeva for engagement in His service, he used the Lord to beg for material possessions that would be finished at the end of one age of Manu. An age of Manu, which is the duration of Manu's life, is calculated to last seventy-two *yugas*. One *yuga* consists of 4,300,000 years, and therefore the duration of Manu's life is 309,600,000 years. The demigods possess their material opulence only until the end of the life of Manu. Time is insurmountable. The time one is allotted, even if it be millions of years, is quickly gone. The demigods own their material possessions only within the limits of time. Therefore Bali Mahārāja lamented that although Indra was very learned, he did not know how to use his intelligence properly, for instead of asking

Vāmanadeva to allow him to engage in His service, Indra used Him to beg Bali Mahārāja for material wealth. Although Indra was learned and his prime minister, Bṛhaspati, was also learned, neither of them begged to be able to render loving service to Lord Vāmanadeva. Therefore Bali Mahārāja lamented for Indra.

TEXT 25

यस्यानुदास्यमेवास्मत्पितामहः किल वव्रे न तु स्वपित्र्यं यदुताकुतोभयं
पदं दीयमानं भगवतः परमिति भगवतोपरते खलु स्वपितरि ॥ २५ ॥

yasyānudāsyam evāsmat-pitāmahaḥ kila vavre na tu sva-pitryaṁ yad
utākutobhayaṁ padaṁ dīyamānaṁ bhagavataḥ param iti
bhagavatoparate khalu sva-pitari.

yasya—of whom (the Supreme Personality of Godhead); *anudāsyam*—the service; *eva*—certainly; *asmat*—our; *pitā-mahaḥ*—grandfather; *kila*—indeed; *vavre*—accepted; *na*—not; *tu*—but; *sva*—own; *pitryam*—paternal property; *yat*—which; *uta*—certainly; *akutaḥ-bhayam*—fearlessness; *padam*—position; *dīyamānam*—being offered; *bhagavataḥ*—than the Supreme Personality of Godhead; *param*—other; *iti*—thus; *bhagavatā*—by the Supreme Personality of Godhead; *uparate*—when killed; *khalu*—indeed; *sva-pitari*—his own father.

TRANSLATION

Bali Mahārāja said: My grandfather Prahlāda Mahārāja is the only person who understood his own self-interest. Upon the death of Prahlāda's father, Hiraṇyakaśipu, Lord Nṛsiṁhadeva wanted to offer Prahlāda his father's kingdom and even wanted to grant him liberation from material bondage, but Prahlāda accepted neither. Liberation and material opulence, he thought, are obstacles to devotional service, and therefore such gifts from the Supreme Personality of Godhead are not His actual mercy. Consequently, instead of accepting the results of karma and jñāna, Prahlāda Mahārāja simply begged the Lord for engagement in the service of His servant.

PURPORT

Śrī Caitanya Mahāprabhu has instructed that an unalloyed devotee should consider himself a servant of the servant of the servant of the

Supreme Lord (*gopī-bhartuḥ pāda-kamalayor dāsa-dāsānudāsaḥ*). In Vaiṣṇava philosophy, one should not even become a direct servant. Prahlāda Mahārāja was offered all the blessings of an opulent position in the material world and even the liberation of merging into Brahman, but he refused all this. He simply wanted to engage in the service of the servant of the servant of the Lord. Therefore Bali Mahārāja said that because his grandfather Prahlāda Mahārāja had rejected the blessings of the Supreme Personality of Godhead in terms of material opulence and liberation from material bondage, he truly understood his self-interest.

TEXT 26

तस्य महानुभावस्यानुपथममृजितकषायः को वास्मद्विधः परिहीणभगवदनुग्रह उपजिगमिषतीति ॥ २६ ॥

tasya mahānubhāvasyānupatham amṛjita-kaṣāyaḥ ko vāsmad-vidhaḥ
parihīṇa-bhagavad-anugraha upajigamiṣatīti.

tasya—of Prahlāda Mahārāja; *mahā-anubhāvasya*—who was an exalted devotee; *anupatham*—the path; *amṛjita-kaṣāyaḥ*—a person who is materially contaminated; *kaḥ*—what; *vā*—or; *asmat-vidhaḥ*—like us; *parihīṇa-bhagavat-anugrahaḥ*—being without the favor of the Supreme Personality of Godhead; *upajigamiṣati*—desires to follow; *iti*—thus.

TRANSLATION

Bali Mahārāja said: Persons like us, who are still attached to material enjoyment, who are contaminated by the modes of material nature and who lack the mercy of the Supreme Personality of Godhead, cannot follow the supreme path of Prahlāda Mahārāja, the exalted devotee of the Lord.

PURPORT

It is said that for spiritual realization one must follow great personalities like Lord Brahmā, Devarṣi Nārada, Lord Śiva and Prahlāda Mahārāja. The path of *bhakti* is not at all difficult if we follow in the footsteps of previous *ācāryas* and authorities, but those who are too materially contaminated by the modes of material nature cannot follow them. Although Bali Mahārāja was actually following the path of his grandfather, because of his great humility he thought that he was not. It is characteristic of advanced Vaiṣṇavas following the principles of *bhakti* that they think themselves ordinary human beings. This is not an artificial exhibition of humility; a Vaiṣṇava sincerely thinks this way and therefore never admits his exalted position.

TEXT 27

तस्यानुचरितमुपरिष्टाद्विस्तरिष्यते यस्य भगवान् स्वयमखिलजगद्गुरुर्नारायणो द्वारि गदापाणिरवतिष्ठते निजजनानुकम्पितहृदयो येनाङ्गुष्ठेन पदा दशकन्धरो योजनायुतायुतं दिग्विजय उच्चाटितः ॥ २७ ॥

tasyānucaritam upariṣṭād vistariṣyate yasya bhagavān svayam akhila-
jagad-gurur nārāyaṇo dvāri gadā-pāṇir avatiṣṭhate nija-
janānukampita-hṛdayo yenāṅguṣṭhena padā daśa-kandharo
yojanāyutāyutaṁ dig-vijaya uccāṭitaḥ.

tasya—of Bali Mahārāja; *anucaritam*—the narration; *upariṣṭāt*—later (in the Eighth Canto); *vistariṣyate*—will be explained; *yasya*—of whom; *bhagavān*—the Supreme Personality of Godhead; *svayam*—personally; *akhila-jagat-guruḥ*—the master of all the three worlds; *nārāyaṇaḥ*—the Supreme Lord, Nārāyaṇa Himself; *dvāri*—at the gate; *gadā-pāṇiḥ*—bearing the club in His hand; *avatiṣṭhate*—stands; *nija-jana-anukampita-hṛdayaḥ*—whose heart is always filled with mercy for His devotees; *yena*—by whom; *aṅguṣṭhena*—by the big toe; *padā*—of His foot; *daśa-kandharaḥ*—Rāvaṇa, who had ten heads; *yojana-ayuta-ayutam*—a distance of eighty thousand miles; *dik-vijaye*—for the purpose of gaining victory over Bali Mahārāja; *uccāṭitaḥ*—driven away.

TRANSLATION

Śukadeva Gosvāmī continued: My dear King, how shall I glorify the character of Bali Mahārāja? The Supreme Personality of Godhead, the master of the three worlds, who is most compassionate to His own devotee, stands with club in hand at Bali Mahārāja's door. When Rāvaṇa, the powerful demon, came to gain victory over Bali Mahārāja, Vāmanadeva kicked him a distance of

eighty thousand miles with His big toe. I shall explain the character and activities of Bali Mahārāja later [in the Eighth Canto of Śrīmad-Bhāgavatam].

TEXT 28

ततोऽधस्तात्तलातले मयो नाम दानवेन्द्रस्त्रिपुराधिपतिर्भगवता
पुरारिणा त्रिलोकीशं चिकीर्षुणा निर्दग्धस्वपुरत्रयस्तत्प्रसादाल्लब्धपदो
मायाविनामाचार्यो महादेवेन परिरक्षितो विगतसुदर्शनभयो महीयते ॥ २८ ॥

tato 'dhastāt talātale mayo nāma dānavendras tri-purādhipatir
bhagavatā purāriṇā tri-lokī-śaṁ cikīrṣuṇā nirdagdha-sva-pura-trayas
tat-prasādāl labdha-pado māyāvinām ācāryo mahādevena parirakṣito
vigata-sudarśana-bhayo mahīyate.

tataḥ—the planet known as Sutala; *adhastāt*—below; *talātale*—in the planet known as Talātala; *mayaḥ*—Maya; *nāma*—named; *dānava-indraḥ*—the king of the Dānava demons; *tri-pura-adhipatiḥ*—the Lord of the three cities; *bhagavatā*—by the most powerful; *purāriṇā*—Lord Śiva, who is known as Tripurāri; *tri-lokī*—of the three worlds; *śam*—the good fortune; *cikīrṣuṇā*—who was desiring; *nirdagdha*—burned; *sva-pura-trayaḥ*—whose three cities; *tat-prasādāt*—by Lord Śiva's mercy; *labdha*—obtained; *padaḥ*—a kingdom; *māyā-vinām ācāryaḥ*—who is the *ācārya,* or master, of all the conjurers; *mahā-devena*—by Lord Śiva; *parirakṣitaḥ*—protected; *vigata-sudarśana-bhayaḥ*—who is not afraid of the Supreme Personality of Godhead and His Sudarśana *cakra;* *mahīyate*—is worshiped.

TRANSLATION

Beneath the planet known as Sutala is another planet, called Talātala, which is ruled by the Dānava demon named Maya. Maya is known as the ācārya [master] of all the māyāvīs, who can invoke the powers of sorcery. For the benefit of the three worlds, Lord Śiva, who is known as Tripurāri, once set fire to the three kingdoms of Maya, but later, being pleased with him, he returned his kingdom. Since that time, Maya Dānava has been protected by

Lord Śiva, and therefore he falsely thinks that he need not fear the Sudarśana cakra of the Supreme Personality of Godhead.

TEXT 29

ततोऽधस्तान्महातले काद्रवेयाणां सर्पाणां नैकशिरसां क्रोधवशो नाम गणः कुहकतक्षककालियसुषेणादिप्रधाना महाभोगवन्तः पतत्त्रिराजाधिपतेः पुरुषवाहादनवरतमुद्विजमानाः स्वकलत्रापत्यसुहृत्कुटुम्बसङ्गेन क्वचित्प्रमत्ता विहरन्ति ॥ २९ ॥

tato 'dhastān mahātale kādraveyāṇāṁ sarpāṇāṁ naika-śirasāṁ krodhavaśo nāma gaṇaḥ kuhaka-takṣaka-kāliya-suṣeṇādi-pradhānā mahā-bhogavantaḥ patattri-rājādhipateḥ puruṣa-vāhād anavaratam udvijamānāḥ sva-kalatrāpatya-suhṛt-kuṭumba-saṅgena kvacit pramattā viharanti.

tataḥ—the planet Talātala; *adhastāt*—beneath; *mahātale*—in the planet known as Mahātala; *kādraveyāṇām*—of the descendants of Kadrū; *sarpāṇām*—who are big snakes; *na eka-śirasām*—who have many hoods; *krodha-vaśaḥ*—always subject to anger; *nāma*—named; *gaṇaḥ*—the group; *kuhaka*—Kuhaka; *takṣaka*—Takṣaka; *kāliya*—Kāliya; *suṣeṇa*—Suṣeṇa; *ādi*—and so on; *pradhānāḥ*—who are the prominent ones; *mahā-bhogavantaḥ*—addicted to all kinds of material enjoyment; *patattri-rāja-adhipateḥ*—from the king of all birds, Garuḍa; *puruṣa-vāhāt*—who carries the Supreme Personality of Godhead; *anavaratam*—constantly; *udvijamānāḥ*—afraid; *sva*—of their own; *kalatra-apatya*—wives and children; *suhṛt*—friends; *kuṭumba*—relatives; *saṅgena*—in the association; *kvacit*—sometimes; *pramattāḥ*—infuriated; *viharanti*—they sport.

TRANSLATION

The planetary system below Talātala is known as Mahātala. It is the abode of many-hooded snakes, descendants of Kadrū, who are always very angry. The great snakes who are prominent are Kuhaka, Takṣaka, Kāliya and Suṣeṇa. The snakes in Mahātala are always disturbed by fear of Garuḍa, the carrier of Lord Viṣṇu, but

although they are full of anxiety, some of them nevertheless sport with their wives, children, friends and relatives.

PURPORT

It is stated here that the snakes who live in the planetary system known as Mahātala are very powerful and have many hoods. They live with their wives and children and consider themselves very happy, although they are always full of anxiety because of Garuḍa, who comes there to destroy them. This is the way of material life. Even if one lives in the most abominable condition, he still thinks himself happy with his wife, children, friends and relatives.

TEXT 30

ततोऽधस्ताद्रसातले दैतेया दानवाः पणयो नाम निवातकवचाः
कालेया हिरण्यपुरवासिन इति विबुधप्रत्यनीका उत्पत्त्या महौजसो
महासाहसिनो भगवतः सकललोकानुभावस्य हरेरेव तेजसा
प्रतिहतबलावलेपा बिलेशया इव वसन्ति ये वै सरमयेन्द्रदूत्या वाग्भि-
र्मन्त्रवर्णाभिरिन्द्राद्बिभ्यति ॥ ३० ॥

tato 'dhastād rasātale daiteyā dānavāḥ paṇayo nāma nivāta-kavacāḥ
kāleyā hiraṇya-puravāsina iti vibudha-pratyanīkā utpattyā mahaujaso
mahā-sāhasino bhagavataḥ sakala-lokānubhāvasya harer eva tejasā
pratihata-balāvalepā bileśayā iva vasanti ye vai saramayendra-dūtyā
vāgbhir mantra-varṇābhir indrād bibhyati.

tataḥ adhastāt—below the planetary system Mahātala; *rasātale*—on the planet called Rasātala; *daiteyāḥ*—the sons of Diti; *dānavāḥ*—the sons of Danu; *paṇayaḥ nāma*—named Paṇis; *nivāta-kavacāḥ*—Nivāta-kavacas; *kāleyāḥ*—Kāleyas; *hiraṇya-puravāsinaḥ*—Hiraṇya-puravāsīs; *iti*—thus; *vibudha-pratyanīkāḥ*—enemies of the demigods; *utpattyāḥ*—from birth; *mahā-ojasaḥ*—very powerful; *mahā-sāhasinaḥ*—very cruel; *bhagavataḥ*—of the Personality of Godhead; *sakala-loka-anubhāvasya*—who is auspicious for all planetary systems; *hareḥ*—of the Supreme Personality of Godhead; *eva*—certainly; *tejasā*—by the

Sudarśana *cakra; pratihata*—defeated; *bala*—strength; *avalepāḥ*—and pride (because of bodily strength); *bila-īśayāḥ*—the snakes; *iva*—like; *vasanti*—they live; *ye*—who; *vai*—indeed; *saramayā*—by Saramā; *indra-dūtyā*—the messenger of Indra; *vāgbhiḥ*—by the words; *mantra-varṇābhiḥ*—in the form of a *mantra; indrāt*—from King Indra; *bibhyati*—are afraid.

TRANSLATION

Beneath Mahātala is the planetary system known as Rasātala, which is the abode of the demoniac sons of Diti and Danu. They are called Paṇis, Nivāta-kavacas, Kāleyas and Hiraṇya-puravāsīs [those living in Hiraṇya-pura]. They are all enemies of the demigods, and they reside in holes like snakes. From birth they are extremely powerful and cruel, and although they are proud of their strength, they are always defeated by the Sudarśana cakra of the Supreme Personality of Godhead, who rules all the planetary systems. When a female messenger from Indra named Saramā chants a particular curse, the serpentine demons of Mahātala become very afraid of Indra.

PURPORT

It is said that there was a great fight between these serpentine demons and Indra, the King of heaven. When the defeated demons met the female messenger Saramā, who was chanting a *mantra*, they became afraid, and therefore they are living in the planet called Rasātala.

TEXT 31

ततोऽधस्तात्पाताले नागलोकपतयो वासुकिप्रमुखाः शङ्खकुलिकमहाशङ्ख-
श्वेतधनञ्जयधृतराष्ट्रशङ्खचूडकम्बलाश्वतरदेवदत्तादयो महाभोगिनो
महामर्षा निवसन्ति येषामु ह वै पञ्चसप्तदशशतसहस्रशीर्षाणां फणासु
विरचिता महामणयो रोचिष्णवः पातालविवरतिमिरनिकरं स्वरोचिषा
विधमन्ति ॥ ३१ ॥

tato 'dhastāt pātāle nāga-loka-patayo vāsuki-pramukhāḥ śaṅkha-kulika-mahāśaṅkha-śveta-dhanañjaya-dhṛtarāṣṭra-śaṅkhacūḍa-kambalāśvatara-devadattādayo mahā-bhogino mahāmarṣā nivasanti yeṣām u ha vai pañca-sapta-daśa-śata-sahasra-śīrṣāṇāṁ phaṇāsu viracitā mahā-maṇayo rociṣṇavaḥ pātāla-vivara-timira-nikaraṁ sva-rociṣā vidhamanti.

tataḥ adhastāt—beneath that planet Rasātala; *pātāle*—on the planet known as Pātāla; *nāga-loka-patayaḥ*—the masters of the Nāgalokas; *vāsuki*—by Vāsuki; *pramukhāḥ*—headed; *śaṅkha*—Śaṅkha; *kulika*—Kulika; *mahā-śaṅkha*—Mahāśaṅkha; *śveta*—Śveta; *dhanañjaya*—Dhanañjaya; *dhṛtarāṣṭra*—Dhṛtarāṣṭra; *śaṅkha-cūḍa*—Śaṅkhacūḍa; *kambala*—Kambala; *aśvatara*—Aśvatara; *deva-datta*—Devadatta; *ādayaḥ*—and so on; *mahā-bhoginaḥ*—very addicted to material happiness; *mahā-amarṣāḥ*—greatly envious by nature; *nivasanti*—live; *yeṣām*—of all of them; *u ha*—certainly; *vai*—indeed; *pañca*—five; *sapta*—seven; *daśa*—ten; *śata*—one hundred; *sahasra*—one thousand; *śīrṣāṇām*—of those possessing hoods; *phaṇāsu*—on those hoods; *viracitāḥ*—fixed; *mahā-maṇayaḥ*—very valuable gems; *rociṣṇavaḥ*—full of effulgence; *pātāla-vivara*—the caves of the Pātāla planetary system; *timira-nikaram*—the mass of darkness; *sva-rociṣā*—by the effulgence of their hoods; *vidhamanti*—disperse.

TRANSLATION

Beneath Rasātala is another planetary system, known as Pātāla or Nāgaloka, where there are many demoniac serpents, the masters of Nāgaloka, such as Śaṅkha, Kulika, Mahāśaṅkha, Śveta, Dhanañjaya, Dhṛtarāṣṭra, Śaṅkhacūḍa, Kambala, Aśvatara and Devadatta. The chief among them is Vāsuki. They are all extremely angry, and they have many, many hoods—some snakes five hoods, some seven, some ten, others a hundred and others a thousand. These hoods are bedecked with valuable gems, and the light emanating from the gems illuminates the entire planetary system of bila-svarga.

Thus end the Bhaktivedanta purports of the Fifth Canto, Twenty-fourth Chapter of Śrīmad-Bhāgavatam, *entitled "The Subterranean Heavenly Planets."*

CHAPTER TWENTY-FIVE

The Glories of Lord Ananta

In this chapter, Śukadeva Gosvāmī describes Ananta, the source of Lord Śiva. Lord Ananta, whose body is completely spiritual, resides at the root of the planet Pātāla. He always lives in the core of Lord Śiva's heart, and He helps him destroy the universe. Ananta instructs Lord Śiva how to destroy the cosmos, and thus He is sometimes called *tāmasī*, or "one who is in the mode of darkness." He is the original Deity of material consciousness, and because He attracts all living entities, He is sometimes known as Saṅkarṣaṇa. The entire material world is situated on the hoods of Lord Saṅkarṣaṇa. From His forehead He transmits to Lord Śiva the power to destroy this material world. Because Lord Saṅkarṣaṇa is an expansion of the Supreme Personality of Godhead, many devotees offer Him prayers, and in the planetary system of Pātāla, all the *suras*, *asuras*, Gandharvas, Vidyādharas and learned sages offer Him their respectful obeisances. The Lord talks with them in a sweet voice. His bodily construction is completely spiritual and very, very beautiful. Anyone who hears about Him from a proper spiritual master becomes free from all material conceptions of life. The entire material energy is working according to the plans of Anantadeva. Therefore we should regard Him as the root cause of the material creation. There is no end to His strength, and no one can fully describe Him, even with countless mouths. Therefore He is called Ananta (unlimited). Being very merciful toward all living entities, He has exhibited His spiritual body. Śukadeva Gosvāmī describes the glories of Anantadeva to Mahārāja Parīkṣit in this way.

TEXT 1

श्रीशुक उवाच

तस्य मूलदेशे त्रिंशद्योजनसहस्रान्तर आस्ते या वै कला भगवतस्तामसी समाख्यातानन्त इति सात्वतीया द्रष्टृदृश्ययोः सङ्कर्षणमहमित्यभिमानलक्षणं यं सङ्कर्षणमित्याचक्षते ॥ १ ॥

śrī-śuka uvāca
tasya mūla-deśe triṁśad-yojana-sahasrāntara āste yā vai kalā bhagavatas tāmasī samākhyātānanta iti sātvatīyā draṣṭṛ-dṛśyayoḥ saṅkarṣaṇam aham ity abhimāna-lakṣaṇaṁ yaṁ saṅkarṣaṇam ity ācakṣate.

śrī-śukaḥ uvāca—Śrī Śukadeva Gosvāmī said; *tasya*—of the planet Pātāla; *mūla-deśe*—in the region beneath the base; *triṁśat*—thirty; *yojana*—eight-mile units of measurement; *sahasra-antare*—at an interval of one thousand; *āste*—remains; *yā*—which; *vai*—indeed; *kalā*—an expansion of an expansion; *bhagavataḥ*—of the Supreme Personality of Godhead; *tāmasī*—related to darkness; *samākhyātā*—called; *anantaḥ*—Ananta; *iti*—thus; *sātvatīyāḥ*—the devotees; *draṣṭṛ-dṛśyayoḥ*—of matter and spirit; *saṅkarṣaṇam*—the drawing together; *aham*—I; *iti*—thus; *abhimāna*—by self-conception; *lakṣaṇam*—symptomized; *yam*—whom; *saṅkarṣaṇam*—Saṅkarṣaṇa; *iti*—thus; *ācakṣate*—learned scholars describe.

TRANSLATION

Śrī Śukadeva Gosvāmī said to Mahārāja Parīkṣit: My dear King, approximately 240,000 miles beneath the planet Pātāla lives another incarnation of the Supreme Personality of Godhead. He is the expansion of Lord Viṣṇu known as Lord Ananta or Lord Saṅkarṣaṇa. He is always in the transcendental position, but because He is worshiped by Lord Śiva, the deity of tamo-guṇa or darkness, He is sometimes called tāmasī. Lord Ananta is the predominating Deity of the material mode of ignorance as well as the false ego of all conditioned souls. When a conditioned living being thinks, "I am the enjoyer, and this world is meant to be enjoyed by me," this conception of life is dictated to him by Saṅkarṣaṇa. Thus the mundane conditioned soul thinks himself the Supreme Lord.

PURPORT

There is a class of men akin to Māyāvādī philosophers who misinterpret the *ahaṁ brahmāsmi* and *so 'ham* Vedic *mantras* to mean, "I am the Supreme Brahman" and "I am identical with the Lord." This kind of false conception, in which one thinks himself the supreme enjoyer, is a kind of illusion. It is described elsewhere in *Śrīmad-Bhāgavatam* (5.5.8): *janasya moho 'yam ahaṁ mameti.* As explained in the above verse, Lord Saṅkarṣaṇa is the predominating Deity of this false conception. Kṛṣṇa confirms this in *Bhagavad-gītā* (15.15):

sarvasya cāhaṁ hṛdi sanniviṣṭo
mattaḥ smṛtir jñānam apohanaṁ ca

"I am seated in everyone's heart, and from Me come remembrance, knowledge and forgetfulness." The Lord is situated in everyone's heart as Saṅkarṣaṇa, and when a demon thinks himself one with the Supreme Lord, the Lord keeps him in that darkness. Although such a demoniac living entity is only an insignificant part of the Supreme Lord, he forgets his true position and thinks he is the Supreme Lord. Because this forgetfulness is created by Saṅkarṣaṇa, He is sometimes called *tāmasī.* The name *tāmasī* does not indicate that He has a material body. He is always transcendental, but because He is the Supersoul of Lord Śiva, who must perform tamasic activities, Saṅkarṣaṇa is sometimes called *tāmasī.*

TEXT 2

यस्येदं क्षितिमण्डलं भगवतोऽनन्तमूर्तेः सहस्रशिरस एकस्मिन्नेव
शीर्षणि ध्रियमाणं सिद्धार्थ इव लक्ष्यते ॥ २ ॥

yasyedaṁ kṣiti-maṇḍalaṁ bhagavato 'nanta-mūrteḥ sahasra-śirasa
ekasminn eva śīrṣaṇi dhriyamāṇaṁ siddhārtha iva lakṣyate.

yasya—of whom; *idam*—this; *kṣiti-maṇḍalam*—universe; *bhagavataḥ*—of the Supreme Personality of Godhead; *ananta-mūrteḥ*—in the form of Anantadeva; *sahasra-śirasaḥ*—who has thousands of hoods; *ekasmin*—on one; *eva*—only; *śīrṣaṇi*—hood; *dhriyamāṇam*—is being sustained; *siddhārthaḥ iva*—and like a white mustard seed; *lakṣyate*—is seen.

TRANSLATION

Śukadeva Gosvāmī continued: This great universe, situated on one of Lord Anantadeva's thousands of hoods, appears just like a

white mustard seed. It is infinitesimal compared to the hood of Lord Ananta.

TEXT 3

यस्य ह वा इदं कालेनोपसञ्जिहीर्षतोऽमर्षविरचितरुचिर-
भ्रमद्भ्रुवोरन्तरेण साङ्कर्षणो नाम रुद्र एकादशव्यूहस्त्र्यक्षस्त्रिशिखं
शूलमुत्तम्भयन्नुदतिष्ठत् ॥ ३ ॥

*yasya ha vā idaṁ kālenopasañjihīrṣato 'marṣa-viracita-rucira-
bhramad-bhruvor antareṇa sāṅkarṣaṇo nāma rudra ekādaśa-vyūhas
try-akṣas tri-śikhaṁ śūlam uttambhayann udatiṣṭhat.*

yasya—of whom; *ha vā*—indeed; *idam*—this (material world); *kālena*—in due course of time; *upasañjihīrṣataḥ*—desiring to destroy; *amarṣa*—by anger; *viracita*—formed; *rucira*—very beautiful; *bhramat*—moving; *bhruvoḥ*—the two eyebrows; *antareṇa*—from between; *sāṅkarṣaṇaḥ nāma*—named Sāṅkarṣaṇa; *rudraḥ*—an incarnation of Lord Śiva; *ekādaśa-vyūhaḥ*—who has eleven expansions; *tri-akṣaḥ*—three eyes; *tri-śikham*—having three points; *śūlam*—a trident; *uttambhayan*—raising; *udatiṣṭhat*—arose.

TRANSLATION

At the time of devastation, when Lord Anantadeva desires to destroy the entire creation, He becomes slightly angry. Then from between His two eyebrows appears three-eyed Rudra, carrying a trident. This Rudra, who is known as Sāṅkarṣaṇa, is the embodiment of the eleven Rudras, or incarnations of Lord Śiva. He appears in order to devastate the entire creation.

PURPORT

In each creation, the living entities are given a chance to close their business as conditioned souls. When they misuse this opportunity and do not go back home, back to Godhead, Lord Saṅkarṣaṇa becomes angry. The eleven Rudras, expansions of Lord Śiva, come out of Lord Saṅkarṣaṇa's eyebrows due to His angry mood, and all of them together devastate the entire creation.

TEXT 4

यस्याङ्घ्रिकमलयुगलारुणविशदनखमणिषण्डमण्डलेष्वहिपतयः सह सात्वतर्षभैरेकान्तभक्तियोगेनावनमन्तः स्ववदनानि परिस्फुरत्कुण्डलप्रभामण्डितगण्डस्थलान्यतिमनोहराणि प्रमुदितमनसः खलु विलोकयन्ति ॥४॥

yasyāṅghri-kamala-yugalāruṇa-viśada-nakha-maṇi-ṣaṇḍa-maṇḍaleṣv ahi-patayaḥ saha sātvatarṣabhair ekānta-bhakti-yogenāvanamantaḥ sva-vadanāni parisphurat-kuṇḍala-prabhā-maṇḍita-gaṇḍa-sthalāny ati-manoharāṇi pramudita-manasaḥ khalu vilokayanti.

yasya—of whom; *aṅghri-kamala*—of lotus feet; *yugala*—of the pair; *aruṇa-viśada*—brilliant pink; *nakha*—of the nails; *maṇi-ṣaṇḍa*—like gems; *maṇḍaleṣu*—on the round surfaces; *ahi-patayaḥ*—the leaders of the snakes; *saha*—with; *sātvata-ṛṣabhaiḥ*—the best devotees; *ekānta-bhakti-yogena*—with unalloyed devotional service; *avanamantaḥ*—offering obeisances; *sva-vadanāni*—their own faces; *parisphurat*—glittering; *kuṇḍala*—of the earrings; *prabhā*—by the effulgence; *maṇḍita*—decorated; *gaṇḍa-sthalāni*—whose cheeks; *ati-manoharāṇi*—very beautiful; *pramudita-manasaḥ*—their minds refreshed; *khalu*—indeed; *vilokayanti*—they see.

TRANSLATION

The pink, transparent toenails on the Lord's lotus feet are exactly like valuable gems polished to a mirror finish. When the unalloyed devotees and the leaders of the snakes offer their obeisances to Lord Saṅkarṣaṇa with great devotion, they become very joyful upon seeing their own beautiful faces reflected in His toenails. Their cheeks are decorated with glittering earrings, and the beauty of their faces is extremely pleasing to see.

TEXT 5

यस्यैव हि नागराजकुमार्य आशिष आशासानाश्चार्वङ्गवलयविलसितविशद विपुलधवलसुभगरुचिरभुजरजतस्तम्भेष्वगुरुचन्दनकुङ्कुमपङ्कानुलेपेनावलिम्पमानास्तदभिमर्शनोन्मथितहृदयमकरध्वजावेशरुचिरललितस्मितास्तद-

नुरागमदमुदितमद विघूर्णितारुणकरुणावलोकनयनवदनारविन्दं सव्रीडं किल विलोकयन्ति ॥ ५ ॥

yasyaiva hi nāga-rāja-kumārya āśiṣa āśāsānāś cārv-aṅga-valaya-vilasita-viśada-vipula-dhavala-subhaga-rucira-bhuja-rajata-stambheṣv aguru-candana-kuṅkuma-paṅkānulepenāvalimpamānās tad-abhimarśanonmathita-hṛdaya-makara-dhvajāveśa-rucira-lalita-smitās tad-anurāgamada-mudita-mada-vighūrṇitāruṇa-karuṇāvaloka-nayana-vadanāravindaṁ savrīḍaṁ kila vilokayanti.

yasya—of whom; *eva*—certainly; *hi*—indeed; *nāga-rāja-kumāryaḥ*—the unmarried princesses of the serpent kings; *āśiṣaḥ*—blessings; *āśāsānāḥ*—hoping for; *cāru*—beautiful; *aṅga-valaya*—on the sphere of His body; *vilasita*—gleaming; *viśada*—spotless; *vipula*—long; *dhavala*—white; *subhaga*—indicating good fortune; *rucira*—beautiful; *bhuja*—on His arms; *rajata-stambheṣu*—like columns of silver; *aguru*—of aloe; *candana*—of sandalwood; *kuṅkuma*—of saffron; *paṅka*—from the pulp; *anulepena*—with an ointment; *avalimpamānāḥ*—smearing; *tat-abhimarśana*—by contact with His limbs; *unmathita*—agitated; *hṛdaya*—in their hearts; *makara-dhvaja*—of Cupid; *āveśa*—due to the entrance; *rucira*—very beautiful; *lalita*—delicate; *smitāḥ*—whose smiling; *tat*—of Him; *anurāga*—of attachment; *mada*—by the intoxication; *mudita*—delighted; *mada*—due to intoxication with kindness; *vighūrṇita*—rolling; *aruṇa*—pink; *karuṇa-avaloka*—glancing with kindness; *nayana*—eyes; *vadana*—and face; *aravindam*—like lotus flowers; *sa-vrīḍam*—with bashfulness; *kila*—indeed; *vilokayanti*—they see.

TRANSLATION

Lord Ananta's arms are attractively long, beautifully decorated with bangles and completely spiritual. They are white, and so they appear like silver columns. When the beautiful princesses of the serpent kings, hoping for the Lord's auspicious blessing, smear His arms with aguru pulp, sandalwood pulp and kuṅkuma, the touch of His limbs awakens lusty desires within them. Understanding their minds, the Lord looks at the princesses with a merciful

smile, and they become bashful, realizing that He knows their desires. Then they smile beautifully and look upon the Lord's lotus face, which is beautified by reddish eyes rolling slightly from intoxication and delighted by love for His devotees.

PURPORT

When males and females touch each other's bodies, their lusty desires naturally awaken. It appears from this verse that there are similar sensations in spiritual bodies. Both Lord Ananta and the women giving Him pleasure had spiritual bodies. Thus all sensations originally exist in the spiritual body. This is confirmed in the *Vedānta-sūtra: janmādy asya yataḥ.* Śrīla Viśvanātha Cakravartī Ṭhākura has commented in this connection that the word *ādi* means *ādi-rasa,* the original lusty feeling, which is born from the Supreme. However, spiritual lust and material lust are as completely different as gold and iron. Only one who is very highly elevated in spiritual realization can understand the lusty feelings exchanged between Rādhā and Kṛṣṇa, or between Kṛṣṇa and the damsels of Vraja. Therefore, unless one is very experienced and advanced in spiritual realization, he is forbidden to discuss the lusty feelings of Kṛṣṇa and the *gopīs.* However, if one is a sincere and pure devotee, the material lust in his heart is completely vanquished as he discusses the lusty feelings between the *gopīs* and Kṛṣṇa, and he makes quick progress in spiritual life.

TEXT 6

स एव भगवाननन्तो ऽनन्तगुणार्णव आदिदेव उपसंहृतामर्षरोषवेगो लोकानां स्वस्तय आस्ते ॥ ६ ॥

sa eva bhagavān ananto 'nanta-guṇārṇava ādi-deva upasaṁhṛtāmarṣa-roṣa-vego lokānāṁ svastaya āste.

saḥ—that; *eva*—certainly; *bhagavān*—the Supreme Personality of Godhead; *anantaḥ*—Anantadeva; *ananta-guṇa-arṇavaḥ*—the reservoir of unlimited transcendental qualities; *ādi-devaḥ*—the original Lord, or nondifferent from the original Supreme Personality of Godhead;

upasaṁhṛta—who has restrained; *amarṣa*—of His intolerance; *roṣa*—and wrath; *vegaḥ*—the force; *lokānām*—of all people on all planets; *svastaye*—for the welfare; *āste*—remains.

TRANSLATION

Lord Saṅkarṣaṇa is the ocean of unlimited spiritual qualities, and thus He is known as Anantadeva. He is nondifferent from the Supreme Personality of Godhead. For the welfare of all living entities within this material world, He resides in His abode, restraining His anger and intolerance.

PURPORT

Anantadeva's main mission is to dissolve this material creation, but He checks His anger and intolerance. This material world is created to give the conditioned souls another chance to go back home, back to Godhead, but most of them do not take advantage of this facility. After the creation, they again exercise their old propensity for lording it over the material world. These activities of the conditioned souls anger Anantadeva, and He desires to destroy the entire material world. Yet, because He is the Supreme Personality of Godhead, He is kind toward us and checks His anger and intolerance. Only at certain times does He express His anger and destroy the material world.

TEXT 7

ध्यायमानः सुरासुरोरगसिद्धगन्धर्वविद्याधरमुनिगणैरनवरतमदमुदितविकृत-
विह्वललोचनः सुललितमुखरिकामृतेनाप्यायमानः स्वपार्षदविबुधयूथपती-
नपरिम्लानरागनवतुलसिकामोदमध्वासवेन माद्यन्मधुकरव्रातमधुरगीतश्रियं
वैजयन्तीं स्वां वनमालां नीलवासा एककुण्डलो हलककुदि
कृतसुभगसुन्दरभुजो भगवान्माहेन्द्रो वारणेन्द्र इव काञ्चनीं
कक्षामुदारलीलो बिभर्ति ॥७॥

dhyāyamānaḥ surāsuroraga-siddha-gandharva-vidyādhara-muni-gaṇair anavarata-mada-mudita-vikṛta-vihvala-locanaḥ sulalita-

mukharikāmṛtenāpyāyamānaḥ sva-pārṣada-vibudha-yūtha-patīn aparimlāna-rāga-nava-tulasikāmoda-madhv-āsavena mādyan madhukara-vrāta-madhura-gīta-śriyaṁ vaijayantīṁ svāṁ vanamālāṁ nīla-vāsā eka-kuṇḍalo hala-kakudi kṛta-subhaga-sundara-bhujo bhagavān mahendro vāraṇendra iva kāñcanīṁ kakṣām udāra-līlo bibharti.

dhyāyamānaḥ—being meditated upon; *sura*—of demigods; *asura*—demons; *uraga*—snakes; *siddha*—inhabitants of Siddhaloka; *gandharva*—inhabitants of Gandharvaloka; *vidyādhara*—Vidyādharas; *muni*—and of great sages; *gaṇaiḥ*—by groups; *anavarata*—constantly; *mada-mudita*—delighted by intoxication; *vikṛta*—moving to and fro; *vihvala*—rolling; *locanaḥ*—whose eyes; *su-lalita*—excellently composed; *mukharika*—of speech; *amṛtena*—by the nectar; *āpyāyamānaḥ*—pleasing; *sva-pārṣada*—His own associates; *vibudha-yūtha-patīn*—the heads of the different groups of demigods; *aparimlāna*—never faded; *rāga*—whose luster; *nava*—ever fresh; *tulasikā*—of the *tulasī* blossoms; *āmoda*—by the fragrance; *madhu-āsavena*—and the honey; *mādyan*—being intoxicated; *madhukara-vrāta*—of the bees; *madhura-gīta*—by the sweet singing; *śrīyam*—which is made more beautiful; *vaijayantīm*—the garland named *vaijayantī; svām*—His own; *vanamālām*—garland; *nīla-vāsāḥ*—covered with blue garments; *eka-kuṇḍalaḥ*—wearing only one earring; *hala-kakudi*—on the handle of a plow; *kṛta*—placed; *subhaga*—auspicious; *sundara*—beautiful; *bhujaḥ*—hands; *bhagavān*—the Supreme Personality of Godhead; *mahā-indraḥ*—the King of heaven; *vāraṇa-indraḥ*—the elephant; *iva*—like; *kāñcanīm*—golden; *kakṣām*—belt; *udāra-līlaḥ*—engaged in transcendental pastimes; *bibharti*—wears.

TRANSLATION

Śukadeva Gosvāmī continued: The demigods, the demons, the Uragas [serpentine demigods], the Siddhas, the Gandharvas, the Vidyādharas and many highly elevated sages constantly offer prayers to the Lord. Because He is intoxicated, the Lord looks bewildered, and His eyes, appearing like flowers in full bloom, move to and fro. He pleases His personal associates, the heads of

the demigods, by the sweet vibrations emanating from His mouth. Dressed in bluish garments and wearing a single earring, He holds a plow on His back with His two beautiful and well-constructed hands. Appearing as white as the heavenly King Indra, He wears a golden belt around His waist and a vaijayantī garland of ever-fresh tulasī blossoms around His neck. Bees intoxicated by the honeylike fragrance of the tulasī flowers hum very sweetly around the garland, which thus becomes more and more beautiful. In this way, the Lord enjoys His very magnanimous pastimes.

TEXT 8

य एष एवमनुश्रुतो ध्यायमानो मुमुक्षूणामनादिकालकर्मवासनाग्रथितमविद्यामयं हृदयग्रन्थिं सत्त्वरजस्तमोमयमन्तर्हृदयं गत आशु निर्भिनत्ति तस्यानुभावान् भगवान् स्वायम्भुवो नारदः सह तुम्बुरुणा सभायां ब्रह्मणः संश्लोकयामास ॥ ८ ॥

ya eṣa evam anuśruto dhyāyamāno mumukṣūṇām anādi-kāla-karma-vāsanā-grathitam avidyāmayaṁ hṛdaya-granthiṁ sattva-rajas-tamomayam antar-hṛdayaṁ gata āśu nirbhinatti tasyānubhāvān bhagavān svāyambhuvo nāradaḥ saha tumburuṇā sabhāyāṁ brahmaṇaḥ saṁślokayām āsa.

yaḥ—who; *eṣaḥ*—this one; *evam*—thus; *anuśrutaḥ*—being heard from a bona fide spiritual master; *dhyāyamānaḥ*—being meditated upon; *mumukṣūṇām*—of persons desiring liberation from conditioned life; *anādi*—from immemorial; *kāla*—time; *karma-vāsanā*—by the desire for fruitive activities; *grathitam*—tied tightly; *avidyā-mayam*—consisting of the illusory energy; *hṛdaya-granthim*—the knot within the heart; *sattva-rajaḥ-tamaḥ-mayam*—made of the three modes of material nature; *antaḥ-hṛdayam*—in the core of the heart; *gataḥ*—situated; *āśu*—very soon; *nirbhinatti*—cuts; *tasya*—of Saṅkarṣaṇa; *anubhāvān*—the glories; *bhagavān*—the greatly powerful; *svāyambhuvaḥ*—the son of Lord Brahmā; *nāradaḥ*—the sage Nārada; *saha*—along with; *tumburuṇā*—the stringed instrument called a Tumburu; *sabhāyām*—in the assembly; *brahmaṇaḥ*—of Lord Brahmā; *saṁślokayām āsa*—described in verses.

TRANSLATION

If persons who are very serious about being liberated from material life hear the glories of Anantadeva from the mouth of a spiritual master in the chain of disciplic succession, and if they always meditate upon Saṅkarṣaṇa, the Lord enters the cores of their hearts, vanquishes all the dirty contamination of the material modes of nature, and cuts to pieces the hard knot within the heart, which has been tied tightly since time immemorial by the desire to dominate material nature through fruitive activities. Nārada Muni, the son of Lord Brahmā, always glorifies Anantadeva in his father's assembly. There he sings blissful verses of his own composition, accompanied by his stringed instrument [or a celestial singer] known as Tumburu.

PURPORT

None of these descriptions of Lord Anantadeva are imaginary. They are all transcendentally blissful and full of actual knowledge. However, unless one hears them directly from a bona fide spiritual master in the line of disciplic succession, one cannot understand them. This knowledge is delivered to Nārada by Lord Brahmā, and the great saint Nārada, along with his companion, Tumburu, distributes it all over the universe. Sometimes the Supreme Personality of Godhead is described as Uttamaśloka, one who is praised by beautiful poetry. Nārada composes various poems to glorify Lord Ananta, and therefore the word *saṁślokayām āsa* (praised by selected poetry) is used in this verse.

The Vaiṣṇavas in the Gauḍīya-sampradāya belong to the disciplic succession stemming from Lord Brahmā. Lord Brahmā is the spiritual master of Nārada, Nārada is the spiritual master of Vyāsadeva, and Vyāsadeva wrote the *Śrīmad-Bhāgavatam* as a commentary on the *Vedānta-sūtra.* Therefore all devotees in the Gauḍīya-sampradāya accept the activities of Lord Ananta related in the *Śrīmad-Bhāgavatam* as authentic, and they are thus benefited by going back home, back to

Godhead. The contamination in the heart of a conditioned soul is like a huge accumulation of garbage created by the three modes of material nature, especially the modes of *rajas* (passion) and *tamas* (ignorance). This contamination becomes manifest in the form of lusty desires and greed for material possessions. As confirmed herein, unless one receives transcendental knowledge in disciplic succession, there is no question of his becoming purified of this contamination.

TEXT 9

उत्पत्तिस्थितिलयहेतवोऽस्य कल्पाः
सत्त्वाद्याः प्रकृतिगुणा यदीक्षयाऽऽसन् ।
यद्रूपं ध्रुवमकृतं यदेकमात्मन्
नानाधात्कथमु ह वेद तस्य वर्त्म ॥ ९ ॥

utpatti-sthiti-laya-hetavo 'sya kalpāḥ
sattvādyāḥ prakṛti-guṇā yad-īkṣayāsan
yad-rūpaṁ dhruvam akṛtaṁ yad ekam ātman
nānādhāt katham u ha veda tasya vartma

utpatti—of creation; *sthiti*—maintenance; *laya*—and dissolution; *hetavaḥ*—the original causes; *asya*—of this material world; *kalpāḥ*—capable of acting; *sattva-ādyāḥ*—headed by the *sattva-guṇa; prakṛti-guṇāḥ*—the modes of material nature; *yat*—of whom; *īkṣayā*—by the glance; *āsan*—became; *yat-rūpam*—the form of whom; *dhruvam*—unlimited; *akṛtam*—uncreated; *yat*—who; *ekam*—one; *ātman*—in Himself; *nānā*—variously; *adhāt*—has manifested; *katham*—how; *u ha*—certainly; *veda*—can understand; *tasya*—His; *vartma*—path.

TRANSLATION

By His glance, the Supreme Personality of Godhead enables the modes of material nature to act as the causes of universal creation, maintenance and destruction. The Supreme Soul is unlimited and beginningless, and although He is one, He has manifested Himself in many forms. How can human society understand the ways of the Supreme?

PURPORT

From Vedic literature we learn that when the Supreme Lord glances (*sa aikṣata*) over the material energy, the three modes of material nature become manifest and create material variety. Before He glances over the material energy, there is no possibility of the creation, maintenance and annihilation of the material world. The Lord existed before the creation, and consequently He is eternal and unchanging. Therefore how can any human being, however great a scientist or philosopher he may be, understand the ways of the Supreme Personality of Godhead?

The following quotations from *Caitanya-bhāgavata* (*Ādi-khaṇḍa,* 1.48-52 and 1.58-69) tell of the glories of Lord Ananta:

ki brahmā, ki śiva, ki sanakādi 'kumāra'
vyāsa, śuka, nāradādi, 'bhakta' nāma yāṅra

"Lord Brahmā, Lord Śiva, the four Kumāras [Sanaka, Sanātana, Sanandana and Sanāt-kumāra], Vyāsadeva, Śukadeva Gosvāmī and Nārada are all pure devotees, eternal servants of the Lord.

sabāra pūjita śrī-ananta-mahāśaya
sahasra-vadana prabhu—bhakti-rasamaya

"Lord Śrī Ananta is worshiped by all the uncontaminated devotees mentioned above. He has thousands of hoods and is the reservoir of all devotional service.

ādideva, mahā-yogī, 'īśvara', 'vaiṣṇava'
mahimāra anta iṅhā nā jānaye saba

"Lord Ananta is the original person and the great mystic controller. At the same time, He is a servant of God, a Vaiṣṇava. Since there is no end to His glories, no one can understand Him fully.

sevana śunilā, ebe śuna ṭhākurāla
ātma-tantre yena-mate vaisena pātāla

"I have already spoken to you of His service to the Lord. Now hear how the self-sufficient Anantadeva exists in the lower planetary system of Pātāla.

śrī-nārada-gosāñi 'tumburu' kari' saṅge
se yaśa gāyena brahmā-sthāne śloka-vandhe

"Bearing his stringed instrument, the *tumburu,* on his shoulders, the great sage Nārada Muni always glorifies Lord Ananta. Nārada Muni has composed many transcendental verses in praise of the Lord."

sṛṣṭi, sthiti, pralaya, sattvādi yata guṇa
yāṅra dṛṣṭi-pāte haya, yāya punaḥ punaḥ

"Simply due to the glance of Lord Ananta, the three material modes of nature interact and produce creation, maintenance and annihilation. These modes of nature appear again and again.

advitīya-rūpa, satya anādi mahattva
tathāpi 'ananta' haya, ke bujhe se tattva?

"The Lord is glorified as one without a second and as the supreme truth who has no beginning. Therefore He is called Anantadeva [unlimited]. Who can understand Him?

śuddha-sattva-mūrti prabhu dharena karuṇāya
ye-vigrahe sabāra prakāśa sulīlāya

"His form is completely spiritual, and He manifests it only by His mercy. All the activities in this material world are conducted only in His form.

yāṅhāra taraṅga śikhi' siṁha mahāvalī
nija-jana-mano rañje hañā kutūhalī

"He is very powerful and always prepared to please His personal associates and devotees.

ye ananta-nāmera śravana-saṅkīrtane
ye-te mate kene nāhi bole ye-te jane

aśeṣa-janmera bandha chiṇḍe sei-kṣaṇe
ataeva vaiṣṇava nā chāḍe kabhu tāne

"If we simply try to engage in the congregational chanting of the glories of Lord Anantadeva, the dirty things in our hearts, accumulated during many births, will immediately be washed away. Therefore a Vaiṣṇava never loses an opportunity to glorify Anantadeva.

'śeṣa' ba-i saṁsārera gati nāhi āra
anantera nāme sarva-jīvera uddhāra

"Lord Anantadeva is known as Śeṣa [the unlimited end] because He ends our passage through this material world. Simply by chanting His glories, everyone can be liberated.

ananta pṛthivī-giri samudra-sahite
ye-prabhu dharena gire pālana karite

"On His head, Anantadeva sustains the entire universe, with its millions of planets containing enormous oceans and mountains.

sahasra phaṇāra eka-phaṇe 'bindu' yena
ananta vikrama, nā jānena, 'āche' hena

"He is so large and powerful that this universe rests on one of His hoods just like a drop of water. He does not know where it is.

sahasra-vadane kṛṣṇa-yaśa nirantara
gāite āchena ādi-deva mahī-dhara

"While bearing the universe on one of His hoods, Anantadeva chants the glories of Kṛṣṇa with each of His thousands of mouths.

gāyena ananta, śrī-yaśera nāhi anta
jaya-bhaṅga nāhi kāru, doṅhe—balavanta

"Although He has been chanting the glories of Lord Kṛṣṇa since time immemorial, He has still not come to their end.

adyāpiha 'śeṣa'-deva sahasra-śrī-mukhe
gāyena caitanya-yaśa anta nāhi dekhe

"To this very day, Lord Ananta continues to chant the glories of Śrī Caitanya Mahāprabhu, and still He finds no end to them."

TEXT 10

मूर्तिं नः पुरुकृपया बभार सत्त्वं
संशुद्धं सदसदिदं विभाति यत्र ।
यल्लीलां मृगपतिराददेऽनवद्या-
मादातुं स्वजनमनांस्युदारवीर्यः ॥१०॥

mūrtiṁ naḥ puru-kṛpayā babhāra sattvaṁ
saṁśuddhaṁ sad-asad idaṁ vibhāti tatra
yal-līlāṁ mṛga-patir ādade 'navadyām
ādātuṁ svajana-manāṁsy udāra-vīryaḥ

mūrtim—different forms of the Supreme Personality of Godhead; *naḥ*—unto us; *puru-kṛpayā*—because of great mercy; *babhāra*—exhibited; *sattvam*—existence; *saṁśuddham*—completely transcendental; *sat-asat idam*—this material manifestation of cause and effect; *vibhāti*—shines; *tatra*—in whom; *yat-līlām*—the pastimes of whom; *mṛga-patiḥ*—the master of all living beings, who is exactly like a lion (the master of all other animals); *ādade*—taught; *anavadyām*—without material contamination; *ādātum*—to conquer; *sva-jana-manāṁsi*—the minds of His devotees; *udāra-vīryaḥ*—who is most liberal and powerful.

TRANSLATION

This manifestation of subtle and gross matter exists within the Supreme Personality of Godhead. Out of causeless mercy toward His devotees, He exhibits various forms, which are all transcendental. The Supreme Lord is most liberal, and He possesses all mystic power. To conquer the minds of His devotees and give pleasure to their hearts, He appears in different incarnations and manifests many pastimes.

PURPORT

Śrīla Jīva Gosvāmī has translated this verse as follows. "The Supreme Personality of Godhead is the cause of all causes. It is by His will that gross and subtle ingredients interact. He appears in various incarnations just to please the hearts of His pure devotees." For example, the Supreme Lord appeared in the transcendental incarnation of Lord Varāha (the boar) just to please His devotees by lifting the planet earth from the Garbhodaka Ocean.

TEXT 11

यन्नाम श्रुतमनुकीर्तयेदकस्मा-
दार्तो वा यदि पतितः प्रलम्भनाद्वा ।
हन्त्यंहः सपदि नृणामशेषमन्यं
कं शेषाद्भगवत आश्रयेन्मुमुक्षुः ॥११॥

yan-nāma śrutam anukīrtayed akasmād
ārto vā yadi patitaḥ pralambhanād vā
hanty aṁhaḥ sapadi nṛṇām aśeṣam anyaṁ
kaṁ śeṣād bhagavata āśrayen mumukṣuḥ

yat—of whom; *nāma*—the holy name; *śrutam*—heard; *anukīrtayet*—may chant or repeat; *akasmāt*—by accident; *ārtaḥ*—a distressed person; *vā*—or; *yadi*—if; *patitaḥ*—a fallen person; *pralambhanāt*—out of joking; *vā*—or; *hanti*—destroys; *aṁhaḥ*—sinful; *sapadi*—that instant; *nṛṇām*—of human society; *aśeṣam*—unlimited; *anyam*—of other; *kam*—what; *śeṣāt*—than Lord Śeṣa; *bhagavataḥ*—the Supreme Personality of Godhead; *āśrayet*—should take shelter of; *mumukṣuḥ*—anyone desiring liberation.

TRANSLATION

Even if he be distressed or degraded, any person who chants the holy name of the Lord, having heard it from a bona fide spiritual master, is immediately purified. Even if he chants the Lord's name jokingly or by chance, he and anyone who hears him are freed from all sins. Therefore how can anyone seeking disentanglement from the material clutches avoid chanting the name of Lord Śeṣa? Of whom else should one take shelter?

TEXT 12

मूर्धन्यर्पितमणुवत्सहस्रमूर्ध्नो
भूगोलं सगिरिसरित्समुद्रसत्त्वम् ।
आनन्त्यादनिमितविक्रमस्य भूम्नः
को वीर्याण्यधिगणयेत्सहस्रजिह्वः ॥१२॥

mūrdhany arpitam aṇuvat sahasra-mūrdhno
bhū-golaṁ sagiri-sarit-samudra-sattvam
ānantyād animita-vikramasya bhūmnaḥ
ko vīryāṇy adhi gaṇayet sahasra-jihvaḥ

mūrdhani—on a hood or head; *arpitam*—fixed; *aṇu-vat*—just like an atom; *sahasra-mūrdhnaḥ*—of Ananta, who has thousands of hoods; *bhū-golam*—this universe; *sa-giri-sarit-samudra-sattvam*—with many mountains, trees, oceans and living entities; *ānantyāt*—due to being unlimited; *animita-vikramasya*—whose power is immeasurable; *bhūmnaḥ*—the Supreme Lord; *kaḥ*—who; *vīryāṇi*—potencies; *adhi*—indeed; *gaṇayet*—can count; *sahasra-jihvaḥ*—although having thousands of tongues.

TRANSLATION

Because the Lord is unlimited, no one can estimate His power. This entire universe, filled with its many great mountains, rivers, oceans, trees and living entities, is resting just like an atom on one of His many thousands of hoods. Is there anyone, even with thousands of tongues, who can describe His glories?

TEXT 13

एवम्प्रभावो भगवाननन्तो
दुरन्तवीर्योरुगुणानुभावः ।
मूले रसायाः स्थित आत्मतन्त्रो
यो लीलया क्ष्मां स्थितये बिभर्ति ॥१३॥

evam-prabhāvo bhagavān ananto
duranta-vīryoru-guṇānubhāvaḥ

mūle rasāyāḥ sthita ātma-tantro
yo līlayā kṣmāṁ sthitaye bibharti

evam-prabhāvaḥ—who is so powerful; *bhagavān*—the Supreme Personality of Godhead; *anantaḥ*—Ananta; *duranta-vīrya*—insurmountable prowess; *uru*—great; *guṇa-anubhāvaḥ*—possessing transcendental qualities and glories; *mūle*—at the base; *rasāyāḥ*—of the lower planetary systems; *sthitaḥ*—existing; *ātma-tantraḥ*—completely self-sufficient; *yaḥ*—who; *līlayā*—easily; *kṣmām*—the universe; *sthitaye*—for its maintenance; *bibharti*—sustains.

TRANSLATION

There is no end to the great and glorious qualities of that powerful Lord Anantadeva. Indeed, His prowess is unlimited. Though self-sufficient, He Himself is the support of everything. He resides beneath the lower planetary systems and easily sustains the entire universe.

TEXT 14

एता ह्येवेह नृभिरुपगन्तव्या गतयो यथाकर्मविनिर्मिता यथोपदेशमनुवर्णिताः कामान् कामयमानैः ॥१४॥

etā hy eveha nṛbhir upagantavyā gatayo yathā-karma-vinirmitā yathopadeśam anuvarṇitāḥ kāmān kāmayamānaiḥ.

etāḥ—all these; *hi*—indeed; *eva*—certainly; *iha*—in this universe; *nṛbhiḥ*—by all living entities; *upagantavyāḥ*—achievable; *gatayaḥ*—destinations; *yathā-karma*—according to one's past activities; *vinirmitāḥ*—created; *yathā-upadeśam*—as instructed; *anuvarṇitāḥ*—described accordingly; *kāmān*—material enjoyment; *kāmayamānaiḥ*—by those who are desiring.

TRANSLATION

My dear King, as I heard of it from my spiritual master, I have fully described to you the creation of this material world according to the fruitive activities and desires of the conditioned souls.

Those conditioned souls, who are full of material desires, achieve various situations in different planetary systems, and in this way they live within this material creation.

PURPORT

In this regard, Śrīla Bhaktivinoda Ṭhākura sings,

anādi karama-phale,
paḍi' bhavārṇava-jale, taribāre nā dekhi upāya

"My Lord, I do not know when I commenced my material life, but I can certainly experience that I have fallen in the deep ocean of nescience. Now I can also see that there is no other way to get out of it than to take shelter of Your lotus feet." Similarly, Śrī Caitanya Mahāprabhu offers the following prayer:

ayi nanda-tanuja kiṅkaraṁ
patitaṁ māṁ viṣame bhavāmbudhau
kṛpayā tava pāda-paṅkaja-
sthita-dhūlī-sadṛśaṁ vicintaya

"My dear Lord, son of Nanda Mahārāja, I am Your eternal servant. Somehow or other, I have fallen into this ocean of nescience. Kindly, therefore, save me from this horrible condition of materialistic life."

TEXT 15

एतावतीर्हि राजन् पुंसः प्रवृत्तिलक्षणस्य धर्मस्य विपाकगतय उच्चावचा विसदृशा यथाप्रश्नं व्याचख्ये किमन्यत्कथयाम इति ॥ १५ ॥

etāvatīr hi rājan puṁsaḥ pravṛtti-lakṣaṇasya dharmasya vipāka-gataya uccāvacā visadṛśā yathā-praśnaṁ vyācakhye kim anyat kathayāma iti.

etāvatīḥ—of such a kind; *hi*—certainly; *rājan*—O King; *puṁsaḥ*—of the human being; *pravṛtti-lakṣaṇasya*—symptomized by inclinations; *dharmasya*—of the execution of duties; *vipāka-gatayaḥ*—the resultant destinations; *ucca-avacāḥ*—high and low; *visadṛśāḥ*—different; *yathā-praśnam*—as you inquired; *vyācakhye*—I have described; *kim anyat*—what else; *kathayāma*—shall I speak; *iti*—thus.

TRANSLATION

My dear King, I have thus described how people generally act according to their different desires and, as a result, get different types of bodies in higher or lower planets. You inquired of these things from me, and I have explained to you whatever I have heard from authorities. What shall I speak of now?

Thus end the Bhaktivedanta purports of the Fifth Canto, Twenty-fifth Chapter of the Śrīmad-Bhāgavatam, *entitled "The Glories of Lord Ananta."*

CHAPTER TWENTY-SIX

A Description of the Hellish Planets

The Twenty-sixth Chapter describes how a sinful man goes to different hells, where he is punished in various ways by the assistants of Yamarāja. As stated in the *Bhagavad-gītā* (3.27):

prakṛteḥ kriyamāṇāni
guṇaiḥ karmāṇi sarvaśaḥ
ahaṅkāra-vimūḍhātmā
kartāham iti manyate

"The bewildered spirit soul, under the influence of the three modes of material nature, thinks himself to be the doer of activities, which are in actuality carried out by nature." The foolish person thinks he is independent of any law. He thinks there is no God or regulative principle and that he can do whatever he likes. Thus he engages in different sinful activities, and as a result, he is put into different hellish conditions life after life, to be punished by the laws of nature. The basic principle of his suffering is that he foolishly thinks himself independent, although he is strictly under the control of the laws of material nature. These laws act due to the influence of the three modes of nature, and therefore each human being also works under three different types of influence. According to how he acts, he suffers different reactions in his next life or in this life. Religious persons act differently from atheists, and therefore they suffer different reactions.

Śukadeva Gosvāmī describes the following twenty-eight hells: Tāmisra, Andhatāmisra, Raurava, Mahāraurava, Kumbhīpāka, Kālasūtra, Asi-patravana, Sūkaramukha, Andhakūpa, Kṛmibhojana, Sandaṁśa, Taptasūrmi, Vajrakaṇṭaka-śālmalī, Vaitaraṇī, Pūyoda, Prāṇarodha, Viśasana, Lālābhakṣa, Sārameyādana, Avīci, Ayaḥpāna, Kṣārakardama, Rakṣogaṇa-bhojana, Śūlaprota, Dandaśūka, Avaṭa-nirodhana, Paryāvartana and Sūcīmukha.

A person who steals another's money, wife or possessions is put into the hell known as Tāmisra. A man who tricks someone and enjoys his wife is put into the extremely hellish condition known as Andhatāmisra. A foolish person absorbed in the bodily concept of life, who on the basis of this principle maintains himself or his wife and children by committing violence against other living entities, is put into the hell known as Raurava. There the animals he killed take birth as creatures called *rurus* and cause great suffering for him. Those who kill different animals and birds and then cook them are put by the agents of Yamarāja into the hell known as Kumbhīpāka, where they are boiled in oil. A person who kills a *brāhmaṇa* is put into the hell known as Kālasūtra, where the land, perfectly level and made of copper, is as hot as an oven. The killer of a *brāhmaṇa* burns in that land for many years. One who does not follow scriptural injunctions but who does everything whimsically or follows some rascal is put into the hell known as Asi-patravana. A government official who poorly administers justice, or who punishes an innocent man, is taken by the assistants of Yamarāja to the hell known as Sūkaramukha, where he is mercilessly beaten.

God has given advanced consciousness to the human being. Therefore he can feel the suffering and happiness of other living beings. The human being bereft of his conscience, however, is prone to cause suffering for other living beings. The assistants of Yamarāja put such a person into the hell known as Andhakūpa, where he receives proper punishment from his victims. Any person who does not receive or feed a guest properly but who personally enjoys eating is put into the hell known as Kṛmibhojana. There an unlimited number of worms and insects continuously bite him.

A thief is put into the hell known as Sandaṁśa. A person who has sexual relations with a woman who is not to be enjoyed is put into the hell known as Taptasūrmi. A person who enjoys sexual relations with animals is put into the hell known as Vajrakaṇṭaka-śālamalī. A person born into an aristocratic or highly placed family but who does not act accordingly is put into the hellish trench of blood, pus and urine called the Vaitaraṇī River. One who lives like an animal is put into the hell called Pūyoda. A person who mercilessly kills animals in the forest without sanction is put into the hell called Prāṇarodha. A person who kills animals in the name of religious sacrifice is put into the hell named Viśasana. A man who forces his wife to drink his semen is put into the hell called Lālābhakṣa. One who sets a fire or administers poison to kill someone is put into the hell known as Sārameyādana. A man who earns his livelihood by bearing false witness is put into the hell known as Avīci.

A person addicted to drinking wine is put into the hell named Ayaḥpāna. One who violates etiquette by not showing proper respect to superiors is put into the hell known as Kṣārakardama. A person who sacrifices human beings to Bhairava is put into the hell called Rakṣogaṇa-bhojana. A person who kills pet animals is put into the hell called Śūlaprota. A person who gives trouble to others is put into the hell known as Dandaśūka. One who imprisons a living entity within a cave is put into the hell known as Avaṭa-nirodhana. A person who shows unwarranted wrath toward a guest in his house is put into the hell called Paryāvartana. A person maddened by possessing riches and thus deeply absorbed in thinking of how to collect money is put into the hell known as Sūcīmukha.

After describing the hellish planets, Śukadeva Gosvāmī describes how pious persons are elevated to the highest planetary system, where the demigods live, and how they then come back again to this earth when the results of their pious activities are finished. Finally he describes the universal form of the Lord and glorifies the Lord's activities.

TEXT 1

राजोवाच
महर्ष एतद्वैचित्र्यं लोकस्य कथमिति ॥ १ ॥

rājovāca
maharṣa etad vaicitryaṁ lokasya katham iti.

rājā uvāca—the King said; *maharṣe*—O great saint (Śukadeva Gosvāmī); *etat*—this; *vaicitryam*—variegatedness; *lokasya*—of the living entities; *katham*—how; *iti*—thus.

TRANSLATION

King Parīkṣit inquired from Śukadeva Gosvāmī: My dear sir, why are the living entities put into different material situations? Kindly explain this to me.

PURPORT

Śrīla Viśvanātha Cakravartī Ṭhākura explains that the different hellish planets within this universe are held slightly above the Garbhodaka Ocean and remain situated there. This chapter describes how all sinful persons go to these hellish planets and how they are punished there by the assistants of Yamarāja. Different individuals with different bodily features enjoy or suffer various reactions according to their past deeds.

TEXT 2

ऋषिरुवाच

त्रिगुणत्वात्कर्तुः श्रद्धया कर्मगतयः पृथग्विधाः सर्वा एव सर्वस्य तारतम्येन भवन्ति ॥ २ ॥

ṛṣir uvāca

tri-guṇatvāt kartuḥ śraddhayā karma-gatayaḥ pṛthag-vidhāḥ sarvā eva sarvasya tāratamyena bhavanti.

ṛṣiḥ uvāca—the great saint (Śukadeva Gosvāmī) said; *tri-guṇatvāt*—because of the three modes of material nature; *kartuḥ*—of the worker; *śraddhayā*—because of the attitudes; *karma-gatayaḥ*—destinations resulting from activity; *pṛthak*—different; *vidhāḥ*—varieties; *sarvāḥ*—all; *eva*—thus; *sarvasya*—of all of them; *tāratamyena*—in different degrees; *bhavanti*—become possible.

TRANSLATION

The great sage Śukadeva Gosvāmī said: My dear King, in this material world there are three kinds of activities—those in the mode of goodness, the mode of passion and the mode of ignorance. Because all people are influenced by the three modes of

material nature, the results of their activities are also divided into three. One who acts in the mode of goodness is religious and happy, one who acts in passion achieves mixed misery and happiness, and one who acts under the influence of ignorance is always unhappy and lives like an animal. Because of the varying degrees to which the living entities are influenced by the different modes of nature, their destinations are also of different varieties.

TEXT 3

अथेदानीं प्रतिषिद्धलक्षणस्याधर्मस्य तथैव कर्तुः श्रद्धाया वैसादृश्यात्कर्मफलं विसदृशं भवति या ह्यनाद्यविद्यया कृतकामानां तत्परिणामलक्षणाः सृतयः सहस्रशः प्रवृत्तास्तासां प्राचुर्येणानुवर्णयिष्यामः ॥३॥

athedānīṁ pratiṣiddha-lakṣaṇasyādharmasya tathaiva kartuḥ
śraddhāyā vaisādṛśyāt karma-phalaṁ visadṛśaṁ bhavati yā hy anādy-
avidyayā kṛta-kāmānāṁ tat-pariṇāma-lakṣaṇāḥ sṛtayaḥ sahasraśaḥ
pravṛttās tāsāṁ prācuryeṇānuvarṇayiṣyāmaḥ.

atha—thus; *idānīm*—now; *pratiṣiddha*—by what is forbidden; *lakṣaṇasya*—symptomized; *adharmasya*—of impious activities; *tathā*—so also; *eva*—certainly; *kartuḥ*—of the performer; *śraddhāyāḥ*—of faith; *vaisādṛśyāt*—by the difference; *karma-phalam*—the reaction of fruitive activities; *visadṛśam*—different; *bhavati*—is; *yā*—which; *hi*—indeed; *anādi*—from time immemorial; *avidyayā*—by ignorance; *kṛta*—performed; *kāmānām*—of persons possessing many lusty desires; *tat-pariṇāma-lakṣaṇāḥ*—the symptoms of the results of such impious desires; *sṛtayaḥ*—hellish conditions of life; *sahasraśaḥ*—by thousands upon thousands; *pravṛttāḥ*—resulted; *tāsām*—them; *prācuryeṇa*—very widely; *anuvarṇayiṣyāmaḥ*—I shall explain.

TRANSLATION

Just as by executing various pious activities one achieves different positions in heavenly life, by acting impiously one

achieves different positions in hellish life. Those who are activated by the material mode of ignorance engage in impious activities, and according to the extent of their ignorance, they are placed in different grades of hellish life. If one acts in the mode of ignorance because of madness, his resulting misery is the least severe. One who acts impiously but knows the distinction between pious and impious activities is placed in a hell of intermediate severity. And for one who acts impiously and ignorantly because of atheism, the resultant hellish life is the worst. Because of ignorance, every living entity has been carried by various desires into thousands of different hellish planets since time immemorial. I shall try to describe them as far as possible.

TEXT 4

राजोवाच

नरका नाम भगवन् किं देशविशेषा अथवा बहिस्त्रिलोक्या आहोस्विदन्तराल इति ॥ ४ ॥

rājovāca

narakā nāma bhagavan kiṁ deśa-viśeṣā athavā bahis tri-lokyā āhosvid antarāla iti.

rājā uvāca—the King said; *narakāḥ*—the hellish regions; *nāma*—named; *bhagavan*—O my Lord; *kim*—whether; *deśa-viśeṣāḥ*—a particular country; *athavā*—or; *bahiḥ*—outside; *tri-lokyāḥ*—the three worlds (the universe); *āhosvit*—or; *antarāle*—in the intermediate spaces within the universe; *iti*—thus.

TRANSLATION

King Parīkṣit inquired from Śukadeva Gosvāmī: My dear lord, are the hellish regions outside the universe, within the covering of the universe, or in different places on this planet?

TEXT 5

ऋषिरुवाच

अन्तराल एव त्रिजगत्यास्तु दिशि दक्षिणस्यामधस्ताद्भूमेरुपरिष्टाच्च जलाद्यस्यामग्निष्वात्तादयः पितृगणा दिशि स्वानां गोत्राणां परमेण समाधिना सत्या एवाशिष आशासाना निवसन्ति ॥ ५ ॥

ṛṣir uvāca
antarāla eva tri-jagatyās tu diśi dakṣiṇasyām adhastād bhūmer upariṣṭāc ca jalād yasyām agniṣvāttādayaḥ pitṛ-gaṇā diśi svānāṁ gotrāṇāṁ paramena samādhinā satyā evāśiṣa āśāsānā nivasanti.

ṛṣiḥ uvāca—the great sage replied; *antarāle*—in the intermediate space; *eva*—certainly; *tri-jagatyāḥ*—of the three worlds; *tu*—but; *diśi*—in the direction; *dakṣiṇasyām*—southern; *adhastāt*—beneath; *bhūmeḥ*—on the earth; *upariṣṭāt*—a little above; *ca*—and; *jalāt*—the Garbhodaka Ocean; *yasyām*—in which; *agniṣvāttā-ādayaḥ*—headed by Agniṣvāttā; *pitṛ-gaṇāḥ*—the persons known as *pitās; diśi*—direction; *svānām*—their own; *gotrāṇām*—of the families; *paramena*—with great; *samādhinā*—absorption in thoughts of the Lord; *satyāḥ*—in truth; *eva*—certainly; *āśiṣaḥ*—blessings; *āśāsānāḥ*—desiring; *nivasanti*—they live.

TRANSLATION

The great sage Śukadeva Gosvāmī answered: All the hellish planets are situated in the intermediate space between the three worlds and the Garbhodaka Ocean. They lie on the southern side of the universe, beneath Bhū-maṇḍala, and slightly above the water of the Garbhodaka Ocean. Pitṛloka is also located in this region between the Garbhodaka Ocean and the lower planetary systems. All the residents of Pitṛloka, headed by Agniṣvāttā, meditate in great samādhi on the Supreme Personality of Godhead and always wish their families well.

PURPORT

As previously explained, below our planetary system are seven lower planetary systems, the lowest of which is called Pātālaloka. Beneath

Pātālaloka are other planets, known as Narakaloka, or the hellish planets. At the bottom of the universe lies the Garbhodaka Ocean. Therefore the hellish planets lie between Pātālaloka and the Garbhodaka Ocean.

TEXT 6

यत्र ह वाव भगवान् पितृराजो वैवस्वतः स्वविषयं प्रापितेषु स्वपुरुषैर्जन्तुषु सम्परेतेषु यथाकर्मावद्यं दोषमेवानुल्लङ्घितभगवच्छासनः सगणो दमं धारयति ॥ ६ ॥

yatra ha vāva bhagavān pitṛ-rājo vaivasvataḥ sva-viṣayaṁ prāpiteṣu sva-puruṣair jantuṣu sampareteṣu yathā-karmāvadyaṁ doṣam evānullaṅghita-bhagavac-chāsanaḥ sagaṇo damaṁ dhārayati.

yatra—where; *ha vāva*—indeed; *bhagavān*—the most powerful; *pitṛ-rājaḥ*—Yamarāja, the king of the *pitās; vaivasvataḥ*—the son of the sun-god; *sva-viṣayam*—his own kingdom; *prāpiteṣu*—when caused to reach; *sva-puruṣaiḥ*—by his own messengers; *jantuṣu*—the human beings; *sampareteṣu*—dead; *yathā-karma-avadyam*—according to how much they have violated the rules and regulations of conditional life; *doṣam*—the fault; *eva*—certainly; *anullaṅghita-bhagavat-śāsanaḥ*—who never oversteps the Supreme Personality of Godhead's order; *sa-gaṇaḥ*—along with his followers; *damam*—punishment; *dhārayati*—executes.

TRANSLATION

The King of the pitās is Yamarāja, the very powerful son of the sun-god. He resides in Pitṛloka with his personal assistants and, while abiding by the rules and regulations set down by the Supreme Lord, has his agents, the Yamadūtas, bring all the sinful men to him immediately upon their death. After bringing them within his jurisdiction, he properly judges them according to their specific sinful activities and sends them to one of the many hellish planets for suitable punishments.

PURPORT

Yamarāja is not a fictitious or mythological character; he has his own abode, Pitṛloka, of which he is king. Agnostics may not believe in hell, but Śukadeva Gosvāmī affirms the existence of the Naraka planets, which lie between the Garbhodaka Ocean and Pātālaloka. Yamarāja is appointed by the Supreme Personality of Godhead to see that the human beings do not violate His rules and regulations. As confirmed in *Bhagavad-gītā* (4.17):

karmaṇo hy api boddhavyaṁ
boddhavyaṁ ca vikarmaṇaḥ
akarmaṇaś ca boddhavyaṁ
gahanā karmaṇo gatiḥ

"The intricacies of action are very hard to understand. Therefore one should know properly what action is, what forbidden action is, and what inaction is." One should understand the nature of *karma, vikarma* and *akarma,* and one must act accordingly. This is the law of the Supreme Personality of Godhead. The conditioned souls, who have come to this material world for sense gratification, are allowed to enjoy their senses under certain regulative principles. If they violate these regulations, they are judged and punished by Yamarāja. He brings them to the hellish planets and properly chastises them to bring them back to Kṛṣṇa consciousness. By the influence of *māyā,* however, the conditioned souls remain infatuated with the mode of ignorance. Thus in spite of repeated punishment by Yamarāja, they do not come to their senses, but continue to live within the material condition, committing sinful activities again and again.

TEXT 7

तत्र हैके नरकानेकविंशतिं गणयन्ति अथ तांस्ते राजन्नामरूपलक्षणतो-
ऽनुक्रमिष्यामस्तामिस्रोऽन्धतामिस्रो रौरवो महारौरवः कुम्भीपाकः कालसूत्रमसि-
पत्रवनं सूकरमुखमन्धकूपः कृमिभोजनः सन्दंशस्तप्तसूर्मिर्वज्रकण्टकशाल्मली

वैतरणी पूयोदः प्राणरोधो विशसनं लालाभक्षः सारमेयादनमवीचिरयःपा-
नमिति । किञ्च क्षारकर्दमो रक्षोगणभोजनः शूलप्रोतो दन्दशूकोऽवटनि-
रोधनः पर्यावर्तनः सूचीमुखमित्यष्टाविंशतिर्नरका विविधयातनाभूमयः॥७॥

tatra haike narakān eka-viṁśatiṁ gaṇayanti atha tāṁs te rājan nāma-rūpa-lakṣaṇato 'nukramiṣyāmas tāmisro 'ndhatāmisro rauravo mahārauravaḥ kumbhīpākaḥ kālasūtram asipatravanaṁ sūkaramukham andhakūpaḥ kṛmibhojanaḥ sandaṁśas taptasūrmir vajrakaṇṭaka-śālmalī vaitaraṇī pūyodaḥ prāṇarodho viśasanaṁ lālābhakṣaḥ sārameyādanam avīcir ayaḥpānam iti. kiñca kṣārakardamo rakṣogaṇa-bhojanaḥ śūlaproto dandaśūko 'vaṭa-nirodhanaḥ paryāvartanaḥ sūcīmukham ity aṣṭā-viṁśatir narakā vividha-yātanā-bhūmayaḥ.

tatra—there; *ha*—certainly; *eke*—some; *narakān*—the hellish planets; *eka-viṁśatim*—twenty-one; *gaṇayanti*—count; *atha*—therefore; *tān*—them; *te*—unto you; *rājan*—O King; *nāma-rūpa-lakṣaṇataḥ*—according to their names, forms and symptoms; *anukramiṣyāmaḥ*—we shall outline one after another; *tāmisraḥ*—Tāmisra; *andha-tāmisraḥ*—Andhatāmisra; *rauravaḥ*—Raurava; *mahā-rauravaḥ*—Mahāraurava; *kumbhī-pākaḥ*—Kumbhīpāka; *kāla-sūtram*—Kālasūtra; *asi-patravanam*—Asi-patravana; *sūkara-mukham*—Sūkaramukha; *andha-kūpaḥ*—Andhakūpa; *kṛmi-bhojanaḥ*—Kṛmibhojana; *sandaṁśaḥ*—Sandaṁśa; *tapta-sūrmiḥ*—Taptasūrmi; *vajra-kaṇṭaka-śālmalī*—Vajrakaṇṭaka-śālmalī; *vaitaraṇī*—Vaitaraṇī; *pūyodaḥ*—Pūyoda; *prāṇa-rodhaḥ*—Prāṇarodha; *viśasanam*—Viśasana; *lālā-bhakṣaḥ*—Lālābhakṣa; *sārameyādanam*—Sārameyādana; *avīciḥ*—Avīci; *ayaḥ-pānam*—Ayaḥpāna; *iti*—thus; *kiñca*—some more; *kṣāra-kardamaḥ*—Kṣārakardama; *rakṣaḥ-gaṇa-bhojanaḥ*—Rakṣogaṇa-bhojana; *śūla-protaḥ*—Śūlaprota; *danda-śūkaḥ*—Dandaśūka; *avaṭa-nirodhanaḥ*—Avaṭa-nirodhana; *paryāvartanaḥ*—Paryāvartana; *sūcī-mukham*—Sūcīmukha; *iti*—in this way; *aṣṭā-viṁśatiḥ*—twenty-eight; *narakāḥ*—hellish planets; *vividha*—various; *yātanā-bhūmayaḥ*—lands of suffering in hellish conditions.

TRANSLATION

Some authorities say that there is a total of twenty-one hellish planets, and some say twenty-eight. My dear King, I shall outline all of them according to their names, forms and symptoms. The names of the different hells are as follows: Tāmisra, Andhatāmisra, Raurava, Mahāraurava, Kumbhīpāka, Kālasūtra, Asipatravana, Sūkaramukha, Andhakūpa, Kṛmibhojana, Sandaṁśa, Taptasūrmi, Vajrakaṇṭaka-śālmalī, Vaitaraṇī, Pūyoda, Prāṇarodha, Viśasana, Lālābhakṣa, Sārameyādana, Avīci, Ayaḥpāna, Kṣārakardama, Rakṣogaṇa-bhojana, Śūlaprota, Dandaśūka, Avaṭa-nirodhana, Paryāvartana and Sūcīmukha. All these planets are meant for punishing the living entities.

TEXT 8

तत्र यस्तु परवित्तापत्यकलत्राण्यपहरति स हि कालपाशबद्धो यमपुरुषैरतिभयानकैस्तामिस्रे नरके बलान्निपात्यते अनशनानुदपानदण्डताडनसंतर्जनादिभिर्यातनाभिर्यात्यमानो जन्तुर्यत्र कश्मलमासादित एकदैव मूर्च्छामुपयाति तामिस्रप्राये ॥८॥

tatra yas tu para-vittāpatya-kalatrāṇy apaharati sa hi kāla-pāśa-baddho yama-puruṣair ati-bhayānakais tāmisre narake balān nipātyate anaśanānudapāna-daṇḍa-tāḍana-santarjanādibhir yātanābhir yātyamāno jantur yatra kaśmalam āsādita ekadaiva mūrcchām upayāti tāmisra-prāye.

tatra—in those hellish planets; *yaḥ*—a person who; *tu*—but; *para-vitta-apatya-kalatrāṇi*—the money, wife and children of another; *apaharati*—takes away; *saḥ*—that person; *hi*—certainly; *kāla-pāśa-baddhaḥ*—being bound by the ropes of time or Yamarāja; *yama-puruṣaiḥ*—by the assistants of Yamarāja; *ati-bhayānakaiḥ*—who are very fearful; *tāmisre narake*—into the hell known as Tāmisra; *balāt*—by force; *nipātyate*—is thrown; *anaśana*—starvation; *anudapāna*—without water; *daṇḍa-tāḍana*—beaten with rods; *santarjana-ādibhiḥ*—by scolding and so on; *yātanābhiḥ*—by severe punishments:

yātyamānaḥ—being punished; *jantuḥ*—the living entity; *yatra*—where; *kaśmalam*—misery; *āsāditaḥ*—obtained; *ekadā*—sometimes; *eva*—certainly; *mūrcchām*—fainting; *upayāti*—obtains; *tāmisra-prāye*—in that condition, which is almost entirely dark.

TRANSLATION

My dear King, a person who appropriates another's legitimate wife, children or money is arrested at the time of death by the fierce Yamadūtas, who bind him with the rope of time and forcibly throw him into the hellish planet known as Tāmisra. On this very dark planet, the sinful man is chastised by the Yamadūtas, who beat and rebuke him. He is starved, and he is given no water to drink. Thus the wrathful assistants of Yamarāja cause him severe suffering, and sometimes he faints from their chastisement.

TEXT 9

एवमेवान्धतामिस्रे यस्तु वञ्चयित्वा पुरुषं दारादीनुपयुङ्क्ते यत्र शरीरी निपात्यमानो यातनास्थो वेदनया नष्टमतिर्नष्टदृष्टिश्च भवति यथा वनस्पतिर्वृश्च्यमानमूलस्तस्मादन्धतामिस्रं तमुपदिशन्ति ॥९॥

evam evāndhatāmisre yas tu vañcayitvā puruṣaṁ dārādīn upayuṅkte yatra śarīrī nipātyamāno yātanā-stho vedanayā naṣṭa-matir naṣṭa-dṛṣṭiś ca bhavati yathā vanaspatir vṛścyamāna-mūlas tasmād andhatāmisraṁ tam upadiśanti.

evam—in this way; *eva*—certainly; *andhatāmisre*—in the hellish planet known as Andhatāmisra; *yaḥ*—the person who; *tu*—but; *vañcayitvā*—cheating; *puruṣam*—another person; *dāra-ādīn*—the wife and children; *upayuṅkte*—enjoys; *yatra*—where; *śarīrī*—the embodied person; *nipātyamānaḥ*—being forcibly thrown; *yātanā-sthaḥ*—always situated in extremely miserable conditions; *vedanayā*—by such suffering; *naṣṭa*—lost; *matiḥ*—whose consciousness; *naṣṭa*—lost; *dṛṣṭiḥ*—whose sight; *ca*—also; *bhavati*—becomes; *yathā*—as much as; *vanaspatiḥ*—the trees; *vṛścyamāna*—being cut; *mūlaḥ*—whose root;

tasmāt—because of this; *andhatāmisram*—Andhatāmisra; *tam*—that; *upadiśanti*—they call.

TRANSLATION

The destination of a person who slyly cheats another man and enjoys his wife and children is the hell known as Andhatāmisra. There his condition is exactly like that of a tree being chopped at its roots. Even before reaching Andhatāmisra, the sinful living being is subjected to various extreme miseries. These afflictions are so severe that he loses his intelligence and sight. It is for this reason that learned sages call this hell Andhatāmisra.

TEXT 10

यस्त्विह वा एतदहमिति ममेदमिति भूतद्रोहेण केवलं स्वकुटुम्बमेवानुदिनं प्रपुष्णाति स तदिह विहाय स्वयमेव तदशुभेन रौरवे निपतति ॥ १० ॥

yas tv iha vā etad aham iti mamedam iti bhūta-droheṇa kevalaṁ sva-kuṭumbam evānudinaṁ prapuṣṇāti sa tad iha vihāya svayam eva tad-aśubhena raurave nipatati.

yaḥ—one who; *tu*—but; *iha*—in this life; *vā*—or; *etat*—this body; *aham*—I; *iti*—thus; *mama*—mine; *idam*—this; *iti*—thus; *bhūta-droheṇa*—by envy of other living entities; *kevalam*—alone; *sva-kuṭumbam*—his family members; *eva*—only; *anudinam*—day to day; *prapuṣṇāti*—supports; *saḥ*—such a person; *tat*—that; *iha*—here; *vihāya*—giving up; *svayam*—personally; *eva*—certainly; *tat*—of that; *aśubhena*—by the sin; *raurave*—in Raurava; *nipatati*—he falls down.

TRANSLATION

A person who accepts his body as his self works very hard day and night for money to maintain his own body and the bodies of

his wife and children. While working to maintain himself and his family, he may commit violence against other living entities. Such a person is forced to give up his body and his family at the time of death, when he suffers the reaction for his envy of other creatures by being thrown into the hell called Raurava.

PURPORT

In *Śrīmad-Bhāgavatam* it is said:

yasyātma-buddhiḥ kuṇape tri-dhātuke
sva-dhīḥ kalatrādiṣu bhauma-ijya-dhīḥ
yat-tīrtha-buddhiḥ salile na karhicij
janeṣv abhijñeṣu sa eva go-kharaḥ

"One who accepts this bodily bag of three elements [bile, mucus and air] as his self, who has an affinity for an intimate relationship with his wife and children, who considers his land worshipable, who takes bath in the waters of the holy places of pilgrimage but never takes advantage of those persons who are in actual knowledge—he is no better than an ass or a cow." (*Bhāg.* 10.84.13) There are two classes of men absorbed in the material concept of life. Out of ignorance, a man in the first class thinks his body to be his self, and therefore he is certainly like an animal (*sa eva go-kharaḥ*). The person in the second class, however, not only thinks his material body to be his self, but also commits all kinds of sinful activities to maintain his body. He cheats everyone to acquire money for his family and his self, and he becomes envious of others without reason. Such a person is thrown into the hell known as Raurava. If one simply considers his body to be his self, as do the animals, he is not very sinful. However, if one needlessly commits sins to maintain his body, he is put into the hell known as Raurava. This is the opinion of Śrīla Viśvanātha Cakravartī Ṭhākura. Although animals are certainly in the bodily concept of life, they do not commit any sins to maintain their bodies, mates or offspring. Therefore animals do not go to hell. However, when a human being acts enviously and cheats others to maintain his body, he is put into a hellish condition.

TEXT 11

ये त्विह यथैवामुना विहिंसिता जन्तवः परत्र यमयातनामुपगतं त एव रुरवो भूत्वा तथा तमेव विहिंसन्ति तस्माद्रौरवमित्याहू रुरुरिति सर्पादतिक्रूरसत्त्वस्यापदेशः ॥११॥

ye tv iha yathaivāmunā vihiṁsitā jantavaḥ paratra yama-yātanām upagataṁ ta eva ruravo bhūtvā tathā tam eva vihiṁsanti tasmād rauravam ity āhū rurur iti sarpād ati-krūra-sattvasyāpadeśaḥ.

ye—those who; *tu*—but; *iha*—in this life; *yathā*—as much as; *eva*—certainly; *amunā*—by him; *vihiṁsitāḥ*—who were hurt; *jantavaḥ*—the living entities; *paratra*—in the next life; *yama-yātanām upagatam*—being subjected to miserable conditions by Yamarāja; *te*—those living entities; *eva*—indeed; *ruravaḥ*—*rurus* (a kind of envious animal); *bhūtvā*—becoming; *tathā*—that much; *tam*—him; *eva*—certainly; *vihiṁsanti*—they hurt; *tasmāt*—because of this; *rauravam*—Raurava; *iti*—thus; *āhuḥ*—learned scholars say; *ruruḥ*—the animal known as *ruru; iti*—thus; *sarpāt*—than the snake; *ati-krūra*—much more cruel and envious; *sattvasya*—of the entity; *apadeśaḥ*—the name.

TRANSLATION

In this life, an envious person commits violent acts against many living entities. Therefore after his death, when he is taken to hell by Yamarāja, those living entities who were hurt by him appear as animals called rurus to inflict very severe pain upon him. Learned scholars call this hell Raurava. Not generally seen in this world, the ruru is more envious than a snake.

PURPORT

According to Śrīdhara Svāmī, the *ruru* is also known as the *bhāra-śṛṅga* (*ati-krūrasya bhāra-śṛṅgākhya-sattvasya apadeśaḥ saṁjñā*). Śrīla Jīva Gosvāmī confirms this in his *Sandarbha: ruru-śabdasya svayaṁ muninaiva ṭīkā-vidhānāl lokeṣv aprasiddha evāyaṁ jantu-viśeṣaḥ.* Thus although *rurus* are not seen in this world, their existence is confirmed in the *śāstras.*

TEXT 12

एवमेव महारौरवो यत्र निपतितं पुरुषं क्रव्यादा नाम रुरवस्तं क्रव्येण घातयन्ति यः केवलं देहम्भरः ॥१२॥

evam eva mahārauravo yatra nipatitaṁ puruṣaṁ kravyādā nāma ruravas taṁ kravyeṇa ghātayanti yaḥ kevalaṁ dehambharaḥ.

evam—thus; *eva*—certainly; *mahā-rauravah*—the hell known as Mahāraurava; *yatra*—where; *nipatitam*—being thrown; *puruṣam*—a person; *kravyādāḥ nāma*—named *kravyāda; ruravaḥ*—the *ruru* animals; *tam*—him (the condemned person); *kravyeṇa*—for eating his flesh; *ghātayanti*—kill; *yaḥ*—who; *kevalam*—only; *dehambharaḥ*—intent upon maintaining his own body.

TRANSLATION

Punishment in the hell called Mahāraurava is compulsory for a person who maintains his own body by hurting others. In this hell, ruru animals known as kravyāda torment him and eat his flesh.

PURPORT

The animalistic person who lives simply in the bodily concept of life is not excused. He is put into the hell known as Mahāraurava and attacked by *ruru* animals known as *kravyādas.*

TEXT 13

यस्त्विह वा उग्रः पशून् पक्षिणो वा प्राणत उपरन्धयति तमपकरुणं पुरुषादैरपि विगर्हितममुत्र यमानुचराः कुम्भीपाके तप्ततैले उपरन्धयन्ति ॥ १३ ॥

yas tv iha vā ugraḥ paśūn pakṣiṇo vā prāṇata uparandhayati tam apakaruṇaṁ puruṣādair api vigarhitam amutra yamānucarāḥ kumbhīpāke tapta-taile uparandhayanti.

yaḥ—a person who; *tu*—but; *iha*—in this life; *vā*—or; *ugraḥ*—very cruel; *paśūn*—animals; *pakṣiṇaḥ*—birds; *vā*—or; *prāṇataḥ*—in a live condition; *uparandhayati*—cooks; *tam*—him; *apakaruṇam*—very cruel-hearted; *puruṣa-ādaiḥ*—by those who eat human flesh; *api*—even; *vigarhitam*—condemned; *amutra*—in the next life; *yama-anucarāḥ*—the servants of Yamarāja; *kumbhīpāke*—in the hell known as Kumbhīpāka; *tapta-taile*—in boiling oil; *uparandhayanti*—cook.

TRANSLATION

For the maintenance of their bodies and the satisfaction of their tongues, cruel persons cook poor animals and birds alive. Such persons are condemned even by man-eaters. In their next lives they are carried by the Yamadūtas to the hell known as Kumbhīpāka, where they are cooked in boiling oil.

TEXT 14

यस्त्विह ब्रह्मध्रुक् स कालसूत्रसंज्ञके नरके अयुतयोजनपरिमण्डले
ताम्रमये तप्तखले उपर्यधस्तादग्न्यर्काभ्यामतितप्यमानेऽभिनिवेशितः
क्षुत्पिपासाभ्यां च दह्यमानान्तर्बहिःशरीर आस्ते शेते चेष्टतेऽवतिष्ठति
परिधावति च यावन्ति पशुरोमाणि तावद्वर्षसहस्राणि ॥ १४ ॥

yas tv iha brahma-dhruk sa kālasūtra-saṁjñake narake ayuta-yojana-parimaṇḍale tāmramaye tapta-khale upary-adhastād agny-arkābhyām ati-tapyamāne 'bhiniveśitaḥ kṣut-pipāsābhyāṁ ca dahyamānāntar-bahiḥ-śarīra āste śete ceṣṭate 'vatiṣṭhati paridhāvati ca yāvanti paśu-romāṇi tāvad varṣa-sahasrāṇi.

yaḥ—anyone who; *tu*—but; *iha*—in this life; *brahma-dhruk*—the killer of a *brāhmaṇa; saḥ*—such a person; *kālasūtra-saṁjñake*—named Kālasūtra; *narake*—in the hell; *ayuta-yojana-parimaṇḍale*—having a circumference of eighty thousand miles; *tāmra-maye*—made of copper; *tapta*—heated; *khale*—in a level place; *upari-adhastāt*—above and beneath; *agni*—by fire; *arkābhyām*—and by the sun; *ati-tapyamāne*—which is being heated; *abhiniveśitaḥ*—being made to enter; *kṣut-*

pipāsābhyām—by hunger and thirst; *ca*—and; *dahyamāna*—being burned; *antaḥ*—internally; *bahiḥ*—externally; *śarīraḥ*—whose body; *āste*—remains; *śete*—sometimes lies; *ceṣṭate*—sometimes moves his limbs; *avatiṣṭhati*—sometimes stands; *paridhāvati*—sometimes runs here and there; *ca*—also; *yāvanti*—as many; *paśu-romāṇi*—hairs on the body of an animal; *tāvat*—that long; *varṣa-sahasrāṇi*—thousands of years.

TRANSLATION

The killer of a brāhmaṇa is put into the hell known as Kālasūtra, which has a circumference of eighty thousand miles and which is made entirely of copper. Heated from below by fire and from above by the scorching sun, the copper surface of this planet is extremely hot. Thus the murderer of a brāhmaṇa suffers from being burned both internally and externally. Internally he is burning with hunger and thirst, and externally he is burning from the scorching heat of the sun and the fire beneath the copper surface. Therefore he sometimes lies down, sometimes sits, sometimes stands up and sometimes runs here and there. He must suffer in this way for as many thousands of years as there are hairs on the body of an animal.

TEXT 15

यस्त्विह वै निजवेदपथादनापद्यपगतः पाखण्डं चोपगतस्तमसिपत्रवनं प्रवेश्य कशया प्रहरन्ति तत्र हासावितस्ततो धावमान उभयतोधारैस्तालवनासिपत्रैश्छिद्यमानसर्वाङ्गो हा हतोऽस्मीति परमया वेदनया मूर्च्छितः पदे पदे निपतति स्वधर्महा पाखण्डानुगतं फलं भुङ्क्ते॥१५॥

yas tv iha vai nija-veda-pathād anāpady apagataḥ pākhaṇḍaṁ
copagatas tam asi-patravanaṁ praveśya kaśayā praharanti tatra hāsāv
itas tato dhāvamāna ubhayato dhārais tāla-vanāsi-patraiś chidyamāna-
sarvāṅgo hā hato 'smīti paramayā vedanayā mūrcchitaḥ pade pade
nipatati sva-dharmahā pākhaṇḍānugataṁ phalaṁ bhuṅkte.

yaḥ—anyone who; *tu*—but; *iha*—in this life; *vai*—indeed; *nija-veda-pathāt*—from his own path, recommended by the *Vedas; anāpadi*—even without an emergency; *apagataḥ*—deviated; *pākhaṇḍam*—a concocted, atheistic system; *ca*—and; *upagataḥ*—gone to; *tam*—him; *asi-patravanam*—the hell known as Asi-patravana; *praveśya*—making enter; *kaśayā*—with a whip; *praharanti*—they beat; *tatra*—there; *ha*—certainly; *asau*—that; *itaḥ tataḥ*—here and there; *dhāvamānaḥ*—running; *ubhayataḥ*—on both sides; *dhāraiḥ*—by the edges; *tāla-vana-asi-patraiḥ*—by the swordlike leaves of palm trees; *chidyamāna*—being cut; *sarva-aṅgaḥ*—whose entire body; *hā*—alas; *hataḥ*—killed; *asmi*—I am; *iti*—thus; *paramayā*—with severe; *vedanayā*—pain; *mūrcchitaḥ*—fainted; *pade pade*—at every step; *nipatati*—falls down; *sva-dharma-hā*—the killer of his own principles of religion; *pākhaṇḍa-anugatam phalam*—the result of accepting an atheistic path; *bhuṅkte*—he suffers.

TRANSLATION

If a person deviates from the path of the Vedas in the absence of an emergency, the servants of Yamarāja put him into the hell called Asi-patravana, where they beat him with whips. When he runs hither and thither, fleeing from the extreme pain, on all sides he runs into palm trees with leaves like sharpened swords. Thus injured all over his body and fainting at every step, he cries out, "Oh, what shall I do now! How shall I be saved!" This is how one suffers who deviates from the accepted religious principles.

PURPORT

There is actually only one religious principle: *dharmaṁ tu sākṣād bhagavat-praṇītam.* The only religious principle is to follow the orders of the Supreme Personality of Godhead. Unfortunately, especially in this age of Kali, everyone is an atheist. People do not even believe in God, what to speak of following His words. The words *nija-veda-patha* can also mean "one's own set of religious principles." Formerly there was only one *veda-patha,* or set of religious principles. Now there are many. It doesn't matter which set of religious principles one follows: the only injunction is that he must follow them strictly. An atheist, or *nāstika,* is one who does not believe in the *Vedas.* However, even if one takes up a different system of religion, according to this verse he must follow the religious principles he has accepted. Whether one is a Hindu, or a Mohammedan or a Christian, he should follow his own religious principles. However, if one concocts his own religious path within his mind, or if one follows no religious principles at all, he is punished in the hell known as Asi-patravana. In other words, a human being must follow some religious principles. If he does not follow any religious principles, he is no better than an animal. As Kali-yuga advances, people are becoming godless and taking up so-called secularism. They do not know the punishment awaiting them in Asi-patravana, as described in this verse.

TEXT 16

यस्त्विह वै राजा राजपुरुषो वा अदण्ड्ये दण्डं प्रणयति ब्राह्मणे वा
शरीरदण्डं स पापीयान्नरकेऽमुत्र सूकरमुखे निपतति तत्रातिबलैर्वि
निष्पिष्यमाणावयवो यथैवेहेक्षुखण्ड आर्तस्वरेण स्वनयन् क्वचिन्मूर्च्छितः
कश्मलमुपगतो यथैवेहादृष्टदोषा उपरुद्धाः ॥१६॥

yas tv iha vai rājā rāja-puruṣo vā adaṇḍye daṇḍaṁ praṇayati brāhmaṇe vā śarīra-daṇḍaṁ sa pāpīyān narake 'mutra sūkaramukhe nipatati tatrātibalair viniṣpiṣyamāṇāvayavo yathaiveheksukhaṇḍa ārta-svareṇa svanayan kvacin mūrcchitaḥ kaśmalam upagato yathaivehā-dṛṣṭa-doṣā uparuddhāḥ.

yaḥ—anyone who; *tu*—but; *iha*—in this life; *vai*—indeed; *rājā*—a king; *rāja-puruṣaḥ*—a king's man; *vā*—or; *adaṇḍye*—unto one not punishable; *daṇḍam*—punishment; *praṇayati*—inflicts; *brāhmaṇe*—unto a *brāhmaṇa;* *vā*—or; *śarīra-daṇḍam*—corporal punishment; *saḥ*—that person, king or government officer; *pāpīyān*—the most sinful; *narake*—in the hell; *amutra*—in the next life; *sūkaramukhe*—named Sūkharamukha; *nipatati*—falls down; *tatra*—there; *ati-balaiḥ*—by very strong assistants of Yamarāja; *viniṣpiṣyamāṇa*—being crushed; *avayavaḥ*—the different parts of whose body; *yathā*—like; *eva*—certainly; *iha*—here; *ikṣu-khaṇḍaḥ*—sugarcane; *ārta-svareṇa*—with a pitiable sound; *svanayan*—crying; *kvacit*—sometimes; *mūrcchitaḥ*—

fainted; *kaśmalam upagataḥ*—becoming illusioned; *yathā*—just like; *eva*—indeed; *iha*—here; *adṛṣṭa-doṣāḥ*—who is not at fault; *uparuddhāḥ*—arrested for punishment.

TRANSLATION

In his next life, a sinful king or governmental representative who punishes an innocent person, or who inflicts corporal punishment upon a brāhmaṇa, is taken by the Yamadūtas to the hell named Sūkharamukha, where the most powerful assistants of Yamarāja crush him exactly as one crushes sugarcane to squeeze out the juice. The sinful living entity cries very pitiably and faints, just like an innocent man undergoing punishments. This is the result of punishing a faultless person.

TEXT 17

यस्त्विह वै भूतानामीश्वरोपकल्पितवृत्तीनामविविक्तपरव्यथानां स्वयं पुरुषोपकल्पितवृत्तिर्विविक्तपरव्यथो व्यथामाचरति स परत्रान्धकूपे तदभिद्रोहेण निपतति तत्र हासौ तैर्जन्तुभिः पशुमृगपक्षिसरीसृपैर्मशकयूकामत्कुण-मक्षिकादिभिर्ये के चाभिद्रुग्धास्तैः सर्वतोऽभिद्रुह्यमाणस्तमसि विहतनिद्रा-निर्वृतिरलब्धावस्थानः परिक्रामति यथा कुशरीरे जीवः ॥ १७ ॥

yas tv iha vai bhūtānām īśvaropakalpita-vṛttīnām avivikta-para-vyathānāṁ svayaṁ puruṣopakalpita-vṛttir vivikta-para-vyatho vyathām ācarati sa paratrāndhakūpe tad-abhidroheṇa nipatati tatra hāsau tair jantubhiḥ paśu-mṛga-pakṣi-sarīsṛpair maśaka-yūkā-matkuṇa-makṣikādibhir ye ke cābhidrugdhās taiḥ sarvato 'bhidruhyamāṇas tamasi vihata-nidrā-nirvṛtir alabdhāvasthānaḥ parikrāmati yathā kuśarīre jīvaḥ.

yaḥ—any person who; *tu*—but; *iha*—in this life; *vai*—indeed; *bhūtānām*—to some living entities; *īśvara*—by the supreme controller; *upakalpita*—designed; *vṛttīnām*—whose means of livelihood; *avivikta*—not understanding; *para-vyathānām*—the pain of others; *svayam*—himself; *puruṣa-upakalpita*—designed by the Supreme Personality of

Godhead; *vṛttiḥ*—whose livelihood; *vivikta*—understanding; *para-vyathaḥ*—the painful conditions of others; *vyathām ācarati*—but still causes pain; *saḥ*—such a person; *paratra*—in his next life; *andhakūpe*—to the hell named Andhakūpa; *tat*—to them; *abhidroheṇa*—by the sin of malice; *nipatati*—falls down; *tatra*—there; *ha*—indeed; *asau*—that person; *taiḥ jantubhiḥ*—by those respective living entities; *paśu*—animals; *mṛga*—wild beasts; *pakṣi*—birds; *sarīsṛpaiḥ*—snakes; *maśaka*—mosquitoes; *yūkā*—lice; *matkuṇa*—worms; *makṣika-ādibhiḥ*—flies and so on; *ye ke*—whoever else; *ca*—and; *abhidrugdhāḥ*—persecuted; *taiḥ*—by them; *sarvataḥ*—everywhere; *abhidruhyamāṇaḥ*—being injured; *tamasi*—in the darkness; *vihata*—disturbed; *nidrā-nirvṛtiḥ*—whose resting place; *alabdha*—not being able to obtain; *avasthānaḥ*—a resting place; *parikrāmati*—wanders; *yathā*—just as; *ku-śarīre*—in a low-grade body; *jīvaḥ*—a living entity.

TRANSLATION

By the arrangement of the Supreme Lord, low-grade living beings like bugs and mosquitoes suck the blood of human beings and other animals. Such insignificant creatures are unaware that their bites are painful to the human being. However, first-class human beings—brāhmaṇas, kṣatriyas and vaiśyas—are developed in consciousness, and therefore they know how painful it is to be killed. A human being endowed with knowledge certainly commits sin if he kills or torments insignificant creatures, who have no discrimination. The Supreme Lord punishes such a man by putting him into the hell known as Andhakūpa, where he is attacked by all the birds and beasts, reptiles, mosquitoes, lice, worms, flies, and any other creatures he tormented during his life. They attack him from all sides, robbing him of the pleasure of sleep. Unable to rest, he constantly wanders about in the darkness. Thus in Andhakūpa his suffering is just like that of a creature in the lower species.

PURPORT

From this very instructive verse we learn that lower animals, created by the laws of nature to disturb the human being, are not subjected to punishment. Because the human being has developed consciousness, however, he cannot do anything against the principles of *varṇāśrama-dharma* without being condemned. Kṛṣṇa states in *Bhagavad-gītā* (4.13), *cātur-varṇyaṁ mayā sṛṣṭaṁ guṇa-karma-vibhāgaśaḥ:* "According to the three modes of material nature and the work ascribed to them, the four divisions of human society were created by Me." Thus all men should be divided into four classes—*brāhmaṇas, kṣatriyas, vaiśyas* and *śūdras*—and they should act according to their ordained regulations. They cannot deviate from their prescribed rules and regulations. One of these states that they should never trouble any animal, even those that disturb human beings. Although a tiger is not sinful if he attacks another animal and eats its flesh, if a man with developed consciousness does so, he must be punished. In other words, a human being who does not use his developed consciousness but instead acts like an animal surely undergoes punishment in many different hells.

TEXT 18

यस्त्विह वा असंविभज्याश्नाति यत्किञ्चनोपनतमनिर्मितपञ्चयज्ञो वायससंस्तुतः स परत्र कृमिभोजने नरकाधमे निपतति तत्र शतसहस्रयोजने कृमिकुण्डे कृमिभूतः स्वयं कृमिभिरेव भक्ष्यमाणः कृमिभोजनो यावत्तदप्रत्ताप्रहुतादोऽनिर्वेशमात्मानं यातयते॥१८॥

yas tv iha vā asaṁvibhajyāśnāti yat kiñcanopanatam anirmita-pañca-yajño vāyasa-saṁstutaḥ sa paratra kṛmibhojane narakādhame nipatati tatra śata-sahasra-yojane kṛmi-kuṇḍe kṛmi-bhūtaḥ svayaṁ kṛmibhir eva bhakṣyamāṇaḥ kṛmi-bhojano yāvat tad aprattāprahūtādo 'nirveśam ātmānaṁ yātayate.

yaḥ—any person who; *tu*—but; *iha*—in this life; *vā*—or; *asaṁvibhajya*—without dividing; *aśnāti*—eats; *yat kiñcana*—whatever; *upanatam*—obtained by Kṛṣṇa's grace; *anirmita*—not performing; *pañca-yajñaḥ*—the five kinds of sacrifice; *vāyasa*—with the crows; *saṁstutaḥ*—who is described as equal; *saḥ*—such a person; *paratra*—in the next life; *kṛmibhojane*—named Kṛmibhojana; *naraka-adhame*—into the most abominable of all hells; *nipatati*—falls down; *tatra*—

there; *śata-sahasra-yojane*—measuring 100,000 *yojanas* (800,000 miles); *kṛmi-kuṇḍe*—in a lake of worms; *kṛmi-bhūtaḥ*—becoming one of the worms; *svayam*—he himself; *kṛmibhiḥ*—by the other worms; *eva*—certainly; *bhakṣyamāṇaḥ*—being eaten; *kṛmi-bhojanaḥ*—eating worms; *yāvat*—as long as; *tat*—that lake is wide; *apratta-aprahūta*—unshared and unoffered food; *adaḥ*—one who eats; *anirveśam*—who has not performed atonement; *ātmānam*—to himself; *yātayate*—gives pain.

TRANSLATION

A person is considered no better than a crow if after receiving some food, he does not divide it among guests, old men and children, but simply eats it himself, or if he eats it without performing the five kinds of sacrifice. After death he is put into the most abominable hell, known as Kṛmibhojana. In that hell is a lake 100,000 yojanas [800,000 miles] wide and filled with worms. He becomes a worm in that lake and feeds on the other worms there, who also feed on him. Unless he atones for his actions before his death, such a sinful man remains in the hellish lake of Kṛmibhojana for as many years as there are yojanas in the width of the lake.

PURPORT

As stated in *Bhagavad-gītā* (3.13):

yajña-śiṣṭāśinaḥ santo
mucyante sarva-kilbiṣaiḥ
bhuñjate te tv agham pāpā
ya pacanty ātma-kāraṇāt

"The devotees of the Lord are released from all kinds of sins because they eat food which is first offered for sacrifice. Others, who prepare food for personal sense enjoyment, verily eat only sin." All food is given to us by the Supreme Personality of Godhead. *Eko bahūnāṁ yo vidadhāti kāmān:* the Lord supplies everyone with the necessities of life. Therefore we should acknowledge His mercy by performing *yajña* (sacrifice). This is the duty of everyone. Indeed, the sole purpose of life is to perform *yajña.* According to Kṛṣṇa (Bg. 3.9):

yajñārthāt karmaṇo 'nyatra
loko 'yam karma-bandhanaḥ
tad-arthaṁ karma kaunteya
mukta-saṅgaḥ samācara

"Work done as a sacrifice for Viṣṇu has to be performed, otherwise work binds one to this material world. Therefore, O son of Kuntī, perform your prescribed duties for His satisfaction, and in that way you will always remain unattached and free from bondage." If we do not perform *yajña* and distribute *prasāda* to others, our lives are condemned. Only after performing *yajña* and distributing the *prasāda* to all dependents—children, *brāhmaṇas* and old men—should one eat. However, one who cooks only for himself or his family is condemned, along with everyone he feeds. After death he is put into the hell known as Kṛmibhojana.

TEXT 19

यस्त्विह वै स्तेयेन बलाद्वा हिरण्यरत्नादीनि ब्राह्मणस्य वापहरत्यन्यस्य वानापदि पुरुषस्तममुत्र राजन् यमपुरुषा अयस्मयैरग्निपिण्डैः सन्दंशैस्त्वचि निष्कुषन्ति ॥ १९ ॥

yas tv iha vai steyena balād vā hiraṇya-ratnādīni brāhmaṇasya vāpaharaty anyasya vānāpadi puruṣas tam amutra rājan yama-puruṣā ayasmayair agni-piṇḍaiḥ sandaṁśais tvaci niṣkuṣanti.

yaḥ—any person who; *tu*—but; *iha*—in this life; *vai*—indeed; *steyena*—by thievery; *balāt*—by force; *vā*—or; *hiraṇya*—gold; *ratna*—gems; *ādīni*—and so on; *brāhmaṇasya*—of a *brāhmaṇa; vā*—or; *apaharati*—steals; *anyasya*—of others; *vā*—or; *anāpadi*—not in a calamity; *puruṣaḥ*—a person; *tam*—him; *amutra*—in the next life; *rājan*—O King; *yama-puruṣāḥ*—the agents of Yamarāja; *ayaḥ-mayaiḥ*—made of iron; *agni-piṇḍaiḥ*—balls heated in fire; *sandaṁśaiḥ*—with tongs; *tvaci*—on the skin; *niṣkuṣanti*—tear to pieces.

TRANSLATION

My dear King, a person who in the absence of an emergency robs a brāhmaṇa—or, indeed, anyone else—of his gems and gold is put

into a hell known as Sandaṁśa. There his skin is torn and separated by red-hot iron balls and tongs. In this way, his entire body is cut to pieces.

TEXT 20

यस्त्विह वा अगम्यां स्त्रियमगम्यं वा पुरुषं योषिदभिगच्छति तावमुत्र कशया ताडयन्तस्तिग्मया सूर्म्या लोहमय्या पुरुषमालिङ्गयन्ति स्त्रियं च पुरुषरूपया सूर्म्या ॥ २० ॥

yas tv iha vā agamyāṁ striyam agamyaṁ vā puruṣaṁ yoṣid
abhigacchati tāv amutra kaśayā tāḍayantas tigmayā sūrmyā lohamayyā
puruṣam āliṅgayanti striyaṁ ca puruṣa-rūpayā sūrmyā.

yaḥ—any person who; *tu*—but; *iha*—in this life; *vā*—or; *agamyām*—unsuitable; *striyam*—a woman; *agamyam*—unsuitable; *vā*—or; *puruṣam*—a man; *yoṣit*—a woman; *abhigacchati*—approaches for sexual intercourse; *tau*—both of them; *amutra*—in the next life; *kaśayā*—by whips; *tāḍayantaḥ*—beating; *tigmayā*—very hot; *sūrmyā*—by an image; *loha-mayyā*—made of iron; *puruṣam*—the man; *āliṅgayanti*—they embrace; *striyam*—the woman; *ca*—also; *puruṣa-rūpayā*—in the form of a man; *sūrmyā*—by an image.

TRANSLATION

A man or woman who indulges in sexual intercourse with an unworthy member of the opposite sex is punished after death by the assistants of Yamarāja in the hell known as Taptasūrmi. There such men and women are beaten with whips. The man is forced to embrace a red-hot iron form of a woman, and the woman is forced to embrace a similar form of a man. Such is the punishment for illicit sex.

PURPORT

Generally a man should not have sexual relations with any woman other than his wife. According to Vedic principles, the wife of another man is considered one's mother, and sexual relations are strictly forbidden with one's mother, sister and daughter. If one indulges in illicit sexual relations with another man's wife, that activity is considered identical with having sex with one's mother. This act is most sinful. The same principle holds for a woman also; if she enjoys sex with a man other than her husband, the act is tantamount to having sexual relations with her father or son. Illicit sex life is always forbidden, and any man or woman who indulges in it is punished in the manner described in this verse.

TEXT 21

यस्त्विह वै सर्वाभिगमस्तममुत्र निरये वर्तमानं वज्रकण्टकशाल्मलीमारोप्य निष्कर्षन्ति ॥ २१ ॥

yas tv iha vai sarvābhigamas tam amutra niraye vartamānaṁ
vajrakaṇṭaka-śālmalīm āropya niṣkarṣanti.

yaḥ—anyone who; *tu*—but; *iha*—in this life; *vai*—indeed; *sarva-abhigamaḥ*—indulges in sex life indiscriminately, with both men and animals; *tam*—him; *amutra*—in the next life; *niraye*—in the hell; *vartamānam*—existing; *vajrakaṇṭaka-śālmalīm*—a silk-cotton tree with thorns like thunderbolts; *āropya*—mounting him on; *niṣkarṣanti*—they pull him out.

TRANSLATION

A person who indulges in sex indiscriminately—even with animals—is taken after death to the hell known as Vajrakaṇṭaka-śālmalī. In this hell there is a silk-cotton tree full of thorns as strong as thunderbolts. The agents of Yamarāja hang the sinful man on that tree and pull him down forcibly so that the thorns very severely tear his body.

PURPORT

The sexual urge is so strong that sometimes a man indulges in sexual relations with a cow, or a woman indulges in sexual relations with a dog. Such men and women are put into the hell known as Vajrakaṇṭaka-śālmalī. The Kṛṣṇa consciousness movement forbids illicit sex. From the description of these verses, we can understand what an extremely sinful act illicit sex is. Sometimes people disbelieve these descriptions of hell, but whether one believes or not, everything must be carried out by the laws of nature, which no one can avoid.

TEXT 22

ये त्विह वै राजन्या राजपुरुषा वा अपाखण्डा धर्मसेतून्
भिन्दन्ति ते सम्परेत्य वैतरण्यां निपतन्ति भिन्नमर्यादास्तस्यां
निरयपरिखाभूतायां नद्यां यादोगणैरितस्ततो भक्ष्यमाणा आत्मना न
वियुज्यमानाश्चासुभिरुह्यमानाः स्वाघेन कर्मपाकमनुस्मरन्तो
विण्मूत्रपूयशोणितकेशनखास्थिमेदोमांसवसावाहिन्यामुपतप्यन्ते ॥ २२ ॥

ye tv iha vai rājanyā rāja-puruṣā vā apākhaṇḍā dharma-setūn bhindanti te samparetya vaitaraṇyāṁ nipatanti bhinna-maryādās tasyāṁ niraya-parikhā-bhūtāyāṁ nadyāṁ yādo-gaṇair itas tato bhakṣyamāṇā ātmanā na viyujyamānāś cāsubhir uhyamānāḥ svāghena karma-pākam anusmaranto viṇ-mūtra-pūya-śoṇita-keśa-nakhāsthi-medo-māṁsa-vasā-vāhinyām upatapyante.

ye—persons who; *tu*—but; *iha*—in this life; *vai*—indeed; *rājanyāḥ*—members of the royal family, or *kṣatriyas; rāja-puruṣāḥ*—government servants; *vā*—or; *apākhaṇḍāḥ*—although born in responsible families; *dharma-setūn*—the bounds of prescribed religious principles; *bhindanti*—transgress; *te*—they; *samparetya*—after dying; *vaitaraṇyām*—named Vaitaraṇī; *nipatanti*—fall down; *bhinna-maryādāḥ*—who have broken the regulative principles; *tasyām*—in that; *niraya-parikhā-bhūtāyām*—the moat surrounding hell; *nadyām*—in the river; *yādaḥ-gaṇaiḥ*—by ferocious aquatic animals; *itaḥ tataḥ*—here and there; *bhakṣyamāṇāḥ*—being eaten; *ātmanā*—with the body; *na*—not; *viyujyamānāḥ*—being separated; *ca*—and; *asubhiḥ*—the life airs; *uhyamānāḥ*—being carried; *sva-aghena*—by his own sinful activities; *karma-pākam*—the result of his impious activities; *anusmarantaḥ*—remembering; *viṭ*—of stool; *mūtra*—urine;

pūya—pus; *śoṇita*—blood; *keśa*—hair; *nakha*—nails; *asthi*—bones; *medaḥ*—marrow; *māṁsa*—flesh; *vasā*—fat; *vāhinyām*—in the river; *upatapyante*—are afflicted with pain.

TRANSLATION

A person who is born into a responsible family—such as a kṣatriya, a member of royalty or a government servant—but who neglects to execute his prescribed duties according to religious principles, and who thus becomes degraded, falls down at the time of death into the river of hell known as Vaitaraṇī. This river, which is a moat surrounding hell, is full of ferocious aquatic animals. When a sinful man is thrown into the River Vaitaraṇī, the aquatic animals there immediately begin to eat him, but because of his extremely sinful life, he does not leave his body. He constantly remembers his sinful activities and suffers terribly in that river, which is full of stool, urine, pus, blood, hair, nails, bones, marrow, flesh and fat.

TEXT 23

ये त्विह वै वृषलीपतयो नष्टशौचाचारनियमास्त्यक्तलज्जाः पशुचर्यां चरन्ति ते चापि प्रेत्य पूयविण्मूत्रश्लेष्ममलापूर्णार्णवे निपतन्ति तदेवातिबीभत्सितमश्नन्ति ॥ २३ ॥

ye tv iha vai vṛṣalī-patayo naṣṭa-śaucācāra-niyamās tyakta-lajjāḥ paśu-caryāṁ caranti te cāpi pretya pūya-viṇ-mūtra-śleṣma-malā-pūrṇārṇave nipatanti tad evātibībhatsitam aśnanti.

ye—persons who; *tu*—but; *iha*—in this life; *vai*—indeed; *vṛṣalī-patayaḥ*—the husbands of the *śūdras; naṣṭa*—lost; *śauca-ācāra-niyamāḥ*—whose cleanliness, good behavior and regulated life; *tyakta-lajjāḥ*—without shame; *paśu-caryām*—the behavior of animals; *caranti*—they execute; *te*—they; *ca*—also; *api*—indeed; *pretya*—dying; *pūya*—of pus; *viṭ*—stool; *mūtra*—urine; *śleṣma*—mucus; *malā*—saliva; *pūrṇa*—full; *arṇave*—in an ocean; *nipatanti*—fall; *tat*—

that; *eva*—only; *atibībhatsitam*—extremely disgusting; *aśnanti*—they eat.

TRANSLATION

The shameless husbands of lowborn śūdra women live exactly like animals, and therefore they have no good behavior, cleanliness or regulated life. After death, such persons are thrown into the hell called Pūyoda, where they are put into an ocean filled with pus, stool, urine, mucus, saliva and similar things. Śūdras who could not improve themselves fall into that ocean and are forced to eat those disgusting things.

PURPORT

Śrīla Narottama dāsa Ṭhākura has sung,

karma-kāṇḍa, jñāna-kāṇḍa, kevala viṣera bāṇḍa,
amṛta baliyā yebā khāya
nānā yoni sadā phire, kadarya bhakṣaṇa kare,
tāra janma adaḥ-pate yāya

He says that persons following the paths of *karma-kāṇḍa* and *jñāna-kāṇḍa* (fruitive activities and speculative thinking) are missing the opportunities for human birth and gliding down into the cycle of birth and death. Thus there is always the chance that he may be put into the Pūyoda Naraka, the hell named Pūyoda, where one is forced to eat stool, urine, pus, mucus, saliva and other abominable things. It is significant that this verse is spoken especially about *śūdras.* If one is born a *śūdra,* he must continually return to the ocean of Pūyoda to eat horrible things. Thus even a born *śūdra* is expected to become a *brāhmaṇa;* that is the meaning of human life. Everyone should improve himself. Kṛṣṇa says in *Bhagavad-gītā* (4.13), *cātur-varṇyaṁ mayā sṛṣṭaṁ guṇa-karma-vibhāgaśaḥ:* "According to the three modes of material nature and the work ascribed to them, four divisions of human society were created by Me." Even if one is by qualification a *śūdra,* he must try to improve his position and become a *brāhmaṇa.* No one should try to check a person, no matter what his present position is, from coming to the platform of a *brāhmaṇa* or a Vaiṣṇava. Actually, one must come to the platform of a Vaiṣṇava. Then he automatically becomes a *brāhmaṇa*. This can be done only if the Kṛṣṇa consciousness movement is spread, for we are trying to elevate everyone to the platform of Vaiṣṇava. As Kṛṣṇa says in *Bhagavad-gītā* (18.66), *sarva-dharmān parityajya mām ekaṁ śaraṇaṁ vraja:* "Abandon all other duties and simply surrender unto Me." One must give up the occupational duties of a *śūdra, kṣatriya* or *vaiśya* and adopt the occupational duties of a Vaiṣṇava, which include the activities of a *brāhmaṇa*. Kṛṣṇa explains this in *Bhagavad-gītā* (9.32):

māṁ hi pārtha vyapāśritya
ye 'pi syuḥ pāpa-yonayaḥ
striyo vaiśyās tathā śūdrās
te 'pi yānti parāṁ gatim

"O son of Pṛthā, those who take shelter in Me, though they be of lower birth—women, *vaiśyas* [merchants], as well as *śūdras* [workers]—can approach the supreme destination." Human life is specifically meant for going back home, back to Godhead. That facility should be given to everyone, whether one be a *śūdra*, a *vaiśya*, a woman or a *kṣatriya*. This is the purpose of the Kṛṣṇa consciousness movement. However, if one is satisfied to remain a *śūdra*, he must suffer as described in this verse: *tad evātibībhatsitam aśnanti.*

TEXT 24

ये. त्विह वै श्वगर्दभपतयो ब्राह्मणादयो मृगयाविहारा अतीर्थे च
मृगान्निघ्नन्ति तानपि सम्परेताँल्लक्ष्यभूतान् यमपुरुषा इषुभिर्विध्यन्ति॥२४॥

ye tv iha vai śva-gardabha-patayo brāhmaṇāḍayo mṛgayā vihārā
atīrthe ca mṛgān nighnanti tān api samparetāl̐ lakṣya-bhūtān yama-puruṣā iṣubhir vidhyanti.

ye—those who; *tu*—but; *iha*—in this life; *vai*—or; *śva*—of dogs; *gardabha*—and asses; *patayaḥ*—maintainers; *brāhmaṇa-ādayaḥ*—*brāhmaṇas, kṣatriyas* and *vaiśyas; mṛgayā vihārāḥ*—taking pleasure in hunting animals in the forest; *atīrthe*—other than prescribed; *ca*—also; *mṛgān*—animals; *nighnanti*—kill; *tān*—them; *api*—indeed; *samparetān*—having died; *lakṣya-bhūtān*—becoming the targets; *yama-puruṣāḥ*—the assistants of Yamarāja; *iṣubhiḥ*—by arrows; *vidhyanti*—pierce.

TRANSLATION

If in this life a man of the higher classes [brāhmaṇa, kṣatriya and vaiśya] is very fond of taking his pet dogs, mules or asses into the forest to hunt and kill animals unnecessarily, he is placed after death into the hell known as Prāṇarodha. There the assistants of Yamarāja make him their targets and pierce him with arrows.

PURPORT

In the Western countries especially, aristocrats keep dogs and horses to hunt animals in the forest. Whether in the West or the East, aristocratic men in the Kali-yuga adopt the fashion of going to the forest and unnecessarily killing animals. Men of the higher classes (the *brāhmaṇas*, *kṣatriyas* and *vaiśyas*) should cultivate knowledge of Brahman, and they should also give the *śūdras* a chance to come to that platform. If instead they indulge in hunting, they are punished as described in this verse. Not only are they pierced with arrows by the agents of Yamarāja, but they are also put into the ocean of pus, urine and stool described in the previous verse.

TEXT 25

ये त्विह वै दाम्भिका दम्भयज्ञेषु पशून् विशसन्ति तानमुष्मिँल्लोके वैशसे नरके पतितान्निरयपतयो यातयित्वा विशसन्ति ॥ २५ ॥

ye tv iha vai dāmbhikā dambha-yajñeṣu paśūn viśasanti tān amuṣmiṁl loke vaiśase narake patitān niraya-patayo yātayitvā viśasanti.

ye—persons who; *tu*—but; *iha*—in this life; *vai*—indeed; *dāmbhikāḥ*—very proud of wealth and a prestigious position; *dambha-yajñeṣu*—in a sacrifice performed to increase prestige; *paśūn*—animals; *viśasanti*—kill; *tān*—them; *amuṣmin loke*—in the next world; *vaiśase*—Vaiśasa or Viśasana; *narake*—into the hell; *patitān*—fallen;

niraya-patayaḥ—assistants of Yamarāja; *yātayitvā*—causing sufficient pain; *viśasanti*—kill.

TRANSLATION

A person who in this life is proud of his eminent position, and who heedlessly sacrifices animals simply for material prestige, is put into the hell called Viśasana after death. There the assistants of Yamarāja kill him after giving him unlimited pain.

PURPORT

In *Bhagavad-gītā* (6.41) Kṛṣṇa says, *śucīnāṁ śrīmatāṁ gehe yoga-bhraṣṭo 'bhijāyate:* "Because of his previous connection with *bhakti-yoga,* a man is born into a prestigious family of *brāhmaṇas* or aristocrats." Having taken such a birth, one should utilize it to perfect *bhakti-yoga.* However, due to bad association one often forgets that his prestigious position has been given to him by the Supreme Personality of Godhead, and he misuses it by performing various kinds of so-called *yajñas* like *kālī-pūjā* or *durgā-pūjā,* in which poor animals are sacrificed. How such a person is punished is described herein. The word *dambha-yajñeṣu* in this verse is significant. If one violates the Vedic instructions while performing *yajña* and simply makes a show of sacrifice for the purpose of killing animals, he is punishable after death. In Calcutta there are many slaughterhouses where animal flesh is sold that has supposedly been offered in sacrifice before the goddess Kālī. The *śāstras* enjoin that one can sacrifice a small goat before the goddess Kālī once a month. Nowhere is it said that one can maintain a slaughterhouse in the name of temple worship and daily kill animals unnecessarily. Those who do so receive the punishments described herein.

TEXT 26

यस्त्विह वै सवर्णां भार्यां द्विजो रेतः पाययति काममोहितस्तं पाप-कृतममुत्र रेतःकुल्यायां पातयित्वा रेतः सम्पाययन्ति ॥ २६ ॥

yas tv iha vai savarṇāṁ bhāryāṁ dvijo retaḥ pāyayati kāma-mohitas taṁ pāpa-kṛtam amutra retaḥ-kulyāyāṁ pātayitvā retaḥ sampāyayanti.

yaḥ—any person who; *tu*—but; *iha*—in this life; *vai*—indeed; *savarṇām*—of the same caste; *bhāryām*—his wife; *dvijaḥ*—a person of a higher caste (such as a *brāhmaṇa, kṣatriya* or *vaiśya*); *retaḥ*—the semen; *pāyayati*—causes to drink; *kāma-mohitaḥ*—being deluded by lusty desires; *tam*—him; *pāpa-kṛtam*—performing sin; *amutra*—in the next life; *retaḥ-kulyāyām*—in a river of semen; *pātayitvā*—throwing; *retaḥ*—semen; *sampāyayanti*—force to drink.

TRANSLATION

If a foolish member of the twice-born classes [brāhmaṇa, kṣatriya and vaiśya] forces his wife to drink his semen out of a lusty desire to keep her under control, he is put after death into the hell known as Lālābhakṣa. There he is thrown into a flowing river of semen, which he is forced to drink.

PURPORT

The practice of forcing one's wife to drink one's own semen is a black art practiced by extremely lusty persons. Those who practice this very abominable activity say that if a wife is forced to drink her husband's semen, she remains very faithful to him. Generally only low-class men engage in this black art, but if a man born in a higher class does so, after death he is put into the hell known as Lālābhakṣa. There he is immersed in the river known as Śukra-nadī and forced to drink semen.

TEXT 27

ये त्विह वै दस्यवोऽग्निदा गरदा ग्रामान् सार्थान् वा विलुम्पन्ति
राजानो राजभटा वा तांश्चापि हि परेत्य यमदूता वज्रदंष्ट्राः श्वानः
सप्तशतानि विंशतिश्च सरभसं खादन्ति ॥ २७ ॥

ye tv iha vai dasyavo 'gnidā garadā grāmān sārthān vā vilumpanti
rājāno rāja-bhaṭā vā tāṁś cāpi hi paretya yamadūtā vajra-daṁṣṭrāḥ
śvānaḥ sapta-śatāni viṁśatiś ca sarabhasaṁ khādanti.

ye—persons who; *tu*—but; *iha*—in this life; *vai*—indeed; *dasyavaḥ*—thieves and plunderers; *agni-dāḥ*—who set fire; *gara-*

dāḥ—who administer poison; *grāmān*—villages; *sārthān*—the mercantile class of men; *vā*—or; *vilumpanti*—plunder; *rājānaḥ*—kings; *rāja-bhaṭāḥ*—government officials; *vā*—or; *tān*—them; *ca*—also; *api*—indeed; *hi*—certainly; *paretya*—having died; *yamadūtāḥ*—the assistants of Yamarāja; *vajra-daṁṣṭrāḥ*—having mighty teeth; *śvānaḥ*—dogs; *sapta-śatāni*—seven hundred; *viṁśatiḥ*—twenty; *ca*—and; *sara-bhasam*—voraciously; *khādanti*—devour.

TRANSLATION

In this world, some persons are professional plunderers who set fire to others' houses or administer poison to them. Also, members of the royalty or government officials sometimes plunder mercantile men by forcing them to pay income tax and by other methods. After death such demons are put into the hell known as Sārameyādana. On that planet there are 720 dogs with teeth as strong as thunderbolts. Under the orders of the agents of Yamarāja, these dogs voraciously devour such sinful people.

PURPORT

In the Twelfth Canto of *Śrīmad-Bhāgavatam*, it is said that in this age of Kali everyone will be extremely disturbed by three kinds of tribulations: scarcity of rain, famine, and heavy taxation by the government. Because human beings are becoming more and more sinful, there will be a scarcity of rain, and naturally no food grains will be produced. On the plea of relieving the suffering caused by the ensuing famine, the government will impose heavy taxes, especially on the wealthy mercantile community. In this verse, the members of such a government are described as *dasyu*, thieves. Their main activity will be to plunder the wealth of the people. Whether a highway robber or a government thief, such a man will be punished in his next life by being thrown into the hell known as Sārameyādana, where he will suffer greatly from the bites of ferocious dogs.

TEXT 28

यस्त्विह वा अनृतं वदति साक्ष्ये द्रव्यविनिमये दाने वा कथञ्चित्स
वै प्रेत्य नरके ऽवीचिमत्यधःशिरा निरवकाशे योजनशतोच्छ्रायाद् गिरिमूर्ध्नः

सम्पात्यते यत्र जलमिव स्थलमश्मपृष्ठमवभासते तदवीचिमत्तिलशो विशीर्य-
माणशरीरो न म्रियमाणः पुनरारोपितो निपतति ॥ २८ ॥

yas tv iha vā anṛtaṁ vadati sākṣye dravya-vinimaye dāne vā kathañcit sa vai pretya narake 'vīcimaty adhaḥ-śirā niravakāśe yojana-śatocchrāyād giri-mūrdhnaḥ sampātyate yatra jalam iva sthalam aśma-pṛṣṭham avabhāsate tad avīcimat tilaśo viśīryamāṇa-śarīro na mriyamāṇaḥ punar āropito nipatati.

yaḥ—anyone who; *tu*—but; *iha*—in this life; *vā*—or; *anṛtam*—a lie; *vadati*—speaks; *sākṣye*—giving witness; *dravya-vinimaye*—in exchange for goods; *dāne*—in giving charity; *vā*—or; *kathañcit*—somehow; *saḥ*—that person; *vai*—indeed; *pretya*—after dying; *narake*—in the hell; *avīcimati*—named Avīcimat (having no water); *adhaḥ-śirāḥ*—with his head downward; *niravakāśe*—without support; *yojana-śata*—of eight hundred miles; *ucchrāyāt*—having a height; *giri*—of a mountain; *mūrdhnaḥ*—from the top; *sampātyate*—is thrown; *yatra*—where; *jalam iva*—like water; *sthalam*—land; *aśma-pṛṣṭham*—having a surface of stone; *avabhāsate*—appears; *tat*—that; *avīcimat*—having no water or waves; *tilaśaḥ*—in pieces as small as seeds; *viśīryamāṇa*—being broken; *śarīraḥ*—the body; *na mriyamāṇaḥ*—not dying; *punaḥ*—again; *āropitaḥ*—raised to the top; *nipatati*—falls down.

TRANSLATION

A person who in this life bears false witness or lies while transacting business or giving charity is severely punished after death by the agents of Yamarāja. Such a sinful man is taken to the top of a mountain eight hundred miles high and thrown headfirst into the hell known as Avīcimat. This hell has no shelter and is made of strong stone resembling the waves of water. There is no water there, however, and thus it is called Avīcimat [waterless]. Although the sinful man is repeatedly thrown from the mountain and his body broken to tiny pieces, he still does not die but continuously suffers chastisement.

TEXT 29

यस्त्विह वै विप्रो राजन्यो वैश्यो वा सोमपीथस्तत्कलत्रं वा सुरां व्रतस्थोऽपि वा पिबति प्रमादतस्तेषां निरयं नीतानामुरसि पदाऽऽक्रम्यास्ये वह्निना द्रवमाणं कार्ष्णायसं निषिञ्चन्ति ॥ २९ ॥

yas tv iha vai vipro rājanyo vaiśyo vā soma-pīthas tat-kalatraṁ vā surāṁ vrata-stho 'pi vā pibati pramādatas teṣāṁ nirayaṁ nītānām urasi padākramyāsye vahninā dravamāṇaṁ kārṣṇāyasaṁ niṣiñcanti.

yaḥ—anyone who; *tu*—but; *iha*—in this lfe; *vai*—indeed; *vipraḥ*—a learned *brāhmaṇa; rājanyaḥ*—a *kṣatriya; vaiśyaḥ*—a *vaiśya; vā*—or; *soma-pīthaḥ*—drink *soma-rasa; tat*—his; *kalatram*—wife; *vā*—or; *surām*—liquor; *vrata-sthaḥ*—being situated in a vow; *api*—certainly; *vā*—or; *pibati*—drinks; *pramādataḥ*—out of illusion; *teṣām*—of all of them; *nirayam*—to hell; *nītānām*—being brought; *urasi*—on the chest; *padā*—with the foot; *ākramya*—stepping; *asye*—in the mouth; *vahninā*—by fire; *dravamāṇam*—melted; *kārṣṇāyasam*—iron; *niṣiñcanti*—they pour into.

TRANSLATION

Any brāhmaṇa or brāhmaṇa's wife who drinks liquor is taken by the agents of Yamarāja to the hell known as Ayaḥpāna. This hell also awaits any kṣatriya, vaiśya, or person under a vow who in illusion drinks soma-rasa. In Ayaḥpāna the agents of Yamarāja stand on their chests and pour hot melted iron into their mouths.

PURPORT

One should not be a *brāhmaṇa* in name only and engage in all kinds of sinful activities, especially drinking liquor. *Brāhmaṇas, kṣatriyas* and *vaiśyas* must behave according to the principles of their order. If they fall down to the level of *śūdras,* who are accustomed to drink liquor, they will be punished as described herein.

TEXT 30

अथ च यस्त्विह वा आत्मसम्भावनेन स्वयमधमो जन्मतपोविद्याचार-
वर्णाश्रमवतो वरीयसो न बहु मन्येत स मृतक एव मृत्वा क्षारकर्दमे
निरयेऽवाक्‌शिरा निपातितो दुरन्ता यातना ह्यश्नुते ॥३०॥

atha ca yas tv iha vā atma-sambhāvanena svayam adhamo janma-tapo-vidyācāra-varṇāśramavato varīyaso na bahu manyeta sa mṛtaka eva mṛtvā kṣārakardame niraye 'vāk-śirā nipātito durantā yātanā hy aśnute.

atha—furthermore; *ca*—also; *yaḥ*—anyone who; *tu*—but; *iha*—in this life; *vā*—or; *ātma-sambhāvanena*—by false prestige; *svayam*—himself; *adhamaḥ*—very degraded; *janma*—good birth; *tapaḥ*—austerities; *vidyā*—knowledge; *ācāra*—good behavior; *varṇa-āśrama-vataḥ*—in terms of strictly following the principles of *varṇāśrama; varīyasaḥ*—of one who is more honorable; *na*—not; *bahu*—much; *manyeta*—respects; *saḥ*—he; *mṛtakaḥ*—a dead body; *eva*—only; *mṛtvā*—after dying; *kṣārakardame*—named Kṣārakardama; *niraye*—in the hell; *avāk-śirā*—with his head downward; *nipātitaḥ*—thrown; *durantāḥ yātanāḥ*—severe painful conditions; *hi*—indeed; *aśnute*—suffers.

TRANSLATION

A lowborn and abominable person who in this life becomes falsely proud, thinking "I am great," and who thus fails to show proper respect to one more elevated than he by birth, austerity, education, behavior, caste or spiritual order, is like a dead man even in this lifetime, and after death he is thrown headfirst into the hell known as Kṣārakardama. There he must great suffer great tribulation at the hands of the agents of Yamarāja.

PURPORT

One should not become falsely proud. One must be respectful toward a person more elevated than he by birth, education, behavior, caste or spiritual order. If one does not show respect to such highly elevated persons but indulges in false pride, he receives punishment in Kṣārakardama.

TEXT 31

ये त्विह वै पुरुषाः पुरुषमेधेन यजन्ते याश्च स्त्रियो नृपशून् खादन्ति तांश्च ते पशव इव निहता यमसदने यातयन्तो रक्षोगणाः सौनिका इव स्वधितिनावदायासृक् पिबन्ति नृत्यन्ति च गायन्ति च हृष्यमाणा यथेह पुरुषादाः ॥ ३१ ॥

ye tv iha vai puruṣāḥ puruṣa-medhena yajante yāś ca striyo nṛ-paśūn khādanti tāṁś ca te paśava iva nihatā yama-sadane yātayanto rakṣo-gaṇāḥ saunikā iva svadhitināvadāyāsṛk pibanti nṛtyanti ca gāyanti ca hṛṣyamāṇā yatheha puruṣādāḥ.

ye—persons who; *tu*—but; *iha*—in this life; *vai*—indeed; *puruṣāḥ*—men; *puruṣa-medhena*—by sacrifice of a man; *yajante*—worship (the goddess Kālī or Bhadra Kālī); *yāḥ*—those who; *ca*—and; *striyaḥ*—women; *nṛ-paśūn*—the men used as sacrifice; *khādanti*—eat; *tān*—them; *ca*—and; *te*—they; *paśavaḥ iva*—like the animals; *nihatāḥ*—being slain; *yama-sadane*—in the abode of Yamarāja; *yātayantaḥ*—punishing; *rakṣaḥ-gaṇāḥ*—being Rākṣasas; *saunikāḥ*—the killers; *iva*—like; *svadhitinā*—by a sword; *avadāya*—cutting to pieces; *asṛk*—the blood; *pibanti*—drink; *nṛtyanti*—dance; *ca*—and; *gāyanti*—sing; *ca*—also; *hṛṣyamāṇāḥ*—being delighted; *yathā*—just like; *iha*—in this world; *puruṣa-adāḥ*—the man-eaters.

TRANSLATION

There are men and women in this world who sacrifice human beings to Bhairava or Bhadra Kālī and then eat their victims' flesh. Those who perform such sacrifices are taken after death to the abode of Yamarāja, where their victims, having taken the form of Rākṣasas, cut them to pieces with sharpened swords. Just as in this world the man-eaters drank their victims' blood, dancing and

singing in jubilation, their victims now enjoy drinking the blood of the sacrificers and celebrating in the same way.

TEXT 32

ये त्विह वा अनागसोऽरण्ये ग्रामे वा वैश्रम्भकैरुपसृतानुपविश्रम्भय्य जिजीविषून् शूलसूत्रादिषूपप्रोतान् क्रीडनकतया यातयन्ति तेऽपि च प्रेत्य यमयातनासु शूलादिषु प्रोतात्मानः क्षुत्तृड्भ्यां चाभिहताः कङ्कवटादिभिश्चेतस्ततस्तिग्मतुण्डैराहन्यमाना आत्मशमलं स्मरन्ति ॥ ३२ ॥

ye tv iha vā anāgaso 'raṇye grāme vā vaiśrambhakair upasṛtān upaviśrambhayya jijīviṣūn śūla-sūtrādiṣūpaprotān krīḍanakatayā yātayanti te 'pi ca pretya yama-yātanāsu śūlādiṣu protātmānaḥ kṣut-tṛḍbhyāṁ cābhihatāḥ kaṅka-vaṭādibhiś cetas tatas tigma-tuṇḍair āhanyamānā ātma-śamalaṁ smaranti.

ye—persons who; *tu*—but; *iha*—in this life; *vā*—or; *anāgasaḥ*—who are faultless; *araṇye*—in the forest; *grāme*—in the village; *vā*—or; *vaiśrambhakaiḥ*—by means of good faith; *upasṛtān*—brought near; *upaviśrambhayya*—inspiring with confidence; *jijīviṣūn*—who want to be protected; *śūla-sūtra-ādiṣu*—on a lance, thread, and so on; *upaprotān*—fixed; *krīḍanakatayā*—like a plaything; *yātayanti*—cause pain; *te*—those persons; *api*—certainly; *ca*—and; *pretya*—after dying; *yama-yātanāsu*—the persecutions of Yamarāja; *śūla-ādiṣu*—on lances and so on; *prota-ātmānaḥ*—whose bodies are fixed; *kṣut-tṛḍbhyām*—by hunger and thirst; *ca*—also; *abhihatāḥ*—overwhelmed; *kaṅka-vaṭa-ādibhiḥ*—by birds such as herons and vultures; *ca*—and; *itaḥ tataḥ*—here and there; *tigma-tuṇḍaiḥ*—having pointed beaks; *āhanyamānāḥ*—being tortured; *ātma-śamalam*—own sinful activities; *smaranti*—they remember.

TRANSLATION

In this life some people give shelter to animals and birds that come to them for protection in the village or forest, and after making them believe that they will be protected, such people pierce them with lances or threads and play with them like toys, giving

them great pain. After death such people are brought by the assistants of Yamarāja to the hell known as Śūlaprota, where their bodies are pierced with sharp, needlelike lances. They suffer from hunger and thirst, and sharp-beaked birds such as vultures and herons come at them from all sides to tear at their bodies. Tortured and suffering, they can then remember the sinful activities they committed in the past.

TEXT 33

ये त्विह वै भूतान्युद्वेजयन्ति नरा उल्बणस्वभावा यथा दन्दशूकास्तेऽपि प्रेत्य नरके दन्दशूकाख्ये निपतन्ति यत्र नृप दन्दशूकाः पञ्चमुखाः सप्तमुखा उपसृत्य ग्रसन्ति यथा बिलेशयान् ॥ ३३ ॥

ye tv iha vai bhūtāny udvejayanti narā ulbaṇa-svabhāvā yathā dandaśūkās te 'pi pretya narake dandaśūkākhye nipatanti yatra nṛpa dandaśūkāḥ pañca-mukhāḥ sapta-mukhā upasṛtya grasanti yathā bileśayān.

ye—persons who; *tu*—but; *iha*—in this life; *vai*—indeed; *bhūtāni*—to living entities; *udvejayanti*—cause unnecessary pain; *narāḥ*—men; *ulbaṇa-svabhāvāḥ*—angry by nature; *yathā*—just like; *dandaśūkāḥ*—snakes; *te*—they; *api*—also; *pretya*—after dying; *narake*—in the hell; *dandaśūka-ākhye*—named Dandaśūka; *nipatanti*—fall down; *yatra*—where; *nṛpa*—O King; *dandaśūkāḥ*—serpents; *pañca-mukhāḥ*—having five hoods; *sapta-mukhāḥ*—having seven hoods; *upasṛtya*—reaching up; *grasanti*—eat; *yathā*—just like; *bileśayān*—mice.

TRANSLATION

Those who in this life are like envious serpents, always angry and giving pain to other living entities, fall after death into the hell known as Dandaśūka. My dear King, in this hell there are serpents with five or seven hoods. These serpents eat such sinful persons just as snakes eat mice.

TEXT 34

ये त्विह वा अन्धावटकुसूलगुहादिषु भूतानि निरुन्धन्ति तथामुत्र तेष्वेवोपवेश्य सगरेण वह्निना धूमेन निरुन्धन्ति ॥ ३४ ॥

ye tv iha vā andhāvaṭa-kusūla-guhādiṣu bhūtāni nirundhanti tathāmutra teṣv evopaveśya sagareṇa vahninā dhūmena nirundhanti.

ye—persons who; *tu*—but; *iha*—in this life; *vā*—or; *andha-avaṭa*—a blind well; *kusūla*—granaries; *guha-ādiṣu*—and in caves; *bhūtāni*—the living entities; *nirundhanti*—confine; *tathā*—similarly; *amutra*—in the next life; *teṣu*—in those same places; *eva*—certainly; *upaveśya*—causing to enter; *sagareṇa*—with poisonous fumes; *vahninā*—with fire; *dhūmena*—with smoke; *nirundhanti*—confine.

TRANSLATION

Those who in this life confine other living entities in dark wells, granaries or mountain caves are put after death into the hell known as Avaṭa-nirodhana. There they themselves are pushed into dark wells, where poisonous fumes and smoke suffocate them and they suffer very severely.

TEXT 35

यस्त्विह वा अतिथीनभ्यागतान् वा गृहपतिरसकृदुपगतमन्युर्दिधक्षुरिव पापेन चक्षुषा निरीक्षते तस्य चापि निरये पापदृष्टेरक्षिणी वज्रतुण्डा गृध्राः कङ्ककाकवटादयः प्रसह्योरुबलादुत्पाटयन्ति ॥३५॥

yas tv iha vā atithīn abhyāgatān vā gṛha-patir asakṛd upagata-manyur didhakṣur iva pāpena cakṣuṣā nirīkṣate tasya cāpi niraye pāpa-dṛṣṭer akṣiṇī vajra-tuṇḍā gṛdhrāḥ kaṅka-kāka-vaṭādayaḥ prasahyoru-balād utpāṭayanti.

yaḥ—a person who; *tu*—but; *iha*—in this life; *vā*—or; *atithīn*—guests; *abhyāgatān*—visitors; *vā*—or; *gṛha-patiḥ*—a householder; *asakṛt*—many times; *upagata*—obtaining; *manyuḥ*—anger; *didhakṣuḥ*—one desiring to burn; *iva*—like; *pāpena*—sinful; *cakṣuṣā*—with eyes; *nirīkṣate*—looks at; *tasya*—of him; *ca*—and; *api*—certainly; *niraye*—in hell; *pāpa-dṛṣṭeḥ*—of he whose vision has become sinful; *akṣiṇī*—the eyes; *vajra-tuṇḍāḥ*—those who have powerful beaks; *gṛdhrāḥ*—vultures; *kaṅka*—herons; *kāka*—crows; *vaṭa-ādayaḥ*—and other birds; *prasahya*—violently; *uru-balāt*—with great force; *ut-pāṭayanti*—pluck out.

TRANSLATION

A householder who receives guests or visitors with cruel glances, as if to burn them to ashes, is put into the hell called Paryāvartana, where he is gazed at by hard-eyed vultures, herons, crows and similar birds, which suddenly swoop down and pluck out his eyes with great force.

PURPORT

According to the Vedic etiquette, even an enemy who comes to a householder's home should be received in such a gentle way that he forgets that he has come to the home of an enemy. A guest who comes to one's home should be received very politely. If he is unwanted, the householder should not stare at him with blinking eyes, for one who does so will be put into the hell known as Paryāvartana after death, and there many ferocious birds like vultures, crows, and coknis will suddenly come upon him and pluck out his eyes.

TEXT 36

यस्त्विह वा आढ्याभिमतिरहङ्कृतिस्तिर्यक्प्रेक्षणः सर्वतोऽभिविशङ्की
अर्थव्ययनाशचिन्तया परिशुष्यमाणहृदयवदनो निर्वृतिमनवगतो ग्रह
इवार्थमभिरक्षति स चापि प्रेत्य तदुत्पादनोत्कर्षणसंरक्षणशमलग्रहः सूचीमुखे
नरके निपतति यत्र ह वित्तग्रहं पापपुरुषं धर्मराजपुरुषा वायका इव
सर्वतोऽङ्गेषु सूत्रैः परिवयन्ति ॥ ३६ ॥

yas tv iha vā āḍhyābhimatir ahaṅkṛtis tiryak-prekṣaṇaḥ sarvato 'bhiviśaṅkī artha-vyaya-nāśa-cintayā pariśuṣyamāṇa-hṛdaya-vadano nirvṛtim anavagato graha ivārtham abhirakṣati sa cāpi pretya tad-utpādanotkarṣaṇa-saṁrakṣaṇa-śamala-grahaḥ sūcīmukhe narake nipatati yatra ha vitta-grahaṁ pāpa-puruṣaṁ dharmarāja-puruṣā vāyakā iva sarvato 'ṅgeṣu sūtraiḥ parivayanti.

yaḥ—any person who; *tu*—but; *iha*—in this world; *vā*—or; *āḍhya-abhimatiḥ*—proud because of wealth; *ahaṅkṛtiḥ*—egotistic; *tiryak-prekṣaṇaḥ*—whose vision is crooked; *sarvataḥ abhiviśaṅkī*—always fearful of being cheated by others, even by superiors; *artha-vyaya-nāśa-cintayā*—by the thought of expenditure and loss; *pariśuṣyamāṇa*—dried up; *hṛdaya-vadanaḥ*—his heart and face; *nirvṛtim*—happiness; *anavagataḥ*—not obtaining; *grahaḥ*—a ghost; *iva*—like; *artham*—wealth; *abhirakṣati*—protects; *saḥ*—he; *ca*—also; *api*—indeed; *pretya*—after dying; *tat*—of those riches; *utpādana*—of the earning; *utkarṣaṇa*—increasing; *saṁrakṣaṇa*—protecting; *śamala-grahaḥ*—accepting the sinful activities; *sūcīmukhe*—named Sūcīmukha; *narake*—in the hell; *nipatati*—falls down; *yatra*—where; *ha*—indeed; *vitta-graham*—as a money-grabbing ghost; *pāpa-puruṣam*—very sinful man; *dharmarāja-puruṣāḥ*—the commanding men of Yamarāja; *vāyakāḥ iva*—like expert weavers; *sarvataḥ*—all over; *aṅgeṣu*—on the limbs of the body; *sūtraiḥ*—by threads; *parivayanti*—stitch.

TRANSLATION

One who in this world or this life is very proud of his wealth always thinks, "I am so rich. Who can equal me?" His vision is twisted, and he is always afraid that someone will take his wealth. Indeed, he even suspects his superiors. His face and heart dry up at the thought of losing his wealth, and therefore he always looks like a wretched fiend. He is not in any way able to obtain actual happiness, and he does not know what it is to be free from anxiety. Because of the sinful things he does to earn money, augment his wealth and protect it, he is put into the hell called Sūcīmukha, where the officials of Yamarāja punish him by stitching thread through his entire body like weavers manufacturing cloth.

PURPORT

When one possesses more wealth than necessary, he certainly becomes very proud. This is the situation of men in modern civilization. According to the Vedic culture, *brāhmaṇas* do not possess anything, whereas *kṣatriyas* possess riches, but only for performing sacrifices and other noble activities as prescribed in the Vedic injunctions. A *vaiśya* also earns money honestly through agriculture, cow protection and some trade. If a *śūdra* gets money, however, he will spend it lavishly, without discrimination, or simply accumulate it for no purpose. Because in this age there are no qualified *brāhmaṇas, kṣatriyas* or *vaiśyas*, almost everyone is a *śūdra* (*kalau śūdra-sambhavaḥ*). Therefore the *śūdra* mentality is causing great harm to modern civilization. A *śūdra* does not know how to use money to render transcendental loving service to the Lord. Money is also called *lakṣmī*, and Lakṣmī is always engaged in the service of Nārāyaṇa. Wherever there is money, it must be engaged in the service of Lord Nārāyaṇa. Everyone should use his money to spread the great transcendental movement of Kṛṣṇa consciousness. If one does not spend money for this purpose but accumulates more than necessary, he will certainly become proud of the money he illegally possesses. The money actually belongs to Kṛṣṇa, who says in *Bhagavad-gītā* (5.29), *bhoktāraṁ yajña-tapasāṁ sarva-loka-maheśvaram:* "I am the true enjoyer of sacrifices and penances, and I am the owner of all the planets." Therefore nothing belongs to anyone but Kṛṣṇa. One who possesses more money than he needs should spend it for Kṛṣṇa. Unless one does so, he will become puffed up because of his false possessions, and therefore he will be punished in the next life, as described herein.

TEXT 37

एवंविधा नरका यमालये सन्ति शतशः सहस्रशस्तेषु सर्वेषु च सर्व एवाधर्मवर्तिनो ये केचिदिहोदिता अनुदिताश्चावनिपते पर्यायेण विशन्ति तथैव धर्मानुवर्तिन इतरत्र इह तु पुनर्भवे त उभयशेषाभ्यां निविशन्ति ॥ ३७ ॥

evaṁ-vidhā narakā yamālaye santi śataśaḥ sahasraśas teṣu sarveṣu ca
sarva evādharma-vartino ye kecid ihoditā anuditāś cāvani-pate
paryāyeṇa viśanti tathaiva dharmānuvartina itaratra iha tu punar-
bhave ta ubhaya-śeṣābhyāṁ niviśanti.

evam-vidhāḥ—of this sort; *narakāḥ*—the many hells; *yama-ālaye*—in the province of Yamarāja; *santi*—are; *śataśaḥ*—hundreds; *sahasraśaḥ*—thousands; *teṣu*—in those hellish planets; *sarveṣu*—all; *ca*—also; *sarve*—all; *eva*—indeed; *adharma-vartinaḥ*—persons not following the Vedic principles or regulative principles; *ye kecit*—whosoever; *iha*—here; *uditāḥ*—mentioned; *anuditāḥ*—not mentioned; *ca*—and; *avani-pate*—O King; *paryāyeṇa*—according to the degree of different kinds of sinful activity; *viśanti*—they enter; *tathā eva*—similarly; *dharma-anuvartinaḥ*—those who are pious and act according to the regulative principles or Vedic injunctions; *itaratra*—elsewhere; *iha*—on this planet; *tu*—but; *punaḥ-bhave*—into another birth; *te*—all of them; *ubhaya-śeṣābhyām*—by the remainder of the results of piety or vice; *niviśanti*—they enter.

TRANSLATION

My dear King Parīkṣit, in the province of Yamarāja there are hundreds and thousands of hellish planets. The impious people I have mentioned—and also those I have not mentioned—must all enter these various planets according to the degree of their impiety. Those who are pious, however, enter other planetary systems, namely the planets of the demigods. Nevertheless, both the pious and impious are again brought to earth after the results of their pious or impious acts are exhausted.

PURPORT

This corresponds to the beginning of Lord Kṛṣṇa's instructions in *Bhagavad-gītā. Tathā dehāntara-prāptiḥ:* within this material world, one is simply meant to change from one body to another in different planetary systems. *Ūrdhvaṁ gacchanti satva-sthā:* those in the mode of goodness are elevated to the heavenly planets. *Adho gacchanti tāmasāḥ:* similarly, those too engrossed in ignorance enter the hellish planetary systems. Both of them, however, are subjected to the repetition of birth and death. In *Bhagavad-gītā* it is stated that even one who is very pious returns to earth after his enjoyment in the higher planetary systems is over (*kṣīṇe puṇye martya-lokaṁ viśanti*). Therefore, going from one planet to another does not solve the problems of life. The problems of life will only be solved when we no longer have to accept a material body. This can be possible if one simply becomes Kṛṣṇa conscious. As Kṛṣṇa says in *Bhagavad-gītā* (4.9):

janma karma ca me divyam
evaṁ yo vetti tattvataḥ
tyaktvā dehaṁ punar janma
naiti mām eti so 'rjuna

"One who knows the transcendental nature of My appearance and activities does not, upon leaving the body, take his birth again in this material world, but attains My eternal abode, O Arjuna." This is the perfection of life and the real solution to life's problems. We should not be eager to go to the higher, heavenly planetary systems, nor should we act in such a way that we have to go to the hellish planets. The complete purpose of this material world will be fulfilled when we resume our spiritual identities and go back home, back to Godhead. The very simple method for doing this is prescribed by the Supreme Personality of Godhead. *Sarva-dharmān parityajya mām ekaṁ śaraṇaṁ vraja.* One should be neither pious nor impious. One should be a devotee and surrender to the lotus feet of Kṛṣṇa. This surrendering process is also very easy. Even a child can perform it. *Man-manā bhava mad-bhakto mad-yājī māṁ namaskuru.* One must always simply think of Kṛṣṇa by chanting Hare Kṛṣṇa, Hare Kṛṣṇa, Kṛṣṇa Kṛṣṇa, Hare Hare/ Hare Rāma, Hare Rāma, Rāma Rāma, Hare Hare. One should become Kṛṣṇa's devotee, worship Him and offer obeisances to Him. Thus one should engage all the activities of his life in the service of Lord Kṛṣṇa.

TEXT 38

निवृत्तिलक्षणमार्ग आदावेव व्याख्यातः ॥ एतावानेवाण्डकोशो यश्चतुर्दशधा पुराणेषु विकल्पित उपगीयते यत्तद्भगवतो नारायणस्य साक्षान्महापुरुषस्य स्थविष्ठं रूपमात्ममायागुणमयमनुवर्णितमादृतः पठति शृणोति श्रावयति स उपगेयं भगवतः परमात्मनोऽग्राह्यमपि श्रद्धाभक्तिविशुद्धबुद्धिर्वेद ॥ ३८ ॥

nivṛtti-lakṣaṇa-mārga ādāv eva vyākhyātaḥ. etāvān evāṇḍa-kośo yaś caturdaśadhā purāṇeṣu vikalpita upagīyate yat tad bhagavato nārāyaṇasya sākṣān mahā-puruṣasya sthaviṣṭhaṁ rūpam ātmamāyā-guṇamayam anuvarṇitam ādṛtaḥ paṭhati śṛṇoti śrāvayati sa upageyaṁ bhagavataḥ paramātmano 'grāhyam api śraddhā-bhakti-viśuddha-buddhir veda.

nivṛtti-lakṣaṇa-mārgaḥ—the path symptomized by renunciation, or the path of liberation; *ādau*—in the beginning (the Second and Third Cantos); *eva*—indeed; *vyākhyātaḥ*—described; *etāvān*—this much; *eva*—certainly; *aṇḍa-kośaḥ*—the universe, which resembles a big egg; *yaḥ*—which; *caturdaśa-dhā*—in fourteen parts; *purāṇeṣu*—in the *Purāṇas; vikalpitaḥ*—divided; *upagīyate*—is described; *yat*—which; *tat*—that; *bhagavataḥ*—of the Supreme Personality of Godhead; *nārāyaṇasya*—of Lord Nārāyaṇa; *sākṣāt*—directly; *mahā-puruṣasya*—of the Supreme Person; *sthaviṣṭham*—the gross; *rūpam*—form; *ātma-māyā*—of His own energy; *guṇa*—of the qualities; *mayam*—consisting; *anuvarṇitam*—described; *ādṛtaḥ*—venerating; *paṭhati*—one reads; *śṛṇoti*—or hears; *śrāvayati*—or explains; *saḥ*—that person; *upageyam*—song; *bhagavataḥ*—of the Supreme Personality of Godhead; *paramātmanaḥ*—of the Supersoul; *agrāhyam*—difficult to understand; *api*—although; *śraddhā*—by faith; *bhakti*—and devotion; *viśuddha*—purified; *buddhiḥ*—whose intelligence; *veda*—understands.

TRANSLATION

In the beginning [the Second and Third Cantos of Śrīmad-Bhāgavatam] I have already described how one can progress on the path of liberation. In the Purāṇas the vast universal existence, which is like an egg divided into fourteen parts, is described. This vast form is considered the external body of the Lord, created by His energy and qualities. It is generally called the virāṭa-rūpa. If one reads the description of this external form of the Lord with great faith, or if one hears about it or explains it to others to propagate bhāgavata-dharma, or Kṛṣṇa consciousness, his faith and devotion in spiritual consciousness, Kṛṣṇa consciousness, will gradually increase. Although developing this consciousness is very

difficult, by this process one can purify himself and gradually come to an awareness of the Supreme Absolute Truth.

PURPORT

The Kṛṣṇa consciousness movement is pushing forward the publication of *Śrīmad-Bhāgavatam,* as explained especially for the understanding of the modern civilized man, to awaken him to his original consciousness. Without this consciousness, one melts into complete darkness. Whether one goes to the upper planetary systems or the hellish planetary systems, he simply wastes his time. Therefore one should hear of the universal position of the *virāṭa* form of the Lord as described in *Śrīmad-Bhāgavatam.* That will help one save himself from material conditional life and gradually elevate him to the path of liberation so that he can go back home, back to Godhead.

TEXT 39

श्रुत्वा स्थूलं तथा सूक्ष्मं रूपं भगवतो यतिः ।
स्थूले निर्जितमात्मानं शनैः सूक्ष्मं धिया नयेदिति।३९।

śrutvā sthūlaṁ tathā sūkṣmaṁ
rūpaṁ bhagavato yatiḥ
sthūle nirjitam ātmānaṁ
śanaiḥ sūkṣmaṁ dhiyā nayed iti

śrutvā—after hearing of (from the disciplic succession); *sthūlam*—gross; *tathā*—as well as; *sūkṣmam*—subtle; *rūpam*—form; *bhagavataḥ*—of the Supreme Personality of Godhead; *yatiḥ*—a *sannyāsī* or devotee; *sthūle*—the gross form; *nirjitam*—conquered; *ātmānam*—the mind; *śanaiḥ*—gradually; *sūkṣmam*—the subtle, spiritual form of the Lord; *dhiyā*—by intelligence; *nayet*—one should lead it to; *iti*—thus.

TRANSLATION

One who is interested in liberation, who accepts the path of liberation and is not attracted to the path of conditional life, is

called yati, or a devotee. Such a person should first control his mind by thinking of the virāṭa-rūpa, the gigantic universal form of the Lord, and then gradually think of the spiritual form of Kṛṣṇa [sac-cid-ānanda-vigraha] after hearing of both forms. Thus one's mind is fixed in samādhi. By devotional service one can then realize the spiritual form of the Lord, which is the destination of devotees. Thus his life becomes successful.

PURPORT

It is said, *mahat-sevāṁ dvāram āhur vimukteḥ:* if one wants to progress on the path of liberation, he should associate with *mahātmās*, or liberated devotees, because in such association there is a full chance for hearing, describing and chanting about the name, form, qualities and paraphernalia of the Supreme Personality of Godhead, all of which are described in *Śrīmad-Bhāgavatam.* On the path of bondage, one eternally undergoes the repetition of birth and death. One who desires liberation from such bondage should join the International Society for Krishna Consciousness and thus take advantage of the opportunity to hear *Śrīmad-Bhāgavatam* from devotees and also explain it to propagate Kṛṣṇa consciousness.

TEXT 40

भूद्वीपवर्षसरिदद्रिनभःसमुद्र-
पातालदिङ्नरकभागणलोकसंस्था ।
गीता मया तव नृपाद्भुतमीश्वरस्य
स्थूलं वपुः सकलजीवनिकायधाम ॥४०॥

bhū-dvīpa-varṣa-sarid-adri-nabhaḥ-samudra-
pātāla-diṅ-naraka-bhāgaṇa-loka-saṁsthā
gītā mayā tava nṛpādbhutam īśvarasya
sthūlaṁ vapuḥ sakala-jīva-nikāya-dhāma

bhū—of this planet earth; *dvīpa*—and other different planetary systems; *varṣa*—of tracts of land; *sarit*—rivers; *adri*—mountains; *nabhaḥ*—the sky; *samudra*—oceans; *pātāla*—lower planets; *dik*—

directions; *naraka*—the hellish planets; *bhāgaṇa-loka*—the luminaries and higher planets; *saṁsthā*—the situation; *gītā*—described; *mayā*—by me; *tava*—for you; *nṛpa*—O King; *adbhutam*—wonderful; *īśvarasya*—of the Supreme Personality of Godhead; *sthūlam*—gross; *vapuḥ*—body; *sakala-jīva-nikāya*—of all the masses of living entities; *dhāma*—which is the place of repose.

TRANSLATION

My dear King, I have now described for you this planet earth, other planetary systems, and their lands [varṣas], rivers and mountains. I have also described the sky, the oceans, the lower planetary systems, the directions, the hellish planetary systems and the stars. These constitute the virāṭa-rūpa, the gigantic material form of the Lord, on which all living entities repose. Thus I have explained the wonderful expanse of the external body of the Lord.

Thus end the Bhaktivedanta purports of the Fifth Canto, Twenty-sixth Chapter, of Śrīmad-Bhāgavatam, *entitled "A Description of the Hellish Planets."*

—Completed in the Honolulu temple of the Pañca-tattva, June 5, 1975

There is a supplementary note written by His Divine Grace Bhaktisiddhānta Sarasvatī Gosvāmī Mahārāja Prabhupāda in his *Gauḍīya-bhāṣya.* Its translation is as follows. Learned scholars who have full knowledge of all the Vedic scriptures agree that the incarnations of the Supreme Personality of Godhead are innumerable. These incarnations are classified into two divisions, called *prābhava* and *vaibhava.* According to the scriptures, *prābhava* incarnations are also classified in two divisions—those which are called eternal and those which are not vividly described. In this Fifth Canto of *Śrīmad-Bhāgavatam,* in Chapters Three through Six, there is a description of Ṛṣabhadeva, but there is not an expanded description of His spiritual activities. Therefore He is considered to belong to the second group of *prābhava* incarnations. In *Śrīmad-Bhāgavatam,* First Canto, Chapter Three, verse 13, it is said:

aṣṭame merudevyāṁ tu
nābher jāta urukramaḥ
darśayan vartma dhīrāṇāṁ
sarvāśrama-namaskṛtam

"Lord Viṣṇu appeared in the eighth incarnation as the son of Mahārāja Nābhi [the son of Āgnīdhra] and his wife Merudevī. He showed the path of perfection, the *paramahaṁsa* stage of life, which is worshiped by all the followers of *varṇāśrama-dharma.*" Ṛṣabhadeva is the Supreme Personality of Godhead, and His body is spiritual (*sac-cid-ānanda-vigraha*). Therefore one might ask how it might be possible that he passed stool and urine. The Gauḍīya *vedānta ācārya* Baladeva Vidyābhūṣaṇa has replied to this question in his book known as *Siddhānta-ratna* (First Portion, texts 65-68). Imperfect men call attention to Ṛṣabhadeva's passing stool and urine as a subject matter for the study of nondevotees, who do not understand the spiritual position of a transcendental body. In this Fifth Canto of *Śrīmad-Bhāgavatam* (5.6.11) the illusioned and bewildered state of the materialists of this age is fully described. Elsewhere in Fifth Canto (5.5.19) Ṛṣabhadeva stated, *idaṁ śarīram mama durvibhāvyam:* "This body of Mine is inconceivable for materialists." This is also confirmed by Lord Kṛṣṇa in *Bhagavad-gītā* (9.11):

avajānanti māṁ mūḍhā
mānuṣīṁ tanum āśritam
paraṁ bhāvam ajānanto
mama bhūta-maheśvaram

"Fools deride Me when I descend in the human form. They do not know My transcendental nature and My supreme dominion over all that be." The human form of the Supreme Personality of Godhead is extremely difficult to understand, and, in fact, for a common man it is inconceivable. Therefore Ṛṣabhadeva has directly explained that His own body belongs to the spiritual platform. This being so, Ṛṣabhadeva did not actually pass stool and urine. Even though He superficially seemed to pass stool and urine, that was also transcendental and cannot be imitated by any common man. It is also stated in *Śrīmad-Bhāgavatam* that the stool and urine of Ṛṣabhadeva were full of transcendental fragrance. One may imitate Ṛṣabhadeva, but he cannot imitate Him by passing stool that is fragrant.

The activities of Ṛṣabhadeva, therefore, do not support the claims of a certain class of men known as *arhat*, who sometimes advertise that they are followers of Ṛṣabhadeva. How can they be followers of Ṛṣabhadeva while they act against the Vedic principles? Śukadeva Gosvāmī has related that after hearing about the characteristics of Lord Ṛṣabhadeva, the King of Koṅka, Veṅka and Kuṭaka initiated a system of religious principles known as *arhat*. These principles were not in accord with Vedic principles, and therefore they are called *pāṣaṇḍa-dharma*. The members of the *arhat* community considered Ṛṣabhadeva's activities material. However, Ṛṣabhadeva is an incarnation of the Supreme Personality of Godhead. Therefore He is on the transcendental platform, and no one can compare to Him.

Ṛṣabhadeva personally exhibited the activities of the Supreme Personality of Godhead. As stated in *Śrīmad-Bhāgavatam* (5.6.8), *dāvānalas tad vanam ālelihānaḥ saha tena dadāha:* at the conclusion of Ṛṣabhadeva's pastimes, an entire forest and the Lord's body were burned to ashes in a great forest fire. In the same way, Ṛṣabhadeva burned people's ignorance to ashes. He exhibited the characteristics of a *paramahaṁsa* in His instructions to His sons. The principles of the *arhat* community, however, do not correspond to the teachings of Ṛṣabhadeva.

Śrīla Baladeva Vidyābhūṣaṇa remarks that in the Eighth Canto of *Śrīmad-Bhāgavatam* there is another description of Ṛṣabhadeva, but that Ṛṣabhadeva is different from the one described in this canto.

END OF THE FIFTH CANTO

The Author

His Divine Grace A. C. Bhaktivedanta Swami Prabhupāda appeared in this world in 1896 in Calcutta, India. He first met his spiritual master, Śrīla Bhaktisiddhānta Sarasvatī Gosvāmī, in Calcutta in 1922. Bhaktisiddhānta Sarasvatī, a prominent devotional scholar and the founder of sixty-four Gauḍīya Maṭhas (Vedic Institutes), liked this educated young man and convinced him to dedicate his life to teaching Vedic knowledge. Śrīla Prabhupāda became his student, and eleven years later (1933) at Allahabad he became his formally initiated disciple.

At their first meeting, in 1922, Śrīla Bhaktisiddhānta Sarasvatī Ṭhākura requested Śrīla Prabhupāda to broadcast Vedic knowledge through the English language. In the years that followed, Śrīla Prabhupāda wrote a commentary on the *Bhagavad-gītā*, assisted the Gauḍīya Maṭha in its work and, in 1944, without assistance, started an English fortnightly magazine, edited it, typed the manuscripts and checked the galley proofs. He even distributed the individual copies freely and struggled to maintain the publication. Once begun, the magazine never stopped; it is now being continued by his disciples in the West.

Recognizing Śrīla Prabhupāda's philosophical learning and devotion, the Gauḍīya Vaiṣṇava Society honored him in 1947 with the title "Bhaktivedanta." In 1950, at the age of fifty-four, Śrīla Prabhupāda retired from married life, and four years later he adopted the *vānaprastha* (retired) order to devote more time to his studies and writing. Śrīla Prabhupāda traveled to the holy city of Vṛndāvana, where he lived in very humble circumstances in the historic medieval temple of Rādhā-Dāmodara. There he engaged for several years in deep study and writing. He accepted the renounced order of life (*sannyāsa*) in 1959. At Rādhā-Dāmodara, Śrīla Prabhupāda began work on his life's masterpiece: a multivolume translation and commentary on the eighteen thousand verse *Śrīmad-Bhāgavatam* (*Bhāgavata Purāṇa*). He also wrote *Easy Journey to Other Planets.*

After publishing three volumes of *Bhāgavatam*, Śrīla Prabhupāda came to the United States, in 1965, to fulfill the mission of his spiritual master. Since that time, His Divine Grace has written over forty volumes of authoritative translations, commentaries and summary studies of the philosophical and religious classics of India.

In 1965, when he first arrived by freighter in New York City, Śrīla Prabhupāda was practically penniless. It was after almost a year of great difficulty that he established the International Society for Krishna Consciousness in July of 1966. Under his careful guidance, the Society has grown within a decade to a worldwide confederation of almost one hundred *āśramas*, schools, temples, institutes and farm communities.

In 1968, Śrīla Prabhupāda created New Vṛndāvana, an experimental Vedic community in the hills of West Virginia. Inspired by the success of New Vṛndāvana, now a thriving farm community of more than one thousand acres, his students have since founded several similar communities in the United States and abroad.

In 1972, His Divine Grace introduced the Vedic system of primary and secondary education in the West by founding the *Gurukula* school in Dallas, Texas. The school began with 3 children in 1972, and by the beginning of 1975 the enrollment had grown to 150.

Śrīla Prabhupāda has also inspired the construction of a large international center at Śrīdhāma Māyāpur in West Bengal, India, which is also the site for a planned Institute of Vedic Studies. A similar project is the magnificent Kṛṣṇa-Balarāma Temple and International Guest House in Vṛndāvana, India. These are centers where Westerners can live to gain firsthand experience of Vedic culture.

Śrīla Prabhupāda's most significant contribution, however, is his books. Highly respected by the academic community for their authoritativeness, depth and clarity, they are used as standard textbooks in numerous college courses. His writings have been translated into eleven languages. The Bhaktivedanta Book Trust, established in 1972 exclusively to publish the works of His Divine Grace, has thus become the world's largest publisher of books in the field of Indian religion and philosophy. Its latest project is the publishing of Śrīla Prabhupāda's most recent work: a seventeen-volume translation and commentary—completed by Śrīla Prabhupāda in only eighteen months—on the Bengali religious classic *Śrī Caitanya-caritāmṛta.*

In the past ten years, in spite of his advanced age, Śrīla Prabhupāda has circled the globe twelve times on lecture tours that have taken him to six continents. In spite of such a vigorous schedule, Śrīla Prabhupāda continues to write prolifically. His writings constitute a veritable library of Vedic philosophy, religion, literature and culture.

References

The statements of *Śrīmad-Bhāgavatam* are all confirmed by standard Vedic authorities. The following authentic scriptures are quoted in this book on the pages listed.

Bhagavad-gītā, 14, 16, 35, 53, 60, 64, 68, 79, 84, 126, 133, 152-153, 176-177, 185, 189, 191, 208, 243, 252-253, 263, 267, 278, 281, 360, 368, 439, 453, 463, 476, 484

Bhakti-rasāmṛta-sindhu (Rūpa Gosvāmī), 66

Brahmāṇḍa Purāṇa, 99-100, 181, 353

Brahma-saṁhitā, 96, 165, 205, 206, 227, 228, 302, 322, 360, 361

Caitanya-bhāgavata (Vṛndāvana dāsa Ṭhākura), 231, 234, 259-260, 421-424

Caitanya-caritāmṛta (Kṛṣṇadāsa Kavirāja), 19-20, 56, 59, 124, 148, 177, 213, 218, 219, 254, 266, 394-395

Chāndogya Upaniṣad, 228

Kaṭha Upaniṣad, 280

Kūrma Purāṇa, 269

Laghu-bhāgavatāmṛta (Rūpa Gosvāmī), 140-141, 224

Muṇḍaka Upaniṣad, 60

Padma Purāṇa, 134, 141, 224

Glossary

A

Ācārya—a bona fide spiritual master who teaches by his personal example.
Acintya-śakti—the inconceivable energy of the Supreme Lord.
Adhibhautika—miseries inflicted by other living entities.
Adhidaivika—miseries caused by natural disturbances such as floods and excessive heat or cold.
Adhyātmika—miseries arising from own's own body and mind.
Ādi-puruṣa—Kṛṣṇa, the original person.
Ahaṅkāra—the principle of ego.
Akāma-bhakta—one who serves the Lord without any motives.
Akarma—Kṛṣṇa conscious activity for which one suffers no reaction.
Akiñcana-gocara—Kṛṣṇa, who is easily approached by those who are materially exhausted.
Aṁśa—See: Viṣṇu-tattva.
Aṇimā—the mystic perfection of becoming so small that one can enter into a stone.
Antarikṣa—outer space.
Arcana—the devotional process of worshiping the Lord in the temple.
Arcā-vigraha—the Deity form of the Lord.
Asuras—demons.
Ātma-nivedana—the devotional process of surrendering everything to the Lord.

B

Bhāgavata-dharma—the science of devotional service to the Lord.
Bhaktas—devotees.
Bhukti—material enjoyment.
Bila-svarga—the subterranean heavens.
Brahma-bhūta—the joyful state of being freed from material contamination.
Brahmajyoti—the personal effulgence emanating from the body of Kṛṣṇa.
Brāhmaṇas—the intelligent class of men.
Brahmāṇḍa bhramaṇa—wandering up and down throughout the universe.
Brahma-saukhya—spiritual happiness which is unobstructed and eternal.

C

Channāvatāra—a concealed incarnation.

D

Daihika—the bodily necessities of life.
Daivī māyā—the external or illusory energy of the Lord who governs the material world.
Dāsya—the devotional process of rendering service to the Lord.
Dhīra—one who remains unagitated even when there is cause for agitation.

G

Grāmya-karma—mundane activities.
Gṛhastha-āśrama—the householder stage of spiritual life.
Guru—a bona fide spiritual master.

H

Hari—Kṛṣṇa, who removes all inauspicious things from the heart.
Hari-cakra—Kṛṣṇa's Sudarśana weapon, the wheel of time.
Hṛta-jñāna—bereft of intelligence.

J

Jagad-īśa—the Supreme Lord who is the proprietor of all the universes.
Jīvātmā—the spirit soul.
Jñāna—knowledge.

K

Kaivalya—the illusion of becoming one with the Supreme.
Karma—fruitive activities and their subsequent reactions.
Karma-kāṇḍa—the division of the *Vedas* which deals with fruitive activities.
Karmīs—fruitive workers.

Koṭi—ten million.
Kṛpaṇa—a miserly man who wastes his life by not striving for spiritual realization.
Kṛṣṇa-prasāda—*See: Prasāda.*
Kṣatriya—the class of administrators and fighters.

L

Laghimā—the mystic perfection of entering into the sun planet by using the rays of the sunshine.
Līlāvatāra—an incarnation to display pastimes.

M

Mahā-bhāgavatas—the topmost devotees of the Lord.
Mahātmā—a great soul, or devotee of Kṛṣṇa.
Māyā—the energy of Kṛṣṇa which deludes the living entity who desires to forget the Lord.
Māyā-sukha—illusory happiness.
Moha—illusion.
Mūḍha—*See: Vimūḍhas.*
Muhūrta—a period of forty-eight minutes.
Mukta-puruṣas—liberated persons.
Mukti—liberation from material bondage.

N

Nakṣatras—the stars.
Nāma-aparādha—offenses in the chanting of the holy name.
Nara-deva—the king, who is an earthly god.
Narādhama—the lowest of mankind.
Naṣṭa-buddhi—bereft of all good sense.
Nirviśeṣa-vādīs—impersonalists who accept an Absolute, but deny that He has any qualities of His own.
Niṣkāma—free from material desires.

P

Pañcarātrika-vidhi—the authorized process of Deity worship.
Paramahaṁsa—a first-class devotee of the Lord.
Paramparā—the disciplic succession through which spiritual knowledge is received.
Parā prakṛti—the superior energy of the Lord.
Pāṣaṇḍīs—atheists; those who think God and the demigods to be on the same level.
Prakṛti—female, to be enjoyed by the *puruṣa.*
Pramadā—the beauty of the opposite sex.
Prasāda—sanctified remnants of food offered to the Lord.
Praśānta—undisturbed by the modes of nature.
Priyatama—dearmost.
Puṇya-śloka—verses that increase one's piety; one who is glorifed by such verses.
Puruṣa—male, the enjoyer.

R

Rajo-guṇa—the material mode of passion.
Rākṣasas—man-eating demons.

S

Sac-cid-ānanda-vigraha—the eternal form of the Supreme Lord which is full of bliss and knowledge.
Ṣaḍ-bhūja-mūrti—the six-armed form of Lord Caitanya.
Sādhu—a holy man.
Sakāma-bhakta—a devotee with material desires.
Sakhya—the devotional process of making friends with the Lord.
Samādhi—trance, absorption in God consciousness.
Sannyāsa—the renounced order of life.
Śāstras—revealed scriptures.
Sattva-guṇa—the material mode of goodness.
Smaraṇa—the devotional process of remembering the Lord.
Smṛti—scriptures compiled by living entities under trancendental direction.

Soma-rasa—an intoxicant taken on the heavenly planets.
Śravaṇaṁ kīrtanaṁ viṣṇoḥ—hearing and chanting about Viṣṇu.
Śuddha-sattva—the platform of pure goodness.
Śūdra—the laborer class of men who serve the three higher classes.
Suras—demigods, devotees.
Svāṁśa—*See: Viṣṇu-tattva.*
Svarga-loka—the heavenly planetary system.

T

Tamo-guṇa—the material mode of ignorance.
Tattva-darśī—one who has seen the truth.
Trivikrama—Lord Vāmana, the incarnation who performed three heroic deeds.

U

Udāra—magnanimous.
Upāsya—worshipable.
Uttamaśloka—Kṛṣṇa, who is worshiped by select poetry.

V

Vaikuṇṭha—the spiritual sky, where there is no anxiety.
Vaiśya—the class of men involved in business and farming.
Vānaprastha—retired life in which one travels to holy places in preparation for the renounced order of life.
Vandana—the devotional process of offering prayers to the Lord.
Vaṇik—the mercantile community.
Varṇāśrama-dharma—the scientific system of four social and four spiritual orders in human society.
Vikarma—sinful work performed against the injunctions of revealed scriptures.
Vimūḍhas—foolish rascals.
Viraha—transcendental bliss in separation from the Lord.
Virāṭa-rūpa—the universal form of the Lord.
Vīra-vrata—fully determined.

Viṣṇu-tattva—the plenary expansions of Kṛṣṇa, each of whom is also God.
Vivāha-yajña—the sacrifice of marriage.

Y

Yajña—sacrifice.
Yamadūtas—messengers of Yamarāja, the lord of death.
Yoga—linking the consciousness of the living entity with the Supreme Lord.
Yogamāyā—the internal potency of the Lord.
Yojana—eight miles.

Sanskrit Pronunciation Guide

Vowels

अ a आ ā इ i ई ī उ u ऊ ū ऋ ṛ ॠ ṝ

ऌ ḷ ए e ऐ ai ओ o औ au

ं ṁ *(anusvāra)* ः ḥ *(visarga)*

Consonants

Gutturals:	क ka	ख kha	ग ga	घ gha	ङ ṅa
Palatals:	च ca	छ cha	ज ja	झ jha	ञ ña
Cerebrals:	ट ṭa	ठ ṭha	ड ḍa	ढ ḍha	ण ṇa
Dentals:	त ta	थ tha	द da	ध dha	न na
Labials:	प pa	फ pha	ब ba	भ bha	म ma
Semivowels:	य ya	र ra	ल la	व va	
Sibilants:	श śa	ष ṣa	स sa		
Aspirate:	ह ha	ऽ = ' *(avagraha)* - the apostrophe			

The vowels above should be pronounced as follows:

a – like the *a* in org*a*n or the *u* in b*u*t.
ā – like the *ā* in f*a*r but held twice as long as *a*.
i – like the *i* in p*i*n.
ī – like the *ī* in p*i*que but held twice as long as *i*.
u – like the *u* in p*u*sh.
ū – like the *ū* in r*u*le but held twice as long as *u*.

ṛ – like the *ri* in *Ri*ta (but more like French *ru*).
ṝ – same as *ṛi* but held twice as long.
ḷ – like *lree (lruu).*
e – like the *e* in they.
ai – like the *ai* in *ai*sle.
o – like the *o* in *go.*
au – like the *ow* in h*ow.*
ṁ *(anusvāra)* – a resonant nasal like the *n* in the French word *bon.*
ḥ *(visarga)* – a final *h*-sound: *aḥ* is pronounced like *aha; iḥ* like *ihi.*

The consonants are pronounced as follows:

k – as in *k*ite
g – as in *g*ive
ṅ – as in si*n*g
ch – as in staun*ch-h*eart
jh – as in he*dgeh*og
ṭ – as in *t*ub
ṇ – as r*n*a (prepare to say the *r* and say *na*).
kh – as in Ec*kh*art
gh – as in di*g-h*ard
c – as in *ch*air
j – as in *j*oy
ñ – as in ca*n*yon
ṭh – as in ligh*t-h*eart
ḍha- as in re*d-h*ot
ḍ – as in *d*ove

Cerebrals are pronounced with tongue to roof of mouth, but the following dentals are pronounced with tongue against teeth:

t – as in *t*ub but with tongue against teeth.
th – as in ligh*t-h*eart but tongue against teeth.
d – as in *d*ove but tongue against teeth.
dh – as in re*d-h*ot but with tongue against teeth.
n – as in *n*ut but with tongue in between teeth.
p – as in *p*ine
b – as in *b*ird
m – as in *m*other
r – as in *r*un
v – as in *v*ine.
ph – as in u*p-h*ill (not *f*)
bh – as in ru*b-h*ard
y – as in *y*es
l – as in *l*ight
s – as in sun
ś (palatal) – as in the *s* in the German word *sprechen*
ṣ (cerebral) – as the *sh* in *sh*ine
h – as in *h*ome

There is no strong accentuation of syllables in Sanskrit, only a flowing of short and long (twice as long as the short) syllables.

Index of Sanskrit Verses

This index constitutes a complete listing of the first and third lines of each of the Sanskrit poetry verses and the first line of each Sanskrit prose verse of this volume of *Śrīmad-Bhāgavatam*, arranged in English alphabetical order. In the first column the Sanskrit transliteration is given, and in the second and third columns respectively the chapter-verse references and page number for each verse are to be found.

D

E

G

H

I

J

U

General Index

Numerals in boldface type indicate references to translations of the verses of *Śrīmad-Bhāgavatam.*

A

Abhijit
as head of the stars, **348**
Abortions
follow unwanted pregnancies in Kali-yuga, 18
Activities
auspicious and inauspicious controlled by Viṣṇu, 279
conditioned soul attains material facilities due to pious, **21**
material as only engagement of conditioned soul, 16
should be used for mission of Lord, 34
those in mode of ignorance engage in impious, **436**
Ādityas
came from Nārāyaṇa, 277
Advaitam acyutam anādim ananta-
verse quoted, 96, 205
Agni
circumambulates Dhruva Mahārāja, **356-357**
Agniṣvāttā
as head of Pitṛloka, **437**
Ahaṁ hi sarva-yajñānāṁ
quoted, 277
Aham tvāṁ sarva-pāpebhyo
quoted, 189, 258
Ahaṅkāre matta hañā
quoted, 13
Air
planets and stars float by manipulation of, 361
Aiśvaryasya samagrasya vīryasya
quoted, 64
Aja
as son of Pratihartā, **75**
Akāmaḥ sarva-kāmo vā
verses quoted, 191, 265
Ākūti
as wife of Pṛthuṣeṇa, 76-77
Alakanandā River
as branch of Ganges River, **128**
course of described, **131**
Aloka-varṣa
located outside of Lokāloka Mountain, **313**
Āma
as son of Ghṛtapṛṣṭha, **294**
Āmi——vijña, ei mūrkhe 'viṣaya'
quoted, 19
Anadhikāriṇo devāḥ
verses quoted, 269
Anādi karama-phale
verses quoted, 428
Ananta
as expansion of Viṣṇu, **410**
beauty of described, **413-415, 417-418**
becomes angry at time of devastation, **412**
main mission of, 416
no end to glorious qualities of, **427**
Anantadeva
See: Ananta
Ananyāś cintayanto māṁ
verses quoted, 191
Andhakūpa
as hellish planet, **452**
Andhatāmisra
as hellish planet, **441, 443**
Animals
cooked alive by cruel persons, **447**

Animals
don't commit sins to maintain their bodies, 444
not subjected to punishment, 452-453
Aniruddha
abode of, 141
Annād bhavanti bhūtāni
verse quoted, 113
Annamaya
as name of moon-god, **347**
Antarikṣa
places of enjoyment for Yakṣas, etc., in, **377**
Antavat tu phalaṁ teṣām tad
quoted, 194
Ante nārāyaṇa-smṛtiḥ
quoted, 68
Anyābhilāṣitā-śūnyaṁ jñāna-
pure devotional service as, 134, 167, 190, 235, 261
Apareyam itas tv anyāṁ prakṛtiṁ
quoted, 201
Api cet sudurācāro
verses quoted, 243
Āpyāyana
as son of Yajñabāhu, **284**
Āryans
strictly follow Vedic principles, **72**-73
Arcye viṣṇau śilā-dhīr guruṣu
quoted, 139
Arjuna
taken by Kṛṣṇa through Aloka-varṣa, **313**
Ārṣṭiṣeṇa
as the chief person in Kimpuruṣa-varṣa, **223**-224
Aruṇadeva
harnesses the sun-god's horses, **331**
looks backward while driving the sun-god's chariot, **332**
Aruṇodā
as river in Ilāvṛta, **106**
Aryamā
as chief resident of Hiraṇmaya-varṣa, **205**
Asi-patravana
as hellish planet, **441, 449**
Association of devotees
frees one from misery, 56
not obtained by unfortunate, **57**
one may become convinced of material futility by, 19
Aṣṭame merudevyāṁ tu
verses quoted, 484
Aṣṭāṅga-yoga
purpose of, 68
Āsurī
as wife of Devatājit, **74**
Āsurīṁ yonim āpannā
verses quoted, 18
Ataeva kṛṣṇa mūla-jagat-kāraṇa
verses quoted, 219
Ataḥ pumbhir dvija-śreṣṭhā
verses quoted, 58-59
Atala
demon named Bala in, **386-387**
Atheism
results of impious activity due to, **436**
Atheists
Buddha preached among, 73
Ato gṛha-kṣetra-sutāpta-vittair
verse quoted, 66
Avaiṣṇavo gurur na syāt
quoted, 134
Avajānanti māṁ mūḍhā
verses quoted, 484
Avarodhana
as son of Gaya, **87**
Avaṭa-nirodhana
as hellish planet, **441, 472**
Avīcimat
as hellish planet, **441, 466**
Ayaḥpāna
as hellish planet, **441, 467**
Ayi nanda-tanuja kiṅkaraṁ
verse quoted, 110, 170, 428
Ayodhyā
as residence of Lord Rāma, 224
devotees of brought back to Godhead by Rāma, **236**

B

Caitanya Mahāprabhu
Kṛṣṇa consciousness movement as mission of, 47
prayers of, 169-170
quoted on accepting *guru*, 6
quoted on being saved from materialistic life, 428
quoted on detachment from gold and women, 109-110
quoted on duty of one born in Bhārata-varṣa, 239, 257, 267
quoted on mercy of Kṛṣṇa and *guru*, 57
quoted on shelter of pure devotee, 59-60
quoted on wanderings of living entities in universe, 133
represented in six-armed form, 236
Cakṣu River
as branch of Ganges River, **128**
course of described, **129**
Cāṇakya Paṇḍita
two kinds of envious living entities according to, 170
Cañcalā
goddess of fortune as, 35
Candra
came from the mind of Nārāyaṇa, 277
Candraloka
Ganges River carried to, **127**
Candramā manaso jātaś cakṣoḥ
verses quoted, 277
Cāraṇaloka
as planet below Rāhu, **376**
Cātur-varṇyaṁ mayā sṛṣṭaṁ
quoted, 453, 460
Catur-vidhā bhajante māṁ
verses quoted, 191
Ceto-darpaṇa-mārjanam
quoted, 171, 175, 238
Chāndogya Upaniṣad
quoted on Paramātmā, 228
Chanting
about Bharata Mahārāja, **69**
Children
compared to tigers, jackals and foxes, 10
Cintāmaṇi-prakara-sadmasu
verses quoted, 165
Cities
compared to forest, 6
Citraratha
as son of Gaya, **87**
Citrarepha
as son of Medhātithi, **298**
Conditioned souls
absorbed in activities for bodily maintenance, **15-16**
attracted by wife as illusion personified, **40**
attracted to little happiness derived from sense gratification, **32**
bitten by envious enemies, **31**
burned by fire of lamentation, **25**
chastised by enemies and government servants, **20**
enter material world for some material profit, **5**
exchange of money causes enmity among, **51**
experience nothing but misery, **38-39**
exploit relatives, **24**
fear of compared to mountain cave, **50**
four defects of, 37
government men turn against, **26**
jump from one body to another, **49**
live lives of lamentation, **36**
must accept one body after another, 167
obliged to gratify their senses, **8**
receive cheap blessings from atheists, **22**
repeatedly strive for material enjoyment, 19
steal money and escape punishment, **35**
take pleasure in mental concoctions, **27**
take shelter of man-made gods, **42**
treat family members unkindly, **29**
Conjugal love
Kṛṣṇa attracts everyone's heart by mellow of, 197
Cows
those in goodness had last animal birth as, 45

D

E

I

M

Stars
enabled to float by manipulation of air, 361
fixed to wheel of time, **348**
reflect sunshine, 91
Stutī
as wife of Pratihartā, **75**
Stutyavrata
as son of Hiraṇyaretā, **288**
Stuvanti munayaḥ sūryaṁ
verses quoted, **334**
Subhadra
as one of seven islands, **276**
Sūcīmukha
as hellish planet, **441, 474**
Śucīnāṁ śrīmatāṁ gehe yoga-bhraṣṭo
quoted, 68, 463
Sudarśana *cakra*
causes wives of demons to have miscarriages, **385**
demons of Rasātala defeated by, **406**
protected sun and moon from Rāhu, 375
Sudhāmā
as son of Ghṛtapṛṣṭha, **294**
Śūdra
falls into ocean of pus, stool, etc., **460**
Kṛṣṇa consciousness movement is trying to elevate, 47
must try to become *brāhmaṇa,* 460
spends money lavishly, 475
Sugati
as son of Gaya, **87**
Sūkaramukha
as hellish planet, **441, 451**
Śūlaprota
as hellish planet, **441, 471**
Sumanā
as wife of Madhu, **87**
Sumati
as son of Bharata, **72**
Sumeru Mountain
axle of wheel of sun-god's chariot rests on, 330
is surrounded by Jambūdvīpa, **274**
is within Ilāvṛta, **98**
township of Brahmā on summit of, **117**
Sun
described as *bhagavān,* 323
holy name compared to, 394-395
inhabitants of Plakṣadvīpa attain the, **276**
is in middle of outer space, **322**
is worshipable, 91
moon is twice as large as, 374
Nārāyaṇa as the, **341**
orbit of, **323-328**
planet and sun-god divide directions of universe, **316**
situated in middle of universe, **314**
Sun-god
as Nārāyaṇa or Viṣṇu, **343**
as reflection of Viṣṇu, **279**
can't deviate from his orbit, 323
chariot of worshiped by Gāyatrī *mantra,* **329-330**
has three speeds, **344**
Yamarāja as powerful son of, **438**
Supārśva
as mountain of Jambūdvīpa, **102**
Supersoul
as director of living beings, 216
Rāma as, **232**
Supreme Lord
as original cause of all natural events, 216
Surocana
as son of Yajñabāhu, **284**
Sūrya
as life and soul of this universe, 317
Sūrya ātmā ātmatvenopāsyaḥ
quoted, 316
Sūrya Nārāyaṇa
as sun deity incarnation of Supreme Lord, 362
Sūrya-somāgni-vārīśa-
verses quoted, 279
Sutala
as residence of Bali Mahārāja, **390**
Suvarcalā
as wife of Parameṣṭhī, **74**
Svadharma-niṣṭhaḥ śata-
quoted, 304

T

U

W

Y

THE CRYSTAL SPIRIT

By the same author

Longford
Blessings
Man From a Far Country
Candles in the Dark

THE CRYSTAL SPIRIT

Lech Wałęsa and His Poland

Mary Craig

But the thing that I saw in your face
No power can disinherit.
No bomb that ever burst
Shatters the crystal spirit.
George Orwell

Hodder & Stoughton
LONDON SYDNEY AUCKLAND TORONTO

British Library Cataloguing in Publication Data

Craig, Mary
The crystal spirit: Lech Wałęsa and his Poland
1. Wałęsa, Lech 2. Solidarność – Biography 2. Trade-unions – Poland – Biography
I. Title
331.88′092′4 HD67357.Z55W34

ISBN 0-340-37200-1

 Printed in Great Britain for Hodder and Stoughton Limited, Mill Road, Dunton Green, Sevenoaks, Kent by St Edmundsbury Press, Bury St Edmunds, Suffolk. Photoset by Rowland Phototypesetting Limited, Bury St Edmunds, Suffolk. Hodder and Stoughton Editorial Office: 47 Bedford Square, London WC1B 3DP.

FOR BARBARA AND ROBIN KEMBALL

and for Janusz, Joasia, Wojtek, Monika, Piotr – and all those others who risk their freedom to keep the crystal spirit from breaking.

ACKNOWLEDGMENTS

To all inside Poland whom I prefer not to mention by name.

To Elżbieta Barzycka; Urszula Grochowska; Irena Grzeszczak; Maciej Jachimczyk; Andrzej, Jadwiga and Krzysztof Jaraczewscy; Barbara Kemball; Ludka Laskowska; Dr Jerzy Peterkiewicz; Dr Jagodziński of The Polish Library, Hammersmith; Antoni Pośpieszalski; Dr Jan Sikorski (Leeds); Jan Sikorski (London); Grażyna Sikorska; Ewa Stepan; Kazik Stepan; Martha Szajkowska.

To Dr Bohdan Cywiński, for the time he gave me, and particularly for his excellent unpublished paper, *The Polish Experience*.

To my friends, Frances Donnelly and John Harriott, whose encouragement and support were invaluable.

To Tim Garton Ash, in whose book, *The Polish Revolution*, I discovered the Orwell poem from which I have taken the title for this book and to the estate of the late Sonia Brownell Orwell and Secker & Warburg Ltd for permission to use it. To the Association Des Philatélistes Polonais en France for their generosity in helping me obtain the stamps.

To Anna Zaranko for her imaginative involvement in the book, for coming to Poland with me, and for some of the photographs. And to Eric Major, Carolyn Armitage and Ion Trewin of Hodder & Stoughton for believing in the project and supporting it.

To Dr Antony Polonsky, Olgierd Stepan and Dr Bogdan Szajkowski, who read the MS and gave me their valuable comments.

And lastly to my husband, Frank, for his unfailing tolerance, assistance and love.

CONTENTS

ILLUSTRATIONS

Lech Wałęsa's birth entry in register[2]
The Wałęsa family[2]
The house in Popowo where Wałęsa was brought up[3]
Wałęsa's school, Chalin[3]
Wedding photograph[1]
Danuta Wałęsa[2]
Warsaw churchyard[2]
Dreams and determination[1]
Occupation strike in Lenin shipyard[1]
Bread for the strikers[1]
Confession on site[1]
Signing of agreement for independent self-governing trade unions[1]
Cardinal Wyszyński at the Gdańsk monument[1]
Western European support for the Poles[1]
The nation unites in support of Solidarity[2]
Martial law[1]
The realist[1]
Father Henryk Jankowski[2]
Father Jerzy Popiełuszko[2]
Wałęsa and Pope John Paul II in Rome[1]
V for Victory[2]
Stamps[4]
The author with Lech Wałęsa[2]
The Wałęsa family, 1981[1]

[1] Reproduced by courtesy of The John Hillelson Agency, London ©
[2] Author's photograph
[3] Reproduced by courtesy of Anna Zaranko
[4] Reproduced by courtesy of the Association Des Philatélistes Polonais en France

ROUGH GUIDE TO THE PRONUNCIATION OF POLISH

The following hints may be useful to the reader:

The vowels *a*, *e* and *o* are short, i.e. as in: c*a*t, b*e*d, b*o*x.
The vowels *i* and *u* are long, i.e. as in f*ee*t, m*oo*n.
ą and *ę* are nasal sounds, *ą* being pronounced like the '*on*' in French *monde*; and *e* like the *in* in French *fin*.
j is a half-vowel, pronounced as *y*; as is *y*, which is pronounced somewhere between a short *i* and a short *e*. Try either.
oj = *oy*, as in b*oy*.
ó is (like *u*) pronounced *oo*.
ów (a frequent combination in Polish) = *oof*.
c = *ts*, as in *tsar*.
ch is pronounced like its counterpart in Scottish *loch* or German *ach*.
c(i) = *ch(ee)*
cz = *ch*
ł = *w*
sz = *sh*. Hence the formidable looking combination szcz = merely shch.
s and *s(i)* also = *sh*. Likewise, believe it or not, *rz*.
w = *v*. There is no letter *v* in Polish, despite the frequency with which the V-for-Victory sign is made.
ź and *z(i)* = *zh(ee)*
ż resembles the -(a)*ge* in French *courage*.
An accent over the *ń*: merely denotes a softening of the sound.

IN POLISH THE STRESS USUALLY FALLS ON THE PENULTIMATE SYLLABLE.

I have tried to keep the use of Polish proper names to a minimum. Of those I have used, most are easy to pronounce. Here, however, are phonetic transcripts of the most commonly used:

BYDGOSZCZ: bid-goshch.
CYWIŃSKI: tse-ween-skee.
CZĘSTOCHOWA: chen-sto-ho-va.
JASTRZĘBIE: yas-tshen-b'ye
MIŁOSZ: mee-wosh.
POPIEŁUSZKO: po-pyay-woosh-ko.
SZCZECIN: shchech-een.

WAŁĘSA: va-wen-sa.
WALENTYNOWICZ: va-len-tě-no-veech
WOJTYŁA: voy-^{łtě}-wa.
WYSZYŃSKI: v^{ĭ}-sh^{ĭ}n-skee.

As with proper names, I have also attempted to avoid sets of initials. Only a few recur with any frequency in the text. They are:

KOR: the Workers' Defence Committee. Later renamed KSS-KOR, Social Self-Defence Committee-KOR.
SB: secret police, usually known as the UB.
ZOMO: units of specially trained, motorised riot police.

FOREWORD

Early one morning, in the middle of August 1980, a thirty-seven-year-old, out-of-work electrician called Lech Wałęsa scrambled over the twelve-foot-high perimeter wall of the Lenin shipyard in the Baltic port of Gdańsk, Poland. The workers there, driven to desperation by endless shortages, were about to go on strike, a shocking possibility in the "workers' paradise" of People's Poland. Standing on a bulldozer, the director of the shipyard attempted to soothe them with golden promises. They were wavering, almost ready to believe the promises that past experience had taught them were never kept. Suddenly, the air became charged with excitement, as Wałęsa, a short, stocky, young man with a huge moustache, climbed on to the bulldozer and from a higher vantage-point than the director, shouted: "Remember me? I was a worker in this shipyard for ten years. But you kicked me out four years ago . . . We don't believe your lies any more, and we're not going to be cheated again. Until you give us firm guarantees, we're going to stay right here where we are."

The director remembered him all right, and the workers' hesitation vanished. Before the next few days were out, Lech Wałęsa would be famous far beyond the confines of the shipyard, the city of Gdańsk, or even Poland. When he climbed over that wall and on to that excavator, he was entering history. The Solidarity movement which flowed from that moment will for ever be associated with his name. To the world at large, no other name is of importance. Lech Wałęsa is Mister Solidarity.

But Solidarity was much more than just another trade union movement, and Lech Wałęsa did not just spring into active life in that August of 1980. The story of the man and of the movement is a complex, interwoven one. And the story does not make any sense to the outsider unless the story of Poland is told, at least of Poland in the last forty-odd years, that is to say in the lifetime of Lech Wałęsa. For Wałęsa, unknown till 1980 outside of Gdańsk, became the voice of Poland, the man who, for all his peasant origins and uncouth accent, was able to articulate the hopes and longings of a nation which, since 1939, has been in bondage to two ruthless totalitarian systems alien to its nature. "Let Poland Be Poland," was the theme song of Solidarity, one of the few genuinely popular and spontaneous revolutions in the whole history of the world. For a brief moment in 1980, it seemed as if the impossible dream might become reality: that there could be a bloodless revolution in the name of Truth, and that Poland could be Poland again.

Wałęsa – Solidarity – Poland: an indivisible trinity. "Go down to the shipyards," says Wałęsa, "talk to any man there. Every man's story is my story." He is Everyman, as far as Poland is concerned, and any attempt to tell his story outside its Polish context, or unsupported by other people's experience of the Polish situation, would be a barren and unworthy exercise. In the monastery of Częstochowa, Poland's national shrine, hangs a portrait in oils of a typical Polish worker. The face is uncannily that of Lech Wałęsa, though it dates from the sixties, and the man who painted it did not even know that Wałęsa existed. To the interested observer, the strange portrait seems charged with prophetic force.

Much has happened since 1980, and the bright hopes have been dimmed. Poland is still scarred by the trauma of martial law, the "war" which General Jaruzelski declared against his own people, in which Polish soldiers and policemen were licensed to kill Polish workers. In Polish eyes, that is the ultimate horror.

Solidarity has been driven underground, its members are proscribed and hunted. Lech Wałęsa, so recently the "uncrowned king" of Poland, is once again an ordinary shift-worker at the Gdańsk shipyards. "A more working-class worker the working-class never produced", someone once said of him. The Polish government prefers him to be a face in the crowd, and refuses to allow him any status at all. He has not been given the chance to prove what he is capable of. But he has an infinite capacity for endurance, and is content to bide his time. Suffering and persecution have long been part of the Polish experience, and the ability to rise above their suffering is one of the glories of the Polish people. In their indestructible courage, their enduring faith, their deep respect for the dignity even of their adversaries, and in spite of catastrophes too terrible to contemplate, there is a powerful message for our Western societies, drowning in a sea of affluence, but short on hope.

My own association with Poland goes back more than twenty years, and I have already spoken of its beginnings in a previous book, *Blessings*. In 1964, when I first went there, Gomułka was in power and had joined battle with the Catholic Church for the minds and hearts of the Polish people. But in those days I knew little of Poland's troubled history, and was more interested in the beautiful stamps she was manufacturing for her thousand-year anniversary, than in the politics of the day. And then for a number of years, I quite simply forgot her. Only in 1978 did I go back, when Hodder & Stoughton asked me to write a biography of Karol Wojtyła, the first Pole ever to be elected Pope. That fateful journey revived my affection and admiration for the country, and led me at last to study her history and learn her language.

In October 1983, I was in Poland when Lech Wałęsa's Nobel Peace Prize was announced. It was spoken of with great pride and joy by the Poles – but behind closed doors and in whispers. For the government regarded this award to its staunchest critic as a slap in the face. Two days later, I was introduced to a young priest in Warsaw, Father Jerzy Popiełuszko. He was delighted about the award and by the fact that Wałęsa was receiving thousands of telegrams and goodwill messages from all over the world. "The prize," he said, "is not just for Wałęsa, but for Poland, who tried to find her own salvation by peaceful means. And it's a prize for the whole movement of Solidarity, which carried on its struggle without shedding a single drop of blood." Solidarity's refusal to use violence in pursuit of its aims surely makes it unique in the modern world. Lech Wałęsa is in the tradition of Gandhi and Martin Luther King, an apostle of non-violence.

A few months after meeting with Father Jerzy, I met Lech Wałęsa for the first time. Nobel Prize or not, he had reverted to being plain Citizen Wałęsa, and had just come off the early morning shift. He no longer gave many interviews to strangers, but had agreed nevertheless to see me. I went to his flat in Gdańsk, and we sat under the huge portrait of the Pope which hangs on his office wall, surrounded by souvenirs of Solidarity. Edgy at first, he soon relaxed and gave me far more time than he had originally promised. Until I talked to him that afternoon, I had not realised what strength of character he had, nor how much that strength derived from his deep religious faith. He was a man who did not talk in confrontational terms: "I don't think in terms of enemies," he said. "Our most vicious enemies are ourselves. We must learn to understand one another better and stop being so suspicious, so afraid of each other." "He doesn't know what it is to hate," Father Jankowski, his parish priest, had told me; and I could see it was true. Lech may be a fighter, but he is a fighter who doesn't want to trounce his opponent but to turn him into a friend.

I left him, feeling that he was quietly confident about the future, hopeful that the government would engage in dialogue with the discredited Solidarity, in order to save Poland from disaster.

When I met him again a year later, the political climate had deteriorated drastically. Jerzy Popiełuszko had been murdered, and many other supporters of Solidarity, priests and laymen, had disappeared in mysterious circumstances, or were being persistently harassed by the police. A trial that same week, conducted without even the semblance of respect for justice and truth, had resulted in long prison sentences for three men whose only crime was that they had tried to humanise the Marxist–Leninist state in which they lived. Wałęsa, under orders not to leave Gdańsk without permission, had been summoned that very morning to the Public Prosecutor's Office for questioning. There he had refused to speak. Instead he had silently placed a written statement on the prosecutor's desk. In the face of such a monstrous miscarriage of justice, the statement said, the only way to retain one's dignity *vis à vis* the courts, prosecutors or police, was silence.

Wałęsa's mood that afternoon, when I met him in a room at St Brigid's, the "shipyard church", was sombre, his face tense and exhausted – like those of most of the people I met. But not defeated, not afraid. Shadowed always by the police, his every movement watched, he can still assert that he is "the free-est man in the world", and mean it. This book is a modest attempt to shed some light on the apparent paradox.

It is also an attempt to present the story of Poland in the last troubled half-century in an easy-to-read form. It is a layman's, not a scholar's book, and I have included only as much detail as seemed to me indispensable to the overall picture. For this reason too I have cut down on proper names and have provided a rough guide to the pronunciation of those which remain. The pronunciation of Polish is not nearly as daunting as it seems.

My aim has been to give some idea of just what the Polish experience has been in this most terrible of centuries; and to clear up some of the many misunderstandings which prevail in the West. Because present-day Poland is a closed society in which information cannot be freely sought, nor interviews freely given, I have for the most part referred to my contributors by name only when they are already well-known; and am unable therefore to acknowledge my debt to them properly. To illuminate their testimonies, I have quoted also from novels, films and poems of the period, which seem to me to convey a heightened perception of a painful reality.

Many years ago, a friend of mine told me she was convinced

that Poland had the spiritual capacity to save the world from itself. I knew nothing about Poland then, and promptly forgot what she had said. But the remark must have lodged in my subconscious, and for the last few years, ever since August 1980, in fact, I have been sure that my friend was right.

MARY CRAIG, September 1985

PROLOGUE

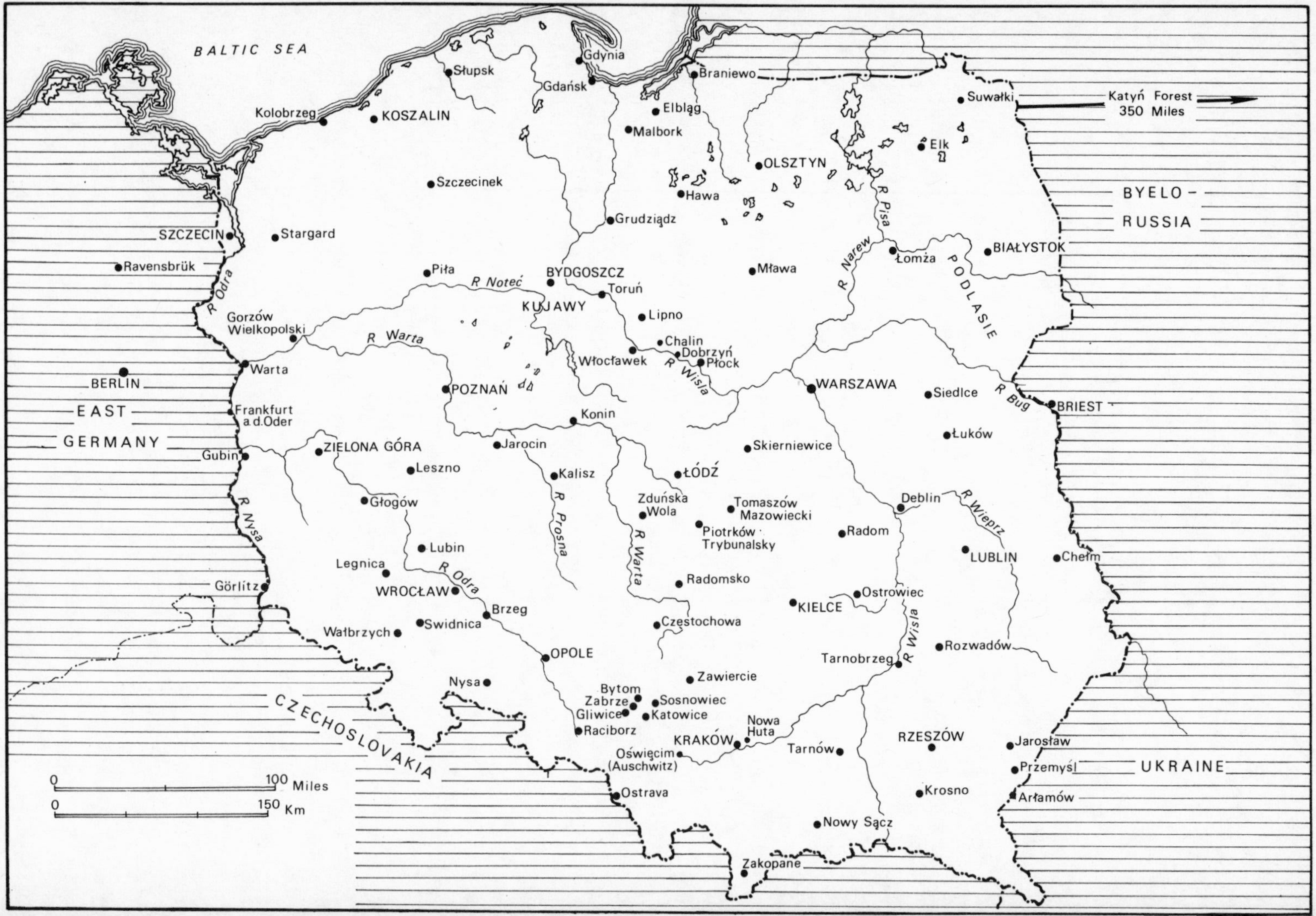
BALTIC SEA
Katyń Forest
350 Miles
BYELO-
RUSSIA
UKRAINE
EAST
GERMANY
CZECHOSLOVAKIA
BERLIN
Ravensbrük
SZCZECIN
Stargard
Kolobrzeg
KOSZALIN
Słupsk
Szczecinek
Gdynia
Gdańsk
Elbląg
Malbork
Braniewo
OLSZTYN
Hawa
Grudziądz
Suwałki
Ełk
Łomża
BIAŁYSTOK
PODLASIE
Mława
Piła
BYDGOSZCZ
Toruń
KUJAWY
Lipno
Chalin
Dobrzyń
Płock
Włocławek
R Noteć
R Warta
R Wisła
R Narew
R Pisa
R Bug
R Odra
R Nysa
R Prosna
R Wieprz
Gorzów
Wielkopolski
Warta
POZNAŃ
Frankfurt
a.d.Oder
Gubin
ZIELONA GÓRA
Leszno
Głogów
Lubin
Legnica
WROCŁAW
Brzeg
Swidnica
Wałbrzych
Görlitz
OPOLE
Nysa
Konin
Jarocin
Kalisz
ŁÓDŹ
Zduńska
Wola
Tomaszów
Mazowiecki
Piotrków
Trybunalsky
Radomsko
Częstochowa
Skierniewice
WARSZAWA
Siedlce
Łuków
BRIEST
Deblin
Radom
LUBLIN
Chełm
KIELCE
Ostrowiec
Rozwadów
Tarnobrzeg
Zawiercie
Bytom
Zabrze
Gliwice
Sosnowiec
Katowice
Raciborz
Nowa
Huta
KRAKÓW
Oświęcim
(Auschwitz)
Tarnów
RZESZÓW
Jarosław
Przemyśl
Krosno
Arłamów
Ostrava
Nowy Sącz
Zakopane
0
100 Miles
0
150 Km

INDEPENDENCE (1918–39)

> I would say this for the Poles: for every stain on the escutcheon of the nation, I can find a concomitant act of unparalleled unselfishness and heroism to lay in the balance. This is no ordinary country – Polish history has decreed it thus. A great and enduring people who have become thus against the most extraordinary of odds – there you have the Poles.
>
> Stewart Steven, *The Poles*

Wałęsa? Even the Poles had difficulty remembering the name when they first heard it in 1980. Polish surnames usually tell you where a person comes from or what his/her occupation is. All those names ending in -ski or -cki are of that sort. But Wałęsa tells a different story. It is based on a Polish verb meaning "to wander about", and suggests a rootless individual, a restless spirit, someone pushed around from one place to another. Someone hunted by the police perhaps? A deportee?

In 1830 a young man named Wałęsa was deported from Russian Poland. And that is where the two stories, of Wałęsa and of Poland, first actually coincide.

* * *

In the monastery at Częstochowa, the shrine which is at the very heart of Polish nationhood, there is a storehouse of priceless treasure. Among the royal regalia, the gold and the jewels, the porcelain of ages past, there is an item from Poland's more recent and tragic experience: an urn filled with ashes – the ashes of those who died in the 1944 Warsaw Rising, or in the concentration camps of Majdanek, Auschwitz, Stutthof and countless other places of horror. "Gold and tears," sighed one of the monks, pointing out these disparate treasures with equal pride. "Gold and tears. That's the story of Poland."

The country lies in the exact centre of Europe, at a dangerous crossroads, prone to sudden attack by enemies to north, south, east and west, and for ever paying the price of her unenviable geographical position. As Igor Stravinsky so graphically put it,

"If you pitch your tent in the middle of Fifth Avenue, don't be surprised if you are run over by a bus."

Poland was a democracy as long ago as the second half of the fourteenth century, when the other great states of Europe – France, England, Germany, Russia and Spain – were all heading in the direction of autocracy and the setting up of absolute monarchies. True enough, Poland's democracy was of the gentry only, but then nowhere else in Europe was there such a large gentry class, comprising about ten per cent of the population.[1]

In the sixteenth century, Poland was a powerful nation, but in the following one she steadily declined from that high point. Her insistence on personal freedom, so intense as to be almost anarchic, was her undoing, and by the eighteenth century, Poland had become ungovernable. Her decline came about just as the Russia of the Romanovs, the Prussia of the Hohenzollerns and the Austria of the Hapsburgs were growing in strength. In 1772, these voracious neighbours proceeded to annex a large part of Poland.

After the success of the French Revolution and the spread of revolutionary ideas in 1789, enlightened spirits in Poland attempted to stop the rot and provide the country with a worthwhile system of government. The Constitution of 3rd May, 1791, was Europe's first and the world's second (after America) written body of law to proclaim the rights of man and of the citizen. If it had been implemented, Poland would have become one of the most progressive countries of Europe. But scarcely was the ink dry on the paper than her three neighbours, alarmed by the revolutionary nature of the Polish charter, moved in to stop the cancer from spreading; and annexed all but a small fragment of Poland's territory, forcing her to abandon her Constitution. Two years later they took away even the bit that was left. For the next one hundred and twenty-three years, Poland was carved up between Russia, Prussia and Austria and disappeared from the maps of Europe. In the history books, these are the years of the Polish Partitions; to the Poles they were rather the *finis Poloniae*, the end of Poland.

Yet, during those years of oppression, when Prussian Poles and Austrian Poles and Russian Poles grew up absorbing different political, social and cultural values into their bloodstreams and had little contact with each other, Polish consciousness somehow refused to die. Whether in the Russian sector where Polish Catholics were actively persecuted by Orthodox Christians; in the Prussian where they were hounded by the Lutherans; or in the

Austrian (known as Galicia) where rule by the large Polish landowners (magnates) preserved an outmoded economic structure which left the majority of the population extremely poor, and exacerbated religious and national tensions between Poles and Ukrainians; it was in the Roman Catholic Church that Poles everywhere could find their common ground. At times even their language was forbidden, and Polish children received their schooling only in Russian or German. But they always learned their catechism, secretly, from the priest, and he taught it to them in Polish. In this way the language and traditions of the old Poland were kept alive.

In the first of the Partitions, it was Prussia who did best out of the deal. But after 1815, the lion's share of Polish territory was acquired by Czarist Russia. As the Russian noose tightened, strangling Polish culture and language, the Poles entered a long period of struggle to preserve their self-respect along with their national identity.

On several occasions the Poles rose in revolt against their oppressors, but the revolts were always bloodily put down; and more repressive measures followed. The first of these brave but doomed insurrections was against Russia and took place in November 1830. It was spearheaded by a number of impecunious gentry who believed they had nothing to lose. The young Wałęsa, ancestor of Lech, was almost certainly one of them.

The Rising was put down by vastly superior Russian forces, and many young Poles fled the country. In the harsh reprisals that followed, many more, about eight or nine thousand in all, and including Wałęsa, were deported by the Russians, who then undertook an even more savage Russification of their part of Poland. Universities were closed down, Parliament suppressed . . . Most of the exiles went to France, where their desire for freedom had aroused the most sympathy. Paris at this time was a haven for many national liberation movements, and now became the centre from which hopes of a free Poland radiated.[1]

* * *

It was not, however, till 1918 that Poland regained her independence. Even then it was no more than an accident, and proved to be little more than a breathing-space. It so happened that her Russian overlords went to war with her German and Austrian masters, and in the course of that war they all three lost their empires. For six years Poland was a bloody battlefield over which their armies advanced and retreated, trampling her underfoot in the process. When the Armistice was signed in the West in November 1918, German troops were still victoriously in place on Polish soil. Then, almost by default and hardly able to believe her good fortune, Poland was declared free. Free, indeed, but still a cat's-paw; a stick with which the Western allies could belabour the defeated Germany. The Treaty of Versailles which restored Poland to the map of Europe aroused deep fury and resentment in Germany and sowed the seeds of the next World War and Poland's virtual destruction. Germany and Russia, Poland's traditional enemies, were for the time being impotent. But they would not long remain so. Poland's resurgence may have seemed like a miracle to the newly-liberated Poles, but in the light of history that resurgence was foredoomed to be short-lived.

Poland in fact was bleeding and helpless from the war which had raged over her and she needed a powerful shot in the arm if she were to survive. But self-interest governed Western policy. It was only French fears of both Germany and newly Bolshevik Russia that had tipped the balance in favour of creating a free Poland as a useful buffer between those two potentially dangerous aggressors. A strong and vigorous Poland was no part of the Allies' post-war strategy. Only reluctantly did they agree to her request for an outlet to the sea, at Danzig, on the Baltic Sea. Then, almost as if regretting such generosity, they made Danzig (known to the Poles as Gdańsk) a Free City, belonging neither to Germans nor Poles, yet inhabited by both. The Prussian part of Germany was now divided into two by what became known as the Polish Corridor. A recipe for disaster, if ever there was one. It was a positive invitation to future German adventurism.[2]

Over the next few years, until 1923, Poland fought six wars to establish her frontiers. French fears were proved to be only too well grounded when, during the Russo-Polish War of 1920–1, the Bolsheviks came near to taking Warsaw, from where they hoped to sweep on over the Oder River and into Germany. A new Communist leadership of Polish revolutionaries was all ready to take power and had begun addressing manifestos to the nation. Anticipating victory, the Russian General Tukhachevsky gloated: "Over the corpse of Poland lies the road to worldwide conflagration. We shall drown the Polish Army in its own blood." Trotsky was certain that Europe was about to be set ablaze. But for once the gods were with Poland. By a miracle (attributed by the Poles about equally to Marshal Józef Piłsudski and the Virgin Mary), the Russian troops were turned back at the eleventh hour, and Europe gained an eighteen-year reprieve. The Battle of

Warsaw, one of history's most crucial battles and known to the Poles as the Miracle on the Vistula, put an end to whatever sympathy Poles might have felt for Russian Communism. The relationship between the two countries suffered a terminal blow. And from now on, Joseph Stalin, the new master of Soviet Russia, would brood on revenge just as ominously as did the Germans.

By 1921, Poland's frontiers were as secure as they were ever likely to be, given her precarious geographical situation, like a nut lying in the hollow of a temporarily out-of-action nutcracker. She could at last address herself to the awesome problem of self-government. As one commentator put it, it was "as though she had been handed a six-inch nail, which she had to bang into a concrete wall with her bare hands".[3] The Western allies left her to it, though she was financially exhausted and lacked all experience of political independence. Government after government fell, as politicians wrangled and failed to find common ground.

The new Poland was a mishmash of ill-assorted ethnic groups with little or no understanding of each other's problems and plenty of ambition and mutual dislike. Ukrainians, Byelo-Russians all dreamed of unilateral independence and resolutely refused the federation that might possibly have saved them.

Frighteningly insecure as she was, Poland became defensive and jittery about the hostile minorities in her midst, and in particular about the Jews, who now represented ten per cent of the entire population (a far higher percentage per head of population than anywhere else in Europe), who seemed to present the biggest threat to Polish autonomy. "Poland for the Poles" became a popular slogan, as the Jews' unpopularity increased.

In earlier centuries, Poland had been renowned for her religious tolerance. No religious wars were ever fought on her territory, and, during the Reformation period, she was a recognised haven for those who were being persecuted elsewhere. Not least for the Jews. Poland, for example, had been the only country in Europe to welcome them, when they were expelled from Spain and Portugal. By the eighteenth century, more than seventy-five per cent of the world's Jews were living in the Polish–Lithuanian Commonwealth.

During the nineteenth-century Partitions, however, Polish Jews had come under more openly anti-semitic rule and were subjected to frequent pogroms by all three occupying powers, particularly by Czarist Russia. It followed that many Poles had been born and bred in an atmosphere which encouraged and provoked anti-semitism. Moreover, many of the Jews in Russian-occupied eastern Poland had joined revolutionary groups, and it was their identification with Russian Bolshevism which was the main cause of their unpopularity in independent Poland. In 1918, the Polish Communists opposed Independence, arguing that the country should remain part of the new Soviet Russia. And as Jews formed the nucleus of this Communist Party, the Poles chose to believe that the entire Jewish community was plotting a Russian take-over. This was unfair, since the Jewish Communists, as avowed atheists, were disliked by their orthodox fellow-Jews almost as much as by the Polish Catholics.

There were economic reasons, too, for the Polish mistrust of the Jews. At a time when the Poles were desperately trying to stave off economic collapse, Jewish control over much of the industrial and commercial life of the country, and Jewish dominance in medicine and law, aroused furious national resentment. During the dictatorship of Marshal Józef Piłsudski (who had assumed emergency powers in 1926 in order to lift the nation out of chaos), the Jews were relatively protected. But after Piłsudski's death in 1935, the "government of the colonels" which succeeded him was obsessed with national unity and became stridently chauvinistic.

A tide of nationalism and anti-semitism was sweeping across Europe, and Poland was not exempt from the madness. Outbursts of anti-semitism became frequent, all too often approved and accepted by the powerful Roman Catholic Church, for whom the Jews were not only Communists but freemasons and secularists bent on destroying the fabric of society. The boycott of Jewish shops and businesses became an accepted part of Polish life.

Four hundred thousand Jews left Poland at this time – with feelings of bitterness which are still strong half a century later. Such bitterness is understandable. Nevertheless, as Isaac Cohen of the Anglo-Jewish Association was later to insist, Jews who believed themselves persecuted in Poland "did not have long to wait for conditions which made Poland look like paradise".

Poland's pre-war intolerance of her minorities would cast a long shadow over her post-war reputation. Angry charges, both justified and unjustified, are laid against her. But it can at least be pleaded in extenuation that in those inter-war years she was struggling to learn democracy the hard way, alone and unaided, after a century and a half of being enslaved; and that she lacked the political maturity to handle wisely those who seemed to threaten her survival. Whatever her faults, and they must not be brushed aside, Polish society was basically healthy, and was a more likely breeding ground for true democracy than for either of the ugly totalitarian tyrannies which lay in wait for her. She needed more time. But time would not be given her.

It is said that, just before his death, Marshal Józef Piłsudski expressed the fear that one day Russia and Germany would unite. And in that hour of mortal danger, he prophesied, Poland would stand alone and defenceless. Britain and France, he was quite sure, would not lift a finger to help her.

[1] Marek Wasowicz, *Idea Demokratyzmu i Tolerancji Religijnej w Historii Ustroju Polski*, Almanach Polonii 1980.

[2] From an article in *Poland One*, January 1985, Volume 1, Number 8, "Polish Independence: How Lloyd George Failed To Stop It", by Józef Gintyllo.

[3] *Idem.*

PART ONE

THE WILDERNESS YEARS

1 A DOUBLE HOLOCAUST (1939–43)

> I think that Solidarity has really been in existence in a latent form since the last war. It was forged in the Polish resistance movement and, to the end, thanks to what you call the "intransigence" of the Poles, it was preserved. Otherwise, we would not have Solidarity today.
>
> Jan Nowak, 1980

Germany had made no secret of its intentions. "Poland's existence is intolerable, incompatible with the essential conditions of Germany's life," wrote a German general in 1922. "Poland must and will go." Taken in conjunction with Russian – by now it was Soviet Russian – resentment of a "bourgeois" Polish buffer between herself and her plans for carrying the revolution into Germany, the signing of the Nazi–Soviet pact in 1939 sounded Poland's death-knell. A new Partition, worse than those of the nineteenth century, was about to overwhelm her. And when the coming war ended, more than six million Polish citizens, including approximately three million Jews, would be dead. That is to say, one in five of the country's population.

Stalin congratulated Ribbentrop, the German Foreign Minister, on the new friendship between the two erstwhile enemies. "A friendship cemented by blood," he called it. By Polish blood. In a speech to the Supreme Soviet on 31st October, 1939, Russian Foreign Minister Molotov bluntly spelled out the nature of this friendship: "A short blow at Poland from the German Army, followed by one from the Red Army, was enough to annihilate this monster-child of the Treaty of Versailles."

By then it was over. Assured of Soviet collusion, Hitler had attacked Poland on 1st September. Barbara N., fifteen years old at the time, remembers: ". . . the paralysing terror, the sensation that the whole world was falling about one's ears, the shock of seeing shot and bleeding people lying in the roads. Everything that once had seemed eternal simply collapsed."

The Polish Army fought bravely, in the belief that they would soon see the British and French launch a counter-offensive across the Rhine. It simply did not occur to them that those two countries, who had finally declared war on Germany on 3rd September, would abandon them to their fate. Earlier that summer the Allies had even prevailed on Poland not to mobilise, for fear of provoking the Germans. As a result of this disastrous decision, Polish volunteers were wandering round in a shocked and futile search for arms and equipment. "Surely we are not going to die for Danzig" summed up the Western attitude, and, as Piłsudski had foreseen, not a shot was fired in Poland's defence by her allies.

Just how hopeless Polish resistance was became clear on 17th September, when the Red Army marched into eastern Poland, on the pretext of liberating those territories which the Russians had never ceased to claim as theirs. To the Poles it seemed like a new variation of the old Russian expansionism.

The Nobel poet, Czesław Miłosz, compared those desperate days to a fire in an ant-hill: "Thousands of hungry and frightened people clogged the roads: soldiers of the beaten army trying to get home, policemen getting rid of their uniforms, women searching for their husbands . . ."

A vicious persecution began, not just of landowners and "class enemies", but of millions of ordinary people. (Not even Polish Communists were safe. Stalin had liquidated all those he could lay hands on in 1936, accusing them of being Trotskyists. The future leader, Władysław Gomułka, saved at that time by virtue of being in a Polish prison, was taking no chances now. Communist or not, he preferred to try his luck in the German zone.)

To the Russians, all Poles were dyed-in-the-wool counter-revolutionaries. Ludka L.'s story is typical of thousands. Her father was a policeman, therefore a "class enemy". Day after day he was summoned by the NKVD (the Russian Secret Police, later called the KGB) and interrogated. Returning home after one of these interrogations, bruised and beaten, with several teeth missing, he confided to his family that he would try to "escape" into the German zone. That was the last they heard of him, until years later they were told that he had died in Auschwitz concentration camp.

Meanwhile, the Russians were arresting army officers, judges, policemen, teachers, civil servants and anyone who might conceivably stand in their way. Children at school were arrested for refusing to stand to attention during the singing of the Internationale. While the prisoners were deported to Siberia, their wives sold everything they could find in the house, to get money for food. Rumours were rife that they were to be deported too, to make room for the families of the Russian soldiers. Ludka takes up the story:

> And then it came, the night of 13th April, 1940. We were in bed when the knocking on the door started and Russian soldiers with guns burst in and told us to pack. We had to leave immediately. My mother was given papers to sign, while the soldiers searched the house looking for guns. They found a little jewellery (not much; she had sold most of it already) and took that . . .
>
> We got to the station by hay-cart. There we saw a long train of cattle-trucks waiting for us. It was a terrible sight. Masses of people and Russian soldiers prodding everyone with their guns. Cries and callings for help and curses. It was a nightmare.
>
> They packed us about sixty to each truck. At each end of the truck there were sort of shelves. Some of us children were told to lie down on these at once, otherwise there would have been no room for others even to stand. There were two tiny windows at the top of the wall, and huge sliding doors at each end. We were kept at the station for two days until all the trucks were full of people. We left at night and travelled for over two weeks. Now and then we stopped to get food, mostly thin soup, bread and hot water. Nobody was allowed to leave the cattle-truck, except the people who were bringing the food. There was a hole in the floor for a toilet. Most of us had either diarrhoea or constipation.
>
> I remember the moment when we crossed the border into Russia. We all cried. Some people had a premonition then that they'd never see Poland again . . .

Their destination was Siberia. From the station they travelled by ox-cart for three days and three nights before reaching the collective farm where they were to stay with a Russian family. At the farm (*kolkhoz*) Ludka slept in one bed with her mother and sister; her brother, Marian, slept on top of a large stove; and the other member of their group slept on top of their combined suitcases. For this accommodation they were ordered to pay forty roubles a month:

> Everyone had to work. Mother made bricks; Mila and Marian worked in the fields (we children had to go to school). We were given bread, skimmed milk and seasonal vegetables in small quantities. At the end of the season we were supposed to be paid, but as we hadn't fulfilled our "quota", there was no money for us and we were told that we owed them for the food we'd received.

> When winter came it was terrible. Our clothes were far too thin, and we were hungry. Mother swapped whatever we could spare for potatoes and bread. When we complained to our work-foreman, he said, "You'll either get used to it or die." We were not prepared for such bitter cold and so much snow. That snow, even our houses were covered with it. Those who died during that dreadful winter had to be buried in the snow and then reburied when the thaw came.

By despatching between one and two million Poles to the arctic wilderness, Stalin could confidently leave typhus, dysentery, starvation and freezing cold to do the work of extermination for him. Of those deported, about a fifth died. A miner, trade unionist, who survived a work-camp in the regions of northern Siberia, described the appalling conditions in which the prisoners worked – in sixty-five degrees of frost, and with no day of rest:

> The prisoners suffered from exhaustion after a very short time and were easily attacked by disease. Yet a man only got sick-leave when he had at least forty degrees of fever and then only if the sick-leave quota for that day was not filled . . . Out of a camp of some ten thousand men, two thousand died every year. Every morning there were some prisoners who could not be roused, having died in the night. In the first two and a half months of my time at Kolyma, out of the total of twenty Poles in my group, sixteen died.[1]

Among the thousands of deportees was a sixteen-year-old high-school boy, Wojciech Jaruzelski, despatched to the north-eastern part of the Soviet Union with his parents.

The towns and villages which the deportees had left behind were being thoroughly bolshevised.[2] The secret police were given free rein, the Polish language was banned, Polish currency abolished, publication of Polish newspapers abandoned. Crucifixes and statues were removed, churches were converted into social clubs. Stalin was seeking to ensure that never again would Poland dare to assert her independence from Russia.

Almost certainly for political reasons, the world has learned little to this day of Russia's part in the crucifixion of Poland. Yet in the first two years of this, one of the most brutal occupations in human history, the savagery of the Russians probably exceeded that of the Germans. The Russians had long experience (in a tradition inherited from the Czars and enthusiastically continued) in the effective application of psychological terror.

* * *

Like Stalin, Hitler wanted his revenge for Versailles; he too wanted to exterminate the Poles. He admitted to his military chiefs[3] that Danzig had been only an excuse for invading Poland: he wanted the destruction of Poland, living room for Germans and a source of cheap labour for the Reich. In a document later read to an International Military Tribune, he suggested killing without mercy "all men, women and children of Polish race or language". Hitler's persecution differed from that of Stalin in that it was along racial rather than class lines: the Jews were confined to ghettos; the Aryans themselves were divided into categories of Reichsdeutsch (those born in Germany), Volksdeutch (those of possible German ancestry) and Nichtsdeutsch (everybody else).

On the western side of the border agreed beforehand with Russia, the Germans established a General Government area with its administrative centre in Kraków; while many areas of Prussia and Silesia were simply incorporated into the German Reich. From Kraków, Governor Hans Frank directed the plunder and exploitation of a captive people. "The Poles," he told his subordinates, "will work. They will eat little. And in the end they will die. There will never again be a Poland." All potential leaders – which meant all those who had received a higher education – clergy, teachers, doctors, dentists, vets, writers, journalists, students, along with landowners and businessmen, were to be liquidated. Blonde and blue-eyed Polish children were kidnapped on the streets and sent to the Reich to be brought up as Germans; hostages were rounded up and shot in scores or hundreds. It was not only the Jews for whom a Final Solution was being prepared.

But the full force of German hatred for Poland had not yet been unleashed. The knell sounded on 22nd June, 1941, when Hitler attacked his erstwhile ally, the Soviet Union, and drove the Red Army out of eastern Poland within a few days. Hitler was at the peak of his power; his grip on Eastern Europe was now complete. He was free to carry out the ambitious social engineering he had planned: where possible, the Poles were to be Germanised; and where it was not possible they were to be expelled to settlements beyond the Urals; a mere residue of the population was to be kept as a pool of semi-educated slaves, their education limited to a little reading and writing, and counting up to ten. "Sub-human" or useless human beings, such as Jews and gipsies, were to be eliminated.

They had already begun to implement these plans in west Prussia where seven hundred and fifty peasants had been driven out to make way for incoming German families; now they began to do the same in central Poland. Within a year they had cleared over three hundred villages with unspeakable lack of humanity. The whole world later heard of the massacre which took place in the Czech village of Lidice in reprisal for the murder of SS General Heydrich; and of Oradour-sur-Glane, the French village whose inhabitants were burned to death. But such massacres were commonplace in Poland, and few outside that country have been told of it.

This "pacification" of more than three hundred Polish villages is a statistic that numbs the mind. Yet even that was only part of the horror. Poland, wrote one historian, became "the home of humanity's holocaust, an archipelago of death-factories and camps, the scene of executions, pacifications and exterminations which surpassed anything so far documented in the history of mankind".[4]

The concentration camps for political and racial enemies of the Reich, which now proliferated throughout Poland, soon became the setting for wholesale slaughter. Life expectancy for a working inmate of Auschwitz, for example, was three months: many were simply killed on arrival. The very name of Auschwitz became synonymous with horror, the distilled essence of man's inhumanity to man. Irena G., a former Polish inmate there, will remember for ever what she saw on the morning after her arrival:

> It was a beautiful morning and as I came out of the barracks opposite the crematoria the sun was shining on what I took to be a pile of firewood. When I drew closer, I could see that in fact it was a huge heap of human bodies waiting to be shovelled into the ovens. As I stood there, dazed with horror, I found myself looking into a pair of imploring eyes, and realised that some of these pathetic "corpses" were still alive. They were putting the sick as well as the dead on those piles.

Like many other survivors of Auschwitz, Irena speaks of "a sky without birds". How could there have been birds, she asks. "There was nothing for them to eat. We prisoners had devoured every last blade of grass, every worm . . ."

The one ray of light was that the two tormentors were now at each other's throats. To the Poles in the eastern territories, the rout of the Russians was welcome; and to the deportees it brought an unexpected release. For the Soviet Union now became devotedly anti-Nazi, and what had once been denounced as the "imperialist war" had now been transmogrified into the "Great Patriotic War", in which the Russians' own survival was at stake. Stalin reached an agreement with General Sikorski, leader of the Polish government which since 1940 had been functioning in exile from London, made up of representatives of *all* the recognised pre-war political parties.

An amnesty was granted for the (non-existent) crimes of the deportees, and Stalin called on all Poles in the USSR to volunteer for a new Polish army unit which he hoped to incorporate into the Red Army. General Anders was released from the infamous Lubjanka prison in Moscow to lead it against the Germans. Thousands poured out of the slave-labour camps in the north and rushed south. Czesław Miłosz wrote: "The corpses of these ragged beggars littered the streets of the cities of south-eastern Russia, and out of the totally exhausted, half-dead people who survived the trek, an army was formed."[5]

Ludka L. and her family could scarcely believe their good fortune when they received the documents declaring them to be free. Eager to do something, anything, they joined the rush to the south in search of the new Army. Ludka's sixteen-year-old brother, Marian, eagerly joined up. They never saw him again; he died at Monte Cassino, fighting the Germans.

Stalin's hopes of bringing this Polish Army under his control came to nothing. It was the London government-in-exile which assumed control. In this lay the seeds of future trouble, for in Stalin's eyes, this was the army of the class enemy, and one day he would declare all who fought in it to be "enemies of the people".* The accusation would tragically blight the lives of their brothers, sisters, uncles and cousins who had remained behind in Poland.

* In March 1942, after much stalling and prevarication on the part of the Soviet authorities, Anders' army, together with the families of the fighting men, crossed into Persia, from where General Anders joined up with another Polish brigade to form the Second Corps. These men fought with distinction alongside the British Army in North Africa. In the ranks of Montgomery's Eighth Army, the Poles fought and died at Gazala, Tobruk, Monte Cassino, Ancona and Bologna. The Second Corps, together with the Polish Armed Forces which were already in the West, made a massive contribution to the Allied cause, one that ought never to be forgotten or undervalued. In the Battle of Britain of 1940, twenty per cent of the RAF's fighter pilots were Polish airmen.

An alarming discovery was then made. Among all the thousands of deportees flocking south, there was no sign of the fifteen thousand Polish officers deported in 1939. These men were, for the most part, reserves, professional men in civilian life: doctors, teachers, scientists, businessmen regarded with special loathing by the NKVD. As the "cream of the class enemy",[6] they had been segregated from the other deportees and sent to three special camps in western Russia.

Two years later, in April 1943, four thousand, three hundred and twenty-one corpses were discovered by the Germans in Katyń Forest outside Smolensk. They were the officers from one of the three camps. Most had their hands tied behind their backs and a bullet in the back of their necks. Goebbels made propaganda out of the discovery; Russia hastened to accuse the Germans. But, whatever the record of Nazi bestiality, few believed that the Germans were guilty of this particular crime. The evidence (the summer uniforms worn by the murdered men; the age of the tiny saplings growing on the mass grave) all pointed to the deed having been done in April 1940 when the area was still in Russian hands, rather than in the winter of 1941 when the Germans had conquered it.

Because no one has ever admitted to the crime, it has remained a great unsolved mystery, a festering interrogation mark over future relations between Poland and Russia. The fate of the other eleven thousand officers can still only be guessed at. But few people doubt that a realistic search would bring to light other Katyńs.

* * *

The Jewish community was already wasting away from terror and near-starvation in the ghettos. In Warsaw, on 4th May, 1942, Chaim Kaplan wrote in his diary: "The hour of twilight is harder to bear than the hour of total darkness. We are on the eve of great events – perhaps decisive ones."[7]

On 30th May he wrote: ". . . outside – annihilation; inside – terror. Woe unto us, for we are lost. You are certain that the death sentences have been drawn up; it is merely a matter of awaiting your turn – your turn to die. Perhaps it will come tonight, perhaps in a few more nights, but you will not escape your fate."

As Jewish settlements all over Poland were being wiped out, their inhabitants murdered, Jews from other cities were being driven into the already bursting ghetto of Warsaw. By July 1942 the deportations from Warsaw had already begun, and Kaplan's diary becomes more and more anguished:

> 27 July . . . the ghetto has turned into an inferno. Men have become beasts . . . People are being hunted down in the streets like animals in the forest . . .
>
> 1 August: Families become frantic. Where will you go? What can you save? What first, what last? They begin to pack bundles in haste and fear, with trembling hands and feet which refuse to do their bidding and to take their belongings outside, for they no longer have a home. Hundreds of women and swollen infants rend the heavens with their cries. The sick are taken outside in their beds, babies in their cradles, old men and women half-naked and barefoot . . .

On that day alone ten thousand people were deported from the ghetto. Jewish Warsaw was in its last agony – the death camps were operating at peak capacity. In April 1943, in a final act of glorious heroism, the survivors of the ghetto went down fighting, as once their ancestors had fought at Masada. Seven thousand Jews were killed in that Ghetto Rising – its fifty-six thousand survivors were transported to instant death at the Treblinka Camp outside Warsaw. Hope died. The insurgents sent a last accusing message to the world outside: "The world is silent. The world *knows* (it is inconceivable that it should not) and stays silent . . . This silence is astonishing and horrifying."[7]

The accusation of silence – and worse – is today often levelled against the Poles; and in some cases the charges are undoubtedly true. There were fanatical anti-semites among them, and there is appalling evidence that some of them rejoiced in this butchery of the Jews. But it is tragically unfair to blame the majority. One woman in Warsaw must surely speak for thousands of decent ordinary Poles when she recalls her horror at what was done: "For me and for everyone I knew, these things put an end, once and forever, to whatever anti-Jewish feeling we had had. I for one felt ashamed even to be alive in a world where such things happened."

People travelling through the ghetto area in sealed trams would throw food parcels out of the tram windows. One woman who worked in a packing factory whose windows overlooked the ghetto also threw out parcels when she had anything to put in them. "It wasn't much," she admits, "but there wasn't much to give. The Jews were starving. But we Poles were not far from starving either."

In providing any help at all to the stricken Jews, every Pole put his life at risk. It is not generally realised that Poland was the only Nazi-occupied country in which even to offer a Jew a glass of water merited instant death – not only for the offender but for his or her entire family too. In the face of such appalling retribution, who can stand in judgment on those Poles who turned away? The amazing thing, however, is that thousands of Poles took the risk, and paid the penalty. If between fifty and a hundred thousand Jews survived four years of Nazi occupation in Poland, it is because many were hidden by individual Poles or by religious orders throughout Poland. Many others actually survived the concentration camps.

Those Poles who were guilty of betraying Jews to the Gestapo were invariably sentenced to death by the courts set up by the Home Army resistance groups, and the sentences were faithfully executed. When Jews were betrayed in this way, not only they but the Polish family sheltering them were shot.

The Home Army resistance movement set up special units to help Jews, and organised various escape routes, a difficult feat with the Gestapo always in evidence. "We got hundreds of children out through underground sewers," says a Home Army man whose home for four years was in the vast Kampinos forest outside Warsaw. "I wish it could have been thousands. But we did our best."

When the Warsaw Ghetto rose in its last defiant stand, the Poles gave what help they could. Later they would be charged with not doing enough, with not, for example, providing the insurgents with enough guns. But they didn't have the guns. The Home Army at that period was not as self-sufficient as it later became; and the only ammunition at their disposal was: what the British managed to send them; what they had managed to save from the September 1939 campaign; and the little they were able to manufacture for themselves. Very occasionally a Polish resistance fighter would manage to persuade a friendly German to supply them with guns; but such an arrangement was dangerous, and discovery always meant death. "Would it have helped," mused a Polish woman, "if all of Warsaw had risen then, in support of the ghetto? I honestly don't think so. The result would have been the same. It might have taken a little longer, that's all."

Outside the ghetto area, Warsaw was surviving, but only just. While the men fought in the Home Army, the women worked to help them and to keep starvation from their families. Not only starvation but fear. "A ring at the door and the sight of the police after curfew terrified us. We were never free of fear." But, afraid or not, they were utterly convinced that one day the Germans would be driven out and Poland would once again belong to the Poles. Faith in the future was strong. The churches were fuller than ever they had been before the war. "For my generation," a young woman said, "it was the time when our religious faith was reborn."

[1] Quoted by Norman Davies in *God's Playground, A History of Poland*, Volume II, Clarendon Press, Oxford, 1984.

[2] Czesław Miłosz, *The Captive Mind*, Chapter 4, Secker & Warburg, 1953.

[3] Nicholas Bethell, *The War Hitler Won*, Allen Lane, Penguin, 1972.

[4] Norman Davies, *op. cit.*

[5] Czesław Miłosz, *op. cit.*

[6] Norman Davies, *op. cit.* Chapter 20: "Golgota, Poland in the Second World War."

[7] *Scroll of Agony: The Warsaw Diary of Chaim H. Kaplan*, Hamish Hamilton, 1966. Found intact on a farm outside Warsaw twenty years after the events it describes.

Reference has been made in this chapter to three papers given at an international Conference on Polish–Jewish Relations held at Somerville College, Oxford, in September 1984:

I. "The Problem of Polish Anti-Semitism," Jerzy Turowicz.
II. "Polish Society in Confrontation with Jewish Fugitives in Hiding 1942–1944," Shmuel Krakowski.
III. "Polish–Jewish Relations in Occupied Poland 1939–1945," Władysław Bartoszewski.

2 WAŁĘSA

For Freedom's battle once begun,
Bequeath'd by bleeding Sire to Son,
Though baffled oft is ever won.

Byron: *The Giaour*

The young Wałęsa who had been deported by the Russians after the 1830 Rising had made the most of his opportunities in France; he had married and bought some land there. But as time passed, the position of the Polish *émigrés* in France changed. Towards the end of the 1870s, as a result of international agreements reached between France and the Russian, Prussian and Austro-Hungarian occupiers of Poland, it became clear, beyond the faintest shadow of doubt, that Poland could not gain her freedom in the foreseeable future. From then on, France no longer made even a pretence of support for the Polish cause. "The Poles in emigration grew older and died," says one historian.[1] Some remained in Paris, brooding on Poland's lost greatness and dreaming impossible dreams. But in some, disappointment bred a new realism. They returned home to Poland, there to work, quietly but doggedly, for the creation of a free Poland at some time in the far-distant future.

It was the son and grandson of that earlier Wałęsa who now returned to Russian-occupied Poland to look for a suitable place to live. The father and his son, whose name was Mateusz, concentrated their search on the area between the Vistula River and the vast Kujawy plain, an area to whose myriad tiny villages the Poles give the collective title of Dobrzyń. "The landscape," wrote Halina Mirowska,[2] over a century later, "is full of Mazovian melancholy which foreigners reared on Chopin call Polishness. White ducks dive sleepily on overgrown ponds, storks, willows weeping into the ditches, and isolated farms among dusty raspberry patches."

It is a lonely area, miles from any large town. "I think my great-great-grandfather wanted to be as far away from the towns as possible," speculates Lech Wałęsa's sister, Izabela. And far away from the secret police who would no doubt be aware of his return. Izabela agrees: "He seems to have been afraid of someone or something, and only in the depths of the country could he feel safe."

Mateusz Wałęsa's father bought the tiny hamlet of Popowo, about fifty hectares, and set himself up as a gentleman farmer. (There are several villages called Popowo in Poland, but this one is too small to feature on any map.) He was minor gentry – not a great landowner, but grand enough to ride to church in his own horse-drawn carriage. A pious man, he walked his fields each day, rosary in hand. The village inn which he owned and rented out did a thriving business, because in those days the busy trade routes from the Baltic ports to the south of Poland ran through Popowo, and the traffic was constant.

Every so often, Mateusz and his father returned to France for a visit. But Poland was now their home, and after a while the visits ceased. When Mateusz married, he had two sons. One of these became one of the first Polish Communists and was disowned by his father. The other son, Jan, Lech Wałęsa's grandfather, inherited the whole estate. Jan was something of a legend in the village. He had twelve sons and twelve daughters; was reputed to have belonged to a Polish military organisation, and to have sheltered Józef Piłsudski, the future Marshal of Poland, in his house. He was a well-informed man, who would not burn a newspaper until he had read it from cover to cover, though he always tore off a corner of it to roll round his tobacco for a cigarette. The First World War rolled over the Kujawy plain, though the destruction there was less than elsewhere. The final outcome of the war, however, the rebirth of Poland in 1918, must have been a deeply moving experience for Jan Wałęsa.

When Jan died, the Popowo property was divided into twenty-four neat but very small parcels. Poland has no law of primogeniture, whereby the eldest son inherits everything, and the others learn to fend for themselves. In a system in which every member of a gentry family inherited *some*thing, the villages of Poland were in those days full of proud but utterly pauperised gentry.

Like his brothers and sisters, Jan's son, Bolesław, who was to become the father of Lech, farmed his inadequate morsel of land. It was not only inadequate but very poor, and nothing would grow there but wheat and potatoes. In addition, he kept a few pigs, two cows and some hens; and travelled weekly to market to sell his butter, milk and eggs. Bolesław, usually known as Bolek, and his brother Stanisław, had learned carpentry from their father, and it stood them in good stead. They were skilled craftsmen, the best for miles around, and were in much demand by local farmers, for building barns and cowsheds.

Bolek married a girl from another Dobrzyń village, Feliksa Kamińska, whose family had lived for generations in the area. Her father, Leopold Kamiński, was a peasant farmer, poor but extremely intelligent, and, despite his lack of education, well-read and a mine of information. In his spare time, Leopold kept the parish records up to date.

After their marriage, Bolek and Feliksa settled down in what was little more than a cowshed on Bolek's share of the Popowo land – a mere hectare and a half (about three acres), barely enough to feed the two of them, and even more woefully inadequate when the children began to arrive. When the war came to blast their lives to hell, the couple had two children, Izabela and Edward, with a third, Stanisław, on the way.

Their part of Poland was incorporated into the German Reich and systematically stripped of all traces of Polishness. Place-names were Germanised, Polish flags burned, Polish books and libraries destroyed, and Polish schools closed. In the country, only the poor farms – like that of Bolek – were left in the hands of the Poles. All larger farms were handed over to German farmers – and the local women were required to work for them on demand. Feliksa Wałęsa (and even her small daughter, Izabela), worked for two farmers, by name Proch and Krempitz. On the whole, the German farmers in this area were kind enough; and only one of them seems to have inspired terror.

But the peasants had to provide food for the Germans. Everything they produced had to be delivered to the Germans at a stipulated time and a stipulated place. In exchange they were given black bread, sugar, oil for their lamps, coupons to exchange for clothes. They were not allowed to keep any of their own grain. If they did so (and most did), they would grind it in a coffee grinder to avoid detection. Possession of a grindstone or quern for grinding wheat was punishable by hanging, or by being sent to a concentration camp. The same fate awaited those foolhardy enough to keep a pig, chickens or geese for their own use. To kill a food-animal was a capital offence.

And if the peasants were unable, by their own efforts, to fulfil the quota set for them, they simply had to acquire the stuff somehow on the open market. No excuse was accepted.

Almost without exception, as in every part of Poland, the peasants either belonged to or supported the Home Army partisans, who lived in the forests by day and came out at night to collect food and sabotage the German communication lines. In sheltering and feeding them, the peasants ran almost as much danger as the partisans themselves, and arrests were frequent. A mass grave for twenty-four unnamed Poles in Sobowo churchyard where the Wałęsa family worshipped, tells its own sombre story.

Izabela Wałęsa (now Młynska) recalls putting out food for the partisans at dead of night. She would be given bread and meat by her mother and told to place them under a certain tree. In the morning they would be gone. The exercise was almost routine for the child. But there is one day in particular which she will never forget. Her father's brother, Stanisław, had been deported to a labour camp in Germany, but had managed to escape, wearing a stolen German uniform. In the late summer of 1943, he had reached Popowo and hidden in Bolek's barn. Someone – perhaps because of the German uniform – must have informed; and next day the Gestapo came. They did not find Stanisław, who had already gone to join the partisans in the forest. He must have gone in the German uniform, since they did not find that either. (It must have been tricky explaining that away to the partisans, and it is a wonder he was not shot on sight.)

But the Germans did not go away empty-handed. Failing to find one brother, they took the other. Bolek was taken away for questioning. At his interrogation, he was beaten so badly that his skull was damaged. Then he was sent off to forced labour, leaving his wife, twenty-six-year-old Feliksa, far advanced in pregnancy, to look after the farm and the family single-handed.

At 9 a.m. on 27th September, 1943, her fourth child, a boy, was born. Stubbornly asserting his Polish heritage, she gave him the old Slavonic name, Lech, after the legendary founder of the Polish race. Perhaps because of the circumstances surrounding his birth, perhaps because of the poverty and hopelessness into which he was born, he would always be her favourite child.

To Feliksa's sorrow, the baby could not be christened in her own church at Sobowo, four kilometres away across the fields. For the parish priest, Father Zaremba, like most of the other priests in the area, had been sent to a concentration camp and had been killed there in 1941. Instead, the christening took place, on 3rd November, at the big church of Mokowo, and a neighbour lent the family a horse and cart for the occasion.

Lech Wałęsa would never know his father. Bolek, seriously injured after his beating, was sent to a labour camp at Młyniec near Toruń, and put to work digging trenches and building bridges.

The work was beyond his strength, and he made little pretence at doing his share. When the job was done, and the other prisoners were moved to another site, Bolek was left behind, to endure the freezing winter of 1944–5 in an unheated barracks, with no more than a sheet to cover him at night. "Can you imagine: to lie on the bed under a single sheet in that cold? Your hair froze to the wall!"[3] It was a death sentence, and Bolek knew it.

[1] *The History of Poland since 1863*, ed. R. F. Leslie. C.U.P., 1980.

[2] Halina Mirowska, *Lechu*, Glos Publications, New York, 1982.

[3] Neal Ascherson, *The Book of Lech Wałesa*, Chapter 1, Penguin, Allen Lane, 1981.

3 THE EDGE OF THE CYCLONE (1943–5)

> Communism for us is not what it is for the great majority of people in the world, an idea, a project, good or bad, true or false, orientated towards the future. It is a reality. A reality which no one in the country chose; a reality imposed on us by force against our will and in spite of our struggles.
>
> Bohdan Cywiński, 1984

The Germans pressed on towards Moscow. But, like Napoleon before them, they had overreached themselves. The six-month battle for Stalingrad proved to be the turning-point of the war. It marked the beginning of the end of the Third Reich; and it was now that to all intents and purposes the post-war period began, as Stalin took out of cold storage his earlier plans for the subjugation of central and Eastern Europe.

Already he had re-activated the Polish Communist Party, which he had determinedly destroyed in 1936. A three-man team, chosen from comrades who had survived the purges in the Soviet Union, was parachuted into German-occupied Poland. In January 1942 this group established itself in Warsaw under the name of the Polish Workers' Party. They were soon to be joined by Władysław Gomułka and others who had never left Poland. Avoiding the name "Communist", so detested by the majority of Poles, and all mention of class war or revolution, the group appealed for a broad national front to defeat the Nazi invaders. For the most part, their appeal fell on deaf ears. The Poles, who already had a perfectly satisfactory resistance movement, were well aware that only since the Soviet Union had been attacked had the Communists (whether they used the name or not) been willing to take a part in the struggle for freedom. By June 1942 only four thousand had joined them, plus three thousand partisans in the Communist militia, the People's Guard.

The Polish Workers' Party continued its conciliatory stance right through 1942 and for the first part of 1943. But after the discoveries in the Katyń Forest, followed by the London-based Polish government's demand for an International Red Cross enquiry, Stalin broke off relations with the Poles, and the Party went on to the offensive. It became stridently hostile to the London government and turned its People's Guard into a People's Army intended to be a direct rival to the London-led Home Army.

By the middle of 1943 it was abundantly clear that Poland would eventually be "liberated" by the Red Army and not by the West. In a bid to keep control of the Polish Communists, Stalin now sent a Polish-born NKVD security police official, Bolesław Bierut, to Poland to keep the Party on the right pro-Soviet lines. Bierut immediately clashed with the Polish leader, Gomułka, who wanted to establish a socialism specifically geared to Polish needs and who, for that purpose, wished to seek help from other left-wing parties. To Bierut such considerations were irrelevant: if support was not forthcoming, then coercion would have to be used.

The Communists now set up a National Council for the Homeland, which claimed to be "the real political representative of the Polish nation", qualified to take power and establish a government when the moment came. But to Gomułka's disappointment, the regular left-wing parties would have nothing to do with it.

Stalin was worried both by the Polish Workers' Party's conspicuous lack of success and by its unwelcome spirit of independence. As an insurance, he set up a rival, more trustworthy, body of Polish Communists in the Soviet Union itself. This group, the Union of Polish Patriots, immediately called for a Polish military force under its control.

So the Kościuszko division of the Red Army, under General Berling, came into being. It was Stalin's own, unlike the Polish armies in the West. For it, he had unearthed Soviet citizens of Polish origin; and large numbers of Polish refugees and deportees, who had not been able to reach Anders' army in time, and who now saw this new unit as their only hope of ever escaping from Russia. Polish Jews, whom Stalin judged unlikely to have much sympathy for the Polish population as a whole, represented by far the largest single group of deportees, and were drafted in large numbers into the political and security sections. Together with the pseudo-Poles (many of them Russians or Ukrainians drafted in their thousands, though they could not speak a word of Polish) and with the Polish Communists who had settled in the Soviet Union after 1917, these inexperienced "soldiers" were to enter Poland with the Red Army and act as a prop for the pro-Soviet government to be established there. Over half of the officers had previously served in the Red Army, and all the highest ranks were filled by Russians. The security police and the Union of Polish Patriots were in overall control. In the ranks of this army was Wojciech Jaruzelski. His father, an agricultural engineer, and his mother, Wanda, had disappeared somewhere in Soviet Russia, and Wojciech had been working as a labourer. In the circumstances, the creation of Berling's Army must have offered him a heaven-sent opportunity of securing a future for himself. He was enrolled into the army as an "orphan soldier".

The people of eastern Poland watched in horror as the Russian tide advanced. They wanted to be rid of the Germans, it is true; but they had always recognised that the enemy had two faces, and that the threat from the east was, if anything, more to be feared. They had no illusions. After all, they had only recently emerged from a century and a half of Russian domination, and memories were still raw: "With the Russians there is no hope. Only the dead hand of oppression, the unrelieved weight of Russian insensibility . . . Do it their way or die . . . Russians can make an entire nation a tomb. They're geniuses at building tombs."[1]

The nightmare began to take shape. On 2nd January, 1944, the Red Army crossed the pre-1939 frontier of Poland, which Stalin was also laying claim to. From this moment the Polish Home Army partisans launched their long-prepared Operation "Tempest". Believing that the Red Army intended to co-operate with them in the liberation of Poland, large groups of Polish partisans (the Home Army had 300,000 members and the peasant battalions at least half that number) began attacking German garrisons and freeing large areas of the country. In these towns and villages they set up a Polish administration. The partisans' success enabled the Russians to advance with lightning speed, encountering little opposition from the already demoralised Germans.

But the Poles' joy was short-lived. NKVD units had entered Poland with the Red Army and immediately on arrival set up a Polish section, the UB security forces. Their only task was to arrest anyone associated in any way with pre-war Poland, especially those who had fought in the underground resistance. All those who had recently assumed administrative duties in the liberated villages were arrested. And the partisan units, far from finding the Russians grateful for their assistance, were disarmed, arrested and sent to concentration camps in the Soviet Union. Many senior officers were executed on the spot.

When an area had been thoroughly "liberated", Soviet-style, hardly anyone was left who might be capable of independent thought. In his novel, *Seizure of Power*, Czesław Miłosz recounts the feelings of a young man who has returned home in this way with the conscript Polish army:

> My country. Everything on a small scale, clutching at bits of land – small fields, small gardens, narrow boundary strips, a peasant with his only horse, an old woman with her cow, an inn, a village shop, neighbours leaning against fences, small girls with bare red feet driving geese – a world innocent of mechanised warfare and books on political theory . . .
>
> What did the peasants think? Their land had been crushed by tanks built in the Ruhr; they had known terror and man-hunts and blue-eyed, fair-haired children taken from their mothers by force . . . Now at last they saw tanks built beyond the Urals. Everything reached them from the outside: a punishment, a calamity, the edge of a cyclone whose centre was always somewhere else, somewhere far away in an unknown country or in the minds of unknown people.[2]

The Red Army's summer offensive swept all before it. But the Stalin-inspired Polish Workers' Party was having much less joy, as neither the peasants nor the political parties in the liberated areas would succumb to its honeyed promises. Then on 21st July, 1944, the Red Army captured Chelm near Lublin, which lay 130 miles west of the Polish border as the Poles knew it, but which in Stalin's eyes was where Poland began. Once again, the glowing promises were dropped in favour of coercion. On the following day, without so much as a nod in the direction of the populace, and without consulting any of the other interested parties, Stalin set up a Polish Committee of National Liberation, composed entirely of Communists and fellow-travellers, though the fact was carefully disguised and it was made to look like a genuine, Popular Front government, with Bolesław Bierut and Władysław Gomułka at its head. Posters proclaiming the Committee's Manifesto had been printed in Moscow beforehand. The Committee's spectacular lack of popular support seemed not to matter, as anyone who opposed it was promptly dealt with by the security forces.

Right up to 29th July, Moscow Radio was calling on the citizens of Warsaw to rise, and on 30th July a Soviet military station called them to arms: "People of Warsaw, strike at the Germans. Help the Red Army cross the Vistula." Soviet planes over Warsaw dropped leaflets urging an immediate uprising. By now, six million Poles had been "liberated" by the Russians. The Home Army resistance forces in the city, under the leadership of General Bór-Komorowski, had a terrible decision to make. It was already clear that Warsaw would make a last stand against the Russians, in order to preserve some sort of base for a future Polish state. The agonising question was: when? But, with the Red Army already at the gates, there was little freedom of manoeuvre. The order was given to start Operation Tempest in Warsaw.

In the first days of August the Red Army and Berling's Polish Army crossed the Vistula in several places south of Warsaw, and then suddenly came to a halt. Few people today doubt that they did so for political reasons. Communist historians claim that the Red Army met heavy German resistance hereabouts and was forced on to the defensive. This claim does not bear much examination: the Russian forces were many times larger than the Germans', and the German defence lines were weak. When, on 1st August, the Rising actually broke out, the insurgents gained some considerable successes in the first few days, liberating most of the city in fact, apart from a few isolated pockets of stiff German resistance. If the Soviets had wished to, they could easily have invaded at that time. But, from the moment that the Rising began, the radio stations went quiet, as did the Russian tanks and guns. They simply stayed on the outskirts of Warsaw, while the citizens, despite their initial success, were systematically butchered by the Nazi troops and the city itself was razed to the ground.

Even at this eleventh hour, the Home Army counted on some sort of help from Britain and America. But the Western allies dared not offend Russia. Relations between them had deteriorated, but Russia's help was still believed necessary for the final defeat of Germany and the continuing war with Japan. At a meeting in Teheran in November 1943, the three wartime allies had already agreed in principle to divide Europe into separate "spheres of influence"; and on a new outline of the Polish–Soviet frontier, which would ratify Russia's present gains and which was to all intents and purposes the same as the Nazi–Soviet demarcation line drawn up in 1939. The Poles did not know it yet, but Britain and America had already left them to their fate. Apart from a couple of attempted parachute drops (see next page), no help was forthcoming to the Warsaw insurgents from the West.

After a few days' silence, Moscow spoke again but this time with a very different voice. On 6th August, an article in the Soviet army newspaper made the absurd claim that the Home Army insurgents were collaborating with the Germans! On the 8th, Radio Moscow said that it was not the Home Army but the Communist People's Army which had sacrificed itself in the slaughter – in spite of the fact that there were only six hundred or so Communist fighters in Warsaw, compared with over forty thousand Home Army soldiers.

Beleaguered and desperate, the people of Warsaw continued to hold out: without water, gas, electricity, food or medicines, reduced to eating dogs and stray pigeons to stay alive. A survivor has left this record:

> German bombers rampaged over the city day and night, burying the living beneath the rubble. People sought shelter from the air-raids in basements, but found no safety there; the Germans dragged them out and conducted mass-executions – of men, women and children. Everyone took part regardless of age or sex. People did not sleep, eat or wash for days on end. No one knew whether he'd be alive five minutes later. Corpses lay about in the streets and the stench of rotting bodies rose from the ruins.[3]

The odds were hopelessly unequal. In that last act of defiance over one hundred and fifty thousand died, and among them were the flower of Poland's youth, the young men and women who might have given leadership in a reborn Poland. Many others, regardless of whether they were resistance fighters or civilians, were rounded up and forced to march to Pruszków, a transit camp about thirty kilometres outside Warsaw, from where they were despatched to Auschwitz and other concentration camps in Poland or Germany. A woman civilian recalls bitterly: "They arrested my mother and me, and said we were bandits. Then they put us in cattle trucks and sent us to Ravensbrück. Well, I came out of there alive, but my mother didn't. She died in the camp at the age of fifty-five."

With some help from the West, in the shape of parachute drops of equipment – largely carried out by the Polish Air Force with much loss of life – the insurgents held out for sixty-three days. But with no help coming from outside, further resistance was hopeless. With despair they heard their commander, General Bór-Komorowski, give the order to surrender. Yet, though this decision was a painful one, the General had wrung one important concession from the Germans. Members of the beaten Home Army were to be treated not as bandits but as regular prisoners of war, in accordance with the Geneva Convention.

All this while, the Russians played a waiting game, watching impassively from the south bank of the river. "They wanted us to die," say the survivors, while, in spite of the official surrender, the Germans, on the express orders of Hitler himself, proceeded to the stone-by-stone demolition of what had been one of Europe's most beautiful cities. Other European cities suffered devastation; but what was done to Warsaw was without parallel. Many had not obeyed General Bór's instructions to come out and surrender to the Germans. They were still there, in their houses, when the Germans started on the final demolition – blowing up the houses, throwing flame throwers or cylinders of explosive gas into the cellars.

What remained was a smouldering moonscape of debris and ash, a graveyard of Polish dreams. When the vandals had done with Warsaw, they had destroyed not only some ninety per cent of the city, but also the nerve-centre of "the most widespread and determined of Europe's resistance movements".[4]

Stalin's ruthless determination had been clearly demonstrated. So too had the Western allies' helplessness. The shock to the survivors cannot be overestimated. They knew that it was all over, that the Communists had only to walk into the city and claim it. The Lublin Committee proclaimed itself the Provisional Government on 31st December, and within it the Polish Workers' Party was predominant. In January, Berling's First Polish Army, under its Russian command, took possession of the stricken shell of the capital, and staged a victory parade amid the ruins.[5]

When the Germans had gone, one hundred thousand people crossed the Vistula River to Warsaw, by boat or over makeshift temporary bridges. Some were returning from Germany, as the concentration and labour camps yielded up their victims; others from different parts of Poland. They came by cycle, by horse and cart, or on foot, walking barefoot and in rags towards what they could not recognise as Warsaw. No streets, no houses, no landmarks of any kind.

> We walked through the snow, with tears streaming down our cheeks, hoping to avoid the unexploded bombs [remembers a survivor], and wherever we looked, there was nothing but rubble and little wooden crosses in the dust. Then, through the curtain of snow, we saw a wisp of smoke and moved towards it. Some enterprising person had started a fire over some planks and was selling hot soup.

Ninety per cent of those who returned would have nowhere to go and no families to find, and a feature of that time was the countless little notes, left on stones or in the porches of surviving churches, giving information about where the writer was to be found.

The Nazis left, convinced that Warsaw would never rise again.

The city looked, as Bolesław Bierut observed, "as though a great earthquake had shattered it". Living in caves, like troglodytes, in holes in the ground, in ditches, sewers, underground tunnels and shelters; in wooden shacks or the staircases of demolished houses, without water or light, roofs, doors or cooking stoves; without transport, schools, hospitals, or communications of any kind, the people of Warsaw were consumed with the desire to rebuild their city as it had been.

But first the Army would have to defuse the bombs. The whole area was a minefield. And next the people must perform what for them was the most sacred of all duties. They gathered the ashes or remains of those who had been executed by the Gestapo, and gave them burial. Only when that was done, could the work of reconstruction begin.

They would rebuild the city. And for the first two years they would do it by clawing the earth with tiny shovels or with their bare hands. Wrapping their hands and feet in rags to keep out the bitter cold, with brick-dust silting up their mouths and noses, the inhabitants of Warsaw set to with incredible vitality. They gathered and sorted bricks, salvaged pieces of wood from charred window-frames. They dug up stones, levelled the earth and took away the rubble in horse-drawn carts. And beneath every heap of stones they would find a corpse.

And when they at last had some sort of roof over their heads, a shelter from the wind and rain, however makeshift, they would ask to rebuild the churches of Warsaw and the mediaeval buildings of its Old City.

[1] James A. Michener, *Poland*, Secker & Warburg, 1983 and Corgi Books.

[2] Czesław Miłosz, *The Seizure of Power*, Abacus, 1985.

[3] Anna Świrszczyńska in *Anthology of Post-War Polish Poetry*, selected and edited by Czesław Miłosz, University of California Press, third edition, 1983.

[4] M. K. Dziewanowski, *Poland in the Twentieth Century*, Columbia University Press, 1977.

[5] Because he attempted to help the Warsaw insurgents in September 1944, General Berling was hauled before his Russian superiors and sent to the Soviet Military Academy for "further education". His post was taken over by someone more "reliable".

Also: "Poland's Aftermath", article by Thomas Field in *Poland One*, 1/12.

4 TOWARDS A BETTER TOMORROW? (1945–7)

> Many people were spiritually prepared to rebuild the system. Had it not been for their narrow atheism, Polish society with its cultural, historically democratic tendencies, would have been a most fertile field for a wise government to work on. Unfortunately, observation proved how little talent for social work this government had; how very much it relied on physical oppression and force. This in itself negated a good part of the positive results, since the people, oppressed, stood up in opposition even against many legitimate goals. If Marxism had come directly from the West, without Eastern intervention, it would undoubtedly have been accepted with greater trust.
>
> Cardinal Stefan Wyszyński: *A Freedom Within*

Letters went out to the men who had fought in the West. "Your country is free. Come back and build the new Poland." But in May 1945, as the men from the Western armies returned, they found all too often that the homes they had left no longer existed. Many of the exiles in Britain and France were unable to return as their home towns and villages were now incorporated into Russia. The harvest of war had been bitter; the people were shattered. One fifth of the population of pre-war Poland had been killed, and of these almost ninety per cent had been shot, hanged, or murdered in the concentration camps. Six million, twenty-eight thousand Polish citizens dead, of whom three million were Jews. In spite of their magnificent resistance, the people had a crushing sense of failure.

"Do you know what it's like to be twenty-five and to find no one who knew you as a child?" The speaker, a returning soldier, had lost twenty-two members of his immediate family: parents, brothers and sisters, uncles, aunts, cousins, friends, all shot in 1940 in the house where they were celebrating a wedding.

Among the half-dead survivors of camps such as Auschwitz and Majdanek, Buchenwald or Ravensbrück, were the "guinea-pig" victims of medical experiments, people like Wanda P. who had bacteria injected into her legs and spine, and petrol into her veins. Or Małgosia K., a child of three subjected to such gross internal experiments that she would spend most of her childhood in a hospital bed. Hanka L., a baby liberated from Auschwitz and delivered to an orphanage, was, like Małgosia, among the many who would never discover who they really were:

> I don't know exactly when I was born [she has said]. My mother was taken to Auschwitz and gave birth to me there. She died in the camp, and my father was executed. It seems from the camp archives that I had an older brother who died from typhus in the camp and it's thought that my family were previously in Majdanek camp. I was prisoner number . . . which was tattooed on my arm by the SS.

As Stalin's winter offensive of January 1945 drove the Germans out of their last footholds in western Poland – the territories they had incorporated into the Reich itself – it seemed as though the "liberators" were even more intent on terrorising the local population than on expelling the Germans. In these lands which were to be taken from Germany and given to Poland, the Russian army wreaked unbelievable havoc: "Arson, battery, murder, group-rapes and family suicides marked the passage of the liberating armies on a scale unparalleled elsewhere in Europe."[1]

The roads were jammed with refugees. The Russians plundered machinery from factories, cut down the dockyard cranes and sent them to the Soviet Union for scrap metal; they confiscated food from the peasants and removed railway works, locomotives and trains. Two weeks after the end of the war, Russian soldiers from the garrison at Lębork went on a drunken rampage and burned down the whole town. Danzig, once again called Gdańsk, was also effectively razed to the ground.

Old familiar landmarks had disappeared – Poland had suffered a sea-change. "Wherever we went," said a survivor of the camps, "it was as though we were in another country." The old territorial boundaries had changed and, enclosed now on three sides by Russia, Poland was effectively cut off from all contact with friendly countries. Her ethnic mix was reduced: the Byelo-Russians and Ukrainians had been absorbed by Russia; the Jews had vanished into the ovens*; her intelligentsia had been liquidated. The whole

* At the beginning of the 1950s, the Jews accounted for 0.2 per cent of Poland's population. A high percentage of Jews had returned from the Soviet Union in 1945 where they had spent the war years. These Jews were former inhabitants of Poland's eastern territories annexed by the Soviet Union in September 1939. This fact saved them from the gas chambers to which their fellow-Jews in Nazi-occupied areas were doomed. *See* Peter Raina: *Political Opposition in Poland, 1954–1977*.

country was a seething mass of migrants, as the hordes of refugees, expellees and repatriates clogged the railways and roads. As millions of hapless Germans fled westward, millions of equally hapless Poles trekked from the east to take their place. Marek Korowicz, returning from the West, described the nightmare journey by slow train from Gdynia and a meeting with some of these refugees:

> At one station we talked for a couple of hours with these unfortunates. Their transport had been on the way for two weeks. For two weeks, women and children, old people and countless adult men had been travelling in cattle trucks on straw. Half of these trucks had no roof. In the cold, rain and snow, people were huddling under sheets; emaciated children were crying; old people, lying on the straw in hopeless apathy. They had to survive as best they could.[2]

In this climate of unimaginable misery, Yalta was perhaps the bitterest pill of all. For it was at Yalta in the Crimea that Poland was handed over to the Soviet Union. In February 1945 the Big Three, Roosevelt, Churchill and Stalin, had met at Yalta to consolidate the understandings reached at Teheran about the fate of Europe and to re-establish the balance of power. Stalin had the upper hand, since Roosevelt believed that he still needed his help against Japan (the A-Bomb had not yet been tested) and did not want to antagonise him. Churchill had his hands tied: "Uncle Joe" Stalin was popular with the British public and there would be an outcry if he was thwarted now. Besides, the West was impatient with Poland for putting "unnecessary" difficulties in the way of a post-war settlement with Russia. In Britain this resentment was increased by a totally unfounded belief that enough British money and energy had already been spent on Poland. The stark truth that, after her initial gesture of declaring war, Britain had not struck one blow in Poland's defence was conveniently forgotten, as was the enormous contribution made by the Poles to the British war effort. (When the Victory in Europe parade marched through London in May, the Poles did not even receive an invitation to attend.) Russia, who had in any case "liberated" most of Poland by this time and was not intending to leave, was felt to have earned a stake in Poland, a fair compensation for her own undoubted sufferings during the war. Westerners did not know or care to recall that, in the course of that war, the Russians had sent over a quarter of a million Poles from the captured eastern provinces to their deaths.

Ignoring the undeniable fact that Russians and Poles are as

different from each other as the proverbial chalk and cheese – the Russians with their long experience of despotic tyranny and their blindly obedient people, the Poles with their fanatical love of independence – Roosevelt and Churchill handed Poland over. In all their history the Russians had never known freedom; the Poles had valued it above all else. Marxist-Leninism would strike at the roots of everything the Poles held most sacred.

Stalin appeared to make a concession to his allies by agreeing to "free and unfettered" elections in Poland, as soon as she had straightened herself out; and by allowing representatives of the London Poles to take part in the government and to be eligible for election. To be fair, Roosevelt and Churchill did not understand the enormity of the threat to Europe's freedom, nor realise that when Stalin talked of "democracy" he did not even know what it meant. They trusted Stalin to be a man of honour on their terms – though Roosevelt died a disillusioned man and Churchill later wondered how history would judge his naïvety. "The Eagle should permit the small birds to sing," he had suggested to Stalin, and foolishly had hoped that the small birds of Eastern Europe would soon be at full throttle.

In spite of Russian claims to the contrary, only a small minority of Poles welcomed the Red Army with undiluted enthusiasm. The huge relief that the Nazis were on the run was tempered by dark fears for the future. "We had gone on telling ourselves," said a survivor, "that if only the Germans would go, then we'd be free. But the day the Russians came meant the end of hope." Irena G., escaping from the death march out of Auschwitz camp*, heard the news as she was hiding in a farmer's hayloft:

> Two soldiers wearing Polish uniforms but with slant-eyed Russian faces, came to the farm, yelling at us to come out. "You're free. The Russians have come," they shouted. I came out of the barn where I'd been hiding, and stood looking at them, tears streaming down my face. But they weren't tears of relief. "No, we're not free," were the words I wanted to say, but dared not.

At the Peace Conference at Potsdam in July 1945, the decisions made at Teheran and Yalta were finally ratified. The Soviet Union was allowed to keep the Polish eastern territories which she had annexed. This meant almost half of Poland's pre-war territory,

* All those who were able to walk were evacuated from Auschwitz before the Red Army could arrive. They were destined for other concentration camps in Germany itself, but many of them died on the way.

and included the cities of Wilno and Lwów, which had played a large part in her cultural and religious history. Compensation was given to Poland in the shape of a huge chunk of territory taken from Germany: land which had once been Polish but which was now overwhelmingly German in population. The Oder–Neisse frontier was accepted as Poland's western border, and the country found itself shifted bodily two hundred miles westward.

With the signing of the peace, the legitimate Polish government in London was written out of existence and the Communist-dominated Provisional government was given legal status as the Polish Government of National Unity, with Bierut as acting President and Gomułka as first Vice-Premier. To keep Britain and America sweet, Mikołajczyk, the left-wing Prime Minister of the exiled London government, with two other London Poles and two non-Communists from Poland, were allowed to join the sixteen hand-picked Communists in the government. But Gomułka made sure that they knew the score: he had no intention of sharing power with them in any real sense:

> . . . We will never surrender the power we have seized . . . If a government of national unity cannot be established, perhaps several hundred people will be killed, but this will not frighten us . . . We will ruthlessly destroy all reactionary bandits. You may cry that the blood of the Polish people will flow, that the NKVD is governing Poland, but it will not divert us.[3]

If free elections had been held in Poland, the vote would have gone overwhelmingly to Mikołajczyk and his Peasants' Party. For Polish society was ready and even eager for some kind of Socialism. Even before the war it was becoming more radical, and there is a distinct chance that, if Hitler had not invaded when he did, there would have been a social upheaval in the country. The war had taken the process further. The Nazis had broken up the old estates and destroyed or scattered the gentry who had owned them. Scarcely anyone was still in touch with his pre-war source of income. Shared danger and suffering in the Occupation years had washed away the old class distinctions and bred a comradeship between the different social groups. As a result, there was now a deep longing to see this comradeship given a lasting political expression. "There was a wonderful unity during those years of Occupation. Anybody at all who spoke Polish was simply a member of the family," says Basia N. Like most countries in war-ravaged Europe, Poland in 1945 was experiencing a lurch to the left, and a real longing for change.

The Communists lacked the imagination to channel this general yearning successfully. Had their policies not been applied by force (and by Russian force at that), matters might have been different. But to the average Pole there was nothing to choose between the Soviet invaders of their country and the Polish lackeys who did their bidding. Gomułka was heard to complain that in the eyes of the Poles, the Party was nothing but an extension of the Soviet secret police. The Polish security force had, in fact, been strengthened and brought under the control of the Party. Repression of political opponents had been stepped up. It seemed that coercion was the only political method that this government understood.

Many of those who now returned from service in the Polish or British Air Forces in the West were arrested as spies and given long prison sentences. But the most shameful treatment was reserved for the resistance fighters of the Home Army. When this army was disbanded by its own High Command in January 1945, the partisans found themselves outlaws. These men and women who had spent years fighting the Nazis and who in normal circumstances might have expected a heroes' return, were now accused of being German spies and of sabotaging the Russian war effort. They were the class enemy, murderers, fascists, traitors, and an instruction had gone out to the UB (Polish security police) chiefs that they must be ruthless in liquidating them. "The Home Army, dribbling reactionary dwarf," sneered a poster.

Thousands of those who came out of the forests and voluntarily laid down their arms were arrested forthwith and deported to the Gulags of Soviet Russia or to concentration camps left empty by the fleeing Germans. In March 1945, a brand-new camp was set up by the NKVD at Rembertów near Warsaw, a transit camp whence prisoners were sent to Russia. In this year alone, fifty thousand Poles were sent to camps inside Russia. Conditions were terrible. In one transport of fourteen thousand prisoners, over three hundred died on the month-long journey to the Arctic. And with supreme cynicism, the Russians frequently put Home Army fighters in the same prison cell as Nazi murderers. Kazimierz Moczarski, for example, a young Home Army lieutenant, shared a cell with Jurgen Stroop, the butcher of the Warsaw Ghetto. Both were equally described as "war criminals".[4]

In June, sixteen leaders of the Home Army, who had been tricked into a meeting with the Russians and had then disappeared, were put on trial in Moscow as war criminals and sentenced to penal servitude in the Gulags. Several of them would die there. There was much anger in the West, but no real protest.

Not all the rank and file obeyed the order to stop fighting, when the new wave of terror struck. Some of the units of the Home Army took to the woods and hills yet again, to fight a new enemy. About 80,000 armed anti-Communist partisans (some of them small semi-fascist groups), were active in the first half of 1945.[5] For them it was a fight for survival, they had nothing to lose. One of these units made a night-attack on the concentration camp of Rembertów and set free eighteen hundred of their former companions who were about to be transported to the Soviet Union.

But the people as a whole were exhausted by suffering and weary of fighting, particularly when it meant that Pole was killing Pole in a civil war which had no future. The novel *Ashes and Diamonds*, published in 1948, caught the confusion and despair of the months that followed, in which "the worst years had passed, but now, at the beginning of a new day, it looked as if so much had been destroyed, so much laid waste, so much crushed down and afflicted, that the destructive force, as though still unappeased, was encroaching upon the present, poisoning even the future".[6]

One reason why so many were prepared to go on fighting, however, was the universal conviction that Britain and America would soon invade, to prevent Russia from swallowing the whole of Eastern Europe. It took at least two years for this illusion to fade and for the heart to go out of the struggle; but with their antiquated (or non-existent) arms the partisans had no real hope. Thousands were killed; thousands more were arrested and forced to sign pledges of loyalty to the Soviet Union. Some caved in and joined the Party; some were deported, others put on trial as bandits and fascist collaborators.

What support the Party had came by and large from the ambitious sons and daughters of the peasants and of the uprooted post-war refugees who needed education and encouragement. The Communists had wooed the peasants from the first moment, by dividing up the old estates and presenting a strip to each peasant. "They'll waste a lot of land that way. On the other hand, the paupers and farm-hands will start to feel human," says an honest idealist in the TV film, *Friends*.[7] But the horses, he said, should be given to the best farmers. And for ideological reasons they were not.

This agrarian reform which was welcomed by almost all sections of Polish society, brought the Communists a certain amount of popularity for a while, although not all the peasants were convinced of the regime's good intentions. Dark suspicions were entertained that the Communists would soon repossess the land and turn it into collectives. And there was never the faintest chance that Polish farmers would willingly join such enterprises. But there was no denying that life was improving for the peasants, with education for the first time freely available for their children, and social advancement a possibility. Seven million of the young and active were persuaded to abandon the villages and to seek their fortunes in the towns, mainly in the returned western territories of Silesia and Pomerania, and along the Baltic seaboard where Poland's economy was being revitalised and efforts were being made to turn her into an industrial nation.

The "better tomorrow" of which the young peasants dreamed was also the dream of a minority of Polish intellectuals who, in the face of much hostility, were hailing the new dawn. In the new society, writers, journalists, media-men, lawyers, were needed as missionaries, to spread the gospel and exert control over vital communications and the judiciary. Czesław Miłosz, a writer who before the war had belonged to radical left-wing literary and political groups, was one of those who wanted a break with the old romantic, tradition-haunted Poland, with its clericalism and extravagant nationalism. In the eyes of Miłosz and his like, Western-type democracy was disgraced or dead; only through the Marxist vision was a new world possible. It was, they believed, not only the best but the only possible solution. The brilliant young philosophy student, Leszek Kołakowski, shared their hopes for a better Poland. "Illusions, to be sure," said Kołakowski, many years later, when exiled to the West, "but not absolutely foolish, I think."

Miłosz watched in horror at the ruthless imposition of the new order, but comforted himself that it might be a necessary first stage: "What's one to do . . . if there's a rock-bottom – of poverty, oppression, humiliation – and if it is only by reaching those depths that people can change the world."[8]

Miłosz and his friends genuinely sought Poland's good; but many others joined the Party for less altruistic reasons: out of fear, weariness, vanity, the desire for power, or for the privileges that went with membership. For good or ill, Poland was going to remain in the Soviet Union's orbit, and that fact in itself caused many of Poland's intelligentsia to throw in their lot with the ruling Party.

Miłosz was soon to realise that reality did not match up to the theory, that paradise was as far away as ever, if not further:

> Our nation [he would write], was going to be transformed into a nation of workers and peasants, and that was right. Yet the peasant was not content, even though he was being given land; he was afraid. The worker had not the slightest feeling that the factories belonged to him, even though he worked to mobilise them with much self-denial and even though the propaganda assured him that they were his.[9]

Everyday life continued in a state of suspension. Fighting continued, the economic situation got worse. There were strikes and demonstrations in towns and cities all over Poland. People survived by bartering whatever goods they still possessed, and small private traders set up in business. Wives frequently had stalls in the market-place, to supplement their husbands' inadequate wage. Marek Korowicz reported the following conversation overheard in Kraków:

> *First man*: What do you live on?
> *Second man*: I'm in the Post Office, my wife's a teacher, one daughter works at the Town Hall, the other's a factory official, and my son's out of work.
> *First man* (horrified): What, you allow your son, a grown man, to be out of work?
> *Second man*: My dear chap, if he had a job, we couldn't possibly make ends meet. He has to earn the money to keep us all. If it weren't for him, we'd all starve.[10]

"Times are hard and are bound to get harder," sighed the heroine of a film[11] set in a small provincial town in 1946, where small-time racketeers and speculators were busy ripping off their helpless compatriots. The Polish authorities complained about this view of post-war Poland as poor, depressed and hopeless. "What about all our efforts to build a glorious Socialist Poland?" they asked. "What about all the optimism?"

* * *

One Polish institution remained intact – the Roman Catholic Church, restored to the affections of the people by its wartime record. Over three thousand priests had been shot or killed in the concentration camps, the most famous of these being the Franciscan, Maximilian Kolbe, who had given his life for another in Auschwitz, and who had already become a national cult figure. The Church had shared the agonies of the people. Its reputation accordingly stood higher than before. The sufferings of the Occupation had broadened and deepened the religious beliefs of the Poles, who now turned to the Church as the champion not only of their religious freedom but of all their freedoms. The shifting of the Polish borders (400 kilometres/200 miles) westward also meant that Poland, for the first time in its history, had lost its ethnic and religious minorities and become truly homogeneous. "A nation of thirty million people," said the wags, "twenty-nine million of whom go to church."

As long as the Church was prepared to go along with plans for rebuilding the country along Socialist lines, the authorities were willing to pay lip-service to the idea of co-existence. They confined themselves temporarily to anti-clericalism – priests, for example, who had belonged to the Home Army, had to change their names or go underground; and to accusing Pope Pius XII of harbouring pro-German sentiments. But the faith itself they left alone. Religion was still being taught in the schools. The Feast of the Immaculate Conception of the Virgin Mary was declared a public holiday. In those days even high-ranking Communist dignitaries went to church on Sundays or at least took part in the annual Corpus Christi procession. Even Bierut, in July 1945, took part in a ceremony during which a statue of Christ was placed in front of the Holy Cross Church in Warsaw.[12] And though Communists took care to address each other as "Comrade", older habits of speech died hard:

> "May God keep you, Comrade." Szczuka opened his mouth to speak but hesitated.
>
> "Thanks," he said. "May God watch over you too."[13]

Some Catholic newspapers were allowed into print and churches were rebuilt with State assistance. On the Church's part, although the hierarchy frequently thundered against the more inhuman aspects of Communism, they agreed with the proposed agrarian reforms and with the drive to turn Poland into an industrial nation. Like their opponents, they were prepared to wait and see. As Cardinal Wyszyński was later to remark, Polish society at this time could have been "a most fertile field for a wise government to work on".[14]

[1] Norman Davies, *God's Playground*, Volume II, *op. cit.*
[2] Marek Korowicz: *W Polsce Pod Sowieckim Jarzmem (1955).*
[3] Dr Antony Polonsky in an article: "Stalin and the Poles, 1941–1947."

[4] Kazimierz Moczarski, *Rozmowy Z Katem*, Panstwowy Instytut Wydawniczy, Warszawa, 1977.
[5] Dr Antony Polonsky in an article: "Stalin and the Poles, 1941–1947."
[6] Jerzy Andrzejewski, *Ashes and Diamonds*, Penguin, 1980.
[7] *Friends*, Telewizyjna Wytwórnia Filmowa, Poltel, 1981.
[8] Czesław Miłosz, *The Captive Mind*, *op. cit.*
[9] Ibid.
[10] Marek Korowicz: *W Polsce Pod Sowieckim Jarzmem (1955)*.
[11] *Year of the Quiet Sun*, directed by Zrzysztof Zanussi.
[12] *Dramatyczny Rok, 1945*, Tadeusz Zenczykowski, Polonia, 1982.
[13] Jerzy Andrzejewski, *Ashes and Diamonds*, as above.
[14] Cardinal Stefan Wyszyński: *A Freedom Within*, Hodder & Stoughton, 1985.

5 THE REVOLUTION THAT NEVER WAS (1945–8)

So often are you as a blazing torch
with flakes of burning hemp falling about you.
Flaming, you know not if flames
freedom bring, or death,
consuming all that you most cherish;
if ashes only will be left and
chaos and tempest shall engulf.
Or will the ashes hold the glory
of a starlike diamond, the
Morning Star of everlasting triumph?

Cyprian Kamil Norwid (1821–83)
Translated by Bolesław Sulik, for
the film *Ashes and Diamonds*

In the late spring of 1945, while Stalin's army rampaged slightly to the north, thirty-seven-year-old Bolek Wałęsa returned to Popowo, to "cough his lungs up" and die. The pneumonia he had caught in the draughty barracks at Młyniec, added to the severe skull injuries inflicted on him by the Gestapo, left the outcome in no doubt. But in the little stone cottage in Popowo, he resolutely clung to life, until his younger brother, Stanisław, should return home from the forests. When Stanisław came, in June, Bolek begged him to take care of Feliksa and the children; and, having extracted the promise, died. He was buried in the little churchyard at nearby Sobowo, where so many of the graves seem to bear the name of Wałęsa.

A year later, Stanisław honoured his brother's last wish, and married Feliksa. "He was our father," says Izabela, the oldest. "We none of us really knew Bolek."

Even with his own piece of land added to Bolek's, Stanisław had to support his new family on only four hectares. It was poor, sandy ground, and nothing would grow there except potatoes and low-grade wheat. On the edge of a little birch wood, Stanisław built a new house for them all, bigger than the tumbledown hut in which Bolek had lived with Feliksa, but still not much larger than a dolls' house. Like his brother, Stanisław was a skilled craftsman, but there could have been few comforts in that little two-roomed stone croft for two adults and four children. And when, before long, three more children, Tadeusz, Zygmunt and Wojtek, were born, the poverty of the family went from abject to unbearable. "We weren't just poor," recalls Zygmunt, "we were paupers."

Bigger than the house was the adjoining cowshed, which Stanisław also built. The two cows, ten pigs and one hundred chickens were the family's ticket to survival. There was no money coming in. They had only what they could provide for themselves.

When he killed a pig, Stanisław would fill a suitcase with joints of pork, butter and eggs, and go off to the nearest market. He was too poor to own a horse, and on these occasions had to borrow a horse and cart from a neighbouring farmer, in exchange for three days' work by himself or his sons.

From the time they could walk, the children had to help "with everything". They would take the cows out to graze, and help with the milking. They worked for the horse-owning farmer, weeded the ground, made hay, and helped their mother make bread and the huge variety of sausage, brawn and black puddings into which Polish country-women convert their slaughtered pigs. They would go into the woods to gather the juniper branches needed for smoking the sausage, and afterwards they would help pack the meat in salt and store it in the large space under the cement floor of the house.

In the woods too there were the delicious mushrooms, which all Polish children learn to identify at an early age. And on winter days, when they were able to borrow the horse (two days' borrowing meant five days' work for the farmer) they would gather firewood and bring it back on a home-made sledge.

"They were difficult times," says Zygmunt, "but we weren't unhappy. It was a different atmosphere then. We respected our parents, and trusted the neighbours. People hadn't started yet to be afraid of each other."

Elsewhere in Poland, armed resistance had almost petered out.* But the people were still restless, and Stalin used the

* Parts of the resistance movement continued fighting until 1948. Some forty thousand are believed to have died on both sides. In July 1985, a monument commemorating members of the security forces who had died in the defence of People's Poland was unveiled in Warsaw. It depicted soldiers, militia, security police, workers and peasants raising aloft the (uncrowned) Polish eagle. The monument is deeply resented by the vast majority of the Polish people, as is the one unveiled earlier in the same year, which, while commemorating the Polish officers murdered in the Katyń Forest, describes them as "victims of Hitlerite fascism". Someone secretly scored out the word "Hitlerite", but left "fascism" in place.

unsettled state of the country as an excuse for postponing the "free and unfettered elections" he had promised the West at Yalta; and to intensify the ruthless Sovietisation of the country. The scales at last fell from Western eyes. This brutal dehumanisation of Polish life was the last straw which caused the breakdown of the wartime alliance with Russia and the start of the Cold War. Churchill spoke of an "iron curtain" descending on Europe and both he and the Americans declared Poland's new western border to be anything but final. This caused great consternation in Poland, where the question of the western frontier was just about the only issue on which government and people were united. A great hopelessness engulfed the country, a state of mind which Gomułka took care to encourage, reminding the people over and over again that Russia was the only true protector of their interests. At this point Stalin exerted pressure on the government to refuse the Marshall Aid from America which was helping Poland in the daunting task of reconstruction.

One way or another, the anti-Communists lost heart and, in the face of the overwhelming odds, decided, for the time being, to bow to the inevitable. Many of them reluctantly threw in their lot with the regime, in the hope of salvaging something from the wreckage of Poland. It was still almost possible, in spite of everything, to believe in the prospect of better things to come. Rebuilding was proceeding at a steady rate. The Russians had sent what Bierut called "fraternal, heartfelt and selfless help", in the shape of some economic assistance.[1] A little basic machinery was now available for the work of rebuilding, and lorries had taken the place of handcarts. The towns were taking shape again. All freedoms were not yet completely abolished. The people could still move about freely, worship where they pleased, choose where they would work, criticise the government in the privacy of their homes, and listen to the radio, even to foreign stations. The opposition Peasant Party, led by Mikołajczyk, was a major political force, with a membership far larger than the combined numbers of the Communists and their allies. Mikołajczyk was genuinely hopeful that Poland might yet become a real democracy, for in a genuine election campaign, the Communists could hope for less than five per cent of the national vote.

But the peasant leader (and almost everybody else) had reckoned without the crucial fact that the Communists could impose their will by armed force. "Was anyone so naïve as to expect that a revolution carried into this land at bayonet point would yield before a ballot-box?" a Party boss later asked a

Western journalist.[2] In that icy winter of 1947, when the Poles had no coal because the Russians had taken it all, the farcical elections took place after a fierce and bloody campaign which was a continuation of the civil war by other means. If the elections had really been "free and unfettered", an overwhelming victory would have gone to the immensely popular Peasant Party. But there was nothing either free or unfettered about them.

The Communists used every trick in the book to keep Mikołajczyk out, secure in the knowledge that at every step of the way they could call on the support of the Russian armed forces. They disfranchised at least a million voters, raided their opponents' offices, cut off telephones, planted weapons, threatened, kidnapped, murdered. They isolated Poland from her friends in the West by setting up a bloody pogrom of Jews in the town of Kielce, four days before the elections. When the results were finally declared, they were quite clearly faked. The popular Mikołajczyk and his party were declared to have received only ten per cent of the vote, and the government bloc eighty per cent. The people received the news with undisguised dismay, understanding too late that they had been tricked, and that their fate was now upon them.

Almost immediately the regime began to tighten the screw, enlarging the security forces, imposing stricter censorship, and staging a long series of political trials designed to crush any remaining opposition. At the end of 1948, the Polish Workers' Party forcibly swallowed up the Socialists; and the pro-regime Peasant Party did the same to Mikołajczyk's party which was far larger than itself and far more representative of the Polish peasants. The peasant leader realised then that no more lip-service would be paid to carrying out social change in accordance with the needs and wishes of the people; and that Poland was to be brought, lock, stock and barrel, into the Russian system. Knowing that his own arrest was a matter only of time, Mikołajczyk fled to the West in October. As Bierut put it, all too clearly, in 1948: "People's Democracy did not arise as the result of an armed uprising, but as the result of victory by the Soviet Union."

Indeed, Poland had had no revolution. Power had passed smoothly and inevitably from the Nazis to the Red Army and from them to the Provisional Government established at Lublin. The Poles had never at any stage been offered a choice. Yalta had handed them over on a platter to the Russians, who had cynically chosen to devour the small birds rather than let them sing.

Gomułka was now intent on developing a specifically Polish road to Communism. Being at once a Pole and a realist, he did not believe that the Polish peasants would ever accept the forcible collectivisation of their land. But his plans for the future were overturned by dramatic events in Yugoslavia. In 1948, Tito's defiant rejection of Russian dominion over his country sent shock-waves through the Communist Parties of Eastern Europe. Stalin clamped down hard, forcing a uniform discipline upon them all, determined to ensure their total obedience, and to prevent the emergence of new Titos. He had never much trusted Władysław Gomułka, who was not one of the Russian-trained and therefore "reliable" Polish Patriots. In the light of Tito's shocking betrayal, independence of mind was not to be tolerated; any man who challenged Soviet supremacy in his own country was a danger to Stalin's grand post-war plan for reshaping the history of Europe.

So, in September 1948, on the grounds that he had been too conciliatory towards Tito and had had the temerity to act as though Poland were an equal partner with the Soviet Union, Gomułka was dismissed as a nationalist deviationist, and his job was taken over by President Bierut. The Revolution, as always, was devouring its own children.

With the purge of all those who shared Gomułka's views, and their replacement by men subservient to Stalin's wishes, Poland's subjugation to the Soviet Union was complete. To underline just how unequal she was, Poland's forces were reorganised on the Soviet model; her soldiers were made to swear an oath of allegiance to the Soviet Union and, bitterest insult of all, the Soviet Marshal Rokossovsky was brought in as Commander-in-Chief of the Polish Army; and all major units were put into the charge of Soviet officers. Such a stinging affront has no parallel before or since, even in the tiniest, most insignificant dependent states, anywhere else in the world! Poland, like the other countries of Eastern Europe, was put on a war footing. Her frontiers were closed, her economy given over to the demands of war. Her shops were empty, her people hungry. And the worst was still to come.

[1] Bolesław Bierut, *The Six Year Plan for the Reconstruction of Warsaw*, Ksiązk i Wiedza Report, 1949.

[2] Stewart Steven, *The Poles*, Collins/Harvill, 1982.

6 ASHES, NOT DIAMONDS (1948–56)

> The Party denied the free will of the individual – and at the same time it exacted his willing self-sacrifice. It denied his capacity to choose between two alternatives – and at the same time it demanded that he should constantly choose the right one. It denied his power to distinguish good and evil – and at the same time it spoke pathetically of guilt and treachery. The individual stood under the sign of economic fatality, a wheel in a clockwork which had been wound up for all eternity and could not be stopped or influenced – and the Party demanded that the wheel should revolt against the clockwork and change its course. There was somewhere an error in the calculation; the equation did not work out.
>
> Arthur Koestler: *Darkness at Noon*

By the end of that year, the circumstances for the Party were particularly propitious. The Church's leader, Cardinal Hlond, the Primate of Poland, had died in October and been replaced by Stefan Wyszyński, the young bishop of Lublin. At a crucial time in its affairs, then, the Church had as leader an inexperienced bishop who had been running a relatively uncomplicated diocese for less than three years.

But even if, in these circumstances, the way seemed open for the Party to destroy its chief rival, in the short term a certain amount of caution was still necessary.

Sooner or later the shaky truce between the Church and the State was doomed to break down; and by 1948 it was already doing so. As Miłosz was to write:

> In its own fashion, the Party too is a church. Its dictatorship over the earth and its transformation of the human species depend on the success with which it can channel irrational drives and use them to its own ends . . . No other church can be tolerated; Christianity is Public Enemy Number One. It fosters all the scepticism of the masses as to the radical transformation of mankind. If, as the Gospel teaches, we must not do harm to others, then perhaps we must not harm the kulaks?[1]

It would be foolish as yet to close down the churches and forbid the practice of the faith, for such a course might provoke the people to renewed armed resistance. Far better to divide and rule, to accuse some of the priests and bishops of being reactionaries and foreign agents, while encouraging the PAX groups of "patriotic" priests sympathetic to the regime.*

PAX did the Church a lot of harm. The "patriotic" priests were few in number, but they were manoeuvred into positions of importance, despite the hierarchy's objections. Meanwhile, a new martyrdom was beginning. Bishops and priests were placed under strict surveillance and a wave of radio and press propaganda accused them of every crime under the sun. By the end of 1950, more than five hundred priests, monks and nuns were in prison, some of them in Siberian work camps.

Still a bit wary of the people, the regime embarked on a campaign to encourage atheism. Atheistic societies were formed, and in schools, colleges, places of work and tenement blocks the Poles were made to listen to interminable lectures on "scientific" Marxism, designed to prove that religion was nonsense. Crosses were taken down from public buildings; and the serving of fish was encouraged on every day except Friday, the Church's traditional day for abstaining from meat: "Today there is fish," remarks a character in a later novel about the period. "That is because it is not Friday. No fish is allowed to be served in restaurants on Friday. You see, they are rather childish sometimes, the people who look after us."[2]

Pilgrimages, processions and all public meetings were banned and Catholic newspapers were forced out of print. *Universal Word*, however, the PAX "Catholic" daily which, in the words of the Polish Primate, "might as well have been written by Stalin", was given all the newsprint it needed. Employees in state enterprises were compelled to work on Sundays, and "voluntary" work brigades were organised to ensure that young people would not get to church. On church feast days, official parades or special

* A pseudo-Catholic group, under the leadership of Bolesław Piasecki, began to emerge as early as 1945. Piasecki, the pre-war leader of the anti-semitic Falanga group, had fought the Russians during the war in his own underground unit. Arrested by the NKVD in 1944, he turned his coat and offered his services to the Russians. He was released immediately and set up the group of pseudo-Catholics which would become known as PAX. Until his death in 1979, Piasecki remained one of the most hated men in Poland.

See Tadeusz Zenczykowski, *Dramatyczny Rok 1945*, Polonia, 1982.

football matches were carefully scheduled to coincide with church services.

Some were taken in by all the propaganda, but a contemporary observer records that on the whole the attacks on religion only provoked resentment. "The threat nourished devotion to the only source of warmth, of spiritual peace, of comfort and of hope that was left."[3]

The Party could hardly fail to be aware that the churches were fuller than they had ever been – not just on Sundays but every day; and not just at the time of religious services. They guessed, probably correctly, that at least in part this fervour was an outlet for a hatred towards Russia and towards Marxism–Leninism, which had no other means of expression. So, in an attempt to trap its arch-enemy, the regime proposed an agreement with the Church. Such an Agreement was signed in the spring of 1950, with the Communists offering more tolerance in exchange for positive Catholic support. It had the appearance of a hopeful charter, but hardly had it been signed than the regime reneged on its part of the bargain and started attacking the Church again:

> Priests are constantly spied on, placed under surveillance, provoked. A whole network of Communist agents surrounds them. Every careless word uttered by a priest is reported, twisted, exaggerated out of all proportion. Because, as a result, priests are cautious about what they say, informers simply invent whatever they please and always manage to provide witnesses.[4]

Whatever good Bierut's regime carried out in the early fifties – the rebuilding of houses, schools and hospitals; industrial development; the provision of social, sports and cultural amenities, of kindergartens and crèches; the loving care with which historic buildings were reconstructed – was lost in the orgy of horror into which the Polish people were now plunged; and which owed less to Marxism–Leninism than to the traditions of the hated Czars.[5] Brute force prevailed. Stalin had once said that imposing Communism on the fiercely independent Poles would be like trying to fit a saddle on to a cow. And so it proved. Where argument had failed, police terror was let loose. It was said[6] that Stalin was addicted to terror and understood that it was most effective when applied in a random, chaotic way, creating an atmosphere in which no one felt safe and everyone was afraid.

The noose tightened; the Party moved to establish control over every aspect of life. Repeatedly told that they did not exist as individuals, that their only function was to work and to serve the

Revolution, the people felt themselves more and more isolated and helpless. Poland was fast becoming an imitation Russia, with red flags and banners fluttering, and compulsory mass parades on vast public squares; while from office walls and hoardings stared outsize portraits of Lenin, Stalin and Bierut. Grey concrete apartment blocks rose from the rubble and hideous, Soviet-style architecture began to dominate the skyline of Polish cities; all the old values – of religious faith, parental authority, patriotism and high moral standards – were denounced and ridiculed. Life became more and more intolerable.

Writers who in the early days of the regime had written pretty nearly what they pleased, so long as they refrained from criticising the Soviet system, were now ordered to give positive support to the Revolution (that never was), to devote their talents to the construction of Socialism. The more cowardly among them began to produce books which were little more than strings of quotations from Lenin or Stalin, and were quite unreadable. The better ones remained silent. Only works which praised Socialism and wrote in glowing terms of its achievements were allowed to be published. An Orwellian "doublespeak" swamped the elegant Polish language. Wherever people went, whether shopping, waiting for a bus or train, or attending one of the unavoidable public meetings, their ears were assailed by a crude propaganda which poured out of the public address system:

> The – train – for – Chelmno – will – leave – from – platform – three – beware – of – bacteriological – warfare – by – the – foreign – imperialists – the – train – from – Kraków – is – arriving – on – platform – number – two – long – live – socialism – and – workers' – unity . . .[7]

All contact with relatives and friends who had remained in the West was a punishable offence, as was any mention of those who had died at Tobruk, Monte Cassino, Arnhem or the Battle of Britain. The singing of patriotic songs such as the popular "Red Poppies of Monte Cassino" was rigorously forbidden. The war was said to have begun only in 1941, and had been won by the Soviet Union alone. Only the Eastern front had been important. While every Polish town had its war memorial to the Soviet dead, there was none to the Poles who had died in the fighting of 1939, or on the Western fronts. As for the Home Army partisans, Stefan D.'s experience was common: "In the Stalinist years," he says, "I had fourteen different jobs. Every time they discovered that

I'd been in the Home Army, the police ordered the employer to get rid of me."

A totalitarian society demands the full, round-the-clock co-operation of all its members. To ensure such co-operation, the secret police were given full rein. They acted on the principle that it is a far, far better thing to punish the innocent than to allow the guilty to go free. In any case, few people any longer knew how to distinguish the innocent from the guilty, since only the Party had the power to decide what was right and what was wrong. Good and evil could be defined only in the context of the Revolution (it was dangerous for a priest to speak of them in the pulpit); conscience was an irrelevance; and the end justified the means, however ignoble. Law had acquired a new meaning – in Humpty Dumpty fashion, it meant whatever the Party wanted it to mean.

This departure from the rule of law increased the uncertainty and fear. People trembled at the mere mention of the UB (the secret police). Eye-witness accounts tell of hundreds of thousands arrested, till the prisons were bursting and the overflow was being crammed into the cellars of ordinary houses. Every word or act was potentially dangerous, even chance remarks made in private could be reported and lead to arrest. The citizen's only duty (he did not have rights) was "watchfulness against the enemies of the people". Denunciations were encouraged: they were the mark of the good citizen. Informers supplied the UB with material for personal dossiers on every single person. These were said to be for reference only, but in fact they labelled a person as politically reliable or unreliable and at the very least determined his chances of a decent job, since almost all personnel officers were under the control of the UB. "At work you were continually watched," said a factory-worker, "who you worked with, who you talked to, what you were talking about."

Tadeusz B., arrested in the early hours of one morning was taken to police headquarters, where he was first of all ordered to write a summary of his life. The investigators wouldn't accept what he wrote the first time, nor the second, nor the third, fourth, fifth, sixth . . .

> This went on for hours [he remembered]. Then I was put into solitary, to "contemplate my destiny". After midnight I was questioned again, and again was ordered to write the story of my life. I sat on a stool placed about two metres from the large table where the interrogators sat. On the table was a reflector with a spotlight trained on my

> face so that I was blinded by the light and could see nothing. The interrogation went on and on until I was totally drained and exhausted. Then, when I was expecting the worst, they unaccountably sent me home. But they sent for me again, and the whole procedure was repeated. It happened several times.

The terrifying pressure of daily life made people mentally and physically ill, and soured their personal relationships. Since nobody knew whom to trust, tensions became unbearable. Uncertainty about whether they would still be free, in work, with a roof over their heads, or even alive, reduced many to such a state of neurotic terror that they were ready to save their own skins by accusing their neighbours or colleagues on demand. In many ways this mental suffering caused by fear, guilt and shame was worse than the Nazi Occupation. In this poisoned atmosphere, "people were rushing to join the Party, take on safe jobs, planning, preparing themselves against some unimaginable Day of Judgment. A movement of their eyes, a sudden blush, an unexpected bowing of the head, betrayed the inner chaos and anguish that inspired their conduct."[7]

One consolation – and this in spite of the risks involved – was listening in to Western radio stations – BBC, Voice of America or Radio Free Europe – for a true account of what was happening in Poland. Many a parent locked himself into the bedroom with the set, away from the prying eyes of the children. Andrzej Gwiazda, a future leader of Solidarity, was a child at the time and remembers his parents keeping a primitive radio set hidden under the blankets.

> I can remember how friends went pale, how their hands shook, if I forgot to switch off the receiver before inviting them into the room. But despite the fear there were many who listened . . . People in the free world will never understand the significance those broadcasts had for us. Only one who has been in prison, hemmed in all round by concrete, can appreciate what the tiny slit in the wall, through which a tree or a passing car can be seen, means to the prisoner. It is proof that a normal world still exists outside the iron bars and the concrete.[8]

In the prisons, beatings, injections, hypnosis, long terms of isolation, day-and-night interrogations under blinding lights destroyed the nerves and will of even the strongest and could reduce valiant men to submission in twenty-four hours. Not many were heroes, not even those who had a record of gallantry in more than one war. It was a leading Communist who in later years was to describe the horror of:

> people who were caught in the streets and released after seven days of interrogation, unfit to live. These people had to be taken to lunatic asylums. Others sought refuge in the asylums to avoid the security police. Men in panic, honest men, were fleeing abroad to escape our system . . . The whole city knew there were cells in which people were kept for three weeks standing in excrement . . . cold water was poured on people who were left in the cold to freeze.[9]

This was the time of those mockeries of justice, the show trials which were being held all over Eastern Europe as Stalin consolidated his hold on his empire. Though less bad in Poland than elsewhere, they nevertheless inspired terror. The courts were corrupt, a great many of the judges being in the pay of the secret police. Pictures of those accused (who would soon be mouthing an abject public confession, whether guilty or not) were printed in the official dailies. When Marek Korowicz saw the picture of a man he knew, he was appalled: "In place of the virile, stocky, rather muscular chap I knew I saw a grey-haired old man, thin as a skeleton. What had they done to him?"[10]

The exemplary trials also included among their victims several well-known clergy. One priest was condemned to death; another to fifteen years' hard labour because photographic equipment, some yards of cloth and a few bottles of wine (the possession of which was not illegal) were found in his house.

No one was exempt from the Terror. Workers who did not fulfil the norms laid down in the Six Year Plan were held just as guilty as those whose crimes were political. In fact the UB eventually succeeded in having this failure to produce the goods pronounced a political crime. The fact that norms were always being raised, so that workers were being paid less and less for more and more work, made no difference. Those who "sabotaged" the Plan were sent to work-camps attached to the coal-mines, stone-quarries or steelworks in the industrial areas. "It's come to this," said a disillusioned worker, "that every steelworks and every mine will soon have its own slaves, and getting coal and steel will cost the authorities almost nothing."

When the regular miners and steelworkers saw the half-starved prisoner-workers embarking on their sentences, the braver among them spat and swore and cursed those who had sent them there. But many of these paid for their temerity by being themselves arrested and sent to similar camps elsewhere.

"He who works eats." In these camps the Orwellian dictum was applied as a matter of course. Whoever did not fulfil his work norms was deprived of food. People would return from those camps pale, nervous, silent, afraid of their own shadows. Suicide became common, but more often the survivors became helpless tools of the UB, informers, prepared, however shamefacedly, to do anything rather than be sent back to the camps.

If, in the early dawn of "liberation", some at least of Poland's industrial workers (including the many thousands of former peasants) believed that a new era of happiness was at hand, they were discovering the hard way that they had been conned. Certainly there were good things: full employment; education for the children – and evening classes for the adult workers; occasional expenses-paid holidays in a rest-home. But, though the increasing productivity of the worker was the basis of the Communist achievement, the worker was not his own man. He belonged to a State, which claimed to know what was best for him, and to speak in his name.

> Workers are told that a strike is a crime. Against whom are they to strike? Against themselves? After all, the means of production belongs to them, the State belongs to them. Such an explanation is not very convincing. The workers who dare not state aloud what they want know that the goals of the State are far from identical with their own.[11]

The unions had no teeth. They had been taken over by the Party in 1949 and their former officials had been purged. The new leaders were quite clear as to their duties: they were taskmasters in the drive for increased production; it was definitely not part of their brief to try to defend their members' interests.

Poland's current Six Year Plan committed her to producing jet planes and spare parts for Russian tanks. Nowhere did it take into account the basic needs of the people. The government set wage-scales over the heads of the unions, increased the working week, passed laws which bound workers to their present jobs and imposed a draconian system of time-keeping whereby even a few minutes' lateness was severely punished. "Heroes of Socialist Labour", super-quota workers akin to the Russian Stakhanovites (and a great many of them fictitious), were urged to perform prodigious miracles of production, so that work-norms might be raised even higher. Since building workers were in such demand, some of them became famous for their efficiency, especially when they began to increase their output by means of teamwork. The incident in Andrzej Wajda's celebrated film, *Man of Marble*, in which one team lays thirty-eight thousand bricks in a single eight-hour shift, is based on a true statistic, which Bierut himself quoted in the Six Year Plan for 1949. For this feat, Wajda's film-hero, the idealistic Mateusz Birkut, is showered momentarily with rewards and bouquets from a grateful Party, and earns the furious loathing of his fellow-workers. The rising work-norms and the accompanying exhaustion and despair caused further breakdowns in health among the workers; and in spite of the strict surveillance and the terrifying punishments involved, absenteeism mounted steadily and standards of work – and honesty at work – went to the wall.

Apart from everything else, the Poles were well aware that the Russians were milking them. Not only were they forced to produce military hardware for the Russian war build-up, but in so many other ways the "fraternal ally" was taking far more than it gave. In the middle of freezing Polish winters, for example, there was no coal, not even in Katowice where it was mined (but from where a railway line ran direct to the Soviet Union). Thank God for our Polish railway workers, went a bitter joke of the period. If it weren't for them, we'd have to carry the coal to the east on our backs. Poland had to import sugar from Czechoslovakia, then sell it at less than half the market rate to the Soviet Union; for railway engines they were paid little more than the cost of materials, and for manufactured cloth not even that.

In George Orwell's satire on Communism, *Animal Farm*, Mollie the mare pines for sugar and is rebuked by Snowball the pig who tells her she doesn't need sugar because under the new dispensation she will have all the oats and hay she needs to keep her alive. Polish women under Stalinism did not even have the human equivalent of oats and hay, let alone the sugar. Frequently they had nothing to eat but potatoes. Badly housed, under-nourished, exhausted, their nerves stretched to breaking-point, housewives forlornly trailed their shopping baskets to empty shops or joined the long queues for bread or meat which started at dawn or even earlier. And as few families could exist on one man's wages, on leaving the queue many of the women would set off for a day's work in office or factory. Sometimes mothers sent their children out to queue. One man, a child at the time, remembers:

> queues for everything . . . In the morning before going to school I had to queue for bread and milk, the essentials which were our staple diet, under different guises, at every meal. My parents who both

queued at different shops would send me to the baker's rather than anyone else, because as a boy I was more likely to wriggle myself to the top of the queue and return home with a loaf of bread and a litre of milk.

Even such items as sewing thread and nails had long since vanished from the shops. In fact the only commodity not in short supply was alcohol. Excessive drinking was officially discouraged; but it was widely believed that the regime preferred the workers to spend what money they had on drink rather than attempt to save it. Not that savings were of any use. Twice in this period currency reform wiped them out altogether; and as prices went up on everything except heavy industry, people joked that the only bargain for the working man to buy was a railway-engine.

Food was strictly rationed but the number of coupons available depended not, as in less inhuman societies, on the age or health of the individual, but on his job status, his degree of usefulness, his political purity. Special-status workers, such as miners, and, of course, the highly productive super-quota workers, received a greater allowance of coupons. In any office or factory the boss received more coupons than his underlings. The Communist slogan, incorporated into the new Soviet-style Polish charter of July 1952, "from each according to his ability; to each according to his work" was cynically interpreted to mean that a full stomach depended on a person's willingness to serve the Party unreservedly.

A new élite had sprung into being, wealthier and far more powerful than its pre-war predecessors. Managers of firms, factories and mines; top civil servants; heads of schools and universities; directors of hospitals; leading members of the judiciary; army officers; media people – all owed their jobs to the Party which had hand-picked them on the basis not of their talent for the job but of their slavish adherence to orthodoxy. These were the urbane, smooth-suited, privileged elect who could be trusted to stick to the rule-book; the grey, faceless men who would never be tempted by compassion to make an exception to the rule. The rewards for such as these were numerous and sweet, and for the greater number of them were the whole *raison d'être* of their loyalty.

Known as the *nomenklatura* (the trusted ones), these were top people, set apart from their countrymen, cut off from real life by the extent of their privileges. They had their own private hospitals, sanatoria, luxury holiday hostels, priority in housing, pharmacies, kindergartens, cinemas. And in this land where even the smallest private traders had been forced out of business, where people were "uniformly grey and uniformly poverty-stricken",[12] the new élite flaunted their special "yellow-curtain shops" – so-called after the yellow-curtained doors which hid their bulging shelves from the hungry passers-by.

Thus was the old quasi-religious Communist fervour corrupted. Thus was "the ethic of war founded on co-operation and brotherhood" transformed into "an ethic of war, pitting all men against all others and granting the greatest chance of survival to the craftiest".[13]

In bringing this new class into being and surrounding it with the luxuries that would inevitably corrupt it, the Party had bought itself servants, and had knowingly created a hydra-headed monster with a vested interest in preserving the system which was so generous to them. These men and women would continue to talk in glowing phrases about the working classes and blame industrial unrest on "enemies of the people". But they no longer shared the experience of the common people and increasingly forfeited their right to speak on their behalf:

> *Jakubik*, a Party functionary: It's not the working classes who are restless. It's the enemies of the people who provoke them.
>
> *Piotr*, his former friend: You don't know a thing about the working classes any more. You only know how to carry out the bosses' orders.[14]

It was the *nomenklatura* who had most to lose if the system came under attack. It was they who made a Communist society possible. It was to protect their privileges that the powers and prerogatives of the UB security police were expanded. Almost thirty years later, it was this same group which saw its lifestyle threatened by Solidarity and which undermined all efforts to create a dialogue between regime and people. By then, of course, the new élite, with the pharisaical morals which characterised it, had become a hereditary caste.

[1] Czesław Miłosz, *The Captive Mind*, *op. cit.*

[2] Frank Tuohy, *The Ice Saints*, Macmillan, 1964.

[3] Flora Lewis, *The Polish Volcano: A Case-History of Hope*, Secker & Warburg, 1959.

[4] Marek Korowicz, *W Polsce Pod Sowieckim Jarzmem*, London, Veritas, 1955.

[5] Nicholas Bethell, *Gomułka: His Poland and His Communism*, Longmans, 1969, Penguin, 1972.

[6] Ewa Fournier, *Poland*, Vista Books, 1964.

[7] Czesław Miłosz, *Seizure of Power*, *op. cit.*

[8] Article: "Radio Free Europe": "A Window on Sanity", in Gdańsk underground publication *Skorpion*, published in UK in *Polish Affairs*, number 110, Spring 1983.

[9] Konrad Syrop, *Poland in Perspective*, Robert Hale, London, 1982.

[10] Marek Korowicz, *W Polsce Pod Sowieckim Jarzmem*, London, Veritas, 1955.

[11] Czesław Miłosz, *The Captive Mind*, *op. cit.*

[12] Ibid.

[13] Ibid.

[14] Film: *Friends* (*Przyjaciele*), dir. Andrzej Kostenko, Telewizyjna Wytwórnia Filmowa. Poltel, 1981.

7 FIGHTING BACK (1951–6)

> The Church in Poland has become synonymous with the Polish nation . . . he who harms the one harms the other . . . So those who criticise the Church . . . for meddling in politics fail to understand that in Poland temporal politics have imposed themselves upon the Church and not the Church on politics. To understand Poland, you must understand that.
>
> Stewart Steven: *The Poles*

When old Cardinal Sapieha died in 1951, half a million mourners lined the streets of Kraków, weeping and singing hymns, while the UB melted into the background and refrained from interference. "They couldn't have stopped us on that day and they knew it," people have said. The Roman Catholic Church continued to be the people's main support – "our help and our rock" – lining up behind those values which would one day be embodied by Solidarity.

With the death of Cardinal Sapieha, the whole fury of the battle fell on Stefan Wyszyński, the new Primate, a tough and pragmatic patriot, a worker-priest who had signed the 1950 Agreement with the regime, in the belief that the Polish Church had already shed too much blood in the Nazi death camps and that a new bloody martyrdom should be avoided if possible. Had the regime not been intent on destroying the Church, it might have been able to reach an accommodation with Wyszyński. But how could aggressive atheism coexist with religion? The smear campaign against the Church had now reached a high peak of hysteria, and Wyszyński was powerless to stop it. His overriding aim was to preserve the unity of the Church, but such unity had to be paid for in the human suffering he had sought to avoid. By the end of 1952, eight bishops and over nine hundred priests were in prison.

A government decree in February 1953 made all ecclesiastical positions dependent on the State. Whereupon the Cardinal and bishops of the "Church of Silence" made an anything but silent protest at this violation of the recent Agreement. They openly opposed the ruthless methods of the regime and defended the nation's right to its own religious tradition. It was "the most energetic and at the same time the most dignified challenge to Communist rule in Poland – a truly historic testimony in Poland's contemporary trial".[1]

The Cardinal's own arrest in 1953 was the government's response. It was intended to be the *coup de grâce* for the Church, but the action did not have the desired effect. Although the shock of the arrest drove many to despair of the Church's chances of survival, it was also salutary. The arrest of the Primate – traditionally the ruler of the Polish people in the interval between the death of one king and the election of another – increased his popularity overnight, alerted the people to the extremity of their danger and gave them a new determination to stand firm against the total enslavement that now threatened to overwhelm them.

That autumn, as the imprisoned Cardinal scribbled in his diary, he recalled that in the first church he had entered en route to being installed as archbishop of his diocese, the people had presented to him a painting of Christ, hands bound, a soldier grasping his shoulder. It was, he now realised, a fitting symbol not only of the Polish Church but of the whole Polish nation: a Christian people must share Christ's way to the cross. They must also follow Christ's example of forgiveness, giving witness to the power of good to overcome evil. When the newspapers, in a frenzy about enemies within and without, had urged the people "to train ourselves to hate more", Wyszyński had responded that "the Poles do not know how to hate, thank God." And when the regime had denied the right of the individual to a private conscience, he had left his congregations in no doubt that "the voice of conscience is the voice of the greatness of man".

Conscience was all the people had left. "Capitalism," went the Polish joke, "is the exploitation of one man by another. Socialism is the reverse." A sense of humour had always, even in the dark days of the Occupation, been a safety valve for the Poles in their struggles with a malign fate. Forbidden to voice any complaint, they took refuge in jokes with a core of political bitterness – like the endless ones about the hated Palace of Culture and Science, the monstrous edifice which dominates the Warsaw skyline and was solemnly presented as a gift to the Polish people by Stalin, at a time when the housing situation in Warsaw was acute. It has been described as "a monument to arrogance, a statue to slavery, a stone layer-cake of abomination".[2] Who's the luckiest man in all Warsaw? went one version of the joke. And the answer: "the caretaker on the top floor of the Palace of Culture. He's the only one who can't see it when he looks out of his window."

This kind of low-key joke was relatively safe and probably made its point better than the serious political articles which could not be written.

By the 1950s armed resistance was out of the question, given the ubiquitous presence of the UB and the nearness of the Russian tanks. Most active opposition had fizzled out, to be replaced by the more passive but none the less heroic tactic of refusing to join the Party. In Poland, no one was ever compelled to join, but every worker was given the chance. To refuse effectively meant an end to all hope of promotion and invited a black mark on to one's personal dossier. It was a high price to pay, and some could not find the courage. "One must live after all," they said. But the majority stood firm, and one should not underestimate the value of this type of resistance to totalitarian enslavement:

> It was a question, really [said a woman from Warsaw], of trying to keep hold of one's interior identity and, even more importantly, that of one's children. You had to choose between bringing them up in a lie, in order to make life easier for them, or in the truth. It was so very complicated. We had to tell them things like, 'Well, that's the truth, but you must not say so at school.' We had to teach them to lead a double life.

In the country areas, resistance took a different form. After Gomułka's removal from office (and subsequent arrest), the regime had launched a full-scale onslaught to drive the peasants into collectives and production co-operatives on the Russian model. Poland, long known as the "granary of Europe", was to be taught to emulate a nation which had never, in all its history, known how to feed itself. Lenin's three-pronged policy for the rural areas: rely on the poor peasants, neutralise the in-betweens and scourge the kulaks (the richer peasants), was about to be put into effect.

"Now was the time of the great post-war degradation of the villages," remembers Bohdan Cywiński:[3]

> . . . when singing brigades of young people from the towns in khaki shirts and red ties rode into the country on open trucks for the so-called summer campaigns, whose aim was the requisitioning of agricultural products. This witch-hunt was dignified by the name of "social work", and a contemporary filmed chronicle showed squads of these noble social workers ransacking barns, dismembering hay-

stacks in search of the sacks of grain or sides of bacon that might be hidden there. The owners stood by and cursed or begged to be allowed at least to keep the seed-grain for the next sowing. In vain. Any peasant who tried to be efficient and plan for the future was lampooned in the press as a capitalist, a "kulak" – and everyone knew what had happened to the kulaks in the Soviet Union.

But the Polish peasants were a tough breed and, after the first shock, they had rallied. All but a few by now regarded the Communists as mortal enemies who had proffered them the carrot of a strip of land and were now intent on taking it back. Not only the "kulaks" but the poorer peasants gave the thumbs down to this rape. When they were forced, like their compatriots in the towns, to attend lectures on Marxist theory and Socialist agriculture, they came and listened in stolid disdain and continued as before.

In the film *Friends*, specially made for Polish TV in the Solidarity era, there is a scene in which peasants are attending just such a meeting. At the first pause in the political harangue from the Party official, one toothless old man breaks in: "Why didn't you bring nails? The war's been over five years and we still have no nails."

The official pours out the usual jargon: "The old expropriators are still in place; the kulaks lord it still in the villages. They'd like to take our bread, starve us out. They're trying to stop us joining co-operative farms."

The man may have been convinced by his own slogans, but the peasants were unimpressed. Mention of the nail shortage releases a chorus of complaint: how can we make bread? There's nothing to light a fire with. Why can't we get buckets? We can't even carry water. There are no saucepans . . .

Since the State paid far less than the market value of their produce, most of the peasants continued to give them only a bare minimum, while continuing to sell their surplus hay, potatoes, meat, milk and eggs on the free market at a much more profitable rate of exchange.

At first the regime was baffled and angry at their attitude, but realising that they could hardly undertake a massive repression of the peasants – the fruit of whose labour was needed for the regular quotas sent to the Soviet Union – they soft-pedalled on collectivisation. As a result, six years later only thirteen per cent of arable land in Poland had come under State control. But the regime did not stop imposing huge fines and prison sentences, managing at one and the same time to turn the peasants into implacable enemies and to send Polish agriculture hurtling down to ruin.

Such was the background to Lech Wałęsa's childhood. For the Wałęsa family too, these years from 1951–6 were the worst of all, though, as Lech's brother, Zygmunt, says, "our land was so poor that nobody even tried to confiscate it." Nevertheless, the brothers remember that "the Communists took our food, and we had to do whatever they told us." Like all peasant-farmers, they had a quota to fill, in accordance with the current Six Year Plan. If they had the audacity to kill a pig, without first fulfilling their quota to the State, they could be sent to prison for five years.

Though their stepfather, Stanisław, was a stern disciplinarian, it was their mother who ruled the household. "Small and round like an apple," a friend described Feliksa, "with that shrewdness which belongs neither to town nor village, peasant nor industrial worker, but which is born of a long apprenticeship to providing bread for the family."

A quiet woman, thrifty, an excellent housewife, is how others describe her. And in the opinion of one of the priests at Sobowo, she was, for all her lack of formal education, "one of the two cleverest women in the parish".

In Feliksa's family tree, the religious tradition was strong. For generations there had been a priest or nun in the family. She herself was very devout – "too devout", says her youngest son, Wojtek, with memories of being dragged unwillingly to church. Refusal was unthinkable. Every Sunday (in two relays because the farm could never be left unattended), the family trudged the four kilometres to Mass in the hill-top church at Sobowo, which massively overlooks the low-lying farmland. And in the evening, when the day's work was done, evening prayers were a ritual that was never dispensed with. The whole family had to say prayers before they were given supper. "And if we said them too quickly, we had to start again from the beginning," remembers Izabela.

Experience had taught Feliksa to expect little from life, and perhaps she had found her only consolation in religion. There were seven children now, all of them crammed into the little stone cottage with its damp earthen floor. Stanisław still went off to market, whenever he could borrow a horse, there to sell his butter, eggs, milk and meat. But there was little enough to keep the family on. Not enough for shoes, for trousers, for exercise books or pencils. A picture of Lech in his first year of primary school shows him with trousers far too long and a jersey far too short.

Ragged they might have been, but dirty never. Feliksa would

no more tolerate dirt than disobedience. Her children would not have dreamed of disobeying their mother, nor of arguing with her edicts. A single glance from those flashing eyes was enough to quell even the bravest. But if any of them was hurt, they ran to her for help, and then it was a different story. Of them all, Lech was most like her. Perhaps both of them had in full measure the characteristic traits of "the land of Dobrzyń". Tough, stubborn and hot-tempered, at the same time the people of Dobrzyń are reputed for their openness, their courage, and above all for their perseverance against impossible odds.

Whatever the reason, the bonds between Lech and his mother were exceptionally close. He loved to bring her presents, mushrooms or hazelnuts, or the last of a batch of apples he had stolen from a neighbouring farmer.

Though he was, according to Izabela, "the most religious of us all", he was a normally mischievous child, who went bird-nesting and caught frogs in the numerous ponds. He played with toy soldiers too and dreamed of becoming an air force pilot. Small for his age, he was always something of a loner. "He walked by himself, like a cat," says Izabela. "He was always different somehow. He used to think about things more than we did." Though close to his older brother, Stanisław, he preferred to be alone and to look at the world with eyes wide open. "Ever since I was a child," he told the Italian journalist, Oriana Fallaci, "I've taken note, listened, watched. I've always spied on life, and I think I've come to know something about it."

From the age of seven he attended the primary school in the village of Chalin, three kilometres away. Chalin is a village out of time. A "proper" village with a recognisable street and a handful of shops; but also a village which plunges the visitor back into an earlier age, where women with kerchiefed heads gather to discuss the day's events; where the cart filled with hay or firewood is a much more common sight than the motor car; and where farmers in blousons and black berets peaceably till the fields with a horse-drawn plough. Nestling among plane trees, Chalin boasts a large and very beautiful lake. Before the war, the mansion house overlooking the lake was privately owned, and the village children have been instructed what to think about the owner. "A wicked man," they say, "he didn't give the villagers anything to eat." But he was driven out by the Germans, and later the Communists took possession of the estate, so that now the house is the village school. For years, it has been falling into disrepair, and the wooden tiles on the classroom floors are rotting away. But a more idyllic setting can scarcely be imagined.

Each day the Wałęsa children made their way in wooden clogs along the sandy cart-track from Popowo, beside waving fields of wheat, punctuated by little ponds with their croaking frogs. In summer it must have been delightful, in the Polish winter, exposed to the cruel winds, a nightmare. At times, when the snow lay too thick on the ground, the school, which was unheated, remained closed.

Lech never played truant. He says modestly that during his first years at school, he was "damn gifted", with a good memory and an intuitive grasp of most subjects. His teachers remember him as no better than average, though they admit that the cramped conditions in the Wałęsa home were not conducive to much studying. That he was better at crafts and sport than at academic work is generally agreed.

Schoolfriends say that, true to his name, he was a "restless spirit", brave but inclined to show off. When, after school, the others would be fooling around with home-made fishing rods, Lech was the one who always caught his fish. "He'd always swim faster and further out into the lake than anyone else. It was as though he had an inner compulsion to succeed."

His bravery, however, had its limits, and did not extend to large dogs. "The trouble was, I was a little kid, and all the dogs were bigger than me. There was one in particular that seemed to know I hated him, and he hated me back."

"Ducks, too," adds Zygmunt with a grin. "He once had a very unfortunate encounter with a duck."

Did he also feel a compulsion to lead? Loner though he was, he seems to have been conscious from an early age of a natural capacity for leadership. "People have always been interested in what I say and think. Somehow, they've always followed where I've led."

For all the grinding poverty, Lech was happy as a child:

> There's a saying that the poor man is a devil without a soul [he smiles]. But we had souls, so we must have been rich. In one sense, we had nothing, but you can't judge poverty by material standards. Prosperity and greed go together. Well, we weren't well-off, and so we weren't greedy. We didn't have television, or even radio, but we had books, and the whole world of nature was open for us to read. We were rich in the things that mattered.

That he was an outspoken child seems fairly clear; and it was a dangerous characteristic in Stalinist Poland. When still quite young, he was warned by a priest that he would end up in prison if he didn't watch his tongue. By 1952, when he was nine, church schools throughout the country had been closed down or taken over by the regime, and the Russian language had become a compulsory subject. No one could escape the indoctrination classes, the classes in citizenship, which began for children at the age of twelve. If the factories, barracks, workshops or sports clubs were centres for political propaganda, the classroom was even more so. For that was where the new generation of Socialist citizens was being nurtured. The main objects of education were three: to make the young aware of the class struggle; to make them good Marxists; and to encourage friendly feelings towards the USSR. Any fact or event that did not portray Russia in the most amiable light was taboo. The Russo-Polish War of 1920, the 1939 Russian invasion of Poland, Katyń or the Warsaw Rising were simply never mentioned. The world, the children were taught, was divided into two: the heaven of enlightened progress that was the USSR; and the hell of reaction and privilege exemplified by the USA.

A syllabus dictated what was to be taught and left no scope to the teachers. Many of the teachers were lukewarm in their enthusiasm for the syllabus, but they had to follow it, if they wanted to keep their jobs. Some confined themselves to lectures on honesty in human relations, or duty to family and country. But there were always a few who were crudely propagandist:

> In my school [said a girl], the history teacher turned the lesson into a vulgar comparison between the "peaceful" Warsaw Pact countries and the "war-mongering" Nato states; between the poverty of the poor exploited workers in the West and the prosperity of our socialist society. Even at our young age, we knew he was talking rubbish. Any and all shortcomings in Poland were blamed on American capitalist plots. And it sometimes seemed that if it rained for the May Day parade, the Americans were to blame.

Even the youngest pupils gathered daily round an enormous portrait of Stalin, twice as large as life, to sing songs about his wise leadership and kindly nature. One of them, sung to a fairly lively tune, contained the lines:

> For ever will live our beloved Uncle, Stalin,
> Whose lips are sweeter than raspberries.

"None of us really believed it," says a contemporary of Lech

Wałęsa, "but it was something we had to pretend about. Otherwise our parents would have received a letter from the school, followed by a visit from the police." A few children were more impressionable. One remembers getting a beating from his father for referring lovingly to Stalin at home as "our grandpa".

This sort of thing did not go down too well with the young Wałęsa, though he liked some of the scarlet and white banners – with slogans like WYWALCZYMY TRWAŁY POKÓJ, We shall fight with all our might for enduring peace – which always festooned the classroom walls. "I had problems with the teachers," he admits. "They taught us Communism and I didn't pay any attention. Once I was sent to the headmaster and he broke a cane over my head. The trouble was, if I could see very well that something or other was white, no one was going to persuade me that it was black."

Later, when he was older, he saw this teaching in a different light: "We were ordered to be atheists, and we were taught atheism, and look what happened. Almost the whole nation is religious. We learned good things in a bad school."[4]

The official Marxist indoctrination of their children was resisted head-on by the peasants. With the tenacity of their kind, they joined the ideological struggle, but not in the way Stalin intended. When the children were taught at school that there was no God; when they learned in biology that Christianity was outmoded and unscientific, and that the whole idea of man being created for a purpose was false; when their history and geography textbooks were discovered to be revamped editions of Russian models, their mothers, fathers, uncles, aunts, grandmothers and grandfathers moved on to the attack. Often unable to read or write themselves, they would explain to the children that everything they had heard during the day – except perhaps in mathematics and physical science – was a lie. Grandparents in particular, highly conservative and regarding all Communists as the brood of Satan, had an answer for everything the children had learned in the classroom.

As a result, the only village children likely to succumb to the propaganda were those who did not receive an alternative education from the family; and some of the cleverer ones who knew well that the best opportunities were open only to those who accepted the Party version of reality.

Feliksa, like most of the village women, sent the children once a week to the church at Sobowo for religious instruction, while at home she set them firmly on the right lines. Life in the villages was slower, closer to the earth than life in the towns. Family life was more intense; and in the long evenings when the oil-lamps were lit, the children gathered round to imbibe a very different philosophy of life from their elders. In both town and country, the real moral and ethical education took place in the heart of the family.

In the Wałęsa family, it was Feliksa from whom they learned. She had never lost the lively, enquiring mind that she had inherited from her father, and she read everything she could lay hands on. "My mother," says Lech, "was the best-read woman I have ever met. I think she had read every book, not only in our house, but in everyone else's, including the church library; and every paper, even old pre-war ones that neighbours had kept."

Feliksa talked to her children about Poland's history, and read aloud to them from the Polish classics. It was from her that Lech first heard the great epic work of Sieńkiewicz, which told the story of the Cossack Wars and praised the chivalry of the Polish knights. As he played with his toy soldiers, did he ever see himself (as later he was most certainly encouraged by others to do) as the Little Knight in that epic – fearless, resourceful and strong, who loved argument and fighting for their own sake rather than for any craving for violence; impatient for action and adventure, but calm in a crisis – "a great soul in a little body"? Was he intrigued by the physical description of the Little Knight, easily recognised by his long, twirling moustaches?

In towns and villages alike, people avoided the Marxist books. Classics, like those of Sieńkiewicz, were in great demand. (As they portrayed the Germans in a bad light, they were among the few classical novels still in print.) At times such as these, there was need to remember that Poland had once been great. Feliksa lost no opportunity of getting the message across to her family. Lech, consequently, viewed the official teaching with mistrust. He was argumentative in class, sometimes giving in when he was getting the worst of it, only to return to the fray next day with fresh ammunition from home. "I always had a lot of problems," he recalls. "You could say that my whole life has been one long turmoil."

[1] O. Halecki, *A History of Poland*, chapter 28, Routledge & Kegan Paul, 1978. "Ten Years of Trial".

[2] Tadeusz Konwicki, *A Minor Apocalypse*, Faber & Faber, 1983.

[3] From an unpublished article: "The Polish Experience".

[4] *Time* magazine, 4.1.82.

8 SPRINGTIME IN OCTOBER (1956)

A Soviet writer asked me what the Poles' real concern was in October 1956. He used the term "petit bourgeois revolt". I answered that the concern was for moral law. "Well, that's a provincial point of view," [he] said, laughing indulgently. "Judaea was a province too," I said, "a little province that gave the world the Old and New Testaments."

Kazimierz Brandys

In March 1953 Stalin died. On the day of his funeral, a three minute silence was observed throughout Poland. Those Poles who had bought the official line that Stalin was a kindly uncle to whom all good things were owed, duly grieved. Grażyna S., four years old at the time, wept, because "we got sweets at Christmas in our kindergarten, and we were told that Stalin had sent them to us. Now, I imagined, there would be no more sweets. My grief was very real."

Outwardly nothing changed. The man was dead, but his system lived on, even though the personality cult he had represented had been repudiated in Moscow, where collective leadership was now the mode. Malenkov ruled for a while in the Kremlin, and when he fell, Krushchev replaced him. It seemed like the mixture as before. Yet underneath the surface, something *was* changing. There was movement under the ice, though nobody could have imagined that within three years the ice would actually crack and give way.

In Poland, the rot set in faster and went further than in any other country in the Soviet bloc. The process began in October 1954 with the broadcast revelations of Józef Światło, a former Lt-Col. in the secret police who had fled to the West the previous December. Światło, the man who had arrested Gomułka in 1948, had organised Department 10 which had kept tabs on the ideological purity of Party members themselves. Accordingly he had a wealth of information about every member of Party and government from the lowest to the highest. He could make or break any or all of those who held power. When he began to tell all he knew on Radio Free Europe he had a fascinated and captive audience among millions of Poles, and what he said instilled terror into the hearts of the powerful. He blew the gaff on corruption and intrigue in high places and on police brutality. He spoke of torture chambers and what was done there. And when he referred to the informer system, he gave chapter and verse, naming names and quoting from actual reports. The portrait of top Communists emerging from these revelations was of "utterly ruthless and utterly dishonest men who stopped at nothing in order to obey the orders of their Soviet masters and to foster their own private interests".[1]

In the first flush of anger, embarrassment and dismay, the regime issued indignant denials. But though the people hated what Światło had stood for, they knew that he was speaking the truth about what was happening in Poland. In the end, the government admitted that mistakes had been made and promised that the guilty would be punished. The secret police apparatus was shaken to the core.

The effects of Światło's broadcasts were earth-shattering. Realising that the Terror must now surely end, people began at last to emerge from the zombie-like trance of fear in which they had been frozen. As life returned, a number of emotions which had been kept submerged for years rose violently to the surface and overflowed.

It was the young people who began it – the new generation that had inherited the Communist paradise. The white hopes of the Party, untainted by the past. They had free schooling, access to jobs, training in sports, medical care, all the things their fathers had dreamed of. But the advantages did not conceal the fact that the life they had to lead was not only bleak, with no outlet for youthful high spirits, but, even more importantly, schizophrenic, with a yawning gap between the official gilded view of reality and the grim reality itself.

In the summer of 1955, the government had staged a Youth Festival for Communist youth from all over Europe. Their aim was to display Polish achievements; but, not surprisingly, the event backfired disastrously. For the first time, the majority of Polish youngsters met their counterparts from the West, and discovered that they had been told a monstrous lie. Far from starving, the Westerners had more to eat than they did; their clothes were more colourful, their music and culture more vibrant and alive. Contrasting the lifestyle of their visitors with their own drab and colourless existence, the Poles were angry at the con-trick that had been worked on them. Ironically, the Youth Festival gave the youth of Poland an impetus to seek change. For the first time since the war, a Western craze, in this instance jazz and rock 'n' roll, seized hold of them.

After the Youth Festival, the authorities began to be seriously alarmed about the young "troublemakers" and "agitators" who were calling for change. They blamed the jazz craze and stamped down hard on its adherents. But there was more to it than jazz. Youngsters began demanding not only more lively entertainment but better food and, in the workers' hostels attached to the new industries and mines, better living conditions.

In the hostels too, a growing number of youngsters, freshly liberated from the restraining influence of parents and parish priests, were showing their frustration by brawling and heavy drinking. Juvenile delinquency in a Marxist state! It was a contradiction in terms, not to be thought of. Or was it an early sign that the morality of that particular kind of Socialism did not work?

Out of curiosity, some younger Party officials set up an enquiry into conditions in the hostels. Predictably they discovered that the buildings were sub-standard, the food inedible and the management inefficient and corrupt.

What had started as a storm in a teacup quickly became a deluge. "Pioneers" on State farms complained about *their* food, pay and housing, while students seized the opportunity to attack the compulsory Marxist–Leninist courses, the fact that entrance to higher education depended on Party membership, and that pro-regime students got the best grants, the best grades and the best jobs.

Young Party activists now took up the cudgels. Writers and journalists who till now had been afraid of repercussions from the police began at last to ridicule the absurdities of the system and to write the truth as they saw it. First in the field was Adam Ważyk whose *Poem for Adults*, published in a literary weekly, had all the force of an earth-tremor. It expressed the disillusionment of the young with the false paradise that had been promised:

> They ran to us shouting
> Under Socialism
> A cut finger does not hurt
> They cut their finger
> They felt pain
> They lost faith.

Ważyk's poem was a protest on behalf of all those whose fingers had bled and festered under the Stalin-directed regime: the hungry, the over-worked, the badly-housed, the boys and girls who were forced to spy on their parents. It ended with a rescue call for a nation that had already known too much suffering:

We should make demands on this earth,
Which we didn't win in a game of chance,
Which cost the lives of millions,
Demands for the plain truth,
For the bread of freedom,
For fiery good sense.
We should make demands daily
We should make demands of the Party.[2]

The mood of the younger intellectuals was made clear in the student newspaper, *Po Prostu*, which proclaimed: "We are a group of the discontented; we want more things, wiser things, better things."[3]

Living conditions in Poland were so bad that even Krushchev, in an address to the Polish Central Committee, had said that something ought to be done to keep the workers sweet. The workers, he said contemptuously, don't care about politics, they just want to live better. "If we don't soon manage to give them better conditions than they can get in a capitalist country, we might as well shut up shop."

A few months later it was Krushchev who dropped a bombshell. In February 1956, at the XXth Party Congress in Moscow, he demolished the Stalin myth. Non-Communists did not need to be told that Stalin had been a murderous lunatic, but to the Party faithful Krushchev's revelations came as a blow between the eyes. Many resigned on the spot, others wrestled painfully with the revelation. In the midst of all this confusion came the news that their leader, Bolesław Bierut, had died of a heart attack while in Moscow. Few would believe that version of events; but few would mourn him either, although attendance at his funeral parade was compulsory, in spite of the freezing cold. The Polish people had always thought of Bierut as an NKVD stooge. In his prison notebook, Cardinal Wyszyński noted wryly that "by now Bolesław Bierut is convinced that there is a God, and that His name is indeed Love", before listing the crimes which could be laid at the dead man's door. Of the hatchet job being worked on the Stalin legend he wrote: "How rapid is the decline of gods wrought by human hands. And it is for such a god that the Living God has to step aside."

Stalin's era in Poland was firmly coming to an end. Hastily, his jovial image was taken down from hoardings and walls. A cartoon in a new satirical weekly, showing an office wall bare except for a nail and the dusty outline of a large portrait, carried the caption: SPACE TO LET. Criticism poured out in a flood, especially within the Party itself, where hard-liners found themselves faced with a majority eager for reform.

In May 1956, thirty thousand were released from prison, and Władysław Gomułka from house arrest. Some of the most resented secret police officials were removed, and their most prominent victims rehabilitated. Among them were the men and women of the wartime Home Army. The Soviet-style history books had continued to denounce the Home Army as a nest of traitors; former Home Army members were still unable to get jobs, places to live or higher education, even if they had not been arrested and sent to one of the special camps reserved for them near the Russian border. At least a partial re-appraisal was called for. The authorities rose to the occasion. While continuing to lambast the wartime leaders as reactionary fascists, they generously admitted that the rank and file may have been inspired by love of their country. And though the subject of Katyń remained utterly taboo, a simple memorial – a tin helmet lying on a stone – was allowed to mark a spot where Home Army partisans had been executed in a group by the SS.

It wasn't a great deal, but it was a big boost to Polish morale. It also released a great wave of pent-up hatred of the Russians, so that it became next to impossible for the regime to go on maintaining that "eternal gratitude and undying love for Moscow fill every Polish heart". Disillusioned Communists led the field. They had most cause to hate the Russians, they claimed, because they knew a lot more about them.

A flood of letters to the papers now demanded the release of priests and nuns from prison. Crucifixes were taken from their hiding places and worn openly to work. In the face of clamorous popular demand, the government began to weaken. Travel restrictions were relaxed; theatres began to offer Western plays and Western music. Jazz became respectable. The Communist press ceased to rave about the exploits of the super-workers, those largely imaginary "proletarian Tarzans who happily carried out the Plan with two hundred per cent achievement". People allowed themselves to hope that a tolerable existence was possible after all! But few realised that what lay round the next corner was a genuine full-blooded proletarian revolution.

Tension had been growing. The new sense of freedom had done nothing to lessen the miseries of everyday life. "The public," wrote one commentator, "was obliged to wait longer, push harder and crowd more, to buy less and less."[4] Life was reduced to an unending struggle for existence. Apart from the chronic shortages and the queues that began at dawn, "too many people lived in dank basements or half-rotting buildings with poor or no hygienic facilities; and it is wrong to imagine one ever got used to it. There was no privacy, no comfort."[4]

"They ask us about the things we promised," says a union member in the film *Friends*, "the washing-machines, fridges, cars. Where are the miracles?"

For a privileged few, hardship and shortages did not exist. The scandal of the packed shelves and the discount prices of the "yellow-curtain shops" became so outrageous that the authorities decided to abandon them and convert them into ordinary State retail outlets. But the gesture did not help the Party, for now its lower ranks, deprived of their special status, were just as under-privileged as everybody else. Their complaints swelled the general discontent.

* * *

June 1956. An explosion of despair and hatred. In Poznań, sixteen thousand workers went on strike and took to the streets, singing religious and patriotic songs, and demanding bread and freedom. Shots were fired and a boy of thirteen was killed. The Army was called in, but refused to shoot at the workers. Some of the soldiers even joined the protestors. The riot was not quelled until the arrival of more politically reliable troops with tanks and heavy artillery. Fifty-four were killed, hundreds wounded, hundreds more arrested. Prime Minister Józef Cyrankiewicz hurried to Poznań and blamed everything on a counter-revolutionary capitalist plot, threatening that "every agitator or madman" who dared lift a hand against "the power of People's Poland" would have that hand cut off. The crassness of such a threat at such a time was an indication of government nerviness in the face of this unprecedented challenge. The old-guard Stalinists were urging a crack-down; the reformers wanted to release the pressure.

In the end, the reformers won the day. In July, the vast majority of collective farms were returned to private ownership. Events moved fast that summer. On 15th August, over a million and a half pilgrims converged on the hill-top monastery of Częstochowa, for the 300th anniversary of the defeat of an all-conquering army (Swedish not Russian) by a handful of resolute Poles. It was perhaps the greatest religious demonstration ever seen, and thousands had walked hundreds of kilometres to get there. In the procession at the monastery on the Hill of Light, the Cardinal's throne, empty but for a huge bouquet of red and white roses, was carried high above the crowd. With passionate intensity the pilgrims prayed for just such a miracle as had happened in 1656. And a few weeks later they were convinced that their prayers had been answered.

* * *

The name of Władysław Gomułka – dismissed and arrested by Stalin in 1948 – was on everyone's lips. His recall was the one subject which united the rival factions within the Party, and even to the people it seemed as if the days of his former misrule had been "the good old days". Everything had been so much worse since then that a golden haze now surrounded the memory of the post-war era. He had the aura of a martyr, punished by Stalin because he had sought a "Polish road to Socialism".

Since the first post-Stalin relaxation, however, the Russian leadership had grown increasingly alarmed and was belatedly trying to stem the tide of change. On Friday 19th October, 1956, Krushchev and a formidable array of Soviet top brass descended on Warsaw to deal with the recalcitrant Poles. Krushchev had been drinking and was purple with rage, refusing even to shake hands with the Poles.[5] At the same time Soviet troops stationed in Poland began to march on Warsaw, while the Soviet fleet staged menacing manoeuvres in the Baltic. A conference took place immediately, with a furious Krushchev accusing the Poles of selling out to the imperialists. The Poles kept cool, told Krushchev there was no crisis, but that some degree of liberalisation was absolutely necessary and long overdue. They referred to the Russian troop manoeuvres and warned that the Poles would fight if necessary. Angry talks went on for hours.

Gomułka stood his ground, insisting that if the Russian troops were not called off, he would personally broadcast to the nation – an action which would have triggered an armed uprising. The people were already out on the streets and their mood was steely and uncompromising. Workers in one factory were preparing to take up arms.

At this late hour, while three columns of Soviet-officered Polish tank units were surrounding the city, Krushchev backed away from confrontation. Ordering the troops not to advance further, he and his delegation went home.

At next day's meeting of the Central Committee, all the hard-liners lost their seats, and Gomułka was formally elected First Secretary of the ruling Communist Party. The internal revolution in the Party had been resolved. Now they had to unite and establish control over the revolution outside.

That afternoon, it was announced that Gomułka would broadcast to the nation. Bogdan S. will never forget that day:

> We clustered round our radio sets in real terror [he recalls]. We knew nothing of the Central Committee meeting, in Warsaw, nor of Krushchev's unexpected arrival. All we knew was that Russian tanks had surrounded all the major cities and were actually on our streets. There could have been nobody in the whole of Poland who did not realise how serious the situation was.

Gomułka's speech to the nation was masterly, one of the most powerful addresses ever given by a Communist leader. He deplored the excesses of the police; promised a return to the rule of law and a certain democratisation of the Party; rejected the imitation-Soviet economy and promised one that was at least partially open to the market forces of supply and demand. To everyone's astonishment, he also admitted the unequal trading arrangements with the USSR, under which the Russians were taking best-quality Polish coal in return for obsolete machinery which had been discarded by the Russian factories.

He promised more, and more truthful, information. The system must be changed, he agreed, even if only gradually. Workers must be given a share in management; peasants must not be forced into co-operatives. He opened his arms wide and begged everyone listening to take a share in creating a new society, admitting that: "It is a poor idea that Socialism can be built only by Communists . . . What is constant in Socialism boils down to the abolition of man's exploitation by man. The roads to this goal can be and are different."

There would, he promised, be no more submission to Moscow.[6]

In the light of hindsight, one can perhaps see that he promised too much. "Maybe we were fools for believing him," says a Warsaw woman, "but we had been so long without hope. We had thought they would go on for ever getting away with all their lies.

Then suddenly there was hope. We believed that Gomułka was an honest man. So we trusted him."

The Cardinal was released forthwith. Giving his support to Gomułka, he appealed to Catholics to stand by the new regime. There was much that divided Gomułka and Wyszyński, much that would soon drive them apart again. But they were both Poles, and both had fallen victim to Stalin. Both were pragmatists who knew that at this hour, Poland's very survival depended on their pulling together.

Carried away by Poland's apparent success, the Hungarians rose in revolt. But Krushchev was not going to tolerate a re-run of what had happened in Warsaw. This time the tanks really did crush the revolution. The mood of euphoria in Poland turned rapidly to stunned dismay as the Hungarians were beaten into submission and the West proved unable to intervene. Plane loads of drugs, provisions and medicines were flown from Poland to the insurgents, every window seemed to be flying a Hungarian flag, and on every wall a graffiti dove shed tears of blood.[7] Once again the Poles returned to the brink of armed revolt which would certainly have been bloody and certainly doomed. It was Wyszyński who saved the situation. In the first sermon he had preached in three years he reminded his countrymen that it is sometimes easier to die than to go on living. "It is that greater heroism that this day calls for, this day so pregnant with events, so full of anxious speculation about the future."

The people allowed the moment to pass. Peace returned to the streets, and hope surfaced again. Though in reality they knew little about him, their enthusiasm for Gomułka bordered on hero-worship, because they believed that he had defied the Russians and got away with it. History had played one of its wry jokes, since for this new Communist regime the Poles were giving vent to an outburst of naked nationalist fervour. Few leaders in history have received such spontaneous acclaim, few have been trusted with so many hopes. And, in fourteen years of rule, few have squandered the opportunity so unimaginatively as did Władysław Gomułka.

[1] Z. J. Błażynski, "The Światło Affair", article in *Poland One* magazine, Volume 1, Number 11, April 1985.

[2] Poemat dla Dorosłych, *Nowa Kultura*, 21.8.55.

[3] O. Halecki, *A History of Poland*, *op. cit.*

[4] Flora Lewis, *The Polish Volcano*, *op cit.*

[5] Peter Raina, *Political Opposition in Poland 1954–1977,* Poets and Painters Press, London, 1978.

[6] Konrad Syrop, *Poland in Perspective*, *op. cit.*

[7] Ewa Fournier, *Poland*, *op. cit.*

9 LOST ILLUSIONS (1956–70)

> A man may have great dreams about coming to power. But when he actually achieves power, he comes up against the triviality of daily life . . . He gets bogged down . . . He gets used to having power . . . Ideals and dreams go by the board . . . You have to administer Socialism and you begin to identify Socialism with the number of screws produced. Oh, don't misunderstand me, screws are very important. But Socialism is also a spiritual idea. And when that is forgotten, discord begins to outrank Truth . . . It becomes a matter of ruling rather than administering. And then even those who are not demoralised by this can at least see that we are facing a crisis.
>
> From *Friends* (*Przyjaciele*) – film shown on Polish Television in 1981

"I was not yet thirteen years old when, in June 1956, the desperate struggle of the workers of Poznań for bread and freedom was suppressed in blood," wrote Lech Wałęsa in his Nobel speech many years later. Even then he had been aware of "all the wrongs, the degradations and the lost illusions" suffered by the majority of the people.

His was the generation on whose wholehearted support the State was counting. Untarnished by the past, they were the regime's stake in the future. Like everybody else, Lech's older brother, Stanisław, had joined the Organisation of Polish Youth, and, at the age of fifteen, was still young enough to retain his youthful idealism about it. Quieter and more stolid than Lech, he had become the secretary of the Organisation in his school; and when it was dissolved in 1956, felt a sense of betrayal. "I was of no use to anyone any more." The oldest of the brothers, Edward, had already left school and was helping his stepfather on the land. But it was frustrating work, with few rewards, and after a year he got a job at a nearby brickworks. Stanisław took his place for a time, before going to the trade school in Lipno to train as a lathe-turner. The Union of Polish Youth helped him out with clothes, money and free lodging, and Stanisław felt a deep gratitude towards them. "People's Poland helped us get out of that village," he said, years later, when he was a long-standing but disillusioned Party member himself: "How can you tell the young about earthen floors, and about there being no work even when you were starving? There *were* achievements then."

Wojtek, the youngest, agrees, though with less enthusiasm: "People's Poland gave us our trades, rescued us from poverty and promised that things would get better. So we were patient and worked as hard as we could. But the better days never came . . ."

Their mother, Feliksa, wanted them all to have as good an education as possible, so that they could get out of the village and have a more rewarding life. These were the days when the young people were deserting the villages in droves for the newly rebuilt Baltic towns. The more ambitious among them would become Party functionaries with some chance of a successful career. The majority would simply join the workforce and become the new proletariat of the Coast.

Lech too was longing to get away and work in the shipyards. He even had hopes of becoming a qualified engineer. For he was now showing promise in maths and physics, and his headmaster had proposed him for the College of Technology, which offered a five year course with a professional qualification at the end of it. The idea was attractive, and the family wanted Lech to go ahead. He took the entrance exams and passed. But in the end, lack of money prevented him. The course had to be paid for in advance, and as Wojtek fell ill with diabetes and needed specialist treatment, the money was simply not available. Lech's plans had to be abandoned.

Bending the rules somewhat, in order to help the family, his headmaster agreed to take him back for the rest of that school year, since it was already too late for other arrangements to be made. So, swallowing his disappointment, Lech returned to school for another year, taking a part-time job at the brickworks, and continuing to work on his stepfather's and other people's farms. But he regarded farm-work with some disgust: "It is hard work but stupid," he says. "You never knew whether something would grow, or whether it would get eaten up by insects or pecked up by birds."

He lost interest in school work, and his marks began to suffer. "I felt less and less like opening the books; there were always so many other things to do." Yet he didn't sulk over his lost opportunity, consoling himself in words that are typical of him: "It isn't really good to be too gifted. I think I prefer to be like the bee, which knows it is perfectly well able to collect the honey, but which doesn't rush headlong for the big beehive, where it could fall in and get stuck."

Leaving school at last, he followed his brother Stanisław to the trade school at Lipno, a small town on the River Mień, twenty or so kilometres away, the nearest town of any size. As number 1488, he registered for the course in mechanised agriculture in September 1959. The then director remembers Lech particularly because even by current standards he was desperately poor, and everybody was very sorry for him. All the teachers knew to make allowances for him, because whatever spare time he had was taken up in farm-work on behalf of the family. The course, which included metallurgy, technical drawing, maths and physics, involved three days' study and three days (paid) in the workshops. The money he earned went to pay his hostel fees.

He seems to have been a quiet, hard-working student, with a reputation for stubbornness. "He was determined. If he set his mind on doing something, he would do it." One teacher describes him as "friendly and open. A bit of a bully but a likeable one." Another recalls his penchant for practical jokes and his complete absence of fear. On one occasion he accepted a dare to go and sit in the cemetery all night. In the end the dare was called off, but Lech had been quite prepared to go.

The present director of the school, then the newly-appointed warden of the hostel, affirms that Lech has stayed in his mind more than any of the others:

> . . . because he had such an amazing gift for organisation. In charge of any group, he was worth his weight in gold. To give you an example: the hostel students had to sweep out the corridors, and each hall took turns, a week at a time. When it was the turn of Wałęsa's hall, the teacher-in-charge would just leave them to it. Lech would wake the others at six each morning, set some boys to washing the floor, others to polishing it. By the time the teacher got up, the floor was shining.

An entry in the hostel conduct book on 17th November, 1960, however, records: "Wałęsa, Lech: troublemaker and smoker." No amount of bad conduct marks cured him of this habit. Three times he was summoned before a disciplinary committee and ordered to stop smoking. But his room-mate reports that to avoid detection, they simply went up on to the roof to smoke.

26th January, 1961: "Lech Wałęsa walks about with his head bare, though he has a cap in his pocket." 17th April, 1961: "I suggest that Lech Wałęsa should receive no more than four points for behaviour." (A somewhat rare mark of disapproval, indicating that he was still the "restless spirit" he had always been.) A report for January 1961 gives him an overall academic assessment of "Fair", declaring him to be "sound in morals and politics", good at economics and sport, fair at Polish language studies. His worst subject appears to have been history – perhaps it was because of the distorted way in which it was taught and with which he refused to go along. But at least he passed the exams each year, and finished the course successfully. "For ten years," a commentator was to write, "the regime had been busy educating the man who would become its most formidable opponent."

Having got his certificate from the trade school – a necessary piece of paper for any Pole wanting to become a skilled worker – he worked for a while as an electrical mechanic at a State Agricultural Machinery Centre, mending electric trailers. Then, in 1963, he was conscripted into the Polish Army.

Poles traditionally have a great respect for their soldiers, a respect only slightly diminished even in People's Poland, where the military was subjected to the Party. Polish conscripts were required to swear an oath of loyalty not only to Poland but to Socialism; and a special political Youth wing of the Party was put to indoctrinating the new recruits. Bogdan S., who was in the Army at the same time as Wałęsa, says that for many of the conscripts the experience was unique:

> It was the first chance they'd ever had of living away from home and of enlarging their horizons. On another level, it was like a fish-tank, where a political indoctrination could be applied very effectively, at a critical stage of one's life. We were told that Germany alone was Poland's traditional enemy, and that the NATO powers were intent on destroying the countries of the Warsaw Pact. Some absorbed the propaganda. After all, the Army offered an opening to a secure and well-paid job, a privileged position in society – for those who were prepared to pay its price.

But, in spite of the pressures, most of the conscripts emerged unscathed, the majority of them being well and truly inoculated by their families and parish priests against such propaganda.

Wałęsa, working as a morse-code operator, enjoyed being in the Army and rose to the rank of corporal. His brother, Stanisław, who was sharing this period of military service, and who had also become a corporal, began to cultivate a spreading moustache, and Lech, always in the shadow of his older brother, followed suit.

Lech loved the uniform. "It fascinated me, just as a kid loves to dress up like a cowboy," he says. He was popular and well thought-of. "A bit of a disciplinarian," said a fellow-conscript, "but human with it. He never harassed anyone just for the hell of it. He liked a joke, and could achieve more that way than others did by shouting. I remember him coming to the cookhouse and asking 'What's cooking?' And we all shouted back: 'Wałęsa's whiskers.'"

One of the officers was keen for him to make a career in the regular Army, reporting that he was "intelligent, keen to learn, determined. Would make a leader. Should be promoted." Had his advice been heeded, history might have been different. But Wałęsa did not want to become a professional soldier. However much he had enjoyed the experience, he had had enough.

It was a tight squeeze in the cottage when Lech returned from the Army. "We couldn't all fit in," says Stanisław. "Some of us had to be farmed out on neighbours."

But they all came together for the big Church Feast Days, as they would continue to do as long as it was feasible. And for New Year. One New Year's Eve, Stanisław and Lech went to a party at a neighbour's house, and Stanisław got very drunk. Realising that his brother was incapable of walking home, Lech heaved him on to his shoulders, threw his sheepskin jacket over him, and began the long walk through the fields knee-deep in snow. But Lech was more than half-sloshed himself, and, somewhere along the road, Stanisław fell off unnoticed. Lech was quite unaware, and even when he arrived home believed he was still carrying his brother. But all he was carrying was the sheepskin jacket. In a panic, Feliksa had to organise a search-party to go back and search for Stanisław in the snow-bound fields. Many years later, Lech would claim that he had been drunk only twice in his life: once, in the Army and once, over a girl. He seems conveniently to have forgotten this other, embarrassing, occasion.

After the Army, Lech's first job was as an electrician in an agricultural co-operative in the village of Lenie. The money he earned was not enough to buy the second-hand motor-bike which he longed for. He had become an expert mechanic and was known locally as "golden hands" for his skill in mending every type of machine, particularly motor-bikes. He had a girlfriend, Jadwiga, from a neighbouring village, but, says Wojtek, the relationship was rather one-sided, since "she wanted Leszek to look at her all the time, but he preferred to sit in her parents' flat and watch TV". Girls "adored" him, claims Izabela, because he was witty and made them laugh. But he treated them all as friends and refused to think seriously about any of them.

Occasionally he wondered if he had a vocation to the priesthood. "It was the uniform again," he jokes. "Well, in fact it was more than that. I always wanted to do some good for people." So why did he not become a priest? "Because I came to the conclusion that when you're a priest you're out of touch with the way ordinary people live. I didn't want that to happen."

The better times hoped for by so many did not come, although the first few years of Gomułka-ism were the most stable that Poland had known since the war. Probably too much was expected of Gomułka. To the people he had assumed the status of Messiah; and inevitably he failed to live up to the role. What the country needed now was a rapid return to the rule of law, some bold economic reform, a recognition of the nation's cultural and religious roots, and a genuine dialogue between the regime and society.

But Gomułka's imagination was limited, and he misread the mood of the people. He was a true, old-fashioned Communist believer, who had never ceased to think that it was possible to create a Communist society in Poland and that Marxism–Leninism would finally triumph there. The "human face" of Socialism, which the Poles were hoping to see, was not part of his plan.

For obvious strategic reasons, he soft-pedalled at the beginning. As Gomułka and the Cardinal needed each other's support, sweeping concessions were made to the Church. Priests and bishops were among the thousands being released from prison; new Catholic newspapers were permitted, and five members of their editorial boards allowed to stand for election to the Sejm (Parliament); religious education temporarily began again in the schools; and the regime limited its control over church appointments to a mere right of veto. In exchange, the Church promised support, and urged Catholics to vote for the regime's candidates at the forthcoming elections. The Vatican took a decidedly cool view of such supping with the devil on the Cardinal's part.

The old unpopular Organisation of Polish Youth was dissolved. Only a few, like Lech's brother, Stanisław, regretted its passing. The Organisation's successor was no less unpopular with the majority, but had the merit of not being compulsory. More popular were the Scouts (mixed, for boys and girls), dusted off and given a new Socialist image, but with the pre-war uniform unchanged. A more relaxed attitude towards the West meant that friends and relatives on both sides of the great divide could now renew contact, without fear of reprisals. Before 1956, a passport was a rarity: the majority of Poles were imprisoned within their borders. Passports (valid only for a single journey) now became possible again, even though the traveller was allowed so little dollar or sterling currency that he invariably had to find someone in the host country to finance the trip.

Travel to the West opened the Poles' eyes to the world outside. No longer was it possible to persuade them that workers in Western Europe were starving. They could see with their own eyes that most workers in the capitalist world actually had cars.

Films and books from the West began to trickle in, though no anti-Soviet, or "counter-revolutionary" works were admitted, and George Orwell and Ian Fleming were both rigorously excluded. This new influx from abroad seemed to release something in the Polish creative spirit, so that there was a new cultural flowering, with the satirical plays of Mrożek, the films of Wajda, the novels of Andrzejewski and the poems of Herbert appearing like life-giving streams in the cultural desert.

Gomułka went to Moscow almost immediately after his election and returned with a satisfactory agreement. From now on the two countries were to treat each other on a much more equal basis, each of them recognising the other's independence and national sovereignty.[1] In recognition of the cheap coal the Russians were getting from Poland and the free maintenance for Russian troops on Polish soil, Krushchev cancelled Poland's huge outstanding debt and promised to pay the troops' expenses themselves in future. Those Poles who were still in the Soviet Union and who wished to return home were to be allowed to do so.

The rumour later gained ground in Poland that at this meeting Krushchev offered to tell the truth about Katyń, and that Gomułka declined, fearing a violent reaction from the Poles. If that offer really was made, then the Polish leader missed a historic opportunity to improve the relations between the two countries. For the heavy shadow of Katyń continues to hang over those relations, and does not diminish as the years pass. There has always been a certain unnamed green square in a Warsaw cemetery, to which flowers have been brought and candles lit to commemorate those who were murdered in the dark forest near Smolensk.

Whatever Krushchev did or did not propose to Gomułka, it is fair to say that by the time Gomułka left Moscow, the relations between the two men were very cordial. Perhaps Hungary had finally convinced Gomułka that Poland's only hope was to remain firmly inside the Russian orbit. From that conviction he would never again waver.

Was it to convince his new friends of his own good faith that Gomułka so soon began to turn on his older ones? In a Party split down the middle it was up to him to hold the balance between the conservative Stalinists and the reformers. But he began almost immediately to veer towards the conservatives. It took some time for the hard truth to sink in – that whereas the reformers, led by Leszek Kołakowski, at that time a Professor of Philosophy at Warsaw University, believed they were on the threshold of change, for Gomułka the revolution was over. A relatively uneducated man, Gomułka had a deep distrust of the intellectuals who had helped him to power. He wanted now to put them in their place.

His about-turn was already obvious in January 1957 when the elections to the Sejm (Parliament) took place. The people hoped that Gomułka would curb the power of the Party and open the elections to genuinely popular candidates. A few extra names were indeed added to the usual list of Party hacks, and it was the people's electoral right to cross off the names of such candidates as they did not want. But at the last moment Gomułka took fright at so much liberty and warned on radio that if Communist names were crossed off, Poland would be swept off the maps of Europe for the foreseeable future. Shades of Hungary yet again! His appeal cut strangely little ice. He himself won handsomely, but many Party candidates came bottom of the list and one lost his seat altogether. In a Communist regime this was unheard of! Furthermore, at the risk of losing their jobs or of being punished in a variety of ways, over one million voters abstained; more than half a million crossed out at least one Party name, and three hundred thousand crossed out every name on the list.

In practice it didn't make much difference. Even with sixty-seven new non-Party members, the Sejm remained what it was – a rubber-stamp for Party policies. It was not allowed to engage in free and open debate, and had no chance of mounting a genuine opposition to the regime.[2]

Gomułka had already begun to bite the hand that had fed him. Early that year he dismissed the whole editorial board of the main Party newspaper, *Trybuna Ludu*; and in May he suppressed the chief student and intellectual paper, *Po Prostu*, which had supported him throughout the previous year. When students called a protest meeting, the police broke it up with tear gas and truncheons. Polish culture was again coming under siege.

A Party purge followed, with two hundred thousand being expelled over the next two years. These men and women were, argued Gomułka at the tenth Central Committee plenum in October 1957, far more dangerous to Poland than the Stalinists, in much the same way as tuberculosis was more dangerous than influenza. Influenza, he said, cannot be cured by contracting tuberculosis: the reformers must be expelled.[3]

When the winnowing was done, the careerists and trimmers, the guaranteed yes-men, remained in place. Gomułka, it was clear, did not want to be argued with. He was revealing himself as the dogmatic Marxist–Leninist he had always been. By the end of the 1950s he was courting his old enemies, the Stalinists. "But by then he had long since discarded the ideals of the Polish October."[4] The security police, though less powerful than they had been, were back in favour, every bit as vigilant as before and just as effective.

The rigid central planning which had been imposed on the country since 1949 simply didn't work, and it was time for a new look at the economy.[5] At last there was to be a slight nod in the direction of housing and consumer goods. At present, people were existing rather than living. In *The Ice Saints*, Rose, a visitor to Poland in the late fifties, was shocked by what she saw: "Most were dressed in little more than rags, jumble-sale clothes. There was no effort to present a façade of prosperity to the world. Each seemed to show a face and figure which said, 'Look, this is me, smashed.'"

A friend of Rose's tells her: "We were lucky to get a new flat. We had to wait many years on a list." Rose had not realised that the flat was new. Its plaster was cracked and it had already taken on the drab, unpainted look of the city.

When later on she watches one of those compulsory May Day parades which dragged on from early morning till mid-afternoon, she is struck by the grey, expressionless faces of the factory workers as they file past the huge floating faces of Lenin, Marx and Gomułka. It felt wrong, she said: "This should have been a march of protest. They should be protesting now because they were so poor, so ill-dressed, so ugly, with their swinging, work-distorted hands."[6]

An American journalist posted to Warsaw in 1958 returned home after a year, having had "a bellyful of the greyness, the dullness, the total absence of mental stimulus which is the essence of a Communist society".[7]

Yet still the people clung to their faith in Gomułka, for he remained the only realistic option available. They joked that Poland, ruled by the nine-man Politburo, was in fact ruled by 100,000,000 – Gomułka and eight nothings. When they realised that the regime was not going to change, they concentrated their attention on the inadequacy of basic living conditions – on food, clothing, housing. The spring of 1957 brought strikes and threats of strikes. When electrical workers sent a delegation to tell Gomułka they would cut off the lights if they didn't get a raise, he retorted unsympathetically: "You cut off the lights, and we'll start cutting off heads."[8]

The strikes petered out, but the underlying causes remained. "Butter costs more, bread costs more, vodka costs more, clothes cost more. The only thing that's plentiful is talk." Difficulties, it was said, were the only permanent feature of Poland's economy. A new suit was a major outlay requiring months of careful budgeting.[9] Food swallowed up most of the wages, and as there was nothing in the shops to buy, the rest went on vodka. "We may not have achieved the Polish road to Socialism," said a woman wearily, "but we're well on the Polish road to alcoholism."[10]

For a brief moment in October 1956 the workers had had some hope. The workers' councils set up in 1956 were officially recognised. But workers' control could not be tolerated by the regime, and the new councils were undermined just as surely as the old ones had been. Forbidden to have links with each other, they were soon merged with the Party committees and trade union councils in individual factories. Once again they were in the hands of opportunists who owed their positions less to innate skill than to favour with the Party, and who were for the most part quite incapable of making responsible or effective decisions.

It was stalemate. But when a group of able economists put forward a feasible plan for revitalising Poland's stagnant economy, a plan which involved a measure of decentralisation and some dependence on market forces, Gomułka would not listen. He returned instead to the old policy of pursuing rapid industrial growth regardless of demand, quality, or the human cost involved. The result was even worse stagnation. "Our production" became something of a national joke:

> PARTY ACTIVIST: All that matters is production. Something that will last.
>
> WORKER: And you think what we produce will last. You must be mad.[10]

In the countryside, Gomułka had kept his promise to abandon forced collectivisation. But the regime was still paranoid about private farmers, and continued to give priority to the State farms and co-operatives (which never made a profit), while starving the individual farmers of supplies and technical assistance. For the most part, the peasants went on using horses, as they could not have access to tractors. They found it difficult to obtain loans for new equipment, or to get fertiliser and other essential items. Though they still managed to sell their produce on the free market, they had little incentive to enlarge their holdings or increase their production.[11] Excluded from welfare benefits and constantly harassed by local Party officials, they, like their counterparts in the factories, became well and truly alienated, while the backwardness of Polish agriculture remained an undeniable brake on the country's economic progress.

Even by the end of 1957 the truce with the Church was coming to an end.[11] The regime had gone back on a number of its promises and it had refused to broadcast the Cardinal's Christmas message (a favour which had been granted for the first time in the history of People's Poland the previous December). This refusal finally brought a sharp protest from the Church; Wyszyński threatened to ask Catholics to boycott the coming elections. Gomułka then accused him of using religion for political ends.

The Hill of Light (Jasna Góra Monastery) at Częstochowa was raided in 1959 by police looking for printing equipment; and pilgrims and police engaged in fisticuffs. In 1960, in Nowa Huta, the steel town built to the glory of New Socialist Man, the people rioted when the government reneged on its promises to allow them to build a church.

Education became a prime bone of contention. When religious instruction had been brought back into the schools in 1956, it was made optional; but as ninety-five per cent of parents asked for it, the schools reverted overnight to being religious institutions. The Party was understandably alarmed, and in 1960 they backtracked also on this, by placing the teaching of religion at the discretion of individual head teachers. RI was then dropped in eighty per cent of the schools. The Church arranged for religious instruction on its own premises after school hours. But in 1961 the Central Committee decided that not only would religion not be taught in the schools, but that out-of-school teaching should be brought under Party control.

For the Church it was the last straw. The Cardinal now went on to the offensive, urging parents to demand a constitutional guarantee of religious freedom: "If a citizen does not demand his rights, he is no longer a citizen but a slave."[12] And just before leaving for the Vatican Council in Rome in September 1963, he addressed the people of Warsaw in terms of unambiguous defiance:

> My dear children,
> Priests throughout Poland are now being subjected to penalties for teaching catechism without registering and without reporting on their teaching. In a short and very carefully worded letter which was read from the pulpits, we explained that we would not make reports on what a priest teaches the children who are sent to him by their parents. When Christ said "Go into the whole world and preach the Gospel," he was speaking to priests and bishops and not to government officials. No one may stand between Christ and his bishops and priests; no secular authority has the right to do so . . . We have to obey God, rather than man.[13]

The Cardinal proposed a nine-year programme of spiritual renewal (which he had worked out during his years of internment) for the celebration of the Polish Millennium in 1966. In the eyes of the Church this meant the thousandth anniversary of the coming of Christianity. The State saw it as an opportunity to celebrate People's Poland as the high-point of the historical process which had started a thousand years earlier.[14] And they complained with some justification that in articles and sermons the Church was attempting to undermine Marxism–Leninism.

The battle waxed fast and furious, with elements of pure farce woven into the struggle. In the run-up to the celebrations, the Church would announce its ceremonies and the State would follow suit, with its own parades or even football matches being timed for the same day and the same hour. Grażyna S. tells how, in her school, tempting special excursions were arranged for the day of the Corpus Christi procession. One year she was awarded a free ticket for an amusement park – valid for that one day only. She was only nine, and the temptation was great. But conscience won: "In the end I didn't go, and I distinctly remember that when I was singing a hymn at the end of Mass I suddenly felt happy, as if for the first time I had the feeling of being in control of my life."

With police cordons and threats of reprisals, the regime would try to force everyone into their parades, and the people would manage to escape and join those of the Church. Microphones would be mysteriously cut off when the Cardinal was about to address a crowd; and cathedral bells were half-drowned by the din of cannon-shots and low-flying aircraft. The Cardinal told the people they could do without a king or a military commander, a prime minister or any other kind of minister. "But this nation has never lived without a shepherd!" Gomułka retorted that if Wyszyński was a shepherd, he was an irresponsible one, since he was "struggling against our people's state . . . forgetting the lessons of history, [forgetting] who brought Poland to ruin and who liberated her".

In the summer of 1965, a million people converged on the Hill of Light at Częstochowa, and replicas of the Madonna were carried in procession in every town and city. When the icon itself was being taken to Warsaw it was forcibly removed by the police from the hands of a bishop and returned to Częstochowa. In a fury the people marched to Party headquarters in Warsaw – and were met by riot police armed with water cannons.

The Cardinal knew how to exploit the Communist actions. He was in the habit of travelling round the country with a framed replica of the Częstochowa Madonna. When the authorities seized the picture, he carried an empty frame instead. The effect was powerful. "The symbolism of that empty frame was stupendous," remembers a Warsaw woman. "Cardinal Wyszyński was a great opposition leader. And the Church was the only opposition party we had." Bohdan Cywiński believes that these experiences of the sixties prepared the Poles for what happened in 1980:

> People began to understand that they could gather together in large numbers for religious purposes, and no harm would come to them, no matter how many riot police surrounded them. They learned to keep calm, to carry on praying or doing whatever they had to do, and pay no attention to those who might want to stop them. It was an apprenticeship – a lesson that even under a hostile regime you can achieve something without violence.

When in 1965 Wyszyński and the Polish bishops wrote to their counterparts in West Germany, offering Christian friendship and forgiveness, they did so as a grand gesture of reconciliation to mark the 1966 Millennium. A cry of rage went up from the regime, which was furious to find the Church stepping on to the forbidden ground of foreign policy. This new move seemed to them a piece of outrageous impudence. Hatred of Germany, and fear for the permanence of Poland's western borders, were almost the only aspects of the official policy to have unqualified public support.

"WE SHALL NEITHER FORGET NOR FORGIVE" proclaimed the government posters, as they sought to reinforce the Polish fear and hatred of German revanchism. If that were to disappear, so might the regime's last shreds of credibility.

Gomułka hit back. He was not going to yield an inch in the battle with the Cardinal. Wyszyński and the bishops were refused passports for travelling to Rome; a campaign of slander against the Cardinal was unleashed; the clergy were subjected to crippling taxes and difficulties were placed in the way of building new churches. Seminarians were called up into the Army, though officially they were exempt as students; Catholic writers were harassed, Catholic books axed. The Pope was refused entry to Poland for the Millennium celebrations. To underline their displeasure, the Government closed the borders for a month, and excluded foreign Church dignitaries from the festivities. As Wyszyński was to write: "Small, proud and arrogant men came and ordered that not a single mention of the Church and its work must be made at these celebrations."[15]

Gomułka had made himself look ridiculous, and at long last the people began to see him as he really was – inflexible, stubborn, humourless, puritanical, without any redeeming vision. For years they had clung to their belief that he was a Pole first and a Communist second, but now they saw that it had always been the other way round. Though he was to stay in power for another four years, he never recovered the ground he had lost when he engaged in battle with the Church. Today the Poles are inclined to sympathise with the dilemma he faced, though their sense of betrayal is still strong. Says one observer:

> I believe he was a fundamentally honest man. And so through him we learned that even an honest man – once he is in the clutches of an ideology – is helpless. Not only because he is not free to make changes, but also because he is no longer free to think. He becomes a *homo sovieticus*, a sovietised man.

1 O. Halecki's *History of Poland*, additional chapter, "The Rise and Fall of Gomułka", by Antony Polonsky. *op. cit.*
2 *The Polish Volcano*, *op. cit.*.
3 *Poland in Perspective*, *op. cit.*
4 Nicholas Bethell, *Gomułka, His Poland and His Communism*, *op. cit.*
5 M. K. Dziewanowski, *Poland in the Twentieth Century*, *op. cit.*
6 Frank Tuohy, *The Ice Saints*, Macmillan, 1964.
7 A. M. Rosenthal in *New York Times* magazine, 7.8.83.
8 Film, *Przyjaciele* (*Friends*), *op. cit.*
9 *The Polish Volcano*, *op. cit.*

[10] *Idem.*

[11] *Poland in Perspective*, *op. cit.*

[12] *Idem.*

[13] From a collection of Cardinal Wyszyński's sermons: *A Strong Man Armed*, A. T. Jordan, London, 1966.

[14] Halecki's *History of Poland*, *op. cit.*

[15] George Błażyński, *Pope John Paul II*, Weidenfeld & Nicolson, 1979.

10 DIVIDED THEY FALL: The Sixties

> Of course Poles were over-optimistic. They had been led by Gomułka out of hell and imagined he would lead them into paradise. When this did not happen they were disappointed and sometimes so ungrateful they forgot what he had done.
>
> Nicholas Bethell: *Gomułka*

As Gomułka turned more and more to the old guard and put the brake on intellectual freedom, some of the radicals in the Party did not give up. In the summer of 1964, two young reforming Marxist scholars from Warsaw University, Jacek Kuroń and Karol Modzelewski, published a ninety-page open letter to Gomułka, accusing him of betraying the workers and suggesting where he had gone wrong. Gomułka did not take kindly to such impudence and had both young men expelled from the Party and then arrested on charges of dishonesty and immorality. But they had voiced the sentiments of the young, particularly the sons and daughters of high-ranking Communists. There would have to be a reckoning.

Next it was the turn of Leszek Kołakowski. When, in a speech to commemorate the tenth anniversary of the Polish October, he contrasted the hopes of those days with the grim reality of the present, he too was expelled.

Then a new and ugly factor came into play: the old anti-semitism in a different guise. Since the war, the percentage of Jews in the country had been around 0.1%, compared to the pre-war figure of ten per cent. But many of these had spent the war years in Soviet Russia as Stalin's loyal servants. Returning to Poland in Berling's Army they had assumed positions of power and influence, and had played a major role in shaping post-war Poland. (Large numbers of the secret police were Jewish.) Their power had not added to their popularity either inside or outside the Party, and those Polish Communists, who, like Gomułka, had fought in the Communist underground in Poland during the war (and who had been deeply mistrusted by Stalin), had long nursed a grudge against them and envied them their lucrative jobs.[1]

The 1967 Arab–Israeli war had the vast majority of Poles cheering for the Israelis, much to the dismay of the government which, like the rest of the Warsaw Pact countries, was officially pro-Arab.[2] Gomułka broke off relations with Israel and made dark insinuations about Zionists stirring up trouble at home. This anti-Zionism was, in fact, thinly veiled anti-semitism, and over the next few months large numbers of Jewish Party officials who had expressed approval of the Israeli victories, found themselves sacked from their jobs and replaced by ambitious young Polish Communists.

Events in neighbouring Czechoslovakia took a hand. The overthrow of the Stalinist leader, Novotny, and his replacement by the more liberal Alexander Dubček, raised the temperature in Poland, where students and intellectuals were already clamouring for change – "we are waiting for our Dubček". Matters came to a head in March 1968 when the authorities banned the performance of a popular nineteenth-century Polish play about Russian atrocities during the Partitions. The play, *Forefathers' Eve*, had been playing to wildly enthusiastic audiences in Warsaw and Kraków, its numerous anti-Russian lines calling forth cheers and applause. When it was taken off, students and academics marched in protest, demanding an end to censorship. The police moved in and laid about them with clubs. Many arrests were made. The discovery of a handful of Jewish students among those arrested gave Gomułka the excuse for a witch-hunt. By the end of the month, three thousand students had been arrested and hundreds injured. Scores were expelled from the universities, with a black mark against their names which would put paid for ever to their career prospects. Kuroń and Modzelewski, newly released from prison, were re-arrested and sentenced to a further three and a half years for being the "spiritual instigators" of the student revolt.

All over Europe in 1968, students had been erupting into violence. But whereas in Bonn or Paris or Rome they were demanding more autonomy, more of a say in university affairs, and an end to traditionalism, in Poland they were appealing simply for freedom of thought, for the right to hold an opinion of their own, and for the right to hold on to tradition. The Polish students did not seek power but the right to self-respect.

To a large extent, the demonstrations in the streets were merely a reflection of the internal struggle rending the Party. For this reason, the Church at first saw it as a fight between two sets of Communists, and was inclined to leave them to it. Yet the Church's attitude slowly began to change. Both Cardinals, Stefan

Wyszyński of Warsaw and Karol Wojtyła of Kraków, spelled out the human rights which were being flouted and condemned this new persecution of the Jews. Increasingly, the Church began to emphasise the wrongs done not only to itself but to society and to the individual. That it should come, however belatedly, to the defence of Marxist intellectuals was a straw in the wind for the future. It looked as though the old bitter antipathy between the Church and the left-wing intellectuals, so intense before the war, was about to come to an end.

For the present, however, Church support was of little use to the victims. In all, nine thousand people, Jews and non-Jews, lost their jobs, and thirty thousand were sent into exile abroad. Among them were some of the country's most able intellectuals of world stature, such as Leszek Kołakowski.

Party radicals went into shock, their hopes of establishing a Communism based on a respect for law and humanity gone, it seemed, for ever. The academics abandoned their dreams of Utopia, and Polish intellectual life entered a new post-Marxist phase. From this time on, notes Bohdan Cywiński, there was little sign of Marxist influence in science, philosophy or the social sciences.[3]

In the prevailing chaos, Gomułka seemed certain to fall. His authority was being challenged by a new group, calling themselves the Partisans, and headed by General Mieczysław Moczar. This profoundly nationalistic and anti-semitic group was intent on achieving power, and used the fact that Gomułka had a Jewish wife as a weapon against him. Gomułka was saved by the Russian invasion of Czechoslovakia, for by sending Polish troops to Prague he ensured that Brezhnev would back him for the leadership. (The Polish people's attitude to the sending of Polish troops to Czechoslovakia was generally one of unmitigated horror.) As a sign of his championship of Gomułka, Brezhnev came in person to Warsaw for that year's Party Congress and there proclaimed his famous – or infamous – doctrine that whenever a Socialist regime is "threatened from within", the Soviet Union and its allies are entitled to intervene militarily.[4]

For Poland, 1968 was a tragic year, in which she drank the dregs of moral degradation. Illusions bit the dust, the bright dreams vanished. But Gomułka seemed immune to feelings of shame. He was by now so remote from the aspirations of the people that he no longer even pretended to consider them. And so he blundered into a fatal miscalculation. For years the authorities had carefully fostered the natural division between workers and intellectuals.

As long as the three sources of potential opposition – the Church, the workers, the intellectuals – remained separate, the government could breathe freely. Real danger would only present itself if these three should unite. Seeing that the workers were largely indifferent to the demands of Party intellectuals for greater freedom of thought, Gomułka gained a false sense of security. He forgot that the workers had their own grievance – they were hungry.

Between the intellectuals and the workers the gulf still yawned, but there were unmistakable signs that the two groups had recognised and identified a common enemy and a common cause. The groping towards mutual recognition was well caught by Wajda in one of the flashback sequences in *Man of Iron*. The students Maciek and Dzidek have sought out Maciek's father, the shipyard worker and former "shock-worker", Mateusz Birkut, who had fallen foul of the Party in the intervening years, and spent many of those years in prison. They ask for the workers' help but Mateusz refuses. It's not the right time, he argues. "So they won't come out?" asks Dzidek bitterly:

Mateusz: Oh yes, they will come – when the time is right.

Dzidek: And have you any idea when that will be?

Mateusz: No lie can maintain itself for ever. But right now, stop this play-acting of yours.

Dzidek: It's not play-acting. Can't you realise, our lives are at stake?[5]

The characters in *Man of Iron* may be fictional but they are based on real people and the events and arguments are real. The students from the Gdańsk College of Technology did ask the workers for help and were refused. They could not have known that government agents had got in there before them, poisoning the workers' minds against what they described as "spoiled brats" and "hooligans". A worker in the shipyards has described how secret police agents disguised as workmen stirred up feelings against the students and even persuaded a number of workers to take violent action against "the hooligans". "Afterwards," he says, "when we discovered the truth, we had to share our shame and bitterness with someone. And that someone was a young electrician called Lech Wałęsa."

Wałęsa, showing the sharp political insight which would mark him out a decade later, had not fallen for the government's line on the students. He had begged his fellow-workers not to attend an official meeting at which the students were to be publicly censored. When it was too late, the others realised that the young electrician had been right.

Wałęsa's growing restlessness had finally driven him to the big city. He had had enough of the countryside with its grinding poverty. "I felt I must get out. Sometimes one knows in one's bones that one is in the wrong place, and that's how it was with me." Once, on a school outing, he had visited Gdańsk and been impressed. But it was to Gdynia that he was making tracks when one day in 1966 he had bought a single ticket on the train. By a quirk of fate, when the train stopped in Gdańsk, Lech was thirsty and got out to look for a beer. The train went off without him; and he decided not to bother waiting for the next one. "I came to Gdańsk and met my destiny," he says cheerfully. "I spent far too long drinking that beer. And in a sense I'm still drinking it."

Gdańsk – "jewel of the Baltic" – once a fine old merchant town, birthplace of Schopenhauer and of Fahrenheit. Here the meandering Vistula River collects a few last tributaries before disappearing into the Baltic Sea, turning the landscape into a little Holland, crisscrossed by rivers as still as canals. Wedged between high wooded hills and the sea, Gdańsk has had a chequered history. As Danzig, it was part of Prussia during the Nineteenth-Century Partitions and it remained a largely German town until 1918 when it became a Free City, belonging to both Poland and Germany. Hitler's determination to get it back for Germany was the nominal cause of the Second World War, though the Führer admitted it had merely been a pretext for the invasion of Poland. From the Polish Post Office, on 1st September, 1939, sixty postal workers, armed with old-fashioned rifles, held out for a whole day against the armoured might of the Wehrmacht. And then the city disappeared yet again into Germany. Danzig/Gdańsk did not survive the fury of war; almost every one of its buildings was reduced to rubble during Stalin's mad rush to the west in the winter of 1944–5. But after 1945 it was rebuilt with style, on the model of the old city. The architecture in Gdańsk is less depressing and dreary than elsewhere, and many Poles say that the Triple Township (Trójmiasto) – Gdańsk, Gdynia, Sopot – is the only urban area fit to live in.

Since the war, Gdańsk has acquired a new population. When the Germans were driven out in 1945, their place was filled by the refugees from the eastern territories seized by Soviet Russia. This huge and ever-increasing influx of new blood gave the Baltic towns a massive infusion of energy and vitality. The people of the Coast (Wybrzeże), coming more often into contact with visiting foreigners, were less stifled by bureaucracy than the citizens of inland towns like Warsaw or Katowice; they lived with a certain spontaneity and independence of spirit. This made them relatively volatile and unpredictable, and the regime, sensing a potential danger in them, watched them warily.

The vast shipyard-in-the-name-of-Lenin, Poland's industrial pride and joy, was built in the 1950s on the site of five pre-war factories. It stands, some distance from the sea, on a tributary known as the Dead Vistula; and its workforce consists of former peasants escaping from the rural areas, and older "expellees" from the eastern territories. Lech Wałęsa, who had found temporary, poorly-paid work at the State Machinery Centre in Gdańsk, began work as a ships' electrician in the yards in May 1967. He had decided to become an electro-mechanic, and had to study for this new qualification as he went along. His team-leader remembers him as a bright, eager young innocent who appeared never to have seen a ship before: "He was disciplined, never late for work. He seemed to like being part of a team and fitted in well. He was talkative, curious about people and things."

Henryk Lenarciak, a fitter in the same team, says that Lech was: ". . . a quiet boy, who didn't stand out in any way at all. Sometimes he spoke at union meetings, but never in a provocative way."[6]

"They were good years," says Lech, "perhaps the best of all. No children, no real worries. The first loves. And another thing – there, in the shipyard, I could feel I was myself at last. I began to understand that inside me was a deep, irresistible urge to go out and change things."[6]

After the cottage in Popowo, even the shared, rented hostel rooms in which he lived seemed spacious; and he revelled in the interesting new acquaintances he found there. For a time, his brother, Zygmunt, shared a room with him. They would lie on their bunks, Lech reading religious pamphlets, and Zygmunt film magazines. Girls came and went. (He was attracted to women, but lacked confidence and was easily discouraged.) One day, after a row with a girl, he went out and got roaring drunk. "It was cold and I was fed up and tired. I looked for some kind of shelter, and all I could find was a church. I went in and sat in a pew. It was warm in there, and suddenly I felt such a sense of inner peace that it was as though my whole life had taken on a new direction.

From then on I became a genuine believer, and acquired a purpose in life."

Something else changed on the day he entered the Orchidea flower shop in Gdańsk, to change some money, and saw nineteen-year-old raven-haired Danuta Gołoś. Her name was actually Mirosława, but right from the first Lech called her Danuta. Like Lech, she had been brought up in the country, on a "middle-sized farm" in the Podlasie region of eastern Poland, where, the saying goes, there is nothing but woods, sands and carp (in Polish: *laski, piaski i karaski*). Like Lech she came from a large family – five boys and four girls. Like him, she had dreamed of escape to the city. "I wanted to get away. I wanted to taste life," she says.

It was love at first sight. He came back later that day just to see her, though neither then nor later did he buy her flowers. "He always thought words should be enough," sighs Danuta. She found him "different from other men, in the way he behaved and in his whole attitude to life", adding that he was "very persuasive". He courted her for a year, mainly at the cinema, where they went every evening, regardless of what film was being shown. There was simply nowhere else to go.

They were married on 8th November, 1969. The shipyard found them a dilapidated little room on the outskirts of Gdańsk. To help pay their half of the rent (the shipyard paid the other half) Danuta found a job in a newspaper kiosk. Until, that is to say, she found herself pregnant. "I stopped work then," she recalls. "We were terribly poor, we were hungry, we had all kinds of problems. But life was very good. I could say that it was the happiest period of my life, because Lech and I were together all the time."

Within the year, their son, Bogdan (gift of God), was born. And Poland was facing the crisis which would set the course of Lech Wałęsa's future life.

[1] *Poland in the Twentieth Century*, *op. cit.*
[2] Nicholas Bethell, *Gomułka*, *op. cit.*
[3] Bohdan Cywiński, *The Polish Experience.*
[4] *Poland in Perspective*, *op. cit.*
[5] *Człowiek z Marmuru*, Cztowiek z Żelaza, text by Alexsander Ścibor-Rylski, Aneks, London, 1982.
[6] *The Book of Lech Wałesa*, *op. cit.*

11 WATERSHED (1970)

> In order to preserve and defend the right to freedom, and so to defend the dignity of man as an intelligent and free being, one must commit oneself and be prepared for sacrifices . . . A man who passively accepts the slavery imposed on him submits himself to the yoke and in a sense ceases to be fully human. And the nation which no longer knows how to fight for its freedom has already fallen, since it has accepted less than its true dignity. There then arises a need for heroic sacrifices and massive shocks to bring about the awakening of the man who no longer fights for his freedom as an intelligent being should; and of the nation which no longer fulfils its obligations in the name of its most important and sacred right – its freedom.
>
> Cardinal Stefan Wyszyński, 1961

Prices rose, shelves emptied, queues lengthened. Drought and bad harvests played their part. Bitterness grew and festered. Gomułka was now unpopular with just about everyone: with the workers because they didn't have enough to eat; with the peasants for overpricing their equipment and making them produce all their own grain rather than dairy produce for the home market; with the students and intellectuals because of 1968; and with the office workers because he was always sniping at their "bourgeois tendencies".[1]

Hoping to recover some of his lost popularity, Gomułka was wooing the government of West Germany, from whom he hoped to obtain not only a guarantee of Poland's western borders but also a massive loan. Herr Willy Brandt came to Warsaw, and a Treaty was signed, recognising the existing borders. It was Gomułka's only foreign policy triumph; but it held a hidden disadvantage. Fear of the German aggression had been a kind of cement bonding the people to their government and to the protective mantle of the Soviet Union. Now that they need no longer fear Germany, the bonding lost its power. The Poles grew restive. When the loan from Germany did not materialise, and Gomułka invited them to tighten their belts even further, they felt the first stirrings of uncontrollable rage.

The explosion came sooner, however, than anyone expected. On 12th December, 1970, less than two weeks before Christmas, which is traditionally the most important religious as well as family holiday in Poland, the Gomułka regime announced drastic increases in food and fuel prices, without any corresponding increase in wages and salaries. (Some members of the Politburo, including Edward Gierek, the member for Silesia, and General Wojciech Jaruzelski, who had become Minister of Defence, had tried in vain to dissuade Gomułka from this suicidal course.)

It was not the actual price rises, however, so much as the unbelievably inept timing of them, which underlined just how remote from the people Gomułka had become. For the workers, that industrial proletariat created by the Communist regime, it was the final insult. The grumblings and mutterings spilled over into an outbreak of pure rage. Unable to stand any more, they erupted on to the streets. And nowhere more violently than in the Baltic towns of Gdańsk and Gdynia.

The 16th and 17th December, 1970, are graven on to the hearts and minds of the Polish people. The memory of them remains raw and painful, as the years have gone by without healing. For Poland, December 1970 marked a definite watershed. For Lech Wałęsa too. From this time onward, he would be "*engagé*", committed to an enduring struggle with an unjust authority.

He claims that he played a leading role in the bloody events, and that some of the responsibility for what happened must be his. Colleagues suggest that his role was a minor one, but they agree that it marked him. "It was enough to be there, to hear the shots, to clear away the corpses, to watch the terrible burials by night. It was enough – to make a man remember for the rest of his life."[2]

"I took part from the first moment to the last," Wałęsa insists. "But I was only twenty-seven. I was inexperienced and didn't know how to handle a situation like that."

On Monday 14th December, two days after the price rises had been announced, a thousand workers from the Lenin shipyard in Gdańsk surrounded the Party HQ in Gdańsk demanding that the rises be withdrawn. No one in authority would agree to discuss the matter with them; but a junior official pompously ordered them back to work. This infuriated the men. Workers from other factories had now joined the shipyard workers and together they marched on the College of Technology, to call out the students.

Once again it is Wajda's *Man of Iron* which catches the undertones of the exchange. Mateusz Birkut, at the head of the crowd, shouts:

> Students, the time has come. The whole Baltic coast is saying "Enough is enough". We left you to fight alone in 1968, and perhaps we were wrong. But you must not make the same mistake as we did. Together we can do much. We want an end to repression, to violence, to lies, to needless suffering. Students, I beg of you, COME WITH US![3]

But the students, remembering their own past humiliation, stayed silent and did not come out – "neither then nor later, when the city echoed with gunfire, and when the first victims began to fall".[4]

In the early hours of Tuesday morning, as cars, buses, trucks and shops blazed against the Gdańsk skyline, a strike was proclaimed at the shipyards, and Lech Wałęsa was elected to the strike committee. Three thousand workers, with Wałęsa at their head, marched to the city, shouting "HANG GOMUŁKA, GOMUŁKA OUT!" Their destination was police headquarters, and by the time they reached there, the mood was ugly. Wałęsa, who believed in protest but hated violence, was already afraid that things were getting out of hand. Climbing on to a telephone kiosk, he appealed for calm. But the men were intent on attacking the jail and releasing the prisoners. As they stormed into the ground floor of the police building and set it on fire, Wałęsa appeared at a first-floor window, still making his appeal for calm, and begging the crowd to call off their planned attack on the prison. Not recognising him, they threw stones at first, until they recognised the familiar, rasping voice, shouting, "It's me, chaps. It's Leszek." They listened to him then, and did as he asked.

Meanwhile the authorities had proclaimed a state of emergency in the entire coastal area, and had given the security forces orders to shoot if necessary. Pitched battles between police and workers were taking place all over Gdańsk. Gomułka, caring little for the workers' misery, said angrily that it was counter-revolution organised by "anti-Socialist elements", and that it must be stopped by even more repressive measures.

The shipyard had been ringed by security police and militia, and now, as more workers left to join the demonstrations, they were fired on. The workers were stunned when they heard the firing. More shots rang out. Three were killed, eleven injured. It was a silent but bitter crowd which gathered to proclaim a sit-in at the shipyard. Throughout the coastal region, workers downed tools.

Events now assumed a terrifying momentum. Ten thousand workers attacked the Party building and set it on fire. As officials slid down ropes to safety, they were beaten up by the enraged crowd below, in no mood for mercy.

All day long the battle raged; and by nightfall, a pall of smoke hung over the city. A curfew was imposed at 6 p.m., and by then six people had been killed, three hundred injured. A Politburo official explained on radio that security troops had been forced to fire in self-defence against "hooligans and social scum".

Tanks and troops moved in overnight. Radio and telephone links with the rest of the country were cut, all flights to and from Gdańsk were cancelled. When the workers gathered at the shipyard, they were warned that the troops were empowered to use force if necessary. They responded with a set of demands: for pay increases, price freezes, tax cuts, and punishment for those responsible for ruining the economy. Deputy-Premier Kociołek went on TV in Gdańsk to say that the demands were impossible and would not be met, and to appeal for a return to work.

Wearily, many workers decided to return. But the last act of the tragedy had not yet been played. Its setting was to be Gdynia. That evening, in the Paris Commune shipyard, matters had got out of hand. The workers had seized control and were issuing ultimata to the authorities. Even as Kociołek was making his appeal, armoured tank units were moving towards the shipyards and security forces had entered the compound, to prevent the workers from sabotaging the ships and machinery. The shipbuilding industry association ordered work in the shipyards to stop forthwith. No one was to be allowed near. Kociołek knew nothing of this till later. When he realised what was happening, he tried to withdraw his appeal, and warnings were sent out to people all over the Tri-City. But the early-morning shift-workers were already en route.[5]

The thousands of workers arriving at the Gdynia railway station early next morning from the surrounding suburbs moved towards the exit, and found themselves faced by tanks. Security troops opened fire immediately, while tear-gas canisters were dropped from police helicopters circling overhead.

An hour later a crowd of five thousand was still fighting a losing battle with militia and security forces outside the now blazing railway station. As tear-gas, gunfire and smoke filled the air, and as the number of dead continued to grow, a column of workers broke from the crowd, carrying the bodies of the victims on railway carriage doors which had been wrenched off incoming trains. Official sources later admitted that thirteen were killed that day – Gdynia's "Bloody Thursday" – and seventy-four were badly injured. Popular sources suggest a much higher figure.[6] And on the same day, street fighting in Szczecin claimed at least sixteen lives.

In no cases were the workers allowed to bury their dead themselves. The anguish of families faced with a rapid identification, followed by a hasty official burial, in the presence of uniformed police and with the glare of spotlights upon them, was poignantly expressed in a little film *Pomnik (The Monument)*, which was shown in Poland only during the Solidarity era, when a monument had at last been raised to the dead of 1970. In a documentary excerpt, a weeping mother relates how a well-dressed man had come to tell her that her son was dead and must be buried within the hour. The family was allowed in to the mortuary at the cemetery to identify the body lying naked on a slab with all the others. (The bodies had all been stripped of their blood-stained clothes.) They were told to bring a fresh set of clothing and dress the corpse for burial. But in the rush they forgot the boy's boots:

> I was very upset and asked my husband to go home for the boots. But the man said no, that couldn't be allowed. He must be buried quickly, and there were others to be buried too . . . It was so tragic, we didn't have his boots. His friend said, "Don't cry. I'll give him mine." He took off his boots and put them on my son's bare feet. My daughter gave him some socks so that he could walk home in the snow . . . The priest came and blessed my son . . . We threw ourselves on the coffin, but they pushed us away. No time for that sort of thing, they said.

Grieving relatives were never able to find the graves again. When they returned to where they had buried their loved ones that night, the bodies had been removed, and all trace of the graves obliterated. It was as if they had never been.

"They've dug him up," says Anna to Maciek, when they have searched in vain for the body of Mateusz Birkut who has been killed in these events. "But why have they taken him away?" asks Maciek uncomprehendingly. "So that we shall not be able to bring flowers," she answers.

Nobody is sure how many died. The government eventually admitted to twenty-six. The people insist it was several hundred. "We tried to find out," says Lech Wałęsa, "we spoke to people, we asked questions, we searched. But they always prevented us from finding out. We were never able to complete our list. But one day we *shall* complete it."[7]

Gomułka, determined to crush this "counter-revolution" at all costs, asked General Jaruzelski whether the Polish Army could be brought in. Carefully the General replied: "The Army will do its duty." Gomułka sensed that in a struggle against Polish workers, a conscript Polish army might refuse to fight. So he turned instead to his Russian ally and asked for military help. Brezhnev refused, telling him curtly to solve his problems by political or economic means but not by force. This was a body-blow for Gomułka who by now was paranoid about the imagined counter-revolution. His frustration knew no bounds.

Within the Politburo, support was growing for his rival Edward Gierek. Forced to call an emergency meeting, Gomułka argued his case, but more and more unconvincingly. The meeting was still in session at 3 a.m. on Saturday, 19th, when Władysław Gomułka suffered a minor stroke which partially blinded him, and he was carried off to hospital in an armoured car.[8] Edward Gierek moved over and sat in the chairman's seat.

A workers' revolution had unseated Gomułka just as surely as an earlier one had brought him to power. He was given no choice but to resign and hand over power to Gierek.

Wałęsa has 1970 constantly in mind. "The biggest mistake I have ever made," he says, speaking of his decision to lead the men into Gdańsk that first day. For years he continued to feel responsible for what happened, ashamed of his own inability to prevent the crowd from becoming a mob. For the next ten years he would brood on every detail and analyse every mistake. "The killings forced me to do that," he says. "I had plenty of time later to think things through, and realise just where we had gone wrong. It was an apprenticeship, a necessary stage. After all, you don't reach the top class without passing through the lowest one."

Lech's sister, Izabela, a member of the Party and hoping to persuade her brother to join too, remonstrated with him for the part he had played. "Why must you always blow against the wind?" she raged at him, using a phrase from their childhood. "You don't understand," he said maddeningly. "But you will – some day."

[1] Bethell, *op. cit.*
[2] Jerzy Surdykowski, *Notatki Gdańskie*, Aneks, London, 1982.

[3] *Człowiek Z Żelazu*, op. cit.
[4] Ibid.
[5] Ibid.
[6] My account of the December events is taken mainly from George Błażyński's *Flashpoint Poland*, Pergamon Policy Studies, Oxford 1979.
[7] Jean Offrédo, *Lech Wałesa, Czyli Polskie Lato*, Cana, Paris, 1981.
[8] Gomułka died in 1982, without ever returning to public office.

The Wałęsa quotations taken from author's own interviews with Lech Wałęsa.

12 THE RISE AND RISE OF EDWARD GIEREK (1970–76)

One man lies wounded, another dying,
Blood has flowed this December dawn.
These are the rulers
Shooting down workers!
Janek Wiśniewski fell.

Workers from shipyards of Gdańsk and Gdynia,
Back to your homes now, the battle is over,
The world stood by, looking on in silence.
Janek Wiśniewski fell.

Do not weep, mothers, these deaths are not wasted,
A black-ribboned flag o'er the dockyard now flies.
For bread and for freedom
And for Poland reborn,
Janek Wiśniewski fell.

Popular song commemorating the events of December 1970. This is the version sung by Krystyna Janda in the film *Man of Iron*, somewhat diluted from the original in order to pass the censor. The original, stronger version was sung during the Festival of True Song held in Gdańsk in the summer of 1981.

Poles had killed Poles. The workers' regime had given orders for workers to be shot in cold blood. "After December," said Anna Walentynowicz, a middle-aged crane driver at the Gdańsk shipyards, "I thought to myself, now there will be changes. After all these horrors, and all this bloodshed, it's just not possible to go back to the way we were."

The workers were in an ugly mood, unwilling to be sweet-talked into submission. Edward Gierek, the new Party Secretary, addressed the nation on television with emotion, determined to bridge the yawning chasm between Party and workers: "Comrades, citizens, fellow-countrymen, I turn to you in the name of the Party . . . I appeal to all Polish workers . . . together let us learn from the painful events of the past week. I beseech you all . . ."

At this point, Wajda's film hero, Maciek Tomczyk, grieving for his murdered father, heaves a chair at the television set and smashes it. (Whereupon he is put into a straitjacket and removed to a psychiatric institute.) The attitude of the majority was less violent but no less cynical. They had been disappointed once too often. One leader, they had learned, was much like another; with each change at the top, life for the workers merely got bleaker.

But it soon began to appear that Gierek might indeed be different. Unlike most of the previous leaders, he was a genuine proletarian, son of a miner and a miner himself from the age of thirteen. He had been brought up in France, joined the Communist Party there, and been expelled for organising a miners' strike in the Pas de Calais.

So now he could legitimately claim to be on the workers' wavelength and to understand their problems. And as, unlike the penny-pinching Puritan, Gomułka, he also believed in raising living standards, he stood a reasonable chance of becoming popular.

First of all, the country had to be restored to normal. Gierek immediately pledged more housing, concessions to farmers, an increase in consumer goods and food supplies. But, while announcing a rise in pensions and child welfare benefits, he also proposed a two-year price freeze, based on the prices which had caused the December riots. This aroused the workers to renewed fury and a fresh wave of strikes (notably one at the Warski shipyards in Szczecin) hit the country in January, accompanied by demands for radical reform of the economy and punishment of those responsible for the massacres in December. The country was once again like a seething volcano. Catcalls greeted Party officials rash enough to try and speak at public meetings, and there was general disgust with the lies and evasions of the official press, which had barely acknowledged the events on the coast, referring merely to a little "sporadic activity" by "hooligans".[1]

Immediately after the riots in Gdańsk, Lech Wałęsa had his first brush with the police. Danuta has described her first experience of a house-search:

> The child opened the door and said, "Mummy, there's a man here with a parcel." There was a group of them at the door. "Where's your husband?" they demanded. I shrieked at them, "Is he some kind of child that I have to keep an eye on him? I've no idea where he is." They said, "Don't shout like that." "What, can't I shout in my own

home? I'll shout if I want." Four of them pushed past me into the flat. They found something – some tapes recorded from Radio Free Europe, I think.

Ignoring the warning, Lech had become an active member of the Gdańsk post-strike committee, and was one of those demanding an official memorial to the dead of December. For him, this was already a Holy Grail, a quest that would preoccupy him for the next ten years. But he was prepared to be patient, having learned the hard way that to be angry was not enough: "A wall can't be demolished by butting it with your head," he was heard to remark. "We must move slowly, one step at a time. If we rush at it, the wall will still be in place, but we shall have our heads smashed in."

When Gierek came in person to soothe the workers of Szczecin and Gdańsk, Wałęsa and an older colleague, the fitter, Henryk Lenarciak, were two of the three Gdańsk delegates chosen to meet him. But in what the press described as "tough, forthright discussions", Wałęsa was a silent partner. It was Henryk Lenarciak who did the talking.

Later, Gierek spoke to the shipyard workers and made promises. Captivated by him, they listened and were won over. They complained to him about the official trade unions, about the lies told by the media and about the inefficiency of management. Gierek was sympathetic and soothing. The December events must never happen again, he agreed. "Never in my life will I shoot at Polish workers." He told them how he had worked in the mines in France and Belgium, and how he had been in trouble for organising a strike in France. It was a marvellous piece of demagoguery, and he finished by stretching out his arms in appeal. Will you help me make a fresh start? he begged. And the workers shouted with one accord, "Pomożemy", "Yes, we will help you." Lech Wałęsa would later recall with some bitterness that he shouted "Pomożemy" as loudly and trustingly as everybody else.

But as long as the price rises remained in force, the strikes (unprecedented in a Communist country) would continue. Only when, after a stormy meeting with the scandalously underpaid women textile workers in Łódź, Gierek withdrew the rises, did peace return to the factories of Poland. Within the East European Communist bloc, Polish workers had made history by forcing their government to make concessions to them. And the victory gave the workers a quite unrealistic sense of their own power.

Confident now of the workers' support, Gierek embarked on

his new policies. First of all, he established unchallenged control over the Party, by a new purge of over one hundred thousand "unreliable" members, and by the political elimination of his personal rivals. Next, he set about increasing the food supply by giving greater incentives to the private farmers. He recognised their rights of ownership to their land, reduced their taxes, admitted them to welfare benefits and abolished the compulsory deliveries to the State. By ceasing to insist on Poland producing all its own grain, and by allowing the farmers to own more livestock, by the end of 1971 Gierek was able to cut down the amount of food he imported from abroad.

But he was more interested in industry than in agriculture, a preference he would one day come to regret. Profiting from the Soviet Union's present enthusiasm for détente, Gierek set about importing modern machinery on easy credit terms from the West, for the updating of Polish industry. In theory, the plan was excellent. The goods produced in the new, high-technology factories would be exported to the West in exchange for the hard currency needed to repay the debt. In practice, it did not work out as planned. The goods were certainly produced, but they were not always of high quality, nor did the West always want them. (As one writer observed, "Polish machine tools and cars will not be bought by anyone in his right mind.")[2] Nevertheless, the defects in the new system were not immediately obvious, and Gierek's optimism was infectious. Poland cultivated friendly relations with Europe and America, and within three years the Polish economy was one of the fastest-growing in Europe.

Living standards improved. Wages rose, while prices remained frozen. Over one million new flats were built, welfare benefits increased, and imported consumer goods began to pour into the country. Poland was transformed. Westerners who visited the country in these years saw a well-fed people, with money to spare, equipped with washing machines, television sets, transistor radios and the like. The hitherto empty streets began to fill with small cars, as Poland acquired a licence to manufacture her own brand of Fiat. Visitors from the Soviet Union looked with envy on the bulging shelves and the luxuries which never came their own way. As for the Poles, they were indulging in an orgy of travel to the more affluent West.

Gierek, it seemed, was living up to his promises. He regained the trust of the intellectuals by relaxing the censorship; and the result was a fresh flowering of creative talent. Radio and TV programmes injected more truthfulness into the reporting of political affairs. The Sejm (Parliament) was given a fraction more scope, and a few more non-Party members. And the immensely popular decision was taken to rebuild the Royal Palace in Warsaw, a move which had always been stoutly resisted by Gomułka.[3]

Even the Church came in for its share of goodwill. In his first policy speech Gierek's Prime Minister had called for co-operation between believers and unbelievers. Cardinal Wyszyński, ever pragmatic, had called for restraint and mutual tolerance. "We must forgive," he said in his 1970 Christmas homily, "because each of us bears responsibility for the mistakes of the past." Gierek gave permission (never fully implemented) for the construction of one hundred and thirty new churches, including one in the steel town of Nowa Huta, where requests for a new church had for long gone unheeded.[4] (But the government still continued its policy of demolishing those churches which the faithful were spontaneously building for themselves without permission.) Relations with the Vatican also improved, and there was much talk on both sides of *normalisation*, though it was not clear that they both meant the same thing by it.

It even seemed as though Wałęsa's desire for a monument to the riot victims would one day be fulfilled. Vague promises had been made, and on the first May Day after the riots, officials laid wreaths at selected cemeteries in honour of the dead. It seemed as though Lech's confident optimism was justified.

Gierek now began to prove that he understood what the workers wanted. Well aware that he must tread carefully for the present, he entered into consultation with small groups, discussing the country's economic and political problems with them. And although he did not go so far as to allow independent trade unions, he did allow the existing unions to hold completely free elections for the first time, and to dismiss some unwanted Party hacks from high office. In February 1971, as the result of such elections, Lech Wałęsa was elected to his section council as a work inspector.

It was exactly what he had wanted. "A job," wrote a friend, "that would let him wander round the shipyard and visit all the ships. He would be able to keep his finger on the pulse of the shipyard and know what was going on."[5]

Lech was almost euphoric, believing that at last the unions were about to become the true champions of workers' rights. "He believed that every word Gierek spoke was sacred," Izabela said later, in a newspaper interview: "Gierek was the saviour who would make the dreams of millions come true. When he promised to turn Poland into the Japan of Europe, Leszek believed he would do it."[6]

Writing with enthusiasm about the free elections, a reporter on *Voice of the Coast* referred to Lech Wałęsa as "a controversial figure":

> He is twenty-seven years old, has read books about crowd psychology, and about spontaneous action. The last months have seen him involved in unexpected and dangerous activity. It so happened that he was at the centre of the events about which everybody is talking. He did not become involved in them for fun, nor from a thirst for adventure, nor a hatred of the people who are responsible for law and order. He quite simply decided that he had nothing to lose, and for that reason became a leader of the shipyard strike.[7]

To this same reporter, Lech spoke of the need to get production moving:

> We must stop talking and get back to work. Talk will get us nowhere. I believe that the section council must stay in close touch with the people and be accountable to them. But we must ensure that nothing interferes with increased production. Even in this area, things are improving, as they are in social conditions. If people will only trust us, we in the trades unions will do what we can for them. We all want things to get better.

On the section council, Lech Wałęsa proved himself active and exceedingly stubborn, determined at all cost to get his point of view accepted: "Sometimes, when we opposed him," said Lenarciak, "he would say he'd go and tell the workers what his propositions were, and they'd be sure to agree with him."[7]

But Lech soon found that the section's activities were being limited to unimportant matters, and that the big decisions were all being taken over the heads of the workers. The unions were being expected to revert to their earlier role as a mere transmission belt for orders from the Party. This was not his idea of what a trade union was for. A year later, when new elections to the section council were held, Wałęsa did not allow his name to go forward.

Shortly afterwards, it became horrifyingly clear that the leaders of the December strike were being sacked – and blacklisted so that they would be unable to find other employment. Wałęsa was reported for having made derogatory remarks about the authorities, and came close to losing his job. On this occasion he was saved by the fact that his work was good and his team one of the best in the shipyard. He escaped with a warning, and a demand that he should learn to keep his mouth shut.

Lech's parents, Feliksa and Stanisław, had for some time been making plans to emigrate to America, and Feliksa was anxious that Lech should go with them. But, whatever his problems, Lech had no desire to live in a capitalist country. As he told his mother: "I am a Pole. I shall never leave Poland. We have to try and make Poland work."

In 1972, the senior Wałesas left Poland for Jersey City in the United States, where Feliksa's sister, Janina, had lived since before the war. It was the fulfilment of a long-cherished dream, and Feliksa was disappointed that she had been unable to persuade her favourite son to share it. As she said goodbye to her other children, it seems she told them, "Try and be more like Lech." None of them would ever see her again. Three years later, as she crossed a busy street in Jersey City, she was hit by a car and died almost instantly. Her body was brought back to Poland, and she was buried next to Bolesław, in the bleak cluttered little churchyard of Sobowo. Today, peonies, lupins and ox-eye daisies grow wild over the unmarked grave, beside which, unaccountably face downward, lie two stone tablets bearing their names.

By the middle of the decade it was only too clear that Gierek had overreached himself and the whole edifice he had built was about to collapse like a house of cards. He had experimented with too many cosmetic changes, without tackling the basic problem, which was the over-centralised, over-manned, hidebound, top-heavy structure of the Marxist–Leninist economy itself.

The external cause of collapse was the OPEC oil crisis and its knock-on effect. The increased oil prices imposed by the Arab oil sheikhs in 1973–4 sent most of Europe dizzying into recession. They finally hit Poland when Moscow, which supplied eighty per cent of Poland's oil, doubled its asking price. Poland had then to divert more of its exports to the Soviet Union in order to pay for the oil. But, as the Soviet Union paid in "transfer roubles" (about as much use as Monopoly money), the Poles then lacked the hard currency with which to continue paying for machinery from the West. Meanwhile recession and inflation in the West caused a drop in the demand for Polish exports. Unable to lay off workers in redundant industries, Gierek had to borrow more from the West, until his borrowings reached the point where what little he earned from exports had to be put to servicing the debt. When, finally, he was forced to reduce his borrowing and cut down on imports, Polish industry began to suffer a serious lack of spare parts for the machinery which kept the factories going.

Gierek's dream-bubble burst with a vengeance. As wages were still rising and food prices still frozen, there was an excessive demand for food which neither agriculture nor industry could supply. So supplies of food, especially of meat, ran short. Five years of bad weather and poor harvests had aggravated the situation, but the main problem was that, while eighty per cent of the agricultural land was owned by private farmers, they were still not given adequate incentive to produce more. It was the other twenty per cent of State-owned collectives which was allotted most of the available fertiliser, fodder and grants for machinery. To obtain low-interest bank-loans or coupons for fertiliser, private farmers had to provide the State with up to seventy per cent of what they produced – at far below market prices. Grain (now imported) was so expensive that farmers were feeding bread to their pigs, because it was cheaper than the wheat from which it was made.

In 1975, as his economic boom began to wane, so too did Gierek's façade of bonhomie. The unions were already disillusioned about the way he had betrayed them. His popularity evaporated. What is the difference between Gierek and Gomułka? went the joke. None, was the answer, but Gierek doesn't know it yet. The scales fell at last from Lech's eyes. Gierek had, in fact, never fulfilled his promise to bring those responsible for the December massacres to justice. Nor, after the first two years, had the officials continued to lay their May Day wreaths at the graveyards. All commemoration of the December events was now banned, and the promised memorial had never materialised.

On 11th February, 1976, the shipyard's section council held an extraordinary meeting, and Lech Wałęsa made up his mind that he would speak at it. He warned Lenarciak, who was the retiring chairman, that he would speak his mind, regardless of consequences. "You are too soft," he said, "you ought to be more determined."[7]

Wałęsa was true to his promise. "He spoke for quite a long time," said Lenarciak. "One sentence I shall always remember. It was that Gierek had misled the nation, hadn't kept any of his promises, and acted without ever asking the working class for their opinion."

The sentence was rapturously applauded, and the workers elected Wałęsa as their representative to the works' Union Conference. This was a step calculated to alarm the authorities, who did not want this troublemaker given the opportunity to stir up more unrest. A high-ranking director who had attended the meeting was furious with Wałęsa and with the organisation's officials for not interrupting him and throwing him out.

A few days later, a letter was sent to the directorate of the shipyard and the works council, informing them that the work contract with Citizen Wałęsa was to be terminated immediately. "This employee is difficult," the letter said. "He makes tendentious and malicious public statements about the section's managerial staff and about political and social organisations; and this creates a bad working climate within the section."

Lenarciak told his successor on the section council to do everything possible to save Wałęsa: "There is no criticism of his work and one cannot sack somebody just because they've been critical at a union meeting."

The section manager, a civil engineer, had received orders to dismiss Wałęsa, but, as he refused to sign the dismissal document, he too was sacked. Lenarciak explains:

> We were told that he'd resigned because of ill-health, but later one of the directors told us that this was not true. This man told us that if the instructions were not obeyed, the manager would not be the only one to be sacked. The new manager signed Wałęsa's dismissal form the day after taking the job. He was not a bad fellow, just cowardly.

The section council would not sign the dismissal notice. It was authorised by the chairman of the works' council and countersigned "by instruction of the directorate" by the manager of the personnel department. Wałęsa was henceforth forbidden to enter the shipyard: "What's the matter with them?" he cried angrily. "I don't drink; I'm honest; I come to work on time. Why are they doing this to me?"[7]

He did not seem to realise that he had broken the first rule of survival in a Communist country – thou shalt keep thy head well down and do as thou art told.

When he appealed against the dismissal, a committee of judges decreed that criticism of the authorities at a union meeting provided quite adequate grounds for dismissing an employee from his work.

* * *

A new ice age had descended on Polish culture, the frostiest since Stalinist days. Ideological pressure was being stepped up, there was a new attempt to catch Poland's youth in the net. School timetables had been redrawn in such a way as to leave no time for out-of-school religious instruction, and not much time for the family either. In some schools, a written profession of atheism was being demanded. Wyszyński complained that this was a violation of the right to conscience guaranteed by the Polish Constitution. Matters came to a head when Gierek tried to have the Constitution itself amended, in order to enshrine the leading role of the Party and "the unshakeable fraternal ties" with the Soviet Union. As this would deny the Poles any right, at any time, to oppose the Party, everybody, workers, intellectuals and Church deeply resented the proposed changes. The bishops led the expressions of universal dismay. The age-old antipathy between the Church hierarchy and the intellectuals was visibly ending. Alarmed by such a united front, Gierek modified the offending insertions.

In the wake of the Helsinki Conference, during which the whole Eastern bloc committed itself to respect human rights and fundamental freedoms "of thought, conscience, religion and belief", the Poles had become more than ever aware of how their human dignity had been trampled on. They – and especially the young – were looking for a way of recovering their integrity. And many of them found it in the Light-Life Movement, a back-to-the-Gospel religious renewal which had been started in the 50s, but which now in the mid-70s seemed to have acquired a new life. All over Poland, young people were dedicating themselves to living the gospel of Jesus Christ, without fear. "One must be able to overcome fear in order to bear witness to and live by the light," wrote the Movement's founder, Father Blachnicki. "A person is free when he has the courage to bear witness to the truth and to live by the truth, whatever the cost in personal suffering."

The idea of living according to one's conscience without fear was immensely appealing. By 1975, fifty thousand people had joined Light-Life. This new and powerful movement within the Church was to have incalculable consequences for the future. For it signified that the young people of Poland were sorting out their priorities, and were finding that Truth came at the top of their list.[8]

Gierek did not yet know that one day he would have to reckon with the young. For the moment he had other problems on his mind. Had it not been for the economic collapse, he might just have been able to contain the intellectuals. But war on two fronts was too much. The cost of maintaining ridiculously low food prices was becoming unbearable. When the government began exporting meat, shortages at home resulted, and disillusionment became general. Already in the summer of 1974 there were strikes in Gdynia, while in spring 1975 housewives, enraged by the meat shortages and the necessity to queue, set fire to a grocery store in Warsaw.[7] The joke went the rounds: why are butchers' shops always a kilometre apart? Answer: to keep the queues in front from getting tangled.

What else could Gierek do but raise the prices? But, with memories of 1970 still fresh, he was understandably reluctant. In June 1976, however, his options ran out, and he finally summoned up the courage to announce that prices must shoot up (about seventy per cent on meat) and the rate of wage increases must slow down.

On the following day, industry virtually ground to a halt. In Warsaw and Radom there were riots. The country was uniting in rage.

[1] Neal Ascherson, *The Polish August*, Chapter 3: "Years of Disillusion", Penguin, 1981.

[2] From Tim Garton Ash's introduction to *The Polish Revolution*, Jonathan Cape, 1983.

[3] Antony Polonsky, Chapter: "Poland Under Gierek" in Halecki's *History of Poland*, *op. cit.*

[4] See present author's book, *Man From a Far Country*, Hodder & Stoughton, 1979 and 1982.

[5] *Notatki Gdańskie*, *op. cit.*

[6] *Japonia Lecha Wałesy*, interview with Izabela Młynska (née Wałesa) in Wiadomości Skierniewickie, 22.1.81.

[7] *Book of Lech Wałesa*, *op. cit.*

[8] *The Light-Life Movement in Poland*, Grażyna Sikorska, *Religion in Communist Lands*, Volume 11, number 1. Spring 1983.

13 COUNTDOWN TO CHANGE (1976–9)

> Our Party, which has a long and fine-sounding name . . . reminds me of a gigantic vacuum-cleaner which sucks in everything within the compass of this ill-fated country's borders. It could also be likened to a cancer which greedily burns its way through every inch of tissue, every cell of the body politic, an infuriated cancer, a cancer in total overdrive, a cancer with a cosmic erection. Perhaps there has occurred, or is now occurring, in Europe, a degeneration in the functioning of states and in their dealings with each other, but there is no way you can imagine the nightmare that has befallen us.
>
> Tadeusz Konwicki, *The Polish Complex*

When the fateful price rises were announced, workers at the Ursus tractor factory in Warsaw tore up the tracks of the Paris to Moscow railway line, which runs through the factory, and blockaded the line so that no trains could enter or leave Warsaw. In Radom, further to the south, workers stormed the Party HQ, and when they saw the huge quantities of food and drink stored there for the privileged few, they divided it amongst themselves and set fire to the building.

Retribution was swift and savage. The UB ran amok, arresting workers right, left and centre, regardless of whether or not they had taken part in the demonstrations. In Ursus, the arrested workers were sacked from their jobs and evicted from their hostels. In Radom, where at least seventeen men were killed, thousands were arrested and made to run the so-called "path of health" – between double lines of militia armed with batons. "They beat us senseless and smashed our bones," reports a survivor.

Within a few hours the prisons were bursting. Next day special kangaroo courts began handing down draconian sentences, making liberal use of false witnesses and manufactured evidence. Heavy fines and long prison sentences were meted out. Scores of workers were thrown out of their jobs and prevented from finding other employment, except of the badly paid, unskilled variety.

Most of the official unions made haste to condemn the "hooligans" and "anti-social elements" in their midst. But there were honourable exceptions. In Bydgoszcz, for example, Stanisław, Lech Wałęsa's brother, who had shared Lech's faith in Gierek, and who was still a loyal member of the Party, resigned as secretary of his union branch, rather than read aloud the speech which had been prepared for him, condemning the "hooligans and firebrands". As a result, he too lost his job.

To Lech, the events of June 1976 were illuminating as well as distressing. "The strike of the workers at Ursus and Radom," he said in his 1983 Nobel speech, "was a new experience, which not only strengthened my belief in the justness of the workers' demands and aspirations, but also indicated the urgent need for solidarity amongst them."

An angry crowd of workers gathered outside the shipyard management offices in Gdańsk, threatening a strike if the intolerable price rises were not withdrawn, and demanding the reinstatement of Lech Wałęsa. The Church, meanwhile, was supporting the workers, though stressing the need for calm. "It is painful," declared Cardinal Wyszyński in a sermon, "that workers should have to struggle for their basic rights under a workers' government." But nothing, he also assured them, was ever solved by violent protest. In Kraków, Poland's other Cardinal, Karol Wojtyła, begged the government to reconsider the price rises and to stop terrorising the workers. At the same time he set up a fund for the families of those arrested or out of work.

Two days later, the rises were called off. The shipyard workers therefore did not strike. Nor did they continue to insist on Wałęsa's reinstatement. On the surface, life returned to normal. But the repression continued. More and more workers were arrested. This new attempt at coercion, however, boomeranged on the government, for the net result was to drive the workers and the intellectuals together at last. On 23rd September, 1976, fourteen dissidents, among whom was Jacek Kuroń, established KOR, the Workers' Defence Committee. It was a milestone in the history of Communist Poland.

> It is a long time [wrote KOR's spokesman, Jerzy Andrzejewski], since reprisals have been as brutal as these recent ones. For the first time in many years, arrests and interrogations have been accompanied by physical terror. The victims can count on no help from the trade unions – whose role has been deplorable. Society's only defence against lawlessness is solidarity and mutual support. That is why we have formed the Workers' Defence Committee.[1]

"We've done it out of shame," said Kuroń. "We were ashamed of the intellectuals' silence in 1970. We need to recover our good name."[2]

KOR brought legal aid to workers who had been at the mercy of corrupt courts; and gave financial help to their families. They collected proof of police brutality and of the crooked photographic evidence that had convicted them. For many they secured an early release. Then, so that everywhere people would understand the enormity of what had been done, they published their findings. In this way KOR effectively nipped in the bud the growing police terror, and raised the level of awareness in Poland, bringing that much nearer the hope of a real change in society.

Gierek, himself a relatively easy-going man, who was, besides, bent on preserving good relations with the West, was anxious to put a brake on police repression, while sorting out some of the more obvious disorders in Polish society. Alcoholism – always the last line of defence against misery – had passed the "biological threat" barrier; absenteeism was rife; the divorce rate was rising and the birth-rate falling. For help in this alarming situation, Gierek sought the goodwill of the Church. Reminding First Secretary Gierek that the government could only hope for good workmanship if it provided the workers with a decent way of life, and observed the human rights of all Poles, believers as well as unbelievers, the bishops nonetheless agreed to co-operate with him in this moral disaster area. They were becoming accustomed to the see-saw nature of their relationship with the present regime.

But however much it might suit Gierek to blow hot and cold with the Church, his attitude to KOR was nothing short of icy. As an illegal organisation, its members were subjected to every kind of intimidation. They lost their jobs, their apartments were ransacked, their belongings seized, and they were frequently attacked either by the police or by unknown assailants. In Kraków, a leading KOR sympathiser was Stanisław Pyjas, a final year philology student. His sudden death in deeply suspicious circumstances in May 1977 sparked off student demonstrations in Kraków, and his funeral was attended by two thousand students who walked in silent protest to the spot where his body had been found.[3] Cardinal Wojtyła gave his support to the students and asked the citizens of Kraków to see to it that they didn't get hurt.

The Pyjas affair, closely followed by the arrest of Kuroń and the young scholar, Adam Michnik,* increased public sympathy for KOR and encouraged the Church to offer qualified support to the former Marxist intellectuals they had once regarded with suspicion. St Martin's Church in Warsaw gave sanctuary to fourteen hunger-strikers protesting about the arrest of KOR members. Cardinal Wyszyński took up the cudgels on behalf of KOR, saying: "Sometimes people demand their rights too violently because they feel the noose tightening around their neck. How can a nation live when basic human rights are denied it? A nation that has no human rights is not a nation, but a collection of soulless robots."[4]

KOR itself was spurred to even greater efforts by Gierek's unblushing announcement in February 1977 that the police had not exceeded their powers after the riots of the previous June and that there was no need for an inquiry into their behaviour.[5]

After three months, Kuroń and Michnik were released in a large-scale amnesty in July, and proceeded to expand KOR's activities. Once they had believed that they could reform the Party from within, but the years had killed that hope. They proposed now to wash their hands of the Party, to let it preserve its empty façade of power, while they themselves created a genuine opposition, the foundations of a new pluralist society representing different social and political ideas.[6] Only in this way could change come about.

KOR (like the growing Light-Life Movement within the Church), had come to the conclusion that the oppressors' greatest weapon was fear. "Once you can rise above your own fear," said Kuroń, "you are a free man." Determined, therefore, to overcome fear, and to live as though they lived in a free society, KOR emphasised the need for everybody to act openly, regardless of possible consequences. In order to broaden their own scope, they changed their name to KSS-KOR (the Committee for Social Self-Defence-KOR), and backed various other audacious social initiatives and activities which were outside the control of the

* As a young university lecturer, aged twenty-two, involved in the 1968 academic disturbances, Adam Michnik was arrested on a trumped-up charge and sentenced to three years in prison. After his release, the doors of the university were closed to him, and he worked as an unskilled labourer in a Warsaw factory. Then the authorities decided that he was a bad influence on the workers, and he lost that job too. In 1976, at the request of Jean-Paul Sartre, he was given a passport and spent several months in France. But he returned to Poland in 1977, knowing that he would be returning to a life of personal danger. A few days later, he was arrested.

Party. One of these, the Flying University courses, reminiscent of the similar educational arrangements during the Nazi Occupation, flouted the Party taboos and provided information on a variety of long-forbidden subjects. The lectures were held in private flats and were frequently disrupted by the police, the teachers and owners of the flats all being arrested. (One story going the rounds told that after a talk entitled "Orwell's Nineteen Eighty-Four and Today's Poland" had been broken up by police, next day a new lecture was advertised with the title "Orwell's Nineteen Eighty-Three and Today's Poland"; the police left the second one alone, and it was allowed to take place unhindered.)

Censorship was as oppressive as it had ever been. Although Wadja's film, *Man of Marble*, which attacked the Stalinist terror and the moral corruption of the years which followed it, was shown in Poland in 1977, restrictions were otherwise abnormal and ludicrous. Partly because of this, there was a flourishing of independent houses which published a vast amount of underground material unacceptable to the censor. Of these, the most important were KOR's Information Bulletin and *Robotnik*, a paper for workers. "The situation was droll," comments Cywiński. "Draconian sentences were being handed out, the security police were violating every known principle of law. And yet here were writers and editors insisting on signing their own names to everything, and people flocking openly to illegal lectures."[7]

As the need to stick together became increasingly imperative, the link between workers and the intelligentsia grew. The towns of the Baltic coast, with their energetic and volatile populations, were particularly receptive to new ideas. On 29th April, 1978 ("about the time when the World Cup was being played in Argentina," he says), Lech Wałęsa was one of a small group of dissidents in Gdańsk who announced the formation of the Baltic Committee for Free and Independent Trade Unions. The first of these groups had, suitably enough, been launched in Radom, for the defence of workers' economic, legal and human rights. "We got wise," said a worker, unconsciously repeating an idea of Kuroń's. "We realised you don't have to burn down Party Committee houses. We have to build our own."

So began a new more overt phase in Wałęsa's long underground struggle for independent unions. "It was my first taste of genuine human solidarity," he says. "The important thing for me was that at last I belonged to a group with whose aims I could identify."

Over the next four years, Danuta complained that she rarely saw him, that his life had become an endless succession of secret meetings, underground activity and all too frequent arrests. Lech claims that in this period he was arrested "hundreds of times" for circulating leaflets, and for distributing clandestine copies of Miłosz's *Captive Mind*. "Hundreds" may well be an exaggeration, but it is true that he spent many an unpleasant forty-eight hours in a police cell. He says he did his thinking in prison and had a much-needed rest. Nowadays he looks back and marvels at Danuta's patience with him, speculating that a lesser woman would have stuck a carving-knife into him long since.

The founder of the Free Trade Union group in Gdańsk was bearded engineer Andrzej Gwiazda, a name that would become famous later on. Others were Alina Pieńkowska, a nurse in the shipyard's medical section; and Bogdan Lis, a twenty-five-year-old Party member. But the undisputed leader and spokeswoman was Anna Walentynowicz, a widow with one son. Anna, whose sacking in 1980 was the spark that set the tinder of Solidarity alight, is a remarkable woman – "pure gold" say her admirers, of whom there are many. Small, dumpy, with ugly, black-rimmed spectacles perched on her nose, she is said to have "the outward charm and gentleness of a Polish granny and the inner strength of a Polish cavalry-man". She was ten years old when the 1939 war broke out; and in the course of that war, she lost her entire family. Pain was so much a part of her life that she could not bear to see anyone making others suffer, and her whole life had been a conscious struggle to defend the weak. Lacking education – she went to school for only four years before the war – she had learned only what she had picked up in lectures for illiterates and in courses on welding at the Gdańsk shipyards where she had worked as a crane-driver since 1966. Tough though she looked, she knew she had cancer, and in 1965 she had been given only five years to live.

Until 1968 Anna worked for the official trade unions. When disillusionment finally set in, she was sacked, ostensibly for "attacking the work of a union collective", but in reality for exposing the corruption rife in the union. The workers protested at her dismissal, and she was re-instated, though not in her old crane-driving job. Then came December 1970 – "that shriek of agony, that blind terror which sent people rushing onto the streets. I thought to myself: the five years have passed and I'm still alive. If God has given me life, there must be something he wants me to do. And I wondered what it might be."[8]

She knew she could not fight alone, so she contented herself with small acts of kindness – heating hot milk and soup during the work-break and serving it to her fellow-workers, to save them the long journey to a distant canteen. When she was told to stop, she tried instead to brighten their lives by planting flowers outside the workshop entrance: "The manager came and asked me if I wanted to be sacked again. 'I don't want anything except to see flowers growing,' I said. But he wouldn't listen and I didn't get my garden."

Shortly afterwards, in 1971, when she had protested about the withdrawal of promised bonuses, she was again given her cards.

"In 1978," she said, "I first heard about free trade unions. I didn't know what they were, but I thought that if we had real unions we should not be so helpless in the face of licensed evil. So I began to look for people who would explain them to me."[9]

She found KOR, and began to share the good news with her fellow-workers. And that's when her troubles started: "The workers were forbidden to talk to me, and the department head made sure that I went straight from the gate to the cloakroom, and from there to wherever I was working. Any step outside the area allotted to me would mean dismissal."

Harassment did not deter her. The Free Trade Union group of which Anna was co-founder did its best to convince people that if only they would act together, their strength would be a match for the security police. The conspirators met in small groups, always in a different place and at a different time, sometimes on a wild seashore, sometimes deep in a forest. Whenever they held larger meetings – to hear Flying University lectures on modern history, work-law, the need for society to organise itself – they were infiltrated by police agents.

When the group decided to produce its own newspaper, *Solidarity* was one of the titles considered. But they settled for *Worker of the Coast*, to link it to the nationally produced KOR magazine, *Worker* (*Robotnik*).[10] The first issue (August) contained a statement of aims:

> We do not have political aims; we do not wish to impose on our members, collaborators or sympathisers any precise political and social views, we do not aim to take over power. We realise, however, that we will be accused of indulging in political activity. The range of matters considered in our country to be political is very wide and encompasses almost everything except excursions to pick mushrooms.

In the September issue, *Worker* published a thousand-word Charter of Workers' Rights. It was signed by sixty-five activists, among them Wałęsa, Walentynowicz and Gwiazda. They called on workers to "throw off all feelings of apathy; stop passively accepting restrictions on our rights and the erosion of our living standards". And they concluded, somewhat prophetically: "Only independent trade unions, with the backing of the workers they represent, stand a chance of providing an effective challenge to the authorities. They alone can become a power with which the authorities will be obliged to negotiate on an equal footing."

Lech had the reputation of a loner in these years. He would sit at the back of the meetings, soaking up the discussions, learning. When each member of the group was asked to produce a blueprint for his or her ideal society, Lech produced an exhaustive list. When he reached point twenty-four, "the director should treat his employees better", the others laughed at his naïvety. None of them saw him as a possible future leader. He was merely the group's postman.[11] (He was also the goalkeeper when they played football. "That's how he always saw himself," said a colleague. "The perfect anchor-man.")

Since May 1976, he had been working in the transport section of the ZREMB building company. Here, at a time when there was a catastrophic shortage of spare parts for almost any machine, Wałęsa made his name as a first-class mechanic who could work wonders with clapped-out cars. He was popular, and his boss turned a blind eye to his more doubtful activities. "Just do your job well and I shan't bother about all the rest," he told Lech.[4]

When he brought clandestine leaflets, posters and copies of *Worker of the Coast* to work, they were snatched up immediately. Others he scattered in the streets, in trains, buses, churches, or distributed to other factories. In the middle of December he put up posters reminding people of the coming anniversary. When a workmate who had angrily torn down such a poster later broke his leg, Lech assured him that the accident was God's punishment for tearing down Truth!

He was frequently taken away by the police. The first time, they treated him as a poor innocent, too naïve to realise he was being used by men cleverer than himself. But when they realised he had actually written some of the leaflets himself, they changed their tune. The UB followed him everywhere. Once after a funeral a friend invited him to his flat for coffee. Lech refused. "I'm being watched," he explained. "If I go to your place they'll come and turn it upside down later." At work his personal dossier was carefully scrutinised by the police.

As a delegate to the Party-dominated "factory Parliament" he once again showed an undesirable outspokenness, and complained moreover that elections to the post of president and secretary were rigged. "Gentlemen," he asked during the election, "what have I come here for? To take part in an election, or just to applaud? What sort of election is it when the result has been decided beforehand?"

After showing his hand like that, it was only a matter of time before they sacked him. All that was needed was a pretext. In the end they fell back on making him redundant, though they did also charge him with "moonlighting", since he repaired his own and other people's old "bangers" on the works premises. (Hardly an impressive charge, since almost everybody did it.)

As from 31st December, the management told the works council in November 1978, it intended to dispense with the services of Citizen Wałęsa. Lech's section-manager spoke up for him, praising his extraordinary skill as a craftsman, the initiative he showed in solving difficult and complicated problems: "Besides he's never drunk, never late for work. He's a disciplined, conscientious worker who has a gift for creating a good atmosphere around him."

The manager's opinion was unwelcome and he was demoted to a store-room job with a considerable drop in wages. The works council could not oppose a dismissal which was supposedly on account of redundancy, so they signed the necessary documents. Only when Wałęsa had appealed against the decision, on the grounds that he was a breadwinner with a wife and four children to support, were they able to ask the directorate to reinstate him. The directors agreed to take him back but only as a sort of general dogsbody in another section. Wałęsa said he had no intention of becoming an errand boy and refused the job. On 29th December, he was sacked again.

Lech's workmates were furious about the way he had been treated, and there were mutterings about a strike. Wałęsa would not hear of it. "Don't make trouble," he advised, "you'll only get yourselves the sack. You've got children too, don't expose yourself to the risk. We're not strong enough yet. But the time will come when we shall be stronger than they are, and that's when we shall act."[12]

"Some of us cried when he went," remembers a fellow-worker. But many, perhaps the majority, still thought Lech was mad for provoking the authorities so often. Years of pressure had resulted in an ostrich psychology which preferred to keep its head down and hope not to be noticed. "My workmates," Lech wrote later, "were full of repressed hatred of the system, but they believed they were powerless. The fact that I was repeatedly thrown out of work was seen by most of them as a confirmation of their own greater realism. There was this deadening conviction that there was no point in doing anything, since nothing could ever be changed."[13]

[1] *Poland in Perspective*, *op. cit.*

[2] John Taylor, *Five Months with Solidarity*, Wildwood House, 1981.

[3] *Dissent in Poland 1976–1977*: reports and documents presented by the Association of Polish Students and Graduates in Exile, London.

[4] Błażyński, George, *Flashpoint Poland*, Pergamon Policy Studies, Oxford 1979.

[5] *Poland in Perspective*, *op. cit.*

[6] Antony Polonsky in Halecki's *History of Poland*, *op. cit.*

[7] Bohdan Cywiński, notes on *The Polish Experience*.

[8] Jean Offrédo, *Lech Wałesa Czyli Polskie Lato*, *op. cit.*

[9] Ibid.

[10] *Book of Lech Wałesa*, *op. cit.*

[11] Ibid.

[12] Ibid.

[13] *Uncensored Poland*, News Bulletin published by the Information Centre For Polish Affairs, London, Number 19/83, 30th September, 1983.

14 SCATTERING THE GRAINS (1979–80)

By 1979, then, there was already the embryo of that tacit alliance of workers, intelligentsia and Church, unprecedented in Polish history, unique in the Soviet bloc, unseen in the West, which was to grow into Solidarity.

Tim Garton Ash, *The Polish Revolution*

That December, for the first time, an illegal ceremony was held outside gate number two at the shipyard, at the spot where the workers had been killed. It was organised by the Young Poland Movement, one of the independent Human Rights groups which had sprung up in the wake of the Helsinki Agreement. Lech Wałęsa, who had placed flowers at the spot every year, spoke to a crowd of about four thousand and vowed: "Next year there will be more of us."

He spoke more truly than he knew. The following year, 1979, there were seven thousand. And part of the reason lay in the electric shock which had galvanised Poland into life when, in October 1978, Cardinal Karol Wojtyła of Kraków had been elected Pope. It was one of those times, like the outbreak of war or the death of President Kennedy, when everyone claims to remember exactly where he was when the announcement was made. Not since the defeat of the Bolsheviks in 1920 had the Polish people known such heart-warming national pride. The winter that followed was freezing and there was no coal; production in the factories was paralysed; queues were longer than ever for less and less; hospitals were closing for lack of drugs and medicines; pharmacies put up "closed for repair" signs; and several cities were without light, heat and water. But everything was somehow bearable because there was a Polish Pope. Hope had been reborn along with self-respect. Perhaps a new society was possible after all. KOR's attempts to make society realise its potential, the frequent flouting of the censorship, the growing demands for free trade unions were all straws in the wind. Suddenly the Poles began to believe that they were not, after all, "abandoned by man and by God", and that a major political change had now become not only possible but inevitable. In the words of Anna Walentynowicz: "When he became Pope, every Pole held his head a bit higher. We were no longer just a nation of alcoholics and work-shy labourers."

In June, Pope John Paul II returned to his homeland in triumph. He had wanted to come in May, to celebrate the 900th anniversary of the martyrdom of St Stanisław, a bishop of his former Kraków diocese, but this was found politically unacceptable. (The bishop, slain in the eleventh century by the king's stooges, was a symbol of human dignity oppressed by the authorities.) So the visit was delayed, and it was on the feast of Pentecost that John Paul arrived to kiss the soil of Poland. Gierek and the Party had hovered between delight and dismay at the time of his election, but had finally settled for a cautious chauvinistic pride in this "son of the Polish nation, which is building the greatness and prosperity of its Socialist fatherland with the unity and co-operation of all its citizens".

They doubtless hoped that the visit of this particular son to his Socialist fatherland might encourage and enhance this unity and co-operation.

Even the weather rejoiced. It was a blazing hot summer's day when he arrived, to be greeted like a king, with garlands, flowers and song. Any of the grey faceless Politburo men would have given his eye-teeth for such a demonstration of love and allegiance. Who could doubt that John Paul was the real leader of Poland? For two weeks the Poles acted out the fantasy that their actual leaders did not exist.

The sight of Warsaw's Victory Square dominated by a huge oak cross draped with a red stole was miracle enough. On that square a quarter of a million people waited for John Paul. The atmosphere was one of carnival. The very fact that so many had arrived in this place without being compelled to go there was in itself memorable. And when the Pope, standing by an altar built on that very Square which had so often witnessed their humiliation, spoke to them of man's need for Christ, they cried out: WE WANT GOD, again and again over the roaring applause that seemed as though it would never end.

On Pentecost Sunday, the students came on foot from miles around. Everywhere he went, the young made it plain that their loyalty was his. Be proud of your Polish inheritance, he told them. Add to it, hand it on to future generations! Do not be afraid of the difficulties. Be afraid only of indifference and cowardice:

"From the difficult experience we call Poland, a better future can emerge. But only if you yourselves are honourable, free in spirit and strong in conviction."

In Silesia, miners, the darlings of the regime, defying a government ban, turned out in their thousands, wearing their traditional dress. The regime knew the baffling humiliation of a quarter of a million miners singing: "Christ has conquered, Christ is king, Christ commands our lives" at full throttle. The media did their best to play down the visit, to give it a minor place in the evening TV bulletins, to limit the film shots to close-ups of old ladies or brass bands. But nobody was fooled, not in Warsaw, not in Częstochowa, not in Gnieżno, not in Kraków, not anywhere. John Paul spoke to the whole of Poland, giving voice to truths that had too long been silenced, convincing the people that social renewal was possible only at the price of their own moral renewal. He was inviting them to change their lives, and it was as though he had opened a locked door, letting in the light. Adam Michnik, listening on radio, said: "When he asked believers never to deny Christ, I felt he was talking directly to me, an unbeliever."

Michnik, like many other intellectuals, had long realised that since 1945 the Church had been the most consistent defender of human rights and freedoms in Poland.[1] Consequently, the Polish left had abandoned its outdated stereotype of a reactionary, right-wing and anti-semitic Church.

It was like the first Pentecost, they said, when the Holy Spirit came down on the followers of Jesus. "The Spirit will come upon you and change the face of this land," John Paul promised, adding, in Kraków, "the future of Poland will depend on how many people are mature enough to dare to be non-conformists!" Everybody heard, everybody was repeating his words. "It was a strengthening of the whole nation and everyone was aware of it," said a man from Poznań. "People wanted to start again, to become authentic human beings. It was an incomparable spiritual experience."

Significantly, throughout the whole visit, perfect order was kept by volunteer stewards, and there was no violence. A voluntary ban on alcohol had been observed. There was a sense of national unity and solidarity such as had not been experienced since the years of Nazi occupation.

The writer and former Communist, Kazimierz Brandys, had come to believe that the Poles cared only about their own material well-being. But the Pope's visit made him realise that:

> . . . as soon as there was but half a chance of regaining an authentic human existence, all the cars, refrigerators and television sets would be tossed onto the barricades. Yesterday somebody said to me: "This is not an outbreak of religious feeling. This is a manifestation of patriotism, a national uprising without a shot being fired. He has come to lift us out of the mud."[2]

A new concept of the nation – as a community – was being born. John Paul "scattered the grains", reflected Bohdan Cywiński, explaining how harvesters used traditionally to make a festive wreath of the grains and take it along to the big house where a celebration would take place. From now on, said Cywiński, people like Lech Wałęsa felt that they were carrying the Pope's wreath, and they lost whatever fear they had had.

Lech had been working since May 1979 with "Elektromontaż", an engineering firm which produced electrical equipment. A senior employee of the firm described him as "the best automobile electrician bar none", and he was much liked. But he was a marked man, and security police shadowed him from the moment he arrived. If he went to repair equipment at a building site, the UB would be on the scene as soon as he had left it, asking what he'd been doing, to whom had he talked and about what. In spite, or perhaps because of this harassment, he won many sympathisers to the cause of free trade unions, both in the works and on the building sites. He brought in leaflets and got discussions going, and he persuaded many to join the organising committee. But when someone asked him whether he had any hopes for the immediate future, he replied: "I'm convinced that one day there will be independent trades unions in Poland. But not in my lifetime."

As the December 1979 anniversary drew near, surveillance was stepped up. One car with police markings was now permanently parked outside the works, and three days before the anniversary a second car joined it: "We were afraid they would arrest Leszek," said Florian Wiśniewski, a fellow-worker, "but we were determined that he was going to be at the wreath-laying ceremony at Number Two gate of the shipyard where his colleagues were shot in 1970. It was unthinkable that he shouldn't be there. So we arranged to smuggle him out in a container truck as soon as the police entered the compound."[3]

The workers kept a round-the-clock watch on everyone entering and leaving. When a group of officials arrived on the day before the anniversary, and went straight to the office, Lech was promptly smuggled out, but in a "Nysa" car, not a container. Too many people had known about the container, and it was all too probable that the information had leaked out.

Next day, Wałęsa did not come to work. He was in hiding. It was the 16th December, and that evening, outside the Lenin shipyard, seven thousand men and women gathered to honour their dishonoured dead. Wałęsa was one step nearer the fulfilment of his vow that one day a monument would be erected in that place. "This obsession with the martyred dead, so much a part of the national psychology," a British journalist was to write, "was the source of his driving anger and his obstinacy. This young electrician is best understood, when all has been said, as Antigone."[4]

In front of that crowd of mourners, Wałęsa was at his best, and many people noticed him for the first time that day. He spoke to them about his own experience of that terrible December, his feelings of responsibility for what had happened. He told them how deeply he had trusted Edward Gierek, and how that trust had been betrayed. And he appealed for them to come forward: "Only an organised and independent society can make itself heard," he said. "I beg you to organise yourselves in independent groups for your own self-defence. Help each other."

And finally he issued an appeal that was also a challenge, that: "next year on the tenth anniversary, each of you must bring a stone or brick to this spot. We shall cement them into place and we shall build a monument."[5]

Almost immediately after this event, the "Elektromontaż" works council was informed that there were to be redundancies. According to Florian Wiśniewski:

> Fourteen people were on the list, all but two of them members of the Free Trade Unions. The idea of redundancies was ridiculous. We were so short-handed that on one building-site we had had to borrow workers from elsewhere. The chairman of the council was under the management's thumb, but the majority would not agree to the dismissals.[3]

To strengthen their case against Wałęsa – "the company's most outstanding electrician" – the management officially reprimanded him for "absence from work" on the day of the ceremony. He appealed to the council. At the meeting which was to hear the appeal, the director and First Secretary of the works' Party branch turned up – an obvious attempt to scare the council members into submission. The members, however, decided that if Wałęsa had stayed away on the day in question, it was because of the police pressure within the factory; and they voted to quash the reprimand. It was a brave gesture, but the dismissals were not revoked. Angrily, the men set up a committee to defend their mates who had been sacked; but though a delegation went to plead with the management, it achieved nothing and the dismissals were put into immediate effect.

Inevitably the workers had lost their battle with authority. But they were determined at least to show their solidarity with the victims. From then on, they held a collection every pay day for their support.[3]

One of the Free Trades Union activists who was dismissed along with Wałęsa was a teenage boy, Jan Szczepański, who lived near him, on the Stogi estate. Not long afterwards, the boy disappeared without trace; and later his mutilated body was found in a canal. His feet had been cut off, his fingernails pulled out. Lech Wałęsa was one of hundreds from Stogi who planned to attend the boy's funeral. But on the night before, police trucks surrounded the estate. A neighbour of the Wałęsas takes up the story:

> At first we thought it was a raid on the amber-collectors who were digging up the coastal forests and doing a lot of damage. The police were all round our apartment block. In the early morning, there were cars standing outside, and I could see two UB at the bottom of the staircase. I guessed they were waiting for Wałesa, so I rushed down to his flat to warn him not to go out. He was getting ready, and there was an enormous wreath in the passage. I told him the police were there, but he said he had to go to the funeral, no matter what. As he left the building, the UB rushed him and tried to get the wreath, but he held on to it. Then another lot rushed out, and there was a scuffle. They tore the wreath out of his hands and pushed him into one of the cars.[3]

It was probably then that his local fame began. Stogi was a clannish district, where neighbours helped each other and shared each other's problems. Before this, Lech had been remarkable chiefly as the chap who put holy pictures in his window on feast days and who regularly every Sunday led his clutch of children to church. Now they saw him in a different light. As Lech was detained more and more often by the police, they developed a system of warning signals for him. Once Lech and his family (five children now) barricaded themselves into the one-and-a-half roomed apartment, to prevent the police from entering.[6] He opened the window and shouted to the policemen through a loud-hailer, while neighbours poured hot water from the windows and threw slippers, buckwheat kasza and anything handy at them. The police withdrew, and next day Lech hung out a huge banner thanking the neighbours for their support.

The Young Poland Movement which had organised the December ceremony had also re-awakened public interest in the 3rd May Constitution of 1791 – the first written constitution in Europe, and inspired by the principles of the Enlightenment and the French Revolution. Before the war, 3rd May had been Poland's National Day, but the Communists had abandoned it in favour of 22nd July, which marked the 1945 Communist takeover. Young Poland planned to revive the earlier tradition, and had issued a leaflet containing the text of the 3rd May Constitution. Wałęsa stuck a copy on the window of his clapped-out old car, and before long found himself under arrest and minus a driving-licence.

Quite clearly he was unafraid. Perhaps also he had decided that he had nothing to lose, being already out of work and hungry. With a family of five to support (and a sixth on the way) he had appealed for help to the Committee for Social Self-Defence – KOR (KSS-KOR). "Kuroń gave me bread," he was to say later. Through KOR, Kuroń also gave him a legal adviser, Jacek Taylor, who found his new client more than he had bargained for: "He had his own ideas about how I ought to defend him," recalls Taylor. "With other clients I could persuade them where their own reasoning was at fault. But not Lech. I could never explain anything to him. There was I, with all my legal experience, confronted by this simple worker – and completely baffled by him."

Lech kept Taylor busy, rescuing him from police clutches. Once they arrested him in the middle of Gdańsk as he was pushing his baby daughter Magda in the pram, brazenly sticking up posters as he went. They bundled him, the baby and the pram into a car, then drove back to Stogi to deposit pram and baby before taking him off to cool his heels overnight in a cell.

* * *

By the late 1970s the economy had skeetered right out of control, like a runaway train on the wrong track. Industrial and agricultural production were plummeting – "only prices, alcoholism and foreign debts were rising in a spectacular manner".[6] Poland was almost bankrupt, the Western banks had run out of patience, no one but Russia was buying Polish exports. Food supplies dwindled. When stale bread was delivered in November to Kazimierz

Brandys's local co-op because the bakery had run out of electricity to make fresh, there were grumblings in the queue. Whereupon the driver who'd made the delivery said, "You'll be kissing the ground for bread like this when winter comes."[2]

Everyone was tired and frustrated with the degrading living conditions. The young had to wait ten or fifteen years for a three-room flat in which the bath was usually out of order because of a lack of spare parts; women rose before dawn to catch a tram into town and be in the meat queue by 6 a.m. (Some of the queues began at 2 a.m.) They would wait for two, three, four hours and then be fobbed off with rubbish. Shortages were such that when anything at all was available – candles, soap, toothpaste, toilet paper, razor blades, shaving-cream – "You rush to buy as much as you can, because heaven knows when you'll get it again." Before the war, went a current joke, you could go into a butcher's shop and find meat. Today the sign outside the shop says *Meat*, but you go in and find only the butcher.

Another joke concerned the man who went into a shop and asked for a long list of foodstuffs which were as scarce as gold-dust. He was quite mad, everyone agreed. "But what a memory," they added admiringly.

Yet for those who had money, there were few scarcities. A Polish Fiat (for which normally there was a four-year wait and cash to be laid down at the beginning of the waiting period) was available for dollars. A plumber could be paid in nylons, veal was on sale in the extremely expensive "commercial" stores. In these stores, opened by Gierek after the food riots in 1976, the better cuts of meat could be found, at three times the usual price. And for those lucky enough to have dollars (the majority were not in this category), there were the hard-currency Pewex stores where Western goods could be bought. Likewise in the PKO shops Polish products were on sale – for dollars only. "We now have three classes in our classless society," said a Polish taxi-driver. "Those who have dollars, those who have złoty, and those who have neither." The black market was a way of life – the good life – in Poland, for those who could afford it.

The privileged ones, those in the *nomenklatura*, "the bosses" – that new class called into being by the demands of the Communist state, valued for their ability to say "Yes" to the Party, holding all the best jobs and well-protected by the police – were insulated from the reality which afflicted everybody else. They were known as "the owners of People's Poland", and they were deeply resented. Shortages were not for them or for their children, who

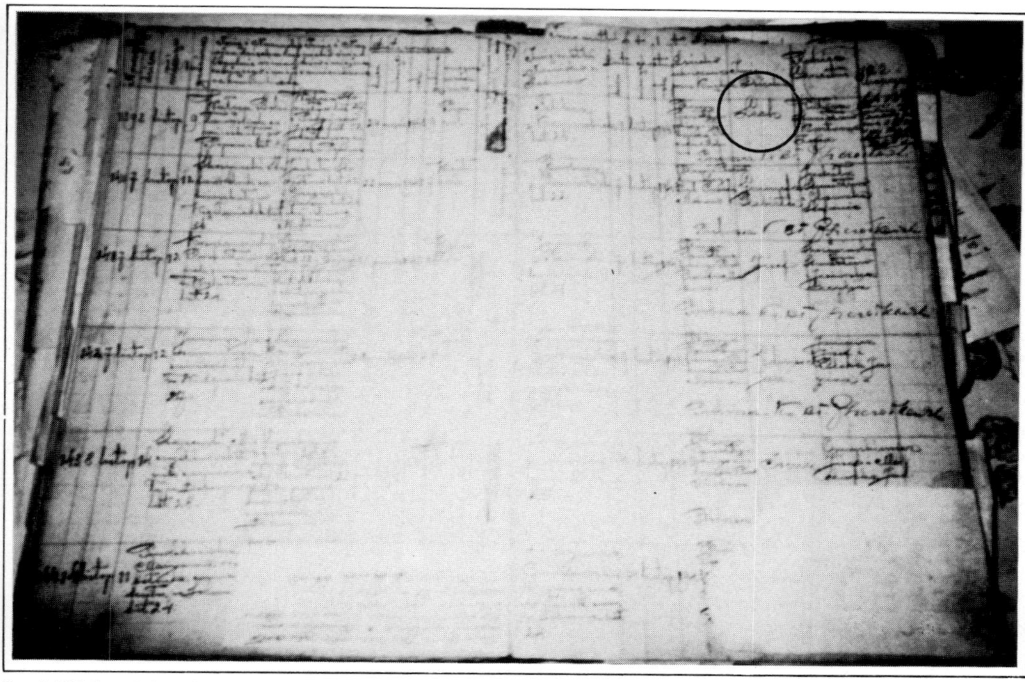

Lech Wałęsa's birth entry in the register of the church in Mochowo – 29th September, 1943.

Lech (third from left) was the fourth of seven children, born into grinding poverty: "We were rich in the things that mattered."

The little house (left) in Popowo where Wałęsa was brought up.

Chalin: the school Wałęsa attended for eight years.

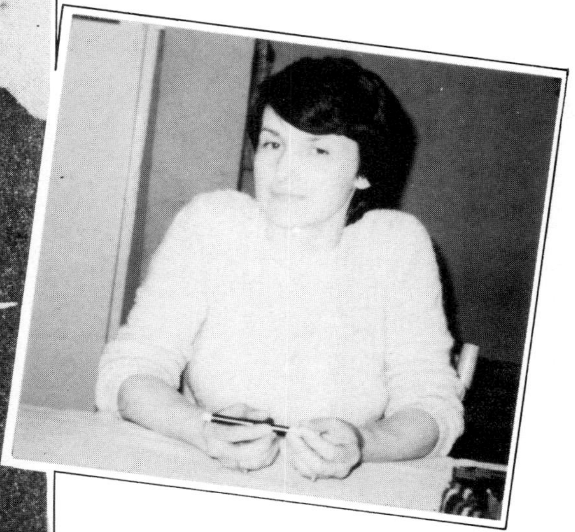

Danuta Wałęsa at home in 1982.

Marriage: 8th November, 1969.

Defiance in a Warsaw churchyard outside St Stanisław Kostka Church where Jerzy Popiełuszko is buried.

Dreams and determination: the vision can become reality.

Occupation strike in the Lenin shipyard and a new leader is born: Lech Wałęsa addresses the crowds.

Bread for the strikers: the nation expresses its overwhelming support.

Confession on site.

31st August, 1981, euphoria and relief as the agreement is signed guaranteeing independent self-governing trade unions.

Cardinal Wyszyński at the Gdańsk monument, finally erected in 1981 to commemorate the tragedy of 1970.

Western Europe rallies to provide food and supplies for the Poles, struggling to survive the winter of 1981 in a shattered economy.

The nation unites in dedicated support for Solidarity.

"War": 13th December, 1981, the tanks move in overnight as the authorities declare martial law.

The realist.

Father Jerzy Popiełuszko, murdered in October 1984.

Encouragement from Father Henryk Jankowski.

Lech Wałęsa with Pope John Paul II in Rome, early in 1981.

V for Victory!

Stamps from the underground.

Mary Craig with Lech Wałęsa at his home in May 1984.

The whole family in 1981. There have been two additions to the family since, both girls.

inherited their parents' privileges. Corruption was rife among them. In this Polish People's Republic, Edward Gierek's friend, TV and radio boss, Maciej Szczepański, was a walking legend by reason of his extravagant lifestyle. He cruised round Warsaw in a huge BMW (he was said to have eight cars), and crossed Poland in his private plane. He had a luxury flat, a sheep farm, a mountain retreat stocked with valuable antique furniture and plentifully supplied with call-girls, and enough ready cash to present Gierek with 5,000 dollars' worth of gifts on his sixty-fifth birthday. He had a yacht and a private cinema complete with nine hundred pornographic films. All that, plus a Swiss bank account. Szczepański was unique, but the corruption was general. "When I grow up," wrote a schoolgirl in a report on children's ambitions organised by the newspaper, *Polityka*, "I want to join the police and have a Rolls Royce." And a schoolboy contributed: "I shall be in the militia and have a house and a Mercedes."

Ideology, and whatever idealism had accompanied it, was absolutely dead. But the regime had to go on using the jargon for the sake of holding on to power. They clung to the rule-book, to the Marxist–Leninist theory, which enabled them to keep the reins in their hands. But it could only express itself as a lie. As everything got worse, so did the government hasten to assert that everything was for the best in the best of all possible worlds. Words like "crisis" or "strike" were taboo. The "propaganda of success" was mandatory. The television evening news was derisorily known as "the prosperity hour", and a TV series which set out to show that life in People's Poland was markedly superior to life in the capitalist West met with the contempt it deserved. Newspapers were still trumpeting of achievements even as the walls were caving in.

The joyous euphoria of the Pope's visit had vanished, but the memory of the pentecostal spirit it had aroused lingered on. It was kept alive not only by the Church but by the efforts of KOR, the Young Poland Movement, the Flying University and other dissident groups. There was a general acknowledgment of the disastrous gulf between society at large and the Party. A questionnaire printed and distributed by the private (KOR) publishing house, Nowa, revealed that the public no longer believed anything their masters told them, not even the bad news. There was an overwhelming contempt for the Party structures which claimed to represent the people, and an overwhelming demand for honesty and openness after years of living with official lies and "double-speak".

Leszek Kołakowski, exiled to the West, claimed that this mendacity had not come about by accident. It was the very essence of the Communist system:

> Mendacity is the immortal soul of Communism. They cannot get rid of it. The gap between reality and the façade is so enormous that the lie has become a sort of normal and natural way of life . . . Because Communism lives on inevitably impossible promises; because its legitimacy is based upon expectations which necessarily will not be fulfilled . . . In order to keep this legitimacy principle alive, they have to keep the mendacious façade, without which they'd fall apart. It is perhaps the most oppressive part of life under Communism. Not terror, not exploitation, but the all-pervading lie, felt by everybody, known to everybody. It is something which makes life intolerable . . .[7]

Whether the government allowed the word "crisis" or not, crisis was confronting them. There was a general feeling that the coming storm would be the biggest yet. Kuroń knew that it was not the dissidents who would provoke it. Only the workers, if they were united and determined enough, would have the power to do so.

In February 1980, Gierek admitted to the Party Congress that the economic situation was out of hand. He tried a change of Prime Minister. The new man, Babiuch, went on TV in early July and told the workers that things were going to get even worse. He did not, in so many words, announce that prices would go up, but it amounted to the same thing when he said that all better-quality meat would be diverted from the state shops (cheap but empty-shelved) to the "commercial" shops (expensive but full).

If the government hoped that the people would be too much absorbed in their summer holiday plans to notice, they could not have been more wrong. And it would be from Gdańsk that the knell would sound for Edward Gierek as it had for his predecessor, Gomułka.

In that city, feelings were already running high. The Young Poland Movement had organised another rally to mark the anniversary of 3rd May, and two of its members had been arrested as they addressed the crowds. A summary court had sentenced them to three months' imprisonment each. (Others, including Lech Wałęsa, who had been distributing leaflets, were detained for forty-eight hours.) Throughout May, daily prayer services were held for the release of the two men. In July, a higher court quashed the sentence and the two were released. But June had already brought a different kind of trouble, when, as the result of an explosion in the Lenin shipyards, eight people died and sixty were injured. There was deep anger among the shipyard workers, and Anna Walentynowicz, who had never ceased to campaign for better safety precautions, stepped up her demands for protective clothing and for less dangerous methods of operation. On 9th July, after thirty years at the Gdańsk shipyards, she was fired, on the grounds of being "too often wilfully absent from work". In her own words:

> The clerk who dismissed me said: "Anna, it's terrible what they're doing. I had to take two pills before I could bring myself to give you your cards." I replied: "Then why have you done it?" "They'll sack me if I don't do as they ask," she said, "and then someone else would come in and do it." "And what if the next person wouldn't do it either? And the next? And then the next? They couldn't sack you all, could they? . . ."[8]

The action was still off-stage, but a new and infinitely more dangerous stage of the Polish Revolution was in the making.

1 Adam Michnik, *Kościół, Lewica, Dialog*. Instytut Literacki, Paris, 1977.
2 Kazimierz Brandys, *A Warsaw Diary 1978 – 1981*, Chatto & Windus, 1984.
3 *Book of Lech Wałesa*, *op. cit.*, Chapter 1.
4 From Neal Ascherson's introduction to the above.
5 *Notatki Gdańskie*, *op. cit.*
6 *Poland in Perspective*, *op. cit.*
7 Leszek Kołakowski, *The Eagle and the Small Birds – The Eclipse of Ideology*.
8 Jean Offrédo, *Lech Wałesa Czyli Polskie Lato*, *op. cit.*

PART TWO

SOLIDARITY – AND AFTER 1980–1985

15 THE CROSS, THE EAGLE AND THE STATUE OF LENIN (AUGUST 1980)

Give over telling us you're sorry,
What guilt for past mistakes you carry;
Look in our faces, weary slaves,
Grey and exhausted like our lives.

Give over calling us the foe
Of all society, of our brother;
Just count our numbers, and you'll know
How strongly we can help each other.

Give over making us eat lies
With lowered heads and tight-shut eyes,
And for our culture, wait before
One vast, monopolistic store.

Stop prising us apart with wedges
Of conduct marks and privileges,
Suppressing facts that do not fit,
And stewing history down to shit.

Put back our words to what they mean.
Words which are empty and obscene,
So we can live with dignity
And work in solidarity.

Give over telling us you're sorry,
What guilt for past mistakes you carry,
Look at our mothers and our wives,
Grey and exhausted, like our lives.

The Twenty Second Demand: anonymous verses circulating during the strike at Gdańsk in August 1980. From a collection of young strikers' poems, published unofficially.[1]

"It was bad enough that there was next to nothing in the shops. But to raise the *price* of nothing took the people over the top."[2]

Ordinary life had become a struggle for mere survival, and Polish women foraged, as animals did, for food for their young.

The first strikes broke out in Warsaw, and the government dealt with them one at a time, forbidding the official media to refer to them. This attempt to keep the workers isolated and ignorant was rudely shattered by KOR who again began monitoring the strikes and telling the world about them. Accordingly, the Polish people heard what was happening by courtesy of Radio Free Europe and the BBC Polish Language Service. Then the whole country seemed to erupt in a rash of strikes, the most serious being that of the Lublin railway-workers who disrupted the lines to the Soviet Union, along which much-needed Polish food supplies were being siphoned off for the 1980 Moscow Olympics. None of this, however, discouraged Edward Gierek from setting off for his annual pilgrimage-cum-holiday in the Soviet Union on 8th August.

Successful revolutions, Lenin once said, are made when popular discontent coincides with a loss of self-confidence within the ruling regime. That collision was at hand. It is fascinating to speculate at what precise moment the routine rumblings about the high cost of food became something qualitatively different: a struggle for the nation's soul with a corrupt and discredited regime. What occurred was spontaneous combustion, an irresistible bush-fire which enveloped everyone in its benign flames. The silent majority, who had for so long been coerced into clapping, cheering and voting to order like so many sheep, found their voice at last. All over the country, Poles were declaring themselves ready to stand up and be counted. Not just for the sake of bread, but for freedom and justice.

The main fire was ignited in Gdańsk, where as yet there had been no strike. And the match that set the tinder alight was Anna Walentynowicz, the crane-driver granny, the "Mother Courage of the Shipyards".[3]

At a gathering of "oppositionists" in Gdańsk on 9th August, the possibility of a strike over the reinstatement of Anna Walentynowicz and Lech Wałęsa was discussed. Wałęsa was present. "See that little chap over there in the corner," someone explained, "that's Wałęsa." "Wałęsa?" said someone else. "Oh yes, isn't he the little guy who sings the national anthem at the top of his voice and out of tune?"[4] He was also the guy who, on the night of 1st August, had been arrested for delivering pro-strike leaflets, just as Danuta was about to give birth to their sixth child, Anna. Danuta had screamed in protest, loud enough to waken the whole block, but the police took Lech away in spite of her. Anna was born at 3 a.m., and Lech was allowed home at 10 a.m. He was not a man to bear grudges, but the humiliation of that night went deep.

Just before dawn on 14th, the Free Trades Unions group smuggled a pile of posters into the shipyard, demanding the reinstatement of Anna Walentynowicz and a thousand złoty rise. The early shift-workers were doubtful at first, but gradually they became more determined to fight. A crowd gathered, work came to a halt. A few wild spirits suggested taking to the streets, but memories of the 1970 carnage were still raw among the older workers, and wiser counsels prevailed.

Nevertheless, a dangerous situation was in the making. The director of the shipyard climbed on to a bulldozer truck and promised that if the men returned to work, something could be arranged. They were wavering, unsure of what they really wanted. And then a stocky little man, with quick, darting eyes, in a jacket far too big for him, climbed on to the bulldozer's roof and towered above the director. "Remember me?" he shouted. "I gave ten years to this shipyard; but you sacked me four years ago. I'm here to tell you we don't believe your lies any more."

Indeed, the director remembered. That flat, foxy face, that flowing moustache that looked as if it had been stuck on, the Charlie Chaplin walk. It was Lech Wałęsa who stood there, tense with the accumulated anger of a decade, and already declaring an occupation-strike by the workers. Minutes earlier he had been helped over the twelve-foot high perimeter fence, in order to be "in the right place, with the right ideas, at the right time".[5]

Why had Wałęsa chosen to act as he did? Because, as he would later tell a French journalist,[6] he had a score to settle. His arrest at the moment of Anna's birth rankled, though his bitterness was directed less against the men who had arrested him than against the system which forced them to act with such heartless insensitivity: "They were only carrying out someone else's stupid orders. It was not their fault but the system's. So when I heard there was trouble at the shipyard, I knew I had to go there and start changing things. So that my children don't go on being humiliated; so that they may have access to the truth."

Some of the men who clustered round that bulldozer had no idea who Wałęsa was. But a great many of them remembered him from his shipyard days and knew that fast-talking and truculent though he might be, he was a fundamentally decent man who had already suffered much for his genuine devotion to the workers' interests. They knew he was to be trusted, and so, if he declared an occupation-strike, they would go along with it. Lech, for his part, had taken the lesson of 1970 to heart. No more marches for him, no more street demonstrations, no more attacks on Party buildings, no more shouting of anti-Soviet slogans. Such activities played right into the government's hands and provoked bloody reprisals. Far better to stay in the place of work and cease production.

Immediately he set about forming a strike committee and arranging for negotiations with management to begin. Although he seemed perfectly relaxed and affable, once the discussions began he revealed a steely determination. On his instructions, the director's car was sent to bring Anna Walentynowicz in style to the shipyard. When Anna arrived and was given a bunch of flowers, and saw the banners demanding her reinstatement, she had difficulty in holding back the tears.

Wałęsa gave the director a list of five demands: the reinstatement of Anna and himself; a pay rise; an increase in the family allowance; a promise of immunity for strikers; and a monument to the victims of December 1970, forty metres high. In vain did the startled director protest that the area chosen by Wałęsa for his monument was already earmarked for a new hospital, a supermarket and a car park. In vain did he suggest that perhaps a plaque . . . A monument, insisted Wałęsa. And the director reluctantly caved in.

Thoroughly alarmed by events in the shipyard, the government (in the continued absence of Gierek) cut the telephone links between Gdańsk and the outside world. (When challenged about this, one government spokesman blamed the lack of contact on a storm which had disrupted the lines from Warsaw!) But by Saturday, the strike was already running out of steam, as the director was flatly refusing to negotiate on any other issue than the pay increase. He offered a raise, and threw in the reinstatement of Anna and Lech as a bonus. The question of the monument had already been agreed. Lacking Wałęsa's wider vision, and against his advice, a majority on the strike committee was ready to take what was on offer. It was all over bar the shouting. About half the striking workers had already left the shipyard, and the relieved director was actually announcing the end of the strike over the works radio when, all of a sudden, the whole picture changed.

What happened was this: following the shipyard workers' example and relying on their powerful support, a number of other concerns like Gdańsk Transport, the Gdynia shipyard and several other enterprises large and small, had also withdrawn their labour. They sent delegates to the Lenin shipyard to see how things were going. When they saw that the strike was fizzling out, their dismay knew no bounds. Transport workers seized the microphone outside the conference hall and protested that they had been betrayed. The woman leader of the tramdrivers, Henryka Krzywonos, cried out: "If you abandon us now, we are lost. Buses can't face tanks."

Wałęsa, leaving the conference hall, was barracked by an angry crowd of workers. In a moment, he sized up the situation and made a lightning decision. "What do you mean?" he asked. "We *are* striking, aren't we?" Promptly commandeering an electric trolley, he drove round the shipyard, shouting through a loud-hailer to drown the voice of the director telling the workers to leave the place forthwith. Fewer than one thousand workers were still there; most of them did as Lech asked, and stayed put. Some of those who were already leaving ignored Lech's appeal, but some turned round and went back in.

Had the moment of confrontation arrived? Would the tanks roll, the security forces move on to the attack? For the men in the shipyard, it was an anxious time. But their numbers began to grow almost immediately, as soon as it became known that though the old strike was over, a new, inter-factory solidarity strike was beginning, with about twenty factories from the Gdańsk area taking part. Significantly, among the strikers at this early stage there was also a small group of non-manual workers from the Young Poland Movement.

Dropping those cautious spirits who had been ready to give in without a struggle, the new strike committee embraced men and women who were concerned with more than the satisfaction of immediate needs. With Andrzej Gwiazda and his wife, Joanna; Anna Walentynowicz; Bogdan Lis and Lech Wałęsa on board, it was hardly surprising when the strike committee scrapped the old list of five demands and replaced it by a new set of twenty-one. It was significant that, though these certainly included the wage rises and demands for a shorter working week common to strikers everywhere, those particular issues did not have top priority. Like a gallant David arming his puny sling for the unequal struggle with Goliath, the committee set forth its ideals, stating in its manifesto: "The workers are not fighting merely for a pittance for themselves, but for justice for the entire nation. We have to oppose the authorities' attempts to break up the unity of our strike movement. We must live up to the words, Man Is Born Free."

Independent trades unions; the right to strike with impunity; freedom of speech and a curb on censorship; access of all denominations to the mass media; reinstatement of workers who had been sacked for taking part in earlier strikes; the release of political prisoners; and a ban on all measures directed against freedom of conscience. These were the issues, the freedoms taken for granted in the West, which had pride of place in the Gdańsk workers' list. They demanded also an overhaul of the economy, and a guarantee that in future managers would be selected for their skills and not for their readiness to toe the Party line.

Taken as a whole, the demands reflected the nation's overwhelming frustration over food shortages, poor medical care, long waiting-lists for houses, cars, fridges; and with the scandalous inequalities which flourished in this supposedly classless society. They were the fruit of all the broken promises of the past, and the disillusionment of a generation whose legitimate hopes had been consistently thwarted. The workers were demanding not just more bread, but an end to the humiliating lies and half-truths with which they had always been fobbed off. "Better the bitter truth than a sugar-coated lie," one of them said. "Sweets are for children. We are adults."

On Sunday 17th August, Father Henryk Jankowski, from the nearby church of St Brigid's, celebrated Mass for about seven thousand workers on a makeshift altar erected by the workers themselves just inside Number Two Gate. "The workers took on the government," said the BBC's Tim Sebastian, "and claimed God on their side."[2] Father Jankowski, tall, ruddy-complexioned, "with a strong voice and the carriage of a retired colonel",[7] would become a familiar figure to the strikers and to Wałęsa, whom he had only recently met. It was Father Jankowski who gave Lech the lapel badge of the Virgin of Częstochowa, which he wore throughout the strike and continues to wear to this day, though he has long forgotten who gave it to him. Lech, in his turn, asked the priest to look after his family, if anything should happen to him.

As the strikers knelt with bowed heads at Mass, many of them must have felt the fear which the priest later acknowledged: "I had seen what happened in 1970, and I was scared. So sure was I that they'd start shooting, I had a New Testament in my hip pocket as I said Mass. We were commemorating the 1920 Miracle of the Vistula that day – and at the end of it, when we were all still alive, I felt we'd lived through the 1980 Miracle of the Baltic."

It was, however, with no visible sign of fear that Father Jankowski blessed a rough wooden cross made by the workers. And with a growing sense that he had been born for this hour, Lech Wałęsa took the cross on his shoulders and, placing it on the spot intended for the Monument, cemented it into place. That night a sheet of paper decorated with a ribbon in the Polish colours and a picture of the Virgin Mary was nailed to the cross. On it was inscribed a new version of some lines by Byron:

> For Freedom's battle once begun,
> Bequeath'd by bleeding Sire to Son,
> Though baffled oft is ever won.

Now, however, to underline that there was to be no more shedding of blood, the word "bleeding" had been omitted. For years, the regime had imposed its will by violence and fear. But violence and fear did not figure in the programme of the Gdańsk strikers.[8]

The numbers inside the shipyard gates had grown to two thousand. As the director made a last, hopeless attempt to insist over the radio that the strike was over, he must have realised that, on the contrary, with that Mass and that cross, it was entering a new and even more dangerous phase.

It was now that, as if by magic, the whole of society swung its weight behind the strikers, as though they were carrying the hopes and fears of the entire nation. "People came from the city," remembers Wałęsa, "by bicycle or on foot; they baked and cooked and carried food and cigarettes. As the news spread, horse carts began arriving at the docks, loaded with potatoes, cabbages, cheese and apples. There was even a cart-load of pigs! . . . Taxis cruised round, offering transport to anyone who was bringing food to the strikers."[9]

"We were all friends. We were together at last," was how many people described the prevailing atmosphere.

Communication with families was only through the railings by the gates. As food was passed in, a team of women prepared it in a hastily improvised strike kitchen. The self-discipline over food and drink was impressive. The workers too had learned from 1970, and would not dissipate their strength in drunkenness. Right from the start the strike committee banned alcohol, and the ban was rigorously adhered to throughout the whole Baltic region – as foreign journalists discovered to their cost. Pickets checked baskets of food for hidden bottles, and emptied their alcoholic contents over the ground. Given Poland's dire reputation for alcoholism, this was something of a miracle in itself. There was a powerful feeling of "We are in our own house and we must behave ourselves." The feeling extended even to swearing and dirty stories. One man who used the Polish equivalent of a four-letter word remembers how "unclean" he suddenly felt!

A song of the moment spoke of:

> those days full of hope,
> filled with talk and heated argument,
> of the nights we hardly slept
> and our hearts that beat so strongly;
> of those who suddenly felt that at last
> they had really come home.

The gates were ablaze with colour, festooned with red, white and gold flowers, bedecked with pictures of the Pope and of the Virgin Mary. Symbols such as the Polish flag – the use of which was allowed only on official occasions – and the Polish eagle made a dramatic reappearance. (At first, it was the crowned "royal" eagle of pre-war Poland, but later, to show that they had no political intentions, the workers sawed the crown off!) Posters and banners appeared all over the shipyard, carrying excerpts from the poetry and song of Poland's heroic past. A number of them bore the words of a song popular during the 1830 November Uprising: "Farewell, my lass, our country calls me from your side." The sun shone and voices over the loudspeaker system reinforced the carnival atmosphere with their non-stop requests: "Will Mr Tadeusz C. please come to Gate Three where his family's waiting. Mr Wojciech G., your sister is at Gate Two. Please don't keep your families waiting, gentlemen. Mietek K., your mother is at Gate Two with your tablets."

And so on. Strikers slept where they could – on the grass, on stone floors, on air-beds, on table-tops, or stretched out on sheets of polystyrene. The fine dry weather made it as much an adventure as a test of endurance.

As each group of new arrivals from other factories came to join in, they were clapped and cheered. By Tuesday, two hundred and fifty factories and firms were taking part, and as their delegates deliberated at long tables groaning under bottles of pop, mugs of tea, flowers and tape-recorders, they stood the debris on the base of the lifesize statue of Lenin, sharing its pre-eminence now with a large crucifix and the Polish flag.

Each evening the delegates returned to their own workplaces with a cassette of the day's discussions. But first, there was Mass at five o'clock. Lech Wałęsa, round his neck a rosary given him by an old woman at the gate, was always there, singing lustily along with the choir of strikers. It gave him strength, he said. "I fear nothing and nobody, only God." At moments of great tension throughout the strike period, he would draw aside to pray. Nor was he alone in this profound religious feeling. With time on their hands, many of the strikers were recalling the ethical and moral values in which they had been reared, and which they had largely abandoned. Father Jankowski worked overtime, hearing confessions.

Lech Wałęsa was the hero of the hour. It was a collective leadership, not a one-man show; but it was his finger that felt the pulse of the strikers. He responded to them with a rare awareness, showing an intuitive grasp of their feelings and needs. The chemistry between the strikers and this emerging "tribune of the people" was like an electric impulse. Not for nothing, said a reporter, was Wałęsa a first-class electrician "who senses currents and can master powerful forces".

Each evening, as he was hoisted on top of the gates to give a run-down of the day's debates, several thousand people chanted LESZ-EK! or WAŁ-ĘS-A! Spontaneous, unconventional, profoundly charismatic, speaking a language they could understand, cracking slightly off-key jokes, he aroused the affection and trust of them all. He was friendly, he was funny, he was a bit of a card. When spirits were low, he tried to raise them, with a mixture of rapid comedian's patter and the harmless vulgarity of the street urchin. "My wife will be furious when she finds out what I've been up to," he clowned. "I already have six children. I guess I'll have to give her a seventh."

When he was sure he had them, there in the hollow of his hand, he would smooth down his thick hair and pat that grotesque moustache; up would shoot both arms, fists tightly clenched in joyous greeting. As he left them, his fingers would spread into the "V" sign.[10]

It was all a far cry from the grey, colourless officialdom to which they were accustomed. He was everything the grey men were not. "I am not your master, I am your servant," he would proclaim. And as he was no demagogue, but palpably one of themselves, they took his word for it. His colleagues within the presidium (the "cabinet" of fifteen which had been chosen to negotiate with whatever team the government might send along) might complain that he was moody, truculent and morose. But out there he was in his true element.

Five hundred firms were represented in the shipyard now. Gierek (who had finally returned from his visit to the Crimea) broadcast once again on TV his shopworn mix of confession, sympathy, and exhortation. Strikes don't solve anything, go back to work – for Poland's sake. The familiar cliches evoked hollow laughter. No one this time felt like shouting "POMOŻEMY". "I think I've seen this before," says a studio electrician in Tom Stoppard's *Squaring the Circle*. "Typical bloody August," agrees his companion ". . . Nothing but repeats."[11]

At about the same time, the chief leader-writer of the Party's *Tribune of the People* issued a dire warning to the Gdańsk strikers: *The Soviet Union is running out of patience. There is a limit which no one must exceed.*

The message was clear: go back to work, or the Soviet Union will intervene directly. It was a lamentable admission that Socialism in Poland could be justified to the workers only in terms of a Soviet military threat. The Polish Party, the "power", had forfeited the people's respect and lost its power even to arouse their fear. One third of the workers were under the age of twenty-five and better-equipped than their predecessors to ask awkward questions and demand answers. They had not lived through the Nazi Occupation nor experienced the Stalinist Terror. They were well-educated, under-employed, disillusioned and alienated. They saw the system for what it was – a hollow sham, dependent for its very existence on lies. The desire for truth exploded. "We've had enough of years of lies," said the workers. "Now we want to clean up the mess."[12]

They did not hate Gierek, but they hated the system which bred him and his like. And the brash little electrician from Gdańsk spoke for all of them when he cried out to an unresponsive TV screen: "But what has any of that to do with us? We have our list of demands, and we shall wait for the government to come to us and discuss them."

[1] Quoted by Neal Ascherson, in *The Polish August*, *op. cit.*

[2] Tim Sebastian, *BBC TV, A Year in Poland*, 21.7.81.

[3] Tim Garton Ash, *The Polish Revolution: Solidarność,* Chapter 1: "Inside the Lenin Shipyard" Jonathan Cape, 1983, Coronet, 1985.

[4] A. Pawlak and M. Terlecki, *Każdy Z Was Jest Wałęsa*, *op. cit.*

[5] Denis Macshane, *Solidarity*: *Poland's Independent Trade Union*, Spokesman Press, 1981.

[6] Jean Offrédo, *Lech Wałesa Czyli Polskie Lato*, *op. cit.*
[7] Jerzy Surdykowski, *Notàtki Gdańskie*, *op. cit.*
[8] Walter Brolewicz, *My Brother, Lech Wałesa*, Robson, 1984.
[9] *The Book of Lech Wałesa*, Chapter 5 *op. `cit.*
[10] *The Book of Lech Wałèsa*, Chapter 3 *op. cit.*
[11] Tom Stoppard, *Solidarność: Squaring the Circle*. Faber & Faber, 1984.
[12] *Robotnicy 80*, film from Polish Film School, 1980.

16 THE FAMILY WE CALL POLAND (1980–81)

Żeby Polska była Polska
So that Poland may be Poland

Refrain of the theme song of Solidarity

And the mountain *did* go to Mohammed: on Saturday 23rd August, 1980, Edward Gierek, after a couple of half-hearted attempts, sent a really competent negotiator, Mieczysław Jagielski, a Deputy Prime Minister responsible for economic affairs.

It was high time. Other industrial cities had followed where Gdańsk had led and set up inter-factory committees of their own. There was one in Szczecin, another in Elbląg. And smaller strikes were continuing to break out in the rest of the country.

One of the KOR advisers in Gdańsk had started up a strike bulletin and called it *Solidarity*, after the word which was constantly on Lech Wałęsa's lips. The first issue of twenty thousand copies sold out immediately. In 1970 the intellectuals had failed to support the workers; in 1976 they came in time to pick up the pieces. But in 1980, they were there right from the start.

Since telephone links with Warsaw were still cut, it was Radio Free Europe which informed the strikers that a group of distinguished academics had addressed an Appeal to the authorities, supporting the strikers' claims and urging the authorities to avoid bloodshed. Late on Friday 22nd, two of the signatories, Tadeusz Mazowiecki, editor of the liberal Catholic weekly, *LINK*, and the mediaevalist professor, Bronisław Geremek, came in person to Gdańsk and gave Lech Wałęsa a copy of the Appeal. "Thank you," said Wałęsa bluntly, "but actions are better than words." "What sort of actions?" asked Mazowiecki, somewhat surprised by this reception. "Well, for a start," replied Wałęsa, "we need experts to help us deal with the government negotiators. We are only workers, after all."

Mazowiecki needed no further invitation. Next day he returned to Gdańsk with a six-man group of advisers, which included Geremek, and the bearded historian, Bohdan Cywiński. "When I arrived," says the latter, "I saw this little man with the moustache, but I'd no idea he was the boss. Yet it soon became clear that what *he* said was what counted." "How long do you intend to stay?" asked Wałęsa. "Till the end, no matter how it turns out," Mazowiecki replied. The answer pleased Lech, and, although some members of the strike committee were unwilling to admit the intellectuals into what was a workers' strike, he successfully overrode them.

It was the advisers' job to check the small print on any document and make sure that the workers were not being tricked. On the other hand, they also had to present the workers' demands in a way that the government team would accept. It was a difficult task, and a round-the-clock marathon, with Wałęsa, as Cywiński recalls, a relentless taskmaster:

> Round about four in the morning, Wałęsa would push back his chair and say, "Right, we can snatch some sleep now till eight, and that will give the experts time to sort something out." Then he would hand us enough work for forty-eight hours. He never actually consulted us. He would listen, yes. But he'd always decide for himself. He never asked *whether* we should do this or that, but *how* it was to be done, and what the consequences were likely to be. And he would trust the judgment of the workers outside. When we came up with a decision, he'd go off to the main gate and tell them about it, then, as often as not, come back and say, "Sorry, they didn't like it." Then we'd have to start all over again.

On Saturday evening, Deputy Prime Minister Jagielski and his team arrived by coach. As the coach tried to edge its way into the shipyard, it was surrounded by a crowd of angry workers, who drummed on the windows and shouted "Get out and walk" and "On your knees". Wałęsa, who had come to meet the government delegation, calmed the crowd and persuaded them to let Jagielski and his men pass through. Twenty thousand pairs of hostile eyes followed them as they strode disdainfully past, to the glass-walled room at the back of the conference building where the talks were to be held. It was a bit like a fish-tank in a zoo, with hordes of workers, newspaper men, observers, photographers, peering through the glass wall. Every gesture and facial expression was visible to those outside the fish-bowl; every word was relayed by loudspeaker to the crowds outside.

> Seated on low easy chairs, the two sides faced each other over a bowl of red and white flowers on a formica-topped coffee table. Jagielski, dapper and trim-suited; Wałęsa scruffy in his usual baggy jacket and trousers. Wałęsa had, in fact, offered to stand down from the talks, in

case his reputation as a fighter should impede progress. But his colleagues had insisted that he remain.

In the rest of Poland, people who had heard about what was happening only through Radio Free Europe were beginning to wonder who this man was. Experience had taught them he might well be a Party stooge, put there to stir things up. Only when the official media began to attack him and insinuate all kinds of terrible things about him, were they reassured that he must be an honest man. The media, in fact, gave little information, referring only to "sporadic interruptions of work", or "certain breaks in production"; admissions still outweighed by the confident assertions that, under the wise guidance of the Party, Poland was "marching towards a better future".

> Yet, how it really was at that time we all know [wrote Lech Wałęsa later]. Millions of people were shedding the invisible veneer of the lie and breaking the equally invisible barrier of fear. It was repeated loudly and thousands of times. Strike! Strike! Strike! – a taboo word, a word they tried to suppress all too unsuccessfully.[1]

After a polite welcome from Wałęsa, the talks began. Without preamble, Jagielski said: "These strikes must stop"; and Wałęsa, puffing imperturbably on his pipe, replied: "They should have been stopped ages ago, but we were waiting for you. So where do you stand on our twenty-one claims?" When Jagielski answered with an expansive: "Allow me to begin by making a few general points," Wałęsa cut him short. "No, I want a solid answer, point by point." To the people outside, listening over the loudspeakers, this was a moment of pure joy. At long last they had a spokesman who would not content himself with evasive answers and the familiar meaningless slogans. Wałęsa's ability to nail Jagielski down to each consecutive point and force him to give coherent answers was one of his most distinctive and important contributions to the success of the August strike.

Nevertheless, the talks did not get off to a promising start, since Wałęsa was insisting on the release of certain KOR activists (including Kuroń and Michnik), who had been arrested since the strike began; and Jagielski refused to be drawn. Before returning to Warsaw that night, he had rejected most of the workers' twenty-one demands.

Next day, yet another Central Committee reshuffle produced a new Prime Minister, the virtually unknown Mr Pińkowski. In the upheaval, Gierek held on as First Secretary, but only by a whisker.

Monday and Tuesday (25th and 26th August) produced much the same stalemate. Jagielski refused even to discuss the matter of free trades unions. Outside, the hours of waiting seemed endless. The strikers took to writing and reciting verse, pinning their own compositions to trees and lamp-posts for all to read. They scoured the Polish classics for suitable quotations, and perhaps most popular of all were the verses which concluded Słowacki's *Hymn of the Confederates*:[2]

> Never shall we league with kings,
> Never bow our heads to force . . .

Then on Wednesday, things began to move, in more senses than one. The government rocked on its heels, when the miners of Silesia and the steelworkers of Nowa Huta not only came out on strike but set up their own inter-factory committees complete with demands. Cardinal Wyszyński chose this moment to appeal for caution and to warn that prolonged strikes could only harm the nation. Delighted with this timely intervention, the evening TV news carried carefully edited highlights of the sermon. But this was one of the times when even such devout Catholics as Lech Wałęsa felt free to disregard the Cardinal's advice.

In any case, the Cardinal's unwelcome caution was more than offset next day by a very explicit statement from the Bishops' Council, spelling out "the inalienable rights of the nation: the right to freedom of worship, to a decent existence, to truth, to daily bread, to a true knowledge of the nation's history".[3] It was a veritable litany of human rights, a gauntlet thrown down by the Church on behalf of the workers.

By Thursday 28th August, Jagielski was conceding some ground – on the liberty of the press and the right to strike. But he was still unhappy to talk about the free trades unions, an unhappiness which reflected that of his masters in Warsaw, and, still more, that of *their* masters in Moscow. The Russian bear was, in fact, positively growling with alarm.

The government was anxious at least to preserve the fable of "the leading role of the Party", which they understandably felt to be at risk. Here was a ludicrous situation: a People's Democracy, with the people on the far side of the barricades. The Politburo was agitated: some wanted an end to the strike by any means at all; others called for a "state of emergency" and for troops to be sent in to the Baltic ports. The official mass media again warned, Cassandra-like, that the situation was like that in the eighteenth century, just before Russia, Prussia and Austria moved in for the carve-up . . . Everyone understood: Prussia and Austria were not part of the present scenario. But Russia . . .![4]

According to one source,[5] the Politburo voted eight to five for military action, but the security and military chiefs would not sanction it, as they were unable to guarantee the loyalty of the troops. "I will not send my army against four hundred fortresses," the Defence Minister, General Wojciech Jaruzelski, is alleged to have said.

Jagielski did not return to the shipyard on the Friday, and the workers were afraid that he would not come back at all. Perhaps they had lost. Perhaps the security forces would move in: there were rumours of paratroopers getting ready to land in the shipyard. Memories of 1970 were never far from their minds. But their solidarity held firm. "We held on to the phrase, 'it is better to die standing than to live on our knees'," said Anna Walentynowicz. Amid the prevailing tension and the need for strong nerves, Lech Wałęsa was superb. He managed to convey some of his own calm to the crowd. "He grew in stature from one hour to the next," said Cywiński.

When tensions threatened to boil over, or spirits were low, he would start up the National Anthem – "Poland is not yet dead, so long as we are still alive" – in full throttle and completely off-key; and the religious hymn, which was almost another national anthem, "God, who protects Poland".

Wałęsa's magnetism never failed:

> It is pure, Polish magic [wrote a British journalist].[6] You know the magician has turned it on, deliberately, almost cynically. Yet as he sings he is transformed: no longer is he the feisty little electrician in ill-fitting trousers, the sharp talker with many human weaknesses; no longer does his authority derive merely from his patter and repartee; now he stands up straight, head thrown back, arms to his side, strangely rigid and pink in the face, like a wooden figure by one of the naïve sculptors from the Land of Dobrzyń where he was born.

Lech Wałęsa had true charisma. In fact his growing authority was deriving increasingly not just from his gift for oratory, but from the fact that he used words honestly, and gave them a truthfulness that years of double-speak had taken from them. Wałęsa, speaking the truth, even though his Polish was rough and ungrammatical, was offering the moral leadership for which Poland hungered.

On Saturday Jagielski came back, in jovial mood. The air had been cleared in Warsaw; a settlement was now possible. Possible, but not yet in sight. The workers had asked for immunity not only for strikers but also for their "supporters". Jagielski knew well that this meant the KOR people. In his avuncular way, he tried to drive a wedge. The "supporters" were irrelevant, he suggested. What were men like Kuroń and Michnik to such as them? An outraged Andrzej Gwiazda stood his ground, demanding either a fair trial or a release. "Are we to be defined as a police state or as a democracy?" he asked. "We do not want to live in a land forced into unity by police batons." Jagielski looked pained, but Gwiazda, Wałęsa and others continued to assert that they had a moral obligation towards those who had helped the workers in the troubles of 1976–7.

Jagielski tried to move on to safer ground, but Wałęsa pursued him like an angry terrier. If the activists were not released, he threatened, there could well be another strike after this one. Jagielski agreed to see what he could do. He was, in any case, preparing to fly back to Warsaw to consult the Central Committee. "It's Saturday," he remarked, "a lucky day." "It's Our Lady's Day," said Lech Wałęsa. "That's right," agreed the disciple of Lenin. "Our Lady's Day, when my parents always used to start the harvest." The strikers cheered ironically. Then, with a reminder from Wałęsa to "stop arresting those KOR people", he went on his way.

Next day there would be a signing. That much seemed sure. Wałęsa was carried shoulder-high to the main gate, and the workers sang the obligatory *Sto Lat* – may he live a hundred years. They were excited, scenting victory. Wałęsa chatted in a relaxed way.

> The atmosphere [recorded Bolesław Fac],[7] was more like that at a picnic than a mass rally. He was at ease. He had the crowd's attention, the sense of oneness with it, the sense of being able to prevail upon it by using exactly the right words. In a place and at a time when anyone else might have felt uneasy, he was consumed with joy. 'And now we'll all go home, take a bath and go to bed. But first let's sing the National Anthem for this country of ours. Oh – and one more thing. Let's sing a hymn to God too, because now we can't go any further without God.'

Film-maker Andrzej Wajda had arrived the previous evening, in search of a sequel for *Man of Marble*. He more than half-expected that the action had run its course and that the workers would settle for what they could get. But the atmosphere in the shipyard changed his mind: "peace, calm, something holy, sublime, extraordinary. I feel I'm witnessing a fragment of history. As a rule, history passes us by, but here I can feel it, see it, touch it."[8]

As for Wałęsa, here, felt Wajda, was the very embodiment of the literary character beloved of the Poles, Sieńkiewicz's Little Knight, "with his moustache, his sense of humour, sometimes even his melancholy; his calm in a crisis; his patriotism. A great soul in a little body."

Wałęsa's first words were: "Mr Wajda, this may be the last chance for our country," and Wajda instantly understood that the strike was more important than he had realised:

> I understood then that this matter could not be considered in the way I had thought of it before; that it must be considered in the context of our national existence, not of the victory of the Gdańsk shipyard over provincial and central authority. I suddenly realised that Wałesa had in himself a much greater sense of historic responsibility, historic importance, than I had. I was impressed by this. No matter what happens to him in future, no matter how the voters assess him, the fact will remain that at a time when nobody had yet thought this was an event of world importance, it was he who gave it that status and imparted it to all those whom he met.[8]

Wajda was in no doubt that he had found the subject for his next film. The *Man of Iron*, suitably disguised, would be Lech Wałęsa. The background would be the true history of those days.

Everyone was dashing around, signing one another's leaflets by way of souvenir and wearing stickers with the new *Solidarity* logo, with its thick red jumbly letters resembling a group of marchers with the Polish flag. "I wanted the marchers to appear to be supporting each other," said the designer, who conceived the idea on top of a crowded tram, "so that they cannot be broken up or forced away from each other."

Yet at the eleventh hour, this precious unity was threatened. The experts had worked out a face-saving formula about the Party's "leading role" *vis-à-vis* the free trades unions. But a girl now burst into the conference room and accused the presidium of betraying the workers and selling them out.[9] Uproar followed this outburst, as tension snapped and the delegates began shouting at each other. Wałęsa seized a microphone. "Listen, all of you," he shouted over the din. "We're going to have our own building, with a large sign over the door, saying IN-DE-PEND-ENT, SELF-GO-VER-NING TRADES UNIONS."

The words, which in Polish have more resonance, rolled off his tongue, and the delegates stopped to savour them. He had calmed them down, even if he had not stilled their doubts. The crucial question was asked – and answered – at the end of the day, by the serious-minded Gwiazda: "Will the new unions be totally free and independent? No written agreement can ensure that. Our only guarantee is ourselves. We know that hundreds of thousands, millions of people think like us. There we have our guarantee . . . We know that the word Solidarity will survive."

As the two teams faced each other for the last time on Sunday, 31st August, Jagielski announced that the KOR detainees were to be freed, and Wałęsa stroked his moustache with satisfaction. He began a prepared speech, in which he spoke of "a success for both sides"; then he jettisoned it in favour of a spontaneous response to this historic moment when, as he saw it – for he was a fighter who loved to make peace – former enemies had been turned into partners:

> Kochani [he said] – beloved friends. Tomorrow, 1st September, we return to work. We know what this date means to all of us. We remember 1939 and think of Poland, our motherland . . . the shared concerns of the family we call Poland. You have trusted me so far, so I beg you to trust me now. We have got all we could in the present situation. The rest we will get in time, because we now have the most important thing of all . . . our IN-DEP-END-ENT, SELF-GOV-ERN-ING TRADES UNIONS. That is our guarantee for the future. We have fought, not for ourselves nor for our own interests, but for the entire country. We have fought for all of you. And now I declare this strike to be over.

"Right to the very end," wrote a Gdańsk docker in his diary,[10] "we were afraid there would be some kind of police provocation . . . And then at last we heard Wałęsa's rough, staccato voice, so different from the smooth, monotonous, woolly speeches of the people in authority. That's why, for all its ugliness, that voice sounds beautiful."

The ecstatic applause in the hall was matched by the cheers – and the tears – of those who waited outside. Everyone rose for the National Anthem, and then the two delegations proceeded to the hall for the signing ceremony. On paper, at least, all the workers' demands had been agreed. There in the hall, flanked by Lenin, the Cross and the Polish eagle, Jagielski repeated that there were "no winners and no losers". "We have settled," he said, "as one Pole with another."

He signed,[11] and Wałesa followed suit, wielding a giant plastic ballpoint pen, tasselled and decorated with a picture of the Pope – a souvenir of the Papal visit in 1979. Then he went outside, to be hurled into the air again and again by the crowd. LESZ-EK, LESZ-EK, they chanted. He gave them the familiar impudent two-fisted salute, shaking both fists like a victorious prize-fighter. Smiling, relaxed, enjoying himself hugely. "Better this way than a long-drawn-out struggle," he said. "But the next stage will be harder, and I'm a bit afraid of it. We'll make mistakes, and there will be those who try to lead us astray. But we'll not let them."

Telling them that Mass was to be broadcast on the state radio from now on, and that the KOR prisoners were to be released, he came at last to the issue closest to his own heart:

> One thing more, even if I do sound like a dictator. I have always felt responsible for the blood that was shed in December 1970. It was partly due to my own incompetent leadership. So I want us to meet here on 16th December always, at this same place. I shall be here, even if I have to crawl on hands and knees. Remember that. And I shall always tell you the truth in this holy place. I shall tell you whether things are going well or badly for us.

He pointed with his hands to the spot where now stood the great wooden cross.

[1] From Lech Wałesa's *Afterword* to Józef Tischner, *The Spirit of Solidarity*, Harper & Row, 1982.

[2] Juliusz Słowacki was a nineteenth-century Polish Romantic poet.

[3] Tim Garton Ash, *The Polish Revolution: Solidarność*, Chapter: "Inside The Lenin Shipyard: Day 15".

[4] Jean Offrédo, *Lech Wałesa Czyli Polskie Lato*, Cana, Paris 1981.

[5] O. Halecki: *History of Poland*, chapter by Antony Polonsky, "From Kania To Jaruzelski". *op.cit.*

[6] Tim Garton Ash, as above, "Day 14".

[7] *The Book of Lech Wałesa*, *op. cit.* Chapter 2, by Bolesław Fac.

[8] As note 7, Chapter 10, interview with Andrzej Wajda.

[9] Tim Garton Ash, as above, "Day 17".

[10] *The Book*, as above, Chapter 9 – extracts from memoirs.

[11] It is typical of the way Communist regimes operate that within a year Jagielski had been demoted and consigned to political oblivion.

17 "OURS IS A MORAL REVOLUTION"

For good or for ill, it was there – in that mass which had learned to be silent and not only to be silent, but to repeat the prescribed slogans – that knowledge was preserved of what was just and what was unjust. It was they – one day in the distant future, when they had become the real owners of the smelting works, of the mines, and of the factories – who would protect with their hands the uncertain light, and without any illusions that they were discovering absolute truth.

Czesław Miłosz: *The Seizure of Power, 1955*

At last the Polish revolution had reached a more hopeful stage. During those days between the signing of the Gdańsk Agreements and the ones signed in Szczecin and with the Silesian miners at Jastrzębie,* the Polish workers were on top – and if what they had had in mind was power, they could have seized it. But their revolution was not about power, any more than it was about hatred of one class for another. The Poles' chief complaint against their rulers was that they had divided the nation against itself. They wanted to reunite society, to break down the barriers which divided Pole from Pole. The demands made by the shipyard workers and miners (the highest-paid of all workers) in August

* It appears to have escaped the attention of most of the writers and analysts of Polish affairs that the most comprehensive of all the Agreements signed during the Solidarity period was that negotiated by the students at Łódź on 19th February, 1981. This Agreement covered such sensitive areas as the banning of the activities of security services within university precincts; students' military training; university budgets and student grants; repression against the activists of the democratic opposition; the teaching of history; the independence of the judiciary from the State; the issuing of passports; the abolition of the *nomenklatura* system; the celebration of the anniversaries commemorating historical events of great significance for the Polish nation; the release of the contents of the Polish-American, Polish-French and other cultural Accords; and the abuses committed by militia and security service functionaries.

This Agreement was the basis of the subsequent law on Higher Education which revolutionised the academic world. The Law was finally repealed in 1985, after a long battle with the academics and students.

1980 gave the lie to Lenin's claim that the working classes could not raise their sights higher than their own immediate wants. Their demands were, as Wałęsa had said, not for themselves but for the nation. For lower-paid workers, for exploited women workers, for pensioners, for the sick. They had no ambitions to overthrow the government, but to make it responsive to the needs of the nation, and answerable for its own larger lunacies.

A massive charge of energy was released by the sudden explosion of hope, and the floodwaters reached even the Party. Five days after the Agreements, Gierek was swept away, with a heart-attack which merely brought forward his inevitable departure from the political scene. Stanisław Kania, a middle-of-the-road *apparatchik*, replaced him as First Secretary, and the "errors and distortions" of the Gierek era were, as was customary, blamed for the shambles Gierek had left behind. Kania made the expected carrot-and-stick broadcast on television. But this time no one was listening.

It seemed, though, that the Party too wanted to put its house in order. Within its ranks there was a noisy clamour for social reform and a more conciliatory attitude towards the workers they had so conspicuously lost. Kania adopted the workers' word *Odnowa* – renewal – and embarked on the gradual removal of many prominent figures who had long been feathering their nest at public expense.

And as the new union, INDEPENDENT AND SELF-GOVERNING, as its banners proudly proclaimed, set up shop in the Hotel Morski, a dingy Gdańsk hotel for shipyard workers and itinerant seamen, some nine hundred thousand Party members joined it. So great was the rush that Kania began to hope that the Party could place itself at the head of the new movement. But first a wedge would have to be driven between the workers and the "wreckers" and "anti-socialist elements" who were presently acting as their advisers.

Alas for Kania's hopes. When, on 17th September, a group of delegates from all the major industrial centres met in the Hotel Morski, Jacek Kuroń was there too, newly released from prison and promptly made official adviser to the new union, *Solidarity*, made up of workers grouped horizontally region by region. A provisional National Co-ordinating Commission was set up and to nobody's surprise Lech Wałęsa became its chairman. Already the new union had three million members.

As if at a hidden signal, similar self-governing unions sprang into being all over the country, taking the place of the old discredited factory branch unions. But the latter did not give way easily, and the new young unionists frequently had a bitter struggle to obtain recognition, not to mention the premises, telephones and cars they needed.

Organising and controlling these loosely knit new groups was a major headache. They came to Gdańsk for advice and reassurance, and to learn about the democratic principles they were so keen to put into practice. They marvelled that things had progressed so far in Gdańsk. Back home, they said, it was "like being behind barbed wire". One delegate from Częstochowa said that people there were paralysed with fright. "They think they are breaking the law. And the press is silent on the matter." "If you don't defend us, they'll flatten us," they told Lech Wałęsa, streaming into his office, where they usually found him sprawled in an armchair, dressed in an open-necked shirt and jeans. On the wall he had hung a large crucifix, but he knew very well that not everyone shared his enthusiasm for religion. "Religion," he said, "is my peace and my strength. I'll just say a short prayer, and that way I'll avoid a coronary. But I don't push God down anybody's throat. I don't want the unions to be churchy, just Polish."

Wałęsa had hoped to go on working at the shipyards, at least part-time, even if it meant going there by taxi. All his old employers were falling over themselves trying to get him back. But the hope was unrealistic. The union needed him to be available. When workers from other regions came, it was Lech they demanded to see. Maria, a girl who worked as a helper there, says that his door was always open, and that nobody else would do: "Right from the beginning, they wanted only him. They came to see him if they'd lost their jobs, or if they were having trouble with their marriages. And they wanted instant answers. No one gave him time to think. He was haunted by people who expected him to work miracles."

In those early days, gratitude spilled over him in cascades. The letters that poured in by the sackload ascribed every virtue to him: courage, integrity, dignity, honesty, compassion, heroism, sincerity and moral rectitude. Though a few were critical to the point of loathing, and one man expressed his intention of shooting him at the first opportunity, the majority saw him as the embodiment of all human values. They wanted him to be a saint, so they made him one. And since they had no king, they made him a king too. At a meeting of Polish writers in Warsaw, a speaker commented on the phenomenon: "When we Poles find ourselves without a king, we immediately begin to look for one. After Poniatowski[1] there was Józef Piłsudski. And now Wałęsa."

The rise from unemployed electrician to unquestioned leader of Poland and a world figure had been truly spectacular. Lech, never a modest man, was flattered by the admiration. He enjoyed being a symbol. But when this meant sitting in an office, he hated it, dreading the loss of spontaneity. He was only truly at home on a factory floor, addressing the workers in his execrable Polish, pouring out crude slang, making grammatical mistakes by the score, contradicting himself constantly, but holding his audiences spellbound by the vibrancy and truthfulness of his speech. "If you want to see what he's really like," said a friend, "go and watch him among people whose hands are as dirty as his own. That's where he's most himself."

Some of those who heard him found him too coarse, a mountebank playing to the gallery, a soapbox orator, a buffoon. A group of students in Kraków, when they heard him for the first time, wondered how such an ill-spoken lout had achieved so much; but when they heard him again they were already under his spell. He was a man of the people, a people's tribune rather than a politician. And he took care, whenever possible, to reassure the government that Solidarity had no political ambitions and should not be seen as a challenge to the "leading role of the Party" or to the system of alliances within the Soviet bloc. Solidarity, in fact, saw its role as that of a permanent loyal opposition, and was content to let the Party be seen to govern, even if only in name. In 1980 most Poles were realistic enough to understand that they could not hope to become independent either of the Party or of Soviet Russia. When an admirer compared the non-violent Wałęsa to Gandhi, Lech replied with a sigh, "Well, his geopolitical situation was simpler than ours."

The whole of society was bursting out of its straitjacket. Private farmers were organising themselves into unions; writers, journalists, teachers, students were in the vanguard of those revising their existing statutes in the search for a new honesty and freedom. As the Gdańsk manifesto had asserted, they were acting out the belief that Man Is Born Free. For the first time in thirty-five years, people began to speak freely, and to stop leading a double life.

The sheer joy and exuberance of those early weeks was described by a young woman assistant in the Warsaw (Mazowsze) branch of Solidarity, led by the charismatic young Zbigniew Bujak, and claiming one million members:

> Hundreds and hundreds of people dropped in every day, with every kind of problem, not just how to set up a factory cell, but divorce problems, housing problems, drink problems. It was chaotic, but it was wonderful, the absolute spontaneity of it all, the fantastic enthusiasm. It was like a huge love affair. We all believed in the same things, we believed desperately. And we were all very young. Older people supported us, but they couldn't cope with the sheer physical hard work, all hours of the day or night. Of course, we had the feeling of making history: we knew that, right from the start.

A volcanic eruption; an earthquake; a dam-burst; something out of the Gospels; Easter; Pentecost. The comparisons were all made, and they all attempted to express the inexpressible, the huge surge of joy and hope, that now the bad times were over, that Solidarity was the new salvation and Lech Wałęsa its Messiah. In October, in the Gdańsk market square, Wałęsa had solemnly sworn the famous oath of Kościuszko before the 1794 Uprising: "I will never abandon my country; I will serve it till the day I die." He believed that he had been chosen for this task; and his vanity was decidedly not all personal.

Solidarity was already working out plans for a better future. Its university members had set up a working-party on how to get the country back on its feet, with *ad hoc* teams discussing work safety and health safeguards; and with a flourishing publicity and counselling department. Could it have worked? Perhaps it could, if the Party had had any intention of keeping the promises it had made. "You don't understand," says a Party boss in Wajda's *Man of Iron*, "no one wins against us." And the journalist, Winkel, in the same film, reflects that though the workers had succeeded in banning alcohol during the Baltic strikes, they would find it harder to bring in the democracy they wanted. "After all, drunks don't have their own army, police and prisons; but the Party has all three," he said prophetically.

The Party's first act of sublime bad faith came in October, when the judge at Warsaw's Provincial Court refused to register Solidarity as a union, without the insertion of a clause recognising the Party's leading role and the system of alliances. Wałęsa and the Solidarity delegates were stunned at this revelation that the judges were still mouthpieces of the Party; and that the Party appeared to be backing out of its promises. The court's action destroyed any belief they might have had in the goodwill of the authorities. It not only increased their resentment but also made it harder for Wałęsa to get his conciliatory line accepted within the union. From this time forward, a new radicalisation of Solidarity was in prospect.

Although Wałęsa was standing firm on the registration issue, he was already considered by many to be too cautious, too ready to seek a compromise; the other union leaders watched him warily. Passions were running high, and a nationwide strike was threatened for 12th November, if Solidarity was not registered by then. The country prepared itself mentally for a showdown.

It was the Party which offered an olive branch: they invited a Solidarity delegation to come to Warsaw for talks. Interpreting this as a sign of weakness, Solidarity immediately raised the stakes, demanding not only to keep their statutes unchanged, but reviving four issues from the summer accords on which no progress had been made. These were: access to the mass media; immediate pay rises; an increased flow of goods to the shops; and an end to the oppression of KOR and other oppositionists. As for an independent union for the peasant farmers, which Solidarity was also demanding, it was unthinkable. Peasants, as private producers, were not eligible to form a trade union at all, let alone a self-governing one. On all these issues, therefore, the government stayed reproachfully silent. But they promised action on the statutes. Unwilling to trust them, Solidarity continued its plans for a strike. And to make an already tense situation even tenser, on 2nd November, All Souls' Day, a large crowd in Warsaw held an open air public service for the victims of Katyń.

The Supreme Court found a compromise solution regarding the statutes; and the tension eased. Wałęsa diplomatically said once again that there were no winners and no losers, but Solidarity on the whole believed it had won a victory. The strike was called off and the nation switched over to a celebratory mood. Wałęsa was guest of honour at a special festival of song and poetry at the Warsaw Opera House. DON'T BE AFRAID; THE NATION IS WITH YOU, said one of the many waving banners. And the nation heard for the first time the song which would become the theme song of Solidarity, the haunting *Żeby Polska była Polska* – so that Poland may be Poland. Or, as some preferred to sing, "so that Poland may be Polish". In the Polish language, it was only a question of adding or removing a final accent.

"My wish," echoed Wałęsa, in a speech later that week, "is that Poland may be Poland; that hope may be real hope, and that all men may be brothers." But hope was already dented, and mistrust of the government's good faith was universal. As the demands for change everywhere came up against a brick wall, the workers began taking matters into their own hands and using the only method that had proved to be effective. After the registration crisis was over, Wałęsa suggested that there was no further need for these wildcat strikes; but they did not cease. In fact the crisis seemed to have triggered more of them, as workers sought to remedy their own specific grievances and rid themselves of their own corrupt and over-privileged officials.

Wałęsa and the other Solidarity leaders found themselves darting from one place to another, putting out the fires of discontent. "No one can deal with the unexpected twenty-four hours a day," grumbled Lech. But that was precisely what they did. Lech travelled the country in a little white Polski Fiat (with an ex-shipyard worker as his bodyguard and driver), catching up on sleep as he went, or listening to rock concerts on Radio Free Europe. His sense of mission was urgent. Face to face with the workers, his magic usually worked, as he tried to calm their growing thirst for revenge and retribution: "Let us forgive one another. Everyone is guilty to some extent. If there was something to take, we took it. It was the rules that were wrong. No one gives up his comfortable armchair without a fight."

And again: "We can't put all the corrupt officials in prison. After all, who would pay for their keep?"

He warned against the dangers of individuals, punch-drunk with freedom, carrying on their personal vendettas against corrupt managers and union leaders. His political antennae told him that this business of settling scores, however understandable, could easily get out of hand and lead to that most dreaded of all evils, civil war. "Let us be human and everything will be all right," he insisted. He believed in reconciliation wherever possible: "I am a believer, which is why I forgive blindly. I can be having a real go at someone, and then all at once I see standing opposite me another human being. Perhaps he acted as he did unwittingly? Maybe my arguments were wrong? I don't believe in other people's badness, only in my own inability to convince them."

Many of the disputes could have been solved by patience and diplomacy. But the workers had run out of patience, and they were low on trust. Wałęsa would later regret that Solidarity did not set out at the beginning to "educate the people". "We should have explained things to them," he said, "and brought them up to a certain common level of agreement." The failure to do this would cost Solidarity – and the whole nation – dear.

The next major crisis followed hard on the heels of the previous one, and while the forest fires were still raging. Solidarity's Warsaw office had got hold of a document from the Public Prosecutor's Office, which outlined tactics for the elimination of "illegal anti-Socialist activity". They were stung by this further illustration of Party bad faith. When police broke into the Solidarity office on the evening of 19th November and arrested Jan Narożniak, a young mathematician helping in the printing section, Solidarity's anger was intense. Zbigniew Bujak, the young Warsaw chairman, threatened a regional strike unless Narożniak was released immediately. For good measure, he threw in five other demands, including one for the investigation of police brutality in 1970 and 1976, and for an overall investigation into the activities of the police and security services. Not only the government was shocked by such demands, which struck at the very roots of the sacred security apparatus on which the Party rested. The more moderate Solidarity leaders like Wałęsa were also shocked. The advisers were shocked. And most importantly, the Soviet Union was shocked.

Alarmed not only by this frontal onslaught on Marxism–Leninism, but also by the possibility of a rail strike which would endanger its routes into East Germany where it had twenty armed divisions, the Soviet Union moved to surround Poland to the north and east. A poignant notice appeared in the window of a Warsaw travel agency: VISIT THE SOVIET UNION BEFORE THE SOVIET UNION VISITS YOU.

It was a cliff-hanger. With only eight hours to go till the strike, and with twenty Warsaw factories already striking, Jan Narożniak was released. But the Warsaw workers refused to call off their action until an assurance was given them, on television, that the investigation into police behaviour would take place. (Though why they should have believed any such assurance on TV is a mystery.)

A cooling-off period was badly needed. Although the strikes had been called off, the Soviet threat remained. It became known that at a December 1980 summit meeting in Moscow, the Warsaw Pact comrades had promised in their final communiqué that the Polish people could rely on their "fraternal solidarity and support" – a nasty threat that was scarcely even veiled. And though the Polish Church was making conciliatory noises towards the authorities (far too conciliatory for some), the belief gained ground – and later became certainty – that Karol Wojtyła had sent a letter to Brezhnev, assuring him that Poland "will help itself" and would manage its own affairs. This letter, which assured Brezhnev of the Church's willingness to continue as mediator, was of crucial importance.

Few people are in a position to know whether the Russians really intended to invade just then, or to what extent these were signals of their desperation. However, all the evidence available would strongly suggest that the threat was more than just an empty one; and it was taken seriously by both the Pope and Wyszyński on the one hand and by the Polish regime on the other. The Pope's intervention seems to have been crucial in avoiding a very major international conflict in the centre of Europe.[2]

The threat from the fraternal comrade to the east, whether real or imagined, had a sobering effect on all sections of Polish society. Subsequently, a joint government/Church commission in December agreed that unity was a top priority, "regardless of differences in world outlook or political views". The Polish bishops appealed to the people to work for the process of renewal and for the "rebuilding of mutual trust".

With Russian warships in all probability only forty miles away on the other side of the Bay of Gdańsk, a new spirit of reconciliation was in evidence on 16th December, as senior members of the government and the armed forces stood in driving icy sleet, with foreign diplomats, bishops, clergy and one hundred and fifty thousand ordinary Poles, to unveil the long-awaited memorial to those who had died in December 1970. On this tenth anniversary, it seemed as if the ghosts of December were at last reconciling the nation. In a three-hour ceremony specially devised by Andrzej Wajda, who was filming a sequence for *Man of Iron*, one of Poland's leading actors read out a roll-call of the twenty-eight officially admitted dead, and paid tribute to "those whose names we do not know". As each name was called, the crowd solemnly intoned, "He is with us still."

Lech Wałęsa, who had for many years worked towards this moment, had begged the people beforehand to welcome every guest, no matter how unpopular. Then he made the worst speech of his career (he was never good with scripted material; a critic remarked that he read aloud like a schoolboy stumbling over a lesson), lit a long oxy-acetylene torch, and a huge flame flared up. It illuminated the spectacular, forty-metres high monument – "we wanted it big," said a worker, "they'll have a job knocking *that* down" – with three steel crosses from each of which hung a black anchor, traditional symbol of hope, and the wartime symbol of Fighting Poland. "The crosses," explained Anna Walentynowicz, "represent the three workers' rebellions of '56, '70 and '76, the three crucified and unfulfilled hopes . . . The monument is tall, because it is a cry to heaven of the people's bitterness."

Beneath the three crosses was an eternal flame to symbolise life, and some emotive lines from the pen of Poland's greatest living poet, Czesław Miłosz, who had that year won the Nobel Prize for Literature:

> You, who wronged a simple man,
> Bursting into laughter at the crime,
> And kept a crowd of fools around you,
> Mixing good and evil to blur the line.
> Though everyone bowed down before you,
> Saying Virtue and Wisdom lit your way,
> Striking gold medals in your honour
> – And glad to have survived another day,
> Do not feel safe. The poet remembers.
> You can slay him, but another is always born . . .
> The words are written down, the deed, the date.
> You would have done better with a winter's dawn,
> A rope, and a branch bent down beneath your weight.

In Wajda's film, Maciek kneels at the spot where his father had been shot by the security forces. "I'm sorry I didn't believe you," he whispered. "But then you didn't believe me either. Now, every one of us in Poland has witnessed the truth for himself, and *nothing* can take that from us."

"For having seen that truth," commented Wajda, "I am indebted to this man with a moustache, whom I did not know before, whose existence I had not even suspected, and who expresses the desires and longings of millions of people."[3]

To which Miłosz added: "What I feel for Lech Wałęsa and the shipyard workers can be expressed in one word – gratitude."[4]

[1] King Stanisław August (Stanisław II), the last king of Poland.

[2] Bogdan Szajkowski, *Next to God . . . Poland: Politics and Religion in Contemporary Poland*. Frances Pinter Publishers. Chapter 3: "The Triumph of Solidarity".

[3] From *The Book of Lech Wałesa*.

[4] From *The Book of Lech Wałęsa*.

For a fuller account of events in this and the following three chapters, see:
Neal Ascherson, *The Polish August*, *op. cit.*
Tim Garton Ash, *The Polish Revolution*, *op. cit.*
Kevin Ruane, *The Polish Challenge*, BBC Publications, 1982.
Bogdan Szajkowski, *Next to God . . . Poland* (see note 2 above)

18 A BASKETFUL OF ANTS

> You think you have passed all danger . . . but now careful deliberation is needed, so that, having escaped one evil, we may avoid another. There is a terrible road before us yet, and God knows what may happen to us.
>
> The "Little Knight" in Sieńkiewicz's *With Fire and Sword*

Fears of immediate Soviet invasion passed – and with them passed December's fragile unity. The government's continuing refusal to honour the Agreements reached in the summer, brought renewed industrial action in January. Wałęsa, for the first time in his life, was out of the country. Having acquired a passport, he had gone to Rome, "as a son to his father", to see the Pope.

When he returned, greeted at the airport with flowers, like a conquering hero, he was plunged straightway into the strike being waged in Bielsko Biała for the dismissal of no fewer than twenty corrupt local government officials. It was a strike that lasted twelve days and almost brought the region's industry to a standstill. Not all Wałęsa's pleading could prevail against it, and only the personal intervention of Cardinal Wyszyński finally brought it to an end.

"The Church is with the workers," the Cardinal assured them. But he was unhappy about all the strikes that were taking place, and was having talks with the Party leader, Stanisław Kania in an effort to defuse the dangerous situation. In return for his mediation, however, he hoped the government would agree to register the new peasant union, Rural Solidarity. In March, the Polish bishops reaffirmed their support for the farmers' organisation:

> The eyes of all honest citizens are on the Polish countryside with sympathy and trust. We are full of respect and admiration for the work of the farmers, who with such determination defend their land and their rights. Our farmers must have the same rights as other workers to form trade unions that would serve their interests and at the same time promote the economic development of the entire

country . . . The Church will continue to support the efforts of the Polish farmer in his patriotic and social service to the nation.[1]

While the argument was still going on, and strikes and stoppages were taking place on behalf of Rural Solidarity, a new crisis blew up over Saturday working and the five-day week which Gierek had promised ten years earlier but never delivered. Struggling with an economic crisis which already threatened to drown it, the government would not concede more than alternate free Saturdays. This did not satisfy Solidarity, although Lech Wałęsa pointed out that in its present parlous state, the country could not afford a shorter working week. His more radical colleagues in the National Commission overrode him and called on union members to stay at home on working Saturdays. After a series of warning strikes had taken place in ten selected cities, the authorities hurriedly agreed that there could be three free Saturdays a month, and in addition that Solidarity might in time be allowed access to the media and have a newspaper of its own. On the issue of Rural Solidarity, however, they refused to budge. This annoyed the Cardinal and provoked an angry protest.

In such a volatile situation, too much pressure was being put on Solidarity. It was being asked for too much and too soon. Everything had to be played by ear, and the union leaders had little experience of democratic procedure. As the authorities were clearly not going to keep their promises unless forced to, the union was constantly having to fight on ground it had already won. It was hardly surprising that they could not agree on the tactics, and that there were frequent squabbles.

Lech Wałęsa had his detractors within Solidarity. Since August he and Danuta, with the union's approval, had moved out of their cramped two-room lodgings (so small that when the six children[2] were put to bed on inflatable mattresses on the floor, the door wouldn't open) and into a larger six-roomed flat-cum-office in the classier Zaspa area of Gdańsk. Inevitably the move aroused envy in some quarters, and there were a few who cut Danuta dead in the street. Others hinted darkly that the flat had been a bribe from the government, although the truth was that in September the government *had* tried a much glossier bribe on Lech, offering him a well-furnished villa in Warsaw if he would take charge of the Central Council of Trades Unions.[3]

The rumours persisted. Lech was being corrupted, they said; he was putting on airs on account of all the publicity, the autograph-hunters, the awards, the doctorates, the Man Of The

Year titles,[4] the films, songs and articles which had him as hero. He had put on weight, they observed, acquired more clothes, taken to wearing a collar and tie at meetings. And, though cigarettes were scarce, he seemed to have an endless supply of them. Power had gone to his head. When a *Who's Who* of Solidarity officials was published and included pictures of Lech's (indispensable) secretary and of his (equally indispensable) body-guard, disapproval reached an aggrieved peak. "Next time they'll have a picture of his dog," someone commented sourly. It had not passed unnoticed that he arrived late for meetings, often appeared to go to sleep in them, or sat there pulling grotesque faces for the benefit of the photographers. His restless impatience with other people's long-windedness was all too obvious, and was taken as a sign of incipient megalomania.

To Wałęsa it seemed different. "You've become public property, haven't you?" a journalist asked him. "You mean a slave, don't you?" he countered wearily. "I haven't got a life. I'm not living at all."[5] He complained of poor health, and of not having much time left (he was always convinced he would die young). He couldn't relax, he felt trapped by his status as star, unable to ogle a pretty girl without everybody noticing. Nor was he under any illusions about his present status. Those who cheered him today might well be stoning him tomorrow. As he told Italian journalist, Oriana Fallaci, in an interview:[6]

> If the worst happens, all the rage of the people will fall on me. The same people who applauded me, erected altars to me, will trample me underfoot. They will even forget that I acted in good faith. If I had any sense, and if I were more selfish, I'd cut off my moustache right now and go and find a job in some shipyard or other. But I can't do it, because there's too much danger ahead. I must stay where I am and try to transform this movement somehow into an organisation.

To keep his feet firmly on the ground, he started each day with Mass – "to defend myself against the power that corrupts, to remind myself to be careful . . . God may not need me, but I need God as my support."

He was a lonely man, with no close friends (except possibly his bodyguard, Henryk Mazul). "I've always been alone and I probably always will be," he said in an interview,[7] adding that he had never in his life been happy. There was a strong streak of tragedy in his make-up, and those who cared to look could see a deep sadness in his eyes.

When Kania brought in General Wojciech Jaruzelski as his new

Prime Minister on 11th February, Wałęsa was pleased. "I like soldiers," he told a French journalist,[8] "I respect him. He's a good Pole." Jaruzelski, slim, ramrod-stiff, his face inscrutable behind heavy dark glasses, was a bit of an enigma. Undoubtedly a loyal Party servant, but one who came from a respectable family with a small amount of land somewhere in eastern Poland. He had spent two years in a lycée run by Marian Fathers. Sending the boy to a private school must have been a considerable drain on his parents' financial resources, and the only way they could pay their son's fees was in sacks of potatoes. His education had been interrupted by the start of the Second World War and the subsequent death of his parents in somewhat mysterious circumstances in the Soviet Union. Although he then went on to the Officers' College in the USSR, most observers, even those most hostile to him, would agree that he was not entirely trusted by the Russian leaders. This may have accounted for the popular view that Jaruzelski was perhaps a Wallenrod, a Polish patriot in disguise.* At all events, the people were willing to give him a chance.

Solidarity's National Commission appealed for an end to the plethora of strikes, and it made its own top-heavy structure more flexible by electing an executive – the presidium – empowered to act for the union in an emergency. General Jaruzelski asked for a ninety-day moratorium on strikes, to give the government a chance to tackle the economic crisis. Solidarity agreed. An air of faint optimism prevailed. Or maybe it was a feeling that a last chance had been offered.

Ninety days, Jaruzelski had asked for. It was neither his fault nor Solidarity's that in the event he was given no more than ten.

At the XXVIth Congress of the Soviet Communist Party held in Moscow immediately after Jaruzelski's accession, the Warsaw Pact Allies fraternally threatened not to abandon Poland in her hour of need. Immediately after the Congress, the Polish delegation had been ordered by the Soviet Central Committee "to remove the peril hanging over the Socialist achievements of the Polish people".[9]

Next morning Jacek Kuroń was arrested again, and Adam

* A character in a verse-novel by Mickiewicz. Carried off from Lithuania as a child by the Teutonic Knights, he becomes Grand Master of the Order. But all the time he is planning the Knights' destruction, to avenge the wrongs of his people. It is easy to see the parallels with the early story of Jaruzelski, who was also carried off by the Russians from Lithuania as a boy. But there the similarities seem to end.

Michnik narrowly avoided a similar fate. By 7th March, when Solidarity's National Commission met again, delegates all contributed harrowing tales of union workers harried by the police. Members of Rural Solidarity were being set upon and intimidated; tear-gas had been loosed on a Warsaw shop where the assistants all wore Solidarity armbands; and the chairman of a Solidarity branch in southern Poland had been found hanged after twenty-four hours in police custody.[10] Eighty-six-year-old Antoni Pajdak, a respected pre-war Socialist and Resistance leader, a founder member of KOR, was attacked by an "unknown assailant" (a euphemism for "secret policeman") and left with a broken hip.

The facts added up to a near-certainty that certain people were determined to prevent a rapprochement between Solidarity and the government. Frustrated hardliners within the Party hated the concessions which had been made to Solidarity and saw their whole way of life threatened by Kania's policy of "Renewal". In a more democratic and less corrupt Poland, they would lose their jobs and the privileges that went with them. So it was in their interests to see that nothing changed; and to provoke a confrontation with Solidarity that might plunge the country into crisis and force the Soviet Union to intervene. One such group (approved by the Russians as "a healthy force" in Polish politics), was the anti-student, anti-Zionist, extremely nationalistic Grunwald Patriotic Union, which was busy spreading rumours that KOR was made up of Jewish intellectuals.

On 14th March, Wałęsa was talking to Solidarity leaders in Radom, asking them to put an end to wildcat strikes and give the government a chance to govern: "With strikes," he said, "we shall simply destroy ourselves. We must all stand together at present. We must . . . behave in such a way that future generations will not curse us. Let's learn to sit down at the same table with government representatives. Let's talk to them."

On that very day, in the western town of Bydgoszcz, a group of Rural Solidarity farmers, with the support of Jan Rulewski, the aggressive and reckless local Solidarity leader, began a sit-in against the authorities' refusal to sanction their union. On Thursday 19th March, while discussions were taking place, two hundred militia and plain-clothes police burst in and ejected the men by force, driving them into the courtyard outside where they were forced to run the "path of health" through police truncheons. Twenty-seven were injured. Three, including Rulewski, were taken to hospital. One of these, the sixty-seven-year-old peasant leader, had suspected brain damage as well as battered ribs.

Wałęsa, rushing to the scene, immediately suspected that this was the work of the hardliners, and stated that the affair was "an obvious provocation against the government of General Jaruzelski". Press and television (always hardline strongholds) at first launched into a fury of invective and innuendo, blaming everything on Solidarity. But as public fury mounted, with angry crowds shouting M-O- (i.e. militia), GE-STA-PO, and outsize portraits of the injured victims being carried through the streets, they changed their tune to one of muted regret.

Solidarity's National Commission called an emergency session for 23rd March and wanted to order an all-out strike without further ado. Professor Geremek warned that this might bring the country to the edge of civil war; and Wałęsa added that it was politically unwise to put all one's cards on the table straight away. He was in favour of a four-hour warning strike to be followed by a general strike if the guilty ones were not brought to justice. (Wałęsa's tactics were those of a poker player. He believed in high stakes, but not so high as to place victory out of reach.) The battle was stormy and went on till three in the morning. Finally, using the technique which would become known as "the Wałęsa effect", he stood up, took off his jacket and strode out, having given the delegates eight hours in which to consider what he had said, and threatening to resign if he didn't get his way.[11] They agreed to hold the warning strike, but they would not forgive him for such undemocratic behaviour.

In the days that followed, moderate elements on both sides desperately sought a solution. Jaruzelski had appointed Mieczysław Rakowski, editor of the respected weekly *Polityka* newspaper and a long-time advocate of reform as Deputy Prime Minister with responsibility for unions. Wałęsa and his team held talks with Rakowski against renewed backstage rumblings from the Warsaw Pact, who had extended their spring manoeuvres, thus re-awakening Western fears that invasion was imminent.

Rakowski accused Solidarity of waging "a holy war against people's power", and suggested that the union was trying to cut its own throat and invite Soviet intervention at the same time. But Wałęsa reminded him that the situation was not of Solidarity's making: "On so many occasions in the past," he said, "in 1956, 1970, 1976, we had situations like this one. In 1980, events would have gone the same way if we'd followed your reasoning. We cannot allow the militia to beat us up."

These first talks got nowhere, and the four-hour warning strike took place. Despite numerous attempts at intimidation, it was the biggest disruption of work ever seen in the Soviet empire. Support for it was absolutely solid, even among the Party members of Solidarity, who had been expressly forbidden by Kania to take part. Solidarity then prepared for a count-down to the General Strike that they believed must follow. Mobilising their ten million members, they set telephones and telexes humming with instructions and contingency plans, which were immeditely rushed into print and distributed to the various factory commissions all over the country. The young radicals in the union approached the coming showdown as though it were the decisive battle between the forces of heaven and hell. They were confident of victory, and they had the nation behind them.

> I don't know what the Warsaw Rising was like [said a girl from the Warsaw Solidarity office], but it must have been something like that. We dossed down on sleeping-bags on the office floor since there was no possibility of getting home. Scouts came in with flowers for us, old men with ration cards for sausages, old ladies with cold drinks, jam and blankets. The whole country was like a coiled spring, we were ready for "them" to do their worst. The spirit was incredible, and the people were one hundred and twenty per cent behind us.

Lech Wałęsa was in the eye of the approaching storm. He was aware of the nation's euphoria, but his own political instincts warned him that to go ahead with the strike meant to plunge the country into civil war. Cardinal Wyszyński and the General had held crisis talks and agreed that the crisis must be speedily defused.

Wałęsa and the National Commission were summoned to the Cardinal's residence, and solemnly warned of their responsibilities by Wyszyński: "Is it right to fulfil the demands of the moment, however just, at the cost of endangering our freedom, our territorial integrity? Is it not better to achieve only some of those demands, and for the rest say: 'Gentlemen, we shall return to this matter later'?"

Rakowski warned that they were on the brink of the abyss, and the advisers all urged restraint. As always, Wałęsa listend to them all, and made up his own mind. (Nobody could have accused him of underestimating his own worth. He claimed that his superiority over the advisers was "that of a decathlon athlete over mere runners"!)

Meanwhile, at a meeting of the Party's Central Committee, a letter from journalist Stefan Bratkowski was read, warning that forces in the Party were working against renewal and that "our hardliners stand for no programme except that of confrontation and disinformation".

Rakowski and Wałęsa reached an agreement, the former promising that those responsible for the Bydgoszcz outrage would be punished, and that a parliamentary committee would examine the question of Rural Solidarity. It was not much, and there were no guarantees, but it was all that was on offer. Wałęsa confronted the Solidarity presidium with the package deal – there was no time to summon the full Commission – and, with one hour to go, the strike was called off. But even then the agreement was reached only after a direct intervention by Cardinal Wyszyński. It had been spelled out to him that unless the strike was called off, a "state of emergency" would be declared on 31st March. As proof of the regime's total seriousness, he had been shown a poster with the proclamation already printed on it. So it was Wyszyński who had begged Wałęsa to call off the strike.

There were sighs of relief in the West, but within Solidarity itself there was grief and despair. Not everyone understood the reasons behind Wałęsa's decision:

> It was the beginning of the end [a girl from Warsaw said sadly], a breaking of the spirit. For three days after that betrayal, I felt physically ill, so depressed I wanted to die. It was such a terrible mistake. I don't think it would actually have come to a strike, the authorities would have backed down. The Russians? They wouldn't have come. It would have meant too bloody a struggle. They knew we'd fight to the death.

It was the old Polish cavalry-versus-tanks romanticism, and it was strong among the young people of Solidarity.

Inevitably, Lech was accused of selling-out, of acting like a prima donna, of being paranoid about Russian tanks, of behaving like a mediaeval king. This last was hurled at him by Karol Modzelewski, who indignantly resigned as Solidarity's press officer. Rulewski and his wounded companions wrote from a hospital bed in Bydgoszcz that "Wałęsa has bungled. We can compromise over supplies of onions, but never over spilt blood." Anna Walentynowicz, who had pleaded for the strike to go ahead, lost her job as the Lenin shipyard's delegate to the National Commission. Henceforth, she and Wałęsa would always be on opposing sides. Gwiazda too warned Wałęsa of the dangers of autocratic leadership. Lech's tendency to decide things for himself offended Gwiazda's passionate concern for democracy. Wałęsa defended himself vigorously, claiming that the result was an achievement:

> Three times I made a storm, three times I whipped things up. But I won't allow things to come to a confrontation. The point is not to smash your head open in one day, but to win, step by step, without offending anyone, not a single person. The world is surprised at us for walking a straight line, and as long as I'm here, that's how we're going to walk, step by step and cautiously.[12]

That Solidarity's precious unity might be lost was Wałęsa's chief dread. If that happened, everything would fall apart: "We are like a basket of ants," he said colourfully. "If the ants stay in the basket, they stay together. But tip them out on the ground, and then look what happens."

But the Bydgoszcz incident, and the subsequent Warsaw Agreement, cast a long shadow over the day when the ants would leave the basket and invite their own destruction. Yet, though Wałęsa had cold reason and commonsense on his side, in one sense the Solidarity Young Turks were right: never again would the country be in such a high state of preparedness, and never again would it be so united. If the government had declared a state of emergency then, in March, it would have met with a great deal of determined resistance. As it was, Solidarity knew that from this time forward their strike weapon had overnight lost much of its power.

For many Wałęsa had lost his cutting edge. Yet it was Rulewski, of all people, who said that he was indispensable. Poland, he said:[13] "has a psychological need for a leader who will allow us to go to bed peacefully in the knowledge that there's someone we trust standing guard over us. For half a century we have had no such man. But now we have Wałęsa, and whatever else we do, we have to stick with him."

> I know [said Lech], that this moment needs a chap like me, a chap who can make sensible decisions and solve problems in a cautious, moderate way. I am not a fool. I am well aware that too many injustices have accumulated over thirty-six years and things cannot change overnight. It takes patience, and it takes wisdom. The rage that people would like to explode like a bomb must be controlled. And I know how to control rage because I know how to argue. I know how far we can go with our demands. I know in what country we live, and what our realities are.[14]

In the annual May Day parade, Kania, Jaruzelski and President Jabłoński actually led the workers in procession, instead of taking the salute from a balcony on high. Two days later, they celebrated the one hundred and ninetieth anniversary of the 3rd May Constitution, the old Polish national day which the Young Poland Movement had revived; and Jabłoński spoke of the need for "a right attitude to our national past".

Thanks mainly to the restraining influence of the Church, April and May were relatively quiet. Lech Wałęsa went off to Japan, where he was given star treatment, his popularity remaining undimmed even when he told the Japanese trade unionists that they had become more like functionaries than true activists. In Poland there were only sporadic incidents, like the one in Otwock outside Warsaw, where a crowd of drunks tried to burn down a police station with the police in it! The situation was saved by Adam Michnik who leaped to his feet, shouting: "Listen to me. I'm what is known as an anti-Socialist element." (They did burn the police station down next day, but by that time it was empty, and the policemen came and thanked Michnik for saving their lives. A situation not without a certain irony, considering that, for the police, arresting Michnik was almost a habit!)

The promised talks about Rural Solidarity really did take place, and the union was actually registered on 12th May. The new atmosphere of mutual goodwill was reinforced by the appearance in April of the new *Solidarity Weekly*, edited in Warsaw by Wałęsa's friend and adviser, Tadeusz Mazowiecki; and by a small ration of radio and TV time bestowed on them early in May.

In his first interview for the new weekly, Lech Wałęsa suggested that before social renewal could take place, people should examine their own personal consciences and start a renewal in their own lives.

There was indeed an increasingly serious attempt to speak and print the Truth – a novelty in a Communist Party-ruled State. School text-books were in the process of being reprinted to give a more realistic and truthful account of history; and the hunger for Truth was such that uncensored publications were snapped up as fast as they were produced. When a public sale of *samizdat* (i.e. underground) literature – the first of its kind for thirty-five years – was staged at Warsaw's College of Technology, all the books were sold out within a couple of hours. Satisfying this ravenous hunger for Truth was one of Solidarity's most tangible achievements.

There was also a thirst for real information as opposed to the disinformation so long ladled out by the Party. The thirst affected the whole of society, and ever since August even the official journalists had started to be more truthful. The queues for weeklies such as Rakowski's *Polityka* were almost as long as those for meat. Only those whose lives had been clouded for so long by lies could appreciate the rare beauty of the new dispensation.

It was all deeply worrying for Kania and Jaruzelski, caught between the old guard and the reformers. The Party had lost one hundred and sixty thousand members since the previous July, and two thirds of those who remained had joined Solidarity and were flouting Party orders. The rank and file members were in open revolt, deluging the leaders with complaints about the hardliners and their provocative tactics. These reformers pushed Kania into holding an emergency Party congress in July, to discuss radical reform. They were already beginning to set up a new kind of party organised on horizontal lines, region by region, and controlled from the base. Lenin, who had insisted on a vertical control line from top to bottom, would have turned in his grave. And it was indeed this grievous heresy of "horizontalism" which alarmed the Soviets more than almost anything that Solidarity might do. The Polish Communist Party seemed all set to become a Social Democratic Party in the Western mould, and this the Soviet Union would not tolerate.

It was widely suspected that the Soviets had been behind the establishment of "Grunwald", with its anti-semitic, anti-intellectual prejudice. And in May 1981, they were surely behind the new ultra-conservative Katowice Forum, which produced a manifesto of which Stalin would certainly have been proud, and roundly condemned Kania for "revisionism" and "counter-revolution".

If hopes had been roused by the registration of Rural Solidarity on 12th May, they were brutally dashed on the following days by news of the assassination attempt on John Paul II in Rome. The death of Cardinal Wyszyński from cancer followed soon after, and with the passing of that "voice of moderation and conciliation", the Poles felt truly bereaved. Hundreds of thousands lined the streets for the funeral procession. Flags stood at half-mast, theatres and cinemas closed, radio and TV programmes reflected the sombre public mood. For the funeral service in Victory Square, a quarter of a million mourners stood before an altar dominated by a cross twelve metres high. And at the Cathedral where the body came to rest, the Cardinal's last will and testament was read, in which he expressed gratitude for the grace which had enabled him to bear witness to truth as a political prisoner; and in which he freely forgave all those who had slandered him.

In view of the people's immense grief, the regime had little option but to join in the general mourning for the Primate. Without precedent in the Communist world, the head of the Roman Catholic Church in Poland was publicly proclaimed "a great statesman, a man of great moral authority recognised by the nation".[15]

But the provocateurs were no respecters of grief, and the incidents continued to multiply. When the Soviet ambassador complained that Soviet war memorials were being daubed with white paint, few doubted that the pro-Soviet hardliners were themselves responsible. Lech Wałęsa, protesting Solidarity's innocence, went out with a bucket of hot water to scrub one of these memorials clean.

On 5th June, Brezhnev made it clear in a letter to the Polish Central Committee that Kania and Jaruzelski had lost control and should be replaced. The hardliners triumphantly called on Kania to resign. But the rest of the Central Committee indignantly closed ranks in the face of this crass interference from outside, and they confirmed Kania in office.

Nevertheless, Brezhnev's letter, with its thinly veiled hints that what had happened to Czechoslovakia on the eve of just such an Extraordinary Party Congress in 1968, could happen in Poland in 1981, caused no little consternation, and rather dampened the Politburo's ardour for internal reform. Their self-confidence took a further knock when the magazine *Kultura* published the results of a nationwide poll to find out which institutions in the country were the most respected. The Church came first, followed by Solidarity, then the Army. The Party came near the bottom of the list, lower even than the police!

Solidarity was being careful not to stir things up during the run-up to this momentous Party congress. Wałęsa told Solidarity meetings all over the country that the union should resist the temptation to play politics. "There has already been too much confrontation," he said. At a ceremony in Poznań, which commemorated the twenty-fifth anniversary of the workers' riots "for bread and freedom", in which sixty people had been killed, he made a further plea for national unity:

> We used to be called troublemakers and vandals and other names that were an affront to our dignity. Today . . . our path lies in solidarity, the solidarity of the world of labour, the solidarity of honest

people against those who are dishonest, who try to keep our mouths shut . . . If we do not want to have any more monuments like this, we must not allow ourselves to be divided or to be set against one another . . . The world of labour is not counter-revolutionary, it is for honesty and truth . . . Let us remember that victory is already within our grasp, provided we do not allow ourselves to be divided.[16]

When the Extraordinary Congress met on, of all days, 14th July, Bastille Day, it was hung over by the Party's own anxieties about unity. And though it was extraordinary in more senses than one, being composed of two thousand freely elected delegates, voting by secret ballot for an agenda chosen by themselves, there was one unforeseen result. Caution led the delegates to avoid *both* extremes, so that although most of the old Central Committee and seven out of eleven Politburo members lost their seats, the men who took their places were middle-of-the-roaders, evenly balanced between conservatives and reformers, it is true, but cautious on the subject of change. Kania was re-elected as First Secretary, and the Soviets sent him a telegram of congratulation. The Party hierarchy which he inherited was collectively something of a eunuch, incapable of filling the political vacuum which now yawned dangerously wide.

1 Bogdan Szajkowski, *op. cit.* Chapter 3.
2 The sixth child, a girl, was born just before the August strike.
3 *The Book of Lech Wałesa.*
4 Wałesa was voted Man Of The Year in West Germany, Denmark and other countries. Elsewhere, he was second only to the Pope.
5 *The Book*, interview with Marzena and Tadeusz Woźniak.
6 Interview with Oriana Fallaci, reprinted in *Sunday Times*, 22.3.81.
7 *The Book*, interview with Marzena and Tadeusz Woźniak.
8 Bernard Guetta, *Le Monde*, 21.3.81.
9 Tim Garton Ash, *op. cit.* Chapter, "The Ides of March".
10 Tim Garton Ash, *op. cit.* Chapter, "The Ides of March".
11 *The Book*, interview with Marzena and Tadeusz Woźniak.
12 Halina Mirowska, *Lechu*, *op. cit.*
13 Dobbs, Karol, Trevisan, *Poland: Solidarity: Wałesa*, Pergamon Press, 1981.
14 Interview with Oriana Fallaci, reprinted in *Sunday Times*, 22.3.81.
15 Bogdan Szajkowski, *op. cit.* Chapter 3.
16 Kevin Ruane, *The Polish Challenge*, BBC, 1982.

19 "CONSCIENCE PLANTS FORESTS"

> It is hard to think of any previous revolution in which ethical categories and moral goals have played such a large part; not only in the theory but also in the practice of the revolutionaries; not only at the outset but throughout the Revolution . . . Moreover, it is an indisputable fact that in sixteen months this revolution killed nobody . . . This extraordinary record of non-violence, this majestic self-restraint in the face of many provocations, distinguishes the Polish revolution from previous revolutions.
>
> Tim Garton Ash: *The Polish Revolution*

"I rack my brains to understand," wrote Kazimierz Brandys, returning to Poland in July, after a brief absence abroad,[1] "how things have come to be stripped so bare, and what people are living on here. Pure spirit? In the course of seven months, goods have almost disappeared and there is talk of hunger. But the crowds . . . inundate the streets, gather in churches to sing 'We Want God' and 'Let Poland Be Poland' and wear ironic badges pinned to their summer shirts – CCR – Creeping Counter-Revolutionary. These are the same crowds about whom six years ago I wrote that they lacked faith, for they were under the sway of material desire and indifferent to the ideas of freedom and justice."

As Father Józef Tischner pointed out, the words most frequently appearing now on posters were those which had for years been lost in the stagnant mud of "newspeak" – words like Freedom, Truth, Equality, Dignity, and Homeland. Human dignity was coming into its own: "Our present defiance," said Tischner, "is not an ordinary mutiny. Rather it is a voice, great and piercing, calling the people to fidelity."[2]

In Solidarity opinion polls, demands for truth in the media and in schools came second only to demands for freedom. Being able to speak the truth, without fear of the secret police, was not only a great relief but meant that they could hold their heads higher. An American professor spoke of "an entire country without alienation". Through Solidarity, hope and a sense of purpose had been reborn. Even the famous Polish jokes had disappeared: they had represented the impotence of a gagged nation and the Poles had other ways of expressing their feelings now. It was striking that the number of suicides and the sales of alcohol both fell dramatically.

Archbishop Józef Glemp who, in July, succeeded Cardinal Wyszyński as Primate, signalled his intention of following where his predecessor had led, "looking at the changing times and listening to what is happening in the nation". He pleaded, as Wyszyński had, for charity and mutual understanding to prevail, for an end to hatred and thoughts of revenge. In churches all over the country, altars of reconciliation were being set up, and every day thousands went to pray for the unity of their country. The churches were fuller than they had ever been. "The conscience plants forests," said Józef Tischner. "Solidarity is a huge forest planted by awakened consciences."

The people had great need of this interior nourishment, for there was precious little of the material kind. That summer the economic situation had gone from bad to worse. The reasons were the usual ones, plus a huge fall in coal exports due to the end of Saturday work and, inevitably, the wage-increases given to the workers. There was now the classic case of too much money chasing too few goods. Under pressure from the Western bankers, who had run out of patience with the Poles, the government now took the commonsense but unpopular step of raising food-prices by over one hundred per cent. As Brandys had remarked, the shelves were almost bare. Many staple foods, among them the humble potato, had disappeared altogether. There was strict rationing of meat, sausage, butter, sugar, rice, oats, flour and buckwheat kasha; but the ration cards were often worthless, since the food was unavailable. There were no cigarettes, matches, petrol, or even vodka.

Hopelessly, Barbara D., a dietician in a big general hospital, confessed that it was impossible to do her job properly: "How can you plan a diet when there is nothing to plan it on? Patients in hospitals have to rely on whatever food their families can scrape together for them."

In many cases, mothers and fathers went hungry in order to give their children what little food there was.

As hunger grew, anger mounted. People were exhausted by the shortages and the endless queues. (On the whole the queues were remarkably good-natured, but quarrels did break out, and fist-fights often took place.) In order to take the potentially violent edge off this anger, local Solidarity groups tried to channel it into relatively harmless hunger marches through the streets of the most afflicted towns. Children carrying I AM HUNGRY, MOTHER banners, housewives holding up empty shopping-bags and saucepans paraded peacefully through the streets.

In the textile town of Łódź, where two hundred and fifty thousand women worked a three-shift system, the women's plight was especially tragic. Most of them had families to look after, and for most it was a question of working all day and then spending the night in a queue, or joining such a queue immediately after coming off the night-shift. Tim Garton Ash has movingly described the drudgery of their lives:

> Young women with complexions ruined by the sweat-shop air, dressed in dirty torn cotton dresses (on their wages they could not afford new ones: washing-powder and thread were unobtainable), told how they joined the butcher's queue in the evening of one day, on the chance (just the chance) that they might get some meat at two o'clock the next afternoon.[3]

Solidarity had appealed for better conditions for these women. On a film released at that time they spoke of hands lacerated by flax, the choking dust, the varicose veins, the exhaustion: "Nothing is done for us here," the women said. "The management wants everything but gives nothing. Look how dirty we are. All we get is two lumps of soap a month like paupers. But take a look at their offices – and just see the luxuries they have."[4]

Only a drastic overhaul of the economy, or a massive and unlikely influx of aid from outside, could have had any effect on this tragic mess. The Solidarity leadership was in a dilemma. They had always imposed a discipline on themselves and deliberately refrained from politics. Their revolution had been a self-limiting one, which did not aim at taking power. But now there was a government which seemed unable even to pretend to govern, while the country slid rapidly downwards towards total disaster. The union leaders stood at a crossroads. With the country looking to them for a lead, and with their own credibility at risk if they did not give one, they took a momentous decision to enlarge the scope of their revolution, and to step into the yawning political vacuum.

At the end of July, they offered to support the necessary price rises and to persuade the people to accept the need for sacrifices, in exchange for information about available food supplies, and access to government stores in order to check how food was being distributed. (It was still widely believed that the privileged few were not going short.) In addition they asked for workers' self-government in the factories, in order to improve production by removing useless and incompetent managers. (Preparations for this had been going ahead in many factories. It must be remembered that most workers were well-educated, and that many of them were well-qualified to take the managerial posts which were currently available only for Party trusties.)

What Solidarity had in mind was a genuine new partnership with the government, a positive programme of regeneration which could save Poland even at this eleventh hour.

For a brief moment, it all seemed possible, and the government offered negotiations. But the partnership got off to a bad start. When the Solidarity delegation arrived in Warsaw for talks, it was to find the whole city brought to a virtual standstill by a transport strike. Rakowski greeted them with a stream of denunciation, and dismissed their proposals as a mere bid for political power. In return, he put forward an impossible list of conditions which would have reduced Solidarity to the state of impotence enjoyed by the old "transmission-belt" official unions.

It is only fair to recognise that in all probability the government, and the Soviet Union, were frightened by the new direction that Solidarity was taking and could not fail to believe that the union's ultimate aim was the overthrow of the Communist regime. This conviction increased the alarm and despondency in an already demoralised Party, and strengthened the hands of those who wanted nothing better than to provoke discord and upheaval. But they were wrong about Solidarity's motives. Though many of the union's rank and file wanted nothing better than to be rid of both the government and the Soviet Union, the majority of their leaders were more clear-sighted:

> Certainly we were setting off in a more political direction [said a member of Warsaw Solidarity], but that didn't mean we wanted to set up political parties and overthrow the regime. The truth is that *everything* in Poland is political. If you want to buy a worker a pair of protective rubber gloves, you have to change the whole system in order to be able to do it.

As the summer wore on, a great many Poles were hungover by a sense of doom. The assassination attempt on the Pope in May, the death of Wyszyński which followed almost immediately, had tragically robbed them of the very two people who had shepherded them through their most difficult and dangerous times, and who had never been more needed than now. Of the three Ws, there remained only Wałęsa, and on him they had to focus all their remaining hopes.

Interviewed on Polish Television, Lech repeated that Solidarity was not seeking power, but "since the government has lost public confidence, it has automatically thrust that confidence and the solution of problems on to us". In an interview for a Western magazine, he added:

> The Party mustn't be allowed to collapse. I don't want that. I'll help the Party once it starts to discredit itself or collapse. There are no other realities here. We cannot overthrow the Party, we cannot take power away from it. We have to preserve it and at the same time tame it and let it eat with us, so that it will come to relish what we create.[5]

But the Party backed away now from the prospect of "eating" with Solidarity. Frightened by the union's new programmes for reform, and by the hunger marches, the government hit back through the media it so powerfully controlled. All the stops were pulled out, as programme after programme accused Solidarity of being the architect of all the nation's ills, responsible alike for rising prices and falling food-stocks. A torrent of disinformation poured out, and Solidarity was given no chance to present its side of the story. Though it had its own newspaper, distribution was slow compared with that of the government papers; and it had almost negligible access to the media.

The Bishops issued a statement to the effect that renewal was bound to be difficult, but that the people were willing to bear hardship if it could be seen to be in a good cause. They insisted that the mass media should serve the general good and that everyone had the right to access to them. Then they pleaded again for mutual tolerance. "Let none of us shake his fist. Let each of us abandon hatred." At Częstochowa, Archbishop Glemp appealed for a month of peace, and said that neither side had a monopoly of virtue: "Tensions and emotions are rising while poverty knocks at the door. Meanwhile the two contestants tell poverty to wait until one of them wins and can drive it away. Let us look at ourselves truthfully. We shall then see our own sins . . . and this will allow us to see the good done by the other side."[6]

Poverty was indeed at the door. "Thirty-six years and still nothing to buy," complained a man in the street.

"I stood in line twenty minutes for bread," noted Brandys in

August, "and succeeded in buying half of the last loaf. The stores are empty, not a single piece of cake, not a single apple to be bought."

Kania warned that if the street demonstrations continued, it could "only be a matter of time" before an explosion occurred. For the moment, people were still blaming the government exclusively. But, in the face of an increasingly hysterical TV campaign against Solidarity, guaranteed to confuse and instil fear, how much longer would they continue to do so?

[1] Brandys, *Warsaw Diary*, *op. cit.*
[2] Józef Tischner, *The Spirit of Solidarity*, *op. cit.*
[3] Tim Garton Ash, *The Polish Revolution*, *op. cit.*
[4] Feature film in *Life on the Shelf*, shown on BBC, 1981.
[5] Interview in *Playboy*, October 1981.
[6] Kevin Ruane, *The Polish Challenge*, BBC, Chapter 12, "The Question of Power".

20 THE TIME OF ROOTING

Friends, to-day is ours
and to-morrow cannot be known.
But let us live to-day as though the century were ours.
Let us create the foundations of peace in this our country.

And if anyone sets our house of friendship on fire,
Then each of us must be ready to defend it.
For it is better to die on our feet
Than to be forced to live on our knees.

Friends – let us be united, for we all have a common aim.

Rough translation of a poem by
Tadeusz Mazowiecki, May 1981

For Solidarity, it was no longer a question of what to do, but how to do it. The desire "to save ourselves by our own efforts", was uppermost in the minds of the delegates to the First Solidarity Congress as they assembled in early September in the Oliwa sports stadium in Gdańsk. It was now twelve months since the summer Agreements had been signed, and the government had carried out scarcely any of its promises.

Was it a coincidence that as the Congress opened in Gdańsk, on the other side of the Gulf of Gdańsk the Soviet Union began a new set of naval manoeuvres? Cardinal Glemp prayed in the Oliwa Cathedral for peace, and Józef Tischner, whose influence on Solidarity both then and later was immense, expressed the feelings of everyone present in his opening sermon: "Nothing like this has ever happened before in this land . . . We all feel it . . . this is a historic place, this is a historic anniversary; something is being built. Here is Poland."

The majority of those present shared Father Tischner's view that Solidarity was not so much a trades union as a way of life deeply rooted in Poland's age-old struggle for freedom. Its true meaning lay in its championship of basic human values: the restoration of truth, the struggle against exploitation, the sacredness of the land, and the importance of satisfying and meaningful work. As regards this last, said Tischner[1]: "Polish work is sick. The volume of work is great, like the Vistula River; but, like the Vistula, it is polluted . . . Let the water in the Polish Vistula become clean and independent – like the water in the Five Lakes in the Tatra Mountains."

It was historic, it was exciting; and the delegates were determined to make it work. There were, of course, differences of opinion amongst them, differences which, in a free country, would have been expressed in membership of different political parties. But they were united in their determination to behave democratically, a new and uncharted experience for them.

Everyone had the right to intervene at any time; and at elections the urns were turned upside down so that everybody could see there had been no cheating. Much of the discussion was about the nature of democracy: should they, for example, choose for themselves a system which would give the regions and their leaders control, or one that would consolidate the power of the already powerful "king" – Wałęsa?

Wałęsa was fairly clear on the matter. He wanted democracy and was prepared to fight for it. But not if it was interpreted as a free-for-all; not now, not when they were in so much danger, and hadn't learned how to cope with democratic freedoms. Look at their meetings, he argued. Speakers droned on endlessly, and nobody seemed to understand that there had to be limits to what was allowed. What Poland needed more than anything else was for Solidarity to be united, not fragmented into dozens of dissident factions, all arguing with each other about democratic procedures. "I have a vision," he had once said,[2] "and I'm capable of putting a lot of things right. I can bring about the kind of Poland we'd all like to see . . . But to do that I'd have to stop dissipating my energy in unnecessary and stupid in-fighting."

Didn't they understand that they faced a power which had the police and the army under its control, and that if they did not present a solid front to that challenge, they were lost? "That's why I am a dictator here," he said stubbornly.

But Solidarity had had enough of dictators, and they had begun to resent this one. Lech was too cautious, too eager to go on talking to the government, too ready to see the good in the other side, and, worst of all, too ready to strike a deal on his own initiative. There was growing pressure from below, from the ten million members, to throw off restraint; and their present sense of mission made them believe in their own power to change things, to make an imperfect world perfect again. They lacked Wałęsa's political vision, the long-sightedness that could foresee what lay ahead. They were youthful (or not so youthful) idealists, he a realist with a strong sense of what was possible and what was not.

Lech Wałęsa, who claimed that in this one year he had aged ten, found himself frequently opposed by Andrzej Gwiazda. It was said that they loathed each other. Like many others, Gwiazda disliked Wałęsa's penchant for acting on experience and instinct, on a poker player's hunch. Wałęsa was a wheeler-dealer, always demanding more at the outset than he knew he could get, quite ready to yield a point here and there, in order to secure his ultimate objective:

> I am a radical but not a suicidal one. I am a man who has to win, because he does not know how to lose. At the same time, if I know that I can't win today because I don't have a good enough hand, I ask for a re-shuffling and then check whether I have got a better hand. I never give up. I'm a radical, I say it again, but I don't walk into a stone wall with my eyes shut. I'd be a fool. There are some such fools, but I'm not one of them.[3]

This sounds like the bravado of an increasingly desperate man. But at the same time, Lech knew when to stop, and would never compromise on the really important issues. Gwiazda, the bearded engineer, more intellectual than Lech, was a political babe-in-arms compared to him. He shunned gamesmanship, disliked taking risks and believed that any compromise at all was immoral. His was an all-or-nothing, cards on the table, take it or leave it approach, which seemed to Wałęsa the height of political unwisdom. "Gwiazda is like a character out of Dostoievsky," says Bohdan Cywiński. "He tends to see things in terms of a cosmic struggle between good and evil, all blacks and whites."

Inevitably, to such as Andrzej Gwiazda, Wałęsa's cocky pragmatism was offensive. And Lech's infuriating technique of bulldozing his own decisions through maddened him most of all: "Andrzej was passionate about democracy, he would insist on everyone having his say," Cywiński adds. "Yet, for all his crude pushiness, Lech was actually the better diplomat. The fact that he was so often proved right didn't make Andrzej like him any better!"

Janusz Onyszkiewicz, Solidarity's new press officer, put the same criticism more gracefully though no less forcefully than

Gwiazda: "Lech is a surfer who rides the waves," he said. "It was his de Gaulle complex that maddened us – his conviction that he and he alone *was* Solidarity, that he alone knew what was best for everyone, best for Poland."

The first part of the Congress ended with a hair-raising exhibition of the sort of "walking into a stone wall with one's eyes shut" that Wałęsa had so deplored. As the government Bill on Workers' Rights continued to insist on State control over hiring and firing (while conceding that workers might be "consulted" about appointments), Karol Modzelewski now proposed that a national referendum should vote on the matter. This provocative idea was carried enthusiastically, and was followed by an even more hot-headed, short but explicit *Message To The Workers Of Eastern Europe*, in which an emotional appeal to join the workers' struggle was addressed to the whole Communist world, including "all the nations of the Soviet Union". A further *Letter To Poles* (i.e. the émigré groups scattered throughout the world) began with the stirring but impolitic words: "Here on the Vistula, a new Poland is being born", and referred to "the homeland and its independence".

A seismic shudder ran through the Soviet leadership, and in the West there were head-shakings and dark murmurs that "Poles are beginning to behave like Poles again". Was Solidarity inciting the Communist world to revolt? Was this the start of World War Three?

Congress, in fact, was surprised by the international fuss. As regards the two *Letters*, they had simply been carried away by their own rhetoric. But about the referendum they were in deadly earnest.

In the fortnight that separated the two parts of the Congress, Lech Wałęsa scarcely slept. Proving that he was indeed a "democratic dictator", he set himself to undo the harm that had already been done. He could foresee only too well the chaos that would result from the holding of a referendum, but he lacked time and patience to explain the possibilities to his more volatile colleagues. Instead, he went direct to Rakowski, persuaded him to change the wording of the proposed Workers' Self-Government Bill, and persuaded an unusually small presidium of four to accept the government's new proposals. (The firebrand Jan Rulewski was one of the four, and he voted against the compromise.) Unfortunately, the government backed away from its agreement the very next day, and went back to its original insistence on the right to hire and fire. At this point, the Sejm refused to "rubber-stamp" the Bill, and forced the government to accept a near-approximation to the Solidarity demands.

It had turned out well, but the Congress delegates were furious with Wałęsa for his high-handed effrontery, and a motion was passed reprimanding him and the two others who had voted his way. Rulewski was praised for refusing to give in to him.

Lech was worn out by all the diplomatic activity. A picture of him taken at the Conference shows him stretched out on two chairs, asleep. Many people were beginning to wonder which would get him first, the government or exhaustion. He was afraid that the movement was falling apart. His own earlier warning, "Our most vicious enemy is ourselves . . . we threaten our existence when we fight each other", seemed to have gone unheard.

Another ordeal awaited him: three candidates – Gwiazda, Rulewski and Marian Jurczyk from Szczecin – were opposing him in the elections for Chairman, and he would have to plead his own cause. Asked what he would do if he failed to be re-elected, he said wearily: "I really don't want power. I'd like to be by myself by some lake, fishing. I'd like to be able to get up, look out of the window, see it's a nice day, go to the station and buy a ticket. Only, damn it, I've no money."

When the elections began on 1st October, he was tense and nervous, ill at ease and in poor speaking form. Each of the four candidates had to make a speech outlining his programmes, and then subject himself to a barrage of questions from the floor. In the first round, the other three were applauded, Wałęsa hardly at all. In the second round he rallied somewhat. Asked what he would regard as the most urgent need of Solidarity, Poland and the world, he replied feelingly that he would like most of all to see peace: "Let us leave our arguments, let us stay together, victory is possible for us. But we really underestimate our enemy. He is strong. Economically, he is weak, but politically he is strong. And let us at least face the fact that he also thinks."[4]

They were still there at midnight, by which time the candidates were supposed to be asking each other questions. Lech said he was too tired to ask any: "Today, ladies and gentlemen, I have answered five hundred questions. Five TV teams have been round since this morning, whether I liked it or not. If I'd sent them away, they'd start saying I'm growing horns. That's why I'm asking no questions. I'm tired of questions."

Perhaps, he added with a flash of his old good humour, turning to the audience with his fists up, they might like to settle the matter with a fight. "Anyone got a pair of boxing-gloves?"

Lech won, but gained only fifty-five per cent of the votes. In spite of the narrowness of the margin, however, there was never any possibility of his losing. As a Warsaw delegate said later:

> Lech has always been our leader and always will be. He's the symbol that keeps the movement together. No one really doubts that, even when they criticise him. But at the Congress, people felt he was getting too sure of himself, and a lot of people voted against him, just to teach him a lesson. Nobody wanted him not to be leader. In a country where lies and censorship still held sway, we had to have a name which stood for honesty and truth. We had to have someone whom everyone knew could be trusted.

When voting later took place for election to the presidium, Lech "moved heaven and earth" to stop Gwiazda and Rulewski being chosen, because he would have found it impossible to work with them. They were dropped. One of his successful nominees, press officer Janusz Onyszkiewicz, was under no illusions about the difficulties that lay ahead. "We are," he said, "like a water-skier who is being pulled by a very powerful boat. Obviously we can zig-zag in order to stay on our feet. But whatever happens, we must not drop the rope. If we do that, we shall sink."

The key question, Father Tischner had said at the beginning of the second part of the Congress, was: "Can we transform our Polish hope into reality? The trees of hope have many flowers, and on those trees flowers bloom easily. The crucial problem is, however, rooting. Now the time of rooting has come."[5]

In spite of all the noisy bickering, the programme which the Solidarity Congress finally produced was a serious attempt at such rooting. It was a masterly blueprint for the sort of society most people in Poland wanted.

> What we had in mind [the preamble stated], was not only bread, butter and sausage, but also justice, democracy, truth, legality, human dignity, freedom of convictions and the repair of the republic. All elementary values had been too mistreated to believe that anything could improve without their rebirth. Thus the economic protest had simultaneously to be a social protest, and the social protest had to be simultaneously a moral protest.[6]

There was no demand to leave the Soviet bloc, to overthrow the system, dislodge the Party or to privatise the means of production. Those planks of the "geo-political reality" were left untouched. What they asked was that Poland should become a pluralist society, with free elections, a representative parliament and a judiciary that was not bent. They made a strong case for workers' control of industry, and for the decentralisation which alone could save the economy. They asked that economic power should not continue to be concentrated in the hands of the Party alone, that "social ownership of the means of production" should mean ownership by groups and individuals and not only by the State.

The programme showed a mature, statesmanlike vision of how to overcome the crises afflicting not only Poland but the whole world: Solidarity's answer lay in sound economic reform accompanied by greater freedom to participate in public life. If their plan owed more to the example of self-management in Yugoslavia, or of liberal Western democracies, than to any wild utopian dream, it was because the Poles had had their fill of what ninety-year-old Professor Lipiński, a respected veteran Socialist, called "this Socialism of rotten economy, this Socialism of prisoners, censorship and police".

The very word socialism, as used in the Soviet bloc, had been discredited, and the accusing phrase "anti-Socialist forces" had no real meaning. "There are forces," said Lipiński, "who demand freedom, who demand conditions of normal life for the Polish nation. And those are *not* anti-Socialist forces."

It was Father Tischner who shed light on this semantic dilemma. Socialism, he said, "is about creating the right conditions in which human brotherhood can come about, and therefore involves a constant struggle against exploitation. But there are two ways of being Socialist and the difference is crucial."[7]

There is "open" Socialism and "closed" Socialism, he explained. Both types identify the main source of exploitation as private ownership of the means of production and resolve therefore to do away with it. To the "closed" Socialist mind, this is the end of the matter: if there is no private ownership, exploitation cannot exist. The "open" Socialist, on the other hand, sees that things are not so simple as that: one form of exploitation may have disappeared, only to be replaced by others. For the "closed" Socialist, a strike is an impossibility, since one cannot strike against oneself. But his "open" colleague would argue that it does not do the workers much good if they are co-owners of a coal-mine, but cannot own a bucket of coal. "Senseless work," argued Father Tischner, "is the most extreme form of exploitation of man by man. It is a direct insult to the human dignity of the worker. When work becomes senseless, the strike is the only kind of behaviour which makes sense."

Between the liberating concept of this "open" Socialism, with its stress on struggle, and the Christian doctrine of forgiving love, there are obvious profound differences. But they are not irreconcilable. "The views are different . . . but the common ground is visible." In Solidarity the views seemed to coalesce. What both Father Tischner and Solidarity deplored was not the lack of consumer goods or of huge profit margins, but the way the worker was treated as a tool, a mere means to an end. As Tim Garton Ash perceptively noted[8]: "Polish Catholicism (the open Catholicism of Father Tischner) and Polish Socialism (the open Socialism of Lipiński) had come a long way from their bitter enmity of half a century before."

Through Solidarity, yet another barrier had fallen. In that thought lay hope. As the delegates rose to sing the closing National Anthem, they might have felt a deeper personal involvement than usual with the ringing words: "Poland is not yet lost so long as we shall live." They had every right to be proud of the programme they had produced, for if it could be put into effect, then Poland had a chance.

[1] Józef Tischner, *op. cit.* Chapter, "Polish Work Is Sick".
[2] *The Book*, *op cit.* Interview with the Wożniaks.
[3] Lech Wałesa interviewed in *Playboy*, October 1981.
[4] Halina Mirowska, *op. cit.*
[5] Tischner, *op. cit.* Chapter, "The Time Of Rooting".
[6] Tim Garton Ash, *op. cit*, Chapter 7: "Noble Democracy".
[7] Tischner, *op. cit.* Chapter "Socialism".
[8] Tim Garton Ash, *op. cit.* Chapter 7: "Noble Democracy".

21 THE BEGINNING OF THE END

I once heard about some kind of giant sea-anemone that commits suicide by swimming right up to the beach. I have this dread that *we* might be doing something similar.

Lech Wałęsa

"Don't worry," a Russian Politburo official is said to have consoled his Polish opposite number. "When we come in, we won't hang you, we'll hang the people who hanged you."

Concern about Soviet intentions had surfaced again in the West, alarmed by the Solidarity Congress's demands for free elections and workers' self-government. As everyone knew, in genuinely free elections, the Communists wouldn't stand a chance. And then what would the Russians do? Solidarity was angrily accused of megalomania, of overreaching itself. In Poland, however, public opinion was solidly behind the union. The Congress had given voice to the Poles' longing for non-violent change.

The trouble was that, though Solidarity had a popular mandate, it had no power to act. How could the workers take control when the system remained unreformed? All around, that system was visibly collapsing: factories stood idle for the lack of spare parts; farm produce rotted before it could reach the consumer; ration cards were a sick joke since there was scarcely any food anyway; and there was a tidal wave of strikes. It was a vicious circle: the failure of the economic system produced the strikes, which in turn made matters even worse.

The authorities were stricken with paralysis. Yet they would not give in to Solidarity, and the people began to clamour for the union to act. "And so both sides stood," wrote Halina Mirowska,[1] "opposite each other, speaking different languages. The authorities, like an hysterical and frightened child clenching its fists and screaming: 'You shan't have it. It's mine'. Solidarity leaning forward, arm outstretched, like a cross but helpless mother."

Half-way through October, Kania resigned, and General Jaruzelski became Party Secretary as well as Prime Minister. For the first time in the history of the Soviet bloc, the two most powerful posts were held by the same person. In addition, he was also Minister of Defence and an army General with more than three decades of military experience behind him. (The people joked that there was only one important post left for him: that of Primate of Poland!) The introduction of the military dimension into the Polish government at this critical stage clearly signalled the arrival of what one British TV commentator called "garrison Communism".[2]

With exceptional power at his disposal, therefore, Jaruzelski faced a situation in which half the provinces of the country were affected by strikes, and Solidarity seemed powerless to stop them. With the traditional admiration for the Polish Army still strong, there was a certain undeniable sense of relief that the Army was becoming involved. The belief that Polish soldiers would never fire on Polish citizens still held good. Wałęsa agreed up to a point. But ever since the Bydgoszcz incident in March, he had known in his heart that the government was preparing for a "state of war". Few of the other Solidarity leaders appeared to share this presentiment of danger.

It was widely believed, however, that the government was allowing things to slide down to perdition, so that Solidarity would be forced to react; and then the police would be able to move in and crush them. Already the police were stepping up their harassment of union activists, as the newly elected Solidarity Commission heard at its first meeting on 22nd October. The young leaders fell in with Wałęsa's suggestion of calling a one-hour general strike on the 28th, mainly as a way of imposing some sort of national control over the wildcat strikes. Though the strike did not generate much enthusiasm, and many grumbled that they couldn't see the need for it, it was nevertheless given total support. Wałęsa could still inspire loyalty. "He still incarnates the spirit of the streets," wrote Brandys in his diary.[3]

One of Jaruzelski's first moves was to send three and a half thousand army officers, conscript NCOs and men into two thousand towns and villages, ostensibly to test the food-distribution system. With hindsight this gesture was an early step in the build-up for martial law. The conscript soldiers also found that their two-year national service period (due to end in December) was extended by two months. In case of trouble in the larger cities, these young men – possible or probable Solidarity supporters – would be safely out of the way. The government was already training other, more politically reliable forces for use in any emergency. The Army Security Service and the ZOMO riot police, carefully selected, well-fed, sumptuously housed, thoroughly brain-washed, would not scruple about the shedding of Polish blood.

For the moment, however, the General was projecting himself as a man of peace. Earnestly he called for a Council of National Accord, which might create a programme for a National Unity Front gathered from all sectors of society: the government, Solidarity, the Church, the official unions, the intellectuals, the peasants, the economists. Wałęsa, who had been asking for a Joint Commission, in which Solidarity and the government would have been equal partners, was suspicious that the Front would mean a general watering-down. Solidarity, after all, had ten million members and could justly claim to represent the whole of Polish society. So why should the union agree to share decision-making about the country's welfare with "the incompetents and hacks – the central planners, the time-servers, the seat warmers",[4] in other words, with the very people who'd created the mess in the first place?

Solidarity's presidium, a much more moderate body than the National Commission, appealed for an end to the wildcat strikes which were eroding Solidarity's authority and giving the union a bad name. They could finish by destroying Solidarity completely, Wałęsa told a meeting of the full Commission. But they rejected his plea, impatient of his caution. And when at the end of this session he announced that he was off to Warsaw to meet General Jaruzelski and Cardinal Glemp for talks, a tremendous row blew up. Lech was not asking his colleagues' permission, he was telling them what he had decided. Not for the first time, he was accused of acting like an autocrat, and of playing into the hands of Jaruzelski. "We want democracy, not dictatorship," shouted one union leader. "Right," retorted Lech, "let's vote that we don't want to talk with the Primate and the Prime Minister. And then you can go out and explain that vote to the nation."

Gwiazda called him a "vain fool" and a "blockhead", with nothing above the famous moustache. But Lech was not going to let insults stand in the way of this meeting with the General, with the faint chance it offered of a better relationship with the government.

The historic Big Three meeting, between the Cardinal, the Solidarity leader and the Prime Minister/Party Secretary, without precedent in the Communist world, went ahead on 4th November and lasted two hours and twenty minutes. It was inconclusive, but further talks were promised on a wide range of social issues. Wałęsa returned to the National Commission, only to find that it had already voted (with Gwiazda in the chair) for a national strike within three months if the negotiations should fail. When Wałęsa told them they were choosing the path of confrontation, he and Gwiazda finally reached the parting of the ways. Playwright Tom Stoppard has illuminated this last argument between the two men in a revealing piece of dialogue:

> WAŁĘSA: Yes, I know. They lie. They cheat. They kick and bite and scratch before they give an inch – but that's how we got this union, inch by inch across the negotiating table!
>
> GWIAZDA: (shouting) We got it by going on strike and staying on strike.
>
> WAŁĘSA: You're wrong. We got it because we could deliver a return to work. We've got nothing else to negotiate with, and if we can't deliver, what have they got to lose? (The applause grows.)
>
> GWIAZDA: They've conned you, Lech! The talks are a sham. Across the table is where they want us – all the time we're talking, they're getting ready to hit us.[5]

With words such as these, Gwiazda and fourteen others resigned from the Commission. Lech Wałęsa's worst fears were coming to pass. Solidarity was moving towards confrontation, which was exactly what the hardliners in the government wanted. As the strikes continued – Wałęsa estimated that there were sixty-five of them – Warsaw TV for once voiced the nation's thoughts, speaking of "a national tragedy taking place in instalments, a conflict between the need to save the nation and the state, and a plethora of irresponsibility . . . There have been various predictions about Poland, but no one forecast the Poles would want to dig their own graves."

Although more talks with the government did take place and continued till the end of the month, events had suddenly assumed a momentum of their own and the direction was all downhill.

Significantly, in view of later events, the authorities announced that the military operational groups which had been working to some effect in the villages were to be withdrawn, and that similar larger groups would soon start work in the cities. The Warsaw daily paper commented that the Army enjoyed great popular support and that it was reassuring for the public "to know there is somebody who can be relied on".[6]

For some, it was a true comment – for the people's patience had snapped at last, and the hungry workers were beginning to make increasingly radical demands. THEY PROMISED US A SECOND POLAND BUT THEY BUILT US INTO A THIRD WORLD NATION proclaimed a banner in Łódź. The people were anxious, confused, hungry and utterly demoralised. "They keep changing Prime Ministers and First Secretaries but I'm still eating nothing but potatoes," complained a man-in-the-street in a radio programme. Women were still getting up at dawn "to buy a pair of shoes the wrong size so that they may have something to barter for a piece of meat which turns out to be rotten".[7]

Fears for the future mingled with a rising exasperation with Solidarity. "The hardest thing for people to bear," wrote Brandys in his diary,[8] "is the fear of a future that appears as a formless gloom." A saviour was needed – and if the saviour wore an army uniform, so be it. Just so long as it was a *Polish* uniform! It was not a universal view, but it was one that was gradually gaining ground.

On 22nd November, the police raided Jacek Kuroń's flat. At the Solidarity Congress in September, KOR had formally disbanded itself as being no longer necessary. Kuroń was now holding an inaugural meeting of a new Club For Self-Government, which might siphon off some of the political activity into which Solidarity was being forced. The police broke up the meeting and arrested him.

A few days later, General Jaruzelski asked Parliament for an Emergency Powers Bill. Before Parliament had considered the request, he acted. ZOMO riot police, landing from helicopters, broke up an eight-day sit-in at the Warsaw Fire Brigade College, by students who were demanding academic reforms: "It looked to me," wrote Brandys, "like a dress rehearsal for a fiery opening night. I have a feeling that the General who donned dark glasses after August will soon be taking them off!"[8]

Wałęsa sent off a telex declaring a "state of extreme emergency" in the union, and the next day the presidium held an emergency debate in Radom. The best they could manage was to threaten a twenty-four hour general strike on 17th December if Parliament actually passed the Emergency Powers Bill, and an unlimited further strike if the emergency powers were used. The government did a "Watergate" on this meeting and recorded what was said. Three days later, Wałęsa's voice was heard on Warsaw Radio announcing (among other carefully edited highlights) "Confrontation is inevitable and it will happen." A government statement accused the Solidarity leadership of breaking the 1980 summer Agreements, and of assuming the role of a political opposition engaged in a struggle for power.

Wałęsa complained that he had been quoted out of context, that the authorities were the ones who were trying to provoke a confrontation – one bloodier even than the one in 1970. For the first time, the government began personal attacks on him. The army newspaper, *Soldier of Freedom*, called him "a great liar", and a "provocateur" who led a group of madmen hell-bent on chaos.[9]

Opening the National Commission meeting next day in the Lenin Shipyard where Solidarity had been born, Wałęsa made a last effort to save the peace, saying: "I declare with my full authority that we are for agreement . . . we do not want confrontation."

But the appeal for a national strike on 17th was endorsed by a majority on the Commission. As the debates wore on, the telex machines in the shipyard began chattering with anxious messages from the regions – stories of unusual troop movements, of Solidarity headquarters being sealed off. The discussions went on. As Wałęsa looked on helplessly, they called for a national referendum on whether the Party was fit to govern; and on free elections to the Sejm. If the referendum brought a vote of no confidence in the Party, then the union should go ahead and form its own provisional government.

Thus did they give the General in dark glasses the perfect pretext for taking them off.

At 12.30 a.m. on the night of the 12th/13th December, as the Commission members reached the end of their discussions, news came in that telephones and telexes had been cut off, that Gdańsk's communications with the outside world had been severed. A voice from the floor expressed dismay but was told not to "play Cassandra". Whereupon Lech Wałęsa stood up, raised both arms in a gesture of despair: "Now you've got what you've been looking for," he said angrily,[10] and, turning his back on them, he went home.

[1] Halina Mirowska, *op. cit.*
[2] Bogdan Szajkowski on ITN News, October 1981.
[3] Brandys, *op. cit.*
[4] Tom Stoppard, *Squaring the Circle*, *op. cit.*
[5] Tom Stoppard, *Squaring the Circle*, *op. cit.*
[6] Kevin Ruane, *op. cit.*

[7] Tom Stoppard, *Squaring the Circle*, *op. cit.*
[8] Brandys, *op. cit.*
[9] *Time*, 4.1.82.
[10] *Time*, 4.1.82.

22 CROW (December 1981)

> "In front of my window there's this dead old tree. Last winter a small bird was perching in its branches, and a big fat one pecked it to death."
>
> Marek Nowakowski: *The Canary*

At about two o'clock in the morning, thirty or forty Solidarity leaders and advisers returned through the frosty snowbound streets to the Hotel Monopol, opposite the Gdańsk railway station. Shortly afterwards Tadeusz Mazowiecki, editor of Warsaw's *Solidarity Weekly*, unable to sleep, looked out of his window and saw a chilling sight – the hotel surrounded by a tight ring of helmeted ZOMO riot police carrying truncheons and riot shields. Mazowiecki felt, he said, "like a mouse watching the cat getting ready to pounce".[1]

Moments later, the cat pounced, and caught almost all Solidarity's leadership in its claws. The ZOMO went to arrest Lech Wałęsa in his flat at about the same time, and flew him by helicopter to Warsaw. The others were flung into police vans and taken off to different destinations.

In Warsaw, the Army and police had started netting Solidarity members and their supporters at midnight, and continued throughout the night. Some were treated courteously enough and given time to collect necessities, like warm underwear. Others were dragged out brutally, their hands tied or manacled behind their backs while they were still half-asleep. Some few were forced out with tear-gas into the waiting arms of the ZOMO wielding new lead-lined truncheons.

All the chairmen of the Solidarity factory committees throughout the country were arrested; all the organisers of peasant protests and Rural Solidarity. Using the element of surprise, and having cut off all methods of communication, the government hoped to trap all the main personalities in Solidarity. In this they were only partly successful: between twelve thousand and eighteen thousand were seized, one thousand of these being from Warsaw alone. But the rest, including Bogdan Lis and Zbigniew Bujak, the Warsaw leader, somehow evaded capture. Some whose names were on the list of those to be arrested were (like Bohdan Cywiński) out of the country at the time; some had actually emigrated. The fact that their names were there, on lists which were printed in the Soviet Union, suggests that the swoop was premeditated long in advance.

That night, the Pope received a telephone call from the Polish Ambassador to Italy, informing him that General Jaruzelski had found it necessary to introduce "temporary emergency measures". A similar explanation was given to the Polish Primate, Archbishop Glemp, but not until much later, only one hour, in fact, before the rest of the nation heard the news.

General Jaruzelski broadcast over Polish radio at six o'clock on that bitterly cold December morning. Poland, he said, more in sorrow than in anger, was "on the brink of the abyss . . . not days but hours away from national catastrophe".

He sighed reproachfully over the recklessness of the Solidarity "adventurists" ". . . the words uttered in Radom . . . the session in Gdańsk"; and asked, with a sublime disregard for the truth of the matter: "How long can a hand outstretched towards agreement meet with a closed fist? . . . Things could have been different in our country; they should have been different . . . The steps we have taken today have as their goal the preservation of the basic requisites of Socialist renewal."

From midnight, the General went on to say, the country was under the control of a Military Council of National Salvation (WRON); the Polish People's Republic was under "a state of war". With whom, asked the Poles, were they at war? That morning, a woman in a taxi heard the news over the driver's radio. "What's all that about?" she asked him. "It's war," he said. "Where's the war?" she asked. "Here in Poland," he replied. "But who on earth can have invaded Poland?" The man was silent.

There was no mention of Solidarity being banned, in Jaruzelski's speech. But any early hopes were dashed in the course of that day as, punctuated by solemn or martial music, a military announcer spelled out what martial law would mean: a curfew from 10 p.m. to 6 a.m.; all gatherings, except for religious services, all demonstrations banned; trade unions and student organisations suspended; the right to strike rescinded; no public entertainments or sporting events; a ban on private motoring and restrictions on all journeys away from home. The use of printing presses was henceforth illegal; all newspapers except the Army's *Soldier of Freedom* and the Party's *Tribune of the People* were proscribed; and all persons over the age of thirteen were to carry identity cards and be prepared for a search of their house or their person at any time. All telephones were officially monitored, and travel abroad was banned for the duration.

Before that day was over, the Poles had realised that all they could now legally do in company with each other was "to work, to stand in a queue and to pray".[2] And if they stood in a queue before the curfew ended at 6 a.m., as many had to, they ran the risk of being arrested.

Many factories and institutions, such as radio and TV stations, were put under direct military rule, and any disobedience was punishable by a long prison sentence or by death. Railways, transport systems, refineries, mines, telecommunications networks all came under this jurisdiction. Military commissars, responsible for discipline, were appointed to schools and universities.

In Warsaw that morning, Hanka G. picked up her telephone and found that it had gone dead. Suspecting the worst, she immediately set about hiding the Solidarity leaflets she had in her flat, before setting out to visit friends. On the way, she passed a truck full of young soldiers. "I smiled at them as usual. But their faces were dead and their eyes full of fear," she recalls.

Next day she went to the laundry to collect a heavy load of washing. "A young woman was explaining to the attendant that the receipt was in her husband's wallet and he had been interned the night before. She was quite matter-of-fact about it. The attendant made her write a statement about the missing receipt, and the long, silent queue waited as though frozen into their silence."

At this stage, General Jaruzelski was hoping to woo the people and the moderate section of Solidarity into some sort of agreement. But the Poles were not fooled. They soon realised, as Leszek Kołakowski wrote, that what was at stake was "not Communism or Socialism, not an idea, not a social order, and not economic problems, but a mortal fear of the privileged clique which suddenly realised that the power they were given by a foreign empire might not last for ever".[3]

Though Jaruzelski had made a point of arresting corrupt and incompetent Party officials – among them Edward Gierek and TV chief, "Bloody Maciej" Szczepański – adding insult to injury by equating these "enemies of the State" with the Solidarity people – there was no doubt that the hardliners had triumphed and that "the owners of People's Poland" were back in business.

It was said that half the Party's three million members resigned in protest, including all the journalists on the magazine *Kultura*, and large numbers of university professors. Despite this unprecedented haemorrhaging, the Party proceeded to deplete its numbers still further by purges. There was no longer any place for "reformers" in the Polish United Workers' Party.

Archbishop Glemp broadcast what seemed to be an appeal for peace at any price. "The most important thing is to avoid bloodshed. There is nothing of greater value than human life."

In a way he was only echoing Wyszyński's words in 1956, after the Hungarian Rising, when the Poles had been on the brink of committing mass-suicide. "It is sometimes harder to live for one's country than to die for it," he had said then. But Glemp lacked Wyszyński's charisma, his sensitivity to Polish culture, his finger on the popular pulse; and his message distressed rather than consoled his listeners. Some, perhaps, contrasted this stress on preserving life at all costs with the "better to die standing than to live on one's knees" creed of Solidarity, the spirit that had inspired the poster which Tim Garton Ash had seen during a Rural Solidarity sit-in: WE DON'T CARE ABOUT LIFE. THE PIG ALSO LIVES. WE WANT A LIFE OF DIGNITY.[4]

It was a moot moral point, and nobody could deny that the Archbishop's position was a difficult one. The kindest explanation is that he genuinely believed what he had been told: that the emergency measures would be short-lived.

Once the first surprise had passed and the full extent of the tragedy had sunk in – *our* army and *our* militia declaring war on *our* workers – the sense of being an occupied country brought to the surface all those latent talents for resistance which the Poles had learned over two centuries. "We survived the Nazi Occupation, so we can survive this," was the general feeling. When Jaruzelski had first referred to the "state of war" – *stan wojenny* which is the Polish phrase for "martial law" – the people had gone into shock. Then, realising that the description was apt, they adopted it, referring thereafter to "the war", as if there had been no other. If the General wanted war with the people of Poland, he could have it.

Active resistance was sporadic. Solidarity's back had been broken, its few remaining leaders had gone into hiding, its superb network of communications had been rendered unworkable. Leaderless now, many of the workers continued to resist the military take-over of their factories. Tension grew as the 16th–17th December anniversary drew near, the date on which only the previous year a monument had been erected in memory of workers killed by police in a workers' state. Now history was about to repeat itself.

At dawn on Wednesday 16th, a group of workers occupying the Gdańsk shipyards were driven out by the Army and police who broke through the gates in tanks. One young woman who had been there since the Sunday said that until then, in spite of the freezing cold and the presence of soldiers and tanks in the streets, they had remained optimistic. "We were frightened all the time. But it was not until the ZOMOs began to attack the yards in force that we understood they had won. Our dream was over. It was terrible."

The remembrance service at the Monument that evening was broken up by ZOMOs with tear-gas and water-cannon. In rioting next day, more than three hundred people were injured.

Similar tragedies were reported all over the country. The following graphic account speaks for itself:

> Armoured vehicles drove through the steel-mill in a show of force. Riot police came out in droves, armed with shields and truncheons and also with tear-gas and gas-masks . . . not everybody managed to run away. The police chased people towards the recreation building and there, against the wall, they beat people, while forcing them to kneel in the snow with their arms raised . . . people were chased out of the factory showers, naked, barefoot, on to the snow, and dispersed in every direction with truncheons.[5]

But the worst news of all came from Katowice where, on the 17th, at the Wujec Colliery, eight miners were shot dead by the police. (There were persistent reports that the casualty figure was far higher than eight.) A tape smuggled out of Poland a year later told a moving story about these miners. It appears that in one of the encounters between them and the riot police, a group of ZOMOs were captured, "put on trial" and found guilty. While the miners were arguing about what to do with them, one miner stood up and reminded them that they had heard Mass and received the eucharist that morning. "Can we take vengeance on these people with Christ in our hearts?" he asked. Ashamed, the men released the incredulous policemen unharmed.[6]

The pattern was always the same: the Army would surround the works and then cajole or threaten the workers into coming out. If they did not, the ZOMO would move in, forcing the workers out and arresting the leaders. At the Katowice steelworks, more than two thousand men held out till 23rd December, but after helicopters dropped leaflets threatening the use of chemical weapons, they finally gave up.

The last heroic stand was made at the Piast mine near Katowice, where on the 14th, thirteen hundred miners had voted to stay underground until the Solidarity leaders were set free and the war was brought to an end. For five days their families were allowed to send down food; then permission was withdrawn. By Christmas Day, the miners were starving and scavenging for food on the pit floor. Two days later they surrendered. The surrender marked the end of all active resistance.

Confusion and insecurity reigned. It took time to adjust to the omnipresence of soldiers and armoured cars and tanks; of militia keeping a constant check on identity papers and swooping on any group of people larger than four. The curfew was strictly, even violently, enforced. Houses were searched, telephones cut off; teachers and students in high schools and universities mercilessly weeded out. Small factories and businesses whose personnel were suspected of Solidarity sympathies were liquidated, their employees then unable to find work elsewhere. And since in a Communist state, there is "no such thing" as unemployment, there is "no such thing" as unemployment benefit either. Hardship was very real.

The courts swung into action, passing summary sentences on all who violated martial law, treating the accused like criminals with no right of appeal. The air of hopeless, incredulous misery was conveyed by a taxi-driver in one of Marek Nowakowski's "snapshots taken in haste" of martial law, smuggled out of the country and published abroad:[7] "The cold is cruel. The old are going under, a lot of funerals about. With telephones cut off, you never get an ambulance in time. Streets full of tanks, police vans, all sorts of army vehicles. Gangs of militia, swarming, nosing. Enough to choke you."

Nowakowski's "snapshots" brilliantly convey the desolation: the police harassment, the house-searches, the danger of making a careless remark in public, the vettings at work; the re-emergence of informers, the petty officials who turn other people's misery to their profit; the monitored telephone conversations; the shortages, the shoe-soles nailed on or held on with wire, the absence of soap; the lying television bulletins, which were now given by poker-faced Army presenters, and which most people tried to avoid hearing. "I switched the telly on for the news. Just pressed the knob out of habit and away we went. Seemed worse than ever somehow. The newsreaders' ugly mugs were solemn, unctuous. They mouthed their words lovingly, uttering slanders, insults and threats with pedantic care . . . Must be two realities: one on the telly, the other in real life. It's unbearable!"[7]

One of the worst things was the pressure to sign a loyalty pledge to the regime – which amounted to a disowning of Solidarity, on pain of losing one's job, or worse. One woman, arrested while at the bedside of her mother dying of cancer, was told[8] "there will not be so much as a lame dog to make your mother a cup of tea". She signed, and was released. Another young mother was threatened with having her children taken away and brought up in a State orphanage. She signed too. Some of those who thus publicly disowned Solidarity were paraded on TV to confess their "errors". An article written by a Solidarity activist and published in an underground newspaper in February, said that because the aim of this "loyalty pledge" was to induce despair, "the act of signing deserves understanding, always sympathy, but never praise. By refusing to co-operate you are preserving hope . . . You know, as you stand alone, bound in handcuffs and with tear-gas in your eyes . . . that 'the avalanche changes course according to the stones over which it passes'. And you want to be the stone that will change the course of events."[9]

The internees – leaders, intellectuals and workers all mixed up together in forty-nine different detention centres – resisted from the start, keeping up a demand for a chaplain, clean clothes, greater hygiene, contact with their families, contact with Wałęsa. (Later they discovered that the prisoners had all been demanding the same things at the same time.) In many of the prisons conditions were inhumane in the extreme. A letter from the Białołęka prison, twelve miles outside Warsaw, revealed that the internees were treated like criminals, kept in close confinement in rat-infested cells, denied proper medical care or hygiene, condemned to exercise in "a very small space in which people can hardly shuffle, surrounded on two sides by walls and on the other two by a net next to the dustbins".[10]

Tadeusz Mazowiecki kept a prison notebook, which provides invaluable information about the life inside.[11] The prisoners weren't allowed to speak to each other, but they found various means of communicating. Three times a day, at a given moment, they sang hymns together, through the windows of their cells, and at midday they recited the Angelus prayer. "It was those hymns, that prayer," said Mazowiecki, "which gave us strength to survive, even though we had no news of our families, our dear ones, our friends. We had to save the most precious thing of all – hope – by our own efforts."

The close contact between workers and intellectuals in prison was mutually enriching. When, therefore, Mazowiecki and some of the other intellectuals were moved to the plushier army camp at Jaworze, they formally protested, believing, probably rightly, that the authorities were trying to drive a wedge yet again between the two groups.

At Jaworze, Mazowiecki realised that the young conscript soldiers who served the prisoners' meals were themselves under great pressure and were closely watched by the regular militia and by the hated ZOMO troops. (One lad who had refused to carry a lead-lined truncheon was sentenced to three years' imprisonment.) The conscripts had been ordered not to talk to the prisoners, but many of them broke the rule, explaining that they were acting under compulsion. One young guard in particular spoke freely, and stirred Mazowiecki's compassion: "One of his remarks remained in my memory because it reflected a bitter truth and also revealed the core of that hellish machine that held us both enslaved. 'There will always be someone to stand up for you,' he said, 'but who will there ever be to stand up for us?' "[12]

The prisoners did not forget their leader, Lech Wałęsa, now being held in solitary confinement. A group from Jaworze wrote to him:

> The blow which the nation suffered on 13th December will not break us. It will not destroy the feelings of unity between the workers and the intellectuals. These bonds will endure. You are the symbol of the values for which we all fought. In solidarity with all those arrested, interned and in hiding, our thoughts and our hearts are with you.[13]

Arriving for interrogation (one of several) before a military procurator in Warsaw on 10th February, Lech had announced to the people who stood outside: "I shall never bear witness against my friends." If the General had hoped to suborn him into co-operating with the military regime, he had far underestimated his opponent. Lech's famed willingness to compromise stopped short of the big moral issues. Lech stood firm, resisting all blandishments, all requests to bless the new official "branch" unions which were now replacing Solidarity but gaining few recruits.

(Many Party members were ordered to join. People on the edge of retirement were threatened with the withdrawal of benefits if they did not join; and already-retired pensioners were drafted to swell the numbers.)

Lech would consider no proposals unless and until martial law was brought to an end and the prisoners were released. Until then, his response would be silence. A silence that became a symbol of Polish defiance. Isolation would not break him, as it would soon break young Jan Kułaj, the Rural Solidarity leader, and lead him to "confess" his crimes on TV. Later he would claim that he acted under duress, but it was too late. As a colleague bitterly said: "Jan gained his freedom, but lost everything else."

Not everyone expected that Lech would hold out. When Andrzej Celiński, his secretary on the National Commission, found himself in a cell in the Białołęka prison, another prisoner jeered: "Well, what price Lech now? I'll bet he'll soon be playing along with the General." Celiński flew into a rage. "You can criticise Lech for all sorts of things. But of one thing I'm certain: he'll never betray us."[14]

Thousands were sacked for their part in the strikes, and the organisers received severe prison sentences of as much as seven years. More Party members resigned. In many factories and offices, bucketsful of returned Party membership cards were collected. It was said that in Katowice, for example, a large trunk was left outside Party headquarters. Fearful that it might contain a bomb, the frightened apparatchiks called in the Army to defuse it. When the trunk was opened, it was found to be full of Party membership cards returned by the last workers still to have belonged.[15]

International support was also forthcoming. (Lech Wałęsa had appealed for help in October 1981 when Poland's plight became desperate.) Seeing a convoy of one thousand lorries leaving in heavy snow for Poland, with a cargo of food, medicines and clothing, a woman in Holland was heard to remark, "Christmas this year is a Polish Christmas." Gifts poured in from West Germany, Austria, Denmark, Sweden, France, the UK, and from all over the world people rallied in their thousands to show "solidarity with Solidarity". It was generally understood that the issues went beyond the simple existence or non-existence of free trade unions in a totalitarian state. It was a battle for human dignity at the very heart of Europe.

On this wave of popular sentiment, governments also gave their support: materially, with shipments of some of their reserves; and politically, with sanctions imposed against the Polish and Soviet governments.*

By now there was no further possibility of active resistance in Poland, but passive resistance, such as Lech Wałęsa now asked for, in a message smuggled out of prison, could be very effective. Notwithstanding Archbishop Glemp's cautious speech on the 13th, it was the Church which took the lead. In fact, now that all legitimate opposition had been stifled, the Church had no option but to become the "voice of the voiceless". It was not so much that the Church stepped into politics, as that politics imposed itself on the Church. Glemp had a difficult tightrope to walk between trying to maintain the spirit of Solidarity and avoiding a head-on clash with the military authorities.

One week after the "war" was declared, the bishops issued a statement, far stronger than the Primate's sermon, calling for a restoration of civil rights, the release of all prisoners and the renewal of dialogue between the government and Solidarity. Then they turned their attention to practical matters. Priests were asked to extend their pastoral work by setting up permanent centres for legal, medical, spiritual and material aid and counselling – to internees, prisoners, those thrown out of work, and their families.

One of the Warsaw priests who threw himself wholeheartedly into this work was the young Jerzy Popiełuszko, an assistant priest at the parish of St Stanisław Kostka. Because of poor health, he was unable to have a parish of his own, but was a very busy medical chaplain in Warsaw. During August 1980, when all over the country workers were striking in support of the Gdańsk shipyard demands, the men from the Warsaw steelworks (Huta Warszawa) had asked Cardinal Wyszyński to find a priest to say Mass for them.[16] He found Father Jerzy – a young man quite uninterested in politics – and the steelworkers adopted him as their chaplain. During the recent sit-in by students at the Firemen's College, he had acted as *ex officio* chaplain, slipping in and out of the besieged school, to bring spiritual and moral help.

* These sanctions partially collapsed in the summer of 1982, when Western European governments decided, against American opinion, to provide the Soviet Union with vital parts for a gas pipeline from Siberia. Later that year, the US government allowed large shipments of grain to be resumed to the Soviet Union. These actions meant that sanctions were more symbolic than effective. They were progressively withdrawn, as some of the repressive measures in Poland were relaxed; and were virtually removed with the amnesty of 22nd July, 1983. It is on record that their removal was publicly recommended by both Cardinal Glemp and Lech Wałęsa.

When "the war" started, many of the steelworkers were arrested, tried and sentenced, and Father Jerzy went to their assistance. "The duty of a priest," he said, "is to be with the people when they need him most, when they are wronged, degraded and maltreated."

He attended the trials of the steelworkers, sitting at the front of the courtroom with their families – so that the men would know that their families had a friend who would care for them. He brought practical help, providing money, food, clothing, much of which came in from well-wishers in other countries. As a medical chaplain, he had been entrusted with medical arrangements during the Pope's 1979 visit; and now in 1981 he was put in charge of the first medical charitable centre in Warsaw – at the church of St Stanisław Kostka, which stored the medical and other supplies coming in from Western Europe and America. At home, Father Jerzy roved far and wide in search of help, persuading the better-off to give, and encouraging the workers in industrial plants and factories to contribute to the support of the old, the sick, large families, and the totally impoverished.

As the Church alone was exempt from the ban on assemblies, it remained the only outlet for public anguish. Already on the first Sunday, a Warsaw church had changed the last line of the hymn, "*God who dost defend Poland*", from the standard, politically acceptable, "Lord, keep our country free", to the defiant version sung in the old days of Czarist oppression, "Lord, return our homeland to us free", the version which the Polish exiles in the West had continued to sing. Much to the annoyance of the authorities, the new version was taken up on all sides, and everywhere sung with passion.

Christmas cribs abandoned tradition in favour of relevance. Sixty-eight-year-old Father Stefan Dzierzek was arrested for politicising the Christian message. His crib showed a Virgin Mary weeping beside a crib which had been overturned by tanks; the Infant Jesus on the ground wrapped not in swaddling clothes but in barbed wire; and, instead of shepherds, eight workers who represented the murdered miners from Katowice.[17] The priest was charged with publicly displaying a crib whose contents "abused freedom of religion and threatened law and order". At his trial he defended himself with spirit:

> What I have tried to stress is that Jesus lives, that He is born today . . . into our circumstances. I have placed Him in the realities of AD 1981–2 in Poland. The police and all those who maintain that Christ

has no right to interfere in the affairs of the contemporary world, reacted violently. For my accusers, Christ is dead. For me, He is eternally alive.

At St Stanisław Kostka in January, Father Jerzy Popiełuszko said the first of his *Masses for Poland* which would make him known and loved throughout the land. With the death penalty facing anyone rash enough to make an "anti-State" pronouncement, the parishioners deluged him with advice and warnings about what to say in his sermon. "The church was packed that night," said Hanka G., "but I could see his face as he spoke – just one sentence: 'Because freedom of speech has been taken away from us,' he said, 'let us therefore pray in silence.' And we stood silent for what seemed an eternity. Those were my first tears of the war. On the way home, I cleared a patch of snow from the windscreen of my car (there was no petrol available for private use) and scraped off the Solidarity sticker with a penknife. I was still crying. 'Dear God,' I prayed, 'just let me stay on the right side of the prison wall long enough to hear his next Mass for Poland.'"

Masses for those suffering under martial law would become a regular feature of life from now on; but the Mass for Poland at St Stanisław Kostka, on the last Sunday of every month, was the most renowned. Workers, intellectuals, artists, actors, university professors, crowded this small church, and stood in their thousands outside. People came to pour out their anguish and sorrow, but also to hear Father Jerzy tell them that the Church could not be neutral in the face of injustice and suffering but must become the true protector of the oppressed.

From "underground", the Solidarity leadership called for some sort of symbolic protest on the 13th of every month – the wearing of armbands and Solidarity badges, lighted candles to be placed in windows. On 13th February, a Mass was said in a large Warsaw church for the intentions of Solidarity and the internees. The packed congregation sang the National Anthem with new words. The old chorus, with its rousing: "March, march, Dąbrowski, from the Italian mainland to Poland", had referred to the country's Napoleonic past; but now the words were changed to:

> Lead us, Wałesa, from the sea-coast to Silesia;
> Solidarity will rise again and be victorious.

They also sang: "to reduce us to silence, you will have to kill us", and a crowd of two thousand chanted: SO-LI-DA-RI-TY . . . WA-ŁĘ-SA. . . BU-JAK.

Outside St Stanisław Kostka, where a similar service was held, truckloads of militia ringed the church, but the people dispersed quietly. Elsewhere in Warsaw, a crowd of three thousand shouting JUNTA OUT were dispersed by ZOMO using water-cannon.

> The Church is a time-bomb [complained the colonel in charge of radio and TV personnel].[17] To me it is clear that the Church's activity all in all is decidedly anti-State . . ., aimed against the current system in our country . . . All the cribs in the churches now have a uniquely political character. Religious symbols of the Home Army, emblems of Fighting Poland, banners spattered with blood . . . Just as it was during Hitler's Occupation.

In fact there was a widespread belief that the authorities now wanted a showdown with the Church, so that the people would be left defenceless. Hostile measures were being urged by the hardliners (known from now on as "*betons*" or "concretes"), with the backing of Moscow which with some justification saw the Church as the prime cause of Socialism's failure in Poland.

It was also the sole source of hope, as the people withdrew into a state of total alienation from the government. Under house-arrest outside Warsaw, the imprisoned Wałęsa appealed for a passive, non-violent resistance. People responded by refusing to read the Party press or watch TV; by going for walks *en masse* at TV news time, or putting their TV sets in the windows facing outwards. Once again they turned to Radio Free Europe and the BBC for a true picture of events; and once again the Polish joke, that cynical expression of impotence and despair which had not been needed in the Solidarity era, became a major popular industry: "What is the numerical strength of your opposition?" General Jaruzelski is supposed to have asked while on a visit to China.

"About thirty-five million people," he was told.

"Ah!" returned the General, "about the same as us."[18]

People drew closer together for mutual consolation, protecting each other from discovery, closing ranks against the oppressors. WRON, Jaruzelski's Military Council, had been immediately dubbed WRONA, which is Polish for "crow". No crow can defeat an eagle, they said. And, to the tune of a patriotic song used during the Nazi Occupation, they sang: "Before us is the crow, green and decked out in uniform. Whoever refuses to caw just like him, has to be put away."

Graffiti appeared on walls: WINTER IS YOURS BUT

SPRING WILL BE OURS; leaflets bore the logo of a snail or of a tortoise, symbols of slow, step-by-step resistance or of go-slow industrial action. Marshal Piłsudski's words, inscribed on his tombstone, "To be defeated and not to surrender, that is victory", became a watchword for the young. All in all, General Jaruzelski's *blitzkrieg* had succeeded only on the physical level. His victory was a hollow one. It must have been an appalling thought for him that the young were almost totally against him. "Polish youth," wrote Norman Davies, "looks neither to Lenin nor to Leftism, but to Piłsudski, Poniatowski and the Pope."[19]

With none but the Party and Army newspapers being printed, the following ironic announcement appeared in a kiosk:

> *Soldier*: plenty.
> *Life* (i.e. the usual Warsaw daily): none.
> *Culture*: suspended.
> *Perspective*: lacking.
> *The Republic*: sold out.

But by March there was an incredible flowering of underground newspapers and literature. About one hundred and fifty independent publications appeared, in spite of the fact that "all" printing materials had been seized by the security police.

It was the underground press which revealed that Archbishop Glemp's nightmare was coming true. They had managed to get hold of documents concerning Operation Raven, which had been put into effect in March to introduce and spread the notion of the "extremist" priest.[20] In view of what later happened to Father Popiełuszko, "Raven" is of exceptional interest. It used set-ups, provocations, scandals blown up out of all proportion to the facts, false accusations – all the classic blackmailing ploys. The priests on the authorities' black list (Józef Tischner was one; Henryk Jankowski another) were surrounded by specially trained informers. "Raven" intended "to set the clergy at variance with each other by singling out those who are 'loyal' and the 'extremists'. The latter are then to be isolated from the churchgoing public and, once alone and at bay, they are to be destroyed. Aim: to prepare the ground for a general confrontation with the Church."

Here were essentially the same plan, the same methods, the same dirty tricks with which the Stalinists in the late 1940s had sought to destroy the Church, and had almost succeeded. That they had failed was largely due to that tough old warhorse,

Wyszyński. But where was a Wyszyński for the 1980s? Few could see Glemp in the role.

Using much the same tactics of "divide and conquer", the authorities poured scorn on the "anti-Socialist garbage" who had joined Solidarity. Ten million of them! Among this "garbage" was, of course, Lech Wałęsa, a man recognised and admired not only in Poland, but by people of many political complexions, creeds and colours. For the Poles, he epitomised strength of conviction, high moral principles and enduring courage. And his stature grew even as his freedom diminished.

After his various interrogations in Warsaw, they had moved Lech to the hunting-lodge of Arłamów, near the Soviet border, where he was given a room thirteen feet square. "It's in a forest," reported Danuta, in an interview for *Spectator*, one of the underground papers. "Wherever you look there's only forest. It's such a lonely place, and terrible for him to sit there with no one for company but security guards who write reports on everything he does and says, and who even keep a camera in his bedroom. But Lech has to talk to them, or he'd go mad."

Lech and Danuta's seventh child, Maria Wiktoria, had been born at the end of January, and the christening at St Brigid's church in Gdańsk in March was attended by fifty thousand people. Lech was not allowed to be there: the authorities feared an insurrection if they let him out. In fact, at this time there was a move afoot to persuade the Solidarity leaders to go into voluntary exile in the West, a move frequently interpreted in the West as a sign of General Jaruzelski's generosity of heart, but deeply resented in Poland. A popular joke showed mistrust as well as resentment. Lech Wałęsa is being interrogated:

"Well now, comrade, where would you rather we sent you – East or West?"

"West, of course," says Wałęsa.

The colonel turns to his secretary and says: "Write it down – West Siberia." (In another variation on this theme, a woman approached a police patrol and asked if there was really a war on, just like Hitler's? "Yes," said the policeman. "In that case," said the woman, "can we please be sent to work in Germany?")

A few Solidarity people accepted the offer of emigration for themselves and their families, but Lech would not even consider it. When Deputy Prime Minister Rakowski raised the matter, he met such an explosion of rage that he hastily retreated from the room.

Lech, with time on his hands, spent much of it reading.

Although he had told Oriana Fallaci that he had never read a book, that was just inverted showing-off. On other occasions he had been more explicit: "I take a book, read two pages, understand what the author wants to say, check the end to see if I'm wrong, and if I am, check the middle to see why. Then I say to myself: well, why read the whole thing when I already know the answer?"

He asked now for Cardinal Wyszyński's prison memoirs, and for a variety of books on the Church's social doctrine, including John Paul II's encyclical on workers' rights and duties. He read these works right through, and when he'd finished with them he passed them on to the guards to read!

The only exercise he took was walking round and round the thirteen foot room, because whenever he went out into the garden, the guards came too. A picture of him taken in April showed him with a bushy beard, a pasty complexion and a paunch. When the guards reproached him with not exercising enough, he told them: "Just open that gate, and I'll show you just how fast I can run." "Your husband is lucky," said a police colonel to Danuta, "he lives in reasonably good conditions." "Yes," replied Danuta, "like a sheep among wolves." Among all the people she talked to, there was no one, she said, who would have changed places with him, for all his supposed "luck".

Yet he said he was never bored, nor did he waste time regretting the past. However gregarious he may have seemed, he had always described himself as a loner. "Internment was good for him," said Father Jankowski.[21] "It gave him the opportunity and the space to think a lot of things out and to learn about people. Much as he may have disliked being surrounded by security police, he is quite incapable of hating anyone."

Lech endorsed this view, saying:

> Forgiveness is always necessary. I don't look on anyone as an enemy, though we may have different aims and purposes, and they may regard me as a pest. In my mind, I always see the cross of Christ. He seemed to lose everything and fail. But He forgave His enemies just the same. And He didn't fail – two thousand years later, he's still winning.[21]

"Internment," he claimed later, "was just one more school of life which it was necessary for me to attend . . . In many ways it was good for me to go through it. We have to take whatever comes to us in life and make the best possible use of it. If we've failed, then we must simply start again. Nothing is ever final. Life is all fresh starts."[21]

Violence grew in intensity. As Underground Solidarity called for a boycott of the May Day parade, a crowd of fifty thousand attended an alternative demonstration of their own in Warsaw's Old City. (And in other cities too.) Two days later, on 3rd May, ZOMO riot squads wearing gas-masks attacked a crowd of demonstrators with firecrackers, missiles and tear-gas. Many were hurt and over a thousand arrested. At midday on the 13th – a day on which there was a "staggered" stoppage of work throughout the country – all traffic came to a halt, and pedestrians wearing Solidarity badges stood still with their hands outstretched in the V-for-Victory sign. During the afternoon, the ZOMO attacked anyone standing around on the public squares with gas, clubs and water-cannon. The most serious incidents were reported in Kraków, Warsaw, Gdańsk and Szczecin, with heavy casualties and numerous arrests in each case.

Although July brought a partial relaxation of martial law, trouble flared again in August, when the anniversary of the signing of the Gdańsk Agreements (31st August) came round. In Przemyśl, for example, a small town in the south-east, people were attacked by police and beaten up on their way to Mass; a man returning peacefully from his vegetable plot was beaten and thrown to the ground; and gas-canisters were thrown at a group of women with prams. Similar events were reported from all over the country. The bishop of Częstochowa complained to the authorities that schoolchildren had been arrested and cruelly ill-treated by militia.[22] More seriously still, in Lubin and Wrocław police opened fire and killed a number of demonstrators; and the official press admitted similar deaths in Gdańsk and Częstochowa. (It was almost impossible to find out the exact numbers, since only those who died in hospital were admitted as statistics. Those killed outright on the streets were removed by the military, and their families were bribed or threatened into silence.)

As a poem circulated by the Underground noted, it seemed as though the government regarded the men in armoured tanks and ZOMO helmets as the only genuine "workers"; while the ordinary man-in-the-street was automatically a "hooligan" or a "scoundrel". The people's bitterness was undeniable. Yet it is significant that they did not offer violence for violence. In Poland there was no terrorism: no bombs, no sabotage. Throughout the world, there were those who interpreted this as a sign of weakness. But to the Poles, it was a sign of honour, a proof that they had learned well the lesson taught them by Solidarity and the Church. They could hold their heads high, even though the happy Solidarity baby of the 1981 I AM ONE YEAR OLD TODAY poster now had a successor, a wretched, sad-eyed little waif who proclaimed AND NOW I AM TWO.

[1] Tadeusz Mazowiecki, *Internowanie*, Aneks, 1982.
[2] Tim Garton Ash, *The Polish Revolution*, *op. cit.* Chapter 9.
[3] Preface to Nowakowski's *The Canary* (see below).
[4] Tim Garton Ash, *op. cit.* Chapter 3, "Inside The Rzeszów Commune".
[5] *Poland Under Martial Law*, a report on Human Rights by the Polish Helsinki Watch Committee 1984.
[6] Grażyna Sikorska, *A Martyr for the Truth*, Fount 1985.
[7] Marek Nowakowski, *The Canary and Other Tales of Martial Law*, Harvill Press, 1983.
[8] Norman Davies, *Heart of Europe*, *op. cit.* Chapter 6.
[9] Norman Davies, *Heart of Europe*, *op. cit.* Chapter 6.
[10] Statement made by the internees of Białołęka and addressed to Amnesty International, The International Red Cross etc. Published by Solidarity Information, Warsaw, 12.1.82.
[11] Tadeusz Mazowiecki, *Internowanie*, Aneks, 1982.
[12] Tadeusz Mazowiecki, *Internowanie*, Aneks, 1982.
[13] As note 1: *Letter to the Solidarity Leader, Lech Wałęsa, From The Internees in Jaworze*, 22.1.1982.
[14] Pawlak and Terlecki, *Każdy Z Was Jest Wałesa*, *op. cit.*
[15] Tim Garton Ash, *The Crow and the Eagle*, *Spectator* 6.2.82.
[16] Grażyna Sikorska, *A Martyr for the Truth*, as above.
[17] *The Church in Poland under Martial Law*, booklet published by Voice of Solidarność, London, 1984.
[18] *Wojna Polsko–Jaruzelska W Karykaturach* I *Rysunkach*, Kopenhaga, 1982.
[19] Norman Davies, as above.
[20] *Wojna Polsko–Jaruzelska W Karykaturach* I *Rysunkach*, Kopenhaga, 1982.
[21] Personal interviews with the author.
[22] Sermon by Bishop Tokarczuk, Częstochowa, 5.9.82.

23 "THERE WILL BE NO RETURN TO ANARCHY" (1982)

> No one expected that they would impose such suffering on the nation during the state of war. They seem to want to impose the maximum suffering on us; they want to see the workers on their knees.
>
> *Danuta Wałęsa*

For a brief moment the scene shifts to Rome, where, on 10th October, 1982, the bells peal out in welcome to hundreds of thousands of pilgrims – mainly Polish – from all over the world. On this day a new saint is to be canonised – the Polish priest, Maximilian Kolbe, who in 1941 had voluntarily taken the place of a man condemned to die of slow starvation in Auschwitz concentration camp. The example of Father Kolbe's heroism had brought new heart to the prisoners and his fame had spread not only throughout the camp but later, when the war was over, throughout Poland and throughout the world. By a strange historical irony, it was the German bishops who, more than any others apart from the Poles themselves, had pressed for Father Kolbe's canonisation. And now the Poles were to have at last their twentieth-century martyr-saint, and their rejoicing should have been great.

Should have been! Coachloads of pilgrims had been given special visas to come to Rome, and the huge Orbis coaches now perched on St Peter's Square, as though keeping a watchful eye on their passengers. But the previous day, the Polish Sejm had outlawed Solidarity, declaring its statutes null and void. It was part of Jaruzelski's "normalisation" programme, which also recreated the old transmission-belt trade unions against which at least ten million people had rebelled. For how could Poland be returned to its "normal" state of subservience to the Party and to the USSR, while a free trades union continued to exist, even if only in name?

Just how "normal" the Poles felt this action to be could be

judged by the tens of thousands who came out on strike in protest. But by now, the strike weapon was scarcely even a paper tiger. It could be easily destroyed by a combination of water-cannon, tear-gas, the threat of dismissal, and the possibility of a five-year prison sentence.

Although the strikes were put down, the situation in Poland remained so volatile that the Primate, Cardinal Glemp, did not feel justified in going to Rome for the canonisation. At a special Papal audience for Polish pilgrims in the Nervi audience hall on the day after the ceremony, the air was electric with emotion,[1] and the applause which greeted the Pope's arrival was tinged with desperation. As John Paul did not fail to notice. Close to tears himself, he addressed his compatriots: "When I was passing through the hall, I heard and saw many tears. What has happened to our country that our fellow-countrymen arrive for the canonisation of a compatriot with their eyes brimming with tears? These were no tears of joy . . ."

Turning to the official government delegation, he said sternly: "Let there be no more tears. Polish society does not deserve the fate of tears of despair and resignation. It deserves something else – to be allowed to build a better future for itself."

It seemed appropriate then that having finished his address, the Pope went down from the rostrum to greet a group of former prisoners from Auschwitz, in their striped twill prison attire and carrying their own flag: a Polish eagle dominated by a cross and a crown of thorns.

Father Kolbe, the new saint, was Jerzy Popiełuszko's ideal, but the young priest was not in Rome for his canonisation. Ever since his first Mass for Poland in January, he had been singled out for special intimidation and harassment by the police. The clergy house where he lived had been broken into and vandalised, his car had twice been smeared with white paint, his telephone was tapped, and two "guardian angels" followed him wherever he went. He was accused of inciting people to violence; and the increasingly popular Masses for Poland, attended by people from all walks of life and from all over the country, were denounced as "rallies hostile to the Polish state".

It was true that the authorities had good reason to fear Jerzy Popiełuszko, in that he was a fearless exponent of the evils that afflicted Poland, and spoke of things which others dared not mention. He spoke openly of "a nation terrorised by military force"; of people detained and brought to trial for being faithful to the ideals of Solidarity; of the beatings and ill-treatment of prisoners, of attempts to send healthy detainees to psychiatric hospitals. He laid bare the sickness of soul from which his country suffered. But he did not, as his enemies alleged, preach hatred. On the contrary. "Let us be strong through love," he pleaded in one of his sermons, "praying for our brothers who have been misled, without condemning anyone, but always condemning and unmasking the evil that they do, Let us pray in the words of Christ on the cross, 'Father, forgive them, for they know not what they do.'"

The crucial need, he said, was to overcome fear, and "we can do this only if we accept suffering in the name of a greater value. If the truth becomes for us a value worth suffering for, then we *shall* overcome fear."

Everyone remarked on the extraordinarily prayerful silence which prevailed at these services. But the authorities saw them as political demonstrations and determined to silence Popiełuszko. They tried first through the Church, asking the hierarchy to deal with this "turbulent priest". When the bishops took no action, they took matters into their own hands. When Father Jerzy in September referred to Poland as "a nation hanging on the cross with Christ", they refused him a passport for Rome, and drew up plans for a new campaign against him.

Like Lech Wałęsa, Jerzy Popiełuszko articulated the hopes and fears of almost an entire nation, and gave them a moral direction. "We are called to the Truth," he said in October. "We have to witness to the Truth with our whole lives." And in February 1983: "Let us put the Truth, like a light, on a candlestick. Let us make life in Truth shine out . . . Let us not sell our ideals for a mess of pottage. And let us not sell our ideals by selling out our brothers."

Witnessing to his own kind of truth, in early November Wałęsa wrote to General Jaruzelski with a new proposal for dialogue: "It seems to me that the time has come to clarify some issues and to work for an agreement . . . I propose a meeting and a serious discussion of the problems, and I am sure that with goodwill on both sides a solution can be found."

His guards at Arłamów had repeatedly urged him to write such a letter, assuring him that it would bring about his release. Wałęsa had consistently refused, pointing out that since he had not asked Jaruzelski for his arrest, he would not ask him for his release either. He had frequently told Father Orszulik, a representative of Cardinal Glemp who was allowed to visit him, that he would stand firm until martial law was abolished, since he had no wish to be released before all the other internees.

However, in November, he wrote the letter asking for dialogue and signed it "Lech Wałęsa, Corporal". Four days later, he was released from internment – an unexpected turn of events which caused many internees to accuse him of buying his way out; especially when they heard about the "Corporal" signature.

It was the first time he had put a foot wrong since martial law began; and, if it was a mistake, it remained the only one. General Jaruzelski was, in any case, considering a partial relaxation of martial law in December, and Wałęsa's release may have been a calculated ploy to convince world opinion that Poland was returning to "normal".

The ordinary people were delighted about his release. When he arrived home, he found the words WELCOME HOME, LESZEK painted in huge white letters on the street in front of his apartment. Banners streamed from the windows of the Zaspa estate: LECH, WE WANT ONLY YOU AND SOLIDARITY. Thousands of supporters gathered to see him, and the police stayed at a discreet distance. He was fatter (there were dark rumours about his having been forcibly drugged in prison); his face was rounder and puffier, his voice weaker. He was obviously a sick man. He greeted the people, but without his usual exuberance. And when he met the press, he asked them to leave him alone to reflect: he had been eleven months out of touch with reality, and needed time to readjust.

The Party newspaper, *Tribune of the People*, carried a non-committal nine-line paragraph about his return, and Jerzy Urban, the government press officer, describing Lech as "the former leader of a former union", added dismissively, "I do not feel called on to comment on any statements made by Citizen Wałęsa, a private citizen." (To underline what the people thought of this cavalier dismissal of their hero as a non-person, a portrait, recognisably of Wałęsa, was soon circulating in Warsaw, entitled, Portrait of Ordinary Citizen With Moustache.)

Wałęsa was well aware of the pitfalls that faced him. As he told a friend: "I have been released on to a tightrope stretched over a prison-yard. The rope is greased, but I do not intend to fall off it."

He was right about the greasy rope. Almost immediately, a Canadian news agency reported that a smear campaign was under way against the unimportant "private citizen". Just before his release from prison, security agents had handed to Church officials pictures of Lech in allegedly compromising pictures with women. For good measure, there were also documents accusing him of financial misconduct.[2] When told about this, Lech was unimpressed. "Attacks like that are a bonus," he shrugged. "Nobody will believe them."

To escape from such sordidness, Lech, with Danuta and a number of other recently-released internees, set off at the end of November on a private pilgrimage to Częstochowa.[3] Presenting to the Prior a bronze medal depicting a bleeding heart and the words *Poland 1982*, he prayed at the shrine:

> My heart I submit to thee from this day forth . . . To thy care, Mother, I commit both myself and Poland . . . Shield us in our strivings to defend the rights and dignity of all who labour. I beg thee to embrace our country with thy care, so that Poland may be truly a home to her people . . . a place where justice, peace, freedom, love and solidarity shall triumph.
>
> Guide me, Mother, that I may be a worthy tool in thy hands, to serve the Church, my country and my neighbour. Look with love upon the workers and peasants of Gdańsk and upon all thy people in Poland. Sustain them and strengthen their hearts in the struggle for justice and freedom.

It was a dreary existence to which Lech had returned, a travesty of his former hectic life. He was out of work, and the authorities would not recognise his status, though his stock was high in the country, and he was still the acknowledged leader. The people did not realise how powerless he now was. For them he was still the saviour, and many of them still beat a path to his door, bringing him all kinds of problems. "The neighbours don't go to the militia when their husbands get drunk and start throwing things," he sighed. "They come to me."

At least he now had a chance to get to know his children. Bogdan, Sławek, Przemek, Jarek, Magda, Ania, and the baby, Maria Wiktoria, knew him mainly as an absentee father.[4] The boys, he said, were all: "awkward buggers, like their father. The oldest one wants to go on strike, and they all want to change the director of their school."

They were, in fact, cheerful, attractive, lively youngsters, but being Wałęsa's children had given them a certain notoriety and often made them aggressive and imprudent. Danuta had her hands full with them, and she was not beyond using the belt to show who was boss. Lech was aware of his inadequacies as a father, and was content to leave the discipline to Danuta. But he did have his ambitions for his children: that they would "learn to distinguish truth from lies, and become real human beings". Danuta shared this hope: "I don't want my children to have the same sort of life as Leszek and I have had. I wish they could live in a free country, without this awful feeling of helplessness."

"Danuta is more of a hero than I am," he would often say. During Lech's long internment, she had shown herself to be immensely competent, strong-minded and good-humoured. "A woman always finds the necessary strength when she is forced to face the unexpected," she says modestly. But Lech did not undervalue her achievement. He had been inclined to take her for granted before, but his admiration for her had grown during the last difficult months. "It's a strange marriage," he mused. "We don't discuss things, and we don't quarrel. People tell me that those who love each other quarrel a lot. Well, we don't. But we do love each other, I think. I have an old-fashioned attitude to marriage: a wife's a wife for ever. She'll bury me, or I'll bury her."

He did not, he said, want a wife who went out to work – "I'd hate to be married to a woman-welder in overalls." For Danuta, with seven young mouths to feed, it was scarcely even a temptation.

Life for women was exceptionally hard, whether they went to work or not. There were few of the labour-saving devices which ease the life of women in the West, and their lives were reduced to a series of "queue, wait, queue, wait, hunt, look, barter, bargain, bribe, queue".[5]

Prices had risen during the "war" by 400 per cent, and many families could not afford to feed themselves. About thirty per cent of all Polish families were living below the accepted minimum standard which was itself not far above the biological survival level.[6] A butcher in Warsaw displayed his entire stock (for a month) of six salami sausages, which his customers bought in thin slices. He was using the meathooks as supports for climbing-plants. Fathers bartered live rabbits for food for their children. Miners in Silesia were exchanging a ton of coal for two tons of potatoes. More and more city-dwellers travelled to the country to deal direct with the farmers, though this was illegal. Farmers and their wives travelled to the cities, with pieces of meat hidden under their coats.

Because of the poor diet, there was an epidemic of viruses stemming from malnutrition. Lack of medicines and of even the most basic facilities for hygiene added to the hopelessness. In the appallingly overcrowded hospitals, patients had to be responsible for their own hygiene. Since detergents and disinfectants were unavailable, hospital laundries were being closed down, and nurses were washing dirty linen by hand in small washbasins in the wards. Many doctors had no surgical gloves, sutures, masks, bandages, plaster of Paris, or apparatus for blood transfusions. Cross-infection was rife, and the danger to life enormous.

Soap was so scarce that not even doctors could wash their hands properly. One of Marek Nowakowski's "snapshots" of life under martial law (later described by Wałęsa as "the best account of that tragic time to have been written") tells of a shop assistant announcing to the queue that there is no more soap:

> The queue started to disperse. Some cursed their luck. The face of the fat woman grew red, and she gasped soundlessly like a fish out of water. With shaking hands she took from her bag a small piece of grey soap wrapped in newspaper:
>
> "It stinks! They allowed us a hundred grammes each at work, and the cleaner won't even scrub the lavatory with it."
>
> She threw the soap down on the pavement and stamped on it in a rage. "Stinks like rotten fish!" she kept saying, her voice hoarse from her exertions.[7]

To combat their tragic demoralisation, the people instinctively turned to the Church as their only hope. Churches were packed day and night. In an effort to reduce tension, the bishops had asked the people to refrain from making the V-sign in church and to hold a cross in their hand instead. The people responded by holding a cross in one hand and making a V-sign with the other! Many churches had their own Solidarity altars where weekly all-night vigils were kept. In Radom, a banner over a church read DO NOT BE AFRAID, FOR BEHOLD I AM WITH YOU. And because a "cultural cold shower" prevented not only foreign but any new Polish books, films, poetry and paintings which did not advance the Socialist cause, the churches had taken to staging exhibitions of Polish culture.

There was, of course, a price to be paid by the Church for this solidarity with the people. The attacks on "extremist" priests were being stepped up. In Gdańsk, Wałęsa's priest, Henryk Jankowski, was subjected to a campaign of vilification in the Party press – "my role is to keep Wałęsa's spirits high," he once said. "And I succeed. That's why the authorities hate me." In Warsaw, on the night of the 13th–14th December, "hooligans" hurled a brick containing a detonator through the window of Jerzy Popiełuszko's room. The bomb did not go off; but the priest now realised the kind of danger he faced. After this, the Warsaw steelworkers organised round-the-clock protection for him.

At the beginning of December, Wałęsa again wrote to General Jaruzelski. The crisis in the country, he wrote, could only be overcome by the whole of society pulling together in an atmosphere of mutual trust. And this could only be achieved on the basis of the Gdańsk Accords of 1980. Three conditions were fundamental to agreement: an amnesty for those arrested during martial law; the reinstatement of those who had been deprived of their jobs; and a recognition that Polish society needed some kind of pluralism. He ended the letter with the words, "I am ready to take part in any work to this end." There was no reply to this letter, but the authorities circulated a scurrilously distorted version of it which made it seem as though Lech was abandoning Solidarity and making a bid for power on his own account.

Wise after the event, Lech would not be caught in the same way again. Before the 16th December, he took the precaution of releasing in advance his intended speech at the Monument. It was just as well he did, as early on that day a group of six armed militia pushed their way into his flat and took him away for questioning. They then drove him up and down the motorway for eight solid hours, to prevent him from keeping his appointment at the Monument. But his speech was read for him. "We have been hurt again," it said:

> But our cause is still alive, and a victory will one day be ours. What can I say, as leader of this great union which officially does not now exist? I say that it exists within us, even within those who seem to have abandoned it . . . I believe we have sown a seed that lies deep. We are not the people that we were before August 1980. We know now what we are striving for. The question is, how do we set about it?

Although he was continuing to keep a low profile, Wałęsa gave numerous interviews to Western journalists in this period. His message was always the same: the demand for an amnesty, the cessation of reprisals, the need for free trades unions, and his own willingness to take part in a dialogue. But by March, when there was still no response to any of his overtures, he was beginning to get exasperated. He realised, moreover, that if he didn't exert some sort of pressure on the authorities, he would soon be losing his own credibility as a leader. The government was making an all-out effort to coerce people into the new unions, and the repression was becoming more severe. It was the trials of two Solidarity leaders: of Anna Walentynowicz; and of six internees which brought him out of his quasi-retirement. Though Walentynowicz had little time for him these days, and openly queried his right to be leader, Lech attended the opening of her trial and later promised some "hard action". As he left the court, passers-by shouted encouragement at him, and gave a hurried V-sign.

The promise was followed by a meeting between Lech and the Solidarity leaders who were still in hiding. When Lech announced that this meeting had taken place, the authorities were furious. But no amount of questioning could make him divulge where it had taken place or what had been said. From now on, however, he would be followed by police wherever he went; a security police family would occupy the floor below his; his telephone would be tapped and a complex surveillance system installed. "My telephone and my walls are all ears," he would warn visitors. "It's not pleasant, but you can get used to anything."

A week later, as he and Father Jankowski drove from Gdańsk to Warsaw, to lay a wreath at a memorial service for the victims of the 1943 Ghetto Rising, they were stopped on the road by the police and held in detention. Presumably the authorities feared that Wałęsa's mere presence at such an emotive occasion would provoke a riot.

So perhaps it was to keep him off the streets that in April – one week before the expected public outbursts on May Day – they gave him back his old job as an electrician at the Lenin shipyard. It said much for his strength of character that this man, so recently the uncrowned king of Poland, admired all over the world, could accept, without any inner turmoil, a return to the role of an electrician working shifts. For all his surface vanity, Lech had never ceased to regard himself as a worker first and foremost:

> I am a worker and that's all I ever want to be. It doesn't mean I have no ambition to learn, or to improve myself. But to the end of my days I shall be a working man. And why? Because, in my kind of work I repair tools old and new, from the East and from the West, from simple hammers to highly complex machines. Now, *there*'s a job which expands a man's mind.

Solidarity had, in fact, *not* asked for any demonstrations to mark May Day. Instead they had asked the people to boycott the parade, and on the 3rd to go to work in their best clothes and observe one minute's silence at some time during the day. But there were some localised protest rallies on May Day: in Kraków, for example, where a demonstration passed off peacefully, and in nearby Nowa Huta, where at least one man was killed when the police moved in to break up the crowd. On the 3rd, spontaneous demonstrations burst out in various cities. It was the largest display of public opposition since the declaration of war over a year earlier. In Warsaw a crowd of eight thousand heading for the Party building were dispersed by water-cannon and many arrests were made. As night fell, a group of security men disguised as thugs raided a convent attached to St Martin's Church and with cudgels beat up a group of volunteer helpers who were making up parcels for the families of internees. Among them was the poet and Solidarity activist, Barbara Sadowska. After wrecking the premises, the thugs took four of the injured to a forest outside Warsaw, and left them to walk home. (A favourite ploy of the police.)

Next day, the official press made a casual reference to "a few isolated incidents" involving "a handful of extremists".

Worse was to come. Grzegorz Przemyk, Barbara Sadowska's nineteen-year-old son, having passed his school-leaving exams, went to a wine bar to celebrate with friends. On the way out he was stopped by the police who kicked and beat him so brutally that he died two days later in hospital. In an open letter to General Jaruzelski, a Polish writer who was also a friend of the family reported that the boy's insides were "a bloody pulp", and that there was "not a centimetre of undamaged intestine". "It is not often that surgeons cry," he wrote, "but these did, as they left the operating theatre."[8]

The people cried too. The Przemyk affair stirred them up again, and ten thousand attended the funeral mass at St Stanisław Kostka. A telegram from Wałęsa stated that: "Every death is painful, but this one is especially brutal. It must not be forgotten." All emotion spent, the mourners walked the two miles to the cemetery, their numbers doubling on the way, their faces frozen in silence. After seeing those faces, an eye-witness confessed to feeling fear: ". . . fear of that stony silence, for what it might mean some day in the blood and death of those young people, when the silent scream was cried aloud."[9]

When Pope John Paul again visited his native land in June to pay tribute at the shrine of Our Lady, Queen of Poland, at Częstochowa, there was none of that hopefulness that had marked the earlier visit. In those long-ago days of 1979, he had persuaded them to pick up their courage and try to save their world. Four years later, they had made the attempt and failed. Hope was in limbo. "Even their expectations are tired," said Józef Tischner. "All they can pray for is a miracle."

Nevertheless, hundreds of forbidden Solidarity banners fluttered in the breeze to greet the Pope, and hundreds of thousands of hands raised in the V-sign showed the world that Solidarity was not yet dead. But, to prevent any spontaneous outburst against the regime large numbers of militia were deployed at every event. The authorities clearly felt even less secure than in 1979, when the policing of the visit was left entirely to stewards appointed by the Church.

It was a difficult journey for the Pope. He too was being asked to walk a slippery tightrope. In government eyes, he was there to bestow authenticity on them, to consult and confer with them as the legitimate rulers of the land. But this he refused to do. Instead he constantly urged Jaruzelski to make good the Gdańsk Agreements, to restore civil liberties and initiate genuine dialogue as the only sure path to social harmony. He was prepared to respect the existence of military rule, but denounced the misery it had inflicted on the people, "the bitterness of disappointment, humiliation, suffering, loss of freedom, injustice, the trampling of human dignity underfoot".

Nearly one million people crowded John Paul's large outdoor Mass in Warsaw, to hear him tell them that "at this particularly difficult moment in the country's history", only a moral victory over themselves could help to heal the divisions in society.

It was a visit which underscored the yawning gap between the entire people and the government which claimed to rule in their name. Yet he did not mention politics, and when he used the word "solidarity", it was in lower-case type, and in the ordinary, human sense of the word. In effect, all he could do was raise morale and preach endurance. It was, said someone, "a call to faith not arms". He did not raise hopes, because he could not. But he did, nevertheless, breathe hope into the people, "not because he suggested that anything could be done, but because he showed us a way of living with the situation, by overcoming hatred and returning good for evil".

To the Polish bishops he threw out a challenge which many of them welcomed. It was necessary, he said, now that the people had no spokesmen of their own, for the Church "to defend every citizen, to protect every life, to prevent any injuries, particularly to the young and weak" – an obvious, even if sideways reference to the police murder of Grzegorz Przemyk.

Lech Wałęsa had been refused holiday leave from the Lenin shipyard for the duration of the Pope's visit. The Pope had asked to see him, but the authorities were most unwilling to give such prominence to this "former leader of a former union", and indeed had been keeping Wałęsa under close surveillance throughout the Pope's visit. John Paul, however, insisted. The two men met in the Tatra mountains near the Czech border and talked for two and a half hours. What they talked about has not been revealed, though an article next day in the Vatican's *L'Osservatore Romano* gave rise to speculation that the Pope had asked Wałęsa to step aside and leave the Church and the authorities to sort things out. Lech himself gave no hint of what passed between them on this score, revealing only a more general comment made to the Pope by himself:

> During my meeting with the Holy Father, I said that our situation is in many ways what we make it. As a nation we Poles are always being forced by circumstances to examine ourselves and our capabilities. This means that we are constantly being driven back to bedrock, to seek and find the most basic truths about ourselves. We have no shoes for our feet, and rarely have enough to eat. But we do ask ourselves questions about what really matters in life. Do other richer nations have such opportunities? In this sense, I believe that Poland is the richest nation in the world.[10]

Meeting the Pope revived at least some of Lech's wounded self-esteem: "I watched him getting in the plane and saw his big shoes and giant clip-clopping stride. Each step seemed to express peace and faith . . . I felt as though I had received an electric charge . . . as though he had passed some of his own peace to me."[10]

But there was not to be much peace in the months ahead. Lech returned to the hurly-burly of a life in which he never had any time left to himself. There was no privacy, and Danuta felt herself a prisoner in a flat where, in spite of the conspicuous police presence outside, people were always dropping in unannounced.

> How can one describe this place [wrote a friend],[10] which for some is a family home, for some a place of work, and for others a cross between a theatre and a zoo? How does the host feel when he returns tired from the shipyard and after a short nap has to divide himself up between his family, the office, visiting journalists, and several million others? How can one calculate the stresses of a life in which if he says something stupid, gets drunk or whispers I love you to his wife, there's a listening microphone to pick it up?

Though he had a better flat than most of his fellow-workers, few of them would have exchanged their lives for his. As he said:

> I have to get up at five to go to work. I can't drive fast because I have a police car on my tail. At home, five hundred letters are waiting to be answered, so I stay up till midnight or later, and then have to be up at five again. Even if I do have more things to eat, I don't have time to eat them. What's more, I never know whether someone is planning to hang me, beat me up or just arrest me.

In July, the "war" officially came to an end. But "there will be no return to anarchy", Jaruzelski warned. By which he meant that there would be as much repression as ever, if not more. New laws required employees to give six months' notice before changing jobs, while facilitating the expulsion of unruly students and dissident academics without any notice at all. The right of assembly continued to be restricted: only church gatherings or meetings of the official unions could be held without prior permission. All printing equipment was to be registered and anyone connected, however remotely, with any underground publication was liable to imprisonment. Those Poles who continued to belong to "secret unions or those that have been dissolved" could be put away for three years.

At the same time, a partial amnesty was announced for all but sixty or so internees and prisoners. Partial, because they were to remain on probation until the end of 1985. Hundreds of internees accepted, for the sake of sparing their families further hardship. Bujak, the Warsaw leader, ignored the amnesty, and preferred to stay underground to ensure the continuance of what was left of Solidarity. As for Wałęsa, he didn't listen to the General's speech, but spent the day fishing.

When he returned to work in August after a break, he was wearing a T-shirt imprinted with the Solidarity logo. By this time, many of the released internees had already been re-arrested for such crimes as scrawling Solidarity slogans on walls. Wałęsa said the new laws meant a return to Stalinism, and the bishops wrote a stiff note to the Sejm to this effect. The Sejm managed to modify a projected new law which would have made "spreading false information" (whatever that might be construed to mean), a crime punishable by prison. But the Sejm's powers were very limited and apart from that one concession, the rope round Poland's neck continued to be pulled tighter.

On the third anniversary of the Gdańsk Agreements, a cordon

of armed ZOMO ringed the shipyards, blocking the path to the monument outside the gate. As Lech and two thousand of his workmates approached the gate, the ZOMO parted momentarily to let Lech through, then immediately closed ranks to keep the others back. Wałęsa, a lonely figure, placed his bunch of flowers beneath the crosses and stood for a minute in silence. But few had come to support him, and fewer still of the shipyard workers had observed the Solidarity call for a go-slow.

The largest response had been, not in Gdańsk, but in the steel town of Nowa Huta outside Kraków, purpose-built as a stronghold of Socialism. Here riot police scattered ten thousand demonstrators with their usual brutality. The ZOMO were now using paint mixed with the water in the cannon. This ruined the clothes and took a week to wash off the face. In Nowa Huta too, militia forced their way into a church where about 300 people had taken sanctuary. Unable to deal with them in the church, the militia went outside again and simply waited till the three hundred came out.[11]

The authorities were jubilant, claiming "a boycott of the boycott". But Wałęsa was reasonably content that, however limited the boycott had been, it had at least proved that Solidarity was still breathing. At the same time he realised that in view of the inevitable reprisals, the time for public demonstrations was past. A new more forward-looking programme of social structures needed to be worked out, covering every area of national life. Doctors, he said, should work out their own programme for a future health service, teachers one for schools, economists for industry: "Sooner or later talks with the government must take place. And whoever represents our side must have behind him a massive, detailed and readable programme of reform. We must be ready and waiting for the new August."[12]

It was a new attempt to show the world that though Solidarity had been stifled, the social conscience which it had awakened lived on. In Warsaw, Jerzy Popiełuszko was making the same point. He too saw the enduring legacy of Solidarity as the awakening of the nation's conscience, the restoration of human dignity to the working people of Poland. He had been impressed by the Pope's references to a "solidarity of hearts". "Solidarity," said Father Jerzy during his August Mass for Poland, "is the unity of hearts, minds and hands rooted in ideals which have the power to change the world for the better . . . Solidarity means that we must overcome the fear that paralyses us . . . and bear witness to what we believe and to the truth which is in our hearts."[13]

Such "anti-State" sentiments were too much for the authorities, who now began legal proceedings against the priest. In September during a workers' pilgrimage to Częstochowa, he had accused the authorities of violating human dignity and depriving the people of freedom of thought and action. Three days later an official investigation was ordered into the priest's "abuse of freedom of conscience and religion".

It seemed as though the authorities had declared open season on their major opponents. For their slander campaign against Wałęsa too was moving into overdrive. Throughout the summer, the media had been indulging in character assassination, endeavouring to portray Wałęsa as an "enemy of the people", who had led the country into bankruptcy and civil war![14] The Party newspaper, *Tribune of the People*, drew public attention to the numerous gifts he had received from Western admirers, and sneeringly dubbed him "the Yank from Gdańsk". In September, with a great deal of advance "hype", a special thirty-minute TV film, *Money*, "exposed" him as a fraud and an embezzler. The film, which reproduced an alleged conversation between Lech and his brother, Stanisław, a year earlier (when Stanisław had visited Lech in prison), claimed to prove that he had over a million dollars-worth of ill-gotten gains salted away in the Vatican Bank. Unfortunately, the tape was of such poor quality that it was impossible to hear who was saying what, so an "interpreter" had to be used. A note of farce was injected into the proceedings when the presenter unctuously warned: "Because the heroes of this programme use vulgar expressions, we ask children and very young people not to watch. We also inform you that we have removed from the conversation . . . remarks which are insulting to the Pope and the Church . . ."[15]

Next day, the specious government spokesman, Mr Jerzy Urban, assured foreign journalists that Citizen Wałęsa was certainly not the target for a propaganda campaign, since he was of no importance in Polish politics. The people had their own opinion about that. They did not need Lech to assure them that the programme had been a tissue of lies, a hotch-potch of various tapes sewn together. At the European Cup-Winners Match in Gdańsk next day (between Lechia Gdańsk and Juventus Turin) about forty thousand soccer fans suddenly realised that Lech was amongst them. Rising to their feet, hands held high in the V-sign, they roared LESZ-EK, SO-LI-DAR-NOŚĆ, LESZ-EK, while the stadium managers turned up the music on the loud-speaker system as loud as it would go, to drown the din. But nothing could have drowned a din as loud as that.

[1] I was there.
[2] *Newsweek*, 29.11.82.
[3] *The Church Under Martial Law*, *op. cit.*
[4] The rumour that the children were not all his, that he had adopted two children of one of the workers killed during the riots of 1970, was absolutely untrue.
[5] A. M. Rosenthal, *New York Times* Magazine, 7.8.83.
[6] *Uncensored Poland*, 22/83.
[7] Marek Nowakowski, *op. cit.* "A Short Street".
[8] Polish Affairs III. Summer/Autumn 1983.
[9] A. M. Rosenthal, as above.
[10] *Każdy Z Was Jest Wałesa*, *op. cit.*
[11] Eye-witness account tòld to the author.
[12] Interview with Lech Wałesa in *CDN* underground publication, 8.9.83.
[13] Grażyna Sikorska, *A Màrtyr for the Truth*, *op. cit.*
[14] *Uncensored Poland*, 16/83.
[15] *Uncensored Poland*, 19/83.

24 GOLD . . . (1983)

> I have always believed it to be my duty to help others and to serve them as far as I can. I did that before August, during Solidarity and still today. Sometimes I can help a large number of people, sometimes only a few. The numbers aren't important. As for rewards – one day they give me the Nobel Prize, and on the next they'll probably put me in prison.
>
> Lech Wałęsa, 1984

Ashes and diamonds, gold and tears. If such dramatic paradoxes lie at the heart of the Polish experience, they were never more graphically illustrated than in the twelve-month period between the Octobers of 1983 and 1984. For it was in October 1983 that Lech Wałęsa won the golden Nobel Prize for Peace and in October 1984 that the murder of Father Jerzy Popiełuszko plunged the nation into yet another deep collective trauma.

Wałęsa had been nominated for the Nobel as early as 1981, and two years later his name was on the short list along with the Pope, Anatoly Scharansky, Philip Habib and Bishop Desmond Tutu. (General Jaruzelski had been on the list of nominees!) Having been unsuccessful earlier, Lech was not particularly hopeful this time; and his own government was extremely anxious that he should fail. On 5th October, 1983, *The Times* (London) carried the following brief paragraph:

> Anticipating the possibility that Mr Wałesa might win the prize, the Polish government spokesman in Warsaw said yesterday that the nominee is still under investigation for illegally holding bank accounts in the West and for evading Polish taxes. It is clear that the authorities in Warsaw are nervous about him winning the prize, for that would undo most of their attempt to discredit him at home.

Warsaw Radio announced on the same day that it was doubtful if the prize would be awarded that year. Presumably the candidates were not of a high-enough standard!

It was a Wednesday. Lech, who had been off work with stomach ulcers, had decided to spend the day in the lake district around Gdańsk, fishing and gathering mushrooms with a few friends. At 11 a.m. they heard the news on the car radio that he had won the Nobel. Passing cars honked their congratulations, and his friends tossed him up in the air with delight. Lech, they noted to their surprise, was "pleased but tight-lipped. Definitely tight-lipped".

Back at the flat, Danuta was being deluged with flowers, telegrams, telephone calls, foreign journalists and camera crews. By 5 p.m. there were two thousand people waiting outside for Lech to return. On the police radio frequencies, voices could be heard discussing this build-up:

First voice: How many are there?
Second voice: A lot. They're standing there, shouting.
First voice: Shouting what?
Second voice: They're shouting: Long live Wałęsa.

When Lech put in an appearance, the cheering began: WA-ŁĘ-SA SO-LI-DAR-NOŚĆ, LE-SZEK. He came to the window, gave a twin-fisted salute, thanked them and shouted: "This prize is for all of us. I didn't consult you, but I've decided to give the money to the bishops for their Private Farmers' Fund."

"Everyone is pleased," he said, at a press conference in the flat immediately afterwards, "but not all are equally so. Many people are in prison, many have been thrown out of their jobs. Many nameless people have deserved this award, and I feel ashamed that at present I am so powerless to help them."[1]

Would the award be a shot in the arm for Solidarity, wondered the pressmen? "Well, winning a prize like this puts us all under an obligation for the rest of our lives. We must never forget why it was awarded." Was he scared by his new international status, asked a French journalist? To which Lech replied: "I'm scared of nothing and nobody but God. I am only a man who belongs to his own time and his own place, and who tries to solve problems as they come along. Unlike some of my colleagues, I believe there's always a solution to every problem, if one tries hard enough."[1]

The official media were less enthusiastic than their foreign counterparts. They did not mention the award until late that night. When they did so, their displeasure was obvious. Mr Urban said the award was nothing but Western propaganda against People's Poland.

Outside of Gdańsk, the people were not sure how to react.

Nobel was the first thought in everybody's mind and heart, but they were not free to give vent to spontaneous enthusiasm. The writer of this book was in Kraków when the news broke, and four times was taken behind closed doors to be told about it – in a muted whisper. *A teraz co?* mused one lady – and now what's going to happen?

In Warsaw, Jerzy Popiełuszko was delighted by the award, which he too saw as an international acknowledgment of Solidarity's admirable record of non-violence. He praised Wałęsa's role since internment: "He does not say so much now, but what he does say is always good and well thought out. He has the appearance of a man with a deep living faith, who gets his strength from God."

Father Popiełuszko was under great strain. He already knew that the State prosecutor was preparing a case against him and would soon charge him with "abusing the role of priest . . . turning churches into places for anti-State propaganda, harmful to the interests of the Polish People's Republic."

It was a charge that could send him to prison for fifteen years. "If they put lies in my mouth, will you tell them in the West that my only concern was the truth?" he asked the author. And in answer to the obvious question about whether he was afraid, he replied: "Yes, I am afraid. But I could not act otherwise. I must continue to protect those who are helpless and have no one else to defend them. That is my pastoral work. As a celibate priest, with no family dependent on me, I must use my freedom on their behalf."

So, what if "they" decided to kill him? He didn't so much as blink. "I live with that risk every day," he admitted. "On one level it terrifies me, the human level. But for the Christian, death is not the end of the story. I would rather die a violent death in the defence of human freedoms, than save my life by opting out of the struggle against evil."

Lech Wałęsa would have agreed that for Father Jerzy there was no real choice. Speaking of the Church's role in society as being "beyond politics", he explained. "The Church may not say that she 'belongs to Solidarity'; but she *must* stand up for the fundamental human values which Solidarity embodies. She may not intervene directly in politics, but it is her duty to speak out in defence of those basic human values."

Since martial law had begun, Lech had spoken in public only a handful of times. That he was able to do so now was almost entirely due to the fact that the world spotlight was on him, and the authorities would not dare prevent his speaking out.

Accordingly, on 14th November, word went out that Lech Wałęsa was to speak at a church hall in a Gdańsk suburb, and about fifteen hundred people made their way through the dark streets in order to hear him.[1]

They saw the same, straightforward honest human being that he had always been, but they saw too that the experience of internment had deepened and matured him. He had always told them the truth, but often in the past his oratory had been stumbling, and his thoughts had lacked the words to express them adequately. But this evening it was obvious that here was a speaker of consummate power. "We had a great and beautiful programme for self-government," he told the audience, "but it was too vague and we used too many slogans. So . . ."

Here he threw the ball right into their unready laps, and refused to take it back again. A new programme must be worked out, and *they* were the ones to do it. They must go home, form small groups, throw ideas around, patiently and slowly.

First of all, he told them, they must decide on the kind of society that was possible. The ideal society was unattainable, but "a better Poland" *could* come about. As they were stuck with a Communist bureaucracy, they might as well try and find a way of humanising it. Next, they must find a way of ensuring that their trade unions were both self-governing and united with each other – acting mainly in their own workers' interests, but capable of acting on behalf of the others. Thirdly, the economy: perhaps it could be made to work, if every work-place was well-run and efficient, and was also geared to the general good. And lastly, Truth. Let them go home and reflect on how to create a community which would preserve Truth and resolve its internal conflicts without resorting to violence.

Sooner or later, insisted Wałęsa, there would be another genuine working-class revolt, and they must be ready for it, with their blueprints worked out. "We are three years older now, and next time round we must do better." No, this did not mean that he was abandoning Solidarity. "This new programme is still Solidarity, a more experienced and therefore wiser Solidarity."

"Every one of you here is Wałęsa," he barked at them, refusing to let them off the hook. "We have been humiliated and insulted. Let us all see to it that we are humiliated no more. None of us has any excuse. Solutions *must* be found. Agreement *must* be reached. Everyone here lives in a family and in a factory. Very well, then, let everyone find the truth about his country in the context of his or her own family or factory. If we can solve our own problems in that smaller sphere, we shall be able to solve them in the larger one."

As the audience sat stunned, feeling they had been turned upside down and shaken, he rammed the point home. "I cannot decide for you. But decisions are vital. Each of us must decide according to our own conscience. And each of us is responsible for what he decides."

There must have been many present that night who had once criticised Wałęsa for being undemocratic. But many also had long ago understood their mistake. Lech's understanding of democracy went beyond the mere licence to pull in a dozen different directions at once; it involved the patient harmonising of many voices. Since martial law, they had realised that Wałęsa was essential to the survival of Solidarity. His patient refusal to give in to the authorities had saved the movement. "If it hadn't been for him," said a former critic, "we'd have had a pseudo-Solidarity today, led by a 'liberal Democrat' like Rakowski. That's what the government wanted, to destroy the movement by taking it over."[1]

But the movement was alive, and Wałęsa had just thrown down a powerful challenge to its rank-and-file. For a moment, said a participant that night, "we could believe that we were living in a free country. Each one of us *was* a Wałęsa. Of course we were."

Between then and the Nobel ceremony in December, the knowledge that the outside world had appreciated their struggle was some consolation in the worsening atmosphere of "normalisation". A letter from Jacek Kuroń,[2] in prison again, spoke of a people which was "hungry, exhausted and poor" and of the "psychological terror" being practised in factories and firms, where every day there were wholesale sackings. One plant manager had lost his job for taking part in a Mass at which the factory's Solidarity banner was blessed; another for being reported in conversation with a former member of Solidarity's National Commission. The pressure to join the new unions was considerable and involved not only threats but bribes – the offer of coupons for washing-machines or colour TV sets, for example. Kuroń begged that both sticks and carrots be rejected. "When the regime tries to persuade us to collaborate with the security police, when we experience doubt and fear, let us remember those who sacrificed their lives, health and youth for our cause."

Wałęsa was in two minds about going to Oslo in person. In the end, two factors persuaded him not to. The first was the possibility of not being allowed to return to Poland; the second the conviction that to go and be wined and dined in Norway while his companions rotted in prison, would be immoral. He decided to send Danuta and thirteen-year-old Bogdan, their eldest son. "When the press find out," he sighed, "they'll say I want Danuta out of the way so that I can play around with other women." Tadeusz Mazowiecki was to go too, to read Lech's Nobel address. But the authorities refused Professor Mazowiecki a passport, and Bohdan Cywiński, now living in Switzerland, stepped into the breach.

On 10th December, at Oslo University, Egil Aarvik, the Chairman of the Norwegian Nobel Committee, presented the $195,000 cheque and the golden Nobel award to Danuta.[3] Lech Wałęsa, he said, had "raised a burning torch . . . and lifted it unarmed", his chosen strategy being that of peaceful negotiation. The determination to resolve conflicts by means of a mutually respectful dialogue was the recognised hallmark of Solidarity. Lech Wałęsa had shown courage when he leaped over that steel fence into the shipyard in August 1980, and his courage had been rewarded by the "millions of Polish workers and farmers who had joined him in the struggle". Mr Aarvik regretted the circumstances which prevented Lech from being present and made it necessary to listen to "a silent speech from an empty chair". But, he asked:

> Is Lech Wałęsa really so silent? Are he and his cause really defeated? Many are of the opinion that his voice has never been stronger nor reached further than at the present moment. The electrician from Gdańsk, the carpenter's son from the Vistula valley has managed to lift the banner of freedom and humanity so high that the whole world can once again see it . . .
>
> . . . Lech Wałęsa has made humanity bigger and more inviolable. His two-edged good fortune is that he has won a victory which is not of this, our political, world. The presentation of the Peace Prize to him today is a homage to the power of victory which abides in one person's belief, in his vision, and in his courage to follow his call.

Danuta, who, as the time for her journey to Oslo had drawn near, had become increasingly nervous, even to the point of praying that she wouldn't be given a passport, rose to the occasion magnificently, reading Lech's acceptance speech with such poise and calm dignity as to win all hearts. Lech, watching a video-recording of the event, on TV in their flat, "fell in love with her all over again", though his friends insist that his admiration was not without a distinct tinge of jealousy.

The theme of reconciliation and of Peace to Men of Goodwill characterised both this and the more important Nobel address delivered next day by Dr Cywiński.[3] The forty years of his own life, Lech reflected, had surrounded him with "violence, hatred and lies". But the lesson he had learned was that "we can effectively oppose violence only if we do not resort to it". The Gdańsk Agreements of 1980 – "a great Charter of workers' rights which nothing can ever destroy" – remained the only possible springboard for a way forward. The Poles, he said, wanted dialogue not confrontation with their government. "Dialogue is possible and we have a right to it . . . But it is impossible to be constructive if frustration, bitterness and helplessness prevail."

Yet, in spite of martial law, about which he preferred not to speak, the people were still vowed to "the defence of our rights and our dignity; as well as efforts never to let ourselves be overcome by feelings of hatred".

A day or so earlier, at a press conference, Wałęsa had called for an end to the Western sanctions against Poland which had been introduced at the time of the imposition of martial law. In this he had the support of underground Solidarity. For the government was now blaming sanctions for the forthcoming spate of price rises and were attacking Solidarity for continuing to support them. Now Wałęsa went further and, as a gesture of good-will towards the regime, asked that Poland should be given a massive transfusion of aid. "We must not close any doors or do anything that would block the road to an understanding," he concluded, making it clear that he was addressing not just Poland but the whole world community. "But we must remember that only a peace built on the foundations of justice and a moral order can be a lasting one."

He might have added, "and based on freedom". That very day, Adam Michnik was writing one of his many letters from prison, this time to General Kiszczak, the Minister of the Interior, accusing: "It was not I who was proscribed that December night two years ago – it was Freedom. It is not I who am in prison today – it is Poland."

Next day, 12th December, Father Jerzy Popiełuszko was ordered to the Public Prosecutor's Office in Warsaw, where he was confronted with "documentary evidence" of his anti-State activities: cassettes of his sermons, photographs, and a video-cassette confiscated from a foreign TV crew. After three hours' interrogation he was taken to the flat which his American aunt from Chicago had recently bought for him and where, by an amazing coincidence the police, within seconds of their arrival, found a cache of gas-canisters, explosives, rounds of machine-gun ammunition, over fifteen thousand copies of underground publications, and leaflets calling for an armed uprising on the 13th and 16th December.[4]

He spent the night in a police cell with a group of convicted murderers, one of whom asked him to hear his confession. Next day, on the intervention of the bishops, he was released – pending investigations. The allegations were on a par with those against Wałęsa, and few believed them. On Christmas Eve, Father Jerzy's parish priest pointed out the absurdity of such accusations against a man who so consistently preached the message of overcoming hatred by love. And on Christmas Day, when Father Jerzy said the December Mass for Poland, the crowd of fifteen thousand who packed the church, the square and the surrounding streets, showed by their mere presence that the attempt to smear a much-loved priest had decisively failed.

[1] Pawlak A. and Terlecki M., *Każdy Z Was Jest Wałesa: Nobel 1983*, *op. cit.*
[2] *Newsweek*, 28.11.83.
[3] *Uncensored Poland*, 24/83.
[4] *Author's Note*: When I met Father Popiełuszko in October 1983, he was fully aware of the case being prepared against him and equally aware of the probability that false evidence would be produced from somewhere. In order to make absolutely sure that there could be no genuine evidence against him, he was going through all his papers and possessions and discarding anything that could be considered even remotely "subversive", in the government's sense of the word. In view of that, it is hard to believe he was so careless as to overlook the large cache of arms etc. which the police later found in his flat – within seconds of their arrival.

25 . . . AND TEARS (1984)

> Let us lie in wait for the virtuous man, since he
> annoys us and opposes our way of life,
> reproaches us for our breaches of the law
> and accuses us of playing false to our upbringing.
> Before us he stands, a reproof to our way of thinking;
> the very sight of him weighs our spirits down . . .
> Let us test him with cruelty and with torture . . .
> and put his endurance to the proof.
> Let us condemn him to a shameful death.
>
> from *The Book of Wisdom*

General Jaruzelski's government maintained a stony indifference. Nobel or not, they did not intend to admit Wałęsa into partnership on *his* terms. The accusations concerning his tax evasions and foreign bank accounts continued, and by pointing to all the money he had gained the government hoped to drive a wedge between him and the ordinary worker.

> The ordinary worker? [snorted a woman in Warsaw]. My God, he earns money but has nothing to spend it on. He has to wait fifteen years for a flat and if he already has one, he can't buy a bigger one because there aren't any. He can't buy a dress for his wife, because they're all so revolting she wouldn't be seen dead in any of them. He can't buy food because it's rationed or because there's none to be had. If his wife has a baby, she'll probably have it without anaesthesia in a filthy overcrowded ward, and when she comes home she won't find a baby food that doesn't make the baby sick. The ordinary worker is up the creek without a paddle. He has no hope.

An article in *Mazowsze Weekly*, the underground Warsaw Solidarity paper with a national circulation, claimed that conditions were now as bad as in the chaotic post-war years, except that then wages had been higher. "We started near the bottom, but we've managed to get even lower."

Many Poles were getting out of Poland if they could. The Stefan Batory boat which plied the Baltic routes was constantly full of "tourists" who had no intention of returning. It wasn't only economic hardship that drove them away. Magda, a teacher in a town in western Poland, sought refuge with her children in West Germany because she had reached the end of her endurance. She and several other teachers at her school had refused to join the new teachers' unions and were being victimised. Magda herself was under investigation for anti-State activities; her flat had been ransacked several times. But it was the bleak prospect for her children which finally broke her. During martial law, her twelve-year-old son, Marek, and many of his friends had been arrested and taken to a state "correction house", where they had to stand to attention for twelve hours at a stretch. Since coming out, Marek had been nervy and unable to concentrate on anything for long. His crime had been to ask for the replacement of the old Stalinist text-books in the school library with newer, more truthful books. "How could I remain in Poland?" Magda wrote from Germany to a friend in England. "The children have no future there. They're already on the police black list, which means that the road to higher education will be closed to them."

Cardinal Glemp continued to appeal for calm and to rely on a successful outcome of his own negotiations with the General. He was hopeful that the Private Farmers' Fund which he had mooted two years earlier* would be operative by the end of 1985. The public were inclined to think he was too soft on Jaruzelski, and that his views coincided too often with government propaganda. Cruelly, they coined a new Polish verb: *glempić* – to glemp, which meant: to say nothing, at great length, but soothingly.

The people's suspicions were deepened when in March the Cardinal was reported as saying, during a visit to Brazil, that though a section of the Polish Church had retained close links with Solidarity, he himself had chosen "a different, more difficult and more just path – the true pastoral path". The Cardinal's remarks caused undisguised fury at home and earned him for some time to come the sobriquet of Comrade Glemp. Devout, elderly ladies on their way out of Mass could be heard wishing to string him up to the nearest lamp-post.

But, if the Cardinal seemed remote from the actual views of

* The Nobel Prize cheque which Lech Wałesa still intends to hand over to the bishops for the fund intended to help private farmers with much-needed equipment and supplies, is still in Norway, since the government has not yet allowed the fund to get off the ground. The diploma and medal etc. were taken by Wałesa to the monastery at Czestochowa where they are being held in trust for the nation.

the people, a large number of parish clergy were very close indeed to those views.

> It was they [wrote Bogdan Szajkowski], who had to cope with the real everyday sufferings of the faithful, the miseries of life in prisons and internment camps, where they went to offer spiritual solace; they who experienced the plight of families deprived for long months of their fathers and of any means of livelihood; they who had to celebrate memorial masses for those killed and injured during the rallies and strikes; and who sheltered the fugitive Solidarity supporters.[1]

At a stormy meeting earlier in the year, Cardinal Glemp was taken to task by a group of about seven hundred younger priests from his Warsaw diocese. But he offered no explanation of his attitude; nor was he prepared to enter into discussion. He merely invited the priests to pray along with him. The special Religious Affairs Office within the Ministry of the Interior now had a black list of eight hundred "subversive" or "strongly anti-State" priests. Their "anti-State" activities covered such misdeeds as organising courses of lectures for workers or for farmers; allowing their churches to be used for performances of underground theatre or for the exhibition of forbidden books or paintings; or even putting on Saturday night discos in the crypt for the young.

Father Henryk Jankowski from St Brigid's church in Gdańsk – which had set up a Solidarity altar and was known as the "shipyard church" – was under interrogation for anti-State activities. As was Jerzy Popiełuszko: between January and June 1984, he was interrogated thirteen times; his friends and even casual callers were threatened; cars parked outside the clergy house were vandalised. When he kept the appointment with the police, a large crowd of well-wishers would escort him to the Ministry of the Interior and wait outside till he was released. This enraged the authorities, who accused him of "using the interrogation as a means of inciting public unrest"!

Troublemakers would regularly be planted in his Masses to try and turn them into the political circuses the authorities declared that they were. Though no one could fail to notice the strain it put him under, Father Jerzy was ready for them and would appeal for self-restraint. No songs or slogans outside church, he begged: "Let us show our maturity and force the troublemakers to go home without achieving what they came for." He would appeal to the provocateurs too: "And you, brothers, who were ordered to come here by others, if you want to serve the truth and regain your self-respect, let the people go in peace."

The ZOMO would be waiting outside, ready to pounce, but the people would disperse quietly, as he had asked. It was said that some of the militia refused to act against him, and that replacements had to be brought in from outside. Perhaps some of the local men remembered that first Christmas of "the war", when Father Jerzy had gone to break the Christmas wafer with the ZOMO patrol outside the church. (The curfew was abolished for Christmas Eve, the traditional time for breaking the wafer, and for midnight Mass.)

"What I do is not political," he continued to insist. "It is my simple duty as a priest. My fight is against hatred and for the dignity of human work; and the only weapons I have are truth and love."

He asked the people to pray for those who had "sold themselves into the service of lies, hatred and violence". There was never any question of his inciting them to violent action. "Jerzy's very careful," a friend in Warsaw assured the author at this time. "He knows how far he can go, and doesn't overstep the mark."

But that was May 1984, and emotions were running high. There was the anger and frustration over the "war of the crosses": the authorities' persistent removal of crosses from schools and public places, no matter how many times the citizens put them back again. Police broke up the resultant protests and sit-ins with truncheons. There was fury over the downward-spiralling living-standards: even the official press now admitted that children were suffering from lack of vitamins and protein. The situation in the hospitals had gone from disastrous to catastrophic. IF YOU NEED AN INJECTION, BRING YOUR OWN SYRINGE, read a notice in one Warsaw hospital; and the spread of scabies and hepatitis was not unconnected with such an appalling lack of basic facilities. The medicine cupboards were all but bare.

A new offensive had been launched against Polish culture, marked by the arrest of Marek Nowakowski for "slandering the State". Once again, only writers who toed the Party line could hope to be published. Add to all that the continued persecution of Solidarity, with scores of Poles being arrested on the strength of their underground connections. "You must realise," Magda had said in the letter referred to above, "there are many supporters of Solidarity, but there are many spies and stool-pigeons too, who track them down and betray them."

Since the much-vaunted amnesty in July 1983, the prisons, with far less publicity, had been quietly filling up again with political prisoners, and there were horrific stories of abductions and torture used to force witnesses to testify against Solidarity. Kuroń, Michnik, two other KOR members and the seven Solidarity leaders – including Andrzej Gwiazda and Bogdan Lis – who had not been released in July, were still awaiting trial after two and a half years. The group was known collectively as the Solidarity Eleven.

Some of those who had been amnestied reported continuing persecution. One man who wrote to thank a Western agency which had helped him with food and clothing, told them:

> I find myself on the right side of the prison wall, but don't be fooled. From the moment of leaving prison, I have been hunted and followed like an animal. I have to move on, changing my address in order to avoid re-arrest and thus jeopardising my sick mother and my brother's family . . . After sixteen years as a miner, I now have nothing, neither a job, nor a home, nor any income, nor freedom. The only freedom I know is carried inside me. Thank you on behalf of my brother's children for the baby food and other wonderful things you sent, which are impossible to get here.

It seemed as though the regime had no idea how to deal with either the economy or the opposition, and resorted to the only procedure they understood: repression. If they could browbeat the people into giving up hope, they might yet numb them into docility.

But May Day killed that hope and brought protest back on to the streets, when thousands of Solidarity supporters infiltrated the official parades. Squeezing themselves in between two factory groups and pretending to be an official delegation, Lech Wałęsa and several hundred Gdańsk supporters disrupted the parade by flashing V-signs, unfurling anti-government banners and chanting FREE THE POLITICAL PRISONERS as they passed the rostrum. ZOMO dispersed them with tear-gas broadsides, rubber truncheons and high-pressure jets of water, whereupon some of the protesters retaliated with stones. That afternoon, the police brought a huge water-cannon, "like some prehistoric animal", and stationed it outside Wałęsa's flat. "I'm surrounded here," he reported on the telephone. "They're chasing people all over the place with water-cannon. They've just hosed my windows down, and they're drenching anyone who attempts to look out."

Near the old Solidarity headquarters in Gdańsk, street-fighting was heavy. Youths tore up stones from the railway tracks to defend themselves against the ZOMO,[2] who, by most eye-witness accounts were more brutal in Gdańsk than elsewhere.

But tensions were just as high in Warsaw – and police scattered a crowd which had assembled after the nine o'clock Mass at St John's Cathedral. The crowd then walked to St Stanisław Kostka to hear Jerzy Popiełuszko speak. After that service too they were assaulted by police. They came back again on the 18th, on the anniversary of the murder of young Grzegorz Przemyk. Those responsible for his death had been arrested and even tried. But the trial had turned into an attack on the murdered boy himself. Two of the four accused were acquitted; the two others were sentenced to a mere two and a half years' imprisonment and were, in fact, released on amnesty in July 1984. On that occasion, Father Jerzy said: "We do not want punishment of the guilty. We yearn for something that stirs the conscience and generates the courage to say, 'It was my fault', and to ask forgiveness."[3]

It was probably two weeks later, during the May Mass for Poland, that Father Jerzy sealed his fate. Local government elections were coming up in June, the first since martial law, and the government was hoping that a high turn-out (however it was achieved) would convince the outside world that "normalisation" was proceeding. Solidarity, on the other hand, called for a boycott. Father Jerzy stepped feet first into the arena, warning:

> We ourselves are responsible for our slavery, when, either through fear or the desire for a quiet life, we elect authorities who proceed to promote evil. If we vote such people into power, then we have no right to condemn the evil that results, as we ourselves are helping to create it and make it legal.[4]

In the event, the government claimed a seventy-five per cent turn-out. (Much less than the usual norm of ninety-eight per cent in a country where the people have much to fear from reprisals. It is no small matter to accept being put back to the bottom of the housing list, for example.) Solidarity, which tried to monitor the results at several polling stations, put the average national turn-out figure at sixty per cent. Whichever way one looked at it (and both sides claimed a victory), between six million and ten million Poles found the courage to boycott the elections, an astonishing figure in a Communist society.[5]

On 12th July, Father Popiełuszko was indicted on the basis of the charges laid against him in December. Ten days later, to celebrate the fortieth anniversary of the Polish People's Republic, General Jaruzelski announced an amnesty for more than six hundred political prisoners, and many common criminals. Father Jerzy was not among them. The following Sunday, his parish priest, Father Teofil Bogucki, took the unusual step of defending his assistant priest from the pulpit: "Just as no one can forbid the sun to shine," he told a packed congregation, "so no one can forbid a priest to speak the truth. Preaching the divine message is not politics."

Father Jerzy, he assured everyone present, was "the best type of priest and the best type of Pole . . . a man who makes people face up to the truth about themselves and society . . . Everyone here knows that he has never preached hatred or revenge . . . On the contrary, he comforts those who are distressed in mind."

Then he added, putting into words the fear that gripped his listeners: "All of us pray night and day for Father Jerzy, trusting in God that no one in Poland will ever do him serious harm."

The 1984 amnesty let General Jaruzelski neatly off the hook as far as the remaining Solidarity prisoners (the Solidarity Eleven) were concerned. Trial dates had been fixed, and indeed the trial of Kuroń, Michnik and company had already started. But it could have been extremely embarrassing to the regime if such fluent and articulate men had been allowed to have their say in court. Attempts had been made to persuade them to emigrate, or to forswear any further political activity. But the prisoners were not to be bought. Releasing them now was the safest course. In any case, they could easily be picked up again, the moment they resumed their "anti-State" activities. They were warned that there would be no leniency, should there be even the slightest return on their part to the "paths of crime". "Urban says I'm free," shrugged Andrzej Gwiazda, "but three police cars follow me wherever I go."

As far as the General was concerned, the amnesty introduced an apparently more normal atmosphere, which permitted him to make overtures to Western bankers again, in the hope of Western credits being renewed. The way was open for Western ministers to begin visiting Poland for the first time since the declaration of martial law. Yet the third report by the Polish Helsinki Committee on Violations of Human Rights in the country told a very different story – of a fierce and bloody struggle against all opposition. The report gave chapter and verse for a horrifying list of kidnappings, beatings, torture of individuals and groups. It also instanced a series of killings by unidentified police officers throughout the year. These crimes *always* went unpunished; and all appeals for justice failed.

It was not until the end of August that Jerzy Popiełuszko learned with relief that his case was after all to be covered by the amnesty.

That week saw the fourth anniversary of the Gdańsk Agreements and also the fortieth of the Warsaw Rising. Lech Wałęsa was allowed to place a bouquet of flowers at the Monument in Gdańsk; but in Wrocław, two members of the recently-released Solidarity Eleven were jailed for two months for making a similar gesture.

The Church marked the anniversaries by calling for a month's abstinence from vodka. Although the sale of liquor before 1 p.m. had been made illegal, there were five million problem drinkers in the country, many of whom manufactured their own hooch, using anything from potatoes to anti-freeze. Solidarity supported the Church's appeal, asserting that alcoholism was one of the weapons with which a totalitarian regime was able to keep a whole people enslaved.[6] Deputy Prime Minister Rakowski marked the anniversaries by warning the clergy not to meddle in politics. In an interview published on the 31st, he said: "One's hair stands on end when one hears what is being said in some pulpits." Jerzy Urban, the government spokesman who wrote for the magazine *Tu I Teraz* (*Here and Now*) under the pen name of Jan Rem, singled out Father Popiełuszko in particular. In an article entitled "Sessions of Hate", he described the priest as "the Savonarola of anti-Communism", "a manipulator of collective emotions" and "a spreader of political rabies".

Adam Michnik was to reproach himself afterwards for not having seen the writing on the wall for Father Jerzy when that article appeared. "If I had had more imagination and had publicly accused Urban of incitement to murder," he wrote, "I might have been sentenced for slandering a minister, but Father Jerzy might still be alive."[7]

In fact, the steelworkers who protected Father Jerzy *were* alarmed, and they asked the bishops to remove him from the scene for a while, for his own safety. The bishops took the request seriously, and plans were made to send him to Rome to study. But the steelworkers had made their move too late. Other people had made plans too. Or perhaps – an even more sinister possibility – these "other people" were so determined to settle accounts with Jerzy Popiełuszko that, rather than let their prey elude them, they brought their own plans forward in time.

The first warning came on 13th October, as the priest was being driven from Gdańsk to Warsaw by his friend and bodyguard, Waldemar Chrostowksi. A man suddenly emerged from the forest bordering the road, and threw a heavy rock at the car. Chrostowksi took successful avoiding action and drove on. Both men decided that the man with the rock was someone deranged.

But that had been Plan One for the disposal of Jerzy Popiełuszko. In the Interior Ministry it had already been decided that the anti-State priests were to be dealt with, and Popiełuszko's name headed the list.

There is considerable confusion about who actually gave the orders and what the orders were. But sadly there is no confusion at all about what was actually done.

Early on the evening of 19th October, Jerzy Popiełuszko took part in a special workers' Mass in the northern town of Bydgoszcz. In the previous nine months, several Solidarity sympathisers had been abducted from the surrounding area. There had, in fact, been so many kidnappings that the oppositionists had nicknamed the area Poland's Bermuda Triangle!

The parish priest of the church to which Father Jerzy had been invited, had been threatened with reprisals if he allowed his visitor to preach. So there had been no sermon. Instead, Father Jerzy prayed with the people after Mass, on the theme of overcoming evil with good. His last words were: "Let us pray to be free from fear, but most of all to be free of the desire for violence or revenge."

Outside, in a Fiat car, his three murderers, Piotrowski, Chmielewski and Pękała, all from the Religious Affairs department of the Interior Ministry, were already waiting. Their executioners' tools were prepared: two clubs hacked from the trees outside Bydgoszcz and wrapped in an old T-shirt brought specially for the purpose; lengths of rope, gauze, sticking-plaster, bags of stones . . .

At ten o'clock, with Waldemar Chrostowski again at the wheel of the VW, Jerzy Popiełuszko set off back to Warsaw. Not far from Bydgoszcz, however, the car was stopped by a "traffic policeman", who ordered Chrostowski out to take a breathalyser test. In the front seat of the police car, he was held at gun-point, bound and gagged. While one man stayed in the car with Chrostowski, the other two returned to the VW to deal with the priest. They ordered him out, dragged him to the Fiat, beat him unconscious with the two clubs, threw him trussed up and gagged into the boot and drove off, telling Chrostowski as they did so to prepare for his "last journey".

Seizing a moment when another Fiat was overtaking them, at a spot where two men were standing by a motorcycle on the left – Chrostowski hurled himself at the car door and threw himself out on to the road, rolling to safety on the verge. The handcuffs came off in his fall, and he managed to escape and raise the alarm.

Had he not done so, the murderers would never have been

caught, for nobody would ever have known what had happened. Father Popiełuszko's body (and Chrostowski's too) would have been fished out of the Vistula dam, and, no matter what anyone might have suspected, would have been attributed to yet another "unfortunate accident". After all, there had been ninety-three such "accidents" since the end of martial law.

The actual events of that dreadful night did not emerge until the trial of the murderers four months later. On the evidence of the accused at that time, Father Jerzy had regained consciousness as he lay tied up in the boot of the Fiat, and began banging on the lid. They decided to stop and tie him more securely, but by the time they had got out of the car, he had somehow got free and was running away calling for help. They caught up with him and Piotrowski began to belabour him with the club on his back and chest. When the priest was unconscious again, they tied him more firmly and pushed a towel in his mouth before putting him face upward in the boot. But again he recovered consciousness and began prising the lid open. Outraged, on his own admission, by such lack of co-operation on the part of his victim (he said aggrievedly in court that "if the priest had obeyed orders, we shouldn't have had to hit him at all"), Piotrowski was "forced" to stop the car and beat him again while he was still lying in the boot. Then, for good measure, he dragged him upright and beat him senseless. Tightening the ropes and pushing the towel further down the priest's throat, he gave orders to drive on a little way, until they came to a wood. Here, they laid their victim on a blanket and tied his legs separately and together in such a way that escape would be impossible. A second rope was attached to his legs at one end and his neck at the other, so that any movement to straighten his legs would have strangled him. That being done, they put more gagging material in his mouth and over his nose, securing the lot with gauze and sticky tape. As a final insurance, they tied bags of heavy stones to his legs, before returning him to the boot one last time.

Waving a phoney traffic pass at a patrol which tried to stop them, they drove straight to the huge dam on the Vistula at Włocławek, where they flung the body into the icy water. Experts who examined the body later said that the priest had already died from suffocation by the time he entered the water.

For ten days after the news of his abduction broke, the people waited and prayed in a kind of stupor. Many spent all their free time, night or day, in the churches, and thousands gathered each evening for Mass in Father Jerzy's Church, St Stanisław Kostka.

Letters of sympathy poured in. Lech Wałęsa came to Warsaw a few days later and warned that "if a hair of Father Popiełuszko's has been harmed, somebody will have a terrible lot to answer for".

It was an explosive situation. The bishops appealed to the authorities to find the missing priest with all possible speed. Thousands of uniformed and plain-clothes police using helicopters and sniffer-dogs scoured the country in search of him. General Jaruzelski denounced the kidnapping and hinted that it was a deliberate challenge to his authority and to his policy of pursuing national accord. Solidarity was convinced that those responsible for the kidnapping had the backing of hardliners extremely high up in the security police who were intent on showing that the General was incapable of keeping order in the country. It was common knowledge that Jaruzelski had lost control over the Party "betons" and the security apparatus which they controlled. The police, it seemed, were above the law and safe from it, just as they had been in Stalinist times.

On 24th October, Polish TV announced that five men were being questioned in connection with the priest's disappearance; and on 27th their identities were divulged. The Minister for Internal Affairs announced the names on television, "with the utmost sorrow", and appealed for public help in the continuing search for Father Popiełuszko.

Throughout the country, the tension was becoming unbearable, and many workers wanted to call strikes or organise marches, in order to relieve pent-up feelings. But Solidarity called for caution. In Gdańsk, Lech Wałęsa persuaded a crowd to disperse quietly after warning them: "We must take care not to be drawn into their internal power struggle. If they want to play musical chairs, they must do it without us."

All over Poland, masses were being said for Father Jerzy's safe return. A banner outside St Stanisław Kostka proclaimed: WHEREVER YOU ARE, JUREK,[8] CHRIST IS WITH YOU, AND OUR PRAYERS.

Then, on the 30th, at eight o'clock, just as the evening mass was finishing, a priest came out . . . "Nobody who heard it," wrote a British journalist who was present,[9] "will ever forget the awful howl of agony that rose from the thousands waiting in the church of St Stanisław Kostka when a priest announced that Father Popiełuszko's body had been found, a cry which went on for many minutes until it was joined by the tolling of the bells."

"Outside," another writer[10] said, "the people . . . were visibly stunned and helpless. They stood with pale, shut faces, with forgotten, folded hands."

There was some pressure on the murdered priest's parents to take his body and bury it quietly in his own home village. But Father Jerzy's mother resisted: "Years ago I gave my son up to the Church. I am not going to take him back now." After much hesitation, it was agreed that he should be buried in Warsaw, where he belonged, in the grounds of St Stanisław Kostka church.

On 2nd November, friends of the family went to identify the body, and then the true horror of his murder was at last exposed:

> The whole body was covered in brownish-grey bruises. The face was deformed. The nose and areas round the eyes were black, the fingers were brown and dark red, the feet greyish. His hair was much thinner, as if some of it had been pulled out. Large areas of the skin on his legs seemed to have been torn away . . . When the mouth was opened, they saw a piece of pulp in the place where the tongue should have been.[3]

"Passivity is no way of combating the present evil," cried Andrzej Gwiazda, calling for a one-hour strike to coincide with the time of the funeral. But Lech Wałęsa, while insisting that the whole truth be told, asked for calm and for a resumption of talks with the government. "This death," he said, "must become the cornerstone from which social peace may be built. Let the silence of mourning reign throughout Poland. But let it also be the silence of hope."

Honest dialogue, he urged, was still Poland's only chance. He begged the Church to give a moral lead at this painful time, and asked the people to trust to the wisdom of Cardinal Glemp. But it was his own influence which carried most weight: "If the Poles stay off the streets in the next few days," suggested a leading article in *The Economist*,[11] "it is because they still give Mr Wałęsa the respect they deny to the government."

Wałęsa's advice prevailed. But the murder had blown a hole the size of a dead priest in Jaruzelski's claims about "normalisation".

Tens of thousands of mourners had been waiting at the church since dawn for the body to arrive. Patiently and sadly they filed past the coffin as it lay in the church. Flowers, candles, lamps were everywhere, and farewell notes were pinned to the surrounding fence. There was one from Solidarity which mourned, "We could not defend the man we most loved"; one from a group of non-believers to say that they too would join the all-night vigil at Father Jerzy's coffin; and one which proclaimed the message he had lived by: FORGIVE US OUR TRESPASSES AS WE FORGIVE THOSE WHO TRESPASS AGAINST US.

The church was cleared at five in the morning. But by seven the crowds had returned, to begin another long wait. With them now were delegations from all over Poland. Every big industrial centre sent its Solidarity delegates. They had hitched a lift or travelled by overnight train, then walked from the city centre, their Solidarity banners held high. It was the largest, most confident Solidarity turn-out since martial law, and it was as if the movement was coming alive again after a long concussion. And in the popular response, there could not have been a more resounding affirmation of support for the banned union which many of them had been forced to abjure.

The funeral Mass was celebrated by Cardinal Glemp with six bishops and six priests on the balcony and over a thousand other priests inside and outside the church. A wreath of thorns lay on the catafalque. The crowd was later estimated at between three hundred and three hundred and fifty thousand, and their self-discipline and restraint were amazing. In the overpowering silence, it was as if the whole assembly had been, as one woman put it, "touched by a visible wave of grace".

During the farewell speeches which followed the Mass, Lech Wałęsa expressed the general emotion when he said simply: "Solidarity lives today because you, Father Jerzy, gave your life for it. A Poland that has such priests and such people has not perished and will never perish."

But the most moving and heart-felt tribute came from one of the steelworkers from Huta Warszawa, whose voice was hoarse with grief as he cried out: "Jurek, our friend, you are still with us . . . Can you hear the bells tolling for freedom? Can you hear our hearts praying? . . . Your ark, the good ship Solidarity Of Hearts drifts along, carrying more and more of us on board . . . You have already won with Christ . . . and that was the victory you most longed for."

When the coffin was sealed, it was carried to the waiting grave. Flowers, wreaths and candles which covered not only the grave but the church, the forecourt, and the squares and streets beyond were indication enough that Solidarity had a new martyr and that the pilgrims were already at his shrine.

* * *

Piotrowski, Pękała, Chmielewski and their immediate superior in the Interior Ministry, ex-Colonel Adam Pietruszka,[1] were brought to trial. That at least was an achievement. And though arguments raged about the whys and the wherefores, most people were inclined to give Jaruzelski the benefit of the considerable doubt. He was, it was agreed, showing his respect for the rule of law, and at the same time showing his hard-liner rivals that there were limits beyond which they could not go. But would the regime really dare sentence four of its security police to death? Or would the whole affair turn out to be the travesty of justice that the Grzegorz Przemyk trial had been? There were grave fears that Father Popiełuszko's death may have been the opening salvo in a new campaign against the Church.

In court number 40 at Toruń, these fears were borne out. The trial took place in a fanfare of publicity, and the four pawns were duly sacrificed as a sop to public outrage. But the question of where the buck stopped was not resolved or even sincerely tackled, and all evidence which might have pointed the finger at anyone higher than Adam Pietruszka was rigorously suppressed. Though ex-Lieutenants Pękała and Chmielewski were visibly suffering from remorse, ex-Captain Piotrowski was unrepentant.[12] Piotrowski was allowed to indulge in an impassioned tirade against the Church in general and Father Popiełuszko in particular, whom he held responsible for all the social unrest in Poland. Ex-Colonel Pietruszka, who was palpably more upset that the good name of the Interior Ministry had been besmirched than by the murder of the troublesome priest, said bitterly that Popiełuszko was one of a number of priests in Poland who "wear a cross on their chests and carry hatred in their hearts". The State Prosecutor suggested that the "extremism" of Father Popiełuszko had given birth to "a no less damaging" (but, by implication, more excusable) extremism on the part of his murderers.

All these attacks were given widespread coverage by the media. But the words of Mr Olszewski, the auxiliary Prosecutor who represented the Church, were not reported at all. Mr Olszewski who was given only a brief time in which to make his reply to these dumbfounding accusations protested that: "This is supposed to be the trial of the murderers of Father Popiełuszko. I never thought I should have to stand in court and defend the innocent victim of the crime."

And, he added heavily: "History alone will reveal whether all the guilty men were in the dock."

The trial lasted twenty-five days. In his summing-up, Judge Kujawa explained that the death penalty was not in order, since the accused had not acted "from base motives" but merely from "excessive zeal" for eliminating "an enemy of the State". Nevertheless, a crime had been committed and he pronounced a sentence of twenty-five years for Pietruszka and Piotrowski (with ten years' loss of civil rights); fifteen years for Pękała and fourteen for Chmielewski.

Severe sentences certainly, but even these could be seen as no more than a symbolic gesture. The manner in which the trial had been conducted caused consternation. Jerzy Popiełuszko's brother said there had been three trials: of the accused, of his brother and of the Church. Waldemar Chrostowski, the driver who had escaped to give the alarm, and whom the State Prosecutor had done his best to dismiss as an unreliable witness, said the trial had been used "to spit on the Church". It was Leszek Kołakowski's opinion that the trial had represented "a clash between two worlds", the one brought up to hate, the other to respect human dignity. "Even now one must forgive," said Lech Wałęsa. "But forgiveness for the cruel and premeditated murder of Father Popiełuszko will make sense only if our determination to resist evil is thereby strengthened."

Cardinal Glemp, in an unwontedly (for him) strong sermon, protested at the implications of the trial and insisted that the Church must have the right to protect the people from injustice.

If General Jaruzelski had hoped that the trial would appease society, he could not have made a bigger miscalculation. The way it had turned out, it had driven Solidarity, the Church and all the independent social forces in the country closer together in a more determined effort and integrated opposition to the regime than at any time since 1981. The war between the General and the Polish nation entered a new and bitter phase.

[1] Bogdan Szajkowski, *Next to God . . . Poland*, *op. cit.*, Chapter 4, "Tribulations Under Martial Law".

[2] *The Times*, 2.5.84.

[3] *The Tablet*, 26.5.84.

[4] Grażyna Sikorska, *op. cit.*

[5] Tim Garton Ash, *op. cit. Postscript 1984*.

[6] *The Tablet* 8.9.84.

[7] Interview with Tim Garton Ash, *Communists Should Not Believe in Miracles*, November 1984.

[8] Jurek is a diminutive of Jerzy.

[9] Neal Ascherson, the *Observer*, 11.11.84.

[10] Tim Garton Ash, *op. cit. Postscript* as above.

[11] *The Economist*, 3.11.84.
[12] All four accused had been demoted after the crime.

Note: On the site where Father Jerzy had been kidnapped, the villagers set up a birchwood cross surrounded by flowers and candles. In April 1985, they applied for permission to build a permanent memorial. Permission was refused on the grounds that "the Toruń trial showed that Father Popiełuszko was not worthy of a monument". The authorities then proceeded to put up road signs forbidding cars to stop anywhere near the site, which is, however, still marked by its wooden cross.

26 "THEY'VE PRACTICALLY DECLARED CIVIL WAR ON US . . ." (1985)

Whereas the seed which falls into the ground but does not die remains alone, without value, the seed which dies when it falls to the ground brings forth great fruit. And the death of Father Jerzy is for us a sign that we have not been mistaken, that we chose the right path, the path which sooner or later will be fruitful. Let us humbly pray God that it will be so.

Sermon by Father Paweł Piotrowski at the church at St Stanisław Kostka, Warsaw, June 1985

The murder of Jerzy Popiełuszko was really only the tip of the iceberg, just one chilling proof that the regime would stop at nothing – not even brutal murder – to stamp out opposition to its policies. In an interview given to an Italian newspaper in February, Adam Łopatka, the Minister for Religious Affairs, insisted that government leniency was responsible for Father Popiełuszko's death: they should have acted against him immediately the cache of arms and leaflets had been discovered. Now, said Mr Łopatka regretfully, they would have to take more rigorous measures against "priests who deliver sermons which violate the laws".

This was no idle threat. 1985 saw a spate of attacks against the clergy. The "war of the crosses" became more vindictive, with participators sentenced to imprisonment, heavy fines and dismissals from work. (Religious tolerance in Poland, said Cardinal Glemp in August, applied only to atheists, and the authorities would not get the support of believers until they began acknowledging their rights. He was speaking at the monastery of Jasna Góra and was cheered by two hundred thousand pilgrims.)[1] Stones were thrown at the car of Father Kazimierz Jancarz,[2] a parish priest in Nowa Huta, as he drove from Gdańsk to Warsaw to take part in a Mass for the Country at St Stanisław Kostka. In April, one of his assistants, twenty-nine-year-old Father Tadeusz Zaleski[3] was attacked in his parents' house late at night, dazed by a chemical spray and burned on his hands, face and chest with

V-shaped burns. The official media put it about that Father Zaleski was mentally disturbed and had inflicted the burns on himself, "by pressing a burning coat-sleeve against his body". But two separate commissions of doctors, one set up by the Cardinal of Kraków, the other by the Kraków medical fraternity, dismissed this possibility as extremely unlikely, and found no evidence whatever of psychological instability in the priest.

At this point it must be explained that after Jerzy Popiełuszko's death, small human rights groups had come into existence to monitor the activities of the police and to collect information about disappearances and unexplained "accidents". These Citizens' Committees Against Violence were known by their (somewhat unfortunate) acronym, KOPPS. They had naturally enough become a new target for police activities and many of them had already been disbanded, their members arrested. The Kraków KOPP was still functioning, however, and now suggested[4] that Father Zaleski had been chosen as a victim because he possessed evidence about the death of a Solidarity activist, which might incriminate the police. The body of this man, a research student, Tadeusz Frąś, had been found in a Kraków street in September 1984. Apparently he had jumped out of the window of a flat belonging to a total stranger! A verdict of suicide was returned. The police made no effort to take photographs of the body or to determine the position in which it was lying. They also conveniently lost the post-mortem documents until well after the suicide verdict had been given. The documents revealed a punctured carotid artery and other injuries which could indeed have resulted from a fall but were just as likely to have been caused by a blow on the head with a heavy object.[5]

Frąś was one of four cases of political dissidents who had met similar deaths in that year. In none of them were suspects either sought or apprehended. The eleven-year-old daughter of Jan Budny, who had died of head injuries after a short spell in police custody, was pressurised again and again to make a false statement about her father's death. The official verdict was that he had sustained the fatal injuries by falling down the three steps leading to his house![6]

Apart from these killings, at least three murders by unidentified policemen had also gone unpunished, while house searches, kidnappings, burglaries and violence against known activists became the norm.[7]

More and more frequent forty-eight hour detentions were followed increasingly by summary court procedures and the conviction of the detainee on trumped-up criminal charges. Maria Jedynak, wife of a member of the Solidarity underground leadership was evicted from her home, and threatened with having her child abducted, with being run over by a car, and with rape, if she refused to divulge the whereabouts of her husband, Tadeusz. In vain did she insist that she did not know where he was; and when she complained to the Ministry of the Interior, she received no reply to her letter.[8]

The political climate had not been more arctic since Stalinist days. In December 1984, riot squads in Gdańsk, armed with truncheons, flares, smoke bombs and the inevitable water-cannon, had squashed a demonstration of about two thousand people at the Monument. Lech Wałęsa, who in 1980 had sworn always to be present at the Monument on 16th December but who had been prevented ever since from keeping his promise, broke through two police cordons, but gave up at the third and dropped the flowers he was carrying at the feet of the police. Gdańsk was "a study in blue" that day, with ZOMO and militia in every niche and opening. Andrzej Gwiazda was arrested at the Monument and sentenced to three months in prison. When he appealed against the sentence, it was not only upheld but extended for another two months.

During February and March, the confrontation between government and opposition intensified, over government proposals to raise food prices on 28th February. (It was an observable fact that as prices went up, quality went dramatically down!) A Solidarity report on the economy noted that the poor were getting poorer and that a quarter of the population lived in grossly overcrowded and insanitary conditions.

On 13th February, just one week after the end of the Toruń trial, and two weeks before the new price rises were due to come into effect, Lech Wałęsa held a meeting with a group of Solidarity activists in a private flat in Gdańsk, to discuss the catastrophic economic situation. There was some talk of calling a fifteen-minute protest strike on 28th February. At this point the meeting was invaded by twenty plain-clothes and uniformed police who detained everybody present. Some, including Wałęsa, were later released, though placed under police investigation. Three were held and charged: Bogdan Lis, Adam Michnik and Władysław Frasyniuk (a bus-driver and Solidarity's regional chairman in Lower Silesia).

In one swoop, the authorities had thereby netted a representative of the three different strands of the opposition. Lis, from the old pre-Solidarity workers' Free Trades Unions groups; Michnik, from the hated KOR; and Frasyniuk, from the younger generation that had come to political awareness through Solidarity itself. The message was plain enough: Popiełuszko trial or no, the secret police were still on top.

Since the Toruń trial, Lech Wałęsa, so restrained at Father Popiełuszko's funeral, had adopted a much tougher stance and was therefore drawing more flak from the authorities. As he wrote, in a letter to the European Trades Union Federation in May[9]: "The demands and goals that Solidarity set for itself are not easily achieved in a country where every single act of independent organisation is immediately thwarted and where every single attempt at social self-organisation is regarded as anti-State agitation."

Interviewed for the underground *Solidarność* in March,[10] he said disgustedly that government propaganda had gone beyond the bounds of common decency and had turned into "a ruthless struggle against any reconciliation or agreement. We are faced with propaganda terrorism . . . They have practically declared civil war on us."

Wałęsa believed that the authorities were using the opposition as scapegoats on whom to lay the blame for the appalling mess the country was in; and also that they were seeking to counteract the shock of the Toruń trial. The frenetic propaganda, the accusations hurled against the social activists were an attempt to distract public attention away from the guilt of Father Popiełuszko's murderers, and indeed to play down the latters' guilt:

> There is a deliberate campaign to equate the crimes of the activists with those of the police. We must clearly and decisively protest against such cynical scheming. This wave of black propaganda must be stopped, not least because the dividing line between psychological terror and actual physical terrorism is a very shadowy one.

Bishops were being asked to remove outspoken priests to country parishes where they could do no harm. This did not mean that the authorities then left them in peace. Father Mieczysław Nowak, whom Cardinal Glemp, as a result of official pressure, had removed from the parish serving the industrial complex of Ursus in Warsaw, narrowly escaped death in July 1985 when the wheel of the car he was driving suddenly fell off. (The mechanic who repaired the wheel said it had been tampered with.) Nor were bishops any more immune than their clergy. The new bishop of Gdańsk was attacked in front of his own cathedral. He managed to reach his car, and the attacker ran off to the police station directly opposite, dropping his identification papers as he ran. Two young girls who had witnessed the incident picked up the papers and took them to the clergy house. As they left, they were detained, charged with prostitution and locked up. They were released when the policeman's identity papers were returned, but neither explanation nor apology was given.

On 23rd April, 1985, the feast of St George, the name day of the late Father Popiełuszko, a crowd of about twenty thousand gathered in or around the church of St Stanisław Kostka for the evening Mass. Outside the church, a huge poster depicted Father Jerzy as St George, plunging a sword into a red dragon. The crowd sang the Solidarity theme song, "Let Poland Be Poland".[11] Father Teofil Bogucki, the parish priest, said that Father Jerzy's death "was intended to extinguish the flame of love for the country that burns in this church. But, on the contrary, it has resulted in that flame spreading all over Poland."

May Day that year brought demonstrations in thirteen cities, described by the authorities as "senseless aggression against the process of normalisation". In Gdańsk, there were thousands of police and soldiers on the streets, and in an angry telegram to the Sejm, Lech Wałęsa asked if this was what "normalisation" was supposed to look like. Police prevented him from joining in the official parade, and marched him home under escort, cheered all the way by people standing in the streets, in doorways or at open windows.

When a march of about ten to fifteen thousand in Warsaw threatened to turn ugly, Jacek Kuroń and Seweryn Jaworski stepped in to cool things down and persuade the marchers to disperse peacefully. Having succeeded, they came forward to negotiate with the police – and were promptly arrested for causing the disturbance! Next day, a court sentenced them both to three months in prison. When they appealed, Kuroń's sentence was quashed, but Jaworski's was not.*

In spite of these disturbances, General Jaruzelski claimed on television that the May Day atmosphere had been much pleasanter than in previous years. "What great things we have achieved. How much calm and hope have come to Poland!" (Did he, one wonders, know of the "souvenir" banknote being circulated by

* In August 1985, the judge who quashed Kuroń's sentence was removed from her post and the Warsaw Prosecutor demanded that the case be re-opened.

underground Solidarity? The note was for "fifty pieces of silver". What, one was supposed to ask, had Jaruzelski done with the other twenty?)

When the trial of Lis, Michnik and Frasyniuk opened in Gdańsk on 23rd May, 1985, the accused, who all faced a possible five-year sentence, were charged with attempting to incite public unrest – though the fifteen-minute strike had been called off after the government had second thoughts about the price rises – and with occupying leading positions in an illegal union.

From the start, the trial was, in Michnik's words, "a classic example of police banditry", lacking even the appearance of legality. Such was the authorities' fear of free expression that no foreign journalists or observers were allowed; counsels were searched as they entered the courtroom; and the court was packed with UB security policemen only. The defendants were not allowed at first to speak with their lawyers privately, away from the ears of the police – so they refused to testify. When that ban was withdrawn, the defendants were repeatedly prevented from stating their case: they were allowed only to answer "yes" or "no". When they tried to do more, they (in particular Adam Michnik) were expelled from the court. Defence lawyers were not permitted to question police witnesses; and all embarrassing questions were disallowed, while prosecuting counsel and police witnesses were given free rein.

Much of the evidence was fabricated, the main case against Bogdan Lis, for example, depending on a recording which was easily exposed as a fake. The judge's sole aim, it seemed, was to have the defendants pronounced guilty and given as stiff a sentence as possible.

By the fourth day, Lech Wałęsa, who was under orders not to leave Gdańsk without permission, issued a statement saying that the trial was "an insult to justice". "The law in Poland has been trodden underfoot," he said. "Its place has been taken by brute force."

When Wałęsa was called as a witness on day seven, he showed his feelings by appearing in court wearing his T-shirt, with the Solidarity logo. Questioned about the meeting on 23rd February, he admitted that he had arranged it, and invited the guests: "Private meetings among friends are considered normal in civilised countries, and the police don't usually go and break them up," he commented.

When asked what sort of people he had invited, he looked pointedly round at the rows of police in the courtroom and said that he wouldn't have considered inviting any of the present company. The judge warned him not to be offensive, and Wałęsa apologised.

Wałęsa's testimony lasted fifty minutes. Towards the end of the session, Adam Michnik asked if he could make a statement in Wałęsa's presence. His request was refused and Wałęsa was escorted out of the courtroom. Michnik raised his fingers in the V-sign and shouted to his retreating figure: "Don't worry, Lech! Solidarity will win in the end."

Whereupon (for the fourth time in the course of the trial), he was expelled from the courtroom.

> Whatever sentence is passed on us [Michnik wrote in his diary], it will be a sentence on Jaruzelski and his cohorts rather than on us. They will incur the odium of the world for their lawlessness; whereas they will have offered us the priceless gift of dignity, which is inseparable from faithfulness . . . The functionaries think that by gagging us they have deprived us of our dignity. But this is the one thing they cannot do.[12]

Frasyniuk got three and a half years, Michnik three and Lis two and a half. With breathtaking mendacity, the judge said this was a criminal not a political trial, for the crimes involved were against public order. The same double vision was exhibited by Major Wiesław Górnicki, a government spokesman being interviewed for a British TV programme.[13] He quite seriously compared the accused, with their call (later rescinded) for a fifteen-minute protest strike, to the Brighton Bombers who, the previous autumn, had attempted to blow up the British Prime Minister and most of her government.

In an eloquent statement smuggled out of prison, Michnik drew attention to the fact that a police note on his file described him as being "of Jewish nationality":

> The staff-sergeant has applied here the very same Nazi criterion which was applied by the Hitlerites when they exterminated my father's family . . . Of course, Communist anti-semitism is nothing new in Poland. Imported from Stalinist Russia, it has always had a dual purpose: to serve as ideology for . . . political police incapable of absorbing anything more complicated, and to blacken the name of Poland in the eyes of the world. A despicable tool.*

* *Uncensored Poland* 17/85. As a matter of interest, by 1985 there were only between three thousand and five thousand Jews still in Poland. It is also worth noting that, in September 1984, Polish and Jewish scholars from all over the world held a week-long Congress in Oxford, England, in an attempt to overcome some of the historical differences which have divided them.

In this same message, Michnik expressed his fervent belief that Jaruzelski's totalitarian regime in Poland was in its death-throes. Unlike the comparable regimes of Hitler's Germany and Stalin's Russia, it was almost totally without popular support, and was thus "Communism with its teeth knocked out". The only course left to it was repression. But "the resistance offered by Solidarity is too strong, the pressure of authentic public opinion too powerful, for the authorities to succeed in the long run."

Lech Wałęsa was no less forthright. When he presented himself for investigation a week later at the Gdańsk Prosecutor's Office, he did not speak, merely bowed and placed a written statement on the Prosecutor's desk. In it he had written that, after such a trial, the only way to preserve one's human dignity when dealing with courts, prosecutors or police, was to be silent.

[1] *Uncensored Poland*, 17/85.
[2] *Uncensored Poland*, 6/85.
[3] *Uncensored Poland*, 9/85.
[4] *Uncensored Poland*, 6/85.
[5] *Uncensored Poland*, 8/85.
[6] *Uncensored Poland*, 17/85.
[7] Polish Helsinki Committee's 4th Report, Sept.–Feb. 1985. See *Eastern European Reporter*, Volume 1, Number 1.
[8] Tadeusz Jedynak was arrested on 19th June, 1985.
[9] *Uncensored Poland*, 11/85.
[10] 23.3.85.
[11] *Uncensored Poland*, 9/85.
[12] As above 17/85.
[13] *Newsweek*, BBC 2. July 1985.

27 THE CRYSTAL SPIRIT

> Reason has won through in Solidarity. The non-confrontational policy has prevailed. It seems to me that in Solidarity the dominant view is that we are already building the framework for an independent and democratic Poland . . . The only alternative would be desperate actions directed against the political banditry of the security apparatus. And that's precisely what I'm afraid of. In my view, we should not pay them back in kind – we should not kidnap, execute or murder our opponents. Let such methods remain *theirs*. We are not fighting for power, but for a democratic form for our country. Any kind of terrorism necessarily leads to moral abasement and spiritual degradation.
>
> Adam Michnik (talking to Tim Garton Ash in 1984)

Wałęsa was warned to stop making public attacks on the authorities – or take the consequences. But threats like that have long been a factor in the equation of Lech's life; his inner resources enable him to take them in his stride. "I am a normal worker, an abnormal husband, the leader of a union that doesn't exist but that is stronger than ever before, the father of seven children, and a man with a load of troubles," is how he introduces himself. If they arrest him, that's just one more trouble. "I do what I have to do, regardless of consequences," he says simply. He believes in facing trouble when it comes, not in meeting it halfway:

> Obviously, some people will not like what I say or do, and may decide to put me behind bars. But if you're free inside yourself, it doesn't matter what they decide. The most important freedom of all is inner freedom, and in that sense I am the free-est man in the world. I say and do what I believe is right. Nobody is free just to act in his own interest; our human freedom is to act within and on behalf of society.[1]

This "free-est man in the world" is followed by police wherever he goes, whether on foot, by bicycle or by car. His flat is bugged, and electronic surveillance monitors his every action. He has no time for himself, no time to get away from it all, to pick mushrooms or go fishing. And he has too little time for his children, though he is quite clear about what it is he wants to pass on to them:

> We cannot behave in the twenty-first century as we did in the nineteenth. That means we should destroy or demolish as little as possible, but build, transform and adapt the present reality to our needs. We should not pass on to our children less than our parents gave to us.

> If your own father gave you a bicycle and taught you how to make the sign of the cross, you should give *your* child a car, and also teach him to say a prayer . . . If you give him a car and don't teach him to say a prayer, you make a fatal mistake.

Though his name appears less in the Western media than formerly, he is "not ready to be a museum exhibit yet". But he does not worry about whether his fame will outlast him: "Will people even know where my grave is? Or will they tear my grave apart because everyone wants a piece of it? Perhaps even then they won't leave me in peace."[2]

Patiently he works on "building, transforming and adapting the present reality", on preparing blueprints for a "better Poland". "We want to change things so that the system becomes more efficient and our lives become more bearable."

The echoes from the distant past are uncanny; the wheel seems to have come full circle. Like his great-great-grandfather who, over a century ago, longed to "build a better Poland", but who was realistic enough to recognise that the moment was not his to choose, Lech also works and waits. If Solidarity ever comes out again into the sunlight, he may or may not be its leader. "I am not irreplaceable," he admits, for all his so-called vanity. "Someone will eventually take over from me." Zbigniew Bujak perhaps? That will be for the workers to decide. For Lech Wałęsa, what the workers want has always been the overriding factor.

"Wałęsa's an extraordinary man," says Father Jankowski (who is himself being threatened with dire consequences, if he does not desist from preaching "anti-State sermons". "He always stresses the importance of human dignity, especially that of the workers. He could have been just a face in the crowd; or he could have bought himself a comfortable life. Instead, he saw that there was a need, and he gave his life to doing something about it."[1]

> It wouldn't have been possible without faith [admits Lech]. Without faith I wouldn't be where I am now, and I wouldn't have the strength to go on. Nothing would have any sense. I suppose it might have been

> easier to have an uncomplicated life. But I have always believed that I'm the steward of whatever talents I've been given and have to use them to the best effect. I'm an average man, a "sinning believer" with many faults. I wasn't prepared for great tasks. But life put me in this situation, and I have had to do what I can with it.[1]

It is above all his simplicity and transparent truthfulness that have made him indispensable. In a world of appalling mendacity, people know they can trust what he says. And what he says now is that Poles must work at their future themselves. "I do not hand solutions out on a gold plate. Everyone must search his or her own conscience and discover how he can best contribute. The community wisdom is the real wisdom."[3]

In a statement issued for the fifth anniversary of the signing of the Gdańsk Agreement, Wałęsa stressed that in 1985, the need was no longer for millions of demonstrators fighting the police – "no one in his right mind is keen to take on tanks with his bare hands" – but for small groups of wise men and women patiently preparing a programme for the future – so that when the time comes, everybody will know what to do. To a French Press Agency, he said: "The biggest battle is yet to come . . . It will be without fireworks, unspectacular, but much more interesting."

It would in fact not be a battle at all, but "a long march into the future". On this march, political and economic concerns would be given equal priority, since "it is hard to be a political militant if you have nothing to eat".[4]

A five-hundred page report issued by Solidarity on 31st August to mark the anniversary and popularly known as the "Wałęsa Report", filled out Lech's statement. Commissioned by him, it was written by lawyers, doctors, economists, sociologists and university professors; and it represented a plea for a new kind of society in Poland. It suggested that the East–West divide brought about by the Yalta Treaty did not mean a stark choice between, on the one hand, abject submission to a totalitarian system, and, on the other, the complete breakdown of social order. In between those two polarities, there was room for the ideas of Solidarity. The report asked for market forces to be allowed to play a role in the economy, and for an end to those piecemeal items of reform which merely get sat on by those who will go to any lengths to prevent change. It asked for the reform of the judicial system, with judges being allowed genuine freedom; for trade union pluralism; and for workers' councils in factories to be free of management (i.e. Party) interference.

As the report pointed out, the 1980s are witnessing an unprecedented decline in the standard of living in Poland. One family in three has no accommodation of its own; and thirty per cent of the population are officially in the poverty belt. Infant mortality has increased by nearly a third, and life-expectancy generally has decreased. Working conditions are more hazardous than ever, and pollution has reached the danger level. The handicapped and elderly suffer from undernourishment, and the whole country lives with bad sanitary conditions and a poor diet which contains few vitamins. Almost all Polish children have some kind of spinal defect and traces of rickets; all young pregnant women develop anaemia; every third drug in circulation is unavailable in sufficient quantities; and every fourth person who enters a pharmacy leaves it empty-handed.[5] Health care is twenty years behind that of the West. In spite of the many heroic doctors who battle against intolerable odds, the medical profession is demoralised, and the patient often bears the brunt. The Church cannot offer the real help it would like to, for even its long-hoped-for agricultural fund has not yet been given the government go-ahead. Polish life is a no-go area; a seed-ground for despair.

Yet for all this, the deepest cause of the Polish crisis, said the Solidarity report, was "the destruction of the elementary mutual trust between people and the authorities".

Lech Wałęsa continues to believe that the search for this lost mutual trust is the only possible path for Poland to tread: "One day, maybe, the authorities will understand that they must choose between two alternatives: ours, which is non-violent; and the other, which is fraught with danger and could lead to incalculable consequences."

Confrontation does not figure in his plans:

> People on our side are convinced that nothing will be achieved by raised voices and violent actions. Some of the other side know it too. When the moment comes for dialogue, we must be ready, and we must be united. We must return to our work-places, for that is where our strength lies. We must struggle there for rights which it will later be impossible to withdraw . . . I am convinced that it is simply not possible for us not to win . . .

Not possible? Is Wałęsa then simply an incurable optimist? 1985 has been a bad year for optimists. The trials, the kidnappings, the police brutality, the unexplained murders. There are between two hundred and two hundred and fifty political prisoners in Poland now and the number increases steadily. The fines imposed get more prohibitive, with the result that many are imprisoned now for debt. There is a clearer than ever dichotomy between "us" and "them", between the vast majority and those who are unequivocally dubbed "the Reds". The system, corrupt to the core, has become psychologically intolerable.

It is the young who are in the vanguard of the revolt. The heirs to the spirit of Solidarity, who did not previously suffer the spiritual desolation of what Miłosz, in Stalinist days, called "ketman" – the survival technique of thinking and believing in one set of values while being forced to act in accordance with another. The young have had better models than that, and they do not want to let them go. They are intelligent enough to understand that a corrupt regime contaminates society with the fall-out of its own corruption. Lies become too easily accepted, for the sake of a quiet life; work is too easily devalued, the natural environment degraded, science and culture dehumanised.

One recent law has tightened censorship; another has made singing hymns outside church a punishable offence; a third has eroded any hope of trade union pluralism for the foreseeable future; and yet another threatens to do away with academic freedoms and reduce the universities to the level of tied Party schools. Professor Bronisław Geremek, a respected member of the Polish Academy of Sciences for thirty years, was dismissed after meeting with the British Foreign Minister, Sir Geoffrey Howe, in April 1985. But Poland, as an industrial nation at the end of the twentieth century, cannot afford to muzzle its universities and research institutes, and thus erode still further its economic competitiveness and render it even more incapable of repaying its foreign debts. Such a short-sighted course is an invitation to economic catastrophe, for the sake of short-term political point-scoring. The "grand old man" of the Academy, ninety-six-year-old Professor Lipiński, goes further in his condemnation. He speaks of a return to Stalinist practices and warns: "The threat to Polish science and learning does not come from 'troublemakers' at the universities but from the numerous attempts made to limit freedom of thought. Science ends when a political muzzle is put on mouths and thoughts."[6]

So does freedom. And trust. And spontaneity. With the return of informers and the increased feelings of insecurity, the Solidarity days of mutual trust have for the moment gone. "What has happened to the days when everyone seemed like a member of the family?" they ask mournfully. Shop assistants are bored and rude; the endless queues and shortages make people short-tempered and weary.

Yet miracles have happened in the past, and the Poles are not beyond hoping for one now. It may even be that one has already happened. As recently as 1977, Adam Michnik remarked disconsolately to a friend in Paris that the Poles were concerned only with their creature comforts and were utterly conformist. Yet today, however grievous the pain of living, what Michnik, Kuroń, Gwiazda, Walentynowicz – and Lech Wałęsa – were working towards then has actually happened. Despite the frustration and the hopelessness – and they are undeniable – the Poles are aware of their situation now, and aware that that awareness is generally shared. 1980 was not a brief interlude but a turning-point. As Wajda said, at the conclusion of *Man of Iron*: we have seen this truth and there is no going back on it. There *is* no going back on August 1980.

However many may now belong to the new unions[7] – said by Wałęsa to be workers' unions in name only[8] – their deeper allegiance is almost certainly elsewhere. The spiritual strength of the people, severely taxed by the grinding everyday reality, cannot be entirely crushed.

The government professes to believe that "normalisation" has been restored. But what is "normalisation"? If, as Wałęsa suggested, it means more troops and police on the streets to maintain the power and privileges of the ruling elite; more people like Adam Michnik behind bars, then indeed normalisation has come about. (Some would perhaps call it pacification!) But it is an illusion. For the true normalisation would be what Lech Wałęsa and his colleagues are still striving for, a dialogue between rulers and ruled, enabling a common effort for the good of Poland.

In many, perhaps the majority of, world societies, it would already be too late. The spiral of violence, in which one violent act begets another even more violent, would already be too tightly coiled, ready to spring back with destructive force. That is the way things have happened in Northern Ireland, in Lebanon, in Uganda, in South Africa. It has come to seem the only possible way out of impasse. But Poland is different. The Poles have shown in the past that they are capable of overcoming their prejudices and of swallowing their wholly-justified grudges. They are romantics, but they have learned realism in a hard school and with it has come maturity. There have been isolated instances of violence in some of the street demonstrations, but these have never been encouraged or condoned by the majority. The record of non-violence in the Polish struggle is impressive. The ultimate crime in Polish eyes is that brother should be killing brother. Where else could one have come across a leading article[9] entitled "How Can We Love the ZOMO?" and justifiably expect it to be taken seriously? The Poles may find it hard to love the ZOMO, but they know the effort is important. "Ours are spiritual values which we can never lose," says Lech Wałęsa, "they form us and explain us, which is why the West finds us difficult to understand."[1]

The people do not want to overthrow the system under which they live; they want to humanise it and make it work. They might want to have more to eat and a reasonable share of the basic consumer goods, but there is no hankering after capitalism in Poland; no desire to return to the pre-war *ancien regime*; egalitarian sentiments are almost universal. There would be no takers for the privatisation of heavy industry, though some call for more private enterprise in other areas. Socialism is what they want, but it must be open not closed Socialism, one with a human face and not the version exported from the Soviet Union.

It follows that they want someone to overhaul their disastrous economy without ideological spectacles on. Such a move would require imagination and courage on the part of the government, because it would involve moving power away from the centre, and this in turn would mean a genuine democratisation of social and political life. The alternative to this – a society perpetually alienated and hostile – may prove too grim to live with, however little the regime seems to care about public good-will. In a stalemate situation, in which the government has power but no popular mandate, while Solidarity has the mandate but no power, something will have to give. Solidarity has gone underground and is biding its time. After all, the Poles are used to waiting. They have waited for two hundred years, and the lessons of those years have not been wasted on them. But how long can a bankrupt regime afford to wait? How much time does it have?

Lech Wałęsa has no doubts at all about the eventual outcome. "Like all the world's major battles, it will end at the negotiating table. Sooner or later there will be an agreement with the authorities. I have held out the hand of friendship, so far without response. But in the end, I shall not have waited in vain."

There are many on "the other side", he claims, who want accord. Even the militia. In so doing, they admit their guilt, but Wałęsa for one will not let past grudges prevail over the need for reconciliation. The revealing and rather touching story is told that one day Lech was found at home drinking vodka with six members of the ZOMO riot police. They were six young conscripts who had hated what they had to do, and this was their last night in the service. They were celebrating by visiting Wałęsa, drinking his health and explaining their conduct.

The incident brings to mind the young prison-camp guard who said to Tadeusz Mazowiecki: "Who will there ever be to stand up for *us*?" The militia men with "dead eyes full of fear" seen by Hanka G. on the day martial law was declared and the internment camp commandant in a moving short story by Andrzej Szczypiorski: a good man whose moral sense has been buried deep with the passing years, yet who is aware of something seriously wrong with his life. He attempts to avoid facing the truth about himself by drinking, but the placebo doesn't work. "Every drink lessened the pain a bit, but after a time it hurt more again. I don't mean a pain in the chest, something more general, maybe not even a pain, more like a burden . . ."[10]

It is Wałęsa's strength, not, as some would say, his weakness, that he can understand the nature of such a burden, and is unwilling to judge anybody as "the enemy". The future will be built by everybody pulling together, or it will not be built at all: "We must forgive. We should listen to everyone we meet, even those we do not like or who do not like us. Every single person has something to teach us, but so often we are deaf and blind to what that something is."[1]

Jerzy Popiełuszko preached that message too. The truth is that the religious faith of the Poles is not just a political safety valve (though it is that too) but a real dynamic force. The gospel of Christ is taken seriously in Poland: not for nothing did a nineteenth-century poet call her the "Christ among nations".[11] The Christmas 1984 crib in St Stanisław Kostka church was a car boot filled with straw, on which lay the mangled body of a young man. The gospel story is a living reality. The Poles understand about crucifixion, because they have lived the experience many times.

But they understand about resurrection too. Today and every day Jerzy Popiełuszko's shrine is visited by thousands, and ablaze with lights and candles. In the church, people pray not for vengeance but for the strength to overcome hatred. The words from the Cross, often repeated by Father Jerzy, FATHER, FORGIVE THEM, still flutter on their banner outside the church. Learning to forgive is an uphill struggle, but if reconciliation is to take place and brother is to stop killing brother, it must be won.

"It's a bit like learning to do the long jump," says Wałęsa

typically. "First a little jump, then a little bit further. We thought we could do more than we were capable of doing, and we were beaten back. But we'll try again. You *must* have hope."

On 31st August, 1985, the fifth anniversary of the founding of Solidarity, workers, farmers, housewives, students, the old, the young, went to church. One poster produced by the underground for the occasion showed a large fist crushing a prison; another showed the defiant five-year-old that the 1981 happy Solidarity baby had become. The crushing grip and the uncrushable defiance: those are the twin realities of Poland today. The defiance may be non-violent, but it is not to be underestimated. A poignant new hymn, popularly attributed to Father Popiełuszko himself, begins sadly and plangently:

> Oh my country, how long you have been suffering,
> How deep your wounds today.

But it ends on a note of hope. The white eagle of Poland, chained now by the foot, will break its chain "when the freedom bell shall ring".

Until that day, the people turn for solace to the source that has never failed them: "Mary, Queen of Poland, grant us freedom, peace and loving hearts, that we may stay true to you and your Son." Listening to them sing, reduced to helpless tears by the passion in their voices, one senses something of the underlying spiritual force as well as the anguish of this much-tried people; the "glory of the starlike diamond" among the ashes of their lives.

As the birthday Mass in St Stanisław Kostka draws to a close, a voice, powerful and resonant, comes through the loudspeakers: "Let us swear to make Solidarity live."

Thousands of fists shoot into the air, and thousands of voices shout as one: "We swear it."

Outside, in front of the banks of fresh flowers which permanently cover the grave of Jerzy Popiełuszko, a group of Silesian miners have laid a wreath in the shape of an anchor. The ancient symbol of undying hope. As Lech Wałęsa says: "You *must* have hope."

[1] Interview with author.

[2] Interview with Lech Wałesa by Aimé Lemoyne, for *La Croix*, October 1983. Reproduced by *Reader's Digest*.

[3] *Każdy Z Was Jest Wałesa*, *op. cit.*

[4] *Uncensored Poland*, 14/85.

[5] Tygodnik Mazowsze, number 129, 16.5.85. Article by member of Solidarity's independent Voluntary Health Commission.
[6] *Uncensored Poland*, 12/85.
[7] The government claims five and a half million, which is still only half the Solidarity figure.
[8] *Uncensored Poland* 11/85.
[9] Józef Tischner, Jak Kochać Zomowca – interview reproduced in Dziennik Polski, 4.8.84.
[10] Andrzej Szczypiorski, *Confession of A Child Of Our Time*, Index on Censorship, Volume 14, Number 4, August 1985.
[11] Juliusz Słowacki, nineteenth-century Polish Romantic poet.

See also East European Reporter, Spring 1985 and Summer 1985.

ENDPIECE

The essential aim of any project of renewal in the world by means of a moral renaissance is not so much the construction of an earthly paradise as the fact of restraining and disarming a rampant evil. In this defence of human life against the evil that threatens it, we can discern the ultimate meaning of those appeals to brotherhood, solidarity, freedom and human dignity . . . Human history is not only a sad procession of human errors and injustices. It is also made up of courageous and wise efforts towards the common good.

The encounter with contemporary evil of an exceptionally aggressive nature awoke in Poland the will to renewal and inclined a large number of people to renounce self-interest in order to defend themselves against the suppression of human rights and against the abasement of human dignity. Their witness will become even more powerful when it moves others to defend the same values, common to us all, in all the diversity of the actual situations which confront us in our own days.

BOHDAN CYWIŃSKI, 1984

BIBLIOGRAPHY

Andrzejewski, Jerzy, *Ashes and Diamonds*, Penguin.

Arendt, Hannah, *On Revolution*, Faber & Faber 1963, Penguin 1973. (Canovan, Margaret, *The Political Thought of Hannah Arendt*, Methuen 1974.)

Ascherson, Neal, *The Polish August*, Penguin 1981.

Ascherson, Neal, *The Book of Lech Wałesa*, Allen Lane (introduction to) 1981.

Barańczak, Stanisław (Wybor), *Poeta Pamieta, Antologia Poezji Świadectwa I Sprzeciwu 1944–1984*, Puls Publications, 1984.

Bethell, Nicholas, *Gomułka, His Poland and His Communism*, Longmans 1969, Penguin 1972.

Bethell, Nicholas, *The War Hitler Won*, Allen Lane, Penguin 1972.

Bierut, Bolesław, *The Six Year Plan for the Reconstruction of Warsaw*, Ksiazka i Wiedza, 1949.

Blażyński, George, *Flashpoint Poland*, Pergamon Policy Studies, Oxford 1979.

Brandys, Kazimierz, *A Warsaw Diary 1978–1981*, Chatto & Windus 1984.

Brolewicz, Walter, *My Brother, Lech Wałesa*, Robson Books 1984.

Bromke, Adam, *Poland: The Protracted Crisis*, Mosaic Press, Canada.

Bromke, Adam, *Poland's Politics: Idealism v. Realism*, Harvard Press.

Charlton, Michael, *The Eagle and the Small Birds: Crisis in the Soviet Empire from Yalta to Solidarity*, BBC, 1984.

Davies, Norman, *God's Playground: A History of Poland*, Volume II, Clarendon Press, Oxford 1981.

Davies, Norman, *Heart of Europe: A Short History of Poland*, Clarendon Press, Oxford 1984.

Dobbs, Michael, K. S. Karol and Dessa Trevisan, *Poland, Solidarity, Wałesa*, Pergamon Press 1981.

Dziewanowski, M. K., *Poland in the Twentieth Century*, Columbia University Press, New York.

Dziewanowski, M. K., *The Communist Party in Poland*, Harvard Press 1976.

Fournier, Ewa, *Poland*, Vista Books 1964.

Garliński, Józef, *Poland, Soe and the Allies*, George Allen & Unwin, 1969.

Garton Ash, Tim, *The Polish Revolution, Solidarity 1980–1982*, Jonathan Cape 1983.

BIBLIOGRAPHY

Halecki, O., *A History of Poland*, with additional material by A. Polonsky, Routledge & Kegan Paul 1978, p/b 1983.

Kaplan, Chaim A., *Scroll of Agony*, Hamish Hamilton 1966.

Kapusciński, Ryszard, *The Emperor*, Picador 1983.

Konwicki, Tadeusz, *A Dreambook For Our Time*, Penguin 1976 and 1983 (with an introduction by Leszek Kołakowski).

Konwicki, Tadeusz, *A Minor Apocalypse*, Faber & Faber 1983.

Konwicki, Tadeusz, *The Polish Complex*, Penguin 1984.

Korowicz, Marek, *W Polsce Pod Sowieckim Jarzmem*, Veritas 1955.

Krzywicki-Herbert and Rev. Walter J. Ziemba (translators), *The Prison Notes of Stefan, Cardinal Wyszyński*, Hodder & Stoughton 1985.

Lane, David and George Kołankiewicz, *Social Groups in Polish Society*, Macmillan 1973.

Lewis, Flora, *The Polish Volcano: A Case-History of Hope*, Secker & Warburg 1959.

Macshane, Denis, *Solidarity, Poland's Independent Trade Union,* Spokesman 1981.

Mazowiecki, Tadeusz, *Internowanie*, Aneks 1982.

Michener, James A., *Poland*, Secker & Warburg 1983.

Miłosz, Czesław, *The Captive Mind*, Secker & Warburg 1953, Penguin 1980.

Miłosz, Czesław, *Native Realm*, Sidgwick & Jackson 1981.

Miłosz, Czesław, *The Seizure of Power, 1955*, pub'd Abacus 1985, (sel. and ed.) *Post-War Polish Poetry*, University of California Press.

Mirowska, Halina, *Lechu*, Glos Publications, New York 1982.

Moczarski, Kazimierz, *Rozmowy Z Katem*, Państwowy Instytut Wydawniczy, Warszawa 1977.

Nowak, Jan, *Courier from Warsaw*, Collins/Harvill 1982.

Nowakowski, Marek, *The Canary and Other Tales of Martial Law*, Harvill Press 1983.

Offrédo, Jean, *Lech Wałesa. Czyli Polskie Lato*, Cana, Paris 1981.

Pawlak, A. and M. Terlecki, *Każdy Z Was Jest Wałęsa: Nobel 1983, Spotkania, Paris 1984.*

Raina, Peter, *Political Opposition in Poland 1954–1977,* Poets & Painters Press, London 1978.

Raphael, Robert R., *Wojna Polsko-Jaruzelska w Karykaturach i Rysunkach*, Copenhagen 1982.

Ruane, Kevin, *The Polish Challenge*, BBC 1982.

Ścibor-Rylski, Aleksander, *Człowiek Z Marmuru, Człowiek Z Żelaza*, Aneks 1982.

Sebastian, Tim, *Nice Promises*, Chatto & Windus 1985.

Sienkiewicz, Henryk, *With Fire and Sword*, London ed. of 1898.

Sikorska, Grażyna, *A Martyr for the Truth: Jerzy Popiełuszko*, Fount, 1985.

Steiner, George, *A Reader*, Penguin 1984.

Steven, Stewart, *The Poles*, Collins/Harvill 1982.
Surdykowski, J., *Notatki Gdańskie*, Aneks 1982.
Syrop, Konrad, *Poland in Perspective*, Robert Hale, London 1982.
Szajkowski, Bogdan, *Next to God . . . Poland. Politics and Religion in Contemporary Poland*, Frances Pinter Publishers, 1983.
Taylor, John, *Five Months with Solidarity*, Wildwood 1981.
Tischner, Józef, *The Spirit of Solidarity*, Harper & Row 1982.
Tuohy, Frank, *The Ice Saints*, Macmillan 1964.
Żenczykowski, Tadeusz, *Dramatyczny Rok 1945*, Polonia 1982.

ARTICLES AND PAMPHLETS

"Dissent in Poland 1976–1977", Reports and Documents in Translation. Assn of Polish Students and Graduates in Exile, 1977.
The Church in Poland Under Martial Law, a voice of Solidarność Publication, London, June 1983.
"Solidarity Underground", A PSC special report, London 1983.
Jak Kochać Zomowca, wywiad z ks. prof. Józefem Tischnerem, Dziennik Polski, 4.8.84.
Uncensored Poland News Bulletin, Information Centre for Polish Affairs (especially 1983–1985, passim)
East European Reporter, Volume 1, Number 1 and Number 2.
Polish Affairs, Spring 1985:
Przemko Maria Grafczyński: Reflections on the Murder of Father Popiełuszko.
Janusz Bugajski: The Dead Victims of Martial Law.
Religion in Communist Lands, II, 1. Spring 1983: Grażyna Sikorska, The Light/Life Movement in Poland.
Poland One Magazine, 1984 and 1985.

INDEX

INDEX

INDEX

INDEX

INDEX